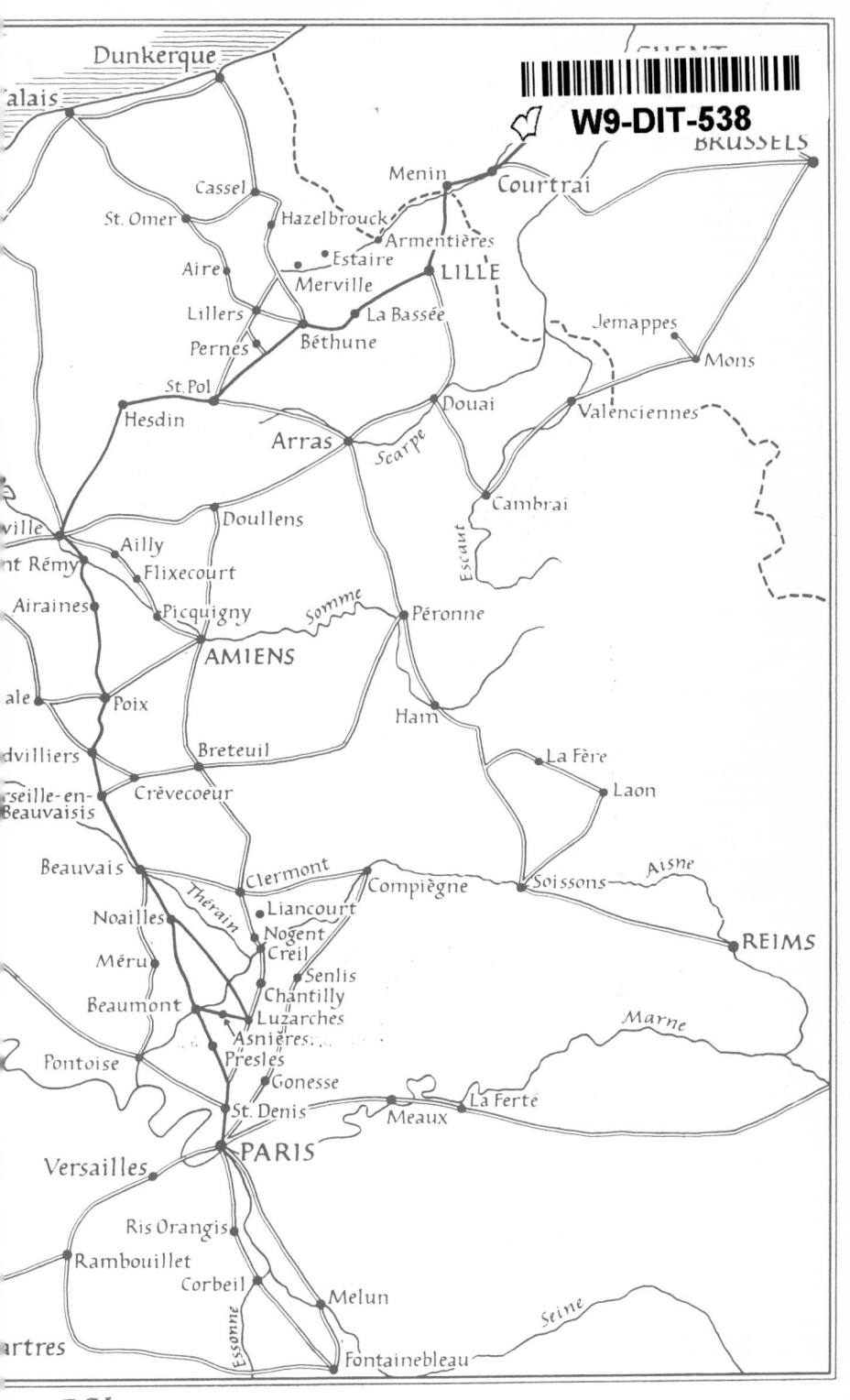

HOLY WEEK

HOLY WEEK

A NOVEL BY

Louis Aragon

TRANSLATED BY

HAAKON CHEVALIER

G. P. PUTNAM'S SONS   NEW YORK

Library of Congress Catalog
Card Number: 61-5679

MANUFACTURED IN THE UNITED STATES OF AMERICA

THIS IS NOT A HISTORICAL NOVEL. ANY RESEMBLANCE TO PER-
SONS WHO HAVE LIVED, ANY SIMILARITY IN NAMES, PLACES,
DETAILS, CAN ONLY BE AN EFFECT OF PURE COINCIDENCE,
AND THE AUTHOR DECLINES RESPONSIBILITY FOR THIS IN
THE NAME OF THE INALIENABLE RIGHTS OF THE IMAGINATION.

A.

Contents

Contents

Principal Historic Characters Appearing in Holy Week

THE ROYAL FAMILY

LOUIS XVIII (1755–1824), Louis-Stanislas-Xavier de Bourbon, King of France and of Navarre from 1814 to 1824, surnamed *le Désiré*. His reign interrupted by Napoleon's return from Elba on February 26, 1815, for the period later called "the Hundred Days," ending with Napoleon's second abdication, June 22, 1815. Grandson of Louis XV, son of the dauphin Louis and of Maria-Josèphe de Saxe, younger brother of Louis XVI. Previously bore the title of Comte de Provence and also known as M. de Lille. One of the leaders of the "emigration" during the Revolution; assumed the title of Louis XVIII as early as 1795, and spent the years of exile successively in Coblenz, Verona, Mitau and finally in England.

CHARLES, COMTE D'ARTOIS (1757–1836), younger brother of Louis XVI and of Louis XVIII. Bore court title of *Monsieur*. First in line of succession, later became King of France under the name of Charles X (from 1824 to 1830).

CHARLES-FERDINAND, Duc de Berry (1778–1820), younger son of the above. Had nominal command of covering operations of all King's troops. Colonel-General of light cavalry and of lancers.

LOUIS-ANTOINE DE FRANCE, Duc d'Angoulême (1775–1844), elder son of the Comte d'Artois, Colonel-General of Cuirassiers and Dragoons.

MARIE-THÉRÈSE DE BOURBON (1778–1851), daughter of Louis XVI, sister of Louis XVII, Duchesse d'Angoulême, married to the above in 1799. Rumored to be the daughter, not of Louis XVI but of Marie-Antoinette's lover, Axel von Fersen. Bore court title of *Madame*. Also known as Madame Royale.

LOUIS-PHILIPPE D'ORLÉANS, the Duc d'Orléans (1773–1850). Heir to the younger branch of the royal family, the Orléans. Also had title of Duc de Chartres. Later King of the French under the name of Louis-Philippe (1830–1848). The son of Philippe-Égalité (1747–1793) who supported the Revolution, was a member of the Convention, voted for the death of Louis XVI and was himself later guillotined. Colonel-General of Hussars.

LOUISE-MARIE-ADÉLAÏDE D'ORLÉANS (1777–1847), sister of the above, bore court title of *Mademoiselle*.

LOUIS-JOSEPH DE BOURBON, Prince de Condé (1736–1818). Member of the collateral branch of the Bourbon family. Emigrated in 1792 and was the organizer, in Coblenz, of the so-called *Armée de Condé*, intended to reconquer France for the royalists. Grand Master of the Royal Household.

LOUIS-HENRI-JOSEPH DE BOURBON-CONDÉ, Duc de Bourbon (1756–1830). Son of the above, father of the Duc d'Enghien whom Napoleon ordered to be shot at Vincennes in 1804. Became the Prince de Condé in 1818 upon the death of his father. Colonel-General of light infantry.

THE BONAPARTES

NAPOLEON BONAPARTE, born in Ajaccio, Corsica, in 1769, died in St. Helena in 1821. Began his political career on his return from the Egyptian expedition by overthrowing the Directory in a *coup d'état* on November 9, 1799 (18th Brumaire of the year VIII by the Revolutionary calendar). First Consul in the triumvirate of the Consulate which he created, then sole consul for life, and finally had himself crowned Emperor on May 18, 1804. Put an end to royalist plotting by the abduction and summary execution of the Duc d'Enghien. Drew up the Civil Code, new financial system, established the Bank of France, a new school system, the University. Made his peace with the Church by signing the Concordat with Pius VII. Most of his reign taken up by a succession of spectacular campaigns which carried his armies to the ends of Europe and which were marked by victories which were triumphs of military art: Austerlitz, Jéna, Eylau, Friedland, Eckmühl, Wagram. . . . Was variously referred to by his contemporaries as the Usurper, the Tyrant, the Ogre, the Enemy of Mankind, *le Petit Caporal, le Petit Tondu, Père la Violette,** and *l'Autre* (That Man).

JOSEPH BONAPARTE (1768–1844), elder brother of Napoleon. King of Naples (1806), King of Spain (1808–1813).

LOUIS BONAPARTE (1778–1846) brother of Napoleon. King of Holland (1806–1810), married to Hortense de Beauharnais and father of Napoleon III.

MARIE-PAULINE BONAPARTE (1780–1825), sister of Napoleon. Married General Leclerc (1801), then Camille Borghese (1803) and was created Duchesse de Guastalla in 1806. Famous for her many love affairs.

CAROLINE-MARIE-ANNONCIADE BONAPARTE (1782–1839), sister of Napoleon. Married Joachim Murat (1800) and became Grande Duchesse de Berg, and de Clèves, then Queen of Naples.

JÉRÔME BONAPARTE (1784–1860), youngest brother of Napoleon. King of Westphalia (1807–1813).

JOSÉPHINE TASCHER DE LA PAGERIE DE BEAUHARNAIS (1763–1814). Married the Vicomte de Beauharnais in 1779 (who died on the scaffold in 1794), then Napoleon Bonaparte in 1796. Napoleon divorced her in 1809.

* After Napoleon was exiled to Elba, his followers predicted that he would return to power by the time the violets bloomed again, and violets became a Bonapartist emblem.

MARIE-LOUISE (1791–1847), Archduchess of Austria, daughter of Francis I, emperor of Austria. Married Napoleon in 1810. The mother of the King of Rome, Napoleon II.

FRANÇOIS-CHARLES-JOSEPH BONAPARTE (1811–1832), son of Napoleon I. Proclaimed King of Rome on his birth and recognized emperor by the joint Chambers upon Napoleon I's second abdication. Spent his whole life at the castle of Schönbrunn with his grandfather, the emperor of Austria, under the name of the Duke of Reichstadt. Nicknamed *l'Aiglon* (the Eaglet) and *le Louvetot* (the wolf cub).

HORTENSE DE BEAUHARNAIS, Duchesse de Saint-Leu, known as *la reine* Hortense (1783–1837). Daughter of the Vicomte de Beauharnais and Josephine, the future empress. Married Louis Bonaparte, King of Holland, by whom she had three sons; the youngest became Napoleon III. Also had an illegitimate son, the Duc de Morny, in 1811, by Auguste-Charles-Joseph de Flahaut.

JOACHIM MURAT (1767–1815), brother-in-law of Napoleon, husband of Caroline Bonaparte, Marshal of France, Grand Duke of Berg, King of Naples from 1808 to 1815. Forced to abandon his kingdom, he attempted to reconquer it, but was captured at Pizzo and shot.

MARSHALS AND GENERALS

LOUIS-ALEXANDRE BERTHIER, Prince de Wagram, Prince de Neuchâtel (1753–1815). General, Napoleon's Grand Army; Marshal of France. Married to Marie-Elisabeth, Princess of Bavaria, daughter of Duke Wilhelm of Bavaria. Had three children. Captain of the Lifeguards, in command of the Fifth Company of the King's Lifeguards in the Royal Household.

HENRI-JACQUES-GUILLAUME CLARKE, Duc de Feltre (1765–1818). Marshal of France, War Minister under Napoleon.

LOUIS-NICOLAS DAVOUT, Duc d'Auerstaedt, Prince d'Eckmühl, Marshal of France (1770–1823).

JEAN-BAPTISTE DROUET-D'ERLON (1765–1844). Marshal of France. Involved with the Lallemand brothers and Lefebvre-Desnouettes in an abortive antiroyalist mutiny at La Fère in early 1815.

RÉMI-JOSEPH-ISIDORE EXELMANS (1775–1852). Created Marshal of France by Louis Napoleon in 1851, one of Napoleon's most trusted generals.

CHARLES DE LABÉDOYÈRE (1786–1815). General. Shot after the Hundred Days for having gone over to Napoleon in Grenoble in March, 1815. Son-in-law of Charles de Damas. Married to Georgine, sister of César de Chastellux.

VICTOR-CLAUDE-ALEXANDRE FANNEAU DE LAHORIE, General (1766–1812). Shot at Napoleon's orders in retaliation for a conspiracy in which he was involved, with General Malet, to overthrow the Emperor during the Russian campaign in 1812.

FRÉDÉRIC-ANTOINE, Baron Lallemand, General (1774–1839). He and his brother involved in the La Fère conspiracy.

HENRI-DOMINIQUE LALLEMAND (1777–1823), brother of the above.

MARQUIS JACQUES LAW DE LAURISTON (1768–1828). General. Grandnephew of John Law, the eighteenth-century Scottish financier. In command of the Gray Musketeers.

CHARLES LEFEBVRE-DESNOUETTES (1773–1822), General. Involved in the La Fère conspiracy.

JACQUES-ÉTIENNE MACDONALD (1765–1840), Duc de Tarente, Marshal of France. Adjutant to the Duc de Berry, in effective command of the royal retreat.

COMTE NICOLAS-JOSEPH MAISON (1771–1840). Marshal of France (1829), Lieutenant-General, Governor of the First Military Division, Paris and vicinity, commander-in-chief of the Seine troops.

CLAUDE-FRANÇOIS DE MALET (1754–1812), General. Plotted against Napoleon, with General Lahorie. Shot in 1812.

AUGUSTE-FRÉDÉRIC-LOUIS DE MARMONT, Duc de Raguse (1774–1852). Marshal of France under the Empire. Fought at Austerlitz, in Portugal, at Leipzig. Beaten by Wellington at Arapiles in Spain in 1812. Withdrew his army corps from Essonnes, near Corbeil, after capture of Paris by the Allies in 1814, treated with the enemy, making Napoleon's abdication inevitable. Captain of the Lifeguards, Commander of the Royal Household. Married to the daughter of Perregaux, banker and partner of Laffitte.

ÉDOUARD MORTIER, Duc de Trévise (1768–1835). Marshal of France. Later war minister under Louis-Philippe, killed by Fieschi's infernal machine in an attempt upon the King's life. Area commander of the Lille region.

MICHEL NEY, Duc d'Elchingen, Prince de la Moskowa (1769–1815). Marshal of France. Made peer of France by Louis XVIII, went over to Napoleon on his return from Elba, March 17, 1815. Convicted of treason for this upon Louis XVIII's return to Paris after Napoleon's second abdication, and shot.

NICOLAS-CHARLES OUDINOT, Duc de Reggio (1767–1847). Marshal of France.

MARIE-ANTOINE (TONY), Vicomte de Reiset (1775–1836), General. Commanded Grammont's (the second) Company of the King's Lifeguards.

NICOLAS SOULT, Duc de Dalmatie (1769–1851), Marshal of France, War Minister under the Restoration. Relieved of his duties shortly before the events related in this novel.

CHARLES-JOSEPH-HYACINTHE DU HOUX, Marquis de Vioménil (1734–1827), Marshal of France (1816). Uncle of the Marquis Victor-Louis de Toustain. In command of the Royal Foot Guard.

OTHER OFFICERS

CÉSAR-LAURENT, Comte de Chastellux (1780–1854). Colonel, Adjutant-Commander of the Light Horse. Married to Zéphirine de Damas.

ÉTIENNE-CHARLES, Comte, then Duc de Damas-Crux, General, Commander of the Light Horse, father-in-law of Chastellux.

COLONEL DRUAULT, Commander of the Law School volunteers.

ÉTIENNE DE DURFORT, Comte, Captain-Lieutenant of the Gendarmes of the King's Guard.

CHARLES-NICOLAS FABVIER, Baron (1782–1855). Colonel, aide-de-camp to Marmont, second lieutenant in the Lifeguards, 6th Raguse Company. Later a general, distinguished himself in the war for Greek independence.

THÉODORE GÉRICAULT (1791–1824). Painter, born in Rouen, second lieutenant in the Gray Musketeers of the Royal Household.

AUGUSTE-PIERRE-MARIE FERRON, Comte de La Ferronays (1777–1842), diplomat. Aide-de-camp to the Duc de Berry.

ADELAÏDE-BLAISE-FRANÇOIS LE LIÈVRE, Marquis de Fourilles et de La Grange, Commander of the Black Musketeers.

ALPHONSE-MARIE-LOUIS DE PRAT DE LAMARTINE (1790–1869). Romantic poet. Second lieutenant in the Royal Household.

COMTE DE MONTBRUN, Lieutenant of the Swiss Guards.

CASIMIR-LOUIS-VICTURNIEN DE ROCHECHOUART, Duc de Mortemart (1787–1875), Commander of the Swiss Guards.

M. DE NOAILLES, Prince de Poix, father of the Duc de Mouchy, Commander of the 3rd Company of the King's Lifeguards.

ARMAND-EMMANUEL, Duc de Richelieu (1766–1822). Grandson of Duc Armand de Richelieu who played such a prominent role at the court of Louis XIV, under the Regency and under Louis XV. First Gentleman of the Privy Chamber, formerly officer of the Queen's Dragoons. Served Czar Alexander I of Russia for 11 years.

COMTE LÉON DE ROCHECHOUART, Brigadier General, Lieutenant in the Black Musketeers. Nephew by marriage of Richelieu, whom he served as major-domo in Odessa, 1804–1811.

VICTOR-LOUIS, Marquis de Toustain. In Wagram's 5th Company of Lifeguards. Nephew of M. de Vioménil.

COMTE DE VERGENNES, Commander of the Gardes-de-la-Porte.

ALFRED DE VIGNY (1797–1863). Poet, novelist and dramatist. A young Musketeer.

OTHER OFFICIALS AND FIGURES

DUC PIERRE DE BLACAS D'AULPS (1771–1839), Louis XVIII's favorite. Secretary of State for the Royal Household.

DUC DE CROY D'HAVRET, Commander of the 1st Company (the so-called Company of Scots) of the King's Lifeguards.

COMTE ALEXANDRE DE LABORDE, Prefect of Liège under Napoleon. Adjutant-Commander of the National Guard. In charge of the Tuileries. Brother of Nathalie de Mouchy.

The DUC and DUCHESSE DE MASSA.

The DUC and DUCHESSE (NATHALIE) DE MOUCHY.

CHARLES-MAURICE DE TALLEYRAND-PÉRIGORD (1754–1838). Bishop of Autun under the former monarchy, president of the National Assembly in 1790, Minister of Foreign Affairs under the Directory, then under the Consulate, and under the Empire from 1799 to 1807. Went over to Louis XVIII after Napoleon's abdication, which he forced. Brilliant, unscrupulous diplomat, who served and betrayed all sides with equal impartiality.

EUGÈNE D'ARNAUD, Baron de Vitrolle (1774–1854). Confidant of the Comte d'Artois, later a minister under Louis XVIII.

POLICE

ANTOINE BALTHAZAR-JOSEPH D'ANDRÉ DE BELLEVUE, known as Monsieur d'André (1759–1825). Director-General of police under Louis XVIII.

LOUIS-ANTOINE FAUVELET DE BOURRIENNE (1769–1834), secretary to Napoleon. Named Prefect of Paris Police, March 13, 1815. Later a minister.

JOSEPH FOUCHÉ (1759–1820). Duc d'Otrante and Minister of Police under the Empire; betrayed Napoleon after the Hundred Days, and kept his ministry briefly under the Restoration. Died in Trieste.

OTHER CHARACTERS

ELISÉE TORLACHON, known as Father Elisée, the King's surgeon.

DUCHESSE DE FRIOUL (MARIA DE LOS ANGELES), widow of Géraud-Christophe-Michel Duroc, Duc de Frioul, Grand Marshal of the Palace under the Empire, killed near Bautzen in 1813. Married Charles Fabvier in 1832.

AUGUSTE-CHARLES-JOSEPH, Comte de Flahaut de la Billarderie (1785–1870), Napoleon's aide-de-camp, natural son of Talleyrand; had a son, the Duc de Morny, by Queen Hortense.

AUGUSTIN THIERRY (1795–1856), French historian.

MADAME GIUSEPPA VISCONTI, wife of the former ambassador of the Cisalpine Republic to France. Berthier's *inamorata*.

MILITARY UNITS AND THEIR COMMANDERS

THE ROYAL HOUSEHOLD (*La Maison du Roi*)
Supreme nominal commander: Charles, Comte d'Artois.
Effective commander: Marmont, Duc de Raguse.
Grand Almoner: Charles-Maurice de Talleyrand-Périgord, Archbishop and Duke of Rheims.
Grand Master: His Serene Highness Monseigneur le Prince de Condé.
Grand Master of the Wardrobe: M. le Comte de Blacas d'Aulps, who was also Minister Secretary of State of the Royal Household.
Quartermaster-General: Baron Denniée.

KING'S LIFEGUARDS
Chief of staff: Le Comte d'Albignac (*major-général*).
First Company, the so-called Company of Scots, under the command of Captain Duc de Croy d'Havret.
Second Company, under the command of Captain Duc de Grammont; his adjutant, Tony de Reiset.
Third Company, under the command of Captain M. de Noailles, Prince de Poix; his adjutant, *sous-aide-major* M. de Fournel.
Fourth Company, under the command of Captain M. le Duc de Luxembourg.
Fifth Company, under the command of Major Prince de Wagram; adjutant, M. le Baron Lascours (*aide-major*).
Sixth Company, under the command of Captain M. le Duc de Raguse; his adjutant, M. de la Marthoris (*aide-major*).
Company of the Hundred Swiss Corps Guards (known as *les Cent Suisses*), under the command of Captain-Colonel M. le Duc de Mortemart.
Company of the Guards of the King's Door (*Gardes-de-la-Porte*), under the command of Captain-Colonel M. le Comte de Vergennes (*major*).
Light Horse of the King's Guard, under the command of Captain-Lieu-

tenant M. le Comte Charles de Damas; his adjutant, M. le Comte de Chastellux (*aide-major*).

Gendarmes of the King's Guard, under the command of Captain-Lieutenant M. le Comte Étienne de Durfort.

Gray Musketeers—First Company, under the command of Law de Lauriston.

Black Musketeers—Second Company, under the command of Captain-Lieutenant M. le Marquis de La Grange.

THE KING'S MOUNTED GRENADIERS, under the command of Captain-Lieutenant M. le Marquis de la Rochejaquelein.

FRENCH GUARDS, OR ROYAL FOOT GUARD, under the command of M. le Comte de Vioménil, Lieutenant-General, with the title of Colonel.

THE NATIONAL GUARD OF PARIS, under the command of Lieutenant-General Dessoles; his adjutant, M. le Comte Alexandre de Laborde.

SWISS GUARDS, under the command of the Comte d'Artois, Colonel-General.

ROYAL VOLUNTEERS, under the command of Colonel Druault.

FIRST MILITARY DIVISION, under the command of Lieutenant-General M. le Comte Maison, Governor of Paris and commander-in-chief of the troops of the Seine.

Translator's Introduction

HOLY WEEK in the year 1815. March 19th to 25th. Seven days. Easter week, that year, occurring just at the point when winter turns into spring. . . .

But before plunging into the whirl of events which was agitating Paris on that fateful morning of March 19th, with the dust of rumors, hopes and fears which it was stirring up, the reader may find it useful to remind himself of some of the things that were uppermost in the minds of Parisians, of Frenchmen, and of Europeans generally, in those weeks that preceded Napoleon's brief return to power— that final bid for empire which was to last barely one hundred days, and which ended on the battlefield of Waterloo.

It is a time of upheaval, a time of decision. One of those moments of history when irrevocable choices must be made—"a tide in the affairs of men," as Shakespeare says, "which, taken at the flood, leads on to fortune; omitted, all the voyage of their life is bound in shallows and in miseries . . ."

Twenty-six years before this story opens—in 1789—the great French Revolution had, it seemed, swept away forever the old feudal order and the monarchy of the Bourbons which had perpetuated it. The heady slogans of freedom, equality and the rights of man had been carried across the length and breadth of Europe, first by the ragged armies of the Revolution, then by the progressively better disciplined, equipped and seasoned armies of Napoleon.

Yet in that spring of 1815 all the questions, all the passions, all the torments that had filled those twenty-six years were being reawakened. Had nothing been accomplished? Had none of the large problems been solved? Would the uncertainty never end?

Most of the characters who play a role in this story have searing memories of those twenty-six years; many of them played a more or less important role in the events that marked them. And for each of them the history of those years is a different story—depending upon background, upbringing, experience, age and sex. Princes of the blood, members of the clergy, the new aristocracy and official-dom of the Empire, the upper and the petty nobility and commoners are moved to decision during this Holy Week by their relation to those past events.

When the Estates-General convened on May 4, 1789, at the invitation of King Louis XVI, in order to seek a solution to the desperate economic crisis which faced the country, there was no thought in the minds of the men representing the three Estates (the clergy, the nobility and the Third Estate) of initiating any fundamental changes. France had been a monarchy for centuries and it seemed in the natural order of things that it should remain one. But the Estates-General became transformed on June 17th of that same year into a National Assembly, which in turn on July 9th assumed the title of Constituent Assembly. The population of Paris emerged as a leading political power in the country, captured the Bastille on July 14th, brought the King and his family by main force from Versailles to Paris on October 6th. The irreconcilable conflict grew in intensity and violence over the succeeding months, with an in-creasing number of the privileged emigrating en masse to neighboring countries, the King himself with Marie-Antoinette and their children attempting to escape on the night of June 20, 1791, and being over-taken at Varennes and brought back to Paris as prisoners. The crisis deepened and the Revolution was progressively threatened by dis-sension within and by invading armies from abroad. There followed the execution of Louis XVI on January 21, 1793, in the square which is now the Place de la Concorde, the Reign of Terror, the setting up of the Committee of Public Safety, the creation of popular armies which beat off the enemy in successive battles of which Valmy, on September 20, 1792, under Dumouriez and Kellerman, was the first decisive one; until a young general, Napoleon Bonaparte, gradually emerged as a military genius and a national hero, and was acclaimed when he returned from Egypt and landed in Fréjus on October 8, 1799. This whole history of ten years of revolution came to a close when Napoleon, by his *coup d'état* on the night of November 9 to 10, 1799, at Saint-Cloud, called the 18th Brumaire from the Revolutionary calendar, put an end to even a semblance of representative government; but it must be carried in the mind of the reader as having been written in blood and anguish on the consciousness of most of these characters.

What was uppermost in the mind of the average Parisian as he awoke on the morning of Palm Sunday, March 19, 1815, was, undoubtedly, Napoleon's return from Elba. He had left the little island on February 26th, landing at Antibes on March 1st. As he marched north, with an initial force of only one thousand men, the successive armies sent by Louis XVIII to destroy him had gone over to his side to swell his army. Peasants and workers, as well as troops, had greeted him with wild ovations in the villages and towns, in Grenoble and Lyons, and now the news had just reached Paris that Marshal Ney, "the bravest of the brave," who had promised the King that he "would bring the Usurper back in an iron cage," had been swept away by the general enthusiasm, had encouraged his troops to acclaim the Emperor and had flung himself into Napoleon's arms at Auxerre.

Where was the Emperor now? How far was he from Paris? The wildest rumors were afloat. And what was the King going to do? Would he remain at his post and "defend Paris with his life," as he had promised the session of the combined Chambers just last Thursday? If not, what was the alternative? All Paris, all France, was breathlessly awaiting Louis XVIII's decision. It is at this point that the story of *Holy Week* begins.

The average Parisian we are imagining, if he was forty years old or more, had witnessed at close hand more sweeping and violent political upheavals than ordinarily occur in several lifetimes, and now history was again facing him with a large question mark. He had been born under a centuries-old and apparently unshakable monarchy, the monarchy of the Bourbons. The year 1789 had set in motion a whole sequence of events that had led to the overthrow of that monarchy and to the complete reshaping of the entire political, economic and social fabric of the country. The very map of France had been changed: the old natural geographical or demographic lines of demarcation discarded, and the country had been divided into eighty-odd departments, each administered by a prefect appointed by the central government. Four successive constitutions had effected a complete administrative, judicial and financial re-organization whose essential features remain to this day. During the ten revolutionary years (1789–1799) the country had been ruled by a succession of provisional or unstable bodies—the Constituent Assembly (July 9, 1789–September 14, 1791), the Legislative Assembly (October 1, 1791–September 20, 1792), the insurrectional Commune (August 10, 1792-September 20, 1792—which *de facto* assumed the responsibility of government for a month and 10 days), the Convention (September 21, 1792–October 26, 1795, which pro-claimed the First Republic (September 25, 1793), and finally the Directory (October 27, 1795–November 19, 1799). During those years the country had been torn by strife within and by assaults from without. Sixty of the newly created departments had been in revolt against the revolutionary government in Paris between 1793 and 1796, while it was being attacked by the armies of Great Britain, the Dutch Republic, Prussia, Austria, Piedmont and Spain. Peasant uprisings in various parts of the country, led by the royalists, of which the most widespread—that of the *Chouans,* and the subsequent Vendée rebellion—controlled for a time large sec-tions of the west, in Brittany, Poitou and Anjou, magnified the general dislocation and unrest. There had been the Terror and the Counter-Terror. There had been the abolition of all feudal rights and privileges, the confiscation of the large landed estates and of all church property, the disestablishment of the church, pillaging and brigandage. And there had been all the things that were not visible or tangible, that could not be weighed or measured—the family rifts, the divided loyalties, the wrenches of conscience; and on the other side the awakening, the hope, the idealism, the fervor, the fanaticism. . . .

Then Napoleon had appeared, to dominate the scene for fifteen years. This undersized man—the second of eight children in a middle-class Corsican family—whose meteoric career ended when he was only forty-six and who came closer to omnipotence in many respects than any comparable figure in the modern world, moved to power with gigantic strides from the moment fortune turned in his favor on the 18th Brumaire. For fifteen years the Parisian had lived under the spell of that man, of his gigantic ambition, of his administrative and military genius, of his conquests. Endless wars had been fought, which had bled France of her manpower. And since the disastrous Russian campaign of 1812, France had experi-enced nothing but reverses and humiliations. Moscow had been the calamitous turning point; the Russian campaign had cost Napoleon nearly one-third of a million men. The exceptional rigor of that winter—with weather at −30° Fahrenheit—had taken a ghastly toll. Of the 290,000 who had originally entered Russia in June, 1812, only 40,000 returned in December. On one of the last nights of the retreat, 12,000 men, in a division of 15,000, near Kovno, froze to death.

The defeat was the signal for all the Allies whom Napoleon had kept at bay over the years to join forces again and to form the Seventh Coalition, composed of Russia, Prussia, Great Britain and Austria. France by now was weakened and demoralized by endless conscription and taxation to finance the military campaigns. Industrial production and trade had fallen disastrously. There was widespread unemployment. The army—more than 300,000 men—which Napoleon was able to muster to meet the forces of the Coalition in Central Europe was composed almost entirely of youngsters of eighteen to nineteen, and had almost no cavalry; he had kept 250,000 seasoned warriors, including his best cavalry, to fight the hopeless war in Spain, which lasted five years (1808–1813) and cost him 300,000 men before Wellington finally defeated him. The defeat, in October 1813, at Leipzig, which has been called the Battle of the Nations, where Napoleon with 155,000 men faced enemy forces of 300,000—feeling acutely his lack of adequate cavalry, and in the end running out of ammunition—was the first of the series of reverses which led to the capitulation of Paris five months later, on March 30, 1814, and to Napoleon's abdication on April 6th.

It was thus less than a year since the Parisian had seen his country overrun and his city invested by foreign troops for the first time in France's history. With his own eyes he had seen Cossacks, Prussians, Austrians and Englishmen take over the thoroughfares of Paris. He had lived through those chaotic days when the Allied armies had marched on Paris while Napoleon had tried to cut off their rear and their supply lines; he had heard the din of the daylong battle of March 30th at the gates of the city, particularly intense at the Porte de Clichy, where the French lost 9,000 men; had heard the reports of Napoleon's lightning return to Fontainebleau whence he was preparing, with 60,000 men, to launch an attack on the Allies. The end had come when Marshal Marmont, Duc de Raguse, his former aide-de-camp, on whom Napoleon had lavished favors, came to an understanding with General Schwarzenberg to abandon the position which the Emperor had entrusted to him and to lead his army corps out of reach of the possible theatre of operations.

Then there had been the betrayal by Talleyrand, Napoleon's foreign minister, who had persuaded Czar Alexander to side with the other Allied sovereigns and restore the Bourbon Monarchy. On April 28, 1814, Louis Bourbon, Comte de Provence, the brother of Louis XVI who had been beheaded in 1793, was proclaimed King of France. And early in May this Prince—fifty-nine years old, huge of bulk, heavy, gout-ridden, ailing, hardly able to move, whom the royalists during the twenty years of his exile had named Louis le Désiré—returned to France from England to ascend the throne as Louis XVIII.

Now, on Palm Sunday of 1815, everything was again being challenged. The return of the Bourbons had solved no problems, healed no wounds. The terms of the peace treaty—the Treaty of Paris—had been harsh and created intense bitterness throughout the country. The saying that "the Bourbons had learned nothing, and had forgotten nothing" applied aptly to Louis XVIII. Perhaps the most important achievement of the Revolution was its creation among the people of a civic sense—for the first time in history they were made to regard themselves as citizens, with duties and responsibilities as well as rights. They had been given a new stature. They were no longer subjects, they were free agents, masters of their fate, with a voice in affairs of state. The sense of nationality, of belonging to a country—patriotism—had been born. In the consciousness of men the principle of rule by divine right had become a relic of the past, an anachronism, a monstrosity. Yet Louis XVIII unheedingly called himself king *"by the grace of God."* He refused to accept the Constitution prepared by the Senate, and instead "granted" a *Charter,* and dated his "decrees" as of *the nineteenth year of his reign,* as though there had been neither a republic nor an empire since 1795. He referred to the events of the Revolution which had made Frenchmen free and equal as "deplorable aberrations" and in every area of the national life he and his government, seconded by the nobility and the clergy hurrying back from exile or coming out of hiding to recover positions and possessions, dedicated themselves to turning back the clock of history.

Whom to follow? What is loyalty? Where does duty lie? By whom will the country's interests best be served? Louis XVIII? Napoleon? Is there a third choice? These are the questions that assail the characters in *Holy Week*—questions to which each one in his own way discovers that there is no simple answer.

HAAKON CHEVALIER

HOLY WEEK

I

The Morning of Palm Sunday

THE only light in the second lieutenants' barrack room came from the candle on the table, and the broken shadows of the card players were cast on the ceiling and the walls. The dirty windowpanes were just beginning to pale.

The second lieutenants' barrack room . . . Actually neither the second lieutenants nor the full lieutenants had their beds here in the Panthémont Barracks, which only two months before had been occupied by Lifeguards, who had since been sent off to the provinces. Even the Musketeers—at least all the Parisians, like Théodore, for example—who had the rank of lieutenants in the army, had slept at home, while a good many provincials had taken hotel rooms. But since the proclamation of a state of emergency the men had crowded in as best they could, without paying too much attention to rank. In the second lieutenants' barrack room, where some of the men were second lieutenants who had been given the rating of lieutenant colonel, personal relations were such that lieutenants who were only Musketeers hobnobbed with second lieutenants who were actually lieutenant colonels. It was more like a school, where the seniors take the juniors under their wing, than cavalry quarters. The officers had a soft spot for Théodore because he was an exceptionally fine horseman, the kind you see at Franconi's circus. Ten days on the alert . . . Ten days of living virtually on top of one another, the old-timers and the raw recruits, without ceremony. Naturally, someone like Théodore slept near the door, where there was still a bed; the Musketeers upstairs had had to make do with straw pallets on the floor. Ten days . . .

Ten days on the alert, which meant ten days since they had last taken off their boots. In the field, that's one thing. But in the Grenelle Quarters! Things were beginning to get on their nerves. At first they had at least been doing guard duty at the Tuileries, but since the 14th the National Guard had been ordered to take over. Under the uneasy idleness lurked all the panic that the newspapers claimed did not exist.

"Did you read yesterday's *Quotidienne?*"

The Gray Musketeer, in a fit of impatience, turned toward Alfred, a young gendarme of the King's guard with whom he had been talking. Alfred had come and sat down on the edge of the bed where Théodore lay stretched out, almost fully dressed, with his boots on and in his red dolman, which he had merely unfastened. The only garment he had removed was his royal blue surcoat, marked with the big white cross and fleurs-de-lis. The breastplate and backplate of his cuirass lay on the floor next to the bed, leaning against each other like two hands joined. For what prayer?

Alfred had come to chat with his friend, young Moncorps, who was standing next to him and looking respectfully at Théodore, who was only half awake. Alfred and Moncorps had gone to the same boarding school. They had run into each other here in the Grenelle Quarters where they were in two different Musketeer companies but on the same dormitory floor. Moncorps was as slender as he was young, but he was better developed than his schoolmate from the Pension Hixe. Alfred with his blond curly hair, his greatcoat thrown over his shoulders, the stiff collar of the dolman jabbing his chin whenever he bent his head, his spurred boots, looked like a girl in travesty, and the hand that held the tall gold-and-black helmet on his knees was still delicate. Théodore stretched and yawned. Time to get up!

The Musketeers' barrack room was in great disorder, and he turned his eyes toward the center table where the light came from. Crillon, Turenne and Comte Gallifet were playing cards with the Marquis de Ganay, who had been a deputy of the Saône-et-Loire under Buonaparte.* At forty-five, already turning gray, he hardly

---

* Originally Buonaparte, Napoleon changed the name, in 1796, to the more French-sounding "Bonaparte." The monarchists, throughout his rule, continued to refer to him as "Buonaparte." In addition to the fact that he was a com-

looked young enough to be a "second lieutenant." Disheveled, all of them, and smoking. The Chevalier de Massilian, standing behind Ganay, was leaning over him to watch the game, the elongated shadows of his athletic shoulders dancing above the players. Houdetot at the far end of the room, against the wall, was still fast asleep; all you could see of him was his heavy buttocks and his hefty legs in the white buckskin breeches. Imagine his having once been a page to the Emperor! He assumed the airs of a protector toward Théodore because he liked the way the young man could ride bareback, and handle horses considered unmanageable. Besides, a cousin of his who wrote verses had spoken enthusiastically about him.

"What's the time?" Théodore asked the youthful gendarme.

"Five," Moncorps had answered.

In the courtyard the cavalry trumpet was already sounding the assembly, yet it was still almost night. The day was overcast. The rain hadn't stopped since the day before. Figures lifted themselves to a sitting position on three or four beds. The Musketeers, yawning, instinctively reached their hands to their hair, one adjusting his dolman, another slipping on his cuirass. A sword fell, clanking on the floor. Suddenly the light increased, danced, streaked the air: someone had climbed upon the bench near Gallifet and lit the oil lamp hanging under its metal shade. Running feet could be heard out in the corridors; men still pink from scrubbing their necks and ears, their cheeks burning from the razor, came in noisily, threw their towels on the pallets, picked up their uniforms from where they had left them. Altogether it was more like a school dormitory than a barrack room. Except that all these horsemen were at least five foot six, and sturdy of build. And alongside two youngsters like Alfred and Moncorps there were men like de Ganay who were past forty, veterans of Condé's army and survivors from the Empire. They made a great din, in the midst of which someone, at the top of his fresh voice, began singing "Charmante Gabrielle."

The two men whose beds were next to Théodore's were coming in again, continuing a conversation: "It was my cousin, Choiseul-Beaupré, who is in the Lifeguards, who passed the information on to me. Clarke announced it two days ago at the Orsay Barracks, which confirms what we read in *Les Débats*. 'You'll be able to take your boots off tonight, sleep to your heart's content,' and so on." "Mean-

---

moner, and that he had usurped his power, they made the most of the fact that he was "not really French." This accounts for the two spellings used throughout the novel.

while," said the other, a tall dark soldier, pipe in mouth, "we go on having sore feet!"

The Chevalier de Massilian turned to them. "I heard Clarke saying the same thing only yesterday in the King's antechamber. We'll end up by taking our boots off, all right. The news is good, and tonight the Spanish Embassy is dining at the Tuileries, and the whole diplomatic corps is invited for a reception and ball on Tuesday evening . . . the day after tomorrow."

Did these chaps need reassurance or what? wondered Théodore, by now on his feet and straightening his clothes. The young gendarme, who might be about eighteen though he looked only fifteen, gazed at him with admiration. What a horseman he was! To say nothing of his mount, a roan named Trick, on which he seemed to lavish all the affection of which he was capable. But Alfred never would have dared show him his notebooks, the things that he wrote in secrecy, though he did show them to Moncorps. Well, he must get back to his company.

Besides, someone in the doorway was calling Théodore, pointedly lifting a flask to invite him to have a swig before boots-and-saddle. Young Alfred was a bit jealous of Marc-Antoine, Vicomte d'Aubigny, a second lieutenant in the mounted grenadiers of La Rochejaquelein. Théodore liked to ride to Versailles with d'Aubigny, who must also be at least twenty-four. He rode an English thoroughbred, a wonderful chestnut jumper—Trick had a hard time keeping up with it. Whenever the grenadier was around, Alfred no longer existed as far as Théodore was concerned.

Marc-Antoine, already in full dress, with his bearskin on his head, was trailing his saber. His gold baldric crossed his gold-braided red dolman, his skin-tight gray breeches with gold stripes girthed his powerful thighs—thighs that seemed at a loss without a horse under them. He had overheard the cavalryman and the other two, for he said in a rather loud and peremptory voice, with the authoritative air of a man of muscle who has nothing to fear, "Your cousin didn't take off his boots. The Lifeguards camped in the Champs-Élysées last night. And so did Monsieur de Vioménil's volunteers. In this rain! They must look a sight! Though of course Monsieur de Croy d'Havre slept in the Tuileries, and the Prince de Poix in the Faubourg Saint-Honoré!"

Charles de Ganay, who had just swept up the cards and the money, got up from the bench by the table, adjusted his trousers and shrugged his shoulders. There were too many things that could be said: this young man was one of these recent Frenchmen whose ancestors had still been Stuarts under Charles VII! * Having served Buonaparte, how could he possibly understand the devotion of a whole younger generation, of all these lads who had come posthaste from their provinces to the Tuileries to rally round the King, and who, when the Comte d'Artois passed in his carriage, would shout that they wanted to march to Grenoble, to block the Usurper's path? . . . What right had he to grumble about the Prince de Poix? Because he himself had not gone and slept at Vauban House where his father the Baron lived?

The Musketeers clattered down the stairs, stumbling in the dark corners. Outside, the wind blew in gusts. It was pouring. Snowflakes whirled among the raindrops. It was cold and nasty. In the vanishing night the city lay still steeped in silence; but there was a din in the courtyard, horses stamping in the stables, and by the flickering light of torches could be seen rows of gray hindquarters, the back of the Musketeers. Théodore was warmed by the alcohol he had taken, but the chill of early dawn made him wrap his cloak around him. The horsemen separated, helmets going one way, bearskins another, each to join his own troop, filling the courtyard with a muffled rumble. Daylight had not yet filtered down from the roofs into this well. In their cloaks, the upturned collars stirring a little like wings on their shoulders, they looked like great birds of prey as they seized the horses by the bridle. Here and there, in the faint glimmer of daybreak, a spark flew from a horseshoe.

Orders rang forth in the dawn. Drill on a Sunday! Were they out of their minds, or what? How long was this to go on? Yesterday the papers said the royal troops had gone back to Grenoble and Lyons. It was one or the other, but the idea of keeping the companies on the alert in this way! Yesterday a review, and drill today. More than the Royal Household troops were used to. And if, as rumor had it, they were really going to join the army of Melun under M. le Duc de Berry and Marshal Macdonald, their having trampled the mud of the Champ-de-Mars on Sunday at the crack of dawn wasn't going to turn the tide when they came to face the army of turncoats marching up from Lyons.

And what if Macdonald were to follow Ney's example?

"Really," said Marc-Antoine d'Aubigny, pivoting in the saddle of his thoroughbred as the Musketeers were assembling after drill, and addressing Théodore, whose horse had paused near the Light Horse,

* Charles VII, King of France 1429–1461, crowned by Joan of Arc at Reims.

awaiting his turn. "Really, they might have let us have Palm Sunday off! Drill on a Sunday, when we'd just had a review for the Duc de Raguse on Saturday! And what's this they're saying now about another review?"

An artillery caisson, being drawn from a ditch by a two-horse team in a crash of wheels and oaths, separated Grenadiers from Musketeers. All were returning to the Grenelle Quarters in small groups. All but the Black Musketeers, in the lead, who were heading for the Célestins. The rain had not abated. Horses and men were drenched, and the cloaks looked black against the scarlet saddles. What an idea, maneuvers in such weather! Although the bearskin on his head made him look small of build, the strapping Vicomte d'Aubigny, sitting stiffly astride his horse, his neck encased in his turned-up collar, was as tall as Théodore, and the breadth of his shoulders threatened to burst their red garment. Théodore, who had had no time to answer him, urged his horse cityward. And because Marc-Antoine's round, freckled face reminded him of Ney, he thought of the Marshal's treason. . . . What did it all mean?

It was barely two months since the companies had been put up at the Panthémont Barracks, called the Grenelle Quarters because it formed the corner of the rue de Bourgogne and the rue de Grenelle. These cavalry quarters, too small to accommodate four hundred and sixty Gray Musketeers, two hundred Grenadiers, nearly five hundred Guardsmen, to say nothing of their horses, had been fitted out first for the Guards, then for the detachments of the companies that formed the patrol around the Tuileries. Two squadrons of Light Horse, recently transferred from Versailles, were quartered at the École Militaire, and two others at the Grenelle Quarters. The Black Musketeers were at the Capucins. As for the Lifeguards, who numbered more than three thousand, they had the Orsay Barracks. Of course quite a few horsemen were still without mounts. Many even lived outside Paris and had reached Quarters only in the last few days. In the Royal Household, an officers' corps, anyone who wanted to could go home at night. Théodore, for example, who would take Trick back to La Nouvelle Athènes, to Monsieur his father's residence. There was a stall in the small court next to their house where he could stable his mount and have it looked after by the porter of the block, who had been a Cuirassier and had fought at the battle of Eylau. Théodore himself slept at home, unless he happened to sleep somewhere else.

The pretext he had used when asking Captain Lieutenant Lauriston for leave, at least until two o'clock, was that it would enable him to make Trick more presentable, since His Majesty was to pass the red and white companies in review at the Champ-de-Mars that afternoon. They had just learned this from one of Marshal Marmont's dispatch riders after they had begun to disperse, and the Black Musketeers had already left. It was then nine o'clock, they were marking time on the drill field, and the devil alone knew how they were to catch up with most of the companies. . . . But they had orders to stand by, worse luck. And Théodore was anxious to go and say good-by to his father, since it was obvious that, whatever happened, they would be leaving the capital. Probably not this evening though, because of the morning maneuvers on the Grenelle drill ground, to be followed by this royal review. Surely they weren't going to make them run their horses again at night? What did it all mean?

As for the captain lieutenant commanding the company of Gray Musketeers, Monsieur Law de Lauriston—a man of Lieutenant de Ganay's age—his people had been English until the time, not of Charles VII, but of Louis XV, for he was the great-nephew of Law, the financier. He had been born in the colonies and had come to France to enter the army of the Revolution at the height of the Terror. It was he who, on Napoleon's behalf, had brought peace to London and war to Kutuzov, he who had decided the victory of Wagram. Such were Théodore's thoughts as he sat astride his mount near the Grenelle tollhouse, before the Farmers-General Wall* with its straight line of trees. Monsieur de Lauriston examined the Musketeer with an approving eye—a handsome lad who seemed to be one with his horse, enormous eyes and reddish-blond hair; one of the few commoners in his company. All right, but be back at the stroke of two, Lieutenant.

What thoughts, Théodore wondered, could be running through the mind of this soldier of '93, of this son of a ruined family, a man who had breathed the intoxicating odor of Napoleonic gunpowder, and who had even named one of his sons after the tyrant? Now he was commanding the Gray Musketeers who formed the actual escort of Louis le Désiré. Théodore suddenly noticed that the tree, over there

---

* The Paris of 1815 was a city of not much more than 700,000 inhabitants (the population of France was about 25 million). The city was bounded on the west by the Invalides and the Champ-de-Mars, on the east by the Bastille, on the north by the present *grands boulevards* (Capucines, Italiens, Montmartre, Poissonnière, St. Denis) and on the south by the Faubourg Saint-Marceau and the present Boulevard Montparnasse, the whole surrounded by the Farmers-General Wall, which was not a defensive wall but marked the administrative limits for the payment of tolls collected at the gates.

behind the *commandant,* was the one d'Aubigny had pointed out to him one day: that was where General de Lahorie had faced the firing squad in 1812.* He saluted with his saber, turned his horse around, and headed toward the city. Lunch. The morning had utterly exhausted him. The rain was letting up, but the mud was ankle-deep.

What a month of March! The violence of the downpours had drenched the fields and the roads, the sudden bursts of sunshine were not enough to dry the Grenelle drill ground. The cavalry maneuvers on the heavy soil had been an ordeal for the animals. On top of which most of the officers of the Royal Household lacked training, many having been only two or three months in the army. On the general staff, to be sure, there were former companions of the Princes, and even officers of Buonaparte's, like Law de Lauriston and the Marquis de La Grange, who commanded the Black Musketeers, and Berthier, Prince de Wagram, captain of the Lifeguards, and General de Reiset in Grammont's company, who had run away from home at eighteen to join Kléber. And there was that strange anomaly, fellows who were really quite old, like the Marquis de Ganay who had been made second lieutenant, men who had come back from exile during the Consulate, having rallied to Buonaparte after the 18th Brumaire, and who had to mark time under the Restoration. There were colonels, even generals, who, in the Royal Household, had only one or two stripes to their trousers. But most of them, Grenadiers, Musketeers, Gendarmes, Guards, all with their purchased officers' commissions, were younger sons of good family whose chief merit lay in the fact that they had never served the Usurper. And if there were going to be fighting, those who were not mounted might be given a gun: fine infantrymen they would make without ever having drilled!

He had to wait for the stream of nearly three thousand horsemen to flow past.

The day after tomorrow it would be spring. Théodore patted the rump of his handsome gray horse. He was glad that the Musketeers were distinguished, not by their uniforms, both companies being dressed in red, but by the color of their animals, gray or black.

* During the disastrous campaign in Russia, Generals Lahorie and Claude-François de Malet, in Paris, taking advantage of Napoleon's absence and hoping to capitalize on the disaffection and gloom created by the catastrophic news, initiated a plot, which had wide ramifications, to assassinate, or at any rate eliminate, Bonaparte. The plot was unmasked and the two generals were summarily shot.

Though it had been difficult for him this winter to find a mount that met this requirement and was also a real cavalry horse. Of course he had wanted an Anglo-Norman, and he had had the devil's own time unearthing one, even with the help of his uncle at Versailles. He had had to go and look for one in Calvados, where he was offered nags that would not have stood the fatigues of army service. He had wanted a real trotter that would ride well and be ready every day to repeat the exploits of the day before. It had been a stroke of luck, coming upon this half-bred horse. He was a descendant of Godolphin Arabian, one of the finest black-coated eastern stallions Normandy had ever bred, and he took after his ancestor—the same clean-cut lines, without an ounce of fat, and a powerful build. *Cap-de-mores* were said not to be sure-footed, but Trick seemed to belie this. Théodore was devoted to Trick, who was the envy of the whole company. At the moment Trick was beaded with sweat and raindrops.

Théodore looked ahead of him at the slate roofs of Paris and, on his left, at the dazzling new gold of the Invalides. This morning had afforded him a gratifying workout, had refreshed him after another night of sleeping fully clad. He enjoyed riding, exercise. But it was like the sky—even the moments of sunshine did not drive away the clouds. For the past ten days an oppressive atmosphere had hung over life. If they had had at least a clear idea of how things stood. . . . At first the rumors circulating in Quarters had seemed sheer inventions: yet they had turned up all over the town. In the cafés, Guards, Light Horse and Musketeers were subjected more and more often to insulting remarks, and duels were increasing: when you're a soldier you're expected to fight.

Until the summer of 1814, with the Allies camped in Paris, the men often fought with the foreigners. Especially Buonaparte's former officers, whose sabers made mincemeat of young Germans, or Russians —as many as you please. But now that they were among Frenchmen again, it was the young ones who were itching for a fight. In the evening they would drink with the victor, at the Royal, on the rue de Rohan. All that tedious talk! All right, so the Corsican had landed at Antibes, so he had some thousand men, and then what? Just another adventure! There was mockery, though, in people's eyes. To be sure, Paris was royalist. But Théodore could not help noticing how his uniform caused people to nudge one another and speak in whispers as he passed. He remembered the girl who had said to him one night when he was drunk, "Too bad you're with the Reds!" There was a restless coming and going around the Tuileries. And then, too, they had raised the volunteers, recalled the soldiers on leave. Since the 9th they had been kept on the alert.

In January Théodore had taken an almost childish delight in having his uniform made: the red coat, the white and the gray trousers, the cashmere-satinette breeches, the scarlet-lined cape. It was a game, trying on the silver and gold helmet with its crest of gilt metal and tuft of horsehair, passing his finger over the black velvet that lined the chin straps. He would caress the white egret with its corolla of curly black plumes. The Musketeers were particularly proud of the black flowing mane that fell from the tuft. This equipment cost a fortune, and although Théodore had inherited from his mother not only his oriental eyes but also an annuity of ten thousand livres, it was his father who had paid for it all, as well as for the innumerable accessories of the outfit—the French-style saddle, the scarlet cover for the horse. It was especially in the animal's trappings, the cartridge pouch, the saber, the gun, that Théo, as Papa called him, took pleasure. *Quo ruit et lethum:* where he rushes in, so does death—the proud legend, featured on the standard of the Gray Musketeers, appeared on each helmet, on the gold grenade ornament on the front of the crest—and Théodore would repeat the motto to himself, *Quo ruit et lethum,* as though it were the legend of his own destiny. It summed up the feeling he always had—a galloping exhilaration—of rushing toward death. The folly he had committed in becoming a King's Musketeer had been something more than the unbridled frivolity in which he often found distraction from his thoughts.

It had, to be sure, created a certain rift between himself and those of his friends who were liberals—or worse. Like Robert. Like Horace. And the officers of the other corps had little liking for the Royal Household: that had been quite evident the week before, at the Babylone Barracks, on the occasion of the Duc de Berry's visit. The reception had been rather cool. His Royal Highness, a coarse, heavy little man subject to fits of temper, had been surrounded by Musketeers. Théodore had heard the mutterings as he passed with the escort. After all, it was understandable: with all the men who had been discharged on the pretext of economy, they could hardly be blamed for wondering if it was not with an eye to replacing them some day that commissions were being given to a bunch of greenhorns fresh out of school, regular young ladies like Alfred, children who had seen neither Austerlitz nor Beresina, just because their families, their loyalty to the dynasty, could be counted on—and because those families of theirs paid! With each man furnishing his own equipment, the King's Household had cost His Majesty little. The horsemen received eight hundred francs pay, but had to be able to show that their families were allowing them another six hundred francs a year.

The barracks had been emptied, everyone was being sent to Melun. Was it their turn now? Well, Melun or some other place. *Quo ruit . . .* what did Théodore care? He had wanted to get a different slant on things, to forget. The best way to do that was through physical exercise. So long as he had a horse . . . On horseback a man was no longer quite the same, both more alone and no longer so alone: his slightest change of mood sent a quiver through the other, the animal. Ah, if only there were this soul-communion between woman and the man who held her in his arms! The horseback rides, the discipline of the army, even the fact that his time was no longer his own—Théodore accepted all this so long as he could come back at the end of the day, utterly spent, and sleep. He no longer wanted to think of that past life, not even of the day before. Of the failure of his dreams. He was a soldier. He had never been anything but a soldier taking the wrong road. Robert Dieudonné had been right, long ago, in urging him to enlist—if only he had listened to him! A soldier is a man who goes to cafés at night, with other soldiers. Who sings and shouts. Who quarrels and chases girls.

A sudden gap in the massed line of Musketeers allowed him to spur his horse forward into an easy trot. Ahead of him the surging mass of gray rumps with their red horsemen had brought Théodore to the edge of the Faubourg, near the Invalides, where they were coming to a halt as the troops ahead entered Quarters, each in turn. In the rue de Bourgogne, Théodore outdistanced his comrades returning to their billets, and before him the road lay empty, free. He reined Trick in to a walk.

All right, these distractions . . . the fun of wearing a fine uniform, this strange army in which colonels had the rank of lieutenants, this scrambling of castes, the novelty—all were things that amused him. Or at least they had, before the beginning of this month of March.

Even the hostility of people, the glances of passers-by, the gibes that fell at his horse's hoofs, had lent a kind of spice to his life. For that matter, among the half-pay officers* and the republican small fry, as well as in a Paris prevailingly royalist, Théodore experienced the

---

* On the pretext of economy, 22,000 officers were retired or put on the reserve list at half-pay under the Restoration of Louis XVIII, and thus reduced to straitened circumstances and even, many of them, to great hardship.

secret thrill of having ideas different from those of other people, of being neither what his uniform signified nor its opposite. Yes, on Marc-Antoine's advice, having rejected Robert's, he had joined the Gray Musketeers; he was magnificently dressed, his breeches became him, he wore the helmet and the cloak, the saber, to perfection. Nothing distinguished him from a Clermont-Tonnerre, or from a Crillon; he had much more of an air than the Comte de Houdetot, the ex-page, who might have been taken for a peasant, or even than the Duc de Berry, with his head sunk between his shoulders. Who would imagine him a commoner so long as he had the five feet six inches needed to be a Musketeer, and this dazzling uniform with all its facings and lappets?

Suddenly, straight ahead, a little to the right, against the dark gray background of the sky above the houses, he caught sight of a rainbow that plunged into the city and seemed to touch the ground over there, not far from the Seine, perhaps at the Carrousel, in that strange district of ill-repute which cluttered about the Court. What bad taste! he thought to himself unexpectedly. And he sneered. Everyone knew that too bright colors were displeasing in painting. It was months since he had visited any exhibitions, since he had been in an atelier—since he had entered the Gallery of the Louvre, there, under the rainbow's arc. Even though he went to the Tuileries every day. But his place there was out in the courtyard with the horses, with those empty-headed youths dressed in scarlet and bedecked with embroidery. Oh yes! He had just remembered that today was the closing day of the 1814 Salon: right over there, behind Saint-Germain-l'Auxerrois. To-night or tomorrow the canvases would be taken down.

Shutters slammed in a gust of wind. Everything suddenly grew dark again. Trick came out on the quay and approached the Louis XVI Bridge.

A tall youth, Théodore, with slightly drooping shoulders and a long face, a discreet fringe of a beard circling his chin from ear to ear, his mustache blonder than his hair which shaded into red, immense eyes, and startlingly feminine lashes—a blend of violence and gentleness. An Anglomaniac, as many of his generation were, by way of showing their opposition to the Empire. They showed it in the pipes they smoked, in the clothes they wore, and by practicing English boxing with grooms and street porters. Théodore was a regular dandy, although he had no English blood on his mother's side as Horace had. Horace, companion of his first outings on horseback, was the son of the old riding master to whom he undoubtedly owed his understanding of the beauty of a horse. And heaven alone knew how many of the dreams that he had nursed in Rouen, behind the windows of the rue de l'Avalasse, had been bequeathed to him by his poor mother. She had never taken to Paris, where she had died in the first days of the century, shortly after the family had settled there. A regular dandy, and for the moment his dandyism found its outlet wholly in horse-back riding. But perhaps it was his Uncle Carruel de Saint-Martin, his mother's brother, even more than Horace's father, who had in-stilled this passion in him. It was through him, with his fine house at Versailles, that Théodore had had access to the stables of the royal château when he was still a little boy. The uncle understood his nephew. They had the same build, the same aristocratic dreams, though Carruel was hardly more than a tradesman who had been appointed collector of taxes.

Was this why Théodore gave the impression that he had been raised in the home of some prince, among equerries and horsemen? And he had been trained in foot boxing as well as in English boxing, was skilled with saber and sword. Yet he had gone only to the imperial *lycée;* had grown up amid the disorder, grime, and stench of urine of the rue Saint-Jacques; and had then spent long years as a boarder at a school on the rue de Babylone to which he had been sent by a father who must have made illicit deals in national property. His holidays, though, had been spent at Mortain, in Normandy, with his uncle— his Uncle Siméon, the regicide.

Crossing the Place Louis-XV, urging his horse forward among the pedestrians (you, there! watch where you're going!), Théodore was thinking that this Sunday morning drill lent color to the rumors. Were they really going to be dispatched to Melun? Anyway, there could no longer be any doubt that Buonaparte was advancing through France with heaven knew how many men. The thousand that had been men-tioned in the first days had proliferated, that was sure: in his stride, the Enemy of the Human Race (as Théodore's comrades called him) was gathering in the royal troops, which were going over to his side bag and baggage.

First there had been the alarm caused by the defection of regiments stationed in the departments of the Nord and the Aisne. Paris had shuddered on learning that Drouet d'Erlon, Lefebvre-Desnouettes, and the Lallemand brothers had begun to march on the capital.* The plot had failed, and the Gendarmes had arrested the two Lallemand

* Immediately upon receiving news of the Emperor's escape from Elba, these four generals, in command of the garrisons of the two northern departments of the Nord and the Aisne, made an abortive attempt, at La Fère, to rally their troops to Napoleon.

brothers at La Ferté-Milon: their treason was obvious. And it was reassuring that everywhere troops were being raised for the Duc de Berry and were being sent south to defend Melun, while the Comte d'Artois, his father, was setting out to meet That Man. But then the news of Ney's defection, still unconfirmed, had reached Paris on the 17th; it had become general knowledge only yesterday.

It was just two days after the joint session of the Chambers over which Louis XVIII had gone to preside, escorted by his Household, acclaimed on the way by cries of *Vive le Roi! À la vie, à la mort!* And Ney, Prince de la Moskowa, had still been thought a guarantee that the Ogre would be stopped at Lyons. Even though he had been one of Napoleon's men. The guard posts at the Louvre had been doubled. The National Guard had replaced the Switzers, who had been sent to Melun. Why had Ney's name struck people more than all the rest? The city had been stunned. The Court, too, it appeared. But not immediately: the news had been kept from the King for a whole day. Hardly believable. Why was the Marshal regarded as the monarchy's chief prop? One of Napoleon's men. Well, what of the Marquis de La Grange then, or Law de Lauriston? And the new Minister of War, Clarke, the Duc de Feltre, another creature of Buonaparte's—he who, on the 17th, had been promising the Lifeguards they would get a chance to take off their boots! On the 17th, when he must have heard of Ney's defection from Baron Clouet who had just arrived from Lyons.

And yet . . . Ney was a traitor. The Ogre had been in Auxerre that night. With or without boots. A traitor like Drouet d'Erlon, the Lallemand brothers. Hadn't they all been together in Spain? Horsemen, for Théodore, meant people like himself. He had often seen General Lefebvre-Desnouettes coming home on horseback to his house on the rue de la Victoire, just two steps from where he lived himself. He, too, rode an Arab horse.

Treason? But when had Ney actually committed treason—yesterday or last year? There was such confusion in all things: a hero of yesterday was a traitor today. And those who changed camps—were they really traitors? Last year, it could have been because they were responsive to the people's will, to the thirst for peace, the weariness. . . . Was a man like Ney now choosing war? Was he different from all those who sneered when the red companies passed, from those former soldiers who fought duels over a word spoken amiss at Frascati's, from many a citizen who read *Le Nain Jaune*? There couldn't be all those traitors. At what rank did treason begin? The soldiers covered with medals, the crippled and the disabled to be seen every-where in their tattered remnants of uniforms, men who had taken cities by storm, conquered Europe at the point of the bayonet—were these traitors? Through the railings over there, on the Terrasse des Feuillants as he followed the rue de Rivoli, Théodore could see people in groups from which one now and again would suddenly break away excitedly. What were they talking about? Still of Marshal Ney?

Théodore remembered a story he had been told. It was while the Emperor was still in Russia, and there had been that extraordinary affair of the conspiracy of Generals Malet and Lahorie in Paris. People swore that the conspirators were in league with the Grande Armée. In that army there had been no lack of republicans who had followed Napoleon out of a kind of military loyalty, for whom marching beneath the Imperial standards had come to mean not so much serving one man's ambition as helping to spread the revolutionary ideas to every horizon. Yet if Malet had succeeded, were they ready for sub-version? It was said that one Marshal, there in the snowbound bivouacs near Moscow, had reached an understanding with the con-spirators and was waiting only for a sign to seize the Corsican. Ney, perhaps. It had been said at the time that it was Ney. But it had been a republican conspiracy. Yet Lahorie was a monarchist, wasn't he? Who was right? Was it better to do it somewhere in Russia than at the gates of Paris, like Marmont, Duc de Raguse, two years later? Or at La Fère, like the Lallemand brothers? And today Marmont was in command of the Royal Household; Lefebvre-Desnouettes was a fugi-tive, the Lallemands prisoners. What did all these people want? The Republic—the Terror, in short! Robespierre. . . .

Théodore had been two, three years old at the time of the Jacobins. What did he know about it except what he had always been told? His father had brought him up on his own ideas, those of a cautious royal-ist letting the storm blow over. There was of course Uncle Siméon, the regicide. But as far back as Théodore could remember, the old man never discussed politics except in terms of conciliation. Siméon had not been consulted about putting his nephew into the Reds. The equip-ment and allowance of a Musketeer had not seemed too expensive to a father whose son's heart always seemed to him to be set on unimportant matters. He preferred to see his fine lad parade in the Royal Household. And perhaps, too, it was a way of passing the sponge over all those years which had had to be lived through. Especially since at the time Théodore had joined the Musketeers, everything had seemed calm and settled . . . but Lyons in Buonaparte's hands! On the Grenelle drill ground Marc-Antoine had managed to bring his horse alongside Trick, and he had whispered to his friend that Sens—yes, Sens—had fallen without resistance. . . . There was no longer a shadow of a regiment between the Adventurer and Paris, no longer a shadow, and he was marching on Fontainebleau.

And just a while ago, speaking to Captain Lieutenant de Lauriston, Théodore had recognized the tree in front of which Lahorie had faced the firing squad. Was Lahorie a traitor? From Law de Lauriston's point of view? Then? And now? When you considered that young Buonaparte and Jacques Law de Lauriston must have been as close friends at the École Militaire as Moncorps and the young Vicomte Alfred de Vigny, who had chattered by his bed this morning. Vigny . . . Was the captain lieutenant thus betraying his youth?

The troops were ordered to stand by, to appear at the Grenelle Quarters at two o'clock. Perhaps the review on the Champ-de-Mars was just a sham and was really an assembly for imminent departure. Because if the King wanted to review them, why hadn't he done so this morning? And those troops encamped on the Champs-Élysées, the National Guard massed at the Tuileries . . . Anyway, Théodore was going back to the rue des Martyrs to have the porter give Trick a rubdown. The important thing was that the horse should be clean, review or no review. Surely they weren't going to make animals which had just come from maneuvering on rain-soaked ground undertake a night march?

No, they must be exaggerating: Lyons, perhaps. But Sens! It's quite a distance from Lyons to Sens. By telegraph it's one thing, for by signals news travels fast. But Infantry! *Infantry:* to Théodore the very word was tinged with contempt. He pressed his knees against Trick and brought the animal to a trot as he turned into the rue du Dauphin. Talking of Fontainebleau already! Scaremongers.

How far was it from Lyons to Paris? More than a hundred leagues* on horseback: at least six days' journey on one animal, and without the relays that enabled the mail coach to do it in three days and two nights! Even for cavalry, a march wasn't a race. As for the footsloggers —they were in Lyons two days ago. If they had reached even Mâcon, they were doing jolly well.

Yet how strange all this seemed. Here he was, an officer of His Majesty Louis XVIII, riding up the rue Neuve-Saint-Roch, and he was trying to reckon how long it would take the Usurper to reach Paris, to reach the Tuileries to which the King would presently return

* The old French *lieue* was 2.76 miles.

after reviewing the troops. Assuming that Buonaparte appeared at the gates, who could be relied on? There was the Royal Household, five thousand officers without men, and not all of them mounted. As for foot soldiers—the Swiss Guards and the Gardes-de-la-Porte—how many of them were there? Not four hundred in all. And from that number must be subtracted the Switzers sent to Melun. The Paris regiments . . . The Musketeers were not alone in their doubts about them: nothing could be more unreliable than that pack, who were still wearing the discarded uniforms of the Empire, whose officers hated the Royal Household and most of whose men had ranged over Europe under the tricolor. Was it possible, in an emergency, to raise any other forces in Paris? Of course there were the Law School students who cried *Vive le Roi!* under the trees in front of the colonnade of the Champs-Élysées. They had been almost alone in responding to the call for a corps of royal volunteers issued ten days ago. Théodore had seen the registers filled with signatures in the Tuileries antechambers. But at Vincennes, where the volunteers were supposed to report, that old fossil Vioménil was wasting away waiting for them. As for the *spontaneous* demonstrations of loyalty in the Paris streets —a Paris so obviously royalist—they were the outbursts of small fanatical groups in empty streets while the citizens hid behind their shutters.

The other day—when was it?—Tuesday, at the Palais Royal, in the garden, Théodore had seen one of these bands passing by, yelling, knocking over chairs, while girls ran for cover in the wooden arcades, and all the people just stood there, watching in silent disapproval. That was Tuesday, and today was Sunday. And just yesterday, Saturday, in the Tuileries itself, in response to cries of *Vive le Roi!* a young man in a long frock coat had taken it into his head to shout *Vive l'Empereur!* They had fixed him, right enough, when the women got going with their umbrellas. He wasn't a pretty sight afterward—a youth of Théodore's age or a little older, lying on the gravel path, his clothes torn, mouth slashed, eye . . . Théodore didn't like to think about that eye. The body had had to be removed before the arrival of the guard, fetched from the Pont-Tournant post. It was that brute Houdetot, the second lieutenant, who had taken charge and hailed a passing soldier, whom he had then recognized as the youth who was such a fine horseman and who slept in his barrack room. "Here, Musketeer, I'll take his arms, you take his feet . . ." You have no idea how heavy a young corpse can be.

To what pound had they carried him, to rot quietly? A man like himself, one who had probably felt the first promptings of the heart at the same time as Théodore, who perhaps had gone out with girls for the first time in this very district. The horseman was approaching that part of the city where he had spent his boyhood, and it made him sentimental.

Why did I get into this? Théodore suddenly wondered. Why, in heaven's name, why? Why did I listen to Marc-Antoine? This wasn't what I was cut out for. Yes, I had begun to have misgivings about myself, but after all! His father, of course, had pushed him into it. To him it had been a game, and there had been the tailor, the armorer, his physique, his love of horses. . . . Now he was caught: what were the Bourbons to him? He should have been a soldier in 1810. Then there was fighting to be done; that had been the great period, the time of victories. His friend Robert Dieudonné had tried to persuade him to join the Guides. Théodore would have none of it. He loathed war. To him, fighting in the name of what? His country was here, not in Austria or Russia. His father had accustomed him to regard the Emperor as a republican; and as for the Republic . . . Dieudonné was a republican. Because of his family. Words, words. It was Paris he was attached to, Paris which held everything he was fond of. For people like him, everything that mattered happened in Paris.

Something plucked at his heart: he had just thought again of those years of his youth, of that wasted enthusiasm, of his blighted hopes. Of what he had abandoned, having ceased to believe in himself. Perhaps that was why he had flung himself into this futility—love of clothes, craze for horses, his own *Quo ruit et lethum*. And then he crossed the rue d'Argenteuil: it was at the other end of the street that the thing had happened.

He had found it quite natural, in 1811, when his father had talked of paying a substitute to serve for him. Théodore had drawn an unlucky number in the conscription lottery. Having no desire to serve, he had said yes. A rather abstract "yes." How could it be arranged? Where would his father find someone? Then one day, there they were together in that small café on the rue d'Argenteuil, two steps from the Pavillon de Marsan: how had it all been arranged? The café owner, a big one-eyed rascal with a pipe and a green apron, had produced a man who was willing. A chap, twenty-five years old, who had served in the army before, a conscript of 1806, ready to go back for the sum that he was asking. He had a way of standing similar to that of the model who posed in the nude at Guérin's, an attitude implying acceptance of whatever happened, including the art students' pranks, so long as he was given enough for a square meal when he left. It was odd, a man selling himself like that. The café-keeper did all the talking, I shouldn't have been surprised if he had said "Feel him!" as though it were a matter of concern to us that the soldier we were giving the Emperor should be good, solid stuff. He was wretched-looking, in dirty clothes which had kept all the body's creases. . . .

What if they really had reached Sens after all? Well, after all, there *was* the army of Paris commanded by Marshal Macdonald and the Duc de Berry! After all. . . .

When I think of it—the corpse we picked up looked a little like the other chap, the substitute. A little smaller perhaps. The details of the arrangement: what was to be paid, and to whom, if he should happen to die. There was that clause in the contract, and I tried to tell Father . . . but he just gave me a shove: never mind, it's all arranged now. He had put up one of our properties in Mortain as security. But when a year later they found out that the man was really dead—dead like the one at the Tuileries—even though it was from sickness somewhere in a hospital in the annexed regions—in the Ruhr, I believe—and not from a shell, a bullet, a fall from a horse . . . Anyway, I hadn't wanted to be one of Napoleon's soldiers. Whatever came over me to make me become one of Louis XVIII's Musketeers? And now where are they going to send us? To the heights of Melun, they say, to block Buonaparte's way. You didn't want to wage war abroad— All right, you'll wage it at home. Why should we put up a better resistance than the rest have, at Grenoble, Lyons, Sens? What if the Duc de Berry's troops go over to the Usurper! There we shall be, three or four thousand officers including mere children, Light Horse, Grenadiers, Guards, and we, Blacks and Grays, our hands on our muskets, and then what? Assuming that we manage to hold the heights of Melun, what is going to prevent them from by-passing us, to right or left? With the connivance of the population. I'll make a corpse like any other. Who, in the end, had actually collected the money when the substitute died at Wesel? Probably the café-keeper. And General Lahorie, under that tree there, what did he look like with a dozen bullets in his hide? Law de Lauriston a while ago—he wasn't thinking about that. I was watching him. That had happened right there. Right there.

As he was crossing the rue Neuve-des-Petits-Champs, Théodore had a vague impulse to turn left: he was two steps from the rue d'Antin. Why not drop in, in passing, and say good-by to Joseph?

But Trick, on his own, had already headed down the rue de Gaillon, as one who knows the way to his feed. Oh well! Besides, if he had seen Joseph he would have had to stop at young Jamar's, on the rue Louis-le-Grand, as well. There would have been no end to it!

Oddly enough, the weather had suddenly turned fine, despite some black thunderclouds to the west which were bearing down on Paris. Before the Gaillon Fountain a water carrier had stopped, mopping his brow as though it were midsummer. A leather hat, a dirty apron, and the yoke with the two full buckets set down in front of him. With expressionless eyes, he watched the Musketeer pass. A team of four horses, which had just emerged from a mansion on the rue Neuve-Saint-Augustin, bore down on him as it approached the crossing and forced him to step back. It was a berlin with all sorts of baggage tied onto its roof. The water carrier chortled softly on seeing them turn west, as if heading into the storm that was threatening. "Not that way!" he shouted. "Coblenz is in the opposite direction!"

Number 8, rue de la Michodière was a building, dating from the previous century, which had been divided into apartments; until 1813, Monsieur Géricault had occupied the beautiful upper-story apartment at the back of the courtyard, with the two wings. Although it was spacious, this home in which his wife Louise had died in 1801 had been to Théodore's father a kind of bachelor's *pied-à-terre*. He had in fact lived there alone most of the time while his son was at boarding school. But since Théo, with his mania for painting, had come home, two rooms had had to be given over to him. Even so, when he had taken it into his head to make those big contraptions of his, the youngster had had to rent a back shop on the Boulevard Montmartre—just at the time Malet and Lahorie had been stood before a firing squad against the Grenelle wall. Speaking of which, Lahorie had been a Musketeer when he was Théodore's age. Anyhow, all the space on the rue de la Michodière was given over to formal rooms.

Passing the house again, the rider brought Trick to a halt and peered into the courtyard through the high carriageway. From his horse he could see only the window ledges of the yellow room. Who lived there now? What did the yellow room look like with its high ceiling, its windows with their inside shutters? When the Géricaults had lived there, all the woodwork had been white, and the heavy furniture had been of mahogany and fruit woods. Long and deep, it extended from wing to wing and had matching windows overlooking the courtyard on one side and the gardens on the other. Théo could visualize the trees which, in this season, stretched black hooked fingers against the white sky in the gardens which extended northward to the boulevard. In the south wing the apartment was divided into two stories, and Théo's room, reached by an inner staircase, looked out from the side of the house onto the stables of No. 4. These extended behind No. 6 on the street right up to the Géricault house. From here the young man could see the stalls, the men who gathered up the dung, could watch the animals which would sometimes rear as they were brought out into the courtyard. The view was partly cut off by No. 6, which had belonged to the Longuevilles.

Perhaps the fact that his son had to go elsewhere to paint had affected Monsieur Georges Géricault. It was at the time when the disasters in Russia weighed heavily on public opinion, not long after the execution of Malet and Lahorie. Théo had just come in from a ride, booted, sweating, having taken just enough time to wash his hands and comb his wild curls. The youngster had never been very careful of the carpets. "Mademoiselle Mélanie, take off the child's boots! Sit down here, make yourself comfortable. . . ."

Mlle. Mélanie was the housekeeper and had probably saved her master from the troubles of a second marriage. She was on the shady side of forty in 1813; she had religion enough for all in a household where no one else had any, and imposed respect not only by the seriousness of her demeanor but by her dress, with its large goffered collar and white cuffs, and her little lace bonnet and bandeaux.

Now, as the scene came back to his mind, Théodore could not resist spurring Trick into the courtyard. Here memory became sharper and more vivid. Less than two years had passed, but it seemed like another life. The fine proportions of the windows . . .

He thought back over that conversation. It is difficult to know your own father. How could Théo have realized that if the old man always made him sit there in that particular armchair it was because it enabled him to see simultaneously both the handsome boy he was so proud of having begotten and Boilly's portrait of Louise, his late wife, with the large dreamy eyes she had passed on to her son? She had died in 1801, in the adjoining room. The father would so have liked to know more about his son than the boy was inclined to confide to him. When a young man is as handsome as that, he has adventures: but on this score Théo was the soul of discretion.

That day's conversation—it had in fact been little more than a monologue, for the father had done almost all the talking. Smaller than his son, and bald, with a strand of hair brushed forward, eyes like a bird's, almost without eyebrows, a chin sunk in a high white cravat, a long nose which gave him a Spanish look (the only thing Théodore had inherited from him), dressed invariably in his puce coat: "In periods of insecurity—you understand, my son, what that means, periods of insecurity?—in periods of insecurity, money goes into hiding. The logical consequence of this is that those who have an urgent need to sell—you follow me? an urgent need—do not find liquid assets, liquid assets. So what they have to offer remains on their hands. But the urgent need persists—"

Théo interrupted him: "Becomes greater, even."

"Becomes greater. Are you making fun of me? Yes, becomes greater. What people have already offered in vain they now offer at a lower price. Nobody wants it. They go even lower. And that is where the difference lies between those who understand the modern world and those who don't. . . . The difference."

Théodore, the Théodore of 1815, began to laugh softly, remembering his father's conversation. He swung Trick around and continued on his way along the rue de la Michodière toward the boulevards. It was raining again, despite the rainbow. There was no longer anything you could trust.

At the corner of the street and the boulevard were the Chinese Baths, and that café opposite where the Conspiracy of Equals* used to meet, as old Géricault—never without a shudder—would remind his son. Everything on this Palm Sunday seemed to turn Théodore's thoughts to conspiracies, to military subversions. Babeuf's men used to gather here to listen to songs. And then one day on that same Grenelle drill ground where I was just now . . . What turn would the world have taken if the Equals had succeeded? People like Robert Dieudonné's father. Bonaparte would not have become Napoleon if the troops that had revolted at Grenelle . . . There would have been no glory, no casualties. How good it would have been to take a bath here now! But the place was closed on Sunday. Everything was closed on Sunday. Théodore swore at religion.

His mind reverted to that earlier conversation of two years before.

* François Émile Babeuf (1760–1797), French political agitator, was the first to propound socialism as a practical policy and the father of movements which played a conspicuous part in the revolutions of 1848 and 1871. After the fall of Robespierre in Thermidor (July 24, 1794), he agitated for the restoration of the constitution of 1793. He gathered around him a small circle of immediate followers known as the *Société des Égaux*. Accused of plotting to overthrow the Directory, he was arrested with many of his associates, including A. Darthé. Both were condemned to death and executed.

"The very ones who hide their money," his father had gone on, "who have created the scarcity of liquid assets that brought about the lowering of selling prices, grow stubborn and miss their chance, you see, whereas others who have a more accurate sense of the mechanism of the market find prices so ridiculously low that they cannot help jumping at the opportunity, and buy. For a mere nothing—or a mouthful of bread. Of course they count on some future stabilization of events, on a fresh rise in prices, and this occurs as money gradually comes out of its hiding places, because it can no longer be kept out of circulation."

Between the tall leafless trees on the Boulevard des Italiens, troops marching in opposite directions were holding up traffic: those horsemen, Dragoons, were probably coming down from the Faubourg Poissonnière barracks and heading for the Champs-Élysées. And in the other direction, gloomy-looking infantry returning to the barracks of the Faubourg du Temple. Marching with rhythmic tread. The scattered crowd cheered the fleurs-de-lis: *Vive le Roi!* The soldiers made no response. The officers on horseback, swords drawn, rode alongside the men, turning around to see if they were keeping in the ranks. There was another halt by the gardens that extended from the mansions on the rue Neuve-Saint-Augustin to the boulevard on his right, past the Chinese Baths.

Over there, beyond this whole district of mansions and gardens, were fields, the Butte Montmartre with its mills, like the background of a Flemish landscape—a scene by Breughel in the rain. Enough, enough of thinking about painting!

In short, what old Géricault had been saying was that since December, since the news of the disaster in Russia had reached France, money had gone into hiding. They had seen on the maps where the French were, and then had learned that there was fighting in April at Lützen*; in October at Leipzig; Bessières killed, then Duroc. It was difficult to follow the shifting movements of the troops that year. It was not as in the days of Austerlitz. What they were witnessing was a post-mortem liquidation. Whether based on rumors or facts, the psychological effect was the same.

"Personally," his father had said, "I attach no importance to it. You understand, you may think what you please about the Emperor,

---

* Lützen, a small town in Saxony, Germany, where Napoleon won a victory over the Russians and Prussians, May 2, 1813. In this battle Bessières was killed. Leipzig, where the "Battle of the Nations" was fought October 15–18, 1813, in which Napoleon was defeated. This was his last great battle before his abdication in April 1814. Duroc was killed near Bautzen in May 1813.

but the interests at stake are too great. You can imagine if the lands had to be distributed, the markets overhauled. That's why Napoleon can't, *can't* be defeated."

Well and good, but the heirs were being very demanding, out of all proportion to the situation, or at least to the prevailing rumors, the market panics. Monsieur Géricault had at the outset offered them a small price which he knew they would refuse. In that way he was taking no risks: if there was a spectacular victory, he would not be obliged to buy. "But when the Battle of Leipzig was lost, and the Saxons deserted us, twenty thousand of our soldiers taken prisoner, Poniatowski drowned, Macdonald falling back on the Rhine, I lowered my own offer. Every day the talk was resumed in the same way. The news from Holland frightened them to death. I closed the deal today at fifty per cent of my original offer."

He had been treating himself to the sly pleasure of not saying what the deal was. It was a piece of property in a district he believed had a future. On the lower slopes of Montmartre; you could almost say in town, behind the Lorette district. "Just a little beyond the Ruggieri garden—you know the marionette theatre there? Yes . . . well, we have a party wall. And I'm giving up the house on the rue de la Michodière."

"For an empty site?" asked Théo.

"Not entirely empty. It's a garden-city with small houses. And ateliers. You know La Nouvelle-Athènes?"

He had let the word out: the ateliers explained the deal. No more need to put up in a back shop on the boulevard. His son could do his work and still remain close to his old father. As a matter of fact, they hadn't been able to move in right away. Because military defeats *do* have disadvantages. On the 1st of January, 1814, the Allies crossed the Rhine and invaded France. It became impossible to find workers to do the repairs. The army was swallowing them all. His father had bought too early after all. So that at the end of summer, when Théo had painted his "Wounded Cuirassier," while his father's house was being got ready, the young painter still had no atelier on the rue des Martyrs and was camping in the attic.

Théodore was growing impatient, Trick was pawing the ground as the soldiers kept marching past. Neither was given to such long, slow-paced reveries as the rider had been driven to this morning. For him there were only two gaits, the walk or, abruptly, even in Paris, a wild gallop. On the boulevard he would have had to keep pace with the troops. He turned in front of Frascati's and plunged into the rue Grange-Batelière, spurring his horse to a gallop, like a tornado, so that people drew back terrified, the market women clutching their little carts as though their vegetables and flowers might be knocked over by the mere passage of the horse. He reached the rue du Faubourg-Montmartre, entered it without slowing down. He did not want to think about painting. He was fleeing from his shame. Galloping made him forget his canvas, his failure. As he passed in front of Saint-Jean, people cried "Madman!" He paid no attention, negotiated the crossing of the rue Coquenard and the rue Saint-Lazare, passed the La Grange mansion, rode the length of the "Coq Hardi" at full speed, climbing the steep street between the garden fences and the street stalls and, turning brusquely, bent over his mount's neck to avoid bumping his helmet as he passed under the carriageway amid a swarm of urchins who ran after him.

How had Trick happened to knock over the young woman in the entrance? Théodore had seen nothing. He had heard the cry, and the dark green mantle, the black velvet hat with its plumes, had slid to his left and struck the ground like a wounded bird.

The rider leaped down, knelt on the grassy paving and picked up the long, supple young body in his strong arms. How light she was— almost without weight! The unknown woman's eyes were shut, she moaned, turned her head; her blond hair slipped down over one shoulder. Hearing the cry, Baptiste and his wife had come out of the lodge, and the urchins were crowding round uttering thrill cries.

"Who is she?" Théodore asked, and the porter said, "A lady who lives at the Rond-Point."

The Musketeer tossed the reins to Baptiste, and headed in the direction of the courtyard with his soft burden. "Take care of Trick," he called back. But the slender neck turned in the goffered linen collar, and the woman, who had let her cheek rest against Théodore's chest, sighed, opened her eyes, did not recognize the person who was carrying her, became terrified, stiffened and began to struggle, striking her captor with a furious little fist.

"Monsieur, monsieur! I don't know you, put me down!"

Slowly, somewhat regretfully, Théodore obeyed. How charming she was! So slender, an adorable mouth, such a fresh complexion, the blondness of a child—there was nothing to fill her voluminous velvet mantle. It almost felt as though he were holding her naked in his arms. He realized that he must have blushed deeply. But once she was back on her feet, she was taken with a kind of dizziness and clutched his arm.

"Allow me, madame, to offer you my arm. You live next door to Major Brack?" The name seemed to calm the young woman for she leaned on Théodore's arm. But she suddenly drew back as though she had only then noticed how he was dressed.

"That uniform!" she exclaimed.

"Does my coat displease you, madame?" asked Théodore.

"I have my reasons, monsieur, for not liking it," she replied, and they walked in silence across the courtyard which was surrounded by a number of heterogeneous buildings, among which the small stable and the kitchen quarters of the Géricault house protruded. Here lived humble folk who raised rabbits and chickens. At the far end the garden began, its trees still stark behind a railing with tall spikes; there was a fountain with a stone column at its center. To the left was the one-story building to which Théodore's atelier was to be added, while his father's house, with the attic Théodore was using for the time being, was on the other side. A large white house with a slate roof. Straight ahead, above a wall between trees, the long low roof of a rustic house could be seen, as well as the chimney on the higher gable of a house behind the tall linden tree. Skirting the lower end of the Géricault property was an oddly placed lane with cottages of every description, some of one story only, others narrow and tall with triangular fronts, or with flat little columns, a terrace or a small turret. On the right, fields climbed the heights, but to the left the lane dipped down again between more or less well-tended trees, into the thickets that extended all the way to the rue Saint-Lazare. Halfway down, the lane widened to form a circle, and here, opposite Fortuné Brack's house, stood a kind of Greek temple, which until recently had been unoccupied. It had a tiny garden in front, with a group of yews trimmed into spheres. Here the unknown woman stopped. The two young people had not spoken a word since their initial exchanges. The air was full of the song of birds. Everything was dripping, although the rain had stopped for the moment. Théodore bowed. "I only hope, madame, that you have forgiven me." She smiled at him and bowed without a word.

On retracing his steps, Théodore felt a certain agitation—less perhaps because of the woman whom he had held for a moment in his arms than because of what she had said. "My uniform!" He uttered the word aloud, and trembled. His red coat had become as odious to him as to the unknown woman. Had he his reasons for this? Before entering his father's house, he passed into the stall behind the pavilion to make sure Baptiste had tied Trick to the big ring in the wall and had fed the animal. "Has the lady been here long?" he asked the porter.

"Four or five days, Lieutenant," replied the man, and then immediately, "Is it true that the Emperor will be in Paris tomorrow?"

Baptiste had always said *the Emperor;* there was nothing astonishing in that. But Théodore, pushing back his drenched cloak, felt his heart pounding very hard under the cuirass and the surcoat. Because of the Emperor or the unknown woman? He did not answer Baptiste's question, and went into the house.

It was the conversation of 1813 all over again. The manservant was off for the day. Mlle. Mélanie, as usual in her styleless dress with collar, cuffs and bonnet, was bustling about. Boilly's portrait was now hanging in this middle-class dining room where the furniture from the rue de la Michodière looked all out of proportion. They were more at home here, however, than in the formal rooms on the ground floor with their woodwork carved in lyres and crowns. The first story was the living quarters, and the dishes were brought up by a lift.

"Thank God you've come, son! Mademoiselle Mélanie, take off his boots. . . ."

She had brought some boxwood from mass at the church of Saint Jean: she excused herself—she was going to put it on the crucifix in Monsieur's room. Besides, Monsieur Théodore had already thoroughly dirtied the carpets; he could do no more harm. The father grumbled, then began to laugh. It was true, the scamp took the house for a stable. Mud-spattered, soaked. He had tossed his drenched cloak on the bench in the entrance hall, hung his belt and saber on a chair in the dining room, and set his helmet on the sideboard. Where did he intend to put the surcoat and the cuirass he was now undoing? The dining room would soon be a military cloak room! Monsieur Géricault never tired of admiring Louise's son, standing there in his red dolman, his breeches of fine leather, with his long eyelashes and beautiful long, pale hands.

"You were at the drill?"

"Yes," said Théodore. "Trick is a bit tired. I've left him with Baptiste. You know what they're saying in town?"

The old man blinked. He knew. But how much truth was there

in all the rumors? After all, the French aren't going to abandon their King, the fleur-de-lis, just like that. There are too many interests involved. No, but can you imagine Buonaparte back? It would bring business to a standstill, unsettle everything, property . . .

"The return of the Bourbons," said Théodore, "certainly hasn't settled anything."

The father cast a frightened glance toward the door.

"You young fool, you're talking like a Jacobin. If I didn't know you! All right, but while I don't doubt the solidity of the throne for a moment, you understand? not for a moment—the French are attached to their Princes—we haven't the right to run even the tiniest risk, not after all the things we've seen in this unhappy country. . . . The *rente* has dropped twelve francs since the beginning of the month."

A lot Théodore cared about the *rente*. He was paying little attention to his father's rambling remarks. Who could that woman be? A friend of Madame de Brack? The little Greek temple had been vacant until just recently. There were apples on the table in a bowl decorated with mythological scenes by Percier-Fontaine. Théodore seized one and bit into it. At M. Géricault's, lunch was served at twelve o'clock sharp. There was time enough to starve to death. What was the old man saying?

"That is to say . . . that is to say . . . that is to say, we must be prepared for any eventuality, even the most improbable—even the return of the Ogre. Yes."

"The most improbable? . . . According to Marc-Antoine the Ogre is at Fontainebleau."

"Don't talk nonsense. If he was at Fontainebleau we should know it. But I haven't waited for that to happen. As far as my liquid assets are concerned. Just imagine what might become of the French currency if, with Buonaparte in the Tuileries, all Europe should show its disapproval by cutting off our credit! Without mentioning the hazards of a war in which the Kaiserlicks* and the Cossacks, to say nothing of the English, won't worry much about private interests in case of invasion!"

"Papa," said Théodore with his mouth full, "are you trying to tell me that you've bought the Butte Montmartre?"

"Don't eat all the apples. Besides, they're no good at this season. You're going to spoil your appetite. What were you saying?

* Slang term for Austrians.

Oh, yes. Here it's actually a question of my liquid assets. Or at least— The fact is, you know, I have a son. . . ."

"So I've been told."

"And this son, I— You're wearing a uniform people might take exception to!"

Théodore gave a start. He no longer heard his father. Again he could feel the unknown woman with the light-blond hair in his arms. For her, too, his uniform . . .

"Mark you, I don't attach great importance to rumors. But when I learned of Ney's treason, it started me thinking. Does such a man commit treason without good reasons?"

Théodore laughed heartily.

"So, Papa, if the Ogre is in the Tuileries tomorrow . . ."

"Well, we'll have to think about it. But you don't really believe . . . ?"

"Who knows? We may not be able to hold him at Melun."

"My son, these jokes do not become an officer of the Royal Household. If Buonaparte . . . That would mean that His Majesty had run away? You must see that's impossible! Why, just on Thursday, before the joint session of Parliament, the King . . . How moving he was! *I have worked for the happiness of my people. At the age of sixty, how could I better end my career than by dying in their defense?* Unforgettable words. His Majesty will not leave the capital. He would rather face death."

"We'll speak of this again, Papa."

"You haven't read today's *Débats*?"

"I must confess—"

"Oh, but it's very important. It's made as much of an impression on me as the Marshal's treason. Of the opposite kind, fortunately. But what's the matter with your commanding officers that they don't show these things to their Musketeers? So you haven't read Monsieur Benjamin Constant's article? Where did I put it? Ah, here it is. Just read this."

The *Journal des Débats* was all crumpled from Monsieur Géricault's nervous hands. Théodore began to read. M. Benjamin Constant's article was certainly not written by someone expecting the Usurper to enter the capital.

"Puts fresh spunk in you, doesn't it?" asked the father, rubbing his hands. "Which doesn't mean that one shouldn't take one's precautions."

Mlle. Mélanie was clearing the table to lay the cloth. She cast a disapproving glance at the bowl, which was two apples short. M. Géricault looked at her. There passed between them the mute exchange of two people who have long been used to each other. Mlle. Mélanie shrugged her shoulders. M. Georges let M. Théodore get away with everything.

"If the Ogre were to return after all . . . however loyal to the Princes one may be . . ."

Théo ignored this remark. His mind was elsewhere, in the garden, the little Greek temple with the sphere-shaped yew trees. A slip of a girl. All at once something his father was saying . . . what was it?

"There are turncoats and turncoats. I've been thinking about Ney. He isn't a scatterbrain like the husband of the lady who has come and perched opposite Major Brack."

What, didn't Théodore know that the little Greek temple was occupied by a person who had arrived on the sly? Not bad-looking, not at all bad-looking, but skinny— You can see the hollows above her collarbones. Who is she? A name that has caused some stir recently. No, she wasn't really a friend of the Bracks, but a Creole, you understand: Baron Lallemand had brought his Caroline from Santo Domingo—where he had gone at the beginning of the century.

"A Creole?" said Théodore. "Blond as she is!"

"Do you think Creoles are Negroes? But have you met her?"

The Musketeer ignored the question. How old could the lady be?

"Why, she's all of thirty! It was General Lefebvre-Desnouettes' wife who brought her to us. She didn't want to keep her on the rue de la Victoire.* Because of the police, you understand. All these people go into hiding in this house or that. Take the Duchesse de Saint-Leu: she disappeared from the rue d'Artois a week ago. Mark you, the Baron's bravery is common knowledge, he's shown it on all the battlefields. Why did he have to get involved in that adventure with Lefebvre-Desnouettes? And why did His Majesty make him prefect of the Aisne? It was tempting the devil. There were too many of Buonaparte's people in the command up there in the north. They say it was Fouché who turned the Baron's head.

* On the rue de la Victoire, which was called the rue Chantereine before the Empire, was situated a delightful mansion (destroyed in 1859), where Josephine and Bonaparte lived, and where the 18th Brumaire—the *coup d'état* of November 9, 1799, which was to overthrow the Directory and give Napoleon power—was plotted. During the Restoration this mansion was considered a hotbed of Bonapartist conspiracy.

You knew Fouché escaped over the wall, just as they came to arrest him a few days ago? He slipped across to his neighbor the Duchess's, who had already skipped, and *pfft!* vanished without a trace. Anyway, Lallemand might well have waited a week before showing off. Their Little Shaver hadn't yet reached Grenoble when General Lallemand and Drouet d'Erlon . . . They say Marshal Soult was in on the conspiracy. Whether he was or not, the King has removed him from the ministry. Well, you know the story: the plan was to march to Paris. But the conspirators got no farther than Compiègne. General Lallemand has been in prison for a week, and he's likely to face a firing party."

"But the lady, Papa . . ."

"What lady? Oh, the Baroness Caroline? It's understandable, poor woman. She had nothing to do with it, but she couldn't possibly remain at the Laon prefecture. She has run away to avoid being pestered by the police. In Paris it always takes them some time to track you down. How could she take refuge with her family? They're in Santo Domingo. She had come to throw herself at the King's feet. Only it isn't so simple as all that, and since neither Madame Lefebvre-Desnouettes nor the Duchesse de Saint-Leu could have introduced her— Besides, what Frenchman would have taken the wife of a condemned man to His Majesty?"

"I!" said Théodore.

His father looked at him and shrugged his shoulders. What had he been saying? Ah yes . . . then an Englishman took it upon himself: he was an intimate of the Orléans family, to be sure, but one of the rue Chantereine crowd* as well. A man named Kinnaird.

"Lord Charles?" asked Théo. "The art patron?"

"So, you know him? Perhaps he gave her the idea—because of the ateliers. She's taken refuge here. You can vanish in La Nouvelle-Athènes like a needle in a haystack. And since Fortuné Brack formerly served under Lefebvre-Desnouettes— Well, it's all the same crowd. They work things out among themselves. And since . . ."

Lefebvre-Desnouettes, Fortuné Brack . . . And what was Fouché's role in this? These names kept going round in Théodore's head. An odd district this, where for the past year everything in life had seemed to lead to bitterness and disappointment. Over there on the corner of the rue Saint-Lazare, which he had passed at a flying gallop, was the house of the Marquis de la Grange who commanded the Black Musketeers. Occasionally he would see groups of officers of the

* See footnote, p. 54.

Royal Household who had come to receive their orders there, or, in the evening, the carriages with a crowd in formal dress, glimpsed in the glistening light which streamed through the open windows from the chandeliers within. The Marquis de la Grange, like Law de Lauriston, was a hero of the Napoleonic wars. Their god had fallen; yet they had lost neither their mansions nor their epaulets, nor the means that had enabled them to live in the whirl of battles and festivities that had been the Empire.

Not more than three paces away, on the rue de la Victoire, which the people of the district still called the rue Chantereine, stood the Lefebvre-Desnouettes house, which had been Josephine's on the 18th Brumaire, and which Napoleon had presented as a gift to his accomplice in the *coup d'état*. And the Lefebvre-Desnouettes house was like the La Grange house; and even though Lefebvre-Desnouettes might be in garrison his wife received a great deal, and humble folk gathered to watch the arrival of society figures who had about them a telltale air of belonging to the opposition, and who wore the same lovely dresses, the same uniforms as ever. With some excitement people would recognize Madame de Saint-Leu, whom they still called Queen Hortense. And that handsome exquisite with her was her lover, Joseph de Flahaut, who was said to be Talleyrand's son.

Lieutenant Dieudonné, Théodore's schoolfellow, the model for that 1812 painting which had made him believe in his talent, in fame—Dieudonné, before the January departure of the 1st cavalry regiment for Béthune, used to be received by the general's wife with his friend Amédée, son of Regnault de Saint-Jean d'Angély, another officer who had served under Lefebvre-Desnouettes and the young Despans de Cubières. Fortuné Brack had told him proudly how these two had presented him at Madame de Saint-Leu's: and he was even prouder of the success he had had there, with that attractive voice of his, than of his campaigns. Théodore was a bit jealous of all these people, the Brumaire nobility and their sons. He was not on an equal footing with them, with their halo of battlefields, wounds, the cross of the Legion of Honor.

M. Géricault probably found it irritating today to talk with Théo before Mlle. Mélanie. He had drawn him into the library, so that the housekeeper could finish setting the table without them. A large room with a view in the other direction. By leaning out of the window a little you could half make out the Greek temple, through the trees which marched two by two, like black soldiers. . . . What was his father getting at? That he should desert?

These soldiers of his own age or a little older whom he met at Frascati's, like Joseph de Flahaut or Lieutenant de la Woëstine, were at home in salons to which Théodore had no access. Marc-Antoine d'Aubigny, for example, was their equal: he could receive them at his father's, on the rue Saint-Honoré, and was separated from them only by his opinions. It was a world of private mansions. It was the world Théodore had tried to paint. People saw only a cavalry officer somewhere at Echmühl, or Tilsit, nothing else. Caracoling, as in the 1812 painting; or a soldier of the Retreat standing by his wounded horse, fallen on the soil of France somewhere near Longwy or Denain, the Cuirassier of 1814. But Théodore knew perfectly well that the cavalry officer with the blond, drooping mustache had Dieudonné's head, and Marc-Antoine's body. Two of the Emperor's soldiers, in other words, and that was all. Only later had he had a sense of having made a hybrid monster of the republican and the Grenadier of La Rochejaquelein as of his own contradictions. Perhaps it had been a mistake to call that painting "Portrait of Monsieur D— Cavalry Lieutenant," instead of making him anonymous, a soldier who had earned his promotion in the thick of battle, amid gunpowder, blood and smoke.

What did this Baron Lallemand look like? Louis XVIII, Théodore knew, had made him a prefect; at twenty he had been in Santo Domingo, at thirty in Spain, and he had been a general when the Allies had invaded the country. She is thinking of him, in that painted brick retreat, among the bare trees of those gardens salvaged from a make-believe countryside. Once again Théodore visualized the Creole woman brought from the West Indies, a kind of frail, trembling bird whom he had held in his arms for a moment. I can imagine what General Lefebvre-Desnouettes's wife must have told her before bringing her here: a queer little spot, my dear; who would dream of looking for you in those shacks, among these humble people who live here with their rabbits and their ducks, small *rentiers* with a few pots of flowers, market gardeners, craftsmen. And then people on our side, you understand, people on our side, like Fortuné who was aide-de-camp to the handsome General Colbert, as well as simple soldiers like that worthy Maubert who goes about on his wooden leg. All kinds of craftsmen, artists' models, painters with their ateliers built of odds and ends; and in the evening you can see the fireworks from the Ruggieri Garden above the walls, hear songs, music. . . .

"What are you thinking about?" asked the father impatiently. "I'll wager you haven't heard a word of what I've been telling you the last fifteen minutes! Come, let's eat! We mustn't keep Mlle. Mélanie waiting."

So that was why the lady had found his uniform so distasteful. Théodore suddenly hated his red coat. Not that he had any inclination to approve of General Lallemand's attempt to turn his troops against the King. But must he leave for Melun? Fight against other Frenchmen? As far as the prisoner's wife was concerned, for the nonce her husband was a hero in his eyes. Théodore had excused himself inadequately. Perhaps she had been hurt. People don't faint like that for nothing.

"You might hide here, you know, until we see how things turn out. La Nouvelle-Athènes is an ideal district for avoiding the police: you enter through our house, and can reach the fields in the direction of Montmartre or go down by the lane toward the rue Saint-Lazare. If they're after you, you can slip along footpaths toward Clichy. Or turn down the rue de la Tour-des-Dames. You make your way to Ruggieri's and you're lost to sight there among the tables, in the blaze of the fireworks. Or you disappear in the crowd at the dance hall by the rue des Martyrs!"

Théodore did not protest. He was not surprised that his father should already look upon the King's Musketeers as outlaws. He only half listened to him. He was saying to himself: Baroness Lallemand . . . Caroline, her name is Caroline. If I were to stay, I should be able to see her every day—and then what? It made no sense. I could do her portrait, he thought. Then, She detests me because I belong to the Reds. . . . And so dinner passed.

"Monsieur Théo," said Mlle. Mélanie, "do you or do you not want some cheese?"

She had been holding the platter for him for some time. He apologized.

II

Four Views of Paris

IT WAS Robert Dieudonné's deep conviction that the Place Louis-XV was the most beautiful spot in the world. Even in the rain. The King's 1st cavalry regiment had piled arms on the square in the late morning. The four hundred and fifty horsemen stood beside their horses with their shabracks of garnet cloth and sheepskin saddles, white for the men, black for the officers, along the Tuileries in the space that separated the stone balconies from the garden walls. It formed a great meadow, this encampment of bottle-green soldiers with their scarlet breeches above their boots, their black pressed-leather helmets trimmed with black horsehair and white plumes, and their white shoulder knots on the right shoulder. Robert, his carrot-red mop brushed down over his forehead, gnawed at his stiff mustache. He had slept like a log after the last march, ten leagues in the dreary wind, and the rain which had caught them near Saint-Denis. They had been on the move since a week ago Friday. No one was sorry to have left Béthune: neither the men, most of them Parisians who had gone there reluctantly, nor the officers, almost all commoners, among whom there was a kind of excitement since they had heard of Napoleon's return.

Unfortunately for Lieutenant Dieudonné, the *capitaine en second* who commanded his company, a Breton, Bouexic de Guichen, a regular Chouan,* was one of the few who were loyal to the King.

* The *Chouans,* named after their leader Jean Cottereau, nicknamed Jean Chouan, were members of the royalist insurrectionary movement that opposed the Revolution and later combined with the La Vendée rising.

Feeling ran high among the lieutenants. By the time they reached Arras, Arnavon, Rochette, Rostant, almost all of them, had begun to hold secret meetings in the inns, to which Dieudonné was admitted as an old-timer from the Emperor's Guides. On the staff itself the colonel, the Comte de Saint-Chamans, was virtually ostracized—according to the doctor, a certain Denoix, who knew the colonel from having shared captivity with him after Leipzig in 1813. There was more than one officer to ten men in that regiment, but the precaution did not suffice. That was obvious from the way the troops had received the colonel's little speech at the assembly at Cambrai before the departure for Saint-Quentin. The newspapers they had found on the way could lie as much as they liked. Enough could be read between the lines for the horsemen in the taverns to begin to drink noisy toasts to the Little Shaver. Only the colonel was in the dark. On Sunday, at Saint-Quentin, the people in the street asked the cavalrymen whether they would fight against Napoleon or join Lefebvre-Desnouettes's men who were marching on Paris with cavalrymen of the Guard, Grenadiers and Artillery.

In the evening, nearly half of the officers debated what they were going to do, since the insurgent regiments were in Ham, only four leagues from Saint-Quentin. Should they join the Guard cavalrymen? Should they go back to the tricolor? It had just been learned that at Grenoble Colonel de Labédoyère had gone over to the Emperor with the entire 7th regiment of the line.

Swarms of Parisians were in evidence despite the rain—any letup in the weather seemed to bring them out of invisible holes to converge upon the square. Their way of circulating in and out among the bivouacs; conversations begun, broken off; women of every kind who, by the way they let their scarves slip down their backs from their shoulders, appeared already to sense the coming of spring; pompous citizens exhorting hilarious cavalrymen to die for the Princes—all this was real in an unreal way. What were they doing here? The King was to review the troops at noon, it was said. You'll see him in my arse hole first, commented Denoix, ill-mannered boor that he was. Someone had brought Lieutenant Arnavon a copy of *Les Débats*: that article of Benjamin Constant's, it made no sense.

Yes, to be sure, Lefebvre-Desnouettes's escapade had failed. Between Saint-Quentin and Ham they had met the Guard cavalrymen heading north. Oh, the fine uniforms, the bearskins with red and green plumes and gold tassels, the scarlet pelisse with black fur over the green dolman and yellow trousers, but what a pitiful state they were in! The "instigators" had been arrested. Lefebvre-Desnouettes was a fugitive. But was the Little Shaver in Lyons or wasn't he? A week had passed. Here they were in the Place Louis-XV, with the horses pawing the ground, between the Tuileries which the King did not seem disposed to leave and the Champs-Élysées edged with fair booths. Over by the Allée des Veuves the Lifeguards were massed, and in the direction of the Seine were the students in their outfits harking back to Henri IV, plumed felt hats and all, like a masquerade. They were sections of Vioménil's volunteers from the School of Medicine and the Law School, hotheads who sang royalist songs. The things the men were saying about them—men who had survived the Russian campaign, who were veterans of Austerlitz and Wagram—were hardly fit for tender ears, and they wouldn't have needed much urging to teach those foolish schoolboys a good lesson.

To say nothing of the carriages fleeing westward. There was no mistaking what they were about—coaches, berlins, even hired cabriolets with their yellow or red painted wheels, all of them loaded, stuffed, with families, trunks, miscellaneous objects made fast God knows how. From time to time a general passed by on horseback as though to persuade the troops to patience. Infantry was massed on both sides of the Pont Louis-XVI, and the Cuirassiers filled the rue Royale-Saint Honoré.

Perhaps His Majesty was hoping the rain would abate. Meanwhile nearly ten thousand men, including the Household on the Champ-de-Mars, were getting drenched. But even with the rain, when you compared the Place Louis-XV to Béthune! Did you miss the billiards at the Hôtel du Nord, with the belfry chimes going ting-a-ling, ting-a-ling, out on the square, which didn't help you to forget that time seemed to stand still? Rochette was guffawing with Schmalz and Delahaye, two second lieutenants who looked as if they had just left their mothers' apronstrings though they had, indeed, distinguished themselves in 1814 in the defense of the Porte de Clichy—a fact which caused them to be frowned upon at staff headquarters. And to top everything, they were famished: the meal they had had at the barracks had got down to their heels by now, along with their stomachs.

"Shut up, you blockhead," said Rochette to Schmalz. He had just caught sight of the colonel and his horse, a dappled bay. The colonel was a handsome rider, although he had narrow shoulders which were filled out by heavy silver epaulets. He was hardly more than thirty-four, and if he carried his head so straight it was chiefly because of that rigid scarlet gorget encircling the black cravat from which the corners of a starched collar protruded and cut into his chin. His hair crisscrossing over his forehead matched his mount's coat, except for the dappling. Since the King had made him a Knight of Saint-Louis, he had ceased to wear his Legion of Honor. He came up to the small group of officers around Robert and asked them if all was well, how their men were taking the long wait.

His childlike eyes clearly betrayed a certain fear that exaggerated their protuberance. He obviously did not approve of the prolonged halt which was being inflicted on the regiment. Especially as there were Parisians among the cavalrymen who were itching to run home. Exiling them to Béthune had been a mistake to begin with. The colonel rode off, followed by his aide-de-camp.

"It's what happened this morning that's worrying him," Schmalz sneered.

Who was this general who had treated them to that ridiculous lecture? They had been on their best behavior, they had made no remarks, but imagine the colonel ordering Captains Riquet and Bouvard to return to Béthune, to the regimental depot!

"He must have found out about the little trip they took to Saint-Quentin," said Arnavon.

Robert was aware that Riquet and Bouvard, believing Lefebvre-Desnouettes's men to be in full insurrection, had gone to Ham during the night to propose to General Lion that they remove their colonel and add the King's cavalry to his command. But General Lion was in fact beating a retreat to Cambrai; he had broken with Lefebvre-Desnouettes and the Lallemand brothers, and had probably denounced the captains. Lion, in whom Napoleon had such confidence! It made no sense. And Clarke had even read General Lion's report to the Chamber and announced that he was being appointed cavalry inspector! On the Place Louis-XV, Riquet and Bouvard had refused to obey. The cavalrymen had overheard them speaking their minds to the unhappy Comte de Saint-Chamans, who looked like a dancer on his highly strung mount, but on such occasions bore an unfortunate resemblance to a naughty schoolboy caught in some misdeed. There had been cries of *Vive l'Empereur!* and the colonel had withdrawn with great dignity, after having capitulated before Bouvard and Riquet.

"He's coming back from the Palace," said Arnavon, his eyes following the colonel. And Schmalz, "What's he got up his sleeve now?

Look at him over there, he's calling his squadron commanders together!"

Godard-Desmarets, the standard bearer, who had made himself unpopular with the other men by his carryings-on with the ladies of Béthune, came riding up to the mounted staff. "I say, Rollet, if you'd been in Riquet's boots, wouldn't you have run off to have another look at your sweetheart Marceline?"

There was a blare of trumpets. To horse! What was the meaning of this? What about the review? Has Little Fatty decided not to put himself out on their account? Mounted orderlies were bringing orders. On the other side of the square the volunteers were watching the King's first cavalry regiment maneuver. They were getting into marching formation. Captain Masson, passing sword in hand, leaned behind Bouexic de Guichen's back toward Lieutenant Dieudonné, who was in the act of mounting his horse. "They're sending us packing," he said. "No direction—Essonnes. The Duc de Berry seems to be afraid of the army. The only troops they're keeping in Paris are their damned Household and the students with their plumes!"

Essonnes! That name meant something to Robert. It was at Essonnes, last year, that the terrible comedy had been played out which had left Fontainebleau exposed and put the Emperor at the Allies' mercy. That night Dieudonné had been galloping on Colonel Fabvier's heels as his aide-de-camp. They were returning from Fontainebleau where the colonel had seen the Emperor. They had ridden through the April night, beneath a weird sky punctured by the moon and masked by great black clouds, had ridden through the forest with its fantastic rocks. Fabvier must have been quite beside himself; he had talked about a woman he loved but who would never be either his mistress or his wife. As people do in shipwrecks, he had poured his heart out, jumbling together the misfortunes of France and his own life, and the blue-eyed lieutenant had listened. Who could the woman be? The way he spoke of her! She was the *perfect woman*. He had known her since 1805. . . .

They had come out on a bare plain, and the sky had darkened. As long as he lived Robert would remember the little winding road, the young trees that slipped past them. Essonnes had been dark and silent. It didn't seem possible that the sixth corps was billeted here. Perhaps a regiment had been moved. Colonel Fabvier wanted to reach the outposts. The Marshal was on his way back from Paris, the Emperor's orders had to be transmitted to him. Over there, somewhere near Orsay, were the Austrians. *The perfect woman,*

Fabvier was saying. Suddenly at a crossing they heard a kind of rumble, the sound of horses, of troops on the march. Forms were outlined against the sky. They had by-passed Essonnes, they must be close to Courcouronnes. What if they were the Austrians? Alas . . . it was the Sixth Corps, moving in the direction of Versailles. What? Are you mad? Turn back to Essonnes! Turn back! See here, Colonel, see here, we're obeying orders. The general. What general? It was General Souham who was beating a retreat to Versailles, in connivance with the enemy, abandoning his post, terrified lest the Emperor discover the dealings that Marmont, he himself, and a few others had had with the Austrians the day before. An unexpected visit by Colonel Gourgaud, His Imperial Majesty's orderly, had pushed him to this extremity. He had thought that the summons to Fontainebleau was a trap. Fabvier—they were on the edge of a stream—was shouting words which Robert did not quite catch, while Souham, across from him, on horseback, kept repeating. "He would have me shot!"

Thus had France been betrayed, along with the Emperor and twenty years of glory. Lieutenant Dieudonné would always remember the name of that stream with bitterness. He had asked a peasant who, aroused from sound sleep, had come half naked to the window to watch the soldiers pass. That stream had an odd name. They called it *Écoute s'il pleut* (Listen if it's raining).

Less than a year had gone by, and Robert Dieudonné was again on his way to Essonnes; they were to sleep there.

And perhaps meet Bonaparte. It was raining. Oddly enough, Dieudonné was thinking of *the perfect woman* even more than of the Emperor. Fabvier had been in love with her since 1805 . . . ten years. All very well, but not for Robert. His youth was dedicated to passing fancies. Who could that woman be?

For the third time that day, Colonel-Baron Charles Fabvier, second lieutenant in the Lifeguards, in the 6th company of Raguse, called by the common people the Judas company, had gone to the Palace. The six-foot colossus—thirty-three, with black mustache, a massive head which was already balding at the temples, enormous eyes, and eyebrows which turned up at the ends, in dress uniform, the cloak attached by the clasp at the collar, the left flap flung over his athlete's shoulder and revealing under his arm the helmet with the sunburst, the royal blue coat with scarlet facings, basques lined with scarlet, and all its silver trimmings—was again coming down the staircase of the Pavillon de Flore in a state of nerves that was aggravated by his disgust at having to force his way through the crowd of shady characters on the police payrolls that congested the steps.

The flight of the courtiers, whose numbers had diminished spectacularly by last Sunday, as was obvious to anyone who had attended the royal mass at the Tuileries, seemed to have encouraged this invasion of civilians carrying cudgels, wearing long green, brown or black frock coats and tall dark hats recognizable a hundred paces away. M. d'André's police were still in evidence, along with Bourrienne's new force, and the unpaid auxiliaries of the Comte d'Artois's counter-police.* It was hard to imagine who might have asked any or all of these groups to come and post themselves here, and they eyed one another suspiciously. It was necessary to elbow a way among all these police agents, a good many of whom were perhaps Fouché's men, ready for some surprise action on Buonaparte's arrival. Yet their presence meant that since Ney's defection the soldiers were no longer trusted. That was evident from the way the Princes up there stared at the other Marshals. Which of them would turn traitor?

It was nearly three o'clock when Marshal Marmont, Duc de Raguse (who had been at the École Militaire while the Royal Household, assembled with great difficulty, was getting drenched on the Champ-de-Mars waiting for His Majesty), had sent for his former aide-de-camp to dispatch him to the Tuileries. It was sheer madness. The King had demanded this review, they had had to scurry in all directions to call back the units that had been dispersed since the call at eight in the morning, to mass them in the rain, and now they were there waiting and nobody came.

At forty-one the Marshal still looked youthful, though he was a bit on the fleshy side. His tall figure and his handsome face, framed in brown hair, a little heavy about the chin, bespoke his aristocratic background. Seeing him in his embroidered uniform with the blue ribbon over the shoulder, and the cross almost at the collar, Fabvier readily recognized the horseman he had known in Spain, still eager to please and to hear himself talk. Today, as on the morning after the battle of Apriles, he was possessed by a morbid compulsion to clear himself of something. Now he kept harping on the accusations

---

* The Comte d'Artois, the King's brother, had his own agents to inform him of his brother's movements and of the activities of the official police. M. d'André was the King's Director-General of Police and Bourrienne had been appointed Prefect of the Paris police just a few days before this (March 13), Fouché had been Napoleon's Minister of Police.

Bonaparte had leveled against him on disembarking at Cannes. How many times the Marshal had lost his temper these last days, speaking with his ex aide-de-camp. "Ah," he said, "*your* Charter!" as though Fabvier had drafted it, as though he alone were responsible for the course of events, for that gross stratagem of Louis XVIII's, who thought he had thereby won over the men of the Empire. And then just look at Marshal Ney! Marmont was for the Comte d'Artois and the Duc de Berry. Although the Duc annoyed him with his way of aping the Little Corporal's mannerisms. There were times when he was sorely tempted to pinch their ears! Size isn't everything.

"Go to the Palace and have a look, Fabvier," he had said. "I don't know what His Majesty is thinking about. The companies must be getting impatient."

And then suddenly he had spilled everything. So it was good-by to the plan the colonel had worked out so elaborately and the Marshal had adopted as his own? What! the King was decamping? A lot of good it had done for him to promise Parliament in its joint session on Thursday that he would remain in Paris even at the cost of his life, only to sneak away on Sunday like a coward! To think that Fabvier had spent two nights on that plan for fortifying the Louvre! All the orders were ready: The Duc d'Angoulême was to hold the southwest, the Duc de Bourbon the west; the Household and the troops before Paris were to be under Macdonald; the Duc de Berry . . . Well, no use going over it again; M. de Blacas d'Aulps, at first on their side, had lost his head the day before: and when Blacas had told the King that he must fly, well, the King, as usual, had accepted that imbecile's advice. What a brave show it would have made, *nom de Dieu,* the King of France remaining in his own capital despite everything—despite treason in the army, the fickleness of the mob; sitting in his armchair before his Palace of the Louvre waiting for That Man, the Usurper, and saying to him, "Well, what now? You're going to destroy Paris? Fire on the Palace? Burn the Tuileries? And when you have killed me, you'll be only a regicide. It won't make you the legitimate heir. That title passes to the Comte d'Artois, the Duc de Berry, the Duc d'Angoulême. A lot of good it will have done you!"

But that he should not hold the review! For you understand, my dear fellow, the review, too, was the King's plan; he would arrive at the Champ-de-Mars, harangue the Household, dictate to it its duty, announce that it was to proceed to Essonnes to block the road to Paris. He himself was bound for an undisclosed destination—the Étoile, the military road. . . .

Essonnes! The former aide-de-camp heard nothing after that word. Essonnes! He looked at Marmont, captain of the Lifeguards, commanding the Royal Household. Was it possible for Marmont to mention that word without trembling? What did it matter to Fabvier that the review was but a ruse by which Louis XVIII would have left the Louvre to make for the Barrière de l'Étoile? And where from there? This morning nobody knew as yet. There were those who wanted the King to proceed to the Vendée and put himself at the head of the Chouans, whither His Highness the Duc de Bourbon had preceded him. A fine way to gain popularity! Others advised Normandy. From Granville they could, if necessary, reach the Channel Islands. The Royal Household could hold out in Le Havre for a long time; and if the worst came to the worst, well, they could slip over to England. The question was whether the navy would remain loyal? The Duc d'Orléans, having managed to escape from Lyons, had reached the North yesterday. Marmont did not really believe the King wanted to join him: sending him to Lille had been rather an act of defiance toward the son of Philippe-Égalité, a sequel to the dismissal of Soult who was considered a hanger-on of the Orléans family rather than a Bonapartist. Orders had been given, too, to refuse horses to the Duchess, who wanted to leave Paris. The Duc de Berry was making scenes because His Majesty insisted on keeping him by his side, thus preventing him from going and hacking the Invader to pieces.

The King's want of resolution though, applied only to men. "This is strictly between ourselves . . ." Lowering his voice, Marmont told Fabvier the story: even before Ney's treason was officially recognized, on Friday, in fact, twenty-four hours after the solemn joint session of the Chambers, the Crown diamonds had been sent off by road. Sent where? To Calais, England—in charge of His Majesty's first valet. Of course a man might put the diamonds in a safe place and still remain in Paris to die, but between you and me . . .

So Fabvier had gone back to the Palace. He had not been able to see the King. But the King was still there and had transmitted the message to him through M. de Blacas—the unsavory M. de Blacas with his Lenten face, long as a wet Sunday, beneath the faded blond wig, his chunky legs attached to a seemingly endless body. His Majesty was still planning to review the Household, but . . . Fantastic!

He had been made to wait in the Marshals' Salon.

Since those at the Palace had begun to quake, this had become a kind of public market; any kind of uniform served as a pass. There were people who came in as though visiting a café; not to mention the ladies on the lookout for Bourrienne, eager to transmit to him personally some information they had picked up. It was a week since Madame de Duras had been seen at Court: she was in on the plot; and her husband, the unfortunate Duke, who was there, with the King.

The antechamber was full of people. Priests, generals, ministers. They came and went, in and out of the King's apartments. Everyone who came out—whether it happened to be M. de Jaucourt or a servant, fat Berthier, pale and drawn, unable to conceal his agitation, or Father Elisée, His Majesty's surgeon, that strange Brother, lean and oily-faced, reeking of lechery—was pounced upon by the mob. How do things stand? Do we leave? Where for? They had lost all decency; had sat themselves down on the benches and, anxious not to lose their places, afraid of missing the moment when they would learn what to do, had come in the morning provided with a bite to eat, or had had chops or herrings wrapped in paper brought in to them. It was sordid, and the room stank like a low eatinghouse. The Pavillon de Flore, for that matter, always smelled of the kitchen. And to have to listen to these ancient courtiers telling one another that His Majesty had eaten four fine pigeons with green peas for his lunch! The sons of Saint Louis had always been addicted to the pleasures of the table!

As he was about to come out on the quay, the colonel encountered an officer of the National Guard with his gold-studded bearskin. He hesitated: wasn't it Alexandre de Laborde, whom he had known in Spain? What he had been doing there was not clear. And then Fabvier had found himself with the Count in 1814 on the commission that had negotiated with the Allies for the capitulation of Paris. They had had a strange conversation one evening then. The Comte de Laborde had talked a great deal, the year before, about his father, who had been guillotined in 1793. Although everyone knew that his mother had had him by an Austrian prince. . . . Alexandre had been an officer in the Austrian army before Thermidor. But what in the world had come over Alexandre de Laborde that evening? They had been somewhere near the Porte de Clichy where the refugee peasants with their carts were camping, and where corpses were being gathered up, not far from the debtors' prison, and Paris was waiting for the Allies to enter. What in the world had come over him to tell Colonel Fabvier how, on returning to France in his youth during the Directory, while painting in David's studio, he had been seduced by dangerous ideas, had joined a group of odd people, known as the Equals? * There are such moments, apocalyptic moments when a man pours out everything to the first comer.

Well, it was Laborde, this former follower of Babeuf, who had been entrusted with the King's safety on this Palm Sunday of 1815. It was true that his sister Nathalie, Duchesse de Mouchy, was the daughter-in-law of M. le Prince de Poix. He commanded the National Guards, who had replaced the Royal Household. General Dessolles had recently made him adjutant-commander of the Guard, and Alexandre had come back to make a tour of inspection at the Palace where he had set up the new guard at noon. He returned the Lifeguard's salute, not at first recognizing him as Fabvier, and walked over to him. "My dear friend," he said to him in a half-whisper, "I'd like to talk to you a moment . . ."

To tell the truth, the *dear friend* was not overpleased at this friendship, but how to escape? They went back up to the first floor. The headquarters of the National Guards had been set up in one of the Royal Family apartments and it was rather odd to see the vestibule and dining room of Madame, the Duchesse d'Angoulême, who was now in Bordeaux, full of Grenadiers, some fifty of them, standing about or sitting on whatever was available—the table and the sideboard, as well as the benches in the lobby—rolling tobacco between their fingers, or pipe in mouth. They snapped to attention as the officers entered. Laborde spoke a few words to them, and they cried *"Vive le Roi!"* They clearly belonged to the common people. Not all of them were freshly shaved.

"They're Grenadiers of the 11th and 12th legions," Laborde whispered to Fabvier, "picked because their captains are reliable." The said captains had the eager look of petty officials when they see their superior approaching. "I've been criticized," Alexandre continued, "because, would you believe it? some of my men on the Pont-Tournant post are from the Faubourg Saint-Antoine. It's a

* See footnote p. 46.

detachment of the 3rd legion, which had been under the command of Richard-Lenoir* for more than a year. So people go and say he's the father-in-law of Labédoyère's brother, which is perfectly possible, but I ask you! Some of the people in the Palace, especially around Monsieur, are hopeless. The people of Paris must be trusted, and I don't need to know anything about the suburb they're talking about. These are National Guards, ready to form a rampart round the Princes with their bodies—that's all. As for Richard-Lenoir, the King hasn't recalled him, and he's done more to bring prosperity to France than most of our ultraroyalists! As for Labédoyère himself, he's the son-in-law of Charles de Damas, the commander of the Light Horse. To hell with them!"

He was drawing the colonel out of earshot. "I've meant to ask you . . . I know you originated the plan for the defense of the Louvre . . . We've taken measures: we've doubled the Pont-Tournant post, the picture gallery is crammed with men, and those manning the inner barricades are prepared to fall back round His Majesty—so much the worse for art! Imagine damaging *Les Noces de Cana!*** But what can we do? Tell me: you've just been seeing M. de Blacas— what a fellow! The way he ignores you, his arrogance. Well, anyway, it's not for him we're fighting. But it seems to me there are changes in the plans. M. de Blacas, we know, has sent his wife off—along with a wagon full of his medal collections, they say! And Mesdames de Duras, de la Ferronays, de Jaucourt, the Princesses of Wagram and of Talleyrand have left France. Our presence here emphasizes Madame's absence. And friends of mine in town have told me . . ."

What was he driving at? Already a rumor was circulating in the Palace corridors that if the King was not going to the Champ-de-Mars, it was because he was getting ready to pack up and flee in broad daylight. M. de Vitrolles was saying the sun need not be a witness to that. . . .

Fabvier looked at the adjutant commander and read in his face the dark anxiety that was obvious wherever you went, on the stairs, in the antechambers. They were all weighing royalty's chances. How many were getting ready to shout *Vive l'Empereur? Morbleu,* in 1814 they had witnessed the thing in reverse. "Monsieur le Comte," said Fabvier,

---

* François Richard (1765–1839) was, with Joseph Lenoir-Dufresne (1768–1806), the founder of the cotton industry in France. After Lenoir-Dufresne's death, his associate took the name of Richard-Lenoir.

** Paul Veronese's famous painting, still in the Louvre, of the marriage feast at Cana at which Christ changed water to wine. The painting measures 35 feet by 20 feet.

"all I can tell you is that His Majesty will review the red and white companies on the Champ-de-Mars in half an hour or so."

This seemed to relieve Laborde. He asked the colonel if he had had lunch: because the post had reserve supplies and could spare him a bite. Here, too, the atmosphere reeked of food. Fabvier thanked him: he was expected at the École Militaire.

With more difficulty than he had had going up, he elbowed his way down the stairs which were cluttered with a masquerade of old men come to offer their services to the King. To judge by their wardrobes they had dug out uniforms dating back to before the flood. People round them were laughing openly, and Bourrienne's policemen nudged one another and made unpleasant comments. Fabvier passed through the crowd as a ship passes through a canal blocked by barges. He was a head taller than most of these people who smelled of beer and garlic. A market woman had managed to make her way into the entrance hall at the bottom of the stairs and was selling Burgundy snails that fouled the air. Beggars had slipped in through the doorway, one exhibiting a stump, another, a blind man led by a poodle.

There was a crowd on the quay, the sky had suddenly brightened, and the Guards were having difficulty in keeping the space before the gate of the Pavillon de Flore open. The fact that the royal carriages had been brought out maintained anxiety at a high pitch. They were waiting for His Majesty and his suite to go to the Champ-de-Mars to review his Household, people were told, but no one believed it. Where were they going? girls kept asking the coachmen. Where were they going? La Rochelle and Boulogne were mentioned. No one was paying much attention to the weather any longer. When a few drops began to fall, it was as if the Parisians had become used to it. Even though spring was at hand, the women had not brought out their straw hats, the weather being so variable. Yet they wore bright dresses and coats in which yellow and green predominated, and the Naples silk on the capes had the tints of early buds. There were entire families; citizens dragging wives and daughters as far away as they could from the soldiers, who were inclined to ribaldry; children who stumbled against your legs; cardsharps, vendors of ointments and creams for the complexion. It was cold enough for furs to be in evidence, but here and there were young ladies who had been imprudent enough to dress in percale, and whose noses in consequence matched their ribbons in accordance with the decree of fashion, violet on yellow dresses. And there were fellows who were no less dangerous to husbands than the soldiers, some booted, others in hose and shoes, all wearing the knitted skin-tight breeches—scarcely fit for the eyes of young ladies, especially in that pink vicuña which the dandies favored; or kersey-mere, which was not much better.

Fabvier had left his horse at the Stables on the other side of the Place du Carrousel and now he passed through the gates where horse-men were standing, and reached the great paved space between the Arc de Triomphe du Carrousel and that semiruined district which so astonished foreigners when they found it here under the very noses of the Kings of France, with the Chapel of the Deanery and the former Longueville mansion, now roofless. From here—from these streets beginning at the Palais Royal and running obliquely to the great Museum gallery separating the Tuileries from the old Louvre, which could just be made out behind the hovels, sheds, tumbledown houses —had been launched the assaults of August 10, 1792, against the Tuileries. What Napoleon had torn down, to give himself more dis-tance before the rabble could reach him, had still left intact a whole quaint district inhabited by secondhand dealers, prostitutes and serv-ants. From it now rose an indecent uproar, for there were cafés and inns where troopers, already drunk, were singing songs by Béranger, and *"Veillons au salut de l'Empire!"*

The Stables, their flat fronts adorned with twin pillars, were just opposite the gates of the Pont des Saints-Pères, like a fragment of an official building forgotten in the disorder of the tall private houses. And there, like a soldier who had stepped forward from the ranks, stood a large six-story cube, with a café on the ground floor and on the mezzanine, the Hôtel de Nantes where the post carriages were usually stationed. But today there were only packages piled on the pavement, for there were no more horses. They had all been seized by fugitives, and no one had come to collect the mail and parcels. Here the crowd was less dense, music could be heard coming from the café, and the people outside were looking in through the windows. There was a great pale rift in the sky, a mock sun.

But suddenly Charles Fabvier trembled. An ill-matched couple com-ing toward him made his heart pound. It was not because of the man, a stranger dressed with a certain elegance, carrying a cape and a greatcoat and not readily identifiable with the glasses he was wearing and the mouse-gray felt hat apparently sitting atop a wig. But he was offering his arm to a lady whose right hand rested on it ever so lightly, while her left held that of a little girl of four or five. The colonel could not believe his eyes. Surely it was a hallucination. He was possessed by this familiar form, he saw it everywhere. Actually he had never seen her in that gray velvet bonnet, turned up in front and pinned on slantwise, adorned with plumes and a bow of ribbons on the side, the edge trimmed with a blond frill, nor in that marten tippet lined with mauve silk, worn over a merino dress decorated with the same velvet as the hat. It was not easy to make out her face, but it was impossible not to recognize the child in her black spencer and white skirt. The little girl with her long black hair hanging down her back, and the big curls hiding her ears, was in half-mourning. She was a bit too plump, and there was a look of suffering in her eyes. It was toward little Hortense that Fabvier now stepped forward, but he was thinking, What is Marie-des-Anges doing here? He looked at her, ignoring her companion.

"Good heavens, madame, you here! On such a day? Isn't it unwise?"

She gave him her gloved hand, and felt the arm on which she had been leaning slip away. Her companion had discreetly moved off a few steps. The lady smiled, and one could see how small and regular were her teeth. Her black hair formed a fringe across her forehead in the oblique opening of the bonnet. At twenty-seven—she had married at fourteen—she was in the full splendor of womanhood. She smiled again, this time for the giant before her, and said, "Charles! It's strange, my dear, how glad I am to see you."

Each time he saw her it was as though he had just discovered her. Today he seemed to notice for the first time the perfection of that straight nose with its sensitive nostrils. And her melodious voice went right through him, with that barely perceptible Spanish accent that even Mme. Campan's school had been unable to eradicate.

"It is very reckless of you, madame," he said, "you might be recognized."

She laughed, making that little shaking movement with her wrist which had become a habit with her even when she was not wearing bracelets: "And suppose I *were* recognized!"

But he was serious. "Political passions are rife today," he went on, "and the courtyard of the Louvre is overrun with agents of the police underworld. It's not hard to imagine someone attempting to attract attention to himself by claiming that he had overheard the Duchesse de Frioul saying I don't know what. . . . Less than three days ago at the Tuileries, I heard your name mentioned by one of the busybodies who hover around the Princes."

"And what did that busybody have to say?" asked the Duchess.

"It doesn't matter. But he linked your name with that of Mme. de Saint-Leu."

"And what harm is there in that? Everyone knows Hortense is my friend—and my daughter's godmother."

"But at this moment, madame, people may remember that she has been a queen. And with Bonaparte already in Fontainebleau . . ."

"You think he's no closer than Fontainebleau? But that's just why I was dying to see what was happening at the Tuileries. Is Monsieur de Lille still there on his throne, cracking broad jokes with his ministers?"

"His Majesty, madame, is going to review the troops, and I am a soldier. But do be careful how you speak, feeling runs high."

"Charles, I would not miss this show for all the gold in the world! Just consider that I'm seeing it for myself, and for Duroc. If he were alive, he'd be on his way to Fontainebleau, not at the Carrousel!"

From her, Fabvier would accept anything. Then she added, "And as for recklessness"—and turned lightly toward the old man hovering in the background—"I have Monsieur Fouché to protect me."

Had the man in the greatcoat heard her? He adjusted his spectacles as though better to conceal his eyes. Fouché! That lean, slightly stooping figure, with an air of the *ancien régime* about him, was Fouché? He whom Bourrienne had tried to arrest, only to have him slip through the fingers of the police. Was Maria-de-los-Angeles completely mad? "I can hardly imagine," he said, "that the Tuileries is a healthy place for M. le Duc d'Otrante."

The colonel had raised his voice, and the other bowed and came forward a few steps. "That depends a little on M. le Baron Fabvier," he said, "and on the use he makes of the name." He had straightened up and it was clear that he was not nearly so old as he had made himself appear. In 1815 Fouché was not more than fifty-two, and had a certain look of youth about him.

Charles eyed him from head to foot with a shade of contempt. "You have nothing to fear, monsieur, since the lips from which I have heard it make it sacred to me."

He bowed to the Duchess, his heart pounding in his ears. He took Duroc's child in his arms, and lifted her into the air. "My precious," he said, "you are to me your father and your mother combined! May life be sweet to you!"

He had poured so much feeling into these unusually solemn words that the Duchess impulsively reached for her daughter and pressed her to her bosom. She had lost her son, her first-born, and was in a constant state of anxiety over this fragile doll. "Charles," she said, so low that Fouché could not hear her, "God keep you, my dear, whatever road you may follow!"

When Fabvier rode out of the Stables again on his horse, Maria-delos-Angeles was no longer in sight. He whipped his animal with his crop and raced through the gates toward the bridge.

Although Marshal Macdonald, Duc de Tarente, had donned civilian clothes at the King's order, the pocketless *tête-de-nègre* coat, the olive breeches, the umbrella, the fawn-colored boots and the tall black hat did not deprive him of his military bearing. He had put on weight, and the upturned nose in his large bony face, which had once given him an air of audacity, had lost its expressiveness through the accumulation of unhealthy fat which marked the man of fifty. Although he tried unsuccessfully to discipline his blond hair, now somewhat darkened by age, it still formed curls, less full than they had once been but springy. He might, at a pinch, have passed for a banker; but who, noticing the mournful look that came so readily into his brown eyes, would have entrusted his money to him?

For there was in him that odd blend of the adventurer, so often found in the men of the Empire—he had been a general at twenty-nine—and of a kind of middle-class fatigue, quite understandable after such a life, when a man already suffered from pains in his toes, especially with these perpetual rains! "Brumaire weather!" he murmured, and looked out through the window at the still-bare trees.

He remembered that morning of the year VIII (1799), at Versailles, when he had gone in the pouring rain to close down a Jacobin club while his colleague was staking everything at Saint-Cloud. He had long been a friend of Josephine's and a regular frequenter of her house on the rue Chantereine. How far off all that was! Sixteen years no less, and a whole wind-swept life. At the moment, the King of France was waiting for him.

Yes, the King had sent word that he was to come to the Palace in civilian dress and on foot, so as to escape notice. The fact that His Majesty knew him only slightly did not seem to diminish the confidence he placed in him; quite the contrary. The Duc de Tarente had been in Paris less than six days. The first contacts last year had been rather unsatisfactory. Louis XVIII had not warmed to this Marshal who took the liberalism of the restored monarchy rather too seriously; and then, too, Jacques-Étienne's forthright character was a handicap to him in his relations with the new sovereign, as it had been not so long before with the Emperor. Before he had joined his government, no one would have anticipated this favor. Since the summer of 1814, he had been living in Bourges—where his division had been set up as a command—or on his nearby property of Courcelles. He had been appointed to Nîmes in early March, and had been diverted on the way to his new residence by a message from the Duc d'Orléans summoning him to Lyons, whence he had been obliged to flee before Napoleon's arrival because of the rebellion of the troops. His Paris house was empty: little Sidonie had remained in Courcelles with her Aunt Sophie, and since his second daughter Adèle had married Alphonse Perregaux in 1815, two years after his elder daughter's marriage, the house on the rue de l'Université had been almost wholly given over to the proliferating concierge couple. In the darkened billiard room Jacques-Étienne had rediscovered his violin, lying in its case with the blue plush lining. It was a long time since he had played it. He did not consider he had any special talent, but it was a love he had inherited, along with his romantic Scots eyes, from his father the Jacobite, a man mad about Handel whom he had known in his blindness.

Before going to the Pavillon de Flore, he had played a little in the big solitary house. The violin had been a part of his charm as a youth. During his first betrothal, at Saint-Germain-en-Laye; when Marie-Constance accompanied him on the harpsichord. It had been perhaps the only time in his life when he had been uncalculatingly in love. Later, his second wife—Sidonie's mother—would make fun of him whenever he picked up his "fiddle," as she called it. She had died after two years, and, left with his two daughters, he had no desire to remarry. Oh, it wasn't only because of the violin! Macdonald now found in it a kind of escape. Too bad he had not worked at his instrument more seriously. On this Palm Sunday he was playing Haydn at sight. It made him forget his rheumatism. And he was meditating on the strangeness of his whole life, on the oddity of this sudden royal confidence. It had been a peculiar week for him.

Having arrived on Monday evening, he had found himself appointed, on Tuesday, as second-in-command of the corps that was being organized at Melun under the Duc de Berry to cover the capital. But he had been kept completely outside this fine organization until Saturday, despite the King's cajoleries. For four days he had cooled his heels in antechambers, sent from one to another, through all the ways and byways of the Court, as though danger had not been at the very gates—for it was obvious from the speech His Majesty had made on Thursday before the joint session of the Chambers that he had no idea of the pressing nature of the peril. On Saturday Macdonald had at last been received by his hierarchical chief, Monseigneur le Duc de Berry, who had been a little cruder and more insufferable than usual —he must be losing his head, his big ugly head, for he seemed on the verge of tears, and furious to have it noticed. And the Marshal had sent the King his resignation, which he had had to retract in the evening.

That was yesterday: the King was then considering retiring to La Vendée. Or to Bordeaux. Macdonald had been the first to recommend Flanders instead, Lille or Dunkirk. This had struck the sovereign as an ingenious notion: but surely he had had plenty of time to think it over? And then, out of the blue, on Sunday morning, this very day, at seven at the Duc de Berry's whither he had been summoned by courier, he had learned from the Prince's lips of Ney's treason. The whole city had known of it two days before, but the Court—although a lot of its people, still not believing it, had already sent their women abroad— had come round to believing it only last night upon the arrival of the generals who had returned to the capital after breaking with the Prince de la Moskowa when he had gone over to Buonaparte at Auxerre. The day before, at least, people pretended to one another not to believe Baron Clouet's heart-rending story.

Perhaps that explained Monseigneur's nervousness yesterday. Macdonald had found the Duc de Berry altogether changed. He seemed to go out of his way to be pleasant to him, as though trying to make amends for the scene of the day before. Suddenly Macdonald had noticed the ethereal quality of Monseigneur's eyes, which counteracted the homeliness of his features. Jacques-Étienne Macdonald stopped playing. From the garden in front of his house came a succession of clear bird-notes. They sing better than I do! he thought.

Ney! I have seen a lot of things in my life. Dumouriez, Moreau, Pichegrue . . . but Ney! I would never have believed it. In 1814, Macdonald had been loyal to Napoleon to the end. Friends of a lifetime, like General de Beurnonville, a member of the provisional government in Paris in 1814 who had run for cover only a little too soon, or—and this was more serious—like Marmont and Souham who, militarily, had been the Emperor's undoing, and Ney when he had rushed over to lead the Bourbons. Yes, all this. But it had not prevented Macdonald from going to Fontainebleau, from being, so to speak, the vanquished Emperor's last card. Napoleon had asked no one to con-

tinue a meaningless struggle. The Duc de Tarente's rallying to the
Bourbons, later—well, a week later—was not disloyalty, but the
natural behavior of a soldier.

It was in Compiègne in late April that Jacques-Étienne had joined
the King. He had accompanied him to the château of Saint-Ouen,
where Louis XVIII was waiting for the ceremonial of the procession
to be decided upon. He had not been out of place as all the Marshals,
or nearly all of them, were there. Had it been only Berthier . . . but
Oudinot, for example. The Princes, in any case, did what they could.
It is true that if the royal safety had rather oddly been entrusted to
Marshal Oudinot on May 3rd, that had been somewhat by chance:
the King had first entrusted the command of the area to that fine
nephew of his, the Duc de Berry. But Charles-Ferdinand had been in
a hurry to enjoy the pleasures of Paris and had handed his duties over
to Oudinot. Thus the Marshals had straightaway become the guardians
of the Monarchy. In the face of defeat, of the folly of hopelessly prolonged wars, a Macdonald does not cast opprobrium on Marmont,
Souham or Ney; he joins them. But Ney's going back on his word now,
after having been sent by the King to bar the road to Bonaparte, and
going over to Bonaparte, *that* he could not countenance: military
honor did not allow *that*. What about the *coup d'état* of the 18th
Brumaire then? you might ask. The two situations were not comparable. Brumaire was a betrayal only of civilians. Bonaparte was the
army.

I really shouldn't play any more, he was thinking. Besides, my eyesight is failing. Soon I'll need glasses to read the notes.

They had decided to send all available troops out on the two roads
to Fontainebleau. Then, with the Duc de Berry and Monsieur, his
father, they had gone to the King. It was at this point that His Majesty
had resolved to go to Lille, but he did not want this to be known. So
they had invented the story of the review to be held on the Champ-de-
Mars. Marmont, who commanded the Household, had made a thousand difficulties about assembling it because he favored resistance in
the Louvre. Madness! The whole day had been taken up by orders and
counter-orders. And so, called to the Palace, Macdonald had put on his
tête-de-nègre coat and his olive breeches. The concierge did not
amount to much as a valet, but his wife was handy with an iron. It
was raining. Jacques-Étienne unfurled his umbrella and slowly made
his way to the quays.

No one would have recognized him as the lieutenant general of the
Melun Camp. No one except Bourrienne's emissary, who was follow-

ing him at a distance and was preparing to make an intelligent report on the Marshal's disguise. He was an ambitious police agent.
In his view, as in everyone's, a Marshal was bound to commit treason,
and he was certainly counting on it as he shadowed this one. His mind
was absorbed by the plot that he was going to uncover; but he was
already wondering to whom he would disclose it. And what items to
put into a small expense account. . . .

Jacques-Étienne was walking in the rain, and he was forgetting that
this was Palm Sunday, in the year 1815, and that Bonaparte was at
Fontainebleau. All his life, in the army, he had seen men go to pieces,
had seen hatreds and personal interests push valuable officers into
internecine strife; and had himself been subjected to these meannesses,
these rivalries. All his life. It had not affected his behavior in the
slightest. He had served the Revolution in all honesty, despite the
suspicions that weighed on him, despite his aristocratic background,
even though he had been thought to be Dumouriez's accomplice, even
though officers of the Convention had threatened him, arrested him,
released him a dozen times. The very rank of general which had come
to him in 1793 had been a snare rather than a joy. He had served
Bonaparte. He had been one of the men who had helped him seize
power on the 18th Brumaire, and then, for five years, he had been discarded.

Heavens, he had still been a young man, after all, and a hot-
blooded one; and General Leclerc's wife, Pauline Bonaparte, had had
her own sweet way with him! Five years, without counting the three
years in Copenhagen as minister plenipotentiary—*he,* just imagine!
For that assignment he had had to remarry; hence the arrangement
with General Joubert's widow who did not like the violin. And even
that marriage had not appeased the Emperor. Afterwards—afterwards
he had gone and buried himself at Courcelles. But how many times
Napoleon himself had thrust him aside. Pauline's shadow had always
loomed between him and the Emperor. All right, Macdonald was
serving Louis XVIII, whose favor he had enjoyed for exactly five days.
But he did not depend upon it. He had his house, his land. He had kept
his funds with Murat in the kingdom of Naples. The Restoration had
changed nothing.

All this seemed perfectly natural to him: he had certainly been ambitious at nineteen, at the Pawlet Institution, when he had imagined
himself to be Achilles. But, becoming a lieutenant in 1791, a colonel
early in '95, and a general that same summer, he had passed through
the hierarchy too quickly, for his ambition not to have vanished with

his youth. He, who had been so often at death's door, now yearned for a quiet life. He remembered a June evening close to the end of the century, between Bologna and Modena, when a stray party of Austrian lancers emerging from a low road had knocked him from his horse before he had caught sight of them. There he was, in the Italian heat, the acrid dust of the road, his head wounded, unable to get up, while frightened horses, abandoned by their riders who were fleeing on foot, passed over him. He had lost consciousness. Then he had not been afraid to die. He had already lost Marie-Constance, and his youth. The return to France, in those jolting carriages, with every bounce of the roads communicating itself to his caved-in chest. He remembered, too, the night of the victory of Wagram, after the charge by Law de Lauriston—who today commanded the Gray Musketeers—had released the fire of a hundred artillery pieces on the enemy, when the maneuver of his troops had broken Archduke Charles's center—that house whose roof had been blown away, still smoking from a fire which had only just been put out, where he had stretched out on a pile of hay on the floor, his knee damaged by a horse's hoof—the frightful pain—the whole July sky full of stars over his head. How he had longed for his violin that starry night, to make him forget his knee! That incomparable night in which so many thoughts had passed through him. Glory makes things easy. Despite pain, despite doubts. That idea within him of a great universal peace, and all the beauty of Italy, the art of antiquity, the music of Germany: everything blending in him and coming back to him, Naples and Vienna, there before them, where Beethoven was. And when in the morning the Emperor entered the ruin to salute him and say, *I name you a Marshal of France,* it had been but a final chord, the resolution of a long nocturnal phrase.

The Palace was surrounded by a noisy crowd; people were pressing round the King's carriages. Only a sprinkling of droplets fell from a sky now turning bright. There was a bustling movement of officers, a feeling of departure; and through the windows people could be seen inside—courtiers, priests, women—bumping into one another, an agitation of wardrobes opened and emptied, trunks being packed. The carriages, which had been standing for hours, increased the public anxiety.

"His Majesty is waiting for you," said Monsieur d'Albignac, chief of staff of the Lifeguards and commander of the Tuileries. He was pale and overwrought. A little violin music, Macdonald reflected, would do him a world of good too. He looked at his watch: a quarter to four.

Someone leaving the King's quarters stepped aside to let him pass: he vaguely recognized Father Elisée, who massaged and tended Louis XVIII. Thank God, the Marshal thought to himself, at least I don't yet need that Jesuit's mint alcohol.

With the Sovereign, besides the inevitable Blacas, was the Prince de Wagram, his old comrade of the 18th Brumaire, furiously chewing his fingernails. Berthier had put on still more fat, looked even older. But he was—how old?—sixty-two, sixty-three; and he had responsibilities, three under-age children, a young wife and an old mistress, the mansion on the rue Neuve-des-Capucines, Chambord and the Grosbois property. Seeing the anguish in his eyes and the perspiration on his brow suddenly made Macdonald feel young, cheerful, in good spirits. A phrase of Haydn's kept coming back into his head, kept coming back . . . And how did it go after that? And what was His Majesty saying?

"This month of March," Louis le Désiré was saying, "I know of nothing worse for rheumatism. And you can image what it would be like on the roads! Tell me, Monsieur le Maréchal, haven't you a son-in-law in Beauvais?"

Seen from the École Militaire to the Seine, the Champ-de-Mars was like an immense aviary behind its bars of rain. At least that was how it looked to Colonel César de Chastellux of the Light Horse, perhaps because the word "aviary" always brought back to him his childhood, the Bellevue palace, home of Louis XVI's aunts, Mesdames Victorie, Adélaide and Sophie, that multicolored paradise full of parakeets and macaws, that hothouse like a novel by Monsieur de Saint-Pierre, full of palm trees and unknown flowers and fluttering with brightly colored birds.

Here the medley of colors was supplied by more than three thousand men and fifteen to sixteen hundred scarlet-saddled horses, a mosaic of uniforms with helmets, bearskins, two-pointed hats, plumes, epaulets, cartridge pouches, bands, sword knots, tassels and buttons, fleurs-de-lis, sunbursts and grenade ornaments, standards, cravats, buckles, shoulder knots, swords and sabers, guns and muskets, all dominated by the white cloaks of the Guards. The entire Royal Household, on the alert in the rain since two o'clock, the companies forming flower beds in which the diversity of arms was augmented by the variety of the dress—for it had been possible to assemble all these men merely by picking them up from wherever they happened to be after the morning's call, except for those units that had drilled on the

Grenelle ground. Some were in full dress, others in riding or town dress; and crowded together in front of the squadrons were all the horsemen who lacked mounts. As César de Chastellux passed, he gave a saber salute to the staff of the Gendarmes of the King's Guard, with his cousin Étienne de Durfort, who was its captain lieutenant.

From the ranks of the Lifeguards there rose an impatient cackling which was further reminiscent of Bellevue; it was among them that disparities in uniform were most marked, and as they composed the great majority, the number of Guardsmen on foot accentuated the impression that the review had been fitted out at some vast rummage sale. Grammont's company, commanded by Tony de Reiset, who was completely absorbed by what his brother-in-law, Baron Clouet, was telling him about events in Lyons, was even more nondescript than the rest, though it was the oldest in point of service and the best mounted. But it had been suddenly swelled by the many sons of nobility who would have considered themselves dishonored to belong to Wagram's company, or Raguse's, which were of such recent date! The blue coats crossed with gold, the black two-pointed hats, amid the black- or red-plumed helmets with the yellow bronzes and the leather, the white cloaks, and the red cassocks with gold frogs and loops were all a little bewildering; but César had a feeling of participating in a kind of melancholy family party. Everywhere there were relatives of the Chastellux', the Damas, the La Rochejaqueleins, the Noailles, the Lorges; a jumble of generations and of ranks, *émigrés* who had returned from Poland or Italy, from England or Austria, and that whole younger generation which had lived for so long in the shadow of the eagles, buried away in crumbling properties, forests and gardens, hidden away in the provinces, dreaming of the return of the Princes. And those sons of nobility who had served under the Usurper because for them to live was to serve, and they could imagine no other calling than the military. Yes, it was an immense aviary of birds with fiery plumage, anxious and rain-soaked, whose embroidered flags with their Latin devices fluttered like wings. There was a rumor to the effect that the story of Ney's treason had proved to be unfounded. There you are! What did I tell you? But look here! Tony de Reiset could still hear Baron Clouet's story ringing in his ears.

César de Chastellux was on his way to join his company. He had left M. le Comte Charles de Damas, captain of the Light Horse and his father-in-law, whose assistant he was, at the École Militaire—had left him with Marshal Marmont, whose orders he was bringing. Thus everything ended here, and the colonel's eyes lifted from across the Seine toward the heights of Chaillot. *Effect a movement in the direction of Saint-Denis.* . . . All day long Paris had been emptied of its troops, some heading toward Villeneuve-Saint-Georges or Essonnes, others sent north of the city. But the Royal Household: so His Majesty was not coming to carry out this review which had been prepared with such great difficulty? Why Saint-Denis? To remain there? And if not, where would they go from there? What were the Princes going to do? Orders to proceed to Saint-Denis had not as yet been given; they were simply to wait for the signal, be ready to effect a movement in the direction of Saint-Denis. . . . But were they abandoning Paris, then? Were they abandoning the King? The Light Horse were all at the other end, along the river, between the Black Musketeers and the Gray Musketeers.

Chastellux kept saying to himself, This is the end, this is the end. Again he remembered scenes of his past, that return, amid the cries of the rabble, from Versailles to Paris in the royal coach in October of '89, when he was not yet ten; and the royal children with whom his sisters and he had played during the last hours; exile, Naples, where he had served until the coming of Murat. Then the return to imperial France, the old family home near Gisors, Le Thil, where Georgine was to meet Charles— César stopped his horse. What was going on? Over there, Musketeers and Light Horse seemed to be getting into marching formation. To tell the truth, the thirty-five-year-old colonel who had refused to serve the Usurper bore the responsibility for that marriage. It was he who had persuaded his family. Had he not badgered his father, irresolute as ever, when he had tried to find pretexts not to marry off his last-born? To be sure, it was because he had had the impression that his sister was smitten with Labédoyère, because he had seemed to read this in the girl's eyes, and he wanted her to be happy. But perhaps also because Charles had won him over, as he charmed everyone. And Georgine . . . poor little sister!

Why yes, his company was executing a movement! He spurred his horse and shouted to the Chevalier de la Marchée, who seemed to be following the maneuver, words to which the other answered by a gesture of denial. The Comte de Lussac, who was in command, turned around and came toward the adjutant commander. What? You're leaving the Champ-de-Mars? They were not the only ones; it was a general order. But as it happened, Colonel de Castellux was bringing Marmont's order: to hold themselves in readiness to effect a movement in the direction of Saint-Denis. Hold themselves in readiness? That meant wait for the order. The order had come. From where? From whom? Was it or was it not the Marshal who had been in command of the Household for the past three days? They did not know where the order came from, but there had been an order. Perhaps from the Palace. Directly from the Comte d'Albignac, chief of staff of the Life-guards, who was in command of the Tuileries . . . or from Lieutenant General Comte Maison, who governed the first military division of Paris and its vicinity. Or from the minister secretary of state of the Royal Household, M. de Blacas d'Aulps; that is to say from the King himself. Or from Monseigneur the Duc de Berry, who was assuming the direction of the operations to cover the capital. Unless it were from Marshal Macdonald, his second-in-command; perhaps from the Duc de Feltre. "Clarke has no right to give orders to the army, damn it! Since when do the troops move at a sign from the War Minister?"

The movement was too far under way to be stopped. And besides, perhaps it was His Most Serene Highness Monseigneur the Prince de Condé, grand master of the Household, who had transmitted the order. Or Monseigneur the Duc de Bourbon. César felt a flush of irritation. In the first place, the Duc de Bourbon had left for La Vendée. When everyone commands, it is as if no one commands. Well, there was nothing he could do! He rode over to the Comte de Lussac and proceeded to head the maneuver.

The whole aviary now seemed to come running, like the dwarf parakeets long ago when he used to scatter bread crumbs. The masses on horseback pivoted, the drums beat, the standards turned in the wind, those on foot (they could hardly be called infantrymen) formed ranks like schoolboys.

César de Chastellux kept repeating to himself, The end, the end . . . And he kept thinking of his little sister in tears, and he accused himself. Was it not he who had forced her marriage through against his family's will, was it not he who last year had recalled Charles de Labédoyère after he had resigned from the army, and had had him assigned to the command of the 7th regiment through the good graces of M. le Duc d'Orléans—on the pledge of Roger de Damas, Pauline's husband? What his Uncle de Lorge had said yesterday about this was simply absurd. He dismissed the thought: the fact nevertheless remained that if he had not enabled Charles to enter the King's service, his brother-in-law could not have gone over to Buonaparte in Grenoble with all his soldiers. César thought of all the members of his family who had died on the guillotine, of those who had died in La Vendée. And it was he and his brother who, in 1814, had called Charles back into the King's service. A traitor in the family! A man must not be afraid of words. Yet César was horribly afraid of words. To César it had been inconceivable that Labédoyère, tied as he was to the Chastellux', should withdraw from the scene when the legitimate sovereign returned.

Being in charge of the mounted guard at that time, César was responsible to Monseigneur the Comte d'Artois, as today he was under the orders of his father-in-law, the Comte de Damas. He accompanied him to the Te Deum in Notre Dame. And even today, everything that ought to separate him from his brother-in-law still did not prevail over the affection he bore him. Charles de Labédoyère—could there be any doubt that Georgine loved him? He was so handsome, so impetuous, so brave. True, he had been an officer of the Empire, but as he used to say so well, *I fight, not for the Emperor, but for France.* And he had not been three weeks at his post when he had handed his regiment over to the Usurper. That such a thing should happen, in our family! The terrible thing to César de Chastellux was that even the horror of treason could not make him hate his brother-in-law. He was haunted by the scene of the day before, in the rue du Bac, with Georgine, who kept the shutters of her room closed, a Georgine dressed in black, passing from tears to prayers, who looked with terror at the child she had had by Charles. . . . His wife Zéphirine had had to let César out on the sly.

The maneuver was being carried out mechanically. These inexperienced youngsters must have it in their blood not to throw everything into confusion. There was no denying the fact that Wagram's company, which had arrived from Meaux the day before, had good form. César saw it all as in a fog. Charles, Charles—"Halt!" They had to let the Grenadiers pass.

At this moment a clamor arose along the quay: a courier ran to see what was happening. The movement of the Royal Household seemed to have stopped of its own accord, troops were surging back. What was going on? The orders flung out seemed to have no effect. The rain was coming down with renewed violence. The horses' rumps backed away before the Grenadiers. Someone over there was waving a sword. All of a sudden the whole fine order was lost. No one seemed to know what he was supposed to do. Horsemen jostled the men on foot; there were shouts, and in no time the whole Champ-de-Mars was one vast congestion of men and horses. Through all this a group of staff officers, loudly cursing, was forging its way toward the Seine, Marmont in the lead, flanked by Colonel Fabvier, both of them having just arrived from the École Militaire.

"What's going on, Colonel?" the Marshal shouted to Chastellux, and did not even listen for the reply. His company, Raguse's Lifeguards, was already over there crossing the bridge, and its vanguard had reached the Allée des Veuves. The Grenadiers, recognizing him, made way for the Marshal, and Chastellux watched him cross over to the other bank.

Then, suddenly, there was an uproar. What were they saying? *The King, the King* . . . what? Chastellux made a sign to the Comte de Lussac, and they overtook the Grenadiers who had re-formed, leaving a passage behind Marmont. What were they saying about the King? Suddenly they understood. They saw the carriage pass. It was approaching along the Quai d'Orsay, a six-horse equipage which they all knew well, preceded by the familiar equerry. Before the van of the moving troops, amid the complete disorder of the Household, His Majesty was arriving from the Tuileries at a good pace. His plump head and gray hair plainly visible in the door, Louis XVIII cried something to the equerry, and, without slowing down, the royal coach turned between the horses of Raguse's company, which drew back with great difficulty, and passed over the bridge in Marmont's wake. As usual without the slightest regard for anything or anyone: people could just get out of the way!

What was to be done? Resume the maneuver? Stop it? The order had been given to proceed to Saint-Denis. . . . Was the King leaving Paris? It was a little after four. The coach was entering the Avenue des Veuves. The Lifeguards, who by this time had been able to mass there, presented arms. The Marshal came to salute the King. And from a distance His Majesty could be seen shouting something to him through the carriage door. Immediately Colonel Fabvier retraced his steps back to the bridge.

He was bringing the counter-order: they were no longer going to Saint-Denis. The King was returning to the Louvre, and we to our barracks. The review? Who said anything about a review?

César was all but beside himself. He asked his father-in-law to be relieved: Zéphirine could not be left alone all this time with poor Georgine sobbing away. "All right," said Charles de Damas, "go and see your wife, Colonel. Kiss her for me, and the child."

Say what you liked, the count cut a fine figure on horseback! When you remembered that he was a good three or four years older than His Majesty! The mania His Majesty had for riding full speed in a carriage, as though to make up for his infirmity! César had heard it was Father Elisée who had put it into his head that racing his equipage produced some physical reaction. I don't know. . . .

III

The Palais Royal by Lamplight

TONIGHT everything that Théodore once believed in had ceased to have meaning.

Through the high windows of the Tuileries he had witnessed the bustle of the servants, the preparations for the feast. His Excellency de Peralada, his Catholic Majesty's ambassador, was the guest of the major-domo of the Palace, his coach was in the courtyard, there were ravishing women, officers and great lords laughing and talking in loud voices. Elaborate dishes were being passed around in the candlelight. Outside it was already dark, and people of every description were drawing near, like thieves, to glimpse what they could of the festivity through the high casements.

The Palace was being guarded by the National Guards, and the men of the Household assigned to the Pavillon de Flore had left their horses under the archways of the Louvre. The intermittent rain did not prevent the rabble from surrounding the Palace like flies drawn by rotting flesh. The crowd quieted a bit at seven o'clock, when someone had the good idea of sending the carriages away. At least nothing would happen before nine o'clock. A small group of Musketeers and Lifeguards remained on guard. The rest could go and dine in the nearby restaurants. Not too far, though—they were sure to be on the move tonight.

Tonight when everything that Théodore once believed in had ceased to have meaning. The Spanish party made a great din—as if wantonly, as if to say to the people: You can see for yourselves that everything is normal; is this the kind of show that precedes a flight?

But where was the King? Where were the Princes? Ministers kept arriving—Jaucourt, Bourrienne, the Abbé de Montesquiou. Certainly they were not bound for the ambassador's banquet, though they rushed upstairs.

A while ago, to be sure, trunks had been carried out to the gate, and people were still saying the King had made no decision. They said a lot of things. Everybody talked. An unhealthy fever prevailed, voices were too loud to be true. Benjamin Constant's morning article was already out of date, and was mentioned with a shrug of the shoulders.

Where was the country's fate being decided? Out there on the roads, where the soldiers were throwing away their white cockades and going over to the Corsican? There was a rumor that the Villejuif garrison had sent its officers packing and raised the cry of *Vive l'Empereur!* An advance guard was said to have reached the Charenton Bridge, which was being defended by the Law School students. Or was the fate of France being decided in Vienna where Talleyrand was playing for high stakes with the plenipotentiaries of Europe? In the corridors of the Palace it was already being admitted that no one there any longer counted on the people of France, or on the army, which was ripe with rebellion. Royalty staked its hopes on foreign intervention. Why hadn't the Prussians and the Russians been called to the rescue? What were they waiting for? The Ogre wouldn't have carried much weight if a few Austrian divisions had been marching on Paris!

Théodore no longer believed in anything, or in anyone.

He had come to defend the Princes, as a soldier who had given his oath, not from any great love for the Princes but because he was forced to it by the elementary notion of duty. Besides, Napoleon was the Napoleon of defeat, the man who had dragged the French armies into the far frozen snows, who had waged that sly, dirty war in Spain; the Napoleon who had made Gros remove from his paintings the generals he was jealous of, and who insisted always on being in the center of the canvas. Théodore respected Gros. He was perhaps the only painter he liked among living French artists. Ah, Gros's drawings for *Les Pestiférés*! But nothing could ever slake That Man's thirst for fame. At the time of his anointing as Emperor he had had a monumental statue on a chariot, a statue of himself, naked and wreathed with laurels, drawn through the streets of Paris. For the Emperor craved also the glory that attaches to the body, perfection of muscle, a fine physique. That little yellow man, whom power had puffed with fat and endowed with a paunch. And everywhere his initial, the N placed like a seal on monuments, on men, on history. This man who was the embodiment of war.

The story went that Duroc, one of his most faithful lieutenants, on the very morning of his death had said in a fit of prophetic despondency, "He will be the death of all of us. Not one of us will return home." And hadn't Junot, whom he had made a duke and driven mad, written to him in a moment of lucidity: *I who love you as the savage worships the sun, want no more of this eternal war that must be waged for you, I want no more of it!* It was d'Aubigny who had told him this, and he had had it also from young Regnault de Saint-Jean-d'Angély. They were very well informed about such things in the rue de Provence, where Regnault's mother lived.

Yes, but today Bonaparte—the Bonaparte whom Gros, Gérard and David had painted—was a man on the roads, driving toward Paris with a handful of soldiers, stirring the people to sudden enthusiasm. He could imagine those halts in mountain inns, the villages as Napoleon passed through them, the towns he entered at nightfall by torchlight. He was already a man of fifty, or almost, with his unbuttoned gray frock coat, his boots, his white breeches. All people remembered was the flags, the symbol of the eagle, the sun of Austerlitz; and they welcomed this man, almost alone, as the negation of everything that had happened to them since 1814— That society returned from exile, those lords of the manor who had emerged from the shadows and passed in hunting parties, of that immense hoary parasitism, the stupid revenges, the humiliations by the shovelful. They had forgotten the immense venality of the Empire, the endowments, the gifts, the pensions. And Théodore opened his eyes wide and visualized the march and the falsehood, the illusions; and in the distant tread of the re-formed armies he heard the nailing down of new, open, avid coffins. But to prefer Louis XVIII to Napoleon! Yet there was only this alternative. What other candidate was there? What Republic?

For him truth was the movement of the horse, the wild ride in which he could expend and exhaust himself—the horse seen in the dark stalls of stables, a shape lighter than the surrounding shadow, the way it stirred, pawed the ground and shied! Never was a painting dark enough for Théodore. Life was like a crime suddenly disclosed, and he dreamed of capturing its image. Between That Man on his forced marches, before whom the dispossessed, as well as the turncoat

Marshals who, having kept their gold braids thanks to the King, seemed suddenly seized with a common madness—between him and this King, with his favorite, his court priests, his councilors, Géricault was like a painter between two paintings. But his only urge was to toss away his brushes. Nothing gave him a sense of exaltation; his throat was filled with the bitterness of deception. Had he been nothing more than a typical young man of his time? Would all the fire in his veins be consumed in the catastrophe of the Empire, and was he that beaten Cuirassier he had painted sitting on his dying horse? This tragicomedy in which one Court drove out another, in which the fine mansions of Paris changed tenants and posts were again redistributed, was a confused spectacle which could not be reduced to any organized principle. One certain thing was that Theodore would never paint a "Return from Elba" with everything composed around the Emperor's conventional pose! Nor would he paint the rottenness that still infested the Tuileries. Feeling in his arms and in his heart a great emptiness that seemed impossible to fill, young Géricault saw a future black as pitch.

His steps had brought him to the rue Montpensier. To the left were cafés whose lights could be seen shining lower down; and to the right the big buildings of the Palais Royal, centers of devouring passion where politics held sway, and the clash of views was accompanied by the banging of fists on tables in the midst of informers and women. Théodore was alone: the company of his comrades had become unbearable. He was not hungry, but he wouldn't mind a drink. Coffee black as his thoughts. There was the Café de Foy where Horace Vernet as a child had painted a bird on the ceiling which could still be seen. He had been seven years old at the time. Géricault was in the mood to go in there and sit down, lift his head, look at the bird and meditate. But it was a café frequented by half-pay soldiers and republicans: it would be foolish, in his red coat, to enter it. He hesitated, shrugged his shoulders. Well, why not? He would despise himself for being afraid. What was a life that depended on a man's entering one café rather than another? Again he remembered the man killed by the mob at the Tuileries. And he was reminded of one of his companions in the Musketeers, whom a colonel of the Empire had left in an alley behind the Palais Royal, stretched out, lifeless. The way he had wiped the sword clean with a handkerchief! *That* was something he could perhaps paint if he had sufficiently handsome models. A picture only gains by darkening. . . .

And speaking of models, if they hadn't had the bright idea of sending his regiment to Béthune in January, Robert Dieudonné might have been there, in that café, and Théodore would have stepped in—that café or another. . . . It might have been Robert who had been insulted. . . .

The smoke-laden café was full, with people standing between the tables, women who had let their shawls slip off their bare shoulders, a crowd that was not the everyday crowd, split into groups but animated by a single loud anxiety which made the talk skirt round what was on everyone's mind. The tricolored cockades, the bouquets of violets, were worn unconcernedly, aggressively. Théodore's uniform immediately caused some great louts to nudge one another, and loud words, hard words, were spoken around him, words surely intended for him. He sat down on a stool only just vacated by an old fellow who had got up to follow two young ladies of the establishment. He paid no attention to the challenging remarks around him as he pulled out his long pipe and lighted it calmly. Beside him another lone customer, a young man with a black-collared brown coat and glasses, was covering a growing pile of sheets of paper in a small, fine hand.

Yet what Théodore had in his mind: how was he to choose? The man for whom war must be endlessly waged, or the one who could reign only by relying on foreign bayonets? Actually this was not exactly the way the question formulated itself in Théo's head: he was hesitating between Marc-Antoine d'Aubigny and Robert Dieudonné. The head or the body . . . The thought remained uncompleted. The threatening looks directed at him by young men with alcoholic breaths, the way they sized him up . . . Théodore did not know whether he would accompany the King in his flight from Paris any more than he knew whether he was going to fight that fellow who was eying him and loudly saying disagreeable things about the Reds. Something in him itched for a fight, he felt cocky and fit, he arched his shoulders, flexed the muscles of his arms; it would not take much to make him leap up. And anyway, why shouldn't he fight? As well be done with it. And in the alleys back there, as had happened the other night, that little fool who had been a poor enough specimen alive, but had made a passable corpse. . . . Where in the world had he seen the man beside him, a young man of perhaps twenty with a studious and passionate air about him?

But suddenly someone had come and sat down at his table.

A man with a gray beard, disheveled hair, an old torn box coat, a magnificent kind of beggar. With a gesture he stopped the youths who were approaching the Musketeer.

"You don't recognize me?" asked the man. "Well, never mind, I'm thirsty. Buy me a drink."

It was Cadamour, the model. He was served some beer. How old was he? Whatever his age, naked he compared favorably with Napoleon. Moreover he had taken part in all the painted battles, all the Greek scenes of the David school. He had posed for Girodet and for Prud'hon. Generations had slaved to picture his deltoid muscles. He had been among the corpses of the Eylau graveyard as well as in the Thermopylae, which David had painted in secret. All his life he had sold his physical beauty. It had not enriched him.

"Let me talk with monsieur," he said to the loafers. "He's a painter; the rags he's wearing make no difference."

Cadamour was known there. He was a republican, and on one occasion he had turned up in this café with Duplay-Jambe-de-bois (Peg-leg), the nephew of the joiner in whose house Robespierre had lived, which everyone, including Cadamour himself, regarded as conclusive proof of his republicanism. Because they didn't know that Peg-leg worked for the police. Fouché's, to be sure. Still, the police. He reported on combinations among the workers. All people saw was that peg he had been dragging around ever since Valmy. To be seen at the Palais Royal with a patriot wounded at Valmy was a reference. Théodore and Cadamour were accordingly left alone. Besides which a wench had climbed onto a table and was singing *"Partant pour la Syrie"*—which was about Queen Hortense. . . .

"I'm not a Bonapartist," said Cadamour. "His troops fired on the people in Saint-Roch."

But this was just to get the conversation going. Apart from the fact that he wanted a little tobacco, all his thoughts this evening turned to art. He couldn't help it. The name of Bonaparte had caused the other man at the table to look up over his spectacles and stop writing. Cadamour, who noticed it, wrinkled his nose and changed his tone.

"You see, Monsieur Géricault, I'm not one to blame you for choosing to wear a red coat. One set of finery or another, they amount to the same thing. But what I don't understand is your having quit painting. That's stupid, and it isn't right."

He had got his information from Dedreux-Dorcy, for whom
he had posed as Epaminondas. The world, for him, revolved around
sculptors and painters. The rest—the Revolution, wars. Perhaps,
at bottom, he was against the Restoration, because this fashion for
pictures of Henri IV left little demand for his nude body. They
had no need of him for the costumed figure.

"You see, young fellow," he said, "I've knocked about the ateliers
a good deal. . . . You pose here and there, and people look at
you as though you were an animal. Hold the pose, sit well, look
into space. All they know about you. . . . They pick me for my
thighs, not for what I have inside my head. But those gentlemen
talk in front of me as if I were a piece of furniture. I've heard
plenty. And, leaving aside the tricks they like to play when they
have it in for you, I know how they talk when they really respect
a person. Oh, they don't go shouting it from the rooftops! Because
of the commissions, the competition . . ."

What was he getting at? The smoke was becoming dense and
its smell mingled with the smell of beer among the customers
crowded elbow to elbow. In spite of himself, Théodore's thoughts
went back to Guérin's studio, to his misadventures, to what made
him wish at times he were dead, the shame he had felt on hearing
certain remarks. On such occasions he would leap on his horse,
gallop like a madman, pass through the Porte des Martyrs, cross
the outer boulevard, circle Montmartre, dash across the plain toward
Saint-Denis or Montmorency. How his heart would beat on his
return! But he would have forgotten his comrades' glances, the
things half whispered, the master's contemptuous remarks.

"What you don't know, Monsieur Géricault, is the way they
talk about you when you're not there. Do you realize that you get
under their skin? Like nobody else. That's your crime. And it
bothers them. Believe me, I've heard them jabber for nearly
forty years. I began young. I can recognize that special tone of voice,
you can't explain it. And *you* think they despise you. You're an
idiot, Monsieur Géricault: they admire you. That's just their way."

Tonight Théodore no longer believed in anything, nor in anyone.
It would certainly take more than a Cadamour to raise his spirits.
For that matter, did it really have anything to do with his painting?—
Tonight, when the fabric of history was being ripped asunder in
the Pavillon de Flore, when discordant voices could be heard in
the darkness, the voices of the forgotten people, settled once and
for all, it seemed, beneath the white flag, the fleur-de-lis, from

whom bursts of song rose at moments out there in the rain, in the
street, where a muffled, incomprehensible agitation prevailed. Tonight
when they were closing the Salon and removing the "Cavalry
officer" who had the body of a King's Grenadier and the face of a
republican.

What was Cadamour saying? He was mixing everything up.
He felt an old tenderness for M. David. If he had anything against
Théodore, it would be that his painting was being used as a
weapon against M. David's painting. "I was there when he came
to the 1812 Salon and posted himself in front of your big what-do-
you-call-it. There was a crowd round him, M. Drolling and M.
Gérard, M. Chinard, a lot of others. If you had heard him say,
'What's that?' I know what it's like when a thing grabs you by the
throat, hits you in the solar plexus. There he was thinking he
knew all there was to see, just moving along—one painting, and
then the next, and the lessons in each case to be drawn from the
one before. And then, bang! there *you* are: a young scamp, where
did he come from, nobody knows, from the first scratch he does
everything topsy-turvy—and you can't just shrug your shoulders
and pass it by. They told him your name, which meant nothing
to him. He got up closer, to have a better look at the brushwork.
Then he stepped back, to get the right distance, and he said,
'It's not like anything I know!' Only there was Gros's canvas,
just across from it, someone pulled him by the sleeve. A fine
canvas, you know, yet he looked at it sort of absent-mindedly.
The King of Naples, on his horse, you remember?"

Bon Dieu! And what were they going to decide, over there at the
Tuileries? When the Spanish ambassador had left, when the windows
were darkened, when the smell of food had evaporated. With this
rain, and the wind that whipped the white flag on the Pavillon de
l'Horloge. Miserable weather. And tomorrow, the day after tomorrow,
it would be spring.

Several tables away, a dark strapping wench who seemed at home
in the place was beckoning Cadamour with her bracelet-laden arm.
The model had at first responded with a slight nod of his handsome
head, then he turned toward Théodore.

"Excuse me, Monsieur Géricault," he said. "Someone is calling
me."

"Good, Cadamour! I wish you well," said the Musketeer with
a smile. "She's attractive. Don't mind me!"

"Ah, you've got the wrong idea! That was with her mother, over

twenty years ago, when I wasn't yet posing as a model of the noble
father for all you fellows. Zélie may be my daughter. I get the
benefit of the doubt, anyhow, and when she has a chance to put
aside a few titbits for me . . ."

As the model was leaving, Théodore noticed that the other man
at his table was eying him persistently. He was really very young,
and the King's Musketeer was annoyed by his stare. He was about
to tell him so when the other rose slightly from his chair, pushed
away his scrawl-covered papers, took off his spectacles and put
them down on the table; then, bowing, he said, "Monsieur Géricault,
you don't remember me?"

He certainly did not. Yet it seemed they had been introduced
by Jamar.

"You know, last year—almost immediately after . . . after . . ."
He wanted to say after the King had entered Paris, and it
embarrassed him as though he were speaking of something slightly
obscene. M. Géricault did not remember? It had been in Montmorency
last year, while the hawthorn was in bloom. There were three of
them of the same age, finishing at the same school in Blois—Jamar,
young Touchard—you know, his father was the director of the
Messageries—and himself, Thierry. At the Hôtel du Grand Cerf,
Mme. Dutocq's . . .

Yes Théodore remembered Jamar's joy when he had arrived on
Trick all winded, lathering, and had come into the inn unexpectedly
and found the young men eating marzipan turnovers. And the
political discussion into which the three fellow students had tried
to drag him. He had refused to let himself get involved. That
was one of Jamar's failings. The trio had seemed to him to have
republican leanings. Perhaps with some reservations . . .

"Why, yes, I remember!" Théodore exclaimed. "You are Monsieur
de Saint-Simon's disciple! Jamar let me read that essay of yours on
the reorganization of European society, in which you advocated
a union of France and England as a means of avoiding a second
revolution in our country. Interesting. But in light of what is
happening tonight, don't those ideas strike you as somewhat out
of date?"

The young man blushed. He explained that while his master,
Monsieur de Saint-Simon, had appealed to the Emperor in 1813
to ask him to promote the reforms necessary for the progress of
humankind, his battle in October 1814, and the thesis with which
he had been good enough to allow his pupil to be associated, was

not that of choosing between Bonaparte and the Bourbons. If Louis XVIII had been willing to listen to reason . . . even a week ago— But tonight, obviously tonight it was no longer clear to whom an appeal could be made tomorrow, who might create a united Europe. Surely institutions were the essential thing, rather than the form of sovereignty?

"Listen," he added with the same passion he put into his writing, "listen to those blatherskites, all of them already won over to the Little Shaver! I'll bet more than half of them are sincere republicans. Don't they realize that their idol has nothing but contempt for the Republic? He's aped the kings, created a nobility of upstarts, allied himself with the Emperor of Austria. Whereas, take the English— for two centuries, with a king more republican than their Cromwell was, they've been living under a charter we can only envy them."

"What are you getting at?" asked Théodore. "You mix everything up, Monsieur Thierry, and for me things are far simpler. All I want to know is whether my horse will be up to making the stretch that it will be expected to cover tonight."

The other was gathering up his papers nervously. Augustin Thierry found M. Géricault's tone all the more disagreeable since he knew from Jamar that this was not his customary manner. The painter was known for the respectful attention he normally gave to those who spoke to him even when they were his juniors, and for his reserve in speaking. Something unusual must be in the wind tonight. Augustin picked up his glasses, put them in a shagreen case and tried to think of a suitable apology for what must have seemed want of tact on his part in introducing himself thusly into the meditations of a table companion who was probably in a mood for solitude.

"*Mon Dieu,* Monsieur Géricault, I didn't mean to offend you— nor to inflict my ideas about politics on you. You must forgive me. I was writing, I've just come out of what I was writing— Yes, I do tend to confuse things. I'm a blunderer."

Théodore smiled at the other's discomfiture. "Let's forget about it," he said. "I'm not myself today, and I should hate to think I gave you the impression . . ."

Young people are quickly reassured, and Augustin looked at Théodore admiringly. How could he have failed to respond to the charm that everyone felt in Géricault's presence?

"I'm a blunderer nevertheless because what I wanted to tell you was something quite different. Just now—you must forgive me:

I couldn't help it, I was listening. Anyway, I heard your conversation with that—that gentleman: is it true that you have given up painting?"

Théodore studied him more closely. He was short, stocky for his age, not handsome, and at twenty already had the heavy features that evidenced his peasant forebears. A curly lock of chestnut hair fell over his left temple, and he had a nervous habit of contracting the muscles of his forehead which brought his eyebrows together over his light brown eyes—a habit due perhaps to the early use of glasses for reading. What was it Jamar had said about him? Something about a ballet dancer at the Opéra? Oh no, that was the other one, the son of the Messageries man, a ladykiller. . . .

"Were you interested in my painting?"

Had Jamar infected him with this enthusiasm? Young Augustin spoke, carried away. Not like an art critic. Not like an enlightened art lover. Did he even know what he was saying? Everything was a bit distorted in his head, as in a dream. He had not seen Théodore's paintings, he had dreamed them. The "Officer of the Guides," of 1812; the "Wounded Cuirassier," of 1814. . . .

"I was seventeen, monsieur, when I saw your 'Chasseur'— seventeen, you understand? I was still at the École Normale. It would have been so wonderful to be able to take everything at its face value. The Emperor was in Moscow, the news from Spain was bad. But who knows? Perhaps all this would still prove to have a meaning. Ah, if Napoleon were to shatter the empire of the Czars, give the land to the peasants, abolish serfdom! The terrible thing was the Spaniards: some of them had turned up in Paris. The things they told! Their hatred of France! Had we made the Revolution just to have everyone hate us? Or for Junot to strut about in Lisbon. And Marmont . . . But perhaps all this was only appearance, apparent contradiction. In the final analysis, our arms were bearers of progress. What made you wonder was the life at Court, the show of wealth, those grasping men and women! And what could official painting do to nourish the restless youth, with its doubts and its resentments, the prospect of conscription? When I saw your 'Chasseur' —a man, not a lay figure, in battle and not posing, the abandoned cannon in the foreground, that cloud of yellow gunpowder enveloping him, and especially the horse! Where the devil did you find that horse?"

"At Saint-Cloud," said Géricault.

"At Saint-Cloud?"

Théodore did not reply. He saw the slope of Saint-Cloud, the big rattletrap loaded with shopkeepers, and the animal—gray, dappled, incommensurable with its fate, with that Sunday jaunt, with that middle-class turnout. That mane, that chest! . . . What had caused it to rear suddenly in the shafts, making the people in the carriage scream? The September storm, a protest perhaps of strength subdued, an animal defiance of ignominious fate. A creature of fire. The image had long haunted him. But Augustin was already talking about something else.

"Have you any idea how the 'Cuirassier' affected us? We—I mean Jamar, Touchard, all of us, the innocents of the imperial drama. Have you any idea? Too young to have the blood of Europe on our hands, or the scars of glory on our bodies! Too old to be unaware, deafened by the cannon, seeking the meaning of this life and of these massacres, do you understand?"

Théodore knew perfectly well where that Cuirassier came from, and it wasn't Saint-Cloud or Suresnes! At that point he could no longer paint a prancing hero, even if he were an ordinary man, Dieudonné or d'Aubigny! The "Wounded Cuirassier" might have fallen on the retreat from Russia, or at Lützen like Duroc and Bessières. But in fact it was the campaign of France—Champaubert, a victory that would give its name neither to a duke nor to a prince, or simply the plain to the north of Paris, anywhere, near Beaumont or Noailles or the Porte de Clichy . . . He had dismounted. He was leading his horse by the bridle, saber in hand. Not a heroic and rearing horse, like the dappled gray of Saint-Cloud, but the horse of a beaten man, an ordinary bay horse. And he, a giant nevertheless, a wounded giant. He was leaving the battle, which continued in the distance in the smoke on a bridge that was being defended uselessly.

"The worst thing," said Augustin, "is the expression in the eyes. Eyes that seek heaven. Empty eyes. . . . If you knew what you have meant to us, to those of my age, would you despair, Monsieur Géricault, would you give up painting? And for what? My God, for what?"

Théodore listened to him and did not believe him. He believed in nothing, on this Palm Sunday night. His Cuirassier was not intended to be a symbol. But a man. Man. The tragic destiny of man. At the end there was only defeat. Others, at the idea of the Eagle's return, might be thrilled again by flags, salvoes, victories.

Not he. Napoleon was returning; but he was an outworn myth, a man at the end of his journey. Whither was he heading, toward what new catastrophe? And for Géricault, this night was the night of the King's anticipated flight, of the black cavalcade, of that thieves' departure in the rain over roads beset with uncertainty. In a first sketch he had given the "Wounded Cuirassier" the pose of Michelangelo's "Thinker." The only light in the world, the only light remaining to eyes already darkened by blood and fever, came from the sheen of the boots, the steel of the cuirass— But to hell with all that!

"I expect you know how those two canvases were received in the Salon that has just closed. Tomorrow they're taking them to my father's, and he'll store them away face to the wall. Failure—"

Young Thierry flung up his arms. Failure! Failure! The word hurt him, revolted him. Could a man of twenty tolerate the idea of failure, especially when he had been through the École Normale and had already co-signed important communications to the Institute with his master, M. le Comte Henri de Saint-Simon?

"Failure!" he said. "How could you expect a society in the process of reforming itself, divided, consisting on the one hand of men elected only yesterday and on the other of people sent packing twenty years ago, to stand that terrible diptych of glory and disaster, that twin exhibit in the 1814 Salon which combined the 'Chasseur' and the 'Wounded Cuirassier.' Look at what M. Gros sent to the same Salon! Why didn't you paint a 'Charming Gabrielle' or a 'Chicken in the Pot'? You would have been praised to the sky! You were Cassandra, going against the current, the bird of ill omen. What failure are you talking about? Don't you understand that tonight is *your* triumph?"

Géricault shook his head. "The misfortune of the Princes, the return of war . . . There's nothing to gloat over. So you've become a Bonapartist?"

Augustin had so much to say that he began to stutter. "W-w-w-why . . . you know p-p-perfectly well I haven't! The King! As if the King had anything to do with it! But he is the same King who signed the Charter. I defend institutions, not men. A family cause has nothing to do with it. For the moment that cause happens to be identical with the cause of the nation. It's the cause of our rights and of our liberty!"

"Listen to them," said Théodore.

The whole café, the women, the civilians, the soldiers, carried away by some mysterious contagion, was singing *"Veillons au salut de l'Empire."* "Look over there," added Théodore. "Look at Cadamour, Cadamour the republican." Standing beside his putative daughter, the old model was singing at the top of his voice.

"I heard him a while ago," Augustin said timidly, "repeating the old story about Bonaparte's firing on the people at Saint-Roch. To think that's the way history will be written! It was Barras who gave the order, not Bonaparte. Besides, it wasn't the people, it was a couple of hundred monarchist conspirators. But there he is, a Bonapartist."

"Let's get out," said the painter. "It might become unhealthy here for you as well as for me, young fellow, and under the arcades of the galleries the air will cool our ideas without our having to worry about the rain."

The gusts of damp wind in the Palais Royal arcades, illuminated by Monsieur Quinquet's oil lamps, did not greatly annoy the strollers. But the arcades that evening were invaded by a crowd of excited people of military complexion, in which were mingled women too elegantly dressed for the place and the hour—feathered hats, embroidered velvets, striking greens, marigold yellows, garnets and, in spite of the wet weather, bosoms daringly exposed by low-cut gowns, glittering with diamonds, genuine or false. Tonight there were so many vagabonds about elbowing citizens, foreigners, tipsy soldiers, ink vendors with their little carts, shopkeepers and clerks out on a spree, a sleight-of-hand artist with bristling hair who swallowed fire, and next to him a laurel-crowned woman who told fortunes from cards spread out in an upturned open umbrella. In short, an exasperating, bantering crowd, in which politics and danger collided with prostitution, men who murmured into your ear invitations to nearby houses, the goddesses of the place saying in loud voices, "What's wrong with the men tonight! Why, I haven't been upstairs three times."

"Let's go on over to the wooden arcades," Théodore said to Augustin.

Here the lights were more widely separated, and a penumbra favorable to the next stage of gallantry attracted a less dense crowd; besides, the rain dripped through the torn canvas roofs of these long arcades of booths, to make ankle-deep mud on the earthen floor. The wooden arcades—called on this side, near the Café de

Foy, Le Four, and on the other, Camp des Tartares—cut the dark garden in two, forming between the opposite blocks of buildings a rickety bridge of stalls, shops, and jerry-built houses in whose upper stories were to be found furnished lodgings, call houses— and police traps. Here Théodore's uniform was less conspicuous, and as most of the women they met were accompanied, the two young men walked on without being accosted and could talk freely.

They made an odd couple—the tall, slender, sturdy Musketeer with his helmet and cloak, and the young short-legged companion he had picked up, a strapping peasant from the region of Blois, curled locks on his left temple, while under the cocked felt hat the hair on the right side was already thinning. Now Théodore alone was talking. He spoke as he never did, as if he were a solitary wanderer in a forest. He would never have spoken thus with those he knew, not even with his closest friends such as Joseph or Horace, or even young Jamar. This Augustin who had dropped from the sky was no more real to him than a reflection, and here as night was falling things suddenly burst from his heart. Beneath the dripping roof of planks and sheets of canvas the two casually met companions paced the wooden arcades, ignoring those whom they jostled, not looking into the milliners' windows where women sat on tall stools working, at this late hour, on rush orders to be delivered in the morning: for whether the King decamped or not, the ladies of Paris needed spring bonnets.

Théodore talked and talked and talked.

What was he saying? Although young Thierry listened with wide-open ears, perhaps he did not really follow the words he heard. It was a little like the first time he had gone to the theatre, as a child. He had been eight years old, and a friend of his father's, Monsieur Métivier, who owned the theatre at Blois, had taken the whole family to his box to see an opera performed by a traveling company of actors. It was under the First Consul, when France had just broken with England. They were playing *Castor and Pollux* by Candeille, who was twenty-two years old and had been pleased to borrow a few airs from the opera by old Rameau.

It was all wonderful. There were forests and rocks, and people in dresses with big hoop skirts, belts decorated with sunbursts, feathers on their heads and lances in their hands, who sang movingly. Never for a moment had the child had the feeling of not under-standing what was going on; everything was linked together in the bright lights. There was a lady who came up to the front of the stage, of whom Monsieur Métivier said that she was a Dugazon. What did that mean? And why did he identify that handsome man by the bizarre name of *Haute-contre-marquée*? Only to add, incidentally, that to his taste Elleviou was much better. Augustin was not too sure which of these befeathered and half-naked seigneurs was Elleviou. But what did it matter? His cheeks were aflame, his head in a swirl; and the music brought gentle tears to his eyes. For there is something admirable about violins.

Tonight, at the Camp des Tartares, Géricault's very language was, for the young Saint-Simonian, full of Elleviou and of Dugazon. Théodore was speaking about painting as a painter, and the paintings in his speech were linked like the scenes of an opera in which, for the listener who has difficulty in following the libretto, music takes the place of logic as it passes from one aria to another without his having time to wonder how they are connected. Augustin heard names of painters punctuating Théodore's reverie, as he had once heard Monsieur Métivier speaking ecstatically to Monsieur Thierry, his father, of Mademoiselle Arnould or of Madame Saint-Hubert. And he remembered that it was said that Mademoiselle Arnould owed her renown to a lesson that she had sung in a Tenebrae service before some princess in a Paris church. In spite of himself, as he listened to Théodore he kept thinking—though the words still failed to assume their true meaning—that he in turn was listening to a lesson of Tenebrae which created a kind of halo of dark rays about the head of the speaker.

About whom was Géricault speaking? About himself or about one of those masters whom he applied himself endlessly to copying, so that it was as though he were slowly and painstakingly learning things about them that he would then proceed to express in his own way on a canvas on which he would work furiously for ten to twelve days and which the critics would describe as scamped? All the evil that he might have thought of Napoleon, of that egotistical tyrant who was responsible for so many deaths, was at bottom of little weight beside the gratitude he felt toward him for the Gallery of the Louvre, and the paintings brought from Italy. So much the worse if they had been obtained by pillage! But the painter about whom he was speaking resembled Théodore as a great shadow resembles the man whose tragic thoughts it betrays, amplifying the familiar gesture. Suddenly for the listening Thierry the painter's remarks assumed greater sharpness, as though a light had been moved.

"What faith can we have in critics?" Théodore was saying. "In some old papers at my uncle's, in Normandy, I've read a few poems by a poet who has been completely lost from sight because of the fate that overtook him. He was Marie-Joseph Chénier's brother. To my mind this unfortunate man, whom the Jacobins guillotined— and there is no doubt he conspired against them—explored the mysterious realm of poetry more deeply than any poet we have. What do the critics say about him? With all the frippery put out by the almanac makers to dress up the return of the Princes, surely there should in justice have been a small place for André Chénier. Not at all. For the rhymesters who represent tradition, and are in the ascendancy, cry out in terror whenever anyone mentions him because of the horrible license of which this Chénier was guilty and, royalists though they are, they prefer Marie-Joseph to him! Poor André, caught between the guillotine and the ultra-royalists of criticism who even in the tomb begrudge him the liberties he allowed himself in his verse forms so that he could say what he had to say! And as for us painters, you should hear them talk about the *grave faults* in our paintings, the lack of finish, our carelessly treated distances, the rough, sketchy character of what we have executed with so much zest."

Augustin understood the bitterness of these remarks. He himself had been furious when he had read the *Salons* of 1814, where the "Wounded Cuirassier" was described as a mere sketch, where the painter was advised to exhibit more moderation and pay more attention to his workmanship. But Théodore's mind was already in Italy, and here he came back to the painter he had spoken of a while back.

"And all the criticisms that were leveled at *him*," he was saying, "faulty workmanship, spontaneity, heaviness, triviality! How many times he was told that his paintings were mere sketches! That his talent, which it was all but impossible not to recognize, lacked correctness. He was blamed for having a gloomy temperament: it was this, they said, that made him weigh his figures and objects with their shadows; he gives them hardly any light, and only from above, and his love of contrasts makes his backgrounds dark. His people have no shading, seem posed on a single plane, on a screen of shadows. The Abbé Lanzi says that his figures inhabit a prison, that he shows neither correctness in drawing nor appreciation of beauty. . . . Because truth suffices for him, because he did not go out of his way to embellish it with a drapery arrangement, with some trick imitated from a Greek statue! It's too black, people used to tell him, life isn't like that.

"There is an admirable canvas by this great painter in the Louvre. 'Mary.' Do you know it? He's never been forgiven for having chosen to represent this dying woman, not as a princess on her tester bed with a graceful curtain arrangement and the mendacious dress of the maidservants, but as a woman of the people, marked by the whole process of the death agony, the sweat which has not been wiped away, the discoloration of the nostrils, the pallor of the flesh, the traces of pain, the body deformed by illness. Her belly is swollen, and the priests said that he had painted a big-bellied woman suffering from dropsy. They refused to put Caravaggio's painting in Santa Maria della Scala, on the altar which in the end was decorated by Francesco Moncini, above a tabernacle of precious stones adorned with columns of oriental jasper. And just think where the painter must have gone to find his model! I'll tell you where he went: to the hospital, where most people end their lives, or to the morgue. That's where a painter can discover the truth about man, not on the fine beds where people of quality make a good end. Too black! And that's what they say about the bitumen of his painted background—and I ask you, what is color, what is light, without that blackness of night?

"But besides the painting, they say that too about what is painted. For if the Virgin must die, the priest would like to see in her very death a hint of the Transfiguration, so that onlookers should feel the airy lightness of the imminent Assumption in her corpse. That is what they expect of us painters, what they reproach us for not giving them. We must be the transfigurers. Of the Virgin or of Napoleon. May the time soon come when people will kiss our hands for having seen an everyday human truth in the market place, a crowd, a hovel! Then the churches, or whatever takes their place, will no longer repudiate violent feeling, rich forms, naked passions, expression that defies decorum and concerns itself only with humanity. Then, before the man who suffers and bleeds, we shall no longer be required to paint Paradise in the eyes of the dying, whether God's, or the idyll of Trianon, or the world of the Napoleonic Code!"

Augustin listened to all this like someone who had wandered through the Louvre with a great deference for art and all those

Dutch or Italian masters, but without quite seeing the difference between the various paintings, all equally well varnished in their rich, heavy frames. He did not remember that "Death of Mary," and the very name of Caravaggio was new to him. He would have liked to know more about him. He said so to his companion.

And Géricault talked on in the half-darkness of the Palais Royal, where everything surrounding them possessed, to the point of caricature, that trivial character whose beauty it is not given to everyone to extract. Augustin saw the threadbare fabrics, the meretricious faces, the blemishes and the vices which marked alike their expression and their features as with a distorting claw; the sated or desiccated bodies, the marks which the mediocrity of their existence had left on the people they passed; the lack of air in their lodgings, the daily grind, the scarcity of water, the price of everything. He saw the intermixture of social effects which placed venal copies of a fallen aristocracy side by side with the disillusioned soldiers of an epic of which nothing remained but the wounds and those shiny frock coats: they were in the palace of the Princes (the next-to-the-last of whom had voted the death of his cousin, the King,* on the spot where the Orléans stables had formerly stood; and it was in this Noah's ark of wooden arcades stretching across the central garden from the Monpensier to the Valois side of the building that thieves, police, humbled glory, revolution and lechery swarmed in the rain-drenched night.

And Géricault spoke of Caravaggio and of his life. How this painter, born among the poor, had at first painted in the taste of his century, and how the Cavaliere d'Arpino who gave him work used him as a journeyman to do the ornaments, the flowers in the paintings that he signed. In Santa Maria della Scala, in the center of the choir, there is a fresco painting of the Virgin by the Cavaliere which has everything that Caravaggio's Virgin lacked. Who knows whether the young apprentice who was to be driven from this church did not work on it for his employer? But when he painted for himself, proudly proclaiming himself a *Naturalista,* a new word full of fury and challenge, he moved away from the Venetian warmth of his first works and, fascinated by contrast and seeing in it the very principle of art and the flesh of painting, retained from Giorgione only the science of shadows.

---

* Louis-Philippe-Joseph, known as Philippe-Egalité, of the Orléans branch of the Bourbon family, father of Louis-Philippe. As a member of the Convention he voted for the death sentence against his cousin, Louis XVI.

"I copied his 'Christ in the Tomb' about 1811," said Théodore, "and that was how I entered into his soul, so to speak. But I don't know what I value most of what he has taught me: this law of contrasts, or the actual choice of subjects. With him everything forms a contrast to those women who attach so much importance to the rouge they put on their cheeks. Beauty is secret, not ostentatious. He painted murders, treacheries in the night, drunkenness, taverns, ruffians at street corners. He did not alter the clothes worn by the people to turn them into seraphs or queens; and his life was a dizzy whirl, like his painting. All of a piece with the dangers to which he exposed himself, depicting the lower depths and being a part of them. What don't they say about him! What were the gangs with whom he really spent his human nights, he who created painted nights in which his lurid companions appear with wolves' teeth and the gleam of flesh in the torchlight? Rome has kept few of these sordid pictures from the brush of her prodigal child. He left Rome because, in the heart of anger, he had killed one of his comrades in the course of a game of tennis. He could not brook cheating. Naples, where he met the child Ribera, his pupil, was at that time dominated by the painting of Belisario Corenzio, the Greek from whom, they say, the Cavaliere d'Arpino had derived his inspiration from early youth.

"But he was forced to leave this Spanish city, where prettiness was the fashion, and even Ribera betrayed him and went in for Raphaelizing. Too black, too black, my poor Caravaggio! Go, take the boat that will carry you to the islands, for there a painter is a boon, people are bored from looking at the sea where sails are scarce! A strange country for him to settle in: I can imagine Malta at the end of the sixteenth century, with its knights-errant who had ended up there between the Spaniards and the Turks, chance masters of a people who had no great love for them but preferred them to the Ottoman invader. When Caravaggio landed, the knights had nothing to do; it was more than thirty years since the Turks had last tried to gain a foothold there. As a result, the people liked them even less. At first the knights took a fancy to the refugee and gave him Moslem slaves. In the course of what game did Caravaggio quarrel with a Templar? If his light was the light of prisons, he now experienced the reality. It must have been something of a feat to escape from a jail on Malta around the year 1600! Caravaggio is said to have possessed uncommon strength, and he was black as his painting, both of hair and beard.

"How did he get to Sicily? He can't have found it to his liking. I don't know of any paintings of his to be found anywhere there. He was too close to Rome, he fell into melancholy, and neither Palermo, nor Messina, nor Syracuse could hold him. But as he was landing from a felucca, somewhere near Porto-Ercole, the Spanish guard seized him, mistaking him for someone else. Again he was to know the dingy prison light that filters down from high up. When he was released, all but naked, and made his way to the seashore to find the boat where his baggage and clothes were, he had already caught the fever then rife in the kingdom of Naples. Here there was no shade. A man alone and desperate, stripped, in the torrid sun from which there was no escape. Uncared for, feverish, he fell on the sand, and delirious, in a world at last fully luminous, such as people of taste would have liked him to paint, he was picked up only to die."

The rain seemed to be persisting out of spite. The jumble of the Palais Royal was made more insane and extravagant by the fact that most of those who came and went beneath the arcades, wet, hair stuck down, clothes crumpled, were creatures torn between the terror and hopes of the morrow. The snatches of conversation overheard formed a hotchpotch of castles in the air and fear of scores to be settled. And there were those who were not yet sure that the moment had come to turn their coats, and those who were afraid they might not succeed in doing so. And people who fish in troubled waters, and those who always have something to avenge, and men in the grip of alcohol, and over all a kind of general hilarity at the never-ending massacre of the powerful.

"All the same," said Augustin, "what are you going to do, Monsieur Géricault? If the King runs away, are you going to follow him?"

The night was whirling in the garden in gusts that swung the lamps in the arcades. Tomorrow morning the "Officer of the Guides" and the "Wounded Cuirassier," which must have been taken down from the walls of the Salon some time ago, would be taken to La Nouvelle-Athènes. When the rain stopped, perhaps Horace Vernet would come to his comrade's, gloating over the return of his Corsican god, but also to hear him speak about painting. And up there, as he was showing Horace out, perhaps—who knows—a young Creole woman out for an airing on the path before the Greek temple might look at them. Caroline . . .

"No," answered Théodore. "Louis XVIII may leave. I shall stay."

IV

The Midnight Farewells

THE valet came in to snuff the candles—those in the big crystal
chandelier as well as those in the lamp with the painted shade
that lighted the card players' table. This did not distract the gentlemen
from their game. You know what the bouillotte* craze is when it gets
hold of people. The ladies commented on it with little titters. The
only male in their group was Mademoiselle Gosselin's young man, a
mute creature whom she had in tow wherever she went. He had curly
hair and mutton-chop whiskers, wore a fine olive-green coat with
goffered jabot tucked correctly into the white piqué vest. He looked
at his watch which had a little chime in its case. "Half-past eleven,"
he said. His chief merit was that at twenty-five he was keeping the
ballet dancer in the manner expected of a man of sixty.

Not so well, to be sure, as Virginie was being kept. Poor Virginie—
she had had to go up to bed! There was certainly a touch of coquet-
tishness in her behavior. She did look ravishing in her churching
dress. But she was having trouble with her milk. And besides, it was
getting late. As a matter of fact, Monsieur and Madame Oreille were
used to receiving in her stead: they lived here, which lent dignity to
the situation. However modest Virginie's position in the ballet she
was an artist, like her father who for twenty years had been the
official hairdresser at the Opéra. She had been barely sixteen when
Bessières had "noticed" her, as they say. Her parents had moved

* French gambling game at cards, similar to poker.

109

in with their daughter when that magnificent lover had been killed at Lützen* and she had gone into mourning. The Marshal had done things properly: the house he had left to Virginie was considered one of the most charming in Paris—here, just next to the alfalfa fields on the slopes of Monceau, two steps from the huge garden Cambacérès had returned to the Emperor at that time because it was too expensive to keep up, and which the King had just restored to the Duc d'Orléans.

How trim the salon was, where the game of bouillotte was in progress! The players sat around an enchanting gate-leg table of rosewood, which came straight from Versailles whence Charles-Ferdinand had had it brought to Virginie. So, too, he had had paintings taken down from the Pavillon de Marsan for her, and had silverware from the Tuileries loaded into her very carriage! Besides the woodwork painted in the best taste of the former reign, and the Greek figures in bas-relief between the doors, there were draperies everywhere, even up to the ceiling, of pleated yellow fabric. A ravishing strip of pale blue silk ran in a festoon round the room, the door frames were trimmed with the same material, and the windows had straw-colored curtains lined with blue, which fell with incomparable softness and broke on the flowered carpet.

Father Elisée formed the only black smudge in this setting. He was not a friend of the family, and it might seem surprising to find him at the home of an Opéra dancer at so late an hour. But there is an explanation for everything. Hadn't he been hidden by her grandmother in 1792, in her house on the rue Saint-Roch, when Marie-Louise, Virginie's future mother, was still hardly more than a child, and he was waiting for an opportunity to get to England? Citizen Torlachon, as he was then called, who had studied surgery with the Frères de la Charité and who had thrown away his frock coat after '89 and done a good deal of wire-pulling behind the scenes, was far from being as important then as he became after the return of the Princes and the endless treatments administered to His Majesty at Hartwell House and ever since. For two or three years he had led a very scandalous life, had been seen everywhere with wenches, as though thereby to prove his attachment to the new ideas. Where had he got all the money he threw out of the window? But the Terror had forced him to go into hiding, then to emigrate.

The Reverend Father sighed: "The flesh is weak!" and took a pinch of snuff from the estimable M. Oreille's snuffbox. He had a

* See footnote, p. 47.

sly, oily face, a lecherous look about him that went oddly with his robe.

It was already more than late, but players are players, and there were the two Alexandres, the inevitable friends of the house, and Uncle Achille, who served Mme. de Saint-Leu's children. M. Oreille was the dealer, and the Jesuit sitting behind him formed a striking contrast to the master of the house who was tall of stature, square shouldered, and wore a cornflower-blue coat, with an old-style wig slightly askew. The holy man was watching the game and making remarks whose aptness M. Maupin, the elder of the Alexandres, who smelled somewhat of his shop, did not always seem to appreciate. Or the spiciness.

The ladies sat around the handsome porcelain stove, which was surmounted by a kneeling cupid: Grandmother Bourguignon knitting babies' vests; her daughter Marie-Louise Oreille, still attractive, with the plumpness that so many women acquire at forty, who was watching the game from afar, and also making conversation with Mlle. Gosselin, a ballet dancer at the Opéra, looking ravishing this evening in a pink and mauve Scotch turban adorned with a bird of paradise, and a white percale dress with a row of little ribbon roses at the bottom. She had to turn around to answer Mme. Persuis, so pleased with her yellow hat trimmed with a bouquet of gray flowers that she had not even wanted to untie the ribbons under her chin. Mlle. Podevin, who was Virginie's age and like her a member of the corps de ballet, sat in front of her on a low stool, intent merely upon acting the child and listening only now and then to what the grownups were saying.

Mme. Persuis was Mme. Oreille's contemporary, or nearly so, but had always remained just a bit provincial. Although she was used to the splendors of the little mansion the Marshal had given Virginie, she could not keep from praising the building and the decoration: ah, there was no architect more elegant than Bellander! Perhaps the Du Roule district was a little out of the way—but how restful compared to Paris! How calm!

"Yes," said Marie-Louise, "it's a bucolic spot."

It was her favorite conceit. Of everything that she had at her table—the eggs, the milk, the poultry—she liked to say, "It comes from the Farm," as though the Monceau farm had been hers and had not belonged to the Orléans family.

"I wonder what would have become of Virginie," said Mlle. Gosselin musingly, "if the Marshal had lived. . . ."

Mme. Bourguignon, who was a trifle hard of hearing, nevertheless caught on to the fact that they were talking about Marshal Bessières. He had meant a good deal to her. She asked to have the remark repeated. But her daughter did not like this kind of conversation and attempted to divert the talk into a different channel. "You know," she murmured, addressing Mme. Persuis, "if it had not been for the Father, His Majesty would not have been able to appear before Parliament last Thursday." Mme. Persuis had no idea what the Jesuit's functions in the Tuileries were, and she opened her eyes wide. But the grandmother was not thus easily to be diverted from her memories.

"I've never understood," she broke in, "I've never really understood what happened. After all, you can't kill off a Marshal just like that!"

"Listen, Mama," snapped Mme. Oreille, "whether or not a man is a Marshal, a bullet is a bullet!"

"And, between ourselves," said Mme. Persuis in her pretty Avignon voice, "that particular bullet may well have been a blessing for Virginie!"

This was probably Mlle. Podevin's opinion, because after all could you compare a Marshal of the Empire with His Royal Highness the Duc de Berry? Mlle. Gosselin gave a slight cough. She thought this chit of a Podevin quite common. But Mme. Persuis, who was too well launched to be easily stopped, went on to develop her idea: "He died like a hero. But if our dear Virginie had not been a widow when the Allies arrived—what would she have done, I ask you? Oh, I'm sure the Marshal would have behaved like a faithful servant of the Princes! He would not have been one to follow the Usurper to his island."

Mlle. Gosselin came to Mme. Oreille's rescue. She spoke of the theatre. Podevin would certainly not disagree, it was a blessing for all those young ladies that Virginie had become what she had become. Modest, unambitious, never dreaming of demanding a role that would be appropriate to her new rank . . . No, but always thinking of others, a good friend.

"You see, Madame Persuis, your husband may beat time up there on the podium and all that—but if we did not have His Highness's protection, what should we dancers do? I mean the young ones: when it's Bigottini who dances we have no objection—talent is talent. But since it's Gardel who does the casting, only his wife, La Miller, has a chance, and that Malfleuroy woman who insults your nose with the perfumes she's always covered with . . . because she is Mme. Boieldieu. Monsieur Persuis wasn't even able to put the dancers he wanted into *l'Epreuve villageoise,* his own ballet which is being rehearsed for next month. They were pressing him to give Mme. Gardel the role of Marton he had promised *me:* he was able to get out of it only by giving it to Bigottini. And I had been half promised at least an entrance for the revival of *Castor and Pollux,* but the old ones are much too jealous! Have you seen La Miller in the *pas de deux?* It's enough to make you weep!"

"That was the last time," said Mlle. Podevin unthinkingly, "Virginie came to the theatre. She was already so pregnant that when she got up in her box to take a bow . . ."

This was worse than talk about the Marshal: all Paris had roared over it, because when the Royal Family had appeared, Virginie, in her box, had imagined that it was she who was being applauded, and she had bowed to the theatre with her seven-months belly. Mlle. Gosselin spoke against Gardel, the choreographer, at great length, and affirmed that if La Malfleuroy used so much perfume everyone knew that it was to hide the bad smells natural to her. Mme. Persuis, nevertheless, was curious about the Jesuit.

"So, His Majesty," she put in. "What does the Father do for him? You can't cure rheumatism with prayers."

Mme. Oreille smiled. Everyone knew that the Father, an experienced surgeon, was a masseur who had no equal. You wouldn't believe it to look at him, thin as he was, but his hands, just look at his hands! Paddles, my dear! When he takes you in those hands, when he molds you, turns you over and gives you a *tapotement* . . . At the Tuileries they can't do without him. He's a most interesting man. He knows everything about everything. And the stories he tells! Very risqué, some of them!

Alexandre Longpré laid down his hand. The others let out loud exclamations. The fellow was sweeping the board. As usual.

"How much did you lose this time?" Mme. Oreille cried to her husband from where she sat.

The door opened, and Philippe-François Touchard entered and went over to pay his respects to the ladies. At fifty-five, the director of the Messageries was still a handsome man, and he had had a good deal to do with M. Oreille since Virginie's father had ceased to be the hairdresser at the Opéra; that is to say since the autumn of 1814. Evil tongues said that his son resembled him and was not fifty-five, and that Virginie found him to her liking. They said that Monseigneur

. . . It must be admitted that the Duke had his adventures at Court. It was not only at the ballet that women fell for him. He had become interested in a lady who belonged to Mme. d'Angoulême's household; only he was jealous, and he had had the lady followed. But when the police report had been brought to him, he was confronted—through the fault of the informer who, having been told *Find out if Monseigneur's mistress is faithful to him,* had shadowed Virginie, so common was the knowledge of their liaison—he was confronted with the proof of favors Mlle. Oreille had bestowed on a lad of her own age who looked as much like the director of the Messageries as François looked like his father. The Duke's reaction can well be imagined: a veritable tempest!

Virginie had been able to turn the thing to her advantage, and M. d'André's police agent had been given the sack. Anyway, all this was just talk circulated by the girls who played small parts or belonged to the corps de ballet. People are horrid; besides, there were Bonapartists in the Royal Academy of Music! No, the main thing was that M. Oreille had put all his savings into horses and carriages. Oh, he didn't do it commercially! He would lend them to his friends for a financial consideration. You have a sudden romance, and no tilbury in which to take a lady to the riverside . . . or you need a discreet berlin for an escapade to Normandy. Oreille's carriages were kept in the Messageries stables.

"You can have my place," said the winner to the newcomer, "I'll go and chat with the ladies." He was really going rather far, leaving the table this way with all his winnings! Philippe-François sat down and greeted the Jesuit. Mlle. Gosselin's young man watched him in despair: how long would the game last? She felt that politeness required them to remain until the master of the house got up. After which, she would be sleepy.

"The news is not good," said M. Touchard. "They say that this very evening the Princes . . ."

He murmured the rest in a half-whisper to the men, so as not to arouse anxiety among the members of the fair sex. The Jesuit, who did not hear well, asked to have the words repeated. No, he refused to believe it! He had spent nearly the whole day at the Palace. He had tended His Majesty at six o'clock, and even as late as eight o'clock nothing had been decided. How could they move without him? It was ridiculous! "Why just today: I lent my carriage— a *dormeuse,* the most comfortable thing you ever rode in—to a monsignor. The archbishop, you understand, felt it would be better for him not to travel by mail coach. He made a small detour through Paris, and is at this moment on his way to one of our houses in Spain. Do you think I would have been so lacking in foresight as to leave myself stranded if there had been something in the wind?"

But Mme. Oreille had risen; midnight had just struck on the large wall clock: feeding time—the infant had to be taken to Virginie. Oh, we must see him! The Mlles. Gosselin and Podevin clasped their hands in an adorable gesture of supplication. It was like a scene out of *La Caravane*! Father Elisée was telling his beads with an air of absorption. In spite of himself, Touchard's stupid remarks had got under his skin. No, it was impossible! It would be treason on His Majesty's part! Why should the King want to get rid of him? Louis XVIII liked off-color stories, and no one could tell them like the Father.

Marie-Louise brought the child. Nothing could be seen of him in the bundle of linen and embroideries. There were shrill outbursts, cascades of laughter—these from the two dancers and Mme. Persuis. But how tiny! You don't realize: he's big for his age! How old is he? Just two weeks tonight, imagine . . .

Mme. Persuis was in ecstasy: "The very image of his father! . . ." And the Jesuit, whose black cassock was now surrounded by the ladies' bright dresses, gave a deep sigh: "Son of Saint Louis, rise to heaven!" The eighth wonder of the world, with Podevin and Gosselin in its wake, was carried upstairs to the bedroom where Virginie lay dozing, propped up on pillows. . . .

Mme. Persuis had remained with Grandmother Bourguignon. "It must thrill you," she said, "to think that your granddaughter's son, when you come right down to it, is the heir to the Throne! The only male offspring in the whole family."

Mme. Bourguignon brought her ear close and cupped it with her hand. She had heard nothing. The master of the house came over to the orchestra conductor's wife and said confidingly, "Yes, he is the first Son of France. . . . Can't expect anything from the Duc d'Angoulême, can we? And confidentially, my son-in-law"— he liked to say "my son-in-law" (only among intimates, to be sure) in speaking of His Royal Highness, the Duc de Berry—"my son-in-law, well, you can imagine for yourselves, he was quite puffed up when it turned out to be a boy! You know, of course—after all, it's no secret—that he has had daughters in England . . . we must be broad-minded, I say. And of course a prince is a prince! Anyway, ever since the end of October my son-in-law has been worrying about it. He has often spoken about it. He would say to me: '*Beau-papa*' (Yes, he sometimes calls me *Beau-papa*!) '*Beau-papa*,' he would say, 'it's a damned nuisance, my cousin having had that baby.' The Orléans, you understand—yes, the neighbors across the way from us—have a male offspring, a Nemours, born on October 25th, and he has been brooding over it. Charles, I mean His Royal Highness . . . brooding over it . . . a threat to the elder branch. . . ."

"What was Monsieur Touchard telling you?" asked Mme. Persuis. "He spoke so low."

"Oh, just a postmaster's idiocies! He was imagining Buonaparte already in Paris!"

"Buonaparte? How perfectly horrible! And what is going to become of us?"

"Well, surely you realize I would be among the first to be informed! To say nothing of Father Elisée! No, it's all because he's been given orders to refuse horses to private persons who want to leave Paris. It's time to put a stop to this absurd panic which the rumor-mongers have created out of nothing."

The servant Ricard entered and came over to his master. Someone was asking for him. M. Oreille left the salon. It was a tall man in a brown Inverness cape and fawn-colored boots. But drenched. The rain could be heard beating against the shutters. The man had come on behalf of Mme. de Chateaubriand: she needed horses. She had her carriage, but she needed horses.

"See here, my friend," said M. Oreille haughtily and, catching a glimpse of his reflection in a small mirror in the antechamber, next to the large candelabrum, he straightened his wig. "Whom do you take me for? I'm not a horse dealer. I have horses, of course. I lend them. As a service. To my friends. I know Mme. de Chateaubriand by name." He bowed. "But at this hour . . ."

Mme. de Chateaubriand needed horses right away.

M. Oreille was losing his temper. "We are at home. My daughter is just up from the child-bed. My grandson . . ."

The man was persistent. Some people are amazing!

"But even assuming that I wanted to oblige Mme. de Chateaubriand," said the ex-hairdresser, "even assuming . . . My horses are at the Messageries, and it so happens that the director, M. Touchard, a friend of mine, is here. He tells me . . . Anyway, it's a royal order: no horses are to be supplied to private persons!"

This made no impression on the visitor. "You have horses here also, monsieur, in the stables, at the end of the garden."

"But," M. Oreille protested, "those are my daughter's horses!"

"Come," said the other impatiently, "your daughter has twelve horses. How much?"

He was a man of no breeding. It would have served no purpose to argue with him. It was better to ask a good, stiff price just to get rid of him. The man immediately agreed to it. Well, what could he do? "Picard!" Picard approached. "Take this gentleman to the stables. He needs four horses . . . you understand?"

Through the door, the rain could be seen coming down in sheets. Lifting the candelabrum high, M. Oreille momentarily lighted the two men as they disappeared into the garden.

The horsemen had left the Louvre in the night and in the rain, immediately after the King's departure, the servants keeping at a respectful distance behind the Prince and his aide-de-camp who rode side by side. Monsieur de La Ferronays was murmuring: it made no sense, going off this way without torches, in this troubled city of Paris which, despite the weather, swarmed with suspicious characters—on the rue Saint-Honoré they had even heard people singing the *Carmagnole*—and someone might recognize them, do His Royal Highness harm.

"Monseigneur should understand—"

"Go to hell!"

Monseigneur had spurred his horse and outdistanced his companion. He was not in the mood for conversation. Monseigneur was short, like all the Bourbons, and rather fat, or at least thick-set. But he was a good horseman, and when he was mounted he did not cut too bad a figure. He pulled his cloak over his thighs. It was cold with this confounded weather. The Duc de Berry was too full of contradictory feelings to listen to La Ferronays' expostulations. Anger, tears, shame, regrets, fears. All this, so utterly absurd! The King, to begin with. He was furious with the King. He knew, of course, that Louis XVIII did not like him any more than he liked his father. He had known it for a long time. They had scenes, they would shout at each other. His Majesty could be heard from the Tuileries right out in the garden. He had relegated them—that is, the Duke and the Comte d'Artois, his father—to the Pavillon de Marsan. And the Pavillon de Flore made its policy, its absurd policy, with no concern for what those on the other side of the courtyard thought about it.

Absurd! In less than a year Louis the fat, the gouty, had brought them to this. His Charter, one of those brilliant ideas—like the time at Mitau, when he had pardoned Philippe-Égalité's son! They were running away like cowards, without fighting, doing nothing, and Buonaparte would come and make himself at home, while they would go to the devil. He had besought the King, who thought only of his rheumatism, besought him to give him a command, to let him march against the Ogre. A fine chance! It was perfectly clear: the uncle was jealous of the nephew, of his possible successor, of the only Bourbon capable of founding a royal dynasty. He had preferred instead to send the Duc d'Orléans and the Comte d'Artois to take charge of the defense of Lyons—the Duc d'Orléans, always under suspicion of conspiracy. He did not want to see his nephew gain authority and prestige on the field of battle.

And then, too, impotent as he was, he must surely detest him, because for him women— The fuss the King had made over every one of his mistresses, on the strength of those damned police reports! A man was not made of wood, after all! Did anyone reproach the Prince de Wagram for having a mistress? And he was married, after all—Alexandre Berthier was married—to a Bavarian princess whom he used to send to take the waters at Balarue in order to be rid of her! Charles-Ferdinand was most disgusted with Louis XVIII when His Majesty would assume a lascivious tone and begin to tell anecdotes culled from the books of the last century, and pretend they were adventures of his own youth. The liar! Aside from which, what kind of a King was this creature forever confined to a chair. He had to be carried, pushed, wheeled. The spectacle it made on the staircases! Not to mention his Jesuit masseur with his pretty tongue. His uncle allowed Elisée to do anything he liked. In Number 27 of the Pavillon de Flore, where he had his living quarters, there were constant intimate dinners, select parties, which must make the large Christ on the cross blush in His place of honor. Right in the Louvre, he had a young woman of about seventeen available at all times—not always the same one, though she was invariably called Mother Elisée.

But this was not all. According to d'André, the scoundrel had inclinations of another sort. It was even insinuated that the great show he made of having girls about was so that the King would not give too much credence to certain rumors that were current. In one way or another, the result was that there were different measures for different weights. And the blackguard was only too familiar with the King's love for Rabelais. Charles-Ferdinand had all possible respect for priests, but to begin with the Jesuit was a Jew. A shady character: he had once lent money to the Princes' army, he had been on the Isle of Yeu with Monsieur. His father's aversion for the surgeon had not escaped his notice: so there must have been some incident . . . But anything even remotely connected with the war in La Vendée made the Comte d'Artois ill at ease. Yet he put up with him: almost as though he feared him. But hadn't the father treated *him* before becoming attached to the King? It was true that he had been with the Prince Regent of England, whose gift of a snuffbox enhanced with diamonds he liked to show off, and Monsieur strongly suspected him of spying for Buckingham Palace. It was hardly to be imagined, for that matter, that the Jesuits would have supplied His Majesty with a surgeon who was not a bit of an informer, a bit of a spy. Had he not, according to Bourrienne, been surprised in the doorway of the Russian embassy?—and Monsieur de Butiaguin was not known to need massage!

Even before Hartwell, Father Elisée had slipped into intimacy with the King. When, exactly? He was certainly already established at the interment of the Comtesse de Provence. Charles-Ferdinand remembered him as he had looked, in the chapel on King Street, ahead of the catafalque, next to the handsome Duc d'Avaray. Odd rumors circulated in London as to the surgeon's ambiguous character: had he not been attached for years to the person of the Chevalier d'Éon,* who had just died? And had he not pretended, up to the last moment, to take him for a woman? Above all, the Duc de Berry could not forgive the man he called the masseur for having been present when, at the beginning of the month, he had come to his royal uncle's begging to be allowed to set forth with his father for Lyons. He had had enough of people saying of him that the only victory he had ever won was over the Opéra ballet. Which, parenthetically, was not true, since during the time when Virginie had been too pregnant he had been going to bed with La Bourgoin, who belonged to the Comédie Française. . . . This

---

* Charles Geneviève Louise Auguste André Timothée d'Éon, known as the Chevalier d'Éon (1728–1810). Man of mystery—adventurer, diplomat, expert swordsman—who wore women's clothes by royal decree to the end of his life, and as to whose sex few of his contemporaries were certain. A post-mortem examination of the body conclusively established the fact that he was a man.

did not affect his sentiments: he always felt a great tenderness for the girls he had got with child. La Bourgoin, who was going on thirty-five, was just to pass the time, though the goddess had a damn fine figure. That lovely throat, like a dove's! And those eyes that all but drove you mad, her voice . . . Just to hear her in *Bajazet*! Not to mention the fact that Lucien Bonaparte had had her—taking their women, away from those people, like their palaces, was only right and proper.

But when everything was collapsing, when he had only a few minutes left to jump on his horse in the rain and the night, he had not dreamed of going to La Bourgoin's apartment. He had not even taken the time to embrace his little bastard daughters whom he loved so much, nor Mrs. Brown, their mother: he had merely sent La Ferronays with the money they would need to get to England, and a message that made it appear he was planning to join them there, though this was but a show of kindness toward Amy on his part. But he was making posthaste toward Le Roule, and he would join the Household, if necessary, at the halt before the Barrière de l'Étoile. The Comte d'Artois, in any case, was not leaving before about one in the morning. He was making posthaste toward Virginie's house—that mansion built by the architect of Bagatelle; and the fact that a Marshal of the Empire had given it to his mistress had always made him feel like a fancy man. He could not bear the thought of not seeing Virginie again this evening, and he could feel tears bursting from his eyes—a weakness inherited from his ancestress, Anne of Austria*—big tears, fully formed, burning, a rain in the rain.

He suddenly remembered how his eyes had filled with tears like this the other day at his uncle's, when he had gone to him on an impulse, and the King had humiliated him in front of his surgeon, the Jesuit. He had caught His Majesty's wink, signaling Father Elisée to stay, as the sly beggar was making as if to leave. Did Louis XVIII want a witness, or what? "We have no secrets from our handsome nephew. Continue, Father." What an ignoble sight! It was as though he were going out of his way to have himself treated in public, exhibiting that disgusting body covered with sores. The Father spread his unguents, made a dressing on the arm, another on the loins. The King had scabs from sitting so constantly

* Anne d'Autriche (1601–1666), daughter of Philip III of Spain, wife of Louis XIII and mother of Louis XIV.

in his chair. The room reeked nauseatingly of medicaments and pus.

After crossing the rue Royale-Saint-Honoré, they entered the rue du Faubourg. Here the mansions were more widely separated; the gardens in the rain already smelled of spring. There was a certain stir in the old stagecoach yard and the approach to it. Grooms who would not pull aside more or less blocked the thoroughfare to the horsemen, and the Duc de Berry was hardly in a mood to tolerate this. He had lifted his riding crop, and there might have been an ugly incident had not a torchbearer lighted up Monseigneur's angry face and recognized it. Under the gateway men and women were bargaining in loud voices for the public carriages. It was like an auction. "One hundred francs!" "I'll double it!" "Enough, messieurs, not even for a thousand!" It was the flight exchange. The little troop re-formed and plunged into the night. La Ferronays murmured something about the Prince's safety. Charles-Ferdinand paid no attention to him.

So they were going to separate him from Virginie. Nothing else mattered. From the child who had just been born, his first son. Charles-Ferdinand had insisted on being present at the delivery. It was the first time he had seen the thing. Mrs. Brown had brought his daughters into the world without him. The experience had been terrible and yet magnificent. He had suffered for the child-mother, he had screamed when the head had appeared. All the horror of the waters and the rest, but God how beautiful she was, so exhausted, covered with sweat; like a small panting animal. He knew that people accused him of having low tastes. But what Duchess, what Queen, could be compared to this girl of the Opéra? Her hair, that mass of glossy black hair which enveloped her tiny head, which no hat could confine and which tumbled down in such extraordinary fashion, like an enveloping cascade, when she got ready for bed. How white she looked in her loosened hair, with that waist, a painter's exaggeration! They were going to separate him from Virginie. Forever.

As he reached Saint-Philippe and Saint-Jacques, and was turning into the rue de Courcelles at the end of the Pépinière, he remembered that first evening—on this which would undoubtedly be the last. Last year. When everything was moving the other way, swept by the intoxication of the return. Charles-Ferdinand had just joined the King at the château of Saint-Ouen; the entry into Paris was to be next day. The day had been spent in feverish negotiations with the representatives of the Allies, the Russian officers, the emissaries from Austria, the Paris delegations. It was just like his uncle to have put him in charge of the safety of the château that evening! He who had come from London as it were into a fairy tale, with all the pent-up feelings of a frustrated boyhood deprived of the Paris he did not know, was dying to discover! And so he had said to himself, To hell with it!

He had handed the command over to Oudinot: this Marshal who had just rallied to the King could jolly well take on the chore! A horse, a horse! He remembered the animal he had been given: a young Arab, a horse for a prince; and how he had headed straight for the Opéra on the rue de Richelieu. How he had dreamed of it, dreamed of the Opéra, over there in Drury Lane! All the *émigrés* spoke of it as of paradise lost. The Opéra! It was as though the Opéra had been his whole life's goal. France reconquered was first of all the Opéra. He entered it a victor; and isn't the victor's first reward a pretty girl? The entire house was wearing the white cockade. The music. The boxes. The crowd. Who had lent him the opera glasses? A lady who was with an Austrian in the adjoining box. At once he had seen her among the dancers, the doe with the mark on her, that child who made a few vague gestures among the others— what was being given that evening? *Les Noces de Gamache,* the ballet of his destiny. Virginie! It was his victory, the return from exile, the triumph of his race.

And what a spring the spring of 1814 had been! In his mistress's garden, near the small house she had been given by a Marshal of the Empire . . . how beautiful the lilacs of Courcelles were that year! The two of them played a comedy that was a continuation of *Les Noces de Gamache,* and of the pleasures of former times from which those *sans-culottes* had snatched him in his childhood! In Monceau they revived Marie-Antoinette's games at Trianon; Virginie would call him "my shepherd"; and when the season came round they would chase one another through the fields of alfalfa, make love right out in the open.

Charles-Ferdinand forgot everything else—the Court, the hunts, politics. Now, when he was again going into exile, Virginie was for him all royalty triumphant—France—and he had forgotten all the others, La Bourgoin—and the old King on his bed, covered with sores, lifting up his shirt and baring his buttocks to the lean Jesuit whose fingers were sticky with a pale unguent.

"François, you're mad. I should never have let you come in. . . . Don't you realize what it is for a woman to just be getting over her confinement? Please go away! No, really, just imagine if someone should come in!"

How adorable she was, and even more adorable for being newly a mother, still exhibiting that trace of fatigue beneath her black eyes, and that whiteness of the arms, of the shoulders, the little palpitating breasts . . . swollen with milk. She was lying with the mass of her hair falling about her, the pillows crumpled, the dimness—the little oil lamps near the dark mirror had been extinguished, there was only a candle which cast a golden glow over the shadow and the flesh. And she was not yet twenty; her birthday was in July. François, the big lout, had been born in December 1795. She had always thought of him as a child. When Monseigneur had made that unearthly scene, she had been able to reply in all innocence, "François? Why, he's just a boy!" She had been pretty frightened just the same, that day.

She looked at François. He really was very handsome. All blond, all fresh, as if he had just been taken out of his box. A big strapping lad who did not yet know his strength. Ah, nothing in common with Bessières, nor with Charles-Ferdinand! She had always known him, all her childhood. She never paid any attention to him, but she would have missed him terribly if he . . . No, she did not take him seriously. It was understood that François loved her, but what of it?

Until that day when she had been told he had been seen at Frascati's with that girl. Strange how badly she had behaved! Why have committed that act of madness? All right, she was already pregnant and perhaps that was what prevented her from calculating. It was in the garden, on the terrace, above the stables that she had suddenly kissed him. The trees were lovely there. And from the street could be heard the cry of the ice-cream wafer vendor. . . .

"François . . . I'm telling you someone might come in at any moment."

"Don't worry," said François. "I've bribed Picard and I've showered gifts on Lise. She'll cough out in the hall if anyone comes upstairs, and I'll hide in the closet as long as necessary!"

Yes, he was handsome, he was young; he was neither a soldier with a red neck like Bessières, nor a heavy-set little man like the Duke with his bulging eyes. Men—it was funny—you'd think just holding their hand was going to give them apoplexy. François was different. I like that little space he has between his upper teeth, she thought. He had come up on the sly, just after the baby had been taken away. He knew the feeding times, all right!

"Nini, this life can't go on any longer. I want you to be mine, just mine."

Oh, good heavens, still the same tune. Was he mad? And who would pay for running the house, the family, the dresses? "A thatched cottage and a heart: is that what you're offering me? Especially since I know your cottage! Can you see me in your father's apartment on the rue Saint-Denis? Besides, you know perfectly well I love my Charles! All right, don't make that face! I like you too—but you understand it isn't the same thing. Now, now, you're not going to weep!"

In such a situation he resorted to extreme measures; he was offering her marriage. He would recognize the child. They would have others, their own . . . She knew the tune. The big idiot! Marriage! How bourgeois he was! The Princes—with them, marriage or no marriage. Mme. de Pompadour . . . Louis XV had married her in the end.

"Besides, when I was born, Papa wasn't married. What does it matter? You make children, and see about it afterwards."

Thereupon he launched into politics. Diatribes against the Bourbons. He was not for Napoleon: because the fellow had his Marshals to seduce innocent girls with words and houses. When they didn't leave them with children on their hands, as Duroc had done La Bigottini . . . No—the Republic! The castles should be given to the people, the Opéra opened to the poor, then you would see how they would applaud. Kings mean foreigners on our soil, and Napoleon means war. What we need is peace, and the Republic. We'll proclaim to the whole world: "Live in peace in your own country! We'll stop burning your towns, ravaging your fields." The Spaniards will have Spain and the Prussians Prussia. The aristocrats can go back to England, the people there like them. No more war, no more emperor, no more king! The power of the nobility, of priests and soldiers, is all over and done with: it's time for the State to pass into the hands of the workers, for those who make the roads, the canals, silk, iron.

"You're talking nonsense, François, and I'm going to get angry! To begin with, your Augustin is ugly and boring. So you want to have me guillotined like Mme. du Barry? And don't forget the baby is a Bourbon! I ought to send you away when you talk like that! No, don't rumple me! Fool! You've hurt my breast!"

Suddenly she sat up, full of anxiety: there were sounds outside, a rapid step, a muffled noise, a cough. Behind the door, Lise's voice: "Madame, Monseigneur is coming up the stairs!"

Monseigneur! Ah, the republican did not stand his ground long: he was already in the adjoining closet. The Bourbons could enter.

"My love," exclaimed Charles-Ferdinand, "they're going to separate us forever!"

Virginie uttered a little cry. She did not yet understand. She saw that His Highness was wearing his Lifeguard uniform; it was one she liked. With the blue and the scarlet. The buttonholes ending in a silver triangle. The silver epaulets. The *aiguillettes* in a clover-leaf design. The gold helmet with black chenille. The white leather breeches. Charlot was, after all, a very different matter from François.

Then she was struck by the pathos of his words. "Separate us? Who? Our uncle?"

He always laughed when she referred to the old King as "our uncle." But not today. He repeated: "Separate us forever and ever, my poor love." She began to exclaim, to work herself up, demanded that he should explain himself, said he shouldn't frighten people like that. And she fell back on the pillow in a way that made her even prettier. The sight of her brought a mist into his eyes. The baby softness of those swollen breasts, the peach-bloom of her shoulder. . . .

"Oh, Charlot, please don't, please don't! You know I'm not well—and besides it's bad for my milk."

He was weeping, with one knee on the edge of the bed, still with those wonderful tears from centuries past bursting from his eyes. "My poor love," was all he found to say. And from the pillows, her head deep in the mass of her beautiful black hair, Virginie looked anxiously at the closet door, which had not quite shut.

When the door to the salon opened, the ladies smothered a little cry, and the bouillotte players looked up over their spectacles. All the money was already stacked in front of M. Touchard.

There stood Monseigneur the Duc de Berry, his left arm supporting Virginie, who clung to him, pale-faced, wearing an all-white house-dress with a big goffered collar. He was straining to look his full height; and the bloodlessness of his lips struck everyone. In the salon they had not been aware of his arrival: he had gone straight up to Virginie's room, leaving M. de la Ferronays under the portico. Everyone later gave a different version of the little speech of which the Duke now delivered himself. Memory readily takes on an heroic tinge; but actually his first words had nothing to do with the situation. "What the bloody hell is that Jesuit doing here on an evening like this?" he shouted. "Whom is he spying for?"

Everyone, stunned, looked at Father Elisée. But His Highness had no time to lose, he was expected at the Barrière de l'Étoile, nor did the answer interest him. The Father had shrunk behind his host, and the general amazement seemed to be conveyed more by M. Oreille's long face than by the words that followed. Besides, what the Prince had to say sufficed to explain the perspiration on that dignified man's face.

"We're leaving Paris tonight and do not expect to return. The King is already on the road. At the moment he has not yet reached Saint-Denis. There is treason on every hand. The army aspires to dictatorship. The ungrateful populace opens its arms to the Corsican brigand. In a single moment it has forgotten the peace brought to the kingdom, the accomplishments and benefits of a whole year. I leave my Virginie, and my child, in your charge. Do not forget that the blood of Henri IV flows in his veins. Alas, alas, my poor love, we shall never see each other again!"

In the general stupefaction, Marie-Louise Oreille was heard to say—not as a question, and to no one in particular, as though speaking to herself—"But where are we going to find the fifteen hundred francs a month?"

Mme. Persuis burst into loud sobs, which seemed the only thing to do. The Mlles. Gosselin and Podevin rushed over to Virginie. M. Oreille, a tall man, raised himself up to his full height, as a result of which the Jesuit behind him was no longer visible. One of the Alexandres shuffled the cards mechanically, the other picked a tooth with his thumbnail. M. Touchard, his hands on the money, had not moved from the table, and Mlle. Gosselin's young man, who was trying to find something to say, found it only the next day. Virginie sobbed softly. And Grandmamma Bourguignon, who had understood nothing of what was being said, asked in a booming voice: "What is Monseigneur saying? Is he going hunting?"

The excitement was so general that no one noticed the scuttling movement of the Reverend Father who, taking advantage of the fact that Mme. Persuis and the Mlles. Podevin and Gosselin had moved toward the young mother and surrounded the couple, had reached the half-open door and slipped out into the vestibule. There he found Picard and whispered a few words in his ear. Picard began by shaking his head and refusing; but the Jesuit, becoming pressing, almost ingratiating, took the valet by the upper arm and kept insisting in a low voice, reaching meanwhile into the pocket of his robe and pulling out a heavy purse. This seemed to decide the servant. "I may lose my situation because of this, Father. But if you can manage with a cabriolet and one horse . . ."

The Jesuit could manage, but he had no time to lose if he was to catch up with His Majesty at Saint-Denis. Who could ever have suspected so much duplicity beneath the fat monarch's good-natured appearance? To have kept that from *him!* Abandoning him when the Corsican was at the gates of Paris! Had Louis, then, wanted to get rid of him? After all that he owed to Father Elisée? Those years of abnegation, his unsparing attention! Not to mention the money that had never been repaid. And even tonight, why was he here on the rue de Valois-du-Roule, if not to serve his King? To come and watch the hairdresser and those shopkeepers at their game of bouillotte, to talk with that deaf-as-a-post old woman and that stupid Marie-Louise, in order to make a report to the Pavillon de Flore on the loves of the handsome nephew—to be willing to do this required a good dose of devotion for which a room at the Palace and ten thousand francs a year could hardly be called a suitable recompense when you considered that that ninny of a Monseigneur gave eighteen to his ballet dancer, to say nothing of that two-horse carriage she would have no use for—just today when his need of it was so great.

V

Saint-Denis

MONSIEUR BENOÎT, mayor of Saint-Denis, had gone to bed early that evening, and when they came to awaken him a little before midnight he let loose his whole repertory of curses. He was all the more furious as the communication emanated from the commander of the National Guard, Monsieur Dézobry, for whom he had little liking, even though their being in the same industry constituted a bond between them. Monsieur Dézobry had been mayor of the town before 1811, and by his stubborn insistence on defending the fortress, as he said, against the Allied armies, he had come close to exterminating the people of the town. His crony in the flour mills, where they had connived at the installation of a new English-type steam engine—a great economy—was obviously taking a sly delight in pulling his monarchist successor from his bed by informing him that the King was about to pass through Saint-Denis. It was Marshal Macdonald's forward detachment, heading north to prepare quarters for the troops, which had notified the garrison, and the colonel of the Light Infantry had in turn told the commander of the Guard.

It seemed as though hardly anyone in the town except the mayor had gone to bed that night.

Monsieur Benoît, making his way to the barracks in the rain, had no idea what was causing all the congestion. Carriages, carriages. The *estaminets* crowded and noisy, foot passengers in heated argument, an incredible number of soldiers: what did it all mean? Weren't they confined to their quarters? Both the rue de Paris and the rue Compoise were completely jammed; people were coming from all directions, vehicles of every description, so that one might have thought not only that Paris was being evacuated, but also that all Normandy was pouring into town.

The lanterns shed inadequate blobs of light over this tangle of people, horses and wheels. The slanting streaks of rain, the damp cold, the muffled anxiety that filled the darkness, the townsfolk behind their shutters awakened by the unaccustomed noise . . . Was it true, then, that His Majesty was fleeing his capital? Upon reaching the barracks and the square, with the pump of the artesian well used to water the coach horses and a small permanent fountain for householders, the mayor was startled by the confusion of soldiers and officers behind the railings. Was discipline dead? Troops, infantrymen, dirty, exhausted by a long march, were coming from the direction of Beauvais, and at the same time, entering by the rue de Paris, the first mounted groups of the Lifeguards, their horses still steaming, and a few riders already dismounting, were marking time at the entrance to the barracks. All this activity had brought out the curious.

Au Postillon was a wineshop across the square from the barracks; there everyone seemed to know what was going on. Monsieur Benoît found a seat and ordered a glass of rum, sugar and hot water. His bad humor was aggravated by the presence of a National Guard picket democratically drinking with his commanding officer. Monsieur Dézobry was obviously enjoying himself at his expense, speaking in a loud voice about Père la Violette and the Comte de Lille. It was hard to understand what he was saying above the loud guffaws of the Guards and the customers at the adjoining tables and at the zinc counter, but his toasts sounded suspect. All this with complete impunity. They had, in fact, too many interests in common for the mayor to think of denouncing his crony. And besides, to whom could he do so—now? There were common people singing seditious airs, and calling to one another from opposite ends of the big room. Tanners with the smell of leather about them and the color of tanners' bark on their hands; dyers who prepared the cloth from which these uniforms, the object of their jeers, were made; enamelers from René Martin's who worked on the mosaics of the Madeleine; cabinetmakers from Graffet's who put together the Opéra stage sets; workers from the soda factory where Nicolas

Leblanc's process was being developed; lower middle-class persons of every description; clerks and shopkeepers. No women, except the waitresses.

On this Sunday night, had all these people lost sight of the fact that tomorrow was Monday and they would have to be at their work? The fact that the wineshop kept open, because of the mail coach, was one thing. Though really, according to the latest ordinance . . .

Outside, despite the rain that was now coming down in sheets, the relay horses were already being prepared. The announcement of the King's imminent arrival only confirmed the rumors that had circulated all day. Lifeguards on foot were beginning to arrive. These were the young officers who were as yet without mounts, and who at the last moment had been armed with guns at the Orsay Barracks. Still they made a good appearance in their drenched cloaks, although they were not used to marching and to carrying a load. But of course they had covered only a bit over two leagues so far; and then there was pride, the point of honor. The Prince de Wagram's company had been sent ahead, at eleven o'clock. It was commanded by Monsieur le Baron Lascours, who went to report to the apartments of Lieutenant General Maison, Governor of Paris and commander-in-chief of the troops of the Seine, who had arrived in the evening from Villejuif, the previous command headquarters, to await at Saint-Denis the troops who were willing to move.

Who were willing! For Maison had no illusions: the news to the south of Paris was bad, and whole regiments had taken to discussing the orders given them. It was an atmosphere that was not altogether unfamiliar to him: he had witnessed the same sort of thing in 1814, at Valenciennes and at Lille. But then Bonaparte had just abdicated, and it had sufficed to cover the roads with cannon to stop desertions. As for orders, just give your own. This is what he replied with an air of utter weariness to Baron Lascours, the aide-major of Wagram's company, who was asking if there were any orders. Whose orders would there be?

Full generals were available by the shovelful—Monsieur le Duc de Berry, Macdonald, Marmont. But who was in command? And don't talk about the War Minister! Clarke was Maison's *bête noire:* he had never forgiven the Duc de Feltre the letters he had sent him when he was the Emperor's War Minister, criticizing his conduct during the French retreat, requiring him to launch absurd offensives in the direction of Antwerp, when his own intention was to protect the frontier by means of skillful movements which he was initiating around Lille. It had taken the fellow only a year to be nagging at him once more, this time as minister to Louis XVIII! Orders? Clarke's orders!

And to think that he had experienced a moment of triumph when Soult had been removed and replaced by Clarke! To be sure, he himself was partly to blame. Soult had persecuted him from the moment he had become minister, even committing the crude blunder of sending the King's Light Cavalry to Béthune, so as to reduce the number of troops at the disposal of the governor of Paris. This Sunday, on the Place Louis-XV, they had seen what that had led to. To say nothing of the bickering between their wives. All for the benefit of a fellow like Clarke! Clarke's orders? Clarke knew only how to criticize, he was incapable of command. He really missed Soult, whom the Princes had thrown out simply on the strength of gossip. And he had contributed his bit.

No one knew anything. The King was about to arrive. Where would he go from here? To Rouen, Boulogne, Dunkirk? The general was bitter. Besides everything else, he had been the first—well, before all the Marshals—to welcome the Princes last year. From Lille where he was in command, he had gone to Boulogne on his own initiative to welcome His Majesty. . . . "Is the Marshal with you?" he asked, again becoming aware of Lascours. What a question! The Prince de Wagram was accompanying the King. He would join them presently, with His Majesty. Maison did not like Marshals, Alexandre Berthier no more than any other. With an air of detachment that shocked the Baron, he asked for news of Madame Visconti: the intrusion of the private life at a moment like this! The Prince de Wagram was not keeping him posted, Lascours replied, but the Princess must be at Gros-Bois. He explained that he had left the Orsay Barracks at about eleven o'clock, and that his officers had been disturbed to learn that instead of being sent to Melun they were made to cross the Seine, pass through the Carrousel courtyard, follow the rue de Richelieu. The excitement as they passed! The orders he himself had received were anything but explicit; he was obeying without asking questions; but what the devil—were they evacuating Paris?

The general did not bother to answer him. Since Wagram's company was here, it had only to wait for the King. He, in any case, had written to Marshal Macdonald that he would be at his disposal at Saint-Denis. Was Macdonald accompanying His Majesty?

"I haven't the least idea," replied Lascours.

Maison was worried. Had he miscalculated, last year? His sole concern had been to safeguard the continuity of the army. At least that was how things looked to him now. For had it been on behalf of the continuity of the army that he had first written to the King of Sweden, his former chief? Or had he been convinced that it would do his own career no harm if Bernadotte were ruler of France? There had been his irritation with the Emperor at the time, an irritation aggravated by Clarke. And there was in him, too— and this went a little deeper—a certain disposition toward liberalism which contrasted sharply with that constant, unreasoning, desperate warfare, with Napoleon's authoritarianism. After having momentarily believed that the Emperor could be replaced by Bernadotte, he had been among those for whom and through whom Louis XVIII had understood the necessity of the Charter. His Majesty had made him a count, a peer of France, lieutenant general and governor of Paris, commanding the first territorial division; that is to say the Aisne, Eure-et-Loir, Loiret, Oise, Seine, Seine-et-Marne and Seine-et-Oise. But it was the army that worried him especially today. What is a general who has the army against him? Not the soldiers, but the army—the officers.

Baron Lascours had been gone less than ten minutes when His Majesty's orderlies were announced. Maison hastened out to the Place de la Caserne, just as the King's six horses and berlin emerged behind a troop of riders, the postillion astride the last horse on the left and two valets, in uniform as at the Tuileries, under the hood of the driver's seat. A lieutenant of his division, who accompanied him with a torch, lifted it when the door opened, and next to Louis XVIII could be seen Monsieur le Duc de Duras; and opposite them, Monsieur de Blacas and the Prince de Poix. A score of carriages followed under the guard of the Gray Musketeers, who rode on the flanks of the convoy. A detachment of Wagram's company had come to meet the Musketeers and line the route. Over there, at the entrance to the town, attempts were being made to divert civilian carriages, both to the right in the direction of the basilica and to the left at the Place aux Gueldres, where they were being turned back. There had even been a few cries of *Vive le Roi!*

In front of the barracks, by the light of the torch carried by a big lumpkin of an infantryman, the travelers, emerging from under their wraps, saw General Maison, bowing, and a Lifeguards officer, helmet respectfully in hand, shaking his head intermittently because of the rain that trickled down his forehead into his eyes. A fellow behind these two was vainly trying to attract attention, but the Lifeguards had pushed him back, not realizing that he was Monsieur Benoît, mayor of the town; who, it would seem, had got out of bed for nothing. From inside the wineshop Monsieur Dézobry, still sitting with his companions, watched his crony's useless contortions with amusement. For the King to alight was out of the question—he would have had to be carried. The others, out of deference, had to forego stretching their legs. And besides, in this rain . . . Also the relay horses were ready, and the ostlers were changing over the harnessing. Maison merely said, "Wagram's Lifeguards have received no orders."

Displeased, His Majesty coughed, and the Prince de Poix leaned over and pointed to the carriages behind: "Well, ask Berthier, General! He's back there somewhere." The Prince de Poix would never have said either the Prince de Wagram or the Prince de Neufchâtel. He had never been able to get used to these revolutionary princedoms. He called Berthier Berthier, and Clarke the Duc de Feltre.

While the postillions were bustling about the royal carriage, Théodore rode off from the troop, looking for somewhere to water his horse. It was not so much those two and a quarter leagues, but the day had been long and full—for the animals as well as the men. He caught sight of the pump and dismounted. But there was no way of reaching it. Buckets were being filled for the carriage horses which were not being changed. Other riders of the escort showed him the way to the watering trough: he would have time if he hurried. Holding their mounts by the reins, a dozen Musketeers were trying to slip back through the convoy in order to reach the rue Compoise. The lanterns shed a fantastic light over everything, and suddenly there was a brief letup in the rain. Overhead, between the clouds, a glimpse could be caught of a wan, swollen moon which seemed to be half asleep.

There are resolutions a man makes, and resolutions that he keeps. When Théodore had left young Thierry, he had been determined to let the Royal Household leave, and to take advantage of the darkness to repair to his bed in the attic at La Nouvelle-Athènes. For all the reasons of 1810 that had reappeared—and for others.

But perhaps especially because he had suddenly thought so intently about painting once again. He imagined pictures to paint, he saw them with painful precision. He suddenly had the urge to backslide—to pay no heed to the advice that had been showered on him, to spurn the criticisms, and instead to reaffirm even more energetically the very things for which he had been reproached.

He had been told a story about a woman dressed as a man who used to pick up travelers near the stagecoach office yard, take them to a hotel where she would pour a soporific into their glass, and then kill them with a hammer and rob them. In his imagination he pictured this modern form of the story of Judith: the Holofernes would be a man of good family who had come from Normandy—there were many such in the region where his uncle, the regicide, lived. He must be young, perhaps a little on the heavy side, but very handsome, to make the crime more abominable—Holofernes, after all, was an old fogey for whom nobody cared. The hotel room would provide the kind of lighting effect he was always after; the murderess, with all her desirable attributes, would be both a shadow effect and a very real woman, a woman of today, perhaps a Creole, with an expression like Caroline's when she had glanced at his red coat. The entire picture composed of those two bright masses, against the commonplaceness, the blackness of the background. And perhaps the pale sheets, from which the half-naked victim attempted to escape, his strength already ebbing as he pushed them off. Hotel sheets, stiff, with accentuated folds. A redheaded, knotty man, the legs of a horseman, and all the frenzy of frustrated desire.

As he was returning to the Court of the Tuileries, thoughts of this kind haunted his mind when it was not imagining a brawl among grooms in a stable lighted by lanterns, amid rearing horses. Then, little by little, he again became aware of his surroundings, the fancies dissolved, he heard the words about him, he became conscious of the people mingled with the soldiers, of their remarks, of their insults. He saw a National Guard fling his gun to the ground, shouting words that the people greeted with rousing cheers as they embraced him and lifted him high on their upstretched arms. He saw tricolor cockades blossoming on jackets and blouses, and on others, bunches of violets to hide the white cockade, and there they were, only two steps from the Pavillon de Flore, from the troops guarding the King.

Those in the courtyard of the Carrousel seemed to be a prey to an agitation that was not explained even by the harangue of a civilian who had climbed onto the railings of the Tuileries and was shouting things that Géricault could not hear. Never had people been more indifferent to rain. The crowd was dense; all the dilapidated buildings that crowded the district at the far end of the square blinked with a thousand candles behind the windows and doors, and there was a disquieting coming and going of sinister-looking men, drunken women, brawlers and furtive creatures. A number of soldiers had lifted their rifle butts high in the air, and there were rhythmic hand-claps as they made for a wineshop on the rue Saint-Niçaise. What difference was there between them and him? Théodore wondered, with a feeling of nausea. He had come here only to fetch his horse, which he had left under an archway. He hurried in that direction.

He was trying to think only of painting. Of the effect of tones. Of the warmth that flesh can assume, even in the yellows. Of what a judicious choice of subject allows, warrants—for example, sickness, death, corroding and denuding the anatomy, thereby achieving a truth that cannot be represented in a healthy man, excusing the painter for deviating from classic Greek beauty which is never touched by decay, never wounded. Between heaven and man there are moments when they are attuned to all the violence of storm and feelings, when lightning rends the sea as the knife the flesh . . . the scalpel . . .

In Saint-Denis, he found it even easier than it had been at the Carrousel to lose himself in this game of shadows and men. Here he had only to look—there was no need to imagine. The road to the watering trough was like a great funeral celebration, a canvas constantly reworked—crowd, torches and lanterns, mean, narrow houses, flicks of shadow with touches of the commonplace in faces and clothes that filled Théodore's heart to overflowing. If he had not had to water Trick, he would have stopped to gaze at that ragged creature standing beside a milestone at the corner of the rue Compoise, who seemed the center of an enormous composition, his face bearing a look of stupor at the happenings on this night which this vast, jumbled, vagrant, incomprehensible crowd seemed to have stolen from him. And at his feet lay a little white and yellow dog whose entire body was trembling.

Earlier, as he was approaching the gateway to the Louvre . . .

He remembered it as though it had happened not four hours earlier, but long ago, in his childhood. He had, so to speak, stumbled upon those two Lifeguards whom he had met by chance some days before in the course of a street fight near the Madeleine. They were coming from the quay. They carried no arms, not even a saber or a sword, and at first Théodore did not realize that he had noticed this. But their walk was erratic, unsure, they were hurrying, and at the sight of the Musketeer's uniform they edged away. There could be no doubt: they were deserting. Théodore spoke to them as though he had understood nothing of this, asking them where they were going.

They were different of build, one tall and lean, the other with the leaden gait of the seasoned trooper. They had recognized Géricault, and could not pretend otherwise. In husky voices and with tears in their eyes, they begged him to let them go on. What, Lifeguards? Deserters! They had each taken the Musketeer by an arm and urged him to understand them. They both spoke at once. Their reasons were lamentable. They were gentlemen from Languedoc, one from Toulouse, the other belonged to a family which had a house in the vicinity of Rodez. They could not agree to follow the King, to abandon everything, perhaps leave France, take ship. Their families had never emigrated, and one of them had a mother and a sister who would be left alone and without money, the other had a fiancée. They spoke ruefully of the vain pride that had made them sign on in His Majesty's Household—even Paris was a kind of exile. Where were they being dragged? Last time it had lasted more than twenty years! How old would they be if they did come back some day? Their whole lives would have been spent. And one of them spoke of his native region as though it had been a woman, of the sun down there, and because of it he could not resign himself to cross over to England. Géricault let them go. They were planning to hide with a *demi-galante* who held gaming parties in her apartment.

Théodore had crossed the parade ground, which was a halting place for fugitives and vehicles. He was skirting the École de la Légion d'Honneur, and before him were perhaps a hundred riders leading their horses to water. Trick whinnied. Patience, patience, my handsome! Théo stroked his neck. In this crush of men who had no compunction about slipping ahead of someone else when they had a chance, he visualized again the portico of the Louvre, the contrast between the night on the square and the pale torches under the gateway, the meeting with the deserters. Everything tonight was a picture, for his eyes and for his memory. At about eleven, suddenly a whirl of flame and sparks had darted from one of the chimneys that rose in sharp black outlines from the roofs of the Tuileries, capping the royal dwelling with a crown of fire; and all at once from all directions the crowd had come running toward the Palace. It was only files of documents and letters that were being burned, but the sparks had rallied people as though they had been hands of fire calling for help. The carriages that had been dismissed at seven o'clock had not returned to the quay, but in the Carrousel courtyard chests of silverware and precious objects were being loaded into vans. Anguished orders had rung out among the Guards, the alerted sentinels surrounded the carriages: probably someone feared that the good people of Paris might seize them. On the quay the Gray Musketeers, mounted, formed a curtain between the mob and the Palace. Yet even then, Théodore was still planning not to follow the King. Painting, art, was different from a sister or a fiancée.

When darkness had again engulfed the roofs, time seemed interminable, and gradually the people wearied. Everything about the Palace grew calm again. The hour and the rain had at last dispersed the crowd. It was black—a blackness that could be cut with a knife. The great trees on the bank of the Seine swayed in the wind, whose lugubrious voice surrounded the horsemen as they continued to guard the approaches to the Pavillon de Flore. About midnight the Musketeers posted before the door of the Pavillon saw the carriages arriving; then, through the suddenly opened door, they saw the King—was it really the King?—coming down the stairs in such obvious pain, leaning on M. de Blacas and on the Duc de Duras like a man who seemed about to fall at every step, old and heavy, suffering from his ailing back, his feet in his canvas boots; and behind him Marshals, Ministers and Princes, surrounded by National Guards who had come running, by Grenadiers, Light Horsemen, and servants. Suddenly Théodore was overwhelmed with pity. He was perhaps the only one who failed to hear the words spoken—words that were to remain historic. He was hardly aware of the general excitement, of the movement of the Guards, of the rush of officials and valets to the fallen monarch. It had become impossible for him to run away. Further calculation was out of the question. He was among those assigned to escort the royal berlin.

The die had been cast.

At about the time when Trick, at last, was drinking long draughts of the subterranean waters of the Groult which supplied the Saint-Denis water trough, in Paris the Duc de Raguse, accompanied on horseback by Baron Fabvier, was giving the signal for departure to the four companies of the Royal Household which had been assembled at the Barrière de l'Étoile since eleven o'clock in the evening.

Monsieur rode in a post-carriage with the Duc de Maillé and the Comte Armand de Polignac, while the Duc de Berry and Marshal Marmont, on horseback, headed the column. The Duc de Richelieu had joined them without having any special assignment. As first gentleman of the Privy Chamber, he had sensed which way the wind was blowing and left the apartment on the rue Royale-Saint-Honoré which the Comte de Rochechouart had rented from Baron Louis and had been sharing since late November with the Duke and his aide-de-camp, M. de Stempkovski, a worthy young officer who had been attached to His Highness since the age of fifteen.

The day before, Ivan Alexandrovich had left for Frankfort, where Czar Alexander the First now was, in the Duke's carriage with M. de Richelieu's valet—which clearly proved that the Duke had no intention of tying his fortune to that of the fugitive King and that today, as yesterday, he looked to the Czar's army rather than to Condé's to remedy the situation. Anyway, this evening, returning from the Tuileries to the apartment at about nine o'clock, he had invited his host, the Comte de Rochechouart, to hold himself in readiness; and just as they were about to separate, the Comte had received the order for the Black Musketeers to assemble at the Étoile. Together they had gone there on horseback, followed by Léon de Rochechouart's cabriolet which would travel with the baggage convoy of the Royal Household. The whole thing gave Léon a funny feeling. It took him back more than seven years, to Odessa, before Stempkovski had replaced him in the service of his uncle, Richelieu. In spite of everything, he was a little jealous of his successor.

Nearly four thousand men, the Comte de La Rochejaquelein's Grenadiers in the lead, got under way in the night beneath torrents of water; they were already drenched to the skin by the repeated fierce downpours of the hours of waiting. Here were most of the Lifeguards; the war squadrons of Grammont's company, which the Duke, being attached to His Majesty, had placed under the command of Tony de Reiset on the 18th; those of the Noailles company, under M. de Fournel of course in the absence of the Prince de Poix; of the company of Scots, under M. de Villiers-Lafaye, replacing the Duc de Croy d'Havret, also with the King; and Raguse's company under M. de La Marthoris who was replacing Marmont. But the King's Gendarmes led by Comte Étienne de Durfort, the Light Horse with Comte Charles de Damas, and the Gray and Black Musketeers under Lauriston and La Grange, formed the main body of cavalry.

It was the men on foot that slowed the march: not so much the professional infantry—reduced to the Swiss Guards who, under the orders of M. de Mortemart, had returned from Melun with four pieces of artillery—as the occasional soldiers on foot of the various companies, especially the Lifeguards, who still had no mounts, and five hundred royal volunteers who had been picked up at the Place Louis-XV and, commanded by Lifeguard officers, were preceded by the Louis de La Rochejaquelein Grenadiers. This long, jogging convoy of horses and men on foot mingled more or less haphazardly, was guarded in the rear by M. de La Grange's Black Musketeers who had arrived later than the others from the Célestins Barracks. They had circled Paris almost in silence. In the blackness of the night, they passed carriages loaded with frightened families. The tread of feet, the tramp of horses, the patter of rain on the drenched ground, formed a dismal, monotonous, singsong symphony in which the thoughts of this mass of men were being molded—men, for the most part, so startled by the turn of events that they were incapable of reasoning or of fear. They kept passing gates, and counted them as though they were the mute stages of a terrible game of parcheesi. Where were they going to turn? Only the unit chiefs knew that they were going to Saint-Denis.

César de Chastellux was one of those who knew, M. de Damas having secretly whispered to his son-in-law the name of the destination, Lille. He could not help trembling, as though it were a stroke of fate, at the King's return in his hour of trial to the city whose name His Majesty had borne until last year. Tony de Reiset, with whom he had exchanged a few words, considered it, featherbrain that he was, to be of good omen! On this Palm Sunday evening they were following in reverse last year's path of glory: they would again pass through the town of Saint-Denis where Louis le Désiré had been presented with the gold keys of the city on a crimson cushion, in the presence of Count Narishkin and his Cossacks. On this Palm Sunday evening the King's passion was beginning. The way of the cross would soon be followed by this whole army which would be required to cover a monstrous stretch tonight. How far would these sons of nobility be able to go, escorting the aged monarch? What was happening behind them, in that enormous, somnolent city over whose spine they were crawling?

One of the Gray Musketeers who had answered the call to assemble at the Étoile, immediately after the King had left the Palace, had told M. de Damas, who knew him—he was the son of an old friend of his, d'Houdetot—that at the very moment when the royal carriages had started moving, a gust of wind had whipped round the walls of the Tuileries, sending all kinds of papers whirling, and a sinister sound had been heard: it was the great white flag falling from the Pavillon de l'Horloge. It would not have to be pulled down.

After leaving the Champ-de-Mars, César had gone home to dine at his house on the rue du Bac. He had had a carriage prepared for his unhappy sister, Mme. de Labédoyère, her five-month-old son, Zéphirine his wife, and his daughter, sending them simply to Bougival, to the château of Mme. de Mesmes, so that the two sisters-in-law should not be in Paris during the uncertain events of the days to come. He was tortured by an idea that his Uncle de Lorge had put into his head: the strange facility with which the Duc d'Orléans had handed the 7th Line Regiment over to Charles de Labédoyère. In vain he repeated to himself that his recommendation, and that of Roger de Damas, had been a factor. No one could tell him that his brother-in-law had taken this regiment with the idea of joining Buonaparte. He knew that if Charles had any kind of political feeling in his heart, he was decidedly more in favor of the Republic than of the Empire. Could there have been calculation on Louis-Philippe's part? Had he made a point of placing men who could be induced to participate in a *coup d'état* at the head of the regiments at his disposal? César remembered the days when Louis-Philippe was still the Duc de Chartres, in Dumouriez's army. Dumouriez and the Girondins had at that time supported his candidacy against Louis XVI, hadn't they? An odd rumor, too, was in circulation regarding the mutiny at La Fère and the real intentions of Generals Lallemand and Lefebvre-Desnouettes. And the King, it so happened, had put his cousin d'Orléans in command of the armies of the North, at whose mercy he would be. Was it true that he was the Baroness Lallemand's lover? People lend only to the rich. . . .

When they had reached the plain of Saint-Denis—a desert from which clumps of trees rose at infrequent intervals along the dirt road, by now nothing but mud, with a sky so black that, on the left, even the outline of Montmartre was invisible—César de Chastellux's thoughts filled him with anguish. He could not forgive himself his responsibility in all this: he exaggerated Charles's role to himself, he was haunted by it. If the 7th Line Regiment had not gone over to the Emperor at Grenoble, who knows whether Ney would have committed treason at Auxerre? And that his brother-in-law should be the cause of it . . . It was not Napoleon's taking possession of the

Tuileries again tomorrow that César found so bitter, but the fact that Labédoyère should return there in triumph.

This plain was haunted by stories of murder. The Royal Household was crossing it, and the horsemen were growing impatient. They had constantly to stop, to wait for those on foot, to form again and set off in more or less orderly units. All these undertrained youths sagged under their loads, and their feet were already beginning to drag. What would it be like in a few hours? The rain came down remorselessly, came down on the Lorges, the Damas', the Mortemarts, the La Rochejaqueleins, on all these men, fathers and sons of families that were linked by blood and women, the long history of the centuries brought to nought. And César urged his horse past the column, retraced his steps. A rider caught up with him and uttered his name questioningly in the dark. It was the Duc de Richelieu, who was seeking a traveling companion. He felt like talking tonight.

"César? Just imagine, my dear fellow, a while ago, at about half past eleven, on the Champs-Élysées, I met M. de Chateaubriand who asked me what I was doing there. He was on his way home like any honest citizen, coming from I don't know where. He had no thought of leaving Paris. He was going to bed, he told me. Besides, at the Pavillon de Flore, Duras and Blacas had assured him—it was well after ten o'clock—that His Majesty would not leave the capital. When I told him that I had quite different information, a word whispered to me by the Prince de Poix at the Tuileries, and that Rochechouart had received orders from the Célestins to report at the Étoile, he swore like a fiend, said this proved nothing, screamed about Blacas, saying at least one-hundredth of the foul things I actually think about him, and announced that he was going home to wait for news, determined not to move without having proof that the King had left. But leaving that aside, where do you suppose he had been? He was coming from the direction of Le Roule, which certainly was not on his way from the Palace to the rue de Rivoli where poor Céleste was waiting for him! How many married men have farewells to make tonight!"

César was not in the least concerned about Mme. de Chateaubriand's marital troubles; and he considered Chateaubriand pretentious and had no liking for him. But what of the Duc de Richelieu himself? He would have had to be a saint to be coming directly from the conjugal domicile, with the wife *he* had! A hump in front, and a hump behind. . . . But César had a notion she had not been in Paris since 1789. He replied out of politeness, "M. de Chateaubriand will perhaps change his mind this morning, when the Ogre appears on the scene."

And the other said, after a silence, "It must be said that he had been unable to find any horses."

Then in a quite different tone of voice, "I don't quite understand what's happening, my dear fellow, but the fact is I'm getting raw as I never do on horseback. I must have put something on backwards or inside out last night, but whatever it is, I'm getting sore."

It was odd, as a matter of fact, for the Duke was reputed to be an excellent rider: there were endless stories about his exploits in the Caucasus where they know how to ride.

They were coming into Saint-Denis and onto a paved road. They crossed the canal and the troops were called to a halt to re-form along the sides of the road, under the double rows of plane trees. César left the Duke and came and posted his horse alongside the Comte de Damas's mount.

While the shadows of the Royal Household filed past, he could not help communicating to his father-in-law the anxiety into which he had been thrown by what the Duc de Lorge, his uncle, had suggested regarding Louis-Philippe's connection with the La Fère rebellion. Was His Majesty informed? Lieutenant General Comte Charles de Damas, captain of the Light Horse, was not a young man, and he knew the ways of the world. But he had enjoyed a long companionship with the Comte d'Artois, and he shared the younger branch's hatred for that of the Orléans'. "Your uncle does not speak lightly, my son," he said. "Anything is to be expected from the Duc de Chartres."

To him, who had commanded Mirabeau's legion in Condé's army, Louis-Philippe would always remain the Duc de Chartres, as he had been called when he wore the uniform of the Republic. An officer of the enemy army. He thought for a moment, then added, "I happen to know—I was there when Lord Charles Kinnaird, who advises him in his purchases of paintings, presented the Lallemand woman to the King. Chartres would perhaps have done it himself, since they say . . . But His Majesty had sent him to Lyons by the time this lady reached Paris. And of course it took an Englishman to make this unseemly move! The men of Condé's army did not like England. And what if Georgine had asked him, César, to take her before the King to implore him to pardon Charles?" It made him shudder. "A pretty present His Majesty had made Monsieur, inflicting such an adjutant on him at Lyons! You'll notice that the Duc de Chartres always happens to be wherever treason breaks out. I can imagine the pleasure it must have been for my brother to see him coming."

Roger de Damas, the Count's younger brother, husband of Pauline de Chastellux, sister of Georgine and César, had been in command at Lyons when Ney's treason had forced the Princes to flee. But was it of Ney's treason to Louis XVIII that the Comte de Damas was thinking, or of the Duc de Chartres's deserting to join the Imperials with Dumouriez in 1793? Betraying the Republic one day, the King the next . . . Yes, he was living in the past, for he added, "Dumouriez: it wasn't mere chance that made him conspire—not so much against the Jacobins as against the legitimacy. He had been an agent of the Orléans faction for a long time. His father Philippe had put him in command of the Cherbourg fortress before '89, for some conspiratorial reason—just as that wretched Charles was put at the head of his regiment by the Duc de Chartres. My poor César, both you and Roger were completely hoodwinked! What's going on?"

Some civilians were trying to get through, and their vehicles were being stopped at the entrance to the town. There was clamor and confusion. "Make way for the Royal Household," an officer was shouting over there in the shadow and the gleam of the lanterns.

Charles de Damas sighed. He had just been reminded of Varennes, where he had accompanied Louis XVI, and of the son of the postmaster of Sainte-Menehould, the too famous Drouet, whose face he would never forget. "Don't you think, my son," he said to César, "that it was something more than chance that brought Drouet's brother into the Lallemands' conspiracy? And how do you explain his recalling his troops on learning of the Usurper's landing, just as General Lion did a few days later, breaking with Lefebvre-Desnouettes?"

"I don't see—" said César. "I was told that it was Marshal Mortier's unexpected arrival in Lille—"

"You don't see? Lion and Drouet d'Erlon are both Buonaparte's men . . . when they realized they were working for the Orléans faction . . ."

Order had been restored. They were entering Saint-Denis.

Father Elisée had not caught up with His Majesty at Saint-Denis. In the first place, it was all very fine to have a horse and a cabriolet. But one also needed a driver. And it had taken Picard more than an hour to find one. Another stroke of luck! A strapping fellow who had haggled endlessly over the price and asked if the Father was armed. Because at night the roads were by no means safe, he was afraid, and especially in times like these anything was possible, and you couldn't count on the constabulary. And then he had had to stop at the Pavillon de Flore to fetch his things. What a sight had met him there! The Palace sealed tight, dark; they had had to make an uproar before they were let in. The National Guards camped in the rooms on the first floor, mattresses on the ground in the Marshals' Salon, an extraordinary disorder, officers talking in whispers in a corner. M. de Laborde had advised the Father to go to the office of Foreign Affairs; there he would find the minister who was to join the King at dawn—as soon as the papers were burned. Father Elisée could do without the company of M. de Jaucourt, and had no intention of waiting till dawn. And suppose they never caught up with the King?

After that, all the roads were so madly congested that Jasmin—the driver's name was Jasmin—had suggested they give up trying to reach Saint-Denis by the direct road, blocked as it was by the Royal Household which made it necessary to move at a snail's pace behind the men on foot. Swept along on a tide of fugitives, they had had to swing west and pass by Saint-Germain. From there they could reach Pontoise and Beauvais direct, via Méru. But there was movement also in the opposite direction—troops were marching on Paris. Officers kept stopping them to ask for news. Most of these officers were bound for Melun or Villejuif. Others did not conceal their excitement or their hopes: "Is the Little Shaver really in Montrouge already?" Perhaps this was a joke at the Jesuit's expense. They turned off into side roads to avoid the regiments with their carriages, the convoys. But these were no less congested with fleeing Parisians. And then, the Oise must be crossed.

It would have been better, after all, to wait for M. de Jaucourt. . . . The night was passing. In the pelting rain, and under the hood of the cabriolet, clutching his slender baggage, Father Elisée noticed that the driver's shoulders were trembling. Handsome shoulders he had, the rascal! But in a funk to match them. . . .

They had been stopped dead by a herd of cattle which several great brutes armed with whips were driving to the slaughterhouse in the capital. This was in a wooded stretch of road, and Jasmin wanted to get down from his seat and fling himself into the thicket—not quite realizing at first what it was all about. At Pontoise he had refused to go any farther. It had taken a lot of persuasion, to say nothing of a tidy sum, to induce him to continue to Beauvais. The road was far from good, but the sky was beginning to pale and the rain seemed to be subsiding. Then they had been caught up in an artillery transport. The artillerymen were displaying the tricolor, and they must have done a good deal of stopping along the way. A number of them were asleep on the caissons, dead drunk. It was a difficult moment: this time the Father was as frightened as his driver. He put his hand on Jasmin's knee and asked him if he would not like to have his watch—a present from His Majesty? Jasmin could not understand why his customer was offering him his watch. It did not occur to him that the Father hoped it might win his devotion in this hour of danger.

The Father did indeed tremble at every shadow, at every creature they passed: he saw assassins everywhere; but he was in such a state of exaltation that at moments he yearned for a violent end, and there formed in his head a blend of prayers and of thoughts which the worthy ecclesiastic would never have dared admit to aloud—diabolical temptations that would undoubtedly have sent him straight to hell had death seized him there in his cabriolet. And he imagined that that farm hand, up before daybreak, leading some horses, was about to come up and fire a pistol point-blank at them. He could see the red and yellow flame, a small horizontal streak as in pictures.

At this same hour M. de Chateaubriand, persuaded at last by his wife to leave, was passing through Saint-Denis from which the last squadrons of the Royal Household were setting out. Wagram's company had waited for the regrouping of the Lifeguards who had come from the Barrière de l'Étoile. After a halt of two hours, it had been drawn up at the side of the road ready to move. But it was close to half-past three before the bulk of the Royal Household had been reassembled, and by the time they had been got into motion it was after four o'clock. The order of departure had been resumed, with La Rochejaquelein still leading, but the mass of the Lifeguards now formed the rearguard, and the Black Musketeers, moving at a trot, had been sent ahead toward Beaumont, where Marmont expected little from the quartermaster corps.

On leaving Saint-Brice, Casimir de Mortemart's artillery had got stuck in the mud and had had to be pulled out by hand, which had thrown the whole column into disorder. Fabvier, unable to resist, had dismounted in order to help in the maneuver. It had reminded him of Persia and the roads that were nothing but trails, with improvised gunners who were as afraid of their weapons as of the storm. The fine plans worked out at Saint-Denis had gone by the board. All the companies had become jumbled, and no matter what was done it would be impossible to sort them out without bringing the column to a halt again. At first it was the volunteers especially who got bogged down in the ditches. Those lads didn't know how to march. Soon they began to abandon their packs in the propitious darkness, not even taking the trouble to toss them out of the way, and Life-guards could be heard swearing as they stumbled on one after another of them. Their fatigue came above all from the mud that clung to their boots, and from the deep ruts in which they got stuck.

Where was the King now, with his line of carriages and his escort of Gray Musketeers? The Comte d'Artois had stopped his berlin in the dark and was waiting for the bulk of the Household which his vehicle outdistanced and periodically lost in the night. He wondered where his royal brother might be at this moment. Before they had left the Tuileries, they had had one of those loud quarrels which periodically reverberated through the Palace and made eavesdropping lackeys stop in the corridors and on the staircases. Where was he? What new vagary had seized the weak and unstable sovereign who considered himself Machiavellian and had confidence in no one, except perhaps Blacas—even that was not certain—or in his con-fessor, M. l'Abbé Rocher? He might have stopped anywhere, seized by a pang of hunger, rung the bell at some nobleman's dwelling and awakened masters and servants in order to have a supper prepared for him. Or, without a care as to who was or was not following, have galloped off with his post horses, all alone, unescorted, along any road. The fact that he had apparently consented to go to Lille, that the countersign had been given to all the Princes, to the generals, proved nothing. The preposterous idea of making for some port or other, Le Havre, Dieppe, or Boulogne, might have seized him again. The King had seemed to rally to his brother's point of view: any-thing, rather than place himself again at the mercy of the Prince Regent of England. Charles's bitter grievances against Buckingham Palace had made him eloquent; he had made a collection of the affronts he had endured during his time at Hartwell, and, as far as he was concerned, never, no *never,* would he consent to go and grow old, end his days, among the English! Better to fall into Buonaparte's hands. There are things one does not do a second time.

Yet if His Majesty his brother—who had changed plans, opinions, objectives and decisions ten times in the past twenty-four hours—had come around to his point of view, the Comte d'Artois was not certain that it was not out of pure weariness. The fact was that in their quarrel that evening Louis XVIII had gone as far as he could go. In shouts, in choking anger, but also in arguments and insults. There was one that marked the extreme limit of their relationship. In the course of the years the King had flung it at his younger brother only two or three times. The worst insult of all. And he knew what he was doing. The occasion had to be exceptional. Charles could never recall it without a sense of infuriating humiliation. M. de Charette . . . M. de Charette's letter! *

The Comte d'Artois could shrug his shoulders, thinking back on it was like a dreadful slap in the face. And what had ever possessed him to advise the King to take refuge in La Vendée? It was offering him the opening, and Louis was itching for it. He would not have missed an opportunity to humiliate his brother for a throne or for a meal: "You, my brother, suggest going to the Chouans? So you think they have forgotten M. de Charette's letter?" M. de Charette was dead and buried, it made no sense, who remembered an unimportant incident? Besides, the letter was a counterfeit, forged by English agents. All right. Charles had proposed Flanders. And Louis, suffocating with triumph and asthma, had no strength to fight another proposal. But on the journey? Suppose the favorite had had one of those ideas of his which only he, with his Provençal imagination, could think up? The devil only knew where the King might be at this moment. If some misfortune were to befall him? Not that Charles took his wishes for fears; but all the same, in the event of a deficiency, a deficiency of fat Louis, did it not devolve upon him to ensure the perpetuation of the monarchy? There would at least be a royal will. . . . Where the devil could the King be?

The King was traveling. He had long since crossed the Oise, at Beaumont, he was two leagues from Noailles, he had fallen into a troubled sleep, shaken, rolling on the cushions against poor Duras, his respiration short, difficult; and Blacas, who was worried sick about his medals which had been sent off the day before by a confidential agent, the Duchess being already in England, was thinking that the Prince de Poix was taking up too much room, especially as he had to be careful not to kick His Majesty who moaned in his sleep, probably from his rheumatism. The window could not be lowered,

---

* In 1795, Charles d'Artois attempted to aid the royalist rising of La Vendée, landing from England at the island of Yeu. But he refused to advance farther and returned to England. For this he was accused of cowardice, and the alleged letter by François Charette de la Contrie relates to this episode.

the King was sensitive to cold. And there was a lack of air, smells. . . .

The road was bad—there had been no time to repair it since the invasion. Beside the royal carriage, with its six horses, trotted the rising and falling shadows of the Musketeers of the escort. Carriages had already been lost on the way. Twenty had started out from the Pavillon de Flore. How many would even reach Beauvais? On the way, Louis XVIII had suddenly given up the idea of going to this town, on which his Household was nevertheless converging. The convoy had headed down the road to Creil. But on changing horses at Luzarches, the postillions had said that on the road to Amiens, somewhere near Clermont, there were rebel troops who had pinned the tricolor cockade on their uniforms. This had sufficed to decide Louis XVIII against taking the road to Creil which leads straight to Amiens. Hence the return by way of Viarmes to Beaumont, Noailles, and the orders left for the Household to avoid Amiens, to pass through Beauvais, Abbeville . . . Blacas was wondering whether His Majesty had not switched back to the English plan, now that the Comte d'Artois was no longer there. Abbeville—that was the road to Boulogne, it would even be possible to embark at Crotoy. The favorite did not share Monsieur's grievances. He had no objection to going to England, returning to Hartwell. And then his wife and his collections. . . .

The second carriage was Alexandre Berthier's, in which rode the Duc de Croy d'Havré, the Duc de Grammont, and the Duc de Luxembourg. The veterans, those who did not ride with their troops.

Beside this carriage, among the horsemen at this stage, were Houdetot who had had as much as he could take, and Géricault, who rode as in a dream, kept awake by the rain and the cold.

Like all young Frenchmen of his generation, Théodore knew the geography of Europe better than that of his own country. However swift the victories, people followed them on the map, anticipated them in their minds, and the enthusiasm of youth understood and foresaw the movements of the armies by the nature of the terrain, imagined the towns, the forests, the rivers. And however absorbed he had been by painting, Géricault had been sixteen in the year of Austerlitz, twenty in that of Saragossa—and glory was contagious. A defeat, on the other hand, was like a stroke of lightning. It first blinded a man and after the flash a little time was needed before the thunder could be heard. The invasion of 1814 had taught nothing to those eager young men, devoured by co-existing hopes and despairs; humiliated and at the same time dazed by the disaster; aspiring to a new and different life, tired and exasperated by all those Agamemnons and Leonidases, by the theatrical character of public life; nauseated by the enormous corruption that was its obverse—nauseated too by the price at which heroism was insolently bought. The Allies had taken less than three months to advance from the Rhine to Paris; moreover the Rhenish and Belgian provinces were but borderlands where retreat itself assumed the character of maneuvers.

For everyone—for a General Maison as well as for a student of the imperial schools, for the idlers of the Boulevard du Temple or the speculators of the Bourse, for a stable boy at Versailles or the painter Géricault—the area extending from the border to Paris, which the invaders needed only to squeeze in their hand to stop all circulation in the great French body, still constituted France's frontier. Yet despite the myth of Empire, the prefects and the garrisons, no one had either the time or the fearful presence of mind to see anything of this whole region beneath the contradictory and hurried news of the Allied advance, the last-minute victories triumphantly announced by the newspapers, the wild glances cast from Champagne to Flanders, the uncertainty as to where the main blow would be struck, the pride, stealthily pursued, that suddenly yields.

For Théodore those departments—the Oise, the Aisne, the Somme, the Nord, the Pas de Calais—were merely dotted lines that had been drawn during his lifetime on the maps of France; they contained only the little administrative circles of the towns. They were but a vast empty void between the world where people spoke foreign languages and Paris which he regarded as the very substance of his existence, a combination of anxieties and discoveries, of ecstasies and disappointments, of tobacco smoked in the back shop where he had painted the "Chasseur" of 1812. . . .

Paris was the scenic railway in the Tivoli Gardens and the Leonardo da Vincis in the Louvre, Franconi's circus, the strange lights of evening in the quarries of Montmartre and the endless arguments on life and art, the pre-eminence of color over form, or the contrary, with Horace Verney or Dedreux-Dorcy—Paris, that blend of squalor and elegance, of palaces and shanties, magnificent and sordid, like a grand opera with innumerable, endless wings, a scene of splendors set in a dump of cripples and refuse, the insolent tawdriness of the

Tuileries and the huddle of dark streets, the jabber of the markets, the dog trainers and bear leaders in the black wells of the narrow courts.

And now he had left all that behind him and was moving in this great void with a soldier's irresponsibility, following in the dead of night itineraries that others had studied for him—if indeed they had had enough leisure. Wearing this red coat that burned him, invisible, the horseman of an infernal hunt. Moving at the dragging trot of an exhausted animal whose sufferings he could feel, its labored breathing, its steps growing uncertain, stumbling against rocks, sinking into the mud, beneath squalls of wind and rain; himself nipped, despite the coat and the sweat and the weight of his equipment, by an icy cold on this eve of spring. Now Théodore Géricault—and look at that line of carriages, at the head of which a gouty King slumbers against the fleurs-de-lis of the cushions and rests his Bourbon blubber lip on the shoulder of the Duc de Duras!—now Théodore, in the fantastic cavalcade of the Musketeers, broken, bruised, their feet bleeding in their boots, their buttocks chafed raw by the stout leather breeches, nearly fifteen leagues without change of pace except for halts in the rain at hamlets whose names hardly anyone knew, or in sudden stops when they were in danger of colliding against one another because a berlin had made an awkward turn or riders had dashed across the path of their own convoy, thinking it suddenly cut by travelers emerging from a country road; now Théodore Géricault was overcome with the dizziness of a man falling, falling, falling, in a void or in a dream—he did not know which: conscious to the point of madness of all the insignificant things of his body and his soul, of all the pieces of his clothing, of every loop of his straps, of the saddle and the stirrup, and of everything he had forgotten to do before leaving; filled with memories exaggeratedly lucid, shuffled like a pack of cards, pursuing an inexpressible anguish, a single idea with endless developments which came back, was lost, repeated itself, broke and rejoined; to the trot, trot of the interminable, choking, icy night, to the rapid and repeated patter of the horses on the drenched ground.

You have no idea of the variations in the nature of a road flooded for hours and hours, the feel of the gravel, the thick clay, the silt as it washes away, the slippery pebbles, the ruts caving in, the hoofs heavy with sticky mud, the sudden puddles as though you are stepping into a brook; the variations of an absent landscape, rises, dips, curves in the road, indiscernible shadows, the spectral presence of the trees, the banks, the few dark houses after passing through long deserts; the feeling sometimes that you have left the road, because of a slope.

Suddenly there were shrubs in front of him; the silence accentuated by the din of the convoy, thoughts pursuing their course, the feeling in all these men of being strangers to one another, no two lives the same, a flight of individual destinies, a jostling of escapades . . . to the trot, trot, trot of a monarchy going to pot, of a world turning backward, in the flight of a false knighthood, with its theatrical costumes, its new standards, its tuppence-colored honor, its fear of comparison, its arrogance as of a child whistling in the dark; a wheel chair for a throne and the Kehl edition of Voltaire beneath the altar; to the trot, trot, and too bad for the axle breaking on the luggage van of the Prince de Wagram, who knew nothing about it and was in the second carriage of the convoy, a casket on his knees, chewing his nails as usual and dreaming of Mme. Visconti; good God, what a scramble it made, a break in the transport. Will you get that shandrydan over into the ditch, goddam it, look at the horses running into one another, halt! halt! and off we go again, we catch up, we string out, at a trot, trot! You will lose His Majesty, lose the thread of History, let the rest of that mock-heroic serial story pass, you blackguard, press on, press on, at a trot! we must not let the panic relax, fears have holds, flight rest; press on, press on, we have only that in common, the wan terror that gurgles in the stomachs of the noble travelers and makes the horsemen's cloaks flutter in the first glimmer of dawn. . . .

Far, far to the rear, well beyond the Oise and less than three leagues from Saint-Denis, bogged down by its foot-sloggers, the Royal Household was barely emerging. All that time lost in Saint-Denis. What a nightmare night! A kaleidoscope in the head. The cavalcade and the disorder, the memories blending with the darkness that stimulated them. And Virginie abandoned, the child of his blood, and his little bastard daughters in England. The affronts and the joys. . . . The Russian marriage the Czar had declined; the scenes the King had made about his private life. For no reason, at all, one spring morning on a hunt in Devon, the eyes of a stag at bay . . . Coming back to that Jesuit: what was that Torlachon doing on the rue de Valois-Monceau? Though he ransacked his memories of Hartwell, he could not quite recall what foul story was linked to this dubious character which explained his connection with His Majesty. Had he not been a doctor in the army of the Princes? What had happened at Quiberon* concerning him? Charles-Ferdinand would ask his father. . . .

It was near Ecouen that the Duc de Berry, who was riding with the Grenadiers, perceived the dawn to the right, above the hill. He stopped his horse. The barren gray landscape stretched out before him; great gusts of wind were sweeping away the clouds. A kind of suffused brightness bathed the fields to the east, while the men still had their feet in the mud and the night. But it was no longer raining. It was odd: after having raged all those hours at the confounded rain, they had grown used to it. Daylight had had to return for them to notice that the rain had stopped. Monseigneur swore horribly. That was it all right. The goddam sun had waited for Buonaparte's return. It was March 20th: in the garden the famous chestnut tree would be in bloom, and they would hear about it till they were nauseated. The rabble loved such stories, and to cap it all it was the wolf-cub's birthday! ** In a childish rage, Virginie Oreille's lover took to wishing the deluge would begin again.

Saint-Denis meanwhile remained the turntable for the flights and the troop concentrations. There were more than seven thousand soldiers in the town at daybreak. How had they assembled there when all the orders were that a certain distance should be maintained between the units from fear of contagion? No one had the least idea. Not even the commanding general, Macdonald, Duc de Tarente, who racked his brain to understand why and how General Saint-Sulpice's battalion of officers, the half-pay officers waiting to be sent back to their homes, happened to be here. Only yesterday this battalion was at Vincennes, side by side with M. de Vioménil's volunteers. Who had given them marching orders? It was no more explicable than the Royal Household, yesterday, on the Champ-de-Mars. These unruly elements would have to be shipped off somewhere, and the road to Rouen was as good as any other; but their general was no longer capable of exacting obedience. Meanwhile, their forage caps on their heads, they had spread through the town. They had had the wineshops reopened, and the frightened waiters, half dressed and half

* A village on the southern coast of Brittany where a small army of *émigrés*, aided by the British, attempted a landing in 1795. They were captured by forces under General Hoche, and 711 of them were stood up and shot in a meadow near Auray.

** A certain chestnut tree in the Tuileries gardens was said to come into bloom infallibly every year on March 20th, which was also the birthday of Napoleon's son—called the "wolf-cub" by anti-Bonapartists.

asleep, were pouring them drinks. Near the barracks others had got into conversations with the soldiers of the garrison, the National Guards. Who had had them sent here?

General Maison, his thick-set figure bulging with the muscles of a gymnast, swore by all the gods that he had had nothing to do with it, and Macdonald left him in his usual state of cold rage. He had been here about an hour and a half, having arrived from Villejuif where, once arrangements had been made in Paris after the royal decision, he had been naïve enough to begin looking for his phantom staff which likewise was in fact not at Saint-Denis, where he had thought he could rejoin it later. He had settled all that remained of it— General Hulot, his chief of staff, who had accompanied him from Paris—in an inn, then had gone to see what was happening in Saint-Denis.

What a rotten state of mind this town was in! A lot of people seemed to have forgotten what sleep meant, but others were already waking up, shutters were banging, voices echoed loud in the dawn. Maison could say what he liked: he had been here since the evening before and had allowed things to degenerate into disorder. The civilians, the fugitives, were one thing. But the military? What was that air of permanent subversion, which could be detected by a mere glance at the steps of the barracks even at this early hour of the morning? The Light Infantry regiment quartered here was out in the street almost in a body, the officers mingling with the horsemen on the roadway, some in fatigue dress, others in uniform. Quite a few of them looked rather the worse for drink.

Macdonald—who, when he went to Maison's for news, had been accompanied by a noncommissioned officer and two mounted men— decided to look over the town with which he was none too familiar, and where he had come to await the troops to which he had given Saint-Denis as a regrouping point. Heaven only knew what trafficking went on here! Hardly more than a straggling village, the houses with frontages on the street and gardens behind, and fields, kitchen gardens, night lingering disquietingly in the vacant plots—a small town crisscrossed by mysterious canals in a network which seemed without plan, plunging suddenly under the houses, the streets, disappearing, reappearing elsewhere. Stepped levels of channeled water for the mills, the tanneries, the dye works.

Next to the church with its double tower like fingers raised in benediction stood an austere building with high walls—the hall of the Legion of Honor where, it was said, the Emperor's influence was secretly maintained. Behind its park was another factory chimney, M. Juval's painted-fabrics plant, revealing the passage of another waterway. All these secret streams carrying colors and refuse in their waters, partly covered, then emerging from reserves of darkness, seemed to Jacques-Étienne the tortuous counterparts of the hidden thoughts of this city of Saint-Denis full of menaces and memories, of dead kings and popular desecrations. What had he been told about the resistance here to the Russians' entry last year? Blood had stained these channels and mingled with the overflow from the factories until it had become indistinguishable from the tannery drainage. And over there where the mills were, that semicircular street formed a grimy little Holland, like a landscape by a master which had darkened with the years. All this in the gray of early morning. Beneath the clouds that were filling with daylight, with gleaming arrows, yonder, toward Gonesse.

This quarter was calm, compared to the center, to the rue de Paris which was congested with vehicles from the capital, families weighed down by baskets and trunks who had set out before daybreak in expectation of a long journey, fugitives on foot, sordid and picturesque, troops arriving from all directions amid a din of kitchens and vans, the men not yet shaved, mounted detachments, soldiers on foot. And the congestion was at its peak in the rue Compoise, which led back toward the parade ground and the church. There stood the inn which the Marshal had picked out as his headquarters, and where Hulot must be sweating over the administrative papers, the guiding plans, the marching orders. Even though he had none of his assistants, who must have installed themselves somewhere else— heaven knew where. Parties were out looking for them.

The Duc de Tarente was returning to the inn, his head crammed with worries. His Majesty had passed through here at about one in the morning; where was he now? And of course he could avail himself of the post relays, and was undoubtedly still traveling; but who could have followed him? He could imagine the state of the Royal Household on the roads, and was probably still far from the truth. With this nightlong rain! Before the doorway of the inn was a dubious-looking gathering. Did it concern him? A group of excited people, among them half-pay officers who fell silent as they recognized the Marshal. What feelings could these people entertain toward him? Whom did they respect in him, the commander of the Melun army, or the soldier who had fought at Wagram?

Jacques-Étienne pretended not to see them and hurriedly entered the inn, whose servants were taking down the shutters. An emergency office had been set up for him on the ground floor. There were papers to sign, quartermasters to echelon ahead. He had to organize the movement of the troops, troops who would not have seen battle, an army with which he had ostensibly been entrusted. Hulot had done a good part of the work. Outside, the street was full of people arriving from Paris whose equipages were piling up in the square and in the street, and who came to ask what road to take, leaving their families and servants in their barouches and berlins. They had located a headquarters, there was no way of holding them back, they were in the entrance. Was the road to Beauvais safe? Was it true that the troops who had mutinied were pursuing the Princes? They already saw themselves with Bonaparte's Mamelukes on their heels. *Émigrés* of yesterday who again had the hunted look and the pleading manner forgotten for a year. By the time they reached Saint-Denis, they had become a new emigration with all the servility, the avidity, of those who look forward to waiting endlessly in antechambers, whose lives henceforth for perhaps another twenty years will be but a humiliating antechamber.

Jacques-Étienne was waiting for a lieutenant, his aide-de-camp, whom he had sent out on an errand. He was beside himself, and he committed the imprudence of sticking his nose outside his office. The pack descended on him and had to be pushed back. There was a lady among them whom they tried to keep from reaching the Marshal, an unknown woman whom he suddenly recognized as Mme. Visconti, all bundled up in a traveling mantle so wet that it was impossible to tell what its original color had been. Macdonald stepped forward and invited the Italian woman to come into his improvised office where a big log fire had been lit. He made her sit down before it, removed her hat to dry it. Giuseppa arranged her black hair as though she had been at the theatre and was about to step onto the stage.

The Prince de Wagram's beloved—"Berthier's blunder," as Napoleon had called her—had changed greatly since the end of the century when Jacques-Étienne had known her in Paris, from which her titular lover, who had had Visconti approved as ambassador of the Cisalpine Republic, was then absent because of the Egyptian campaign. Macdonald had been widowed of his first wife, Marie-Constance, for eighteen months, and on returning from Italy, still not fully recovered from his wounds and threatened with phthisis, was living on a diet of sago, then recommended by the doctors, and milk foods. This gave him an interesting pallor, and with his turned-up nose he had appealed to Mme. Visconti, who could scarcely be satisfied with letters from Egypt, even with the little obscene sketches that Alexandre Berthier drew in the margin of his confidences. With her, Jacques-Étienne had been able to forget an unpleasant adventure with General Leclerc's wife, Pauline Bonaparte, which was later to cause his long disgrace. Giuseppa was already in her maturity then, but she was no less dazzling than the nineteen-year-old Pauline. That was sixteen years ago. The years had added a heaviness to Giuseppa's Roman beauty, and her face showed an unhealthy pallor in the early morning. But she had lost nothing of the charm that had subjugated that little man, Berthier, forever.

She had a slight limp, and a swelling neck—evidence of a goiter in its initial stages—which awakens a good many men's desire and attracts painters by its fullness. At nearly fifty-five, she did not show a wrinkle. Perhaps this had to do with a certain immobility of the face which was the only trace of a little accident she had had the year before. And a slight awkwardness in the use of her left hand. The doctor said it was because she tightened her corset too much. . . .

She had removed her long, rain-soaked gloves and was holding them out to the flame. If she had followed her first impulse, she would never have left Paris. But the Prince de Wagram—she never called Berthier by any other name, except in intimacy when she addressed him as Sandro—the Prince de Wagram—since he had lost the principality of Neufchâtel, he could no longer be called His Most Serene Highness—the Prince de Wagram had come to the house on the rue Neuve-des-Capucines in a great rush. It was past nine in the evening, and what's more, he had not come to her house on the Boulevard next door at once—he had papers to put in order, personal affairs.

It must be said that he had packed Marie-Elisabeth and the children off to Bamberg the previous Tuesday. Mme. Visconti always said Marie-Elisabeth, never the Princesse de Wagram or the Princesse de Bavière—not out of jealousy, heavens no! But she was not averse to reminding people of the excellent relations that united her to a king's niece and to her old lover's young wife. People talked about it. And about the fact that she lived on the Boulevard des Capucines, in a house adjoining the Marshal's palace so that he had only to pass through a small door at the bottom of the garden to visit her. Well, let people talk! Napoleon had not been able to separate her from him, even by marrying him to a girl of twenty-four when he was fifty-four. So Marie-Elisabeth had taken the mail coach on Tuesday with the children and the governess. She must have arrived if all had gone well. The Prince de Wagram could not have left in Paris a woman who had just given birth to her third child when the Melun camp was being formed. Yes, a love of a little girl. Elisabeth, like her mother. The boy was five, the other little girl three. You could understand they would be better off at her parents' home.

"We had five evenings to ourselves, the way we used to. Elisabeth and I, you know, are very good friends. When the three of us are together we play a game of whist. But anyway! Five long evenings, with the bad weather outside, the wind in the trees of the garden. We were like peaceful old married people. I had almost forgotten my grief. . . ."

Macdonald bowed as though to say, "I know, I know." It was a little over a year since she had lost her son Louis, the Baron Sopranay, who had died of his wounds at Leipzig. It was perhaps that, rather than the corset—but doctors don't believe in the influence moral suffering can have on the heart.

"If you knew," Mme. Visconti went on, "what it had become to me during this last year—my apartment on Les Capucines! Upstairs, above my head, were Louis's bachelor quarters. If you knew the kind of lad he was! Yes, you knew him as an officer, his magnificent conduct. . . . When I think there are people wicked enough to claim that if it had not been for the Prince de Wagram and his pushing him, he would never have become a general!"

"Oh, that," said Macdonald. "Certainly none of those who were at Austerlitz when he captured the Czar's aide-de-camp! Or at Ucles, in 1809, where he brought seven flags and over five thousand prisoners back to Marshal the Duc de Bellune."

"Yes, and then people . . . It's true he worshiped the Prince, looked upon him as his father. He had scarcely known M. Sopranay. But his little corner at home, on the Boulevard des Capucines . . . Just think, when he was in Russia, in 1812, wounded. That's what he would write to me about. He would make arrangements for improving the way the rooms were laid out, hanging new curtains, and all that way away he would change decorators. He would have books bound English-style, specifying the yellow edge, with a handsome glazed marbled paper. Ah, my dear friend, now, when I go into his empty room, and absent-mindedly open a book . . . You know, he had a passion for stereotypes. Yes . . . the yellow edge. . . ."

An orderly brought papers from General Hulot to be signed.

"Still nothing?"

"No, Monsieur le Maréchal."

He turned toward the fire. The flames cast a rather tragic light on the visitor's features.

"So, Alexandre asked you to leave?"

"Oh, no. He didn't even think of it. He was leaving as always when there was a war, a campaign, as he did for Russia with the Emp"—she bit her tongue—"with Bonaparte, and God knows how I worried—I mean how we worried, Marie-Elisabeth and I, when he had his terrible attacks of rheumatism! You must know what it's like yourself!"

"It's the malady of our time," said Macdonald. "The King has it too. But he didn't get it on the Beresina. Nor did we, for that matter. I think it's an Italian memento—or a Dutch one. Still, Berthier didn't always leave you so easily, not even for a campaign. I remember Napoleon's fury when he had to beg him to go to Egypt!"

"We were younger then. You too," she said; and after a silence: "But when will he come back this time? How is he going to live? Between ourselves, I forced him to take my diamonds; he can always manage with them. Of course, he can take refuge in Bavaria with Marie-Elisabeth's parents, if the King . . . Do *you* believe that the King . . ."

Macdonald made an evasive gesture. It amounted to an admission. "Ah?" said Mme. Visconti. She reflected for a moment, then plunged back into that torrent of words. For if it was a matter of living, of *living!* Not for a few days, for life! Leaving him alone, after seventeen years—yes, it added up to seventeen years. Last night he had told her that even if he went to Bamberg, he would not be able to stay —nor would Marie-Elisabeth for that matter; she would suffocate in the provincial atmosphere of Bavaria! They would return as soon as possible, to Gros-Bois or to Chambord, to their estates. But would they be allowed into the country? That was the question! As for herself, at first she hadn't dreamed of going with him. The idea of leaving the Boulevard des Capucines! His Majesty was leaving at midnight. How could she possibly manage it between now and then—her trunks, her dresses! Besides, she could not set out on the road at such an hour, it isn't done. And then, too, she was one of those creatures who need sleep, and she was incapable, utterly incapable, of sleeping in a chaise! She had let the Prince de Wagram leave, with er jewel case and a carriageful of baggage which was to join the royal train at the gate to the Palace.

But the moment he was no longer there, she had thought things over. The future. She couldn't do that to him—leave him alone, leave them alone—in such circumstances. That was why she had come to join the Prince, wherever he was going—because after all he wasn't in Bamberg yet, was he? She had suddenly made up her mind in the night. She had waited for daylight, and daylight had only confirmed her in her resolution. But why Lille? A horrible town! His Majesty wasn't going there in a single stretch, for heaven's sake! Where had the Court stopped for the night?

Macdonald was seized with a hilarity which he managed to hold in check. The Court! Two dukes, one prince and two valets—because the rest of the carriages must have been dispersed on the way for lack of relay horses. Could you call that a Court? "I don't know, madame. It may have depended on a good many things, the state of the roads, the post horses. His Majesty originally had in mind spending the night at Amiens, but he may have changed his mind on the way. We're not very sure of our prefect of the Somme, M. de Lameth, you know. If I were you, madame, I should make haste toward Lille without considering the stages. You will find Alexandre easily at Lille."

She had a favor to ask of Jacques-Étienne. Surely he would do it for her. . . . What was it? She had her maid in the carriage, she would like to bring her in. Where was the carriage? Macdonald opened the door of the small room. In the corridor, the din of people clamoring to speak to the Marshal personally. He went out to calm them, leaving Mme. Visconti alone.

He was the one who needed soothing, harassed as he was because of the disappearance of his staff. All right, Maison had let him know that he was joining his troops at Saint-Denis since the Duc de Berry had told him they would be withdrawn to that town. But what about the others? He had been appointed general in command and promptly everyone commanded, made decisions, disposed of the troops, took a carriage, went wherever he pleased. Of course the army of Melun was to fall back to cover the royal journey. But when it was ordered to, *nom de Dieu!* when it was ordered to! Jacques-Étienne had gone to fetch his staff where he had left it, at Villejuif. And lo and behold, by eleven in the evening there had been no one in Villejuif. No one—except Generals Haxo and Ruty, lost in a big house with three cannon in a meadow next door, and

a detachment of sappers drunk as lords in the nearby wineshop
He had taken Ruty along with him to Saint-Denis: no more sig
of a staff here than at Villejuif. Just Hulot, who had come with
his baggage and was as much at a loss as himself. Yet he had
received indications as to the existence of staff administrative
offices with a captain somewhere here in a requisitioned building
it was on receipt of this news that he had dispatched his aide-de-
camp for information.

His aide was returning as the Marshal was being besieged by
fugitives at the entrance to the inn, surrounded by a tenor from
the Opéra-Comique who believed he had everything to fear from the
Emperor's return, half a dozen ladies and old gentlemen dressed
in the manner that had been fashionable at Hartwell about 1810
or even five years earlier in Mitau, whole families sitting on sacks
weeping children, young ninnies making remarks about the Ogre—
which last brought forth growls from the half-pay officers in the
doorway.

"So," said Jacques-Étienne, "what did that captain tell you,
Lieutenant?"

The aide-de-camp did not want to speak in the presence of all
those people. They withdrew to the small office.

"It's sheer madness, Monsieur le Maréchal," he began, "all those
generals, those colonels . . . *pfft!* . . . vanished as if they had
been blown away! But not before they—" He broke off on seeing
a lady by the fireplace.

"You may speak before Mme. Visconti," said Macdonald when he
noticed suddenly that she had collapsed in her chair, her gloves
fallen into the fire and beginning to burn. "My God," he cried,
"what's wrong, Giuseppa?" He had called her by her first name as
he once used to. She did not hear him. She had fainted. They
chafed her hands and she moaned, opened her eyes, but without
seeming to see them. "Quick, a doctor!" said the Marshal, and the
lieutenant ran outside.

It was ridiculous and awkward at such a moment to have a
woman faint in one's office. He avoided thinking that it might be
serious: not that he had any excessively strong feeling for Mme.
Visconti or for Alexandre. But even if there were people to whom
it brought a smile, their romance, well, it had been one of the few
long fidelities of the Empire, in spite of Giuseppa's passing affairs,
Alexandre's marriage at the Emperor's orders. Berthier had complied
as though he were signing his own death warrant, and with a surge

of emotion Macdonald remembered his woebegone expression when Giuseppa's husband, the ex-Ambassador Visconti, had died just two weeks after the Marshal had obeyed Napoleon and, sick at heart, married the Princesse de Bavière. And love, after all, love—if people treated it lightly today, perhaps it was because they had become incapable of it, completely devoted as they were to the quest for money, business. They, the soldiers of Jemmapes, invested everything with greatness. Meanwhile, here he had this sick woman on his hands; and the troops that never came! Should he remain here waiting for them? And what about Monsieur, Monseigneur and Marmont? Where were they now? Where was the King?

The doctor appeared with surprising promptness: he must have been in the house where Mademoiselle, who was on her way to join her brother, the Duc d'Orléans, at Lille, had abandoned one of her companions in the early evening as she was taken with the first pangs of childbirth. He reassured the Marshal: Madame Visconti had had a slight heart seizure, but nothing serious—at least not this time. He had her carried up to a room on the first story. "Fetch Mme. Visconti's maid!" Macdonald ordered. "She must be in a carriage in front of the door." And turning to the aire-de-camp, "What were you saying, Lieutenant? You were interrupted . . ."

The young officer blushed. He had been struck by Mme. Visconti's beauty. He liked mature women, and then he had heard about Marshal Berthier's great love for the Italian woman he had brought back to Paris, and he was romantically inclined. That fainting spell . . . that beautiful swelling neck . . . "What was I saying? Ah yes—well, the generals and colonels have all been through here, imagine, Monsieur le Maréchal. And they signed their passage! I saw it, the captain showed me."

"Signed their passage? What are you talking about? I don't know if it's fainting ladies which put you in such a state, Lieutenant, but you strike me as being strangely agitated!"

The other tugged at his mustache: it was not Mme. Visconti who affected him in this way, but indignation. Before dispersing on the evening of the 19th, the entire staff had visited the office for their pay and had even—this was the hardest to swallow—had even collected the *initial campaign indemnity!* Yes, precisely. Where were they? Probably on the roads, making for the frontier or the ports in carriages after having provided themselves with the sinews of war!

"All right, Lieutenant," said Macdonald, "learn not to judge your superiors. Some day those officers will have to give an account of themselves. To whom? That's another matter. But are we going to stay here all our lives? Take my advice; after you inform General Hulot, go get some sleep; there's a couch in the next room. You've been up all night, young fellow, and we have a long day ahead of us. I still have a lot of papers . . ."

Alone again, he suddenly felt very weary. Day seemed to have reawakened his rheumatism. There was a numbness in his arms and legs. He decided to take off his boots. But then he thought better of it. If he took them off, he would never be able to get them on again. In spite of himself, his eyes were shutting. Having sanded his first signatures, he felt himself swaying as he sat in the arm-chair before the table. His nose dived toward the table; he recovered himself with a shudder, wrote some more signatures. It humiliated him. He would not yield. It was age. He had caught himself making fun of General de Beurnonville to whom this often happened. Beurnonville . . . Dumouriez . . . faces of aging military men came between him and his work. Dumouriez had betrayed the Convention. And delivered Beurnonville to the Austrians. Beurnonville, dear Beurnonville, had abandoned the Emperor in 1814. Perhaps it was age, perhaps fatigue, that made his nose dive. Yet Pichegru had been thirty-four, like Jomini, at the time of that sordid affair . . . and Moreau forty when the other had betrayed him. As for Jomini, he was nothing but an intriguer, a man impelled by base ambitions, furious at being only a brigadier general at thirty-four! Ah, *nom de Dieu,* how this swaying annoyed him! And Beurnonville had been right, last year. A little too early. That was all. . . .

He had barely gone to sleep when Hulot had him awakened. M. de Jaucourt had just arrived. He had managed to doze in his chaise between Paris and here. He said this, convinced that the Marshal had been taking it easy. He had had to advise the ministers that His Majesty begged them to go to Lille. Then run after the ambassadors and give them the same message, more or less: *find them!* He had sent them a circular letter, then worked all night at the ministry with two men to help him, the one to write, the other to destroy. All this had gone on until five o'clock, and he had allowed himself only one hour for his personal affairs. At six in the morning he had left the rue de Varennes. It was now seven: where was the King?

Macdonald had tried to be polite. Jaucourt was already on the road again.

Then the Marshal went out in the hope that fresh air would bring him back to himself. He was haunted by the memory of Dumouriez. Could the victor of Valmy be a traitor? When they told the story they put the whole blame on Kellermann, but after all . . . who had been in command? Macdonald remembered the answer given by an army commissary: "Dumouriez . . . Kellermann . . . the victor of Valmy is the people!" The people! When they had said the people, they had said everything! Jacques-Étienne had seen the people take to their heels more than once, as at the Pas de Baisieux where the soldiers fell back on Lille and murdered their general. The people! It was generals who won battles. The people! When I took command of the Picardy regiment on the roads of Belgium, they were turning tail and singing heroic tunes popular in Paris!

In his waking reverie the Marshal was confusing days, faces. He was roaming in that northern plain where greatness had begun for him, a lieutenant colonel on the morrow of Valmy, a colonel after Jemmapes. It was at Jemmapes that he had first seen that magnificent twenty-year-old lad, a volunteer of the year II, covered with powder, mud and blood, who had just recaptured his battalion flag from the enemy and whose name was Nicolas Maison—the same who, as a general, had greeted him last night, here in Saint-Denis, with a look of bewilderment. And actually, who had won the victory at Jemmapes? Some young Maison or other, or Dumouriez, or the Duc de Chartres. Victories were quickly forgotten, a Nerwinde sufficed to make people forget about either Valmy or Jemmapes. The Picard colonel had had a close shave when Dumouriez had handed the commissaries of the Convention over to the Imperial forces and gone over to the enemy with the young Duc de Chartres. He was suspected of conspiracy. This was at Lille. It had been—how long ago? Twenty-two years. Here he was now, returning to the same spot in 1815. Today it was no longer possible to understand the things of that time—the institutions or the men. But at that time, what would he have thought about the situation in which he was today?

Anyway, the situation in the street was untenable. There were the half-pay officers as well as travelers and onlookers of every description. Ah, he should have been in civilian clothes, as he had been yesterday when he had gone to see the King! He went back into the inn and was no sooner in his armchair than he fell into a deep sleep.

Painted houses beside black water, with stepped roofs, and at the windows little white curtains with pompons; men trudging past carrying loads of wood in baskets; far in the distance flights of eider ducks below the shredding clouds; a boat that could be half made out behind the gray slips by the flags it flew. Mme. Maison, wife of the major general, was still a little girl, or almost; light on her smooth legs, marveling at her newly formed breasts, at the blond flesh of her arms, she went out of her way to be charming to her Van der Meulen girl-cousins. Why were French soldiers passing behind the courtyard gate in rags, arms in slings, limping, falling from exhaustion, one of them with a star of blood on the shoulder of his shirt? The Flemish jewels had been hidden under the heavy folded sheets in the Spanish chest, and at nightfall the neighbors threw notes tied to a stone over the wall—plots or love missives. The men were redheaded, the women wore starched chemisettes. Everything that once had been the day's main concern seemed to have vanished, the great book full of figures had been put aside, no mention was made any longer of scheduled ships—it was as though the tide had gone out forever. People no longer went to church. What would be the use? God looked the other way. Everyone grumbled; doors must be locked, for people were thievish.

Suddenly the landscape whirled like a mill, and the weight of her body seemed to be sinking into a hammock or a haystack that gave way, an enormous cushion of feathers. The child was no longer alone with her blond arms, her round figure, and the secrets of her womb. When she stirred in her sleep, the whole length of her came up against a black mastiff with a short nose, a moist breath. She knew she could no longer push him away now, it made no sense—a warm, hard mastiff, with arms of leather like the collar he had removed before getting into bed, a beast, a beast—and the girl had developed a taste for this strange intimacy. She reached for the dog in the dark, fumbling, with all kinds of pet names to please him, and a vague unaccountable flutter. . . . Where are you? Where are you?

"Ssh!" said the general, sitting up in bed, naked. Daylight already showed through the slats of the shutters. Someone was knocking at the door—an anxious voice. What was it? Was it the dream continuing? Maison got up; he swore under his breath at not finding his slippers, he put on a shirt and waved his raised arms in fury; he knocked over a chair. "Nick, what time is it?" said the voice in the depths of the alcove, and he continued to swear and did not answer. The breeches, the boots. More knocks on the door. Two or three times. The mastiff barked. "You might wait a bit, *nom de Dieu!*"

It was his orderly, and he informed the general that there were some officers here who wanted to see him immediately and would not listen to reason, saying if he's asleep wake him up. Very excited. They had, in short, made a bad impression on the soldier on guard, who had not dared to bar the door with his gun. Besides, there were ten of them.

"At least they'll let me give my face a splash of water, I hope!" Maison said viciously. He had just caught a glimpse of himself in a mirror, his hair rumpled, his open shirt revealing the black hair on his chest. He looked at his fingernails: "Tell the gentlemen I'm coming."

They were half-pay officers, awaiting the governor general of Paris in the office at the entrance to the apartment. They had refused to wait downstairs in the courtyard of the barracks. By their attitude, their lack of respect, it was possible to see at once what was on their minds—one of them at the window, another sitting on the edge of the table hitting the papers with a cane, all of them wearing forage caps, and the Hussar with a pipe in his mouth. Nevertheless, out of habit, they sprang to attention and saluted.

"What do you want, gentlemen?"

They were lieutenants, captains, and my word!—a major. Their uniforms, all different, a medley of colors, one with a small fur-edged jacket flung over his shoulder, the next with a dolman covered with braid from which a silver button was missing, a third in a cavalry cloak. Greens, blues, yellows and reds—a kind of sampling of tin soldiers with the paint chipped, not all well shaved, but all with a look of arrogance. The major spoke. He introduced himself: "Major Latapie."

They had come to solicit—to so-li-cit—of the general that he order the garrison to march immediately on the capital to join His Majesty the Emperor and King. It was to be feared that disorders might break out in a Paris abandoned by the Bourbons, and for their part they intended . . .

"I don't understand such language. You are forgetting yourself, Major."

Maison looked out of the window. The rain had stopped and a pale March sun shone on the low roofs of the barracks. The slates sparkled in the light. The general blinked, his eyes still dimmed by the night. His brief speech, sharp as the crack of a whip, fell completely flat. One of the captains stepped forward, paying no attention to the major who had started to speak again. "*Mon général,* last year, at Lille . . ."

Maison recognized him. "Ah, it's you—Captain Absalon. So we meet again!" They were face to face, sizing each other up. Between these two men there was no longer any question of rank. Captain Absalon had been among those who had led the revolt when the general, then in command of the fortress of Lille, had launched his proclamation to the troops recognizing the provisional government.

"*Mon général,* at Lille, last year, you told us . . ."

Maison knew what he had told them at Lille last year. Turn the thing any way you liked, only one point made sense: soldiers and their officers were not called on to engage in politics; it was no more up to them to judge whether they took orders from this or that government than to decide troop movements. The army was the army: it did what the higher command ordered, and that was that. The Hussar pulled his pipe from his mouth to sneer. He was a lieutenant, an adolescent giant: "The army—that's all very well!" he said with lofty disdain. "But don't you give a damn for France, *mon général?*"

Maison was surrounded by the group of officers. He was like a stag at the kill, but a stag still able to use his horns. At this moment the door opened. All turned around.

Mme. Maison had come to see what was going on. She had gathered up her long blond hair hastily, and not altogether successfully, into a goffered linen bonnet and wrapped herself in a purple velvet dressing gown. "Excuse me, Nick—"

"What are you doing here? Get out," the general exploded. The last thing he wanted was to have his wife on his hands in such a conversation, and besides he did not want her to see him in an awkward situation. He would have done better to leave her in Paris; yet if the King *were* to leave France . . .

Captain Absalon saluted Mm. Maison. He knew her from the time when he had been in the 1st Corps during the movements on the frontier in 1814. She was a handsome woman of forty, but stout, heavy under the chin, with porcelain eyes. Maison had met her at the time of the first occupation of Belgium when there had been disturbances because the common people were against the French and were secretly arming themselves. Pushed by poverty, lack of work . . . The major spoke again.

"*Mon général,* the Tuileries telegraph has just transmitted the message that the Emperor is entering Paris at the head of the troops that had been sent against him. The message says the civil and military authorities are advised of this so that they will cease to obey any other orders but his, and hoist the tricolor immediately."

Mme. Maison looked at her husband terror-stricken. He looked more than ever like a black mastiff. She beat a retreat. And from behind the door she heard him say, "All opinions, Major, must defer to the pressing call of patriotism. To avoid the horrors of civil war, all Frenchmen must rally to the King and the Constitutional Charter." And she thought to herself, Revolution is revolution. I knew that was what they were after, that frightful fat German Duchess and her traitor of a husband, Soult, whom she was egging on against my poor Nickie!

It was past noon when Macdonald was awakened. He was full of aches and pains and his mouth felt like cotton wool. No, there was nothing new, no sign of the troops that it had been decided to pull back from Villejuif to Saint-Denis. Really, no one? Where had the troops of the Comte de Valmy, Kellermann's son, gone? No news of Girardin? In the report that he had sent, he had mentioned the order given Colonel de Saint-Chamans to proceed to Saint-Denis by way of Villeneuve-Saint-Georges. That was last night, and still no one? At this point a dispatch was delivered notifying the Marshal that some artillery was arriving from La Fère.

It was a part of the general movement, set in motion several days before, of troops that were to concentrate at the Melun camp. The movement was continuing mechanically, and no one was doing anything to stop it. Regiments continued to descend on Paris, as though the intention had been to furnish contingents to Napoleon. These artillerymen would have to be stopped on the way and sent back to La Fère. My word, the Lallemands had been thrown into prison because they had been doing what the royal orders were causing all the garrisons of the North to do, at the very moment when the King was taking refuge in Lille! What an absurdity! Ruty? Where was he? General Ruty entered. "Go tell the commander of the artillery group not to enter Saint-Denis. Send him back where he came from!"

As a matter of fact, it was a little late; the pieces and the caissons could be heard rumbling over the cobbles of the rue de Paris, and as General Ruty, passing among the half-pay officers massed on the corner of the rue Compoise, tried to stop the column, there was a sudden flare-up: General Saint-Sulpice's officers rushed out into the rue de Paris in a body, seized the horses by the bridle, shouted orders, jumped into the carriages—and Ruty had to take to his heels in the general confusion. Macdonald, with his skeleton staff and a few men, arrived only in time to see the artillerymen moving on toward the capital. He raised his arms to heaven. What was to be done? All the thoroughfares were overflowing with people, there was an inextricable congestion of carriages and regiments, of fugitives from Paris who were growing impatient over the priority given to the troops. And thereupon, to cap the confusion, a whole line of vehicles and horses—Monseigneur the Duc de Berry's train which had waited endlessly for him in Villejuif where they had only belatedly received the order to fall back to the North— were crossing Saint-Denis in a northerly direction, and making a devil of a hullabaloo about it.

Windows opened, terrified women stopped their ears. Word came to Macdonald—by the same aide-de-camp whom he had sent to the staff captain—that General Maison had fled from his apartments, that his division was threatening to do him harm. Good God! Fortunately the King had passed through ages ago. But now suddenly the half-pay officers, like a band of devils, proceeded to attack the train of vehicles, jumping on the horses, shouting, striking them, tossing the drivers off their seats. They took control of the column and turned it back toward Paris amid a general pandemonium, people on foot getting out of the way as best they could. The air rang with oaths and guffaws, *gee-up horses!* An insane indecent caval- cade—French officers, in uniform! A major on a rearing chestnut was in command of the movement: the same Major Latapie who had appeared at Maison's.

The Marshal was an impotent witness to the spectacle. Those people were drunk! And it was still morning. Jacques-Étienne felt the blush of shame rise to his cheeks. He went back into the inn and told Hulot to pack, passed on the orders to a colonel who had just arrived with his regiment from Rouen and who tried in vain to tell him that the objective he had been given was the Charenton Bridge. But without listening to him the Marshal collected his small group, jumped on his horse and headed full speed down the road to Beauvais. They would have lunch somewhere further on. He was fed up with Saint-Denis! He had done everything that it was his duty to do: after all, he could not be expected to wait for troops that had gone over to Bonaparte, could he? His role was to go on ahead, to organize the positions: next staff headquarters, Beaumont-sur-Oise. It was one o'clock in the afternoon and when the Marshal left the inn he experienced a moment of anxiety because of the crowd of half-pay officers in front of him. But they stepped aside and let him pass.

While Macdonald's carriage was traveling rapidly in the direction of Beaumont-sur-Oise, the officers who had taken the artillery from La Fère on toward Paris, the Duc de Berry's train, some Cuirassiers encountered on the way and an infantry company met a picket of horsemen and a general in full dress with the tricolor on his hat coming out of the suburb. Major Latapie spurred his chestnut on ahead to meet him, and stopped squarely before him, saluting him with his saber. "Is that you, Albert?" exclaimed the general. "What the hell are you doing here?"

It was the notorious Exelmans, on his way to Saint-Denis to win the troops over to the Emperor. Less than four months ago this general, relieved of his command for having written to the King of Naples and sent on half-pay to Bar-sur-Ornain by Soult, had resisted the police in his apartment in Paris, where he had tried to blow his brains out. Now he had turned up on the road to Saint-Denis. But there was no longer any reason for him to continue on his way. He signed to Latapie to ride beside him and proceeded to bring the rebel units back in triumph along the boulevards in the direction of the Place Louis-XV and the Tuileries, where the tricolor flag was already fluttering on the Pavillon de l'Horloge.

VI

Beauvais, March 20th

IT IS both difficult and painful to imagine at the present time what Beauvais was like on that 20th day of the month of March 1815. Abandoning his reserve, the author here invites the reader's cooperation. For since the last war swept through it, nothing, or virtually nothing, remains today of this town, of what lent it its charm and its beauty. You must shut your eyes on these structures hastily thrown up in rows, on these modern shanties, on the empty lots, the open mesh of a town plan marked here and there by temporary buildings, streets indicated by surveyors' tapes, the whole past destroyed, centuries of human deposits, traces of thought and customs, the setting of vanished lives. Nothing remains of that long moment in France's life—neither the gabled houses, nor the overlapping roofs; and the great tapestry factory, now no more, will never again weave in wool and silk the pastorals and landscapes in which the skill of diligent fingers was enhanced by the special quality of sweetness—*douceur*—of the Beauvais region, the sweetness of the vines that carpet the basin in which the town slept indolently among the mists, the Marissel cherry trees, the fields streaked by flights of birds. Nor does anything remain of the Savignies china and the Voisinlieu earthenware, of those humble Picard treasures—cupboards, chests, headdresses, terra-cottas, naïve paintings. What has become of the old sign of the grocer-and-mustard dealer? Where is the sword the executioner once wielded? Nothing

remains of the dreams of yore. The books accumulated by generations have been burned. It is like a family that no longer knows where
it comes from, camping in its own ruins; and no one remembers
that this still standing flight of stairs led up to an attic where
children used to play; and the wrecker's pick scatters nondescript
stones which once were the street corner where lovers used to
meet.

On this 20th of March, 1815, in the deep cup of Beauvais into
which the road descends from Warluis through the first chalks of
Picardy, where the Thérain in its narrow course between deep banks
makes a loop that embraces the town south and west between
Mount Bourguillemont and Mount Capron, the shrunken sun,
frowning in a sky cut by clouds like laundry hanging out to dry,
shone down on the low mists straying over the roads, the slopes and
the town. Merely to look through the window made a man's joints
crack. At the Hôtel de la Préfecture—become in our day the Palais
de Justice—there had been an anxious coming and going since
morning, a panic in the servants' halls where the domestics were
refusing to obey. Before the cathedral of Saint-Pierre worried
crowds could be seen gathering, and over toward Saint-Barthélemy
there were conglomerations of carts and carriages.

Although it was two years since her husband had been appointed
to the prefecture, Nancy had never got used to living in the shadow
of the cathedral in this Gothic house with its buttresses and its
pepper-box turrets. Everything was damp and severe. The young
Duchesse de Massa had come and shut herself up here at twenty-
one, immediately after losing her first-born at the age of twenty-
two months. Here, last year, she had brought her second son Alfred
into the world—she had insisted on giving him the name of the
dead child—while everyone was trembling at the news of the
invasion, and Sylvestre, her husband, was saying fine things about
loyalty to the Emperor, the foreign hordes. He had completely
changed his attitude toward the Bourbons; and for some weeks a
new baby, little Nanette, with her mother's turned-up nose, had
been sucking her thumb in this austere building where the Duc de
Massa, still wearing mourning for his father who had died of grief
and shame shortly after Napoleon's fall, had this morning received
His Majesty Louis XVIII fleeing no one knew where—England,
they said, since he had left Beauvais by the road to Calais—so that
it was all for nothing that the big tapestried chamber at the prefecture
had been prepared.

No one really knew exactly what was happening: only a few days ago they had learned that the Ogre was on his way back to turn life topsy-turvy, had landed at Cannes—but that was so far away! And then, here the King had passed through Beauvais, pausing just long enough to change horses, leaving behind him an exhausted escort, young men collapsing with fatigue who fell asleep without waiting for rooms to be allotted to them, horses dropping on the pavements and in the gutters that ran down the center of the streets. Some of these horsemen, it was said, were among the very ones who had quartered here last year when they were training under the Prince de Poix. People were divided about them: a good many of them were sons of good families who were received with pleasure in society, but the middle-class merchant families which were in the majority here claimed that they were arrogant, brutal, often drunk, elbowing people in the streets, taking up the whole pavement. The truth of the matter was that while people here were royalists, they did not much care for the Royal Household—at least what they could observe of its members. There were continual incidents on the narrow and (it must be admitted) evil-smelling streets because these young dandies, holding their noses, would overwhelm the householders with whom they were lodged with exasperating demands and recriminations.

Meanwhile, what was she to take with her in her trunk? Nancy was emptying it for the third time. The trouble was that she was constantly being interrupted, and she no longer knew what she had put in or forgotten. They had of course had to give hospitality to Marshal Marmont when he had arrived, having driven ahead of the Royal Household all night. It was between noon and one o'clock: the Duchess had given him the room that had been prepared that morning for His Majesty. He must be sleeping in it at this moment. At least she hoped so, for she did not feel at home in big rooms like that—felt as if she needed a carriage to go from the bed to her mirror. Should she leave her fur coat or take it? It was already spring, but it was not warm. Still, that might change in two or three days.

There was still something childlike about the Duchess's face. To her husband, watching her, she looked fresher, fairer than ever, after her third confinement! Here she was, passing her hazel eyes over everything, at her wit's end. She didn't know what to leave and what to take, especially as she didn't know what was to become of her, whether she would be returning, whether she was going to be separated—oh, *mon Dieu!* Sylvestre, Sylvestre, why don't you come with me? A prefect cannot abandon his town and flee with his wife and children. That is understandable. But when you don't know which side to take? We don't even know what Papa has decided. Because Sylvestre can't be in one camp and Papa in the other! For the moment the Duc de Massa was firmly decided on remaining loyal to the King. But tomorrow? After all, he had been a Count of the Empire, pensioned at an age when others are running after girls, councilor of State. . . . It is true, my darling, you are so serious! On the one hand Nancy greatly preferred Paris to Beauvais. But Paris without Sylvestre! She could not see herself all alone at the Hôtel de Massa, or with her sister Perregaux in the country. Sylvestre said that she could certainly not remain here. Since the King was entrenching himself in the North, whether he stayed or merely passed through on his way to England or Belgium, Picardy might well become the military stake between the loyal troops and Napoleon's army. And then the Allies could not be expected to stand by with their arms folded. If there was a second invasion . . . Not that he wished it, but—it was a logical possibility. Logical. If Nancy had been alone, fine. But with two nurslings! Don't forget to take warm things. Downstairs someone was calling for M. le Préfet. All right, I'm coming.

The terrible thing was that the telegraph no longer functioned. Impossible to find out how things stood. Baron Avice, who commanded the military subdivision of Beauvais, was surprised not to have received any message from his direct superior, General Maison, and did not know where to turn. Some of the troops had been quartered at the Saint-Lazare Leper Hospital, others at the great seminary or in the almshouses. Some had even been bedded on straw in the disaffected churches, in Sainte-Marguerite, in the Madeleine, which had been freed last year by the closing of the carpet factory. But more horsemen kept coming. And in what state, seigneur! If the regiments that had gone over to Bonaparte were to surprise them here, what would they do? The information obtained from travelers or dispatches about several garrisons—of Amiens, Clermont, Peronne—was far from reassuring. Rumors had spread through the town and it was impossible to feel any confidence that the more irresponsible elements of the population might not be affected. There were always people ready to fish in troubled waters, so the prefect said.

To tell the truth, the rumors of the Emperor's return were received rather coolly in Beauvais. Not only by the high officials, or the nobility—take for example M. Clermont-Tonnerre, who owned that pretty château a little before you reached Marseille-en-Beauvaisis and who had dropped in to the prefecture for news. But all the manufacturers, the people, their families—out of thirteen thousand inhabitants, more than half were manufacturers. It was a peace-loving city. And Bonaparte's return meant conscription, the levying of men, the blood tax. It must not be forgotten that in 1812 and 1813 there was scarcely a house which had not concealed deserters or absentees up under the roof or in the cellar. 1789 had, of course, brought to the people who worked here in factories making tapestry and calico broadcloths and woolens, ratteens, flannels, cottons and unbleached linens, Utrecht velvets, who labored in the bleaching works, the tanneries, the dye works, the mills, and the ferrous sulphate shops, those same illusions that had taken hold of Frenchmen almost everywhere. But that was long ago. They had also welcomed the First Consul gladly, as a promise that the Terror would not return. They had reckoned without war. And, even worse than the draining off of young men, war had brought stagnation to industry.

For the working people, the Empire had meant above all the collapse of business. Every year more men were laid off; more than a third of the workers in the cloth industry had been reduced to begging—eleven to twelve hundred men. They had never really recovered from the slump of 1811. So people had sighed with relief when the Bourbons had returned; not that they were really so royalist as all that, but order, the Monarchy—if, along with peace, it brought a return to normal life. In other words, work!

Good relations with other countries were needed, people said then, in order to sell the products made at home. There was a great dearth of markets. Apart from a few orders for tapestries to furnish Malmaison, Saint-Cloud, Compiègne, what had Napoleon brought them? The employment of forty workers in the tapestry factory had not been anything like enough to eliminate the category of "poor workers"! Especially since the carpet people had had to shut down during the last days of the Empire—which was not compensated by the setting up of a wood-engraving plant on the rue de la Taillerie, like the one at Épinal. Still, people used to cry *Vive le Roi!* and even unbelievers were fond of the processions in the town, forgetting that it was the Emperor who had re-established them; and the young girls in the July celebration carried banners as they sang, and people stepped aside for them in memory of

Jeanne Hachette,* even though they might belong to poor families.

As a matter of fact, one year of royalty had brought no change in trade, nor in hard times. The end of the continental blockade had brought English competition instead of markets. On the first day of their return, with a single stroke of the pen, the Bourbons ruined the wool industry, brought to nought long-term efforts to improve the sheep stock, plans to create artificial meadows, all of which had had Napoleon's constant support! And so hard-pressed manufacturers kept the Emperor's picture in closets, and there were seditious conversations with persons who had come from Paris. Yet people trembled at the prospect of the return of the Empire with its conscription of men, its insolent luxury. In the town, people had not felt the reign of the *émigrés* as they had in the villages: the seigneurs had no occasion to venture into those narrow stinking streets where the sky was reflected in the gutter, to use polite language.

There were nice officers among them, like the one they had been so sorry to lose who had lived on the Grande-Rue Saint-Martin in the Picardy suburb, at Madame Durand's, the grocer-woman. This M. de Prat-something-or-other was a handsome lad, well built and well spoken, magnificent in his helmet and cuirass; it was not too clear why, blond as he was, he kept insisting that he was of Saracen origin. And orderly in his habits as well, not coming in late, not hanging around the Café des Gardes-du-Corps, where persons of ill-repute gathered. Actually they were a little embarrassed about the miserable room which was all they had to offer him. It had been the loft above the grocery shop when the Durands had first set up housekeeping, before they bought the house next door where the widow was now living with her daughter. The trouble was that everything was so old they were afraid the buildings would collapse, so that during Joseph Durand's lifetime they had never dared to cut through the thick wall between the house and the shop. Thus up to now, in order to go to her counter, Mme. Durand had had to go out into the street, leaving her felt slippers behind her in her house with its well-waxed tiled floors and putting on her wooden shoes at the front door like any peasant. And as for M. de Prat's room, the only way to climb into it from the shop was by means of a ladder through a trap door. Mme. Durand had made an arrange-

---

* Heroine of Beauvais, in the defense of the city besieged by Charles the Bold in 1472. According to legend she felled the Burgundian standard bearer with her hatchet.

ment with the young Guardsman—he couldn't be very rich, M. Alphonse—for forty sous a day, which included his food. It was rather frugal, to be sure, but Denise, the little girl, used to take him his meals and talk with him. He used to read her verses which he claimed he had written himself. And then, too, the fields could be seen through the dormer window, since this was at the end of the town, along with more sky than anywhere else in Beauvais.

As soon as it became known that the Royal Household was arriving, Denise had gone into town in the secret hope of meeting Alphonse. She had just turned sixteen, and for seven months she had been dreaming about the boarder who had always treated her as a child. She imagined how astonished he would be to see her so completely transformed, with a corset that pushed up her young breasts. She was a blond girl with an unbelievable complexion to which a mere nothing would bring a blush, long lashes like the finest silk, and wonderfully slender in the frightful get-up that her mother made her wear which was modeled on the garb the worthy woman herself wore and would have disfigured a beauty of twenty. But on Denise it looked like a disguise stolen from her mother's wardrobe. The round, gathered bonnet of coarse linen, held together by a bedraggled black ribbon, fell with unrelieved symmetry round her face, concealing her clear brow and fair hair; yet it made her all the frailer and fresher, as did the ill-fitting bodice in which her little body danced, proud to wear the corset, and the fringed white woolen fichu around her shoulders that crossed over the small breasts; and that pleated skirt of thick brown homespun which would have made a pin look as fat as a tower. Unused as she was to this dangling bell of cloth which reached to her feet, she had to lift the heavy, bulky skirt with both hands to leap over the Beauvais gutters. It was less than three months since her mother had decided that she was of an age to be dressed up in this way. This was the kind of clothes Mme. Durand had worn for more than twenty years, and she saw no reason to dress her daughter differently. As best she could, she had made over garments of her own that were too worn, to Denise's size; a good yard of fullness removed from the skirt had eliminated the most-worn parts, and now it did not fit her child's little figure too badly.

So, picking up her skirts, Denise made her way in the rain through the streets full of soldiers, whose minds were on other things than noticing how pretty she was. She examined all of them quite brazenly, those, that is, who were five feet six inches or taller, hoping to see M. de Prat in each of them. But before long, what she saw had dampened this hope. The fact was that the handsome horsemen were no longer on parade; some, having dismounted, were dragging an exhausted animal behind them by the lead rein; others were arriving, still mounted but slumped over their horses' necks; still others on foot, their mounts abandoned, spent, left to shift for themselves somewhere along the highway. And then there were those who, having a little money and having considered by the time they reached Beaumont-d'Oise, that eight leagues at night was enough in such weather, had hired carrioles, rattletraps, and were arriving in bands, having saved what they could of their equipment, no longer looking as if they belonged to a military unit, with a little carpet bag on their knees, or wrapped up in blankets, some of them even snoring on the coachman's shoulder. How were these troops going to re-form, go on, even resume the appearance of men? Some were covered with mud from head to toe: where had they been rolling? Rain-drenched, dragging their feet, begging for a room.

And this was how Denise forgot about M. de Prat and, out of pity, brought home a big redheaded lad who claimed to be a Gray Musketeer—you could hardly tell any more—and to answer to the name of Théodore. It was ten o'clock in the morning, and he was still sleeping like a top up there in the loft room, his soaked and dirty clothes thrown on the floor, his mud-caked boots pulled from his feet with great effort: unwashed, naked and exhausted beneath the sheets and the red eiderdown, while Mme. Durand downstairs was, as the sign announced, selling mustard and salt— and walking on tiptoe saying hush! to the customers, as though thunder itself could have awakened M. de Lauriston's Musketeer before nightfall! And even though the room was classified as being in the fourth category of troop lodgings, which in normal times was to the widow's disadvantage, today they had come at least ten times to ask her to put up officers. One of them in fact—a king's Grenadier—had simply plumped himself down on some boxes in the storeroom, and there was no way of getting him to budge. The people who came into the shop all went to look at him as he slept, his bearskin set down by his side, and they were divided between pity and hilarity because he had assumed a position in his sleep which was a little embarrassing, on account of Denise, who turned her eyes away.

And still they kept coming!

Some were washing under the pumps. Others, half-naked in the courtyards, were having hot water, bought for five sous from the bath-water carriers, thrown over them. Heroes! Some were shaving. Some, holding on to their haversacks, their sabers between their legs, had just slumped down in front of the stagecoach station on the Grande-Rue Saint-Martin amid the rough Picard voices. Others were sneezing like mad. Seeing them, people could not help wondering what had driven them through the wind and the rain, for it was impossible to take these poor creatures for a troop, regular cavalry, an army. More like an upturned beehive, a boarding school let out at the end of term, disobedient scamps who had lost their way in mountain or swamp. True enough, they had come where they were led, commanded, marching under orders, but it was unbelievable: they looked like fugitives, deserters. And Beauvais, accordingly, was cordial to them, because they knew all about deserters here. Workers' wives were treating these marquises and viscounts maternally, and it must be said that in the state they were in they could easily be taken for workers, for people like themselves. They were taken indoors, given something to drink, made comfortable. And because of all this, many of them were moved to tears, and they said, ah, here was a town, people loyal to the monarchy, to the King, to the nobility! In the state they were in, it was too difficult to explain anything to them, and besides, to tell the truth, nobody really thought about it, nobody had puzzled it out, nobody even knew exactly what was going on, what he thought, what was coming after—except that there was something appealing about soldiers who ran away, because then they didn't fight. And that was the thought uppermost in their minds: above everything, that there should be no fighting in Beauvais!

Which was not so stupid.

As the carriage conveying Nancy de Massa, her children and their nurse came out of the prefecture on the Place Saint-Pierre and into the deep shadow of the cathedral, there approached a kind of barouche carrying a quartet of gentlemen. Among them the Duchess recognized M. de Toustain, a Lifeguard she had met the month before at Meaux when, immediately after her confinement, she had been visiting an aunt of Sylvestre's, to show her the children.

The Guards of Wagram's company had found Meaux excruciatingly boring, and M. de Toustain had paid court to the Duchesse de Massa, who had not at the time been particularly interested. But suddenly seeing her former suitor again at such a moment, she had a feeling that she was living world history. Not, however, to the point of stopping her carriage. But through the back window she could see the barouche heading into the prefecture she had just left. She rubbed her little turned-up nose and began to imagine the conversation between the Marquis de Toustain and Sylvestre. *Mon Dieu,* small the world is! Everything happens as in a play: all the characters are listed beforehand on the program, not one more can appear on the scene. Then, suddenly, she struck her forehead. "What has Madame forgotten?" asked the nurse as she pressed a thumb-sucking Nanette to her bosom.

"Nothing, nothing, girl. On the contrary I've just remembered something. That tall man, facing M. de Toustain, under the top—"

"What do you mean?" said the nurse gaping through the door in an effort to see this Toustain.

"Why, surely, it's the Duc de Richelieu! And I shan't be there to receive him! They say he's such a pleasant man! And tells such wonderful stories about Russia!"

It was in fact the Duc de Richelieu, sitting all askew because of the genuine sores he had on his buttocks. On hastily leaving the rue Royale-Saint-Honoré, he had taken with him ten thousand francs in gold louis which he had drawn on Saturday from Messrs. Laffitte and Perregaux on the rue du Mont-Blanc. He had fitted the money into his belt, but by mischance had put the belt on upside down and the pieces had escaped from the little pockets, so that all the way from Paris he had trotted and galloped with the gold coins slipping down through his drawers, his breeches, and even into his boots, without at first realizing what was happening. When he at last understood what was causing his discomfort it was too late: he could not halt, undress in the torrential rain, and exhibit his gold like that in the dead of night. Well, in this state he was certainly no longer a menace to the ladies! He could not put up just anywhere; he needed a surgeon to attend him: he had come to ask the prefect for one, and he was bringing his carriage companions with him. Lucky enough to have found this ramshackle vehicle and to be sharing it with the Marquis de Toustain; Léon de Rochechouart, his nephew by marriage, who had been his majordomo at Odessa and was for the moment a Black Musketeer; and de Rochechouart's aide-de-camp, M. de Montpezat. The time was about half-past two.

At this same hour, Marshal Macdonald had reached a section of the road he knew well, because here on the left was the turning that led to the country house of Regnault de Saint-Jean-d'Angély. Scattered here and there in this region were dwellings such as this which bore witness to a stable world; a world to which the Duc de Tarente had belonged and which he was perhaps in the process of abandoning. Where was this flight behind the King leading him? Would he really have to leave France? He could not bring himself to do so. He was uncommunicative and replied neither to Hulot nor his aide-de-camp, who from time to time put his nose to the window and talked about the landscape. Or said suddenly, "I wonder what has become of the Italian lady."

Jacques-Étienne was troubled most of all by not knowing where the King might really be at this moment: he feared His Majesty might have changed his mind on the way, and instead of making a dash for Lille . . . There was that story of unfavorable news coming from Amiens, and yet nothing could be less reliable. For that matter, what could a prefect do? Attack the Royal Household? What officers would lift their hands against a sovereign to whom they had sworn loyalty? It made no sense. And if Louis XVIII was taking the road to Calais after all, there was the attraction of the coast, of the sea, and even if he did not want to emigrate, everyone would think he was making for England. How long would it take the troops who had gone over to Napoleon to set out in pursuit? It was certain that the Emperor would sleep at the Louvre tonight.

The road dipped almost suddenly into a narrow valley, between tall trees, country properties. They were approaching Presles, which, dominated by a hill, extended for a quarter of a league. For a moment the Marshal wondered if he should not stop at Laneuville's. Laneuville was his broker, and the Marshal would certainly have orders to give him. Because even if he had to leave France, he would be leaving money behind which must not remain idle. Laneuville could get in touch with Alphonse, his son-in-law Perregaux, Adèle's husband. There, just ahead, was where they would have to turn off to the right; M. de Laneuville's château was a third of a league off the road, at Nointel—an admirable spot, with a park whose groves and ponds were beyond anything that could be imagined. But was Laneuville at Nointel? The Marshal did not give the order to turn. As a matter of fact, what *had* happened to Madame Visconti? After all, it was her second attack. . . . He said aloud, "She must be back at the Boulevard des Capucines by now."

The aide-de-camp stared at him. It was at least twenty minutes since he had mentioned her, and he had forgotten about it. Besides, he had not known that the Italian woman lived on the Boulevard des Capucines. But he realized that he must ask the Marshal no questions: Jacques-Étienne was again absorbed in his reveries, gripped by an obscure fear.

Thinking of Laneuville, of Alphonse Perregaux, had led him straight to Alphonse's sister—his daughter Adèle's sister-in-law—the Duchesse de Raguse, and thus quite naturally to Marmont, the Duc de Raguse himself. Where was Marmont, where were the Princes? They had certainly not followed in the train of the royal carriage. One had only to look at the road, at the stragglers they were overtaking, the tag-end of the Royal Household. Some were sitting in the ditches, nursing feet from which they had removed their boots; others were sleeping on their outspread coats. Abandoned horses roamed by the roadside, packages were strewn about, bottles, even weapons. As they approached Beaumont, the stragglers became more numerous; there were even groups of them. They were passing carts in which volunteers dressed in the style of Henri IV lay fast asleep on the hay; they caught up with exhaused wretches who were still making a semblance of marching, and with others who stared at them vacantly or had manifestly given up. Some had thrown away their boots and were marching barefoot in the mud. Others were using their muskets as walking sticks. And horsemen who had dismounted and were talking to their stubborn, exhausted horses, trying in vain to persuade them to go on. . . .

Beaumont d'Oise had a population of perhaps two thousand souls, a small town set on a slope overlooking the river, terraced, with a flat promenade between a tall church and the ruined tower of the ancient château. It lived on trade in grain and flour, and on the traffic of the road to Calais. At the postmaster's, as they were about to change the horses on the Marshal's carriage, it was discovered by a miracle that a shaft was on the point of breaking. An accident had barely been avoided. There was no time to wait for repairs. The mail coach was about to leave. Macdonald gave his orders to the quartermasters who had been waiting for him here, arranging billets; and abandoning his escort, and Hulot who was to wait for the repairs to be made, got into the coach with his aide-de-camp. No need of billets, since there was no army! Nothing had followed the Royal Household, not a regiment, not a service corps. Macdonald had expected General Ruty to arrive in Beaumont straight from Saint-Denis, from which he had been driven by the half-pay officers, and had also expected that he would pick up the service corps as he moved on Beauvais. But not a trace of Ruty! *His* loyalty had not survived Saint-Denis and the fright the half-pay officers had given him. Too bad! Macdonald would leave a post with orders as at Saint-Denis, in case a regiment should turn up.

In all history there had been no such adventure: a general without a single soldier, following with only his aide-de-camp the route marked in advance with red pencil on the guiding plans. And in a public conveyance too. It was simply a question of joining the Princes; no one gave any further thought to the army of Melun. There was the Royal Household, under Monsieur, and Marmont; farther ahead, the eldest son of the Church with the Prince de Poix, Blacas and, if he were lucky, behind him the rattletrap carriage in which Berthier was chewing his nails and holding on his knees the casket containing Mme. Visconti's diamonds. And Beurnonville's berlin, with its postillion. What exactly was Beurnonville thinking at this moment?

As for the Prince de Wagram, he could not be taking much interest in the conversation of the Duc de Grammont and the Duc de Luxembourg, which could hardly be more than a dialogue between deaf-mutes in which the first would wait for the second to finish his anecdotes of Condé's army in order to slip in his own reminiscences of Portugal. As for the Duc de Croy d'Havret, who mentally had never left Versailles—he was certainly dozing alone with his past, his powdered hair drawn back in a knot.

In the mail coach in which Macdonald was sitting were a horse dealer, two traveling salesmen, a blind old lady with her housekeeper, a whole family who had come from Paris, a little girl holding a cat in her arms, and an Englishman who from time to time noted something down in a little notebook. All these people had crowded together, dismayed by the entrance of the military men. Who was this general? A general, in any event. They looked at him and remained mute. Since Paris, it was true, they had seen nothing but officers—but none had taken the stagecoach. Were generals now traveling by coach like everyone else? Then little by little they calmed down. The salesmen spoke to one another in low voices. The atmosphere was not conducive to general conversation. To begin with, the landscape here offered few resources—this whole long plain past Chamblay with its tall church, then the slight climb leading to the Thelle country and the windy plateau where the rain overtook them again.

It must have been close to five when the coach began to descend into the vale of La Gobette where the plateau slopes down to Puiseux-le-Hauberger. There they were to change horses. The Marshal listened with half an ear to the horse dealer, who was pointing out a château of the previous century to the left and naming the owner. They manufactured fans there. Or at least fan frames. Odd, a countryside living by that—a little gesture of coquetry rather than of necessity. Jacques-Étienne remembered having once given Pauline Leclerc a fan, which he had been told was "a fan from Mme. de Bruant." Wasn't that the name he had just heard attached to the château? La Paolina had the daintest hands in the world, and the fan seemed to be a continuation of her perfect fingers. Strange to remember that today! In this village of less than a hundred hearths, through which a detachment of Wagram's company was passing on foot, officered by weary horsemen who put up their collars and looked reproachfully up at a sky growing ever more leaden. Today when That Man would be returning to the Louvre, crossing the Salon des Maréchaux as he had done not so long ago, his hands behind his back, stopping abruptly to speak to a soldier— You, I've seen you somewhere . . . *Comédien! Comédien!* And when he entered the Salon de la Paix, who would be there to welcome him? Which of the old comrades—of those who last year had sworn loyalty to the King? Macdonald visualized well-known faces, he could see the postures, the same salute, the women curtseying ceremoniously: Queen Hortense, Mme. Regnault de Saint-Jean-d'Angély, the Duchesse de Frioul. And suddenly he felt a tug at his heart: Pauline who had been on the Isle of Elba— had she returned with him? He shook himself. One might have thought that he had been in love with her all his life! He had long ago forgotten General Leclerc's wife, who had made a laughing-stock of him in front of his best friends. And what after all was the Princesse Borghese to him? Less than nothing.

A hopeless, penetrating drizzle. Mud, endless mud. They passed a group of buildings that couldn't be called a village. It had grown up by the roadside. Some soldiers had stopped near a door and were begging for shelter. And there were others, on foot, on horse-back, straggling on—where would they sleep tonight?—the whole unraveled skein of the Royal Household, Gendarmes, Guards, Light

Horse, Grenadiers—in parade uniforms that had never seen the smoke of battle, but had darkened in this ordeal by water. Cloaks, greatcoats, leathern breeches: there was something ironic about the fact that they were popularly called the Reds! But actually, even with the Musketeers and the Swiss Guards, how many of them were there? Not five thousand. But like this, lost, on these endless roads, in the disorder and fatigue, they might have been Xenophon's Ten Thousand at least. A whole army. The exodus of a world. The end of time. The enormous confusion of all concepts of greatness. The caricature of devotion and heroism. A legend which had miscarried. The incredible mixture of a poor little pale-blooded nobility and the conquerors of Europe. Lauriston, La Grange, Marmont, Macdonald with the Grammonts, the Noailles', the Damas', and the Dombidou de Cruseilles, the Le Large de Lourdouniex', the Bourbon-Bussets, the Gallis de Menilgrand, the Forbins des Issarts, the Gaultiers de la Clopperie. An entire stable of *vidames* and soldiers of Napoleon's Old Guard, with flags bearing Latin mottoes, a wardrobe with gold and silver braid looted from abandoned service wagons, old or new loyalty oaths repudiated or stubbornly honored, wallowing in the mud in the interminable panorama of poor farms and fine houses resold, passing from hand to hand, from a military feudalism to titled merchants, bartering armor for fans or mother-of-pearl buttons, cloth, money, factories. . . . And in the Puiseux forge, a tall dark lad in the uniform of the Gardes-de-la-Porte was waiting for his horse to be reshod, although he himself could no longer keep on his feet.

The Marshal had stepped down from the mail coach into the drizzle to stretch his legs when a carriage, drawn by four horses and coming from the direction of Beauvais, stopped in front of him. Suddenly he heard cries and recognized Nancy's voice: "Papa! Papa!" And he saw his daughter's little turned-up nose and hazel eyes. She resembled him as a cat does a tiger, as a cherry resembles a cannon ball. But her voice was that of Marie-Constance at Saint-Germain-en-Laye. Marie-Constance, his only love and his youth.

"What are you doing here, my Duchess?" he asked, embracing her tenderly. "Have you taken to the road without your prefect? And with this whole carriageful?"

He pointed to his grandchildren, whimpering in their swaddling-clothes, blowing bubbles of saliva, the little bent fingers waving toward the gray sky, and the nurse in her black wool dress who never stopped wiping them. Nancy explained that her husband was sending them to Paris.

"Paris? Well, madame, you must do me the pleasure of accompanying your father to Beauvais!"

Sylvestre could have understood nothing of what was happening. And Sylvestre had, indeed, understood nothing of what was happening. War in Picardy? Did he think he was living under Louis XIV! But to leave Beauvais for Paris was worse than from Charybdis to Scylla! In the first place—even making all kinds of allowances— Paris wasn't just next door, and the roads these days . . . after what he had seen in Saint-Denis! No, no, my girl, about face! Apart from which, did she know where the King was going? Had she seen him in Beauvais?

They had indeed seen him in Beauvais. He had left by the road to Calais. The others— What, Calais? Not Amiens? Not Amiens. Ah, so it was continuing! Of course, he may very well turn in some other direction on the way: Louis XVIII changes his mind every ten minutes. From Poix a road runs straight to Amiens . . . What is so embittering is that this gives everyone the impression he actually wants to go to England.

"And why shouldn't he go?" asked Nancy.

Ah, but he's not going there! He's *not* going there. Only, that road, even if he should turn north at Abbeville, gives the impression— yes, it gives the distinct impression . . . and it can discourage those who most favor the Monarchy, of whom there are many in Picardy and in Artois. How can you expect them to resist, to leap into the fray, if the sovereign runs away? "You know this big dolt?" This was by way of introducing his aide-de-camp to his daughter. The other bowed. "Imagine, he's in love with an Italian woman who's going on sixty!" The denials, the blush that came to the aide's cheeks, lent an appearance of truth to this farce. But the mail coach was about to depart again.

On the stroke of six they reached Noailles, where the Princes were. Leaving the mail coach to continue on its way to Beauvais, the Duc de Tarente had settled his daughter and his grandchildren in the home of a family loyal to His Majesty who had been recommended to him; and with the carriage which they had placed at his disposal he betook himself to the Château de Mouchy, less than a league away, where Monsieur, Monseigneur, their suite and the company chiefs were to spend the night. Marmont had gone on ahead of them to Beauvais. The Duc de Mouchy and his wife, Nathalie—sister of that Alexandre de Laborde who had been left in charge of the Tuileries between Louis XVIII's departure and Napoleon's arrival—had arrived during the day, having left Paris on the advice of the Duke's father, the Prince de Poix, just after M. de Chateaubriand, who had spent the evening at their house, had taken his leave. All this crowd was about to sit down to table when Marshal Macdonald arrived. The odors wafted from the kitchens were enough to turn your head and your stomach topsy-turvy. All the Bourbons are alike: to them the table is an affair of state.

There had been a considerable slaughter in the poultry yard; there were perhaps thirty people for dinner and the Duchesse Nathalie had spared nothing. There would be guinea fowl on the spit. The sauce that was to accompany them was being described in advance, a recipe from Méréville; that is to say, from the Laborde establishment. Macdonald was famished—he had had nothing since that quick bite at Saint-Denis; but he couldn't sit down to table, his daughter was at Noailles. . . . There were exclamations, the Duc de Mouchy said that they would send half a guinea fowl and sweets to Mme. de Massa—he had to make an effort to avoid calling her Mme. Régnier—right away. She liked Burgundy, didn't she? In short, everyone proved so charming that the Marshal sat down and gratefully ate a monstrous quantity of the marvels which kept following one upon another. He was disappointed at the absence of Marmont, with whom he could have explored the situation more thoroughly from a military point of view. For there was no possibility of discussing it either with Charles de Damas, commander of the Light Horse, or with the Comte de Vergennes, commander of the Gardes-de-la-Porte, both of whom questioned him with polite interest, but neither of whom was exactly of a military turn of mind, despite their service in Condé's army. How was it that Étienne de Durfort was not with them? But the cordiality of the Princes, the hospitality of the Duchess, still very beautiful after twenty years—when Macdonald had met her, still a young girl, she had been studying painting in David's studio, and it was easy to understand how M. de Chateaubriand . . .

All this created an enveloping warmth after the frightful night, the road and the rain. They had not yet come to the guinea fowl: the Duc de Mouchy had an incomparable fishpond from which they had fished trout, but this recipe was not from Méréville—only the

Noailles knew how to prepare them in this way; and it was the custom after this to drink a Spanish wine with a name the Marshal had never before heard in his life. He looked at the paintings, at the crystal of the glasses—and suddenly he felt deep down that he was only an upstart. He remembered his childhood at Sancerre when his parents—having settled there with other Scots because of the low price of food and the excellence of the wines—intended him for the Church. He felt himself blush, and turning to the Comte d'Artois, he proceeded to deliver his report on the events of the night and the disappearance of the Royal army.

Monseigneur the Duc de Berry who, technically speaking, was his hierarchical chief, having the same relation to the Duc de Tarente as Monsieur to the Duc de Raguse—that is to say, he was nominally in command of the army, with Macdonald under him— became considerably vexed at the Marshal's addressing his father, who commanded only the Household, through Marmont. But what could he do? In the King's absence, Monsieur represented the Monarchy. And as for his army—where was his army? At the thought he felt Anne of Austria's tears welling into his eyes.

Marmont had wakened in this bed of state, in the immense dark room whose walls were decorated with tapestries bought back at a discount from a M. de Boicervoise when Lucien Bonaparte, in the year VII (1798), had refused to allow the prefect of Beauvais to get his furnishings free of charge from the factory. They were rather moth-eaten tapestries which repeated four of the six panels of Boucher's *La Noble Pastorale*. The succeeding prefect, the Comte de Belderbusch, was more lavish by nature and to go with them had added a sofa with bouquets of white flowers on a blue background, six armchairs that did not match, big valances with arabesques on the bedposts and matching draperies at the windows. Marmont had only half undressed and his things were piled on the floor. He could not have slept very long, judging by the light through the heavy curtains which he drew aside. Ah, he would have something to change into: his trunk had been brought into the room while he slept. A Spanish leather trunk studded with big nails which had been through a lot. He looked absent-mindedly at *La fontaine d'amour* and *La pipée aux oiseaux* and found them rather old-fashioned. There was a big bell cord at the head of the bed. A valet entered bringing hot water, and the Marshal washed and dressed himself. He gazed critically at his reflection in the mirror: at his legs, his thighs: "I'm getting soft." And what were those little black spots there, by the left nostril? He still felt very weary. Less from this night and having had only three or four hours in bed than from everything that had gone before, those last days in Paris, the King's vacillations, the half-measures, the news from the South. The substance of Bonaparte's statements on landing at Cannes had become known rather quickly. The accusations that the Emperor had brought against him, Marmont . . . He thought about them constantly.

It relaxed him a little to be shaved by the barber who was sent up to him. The Duc de Raguse passed his hand over his fresh cheeks, paying little attention to the wigmaker's chatter or to his compliments on the Duke's physique. As though his mind were on such things! This campaign—if this flight could be called a campaign —was not like Spain, where nothing relaxed you better than making love. Beauvais for him was not a garrison city but a stopping place, and presently, tomorrow, the enemy would be here. Frenchmen, worse for him than the *guerrilleros* of the Peninsula. If he were to fall into their hands, his fate would be that of the Duc d'Enghien. Was it this, as much as the hazards of war, that his wife had been thinking about when she had asked to see him again last Saturday, after so many years? He never thought of the Duchesse de Raguse without bitterness; of Mlle. Perregaux, as he called Hortense to himself since she had said she would no longer bear his name after the events of 1814. In fact, they had not been husband and wife since 1810, and while he was fighting on the battlefields of Europe she had never even had the simple decency not to flaunt her lovers. It was as though she had repudiated him for his infidelity toward Napoleon, whereas it was he who, on his return from Illyria, had driven her out of his house on the rue Paradis. Well, since she had wanted to see him—he had seen her. He had gone to her house on the rue Cerutti.

Nothing had enabled him to appraise the situation better than this move of Mlle. Perregaux's while the whole Court was plunged in indecision. She had come right out and proposed to him that before he leave he make her his residuary legatee. In the light of their relationship, such a proposal betrayed not simply insolence, but a virtual certainty on her part as to the fate that awaited him. He could have refused, laughed in her face. But suddenly there had come back to him some haunting impression, a kind of perfume, attached to the early period of their marriage like an interrupted piece of music, a melody that carried you with it although you had never known more than the first bars. After all, even if he were to die, there had to be a Duchesse de Raguse. He had not obtained a divorce when Napoleon had urged him to, and divorce was in fashion. So whether he died or lived on, she would remain his wife, since divorce was now ruled out. It seemed to him that generosity was the only possible revenge on this woman, and on the Emperor, and on life. And besides, he was paying for information of the highest importance—with all his property, his name, his houses, his fortune: Mlle. Perregaux's move proved that her brother and his associate, the banker Laffitte, were convinced of the favorable turn events would take for Bonaparte. Who could be better informed? MM. Laffitte and Perregaux, the son after the father, always played safe. If they were becoming Bonapartists these days, they knew what they were doing. After all, it had been Laffitte's remarks, at the time of the provisional government of 1814, that had made M. de Talleyrand decide to gamble on the return of the Bourbons. . . .

Marmont had fresh cheeks and a heavy heart. He had learned from the barber that the Duc de Richelieu had arrived at the prefecture while he was asleep, and he decided to go and pay his respects to this gentleman. He had seen very little of him in the six months or so since the Duke's return from Russia, for Richelieu had quite deliberately kept aloof from affairs and had constantly refused the posts that Louis XVIII had proposed to him. But the Marshal felt a lively curiosity about this great nobleman whose biography was singular, and who, at the age of forty-nine, had to his credit nearly a quarter of a century of service to His Majesty the Emperor of all the Russias. Not an *émigré* like the others, he had left France in 1791, on the special authorization of the Constituent Assembly, and this was held against him at the Pavillon de Marson— as much as was the reason for his voluntary exile, which, as everyone knew, was the marriage his family had imposed on him in his early youth to a woman, a Rochechouart, so deformed as to be unpresentable. Although his own situation was quite different, Marmont felt a certain kinship with the Duc de Richelieu, since both of them had lived nearly all their lives apart from their lawful wives. For that matter, there are moral deformities which are every bit as bad as a hump. Not that the Marshal had observed the almost saintly aloofness toward women of M. de Richelieu, who had married before the Lord. But had he not for a very short time—the Emperor ironically called him Marmont the First—reigned over Illyria with the same powers that Richelieu had exercised at Odessa for eleven years? His curiosity had its roots less in the parallel of their private lives than in a retrospective nostalgia for that vice-royalty of which he had had no more than a taste, but which had left him with a terrible habit of spending what was no longer backed by a public treasury.

He found the former governor of New Russia being treated for the untoward wounds he had suffered from the louis-d'or that had slipped out of his money belt. His Majesty's surgeon, Father Elisée, had arrived in Beauvais almost at the same time, and had immediately betaken himself to the Duc de Massa's residence to inquire as to the road the royal carriage and its escort had taken. The prefect had said to him, "You've turned up most opportunely!" and had placed the first gentleman of the Privy Chamber in the Jesuit's expert hands.

Elisée was in a hurry to be done and on his way to Abbeville—if indeed it was for Abbeville that Louis XVIII was heading. His coachman had abandoned him here, no longer in the least frightened, talking loudly, even banteringly, and on the pretext that he had a "fiancée" in Paris had turned his cabriolet around, but not without having first relieved his half-angry, half-consenting passenger of a considerable sum. No carriage being available, the Father had secured from M. de Massa a place in the improvised coach which was to take on to the King of France a dispatch that could no longer be transmitted by signals, Louis XVIII having somewhat belatedly ordered the dismantling of the telegraph. Messengers on horseback were carrying news as far as Amiens, from which point the telegraph was still working. And the news was not very encouraging: Napoleon was expected at the Tuileries from one moment to the next; Paris was in the hands of the Bonapartists; M. de Lavalette had reassumed his title as director-general of the Imperial Posts and replaced M. le Comte Ferrand on the rue Jean-Jacques-Rousseau.

Though no longer endowed with the charm of his youth when he had been an officer of the Queen's Dragoons at Trianon, Armand-Emmanuel de Richelieu had, despite a slight stoop, kept the figure of a young horseman, a fact accentuated by his state of undress. He had, indeed, been extremely thin, and this no doubt accounted for the fact that he was still as slim as when, with Prince Charles de Ligne and the Comte de Langeron, he had taken part, under Suvorov's command, in the assault on the fortress of Ismaïla. Marmont, who was eight years his junior, felt heavy in his presence and was even a little jealous of that physique which, in contrast to the prematurely white hair, retained its tawny freshness. He no doubt owed his physical condition to the ascetic life he had led—so surprising in the grandson of the famous libertine of the previous century whom he resembled strikingly in looks and not at all in morals. Emmanuel was as tall as the Marshal, but very differently proportioned. His head looked small, due rather to the fullness of his chest and the length of his neck than to its actual dimensions, and his legs were inordinately long, with something about them suggesting the dancer. Not an ounce of fat, and fine muscles. His abundant wavy white hair tumbled over his forehead and ears, and had, paradoxically, a good deal to do with his air of youthfulness, despite his rather long nose and the large mouth; and there was something slightly feminine about his very regular features and dark skin, almost the complexion of a gipsy, with well-defined eyebrows above the dark, luminous eyes. Yes, Marmont looked upon him as the embodiment of everything he himself would have liked to be, with that jealousy men often feel for a masculine type quite different from their own. But also for quite other, deeper reasons, for everything that sometimes kept him from sleeping, and seized his heart as with claws. . . .

It was extraordinary—a long adventurous life, war, travels, virtual sovereignty for eleven years over a region extending from the Caucasus to the Danube, the terrible days of plague when he had spent himself unstintingly in that Odessa which was his creation, and those immense surrounding steppes—all this had passed over the Duc de Richelieu without leaving the slightest mark on him. Whereas Marmont—of whom, at forty-one, people said that he was *still* attractive—felt all the weight of the campaigns under the Empire, the sun of Illyria and Spain, the snow and wind of Germany and Russia, marked as he was by fatigue, doubt, ambition, anger. And regret for the power he had merely tasted at Leybach, at Trieste.

While Father Elisée was gathering up his kit, his pots of ointment, rolling his bandages and continuing the recital of his misadventures on the road between Pontoise and Beauvais, Marmont suddenly noticed, sitting a little to one side, a young man wearing the uniform of the Musketeers who had stood up for a moment when he entered. He had not immediately recognized this simple lieutenant of the Royal Household as Brigadier General de Rochechouart—a nephew by marriage of the Duc de Richelieu, and like him a Russian officer—whose strange fate it had been to be made commander of the fortress of Paris by the Czar on the entry of the Allies in 1814.

Léon de Rochechouart, who was only twenty-seven years old, looked rather cramped in his clothes, for although he was small of stature he was chubby, with a round, irregular face, and chestnut hair which had obviously been curled with an iron. He had been Richelieu's majordomo in Odessa, and the Duke, whose household he had managed for seven years, had wanted to make him his heir, at least to his Russian properties—until he replaced him, in his will, by M. de Stempkovski. When Father Elisée was ready to leave, M. de Rochechouart got up and accompanied him to the door.

"I must have been devilishly in need of a surgeon, as you can imagine, Monsieur le Maréchal, to let that odious creature in the black robe come near me. I cannot understand how a sovereign who certainly understands the necessity he is under to restore the Altar as well as the Throne can permit everyone to observe in his entourage a figure so propitious to the propagation of atheism. It gives ugly grounds for the suspicion that some secret exists between them—and that is calumny as well as lese-majesty. . . . Well, if you want to go and see your cousin, my dear Léon, you leave me in good hands!" This last remark was addressed to M. de Rochechouart with a wave of the hand indicating Marmont. The lieutenant of the Black Musketeers bowed, and explained to the Marshal that the Marquise de Crillon, nee Mortemart, had just arrived in Beauvais and was going to her father's château; he apologized for taking his leave just when the Duc de Raguse . . . "I'm taking Montpezat with me—my cousin has a weakness for him."

Since Léon de Rochechouart had made him his aide-de-camp just before the fall of Paris, Montpezat had not let him out of his sight. Young General de Rochechouart betrayed a rather bizarre mixture of obsequiousness and effrontery. It was said that when Madame his mother had had to flee France, she had entrusted him and his brother to people who had made bathhouse attendants of them at the age of seven or eight, at Caen. Well, something of that still showed.

The Duke watched him leave; then turned to Marmont and said, "You know, Monsieur le Maréchal, people are astonished that the Revolution and the Empire brought out talent in such young people. They marvel at the youth of generals promoted on the battlefield. This was true on both sides. Take a youngster like the Comte de Rochechouart: at twelve—*twelve,* mind you—he was an officer in the English army in Portugal, and at sixteen he crossed the whole of Europe to join me in Odessa, where his brother was already with me. I saw him, at nineteen, under Turkish fire on an island in the Danube. The same year he was at my side when we entered Anapa, a town in Circassia, which was in flames and where our sailors and our Cossacks fired on one another in the confusion. And then, at his request, he led a punitive expedition against the small princes of the Caucasus who were continually ravaging and pillaging the villages of the Zaporog Cossacks. Just think, he wasn't yet twenty when he went into those Tartar *aouls,* ordering searches and punishment amid the houses his men had set on fire and pillaged. He was not much older when I assigned him to go from village to village between Odessa and Moscow and punish with twenty-five blows of the knout on the belly those Cossack detachments whose duty it was to carry messages from New Russia to His Majesty the Emperor and who were answerable for the disappearance of several mail convoys.

"Imagine that this terrible scourge, this Archangel Michael, was at the same time still enough of a child in 1811 for Mme. Narishkin —whose husband you may have met when the Allies entered Paris— for Mme. Narishkin to take him, dressed as a girl, to visit a harem at Bakhchi-Sarai without causing any alarm except to himself, such was the beauty of the women who innocently admitted him to the privacy of the harem. And I don't even mention his role during the battles in the Kuban in 1811, or his devotion at the beginning of our fight against the plague in 1812, when I didn't try to keep him, since Napoleon was marching on Moscow, preferring as I did to have him face the dangers of war rather than those of the epidemic. Especially since I had young Vanya Stempkovski to make up for his absence. But do you suppose the Russian campaign was less hard for the soldiers of the Czar than for those of Napoleon? All of you here, even those loyal to His Majesty, have a tendency to see heroism only in the French armies. There was a Rochechouart in the French ranks, and a Rochechouart in the Russian ranks, each the aide-de-camp of one of the Emperors. Didn't they suffer the same cold, the same hunger, the same perils? In the Russian campaign there was a kind of tacit understanding between the two armies: the French burned the villages as they retreated but left Napoleon's billets intact, and Alexander promptly occupied them. Just imagine that beyond the Beresina, in Langeron's division, Léon de Rochechouart regularly occupied the room his Cousin Casimir de Mortemart had just abandoned and which still bore his name in chalk on the door— The very same Mortemart whose cannon last night were getting stuck in the mud of the road a little beyond Saint-Denis. Too little thought has been given to the causes that have led to this strange division of the French nobility, where we have seen brothers and cousins in opposing ranks! How old were you when you were made a general officer? Roche-chouart was twenty-six. . . ."

Whereupon Emmanuel de Richelieu made an ugly grimace: completely carried away by his talk, he had forgotten the wounds on his legs and buttocks, and had hurt himself as he turned on the couch. Marmont, unprepared for this flood of words, nevertheless to his surprise found in them ideas parallel to those of his own private reveries. Rubbing his lower lip mechanically between fingers and thumb, he said: "Monsieur le Duc, may I ask you this? It's a question I've asked myself many times since your return. Why, basically, were you never willing to take your share in the work of reconciling the French which the Princes undertook on their return?"

"The Princes?" Richelieu repeated with a tinge of irony. "That, my dear fellow, is a long story. Did you have a good sleep? And your army doesn't claim your presence? Then I could perhaps explain it to you. . . ."

Whereupon he lit his pipe.

VII

The Last Winter Vigil

WHILE the Duc de Richelieu was explaining to Marmont how he had become a stranger to his own country and was telling him about southern Russia, where he had lived for eleven years, Charles, Baron Fabvier, the Marshal's aide-de-camp, slept a sleep of utter exhaustion in the attic of the prefecture where a bed had been put up for him. Lying on his belly, his arms flung out, he dreamed of Persia where, with this same hand that was drooping on the sheet, with these same muscles strained by eighteen leagues on horseback in one stretch, he had once made cannon for the Shah, casting them himself in the sand, in the depths of that Vulcan's forge—he could see himself back there, helped by three brutes with shaved heads—so that the Persians could invade Georgia and use these cannon against the troops commanded by Armand-Emmanuel de Richelieu, governor of New Russia. . . .

In full daylight—for he had not taken the time to draw the shabby curtain on the dormer window—the thirty-three-year-old colonel stirred vaguely and moaned. His mouth pressed against his shoulder, he murmured a forgotten name. In the implacable sun that beat down on that land of dust, where the poetry was all about fountains and nightingales, he again felt beside him the presence of that white-skinned, black-haired Circassian girl, bought in the market of Chiraz, who spoke no known language except tears. Charles had taught her only the few words necessary for love, words whose violent pre-

195

cision on those tender young lips contrasted with a resemblance that
haunted him even today in this dream at Beauvais, a resemblance
found at the opposite ends of the inland sea—in the girls of Spain and
those of the Caucasus. He used to call this slave of his arms and of
his pleasure by a secret name which she herself could not understand:
Marie-des-Démons.

The rain outside had begun to fall again, harder than ever; a sheet
of whirling water was descending on Beauvais, and the wind made
the doors bang. The whole town was on the watch and seemed to
tread on delicate ground, both because of the uncertain news and the
new arrivals, and because of the guests accommodated in every spare
corner of the houses that had, one after another, settled down for the
night. The gray light, pierced occasionally by a ray of pale sunshine,
contrasted with the vast whispering hum of the local people who came
and went like visitors in a cemetery among the daytime sleepers in
their houses, whose breathing could be heard behind the doors.

At the perfumer's on the rue du Théâtre, for example, the masters
of the house had given their own bed to their guest, a Guard of
Wagram's company—there had been no room for him at the prefecture where he had left the Duc de Richelieu; and with him a youngster belonging to Mortemart's regiment, a former comrade of his in
the English army in Portugal. He was dreaming about Portugal because of this fresh encounter with Léon de Rochechouart who, at
twelve, had then been a second lieutenant in the Val de Freiro Barracks (red coat faced with black velvet, white wool braid and silver
buttons, red felt helmet with black fur crest, and the white cockade).
He, Toustain, had been the same age then as Léon was now. Already
at twenty-seven he had had behind him all the years of Condé's
army, with its internal strifes, rivalries and treasons; the humiliations
inflicted on the French by the German princes; the terrifying proximity of the red cloaks, Croat, Serbian and Dalmatian, those adventurers of gigantic appearance, plunderers who burned their French
prisoners alive; and exile, under the command of his Uncle de Vioménil, in the Russia of Paul the First who had sent them to Siberia,
on the Inchon, to the fortress of Petropavlovak in those endless
steppes across which Tartar hordes used to roam—steppes that reminded him of what the earth must have looked like at the time of
creation. . . .

Suddenly he plunged into that kingdom of feasts and operas, that
Lusitania which thinks itself an empire, where the Portuguese ministers—in the very boxes, in the theatre itself, as La Catalini is singing

Cleopatra—must kneel if they have to speak to the princes and princesses covered with sapphires and diamonds. The chandeliers on the ceilings and the balusters are as numerous as the diamonds on the women's shoulders, and music pervades a life gorged with acts of brigandage, murders, refuse in the dark streets where parties of gentlemen going to gaming houses or wineshops are preceded by torchbearers, and somewhere up there above the enormous, slow-winding Tagus, up above the plain, on the wooded heights where regiments wearing the white cockade pass, Mortemart, Castries, Loyal-Emigrant . . . people dance—their women are beautiful—dance in the village squares; and boys sing deep-throated *modinhas.* And in Lisbon, dead animals—cats, horses, mules—lie in the street, devoured in broad daylight by an army of wild dogs—dogs, thousands of dogs hovering over carcasses covered with flies, thousands of flies . . . oh, the flies, black swarms of buzzing flies surrounding, touching, polluting one! The sweeping gestures the man was making attracted the attention of the dogs, which flung themselves against his legs, snapped at him, tore him to pieces, thousands of dogs. . . .

Victor-Louis de Toustain struggled, pushed the dark away, braced his hands against the dark with an odd feeling of encountering nothing before him—and opened his eyes. What room was this with this unknown bed, this fireplace, this chest of drawers cluttered with knickknacks and doilies, this Saint Joseph on the wall? On a small rug near the bed lay two boots which a while ago he had had to slit right up the back in order to get them off, a disastrous sacrifice, for how now was M. le Marquis de Toustain going to be able to follow in the wake of the great royal collapse?

The whole town of Beauvais was full of dreams, stranded there since the morning and thrown haphazardly into the houses and alleys. Order and discipline were out of the question, since these were not regiments or companies which were arriving, but chance advance remnants of all that was left of the Royal Household. These horsemen of the first escort, the advance guard of all the formations, had exhibited exceptional endurance. Most of them had learned, whether in the armies of the Empire or those of the emigration, to rise above themselves, to endure excessive fatigue, bodily pain, and severe weather. They were arriving, clusters of them, isolated stragglers. No preparations had been made for them, no billets allotted, no quarters provided. Neither in the houses nor in dreams.

In the fading light of March, here were wagons and carriages of every description with gentlemen's valets and the things they had brought from their homes—clothes, works of art, personal arms, cases of miscellaneous objects; and the servants did not know whether or not they had outdistanced their masters, where they were, whether they should go on. How could M. le Comte Étienne de Durfort's coachman find his master in the pit of dreams into which the captain-lieutenant, commander of the Gendarmes of the Guard, had fallen at the house of the Comte de Belderbusch, a former prefect who had more or less ruined himself in the carpet-making business? On arriving in town accompanied by Armand-Céleste de Durfort, his nephew and a lieutenant in his company, Étienne had run into his own son, a second lieutenant in Noailles's Guards. In the general disorder, all three of them collapsing with fatigue, the son had taken his father and his cousin to the householder on whom he had been quartered the previous year when the Prince de Poix's company had been garrisoned at Beauvais. But M. de Belderbusch, nonplused by the arrival of these three Durforts, had been unable, or unwilling, to give them more than the room he usually had available and a dressing room adjoining it. A sofa had been made up in the small room for the captain-lieutenant, while the two cousins shared the bed.

But what was wrong with Céleste? His cousin lying next to him heard him sigh, toss about—which did not prevent him at first from plunging into an oblivion resembling death. But once or twice, through this first sleep, he heard a groan, even a cry. He raised himself, came to the surface for a moment, having forgotten everything—the place, the circumstances, who this man next him was. Then he dropped back exhausted, having grasped at some explanation or other which blended with a dream. And Céleste was left to struggle against the obsessive nightmare that had returned to strangle him a hundred times since December of 1812.

In a kind of closed lean-to backed up against the whitewashed brick walls of a barn, its only outlook—through an opening adorned with icicles—being across a snow-covered court where a *dvornik* was splitting wood, Céleste found himself among a pile of bodies which choked him with a frightful stench of wounds, excrement and blood. The shed was only a few feet square and some hundred prisoners had been thrown into it by the Russians who had retaken Vilna; more than half of them were dead, the others were dying, their feet frozen, suffering from both lack of air and cold, most of them bereft of coats and tunics. They were so tightly packed together that they could feel the hearts of the men next to them beating or giving out; and those who fell were perforce trampled on. They had no reason to hope; several had already gone mad. They had had nothing to eat for more than three days. It was then that he had learned once and for all that man is an animal. And now he was again living through this horror —the close contact with others, their breath, their skin, their hair, the saliva, the urine. . . .

Suddenly, in this Gehenna, at the peak of disgust and suffering, he recognized the body falling on him, threatening to choke him if it did not itself perish. What? Impossible, and yet it was . . . "Olivier!" The other could not turn around, but he felt him trying to make himself smaller, to draw away as far as this revolting proximity allowed. "Olivier!" No answer. He could not be wrong, it was his young friend, his little brother, to whom he had taught swordsmanship and horseback riding when he was a mere child. Olivier.

"Don't you recognize me? I'm Céleste. Are you deaf, are you insensible, Olivier, my Olivier?" And the other replied, "I don't know you, I'm not your Olivier. My name is Simon Richard, Captain Simon Richard." Strange dialogue of hell; was his mind becoming foggy, was it an illusion? But no, he was sure it was Olivier. "My name is Simon Richard."

Even that full beard, even the years that had left their bitter mark on his lip, made those wrinkles on his brow . . . "Olivier! Don't deny your identity! At a moment like this, can you imagine I believe you? There on your bare arm is the scar I gave you playing swords when you were eleven. Here, through your torn shirt, the little red birthmark below the left nipple that identifies you . . . Olivier!" The other looked at him with Olivier's eyes, but with a hostile expression. He could barely move his head to indicate no. The others pressed on them, Céleste's mouth was against his ear: "It's no use lying to me, Olivier, it's no use." Good God! In that hell, that hell— or was he out of his mind? Ten years, it was ten years since he had disappeared, and they had thought him dead. It would have been so natural for him to have been killed somewhere—thrown into a river, like a shirt with the label removed—after that tragedy. "Olivier. It's you, alive!" "My name is Simon Richard." He either could or would say nothing else.

In this atrocious shed in the depths of Russia. Captain Simon Richard. Céleste recalled the entire drama of eleven years before. Olivier had everything a man might dream of: the bearer of one of the greatest names of old France, son of a man who held the office of Emperor's master of ceremonies, rich, overwhelmed with honors, a sub-prefect at twenty-five, then summoned to Court to take an unexpected office, with two children and the most beautiful wife in the world, his cousin, a childhood romance. That had in fact been the misfortune. In that pit of living and dead men at Vilna, Céleste saw the Countess's immense eyes, the velvet of Blanche's eyes. One day an anonymous letter. Olivier learned the truth. Betrayed in that garrison town where Blanche found the life of the subprefecture boring, that handsome, brainless officer, that imbecile Tony de Reiset . . . He might have killed him, killed her. He chose to disappear. Ten years. No one knew where he was. And he was here, they were going to die.

"Olivier, in this final moment, don't lie. Listen: your two children, Olivier. Olivier, I assure you she lives alone, with dignity, in attendance on the Empress Josephine at Malmaison. Alone and unhappy. She loved you . . . your children."

The other paid no heed. He was like a log of dead wood in Céleste's arms. He could not draw away, had no room for a gesture, not even room for hatred. "I am Captain Richard . . . Simon Richard."

Céleste's eyes blurred. The abominable stench. All this was but a bad dream. He could no longer see the man who kept repeating, I am Captain Richard.

At the barracks where his valet asked for him, they could not say whether or not M. le Comte de Durfort was in Beauvais. No one knew where he was, nor that he had just awakened with a start in an unfamiliar room amazed at the noise coming from next door . . . his son, or Céleste? Either way, what a poor sleeper! But what could Céleste be dreaming about? The Prisoner of Vilna was screaming in the dark. "Did you hear that?" Mme. de Belderbusch asked her husband. Vaguely, yes; for he was lying there brooding over the ruin of his business, over the stagnation that gripped the rug industry—forty workers and their families in distress since 1814, the Madeleine abandoned. Those ultraroyalists stampeding through the town were responsible, these people he had had to find beds for. Perhaps, with Napoleon back . . . He was no longer young enough to become a prefect, but business might pick up.

In the attic room above the Durand grocery shop the red eiderdown had slipped to the floor, and it was already dark. Théodore was so completely unconscious that he would never know whether or not this whole long day—between the new sheets Denise had got out

for M. de Prat's bed—was a dream. Coarse, yellow sheets, stiff as
cardboard, not yet made supple by use, by laundering. The big
naked youth pulled the bedclothes up over him and sank into the
hollow that other transients had made in the hard mattress. Was
he dreaming—or not? What did those sudden contractions of the
legs mean, and the way he was turning around? At times the face of
the sleeping man revealed an expression of suffering which perhaps
waking consciousness only masked, which torpor allowed to rise like
a jellyfish in the waters of the sea. What did those closed eyes
see, what were those lips murmuring? Surely those movements
belonged to some invisible landscape, that shoulder was avoiding
a traveler encountered in a forest or on a road, in a prison or a
church. . . . This being locked in a tomb of dreams, this shivering
corpse, when it emerged from the foam of the sheets, when the room
resumed its actuality and its place in a house above a grocery
shop in Beauvais, would be called Théodore, and he would know
that it was he whom that sound designated. But for the moment
neither his name nor any human speech could draw him from that
deep dialogue of the darkness in which something had just made
him tremble. He pressed one leg against the other, his hand sought
refuge beneath the pillow. His mouth was open—perhaps only to
draw air past the swollen tonsils, the panting nostrils. But perhaps
also some Ondine was dragging him to the bottom of a river, or
he wanted to shout before the Moors entered the defile, or he was
calling to the Underworld for some Eurydice of whom only the veil
could be seen fluttering over the marshes.

It was not light enough to distinguish the veins in the arm that
emerged from the bedclothes. He was no figment of the imagination,
no figure from antiquity, but a man of flesh with marks on his skin,
hairy for his age, his chest burned a deep chestnut. His muscles
were contracting spasmodically, not for the moment contributing to
the pattern of a purposeful movement or gesture, but leaping or
relaxing for reasons that would have eluded an onlooker, their
reflex actions linked to invisible things, like fish in a grass-covered
pool suddenly streaking under the young, tired skin beaded with
sweat. Perhaps at this moment he was the Holophernes he wanted
to paint in the net of a Judith of the crossroads, and it was no
longer a tale but some forgotten encounter, and this woman was
not thinking of murder in the hotel room where he had had a
meal served that stood neglected on the tablecloth; but at the last
moment, when she had stripped off everything except her black hair

and her white stockings held up by blue garters, he had suddenly felt incapable of desire for this perfect beauty—perfect, and tedious as perfection. . . . His hand clutched the sheet: he had pulled the tablecloth, and glasses, silver, everything was falling, the red apples rolling, the paleness of the grapes. . . .

At the noise that this made, Théodore suddenly sat upright in the shadow of the bed: and he saw that a kind of light rose fantastically from the floor toward the middle of the room. Where was he? What was the meaning of that subterranean sun? He realized that he must cover himself with the sheet—it had slipped away with the movements of his body—before he understood that it came from the trap door in the floor, which was being pushed up from the lighted grocery shop below by a fair and slender arm. Denise was climbing up the ladder carrying a tray which she deposited on the floor, next to a lighted candle. So that the effect was pitch black with crimson glints, and the central motif at the bottom of the canvas was a simple red-chalk drawing on a pale background.

"Are you awake, Monsieur l'Officier? I have your dinner," said a fresh voice, and the girl loomed up in that strange light which inverted the values and the shadows.

Sitting up, leaning back against the pillow, his knees drawn up, the sheet pulled over him, M. l'Officier watched the miracle happen. He stammered a few words of thanks, and she proceeded to arrange the things on the table. As her back was turned, he quickly smoothed his hair, then plunged his long bare arms back under the covers to encircle his legs.

"I've brought some leek soup for you," said Denise. "I hope you like it—it's what we had this evening. And some veal blanquette— Mama makes very good veal blanquette. You must tell me if you want more bread. And a bit of cheese. It's Picard cheese which the peasants bring in to the market. My poor papa used to think it wonderful, but as far as I'm concerned— Instead of beer I managed to sneak a big glass of Marissel wine for you. Monsieur de Prat was very fond of it. I've done everything the way I did it for Monsieur de Prat."

"And who is Monsieur de Prat?" the Musketeer inquired.

"He was the officer of the Noailles Guards who stayed with us last year, I used to bring him his meals, his breakfast. He was a handsome young man!"

"Ah, ha! A handsome young man! And you used to sit at the

foot of his bed like this, young lady? Monsieur de Prat must have flirted with you a little, didn't he?"

"Oh, no!" Denise said, laughing heartily, not noticing the sarcasm. "After all, last year I was only fifteen!"

"Which means you now are sixteen—and Monsieur de Prat's successors are a little less blind than . . ."

"To begin with, Monsieur de Prat wasn't at all blind. And besides, no one has stayed here since he left."

"In other words, I'm the first to see you as you are now—all grown up."

"Don't talk nonsense! I'm sorry, I shouldn't have said that! But everyone can see me as I am—in the street, at church—"

The light of the candle behind her made her bonnet appear less heavy, especially as the fine blond hairs that refused to stay in place formed a golden haze beneath it. Géricault looked at the child and wondered if she were brazen or naïve. How she was gotten up! It was just like a provincial shopkeeper to dress her that way. What part did religion play in it? But the whole get-up the girl was wearing looked as if it did not hang on her body. What would she look like with all that removed? He remembered the other one, with her blue garters, and felt himself blush. This snip of a miss was not exactly perfect.

"But then what *did* Monsieur de Prat talk to you about when you brought him his breakfast if he didn't flirt with you?"

"About Italy!"

She let this out without thinking, and as Théodore laughed, she lowered her head in confusion. "And about other things, too, of course," she added. Now he could not see her as well, because she was between him and the light, and at moments she was outlined by the contours of her garments, appearing no longer a little girl in disguise but a lady of imposing proportions. Mme. Durand, for example. She would have only had to take snuff to resemble her.

"Indeed," Théodore went on, ignoring the qualification, "Monsieur de Prat talked to you about Italy, did he? This handsome young man talks about Italy to young ladies who sit on his bed— I can just see it! And what did he have to say about Italy? Had Monsieur de Prat ever been to Italy?"

"Why, of course he'd been there!" Denise said heatedly, and she adjusted her fichu about her shoulders. "And how he talked about it. About the sky—and the mountains, the sea. The light especially, he said it's especially the light."

"Especially the light? A lot that helps us! And as far as you yourself are concerned, leaving Monsieur de Prat out of it, what is Italy?"

"Oh, you're making fun of me, Monsieur l'Officier! What do you expect me to say?"

"Not at all, I'm not making fun: I'm asking you what you had heard about Italy before Monsieur de Prat spoke to you about it."

"Your soup will get cold, monsieur, you'd better eat it. Do you want me to bring it to you? Or do you want to get up?"

The big body stirred a little under the sheet which slipped, revealing a bare shoulder. "Oh!" said Denise. "Why, you sleep naked!" And she began to laugh, clapping her hands together.

"You'd better throw me my shirt, there on the low chair, and turn around long enough for me to put it on! That's it. Thank you."

"Can I turn around?" she asked.

"Not yet, my lovely child. Lower your head a little . . . yes. Did anyone ever tell you you have a pretty neck?"

She straightened and pivoted to face Théodore.

"How stupid of you to say things like that! Italy is the land that chimney sweeps and musicians come from. A country full of sunshine, where the nights are all bright—with terraces. I was too little to remember when our soldiers conquered it, and all the women, who are wonderful there, kissed them, and would have nothing more to do with their husbands. And then there is Rome, where our Holy Father the Pope lives." She crossed herself.

"But after all, what *did* Monsieur de Prat say about Italy?"

"The sky, I'm telling you, the sea . . . The women . . . He spoke about the women too sometimes. At least, about one girl. He said she was all sunburned, her skin hot and smooth—like pottery. I don't think that's very pretty myself, for a girl!"

"And what else?"

"The sea, the sky, the mountains . . . First he saw the north of the country, and he thought nothing could be more beautiful. What's that town called? Florence—that's it. He was sorry to leave it for Rome and Naples: there is so much to see in Florence, and in all the other towns of the north. The houses—they're not like ours here, they're beautiful. And then there were the paintings, the statues . . ."

"So?" said Géricault, suddenly becoming interested in this Noailles Guard.

"People had told him that in Rome, in Naples, there was nothing to look at. He had believed it. And then!"

"Yes? What about Rome? And Naples?"

She said nothing more, indeed she seemed to be elsewhere. Perhaps she was still listening to M. de Prat talking about Rome, about Naples. She simply said, "How he talked of them!" and suddenly Théodore became aware that he felt a certain resentment against that talkative young man. Besides, having got comfortably settled, he had eaten his soup, enjoying it.

"The wine," he said. She brought it half guiltily, the glass filled to the brim. The quality of the Marissel wine was indifferent.

"Do you like it?" she asked anxiously.

"Oh course, of course. Give me the blanquette, and let's get back to Italy."

"Forgive me," Denise said, and when she had brought the forgotten knife, went on. "You men, you soldiers, are lucky. You travel. You see countries, cities . . . Me, I'll never go to Italy!"

There was so much despair in these last words that Théodore suddenly abandoned the bantering tone he had maintained until now. He asked her gently, "And would you have liked to go to Italy, mademoiselle?" Perhaps she was weeping. How the devil was a man to tell with that wretched candle?

"You," she said. "You go off! Here today, gone tomorrow. Think, Paris, just Paris—they say it's so beautiful, so big! Shall I ever see Paris? It's too far away."

"Don't be silly! We were there just last night. And by the mail coach—"

"It's eighteen leagues. That costs a lot. And then what would I do there? A girl alone there is lost. I haven't even been to Amiens."

"But then. . . . You don't know anything of the world? Only Beauvais?"

"Oh, no! I've been everywhere around here. I'm a good walker. And even once as far as Saint-Germer. And when my father was alive, he took me to Clermont by carriage. . . . But I would so have liked to go to Italy!"

What was there to say? That the Beauvais sky also had its charm? The blanquette certainly was good. Now the cheese—it ought to be as good as Gorgonzola. Denise had begun to talk as though she were dreaming. And a person who dreams is alone: no need to stop for the other to talk in his turn:

"You're so lucky—I would have liked to be a boy! You haven't been to Italy?—no?—but you'll go, I'm sure you will! People there are different from anywhere else. The carnival in Rome . . . I've asked a thousand questions, I've had a thousand answers: well, I still have no idea what it's like. They talk and talk about it, talk endlessly. Is it like the July celebration, the Jeanne Hachette procession? No more than Beauvais is like Rome, I'm sure. It's funny, there are words that keep coming back in the things they say about Italy, or perhaps it's the verses, the poetry. Monsieur de Prat wrote poems about Italy: *the vine branch . . . marrying the vine to the elm . . .* How did it go?" She tried to remember the verses, tilted her head and recited:

> "Qu'êtes-vous devenus, magnifiques rivages
> Ou la mer de Tyrrhene, a l'abri des orages
> Entoure Naples de ses flots?" *

She fell silent a moment, then went on hurriedly, "He said that in the mountains the shepherds dressed in black velvet with pointed hats—how strange! Sometimes I think about it when there are people in the street playing the violin. Do you like the violin? I could spend my life listening to violins. . . . How stupid of me! I haven't brought you any dessert! What kind of sweet would you like?"

He reassured her. He didn't care much for sweets. The cheese was excellent. And by way of dessert, she spoke so well about Italy: "You're making fun of me!" she said, and immediately resumed her reverie aloud. She was not saying anything, really. Words for her had so much power, such novelty. They sufficed her, without embellishment. When she said *the sea,* for example. She had never seen the sea, she had never been taken to it. But when she said the sea, a host of things were crammed in those two little words, most of them perhaps having nothing in common with the sea that the eye beholds, but which were the sea she saw. And it was the same for almost all words, because her world, the world with which she was familiar, Beauvais, the grocery shop, could be expressed in just a few words, and any further unknown, or simply only half understood, word could start her dreaming, dreaming . . . Géricault suddenly felt very old, very bitter, withered; and he envied the freshness of this child who envied him.

* What has become of your splendid shores
  Where the storm-sheltered Tyrrhenean Sea
  Encircles Naples with its waves?

"What kind of a life do girls have? Everything is settled for them. Nothing can happen. I shall always go from here to there, and no farther. All my life the same things. I'll never go to Italy, I know that perfectly well. Nor anywhere else. Get up every day at the same time, help with the housework, take care of the shop— The people I see, I know beforehand what they're going to say. There is only Saint-Pierre . . . and prayer."

"You're religious?" he asked in spite of himself, with an edge of skepticism in his voice. She did not notice it—she was probably already in the great cathedral with the organs and the incense.

"I don't know why," she murmured, "Monsieur de Prat said that Saint-Pierre was a failure as a church—they had been too ambitious, it dwarfed the town, and then they had stopped halfway. It was never finished. *I* think our cathedral is beautiful—no, beautiful isn't the word. Beautiful is what you say about a woman, about anything. It's better than beautiful, it's . . . I don't know, it's immense. It doesn't weigh on you, it goes upward, and you're there on the prayer-stool, and your thoughts have room. Nothing stops them up there. The tapestries on the wall, the stained-glass windows—have you seen our stained-glass windows? All the colors they have, and it's never the same. At different times of the day the colors dance, they come down to you with the sunlight that filters through, that sundust, and all the dark around, red, blue, orange. I can't understand why they say bad things about Saint-Pierre. There you can believe in the Saints, the Virgin . . ."

"You're a believer?" he asked, and perhaps this time she did notice the irony in his voice. She looked at him in the half-darkness of the alcove. He was not M. de Prat, but he wasn't bad, even though he was redheaded. He had big, gentle eyes. Then she said, "*You* will be God knows where tomorrow. You will see Italy, and more than Italy. Prayer is all we women and girls have to take the place of travels."

All men are alike. Théodore sitting in his bed, the dishes set aside, the shirt about his shoulders open on his hairy chest, a shirt stale from traveling though it had got an airing while he was sleeping. He felt a kind of responsibility toward this little girl who was so unhappy over her fate. Besides, he had forgotten his aches, his limbs felt fit, he had energy to expend, he stretched his legs under the sheet and spread out the toes of his right foot.

"No, little girl," he said, "even if you never go to Italy, there will be something more to life for you than prayer. Everyone won't be so stupid as your Monsieur de Prat. Sooner or later girls meet a man, and *that,* not the *Ave Maria,* is their great journey."

She broke in: "They'll marry me off, and then what? Still the same thing except, if I'm lucky, I'll have my own house."

All kinds of books—the ones he had read in the long summers in the attic of the house of his uncle the regicide in Normandy—returned to Théodore's memory, and he abruptly had the impression that this room, he in his bed, the guileless girl sitting on its edge, all this was like a picture from the previous century in which gallantry was uppermost in people's minds, and he remembered novels that had as heroes corrupters who were later converted to piety by gout and their bald pates. He felt a great physical well-being, and a kind of power long held in leash within his body. But he must not rush things. Pleasure, to be complete, must be savored slowly.

"You'll be married, little girl, you'll be married. That's the thing. Listen, you enjoyed being here, beside Monsieur de Prat, listening to him, didn't you? You enjoyed that. He spoke well, I must say. But he was also a handsome young man?"

"Yes," she said, "there's no denying that!"

"If he had been less handsome, he might still have talked well—and yet he would have talked less well, believe me! When he spoke to you, of course you listened to him, but you used to look at him too?"

"Yes," she said, "it seems to me that did happen."

"Some day, without realizing it, you will completely lose the thread of what a handsome young man is telling you, one who may not be as handsome as Monsieur de Prat . . . more than likely he won't be. But don't let that worry you! Believe me, the most interesting men aren't always the handsomest, or at least not those you think are the handsomest when you're fifteen! Those good looks of Monsieur de Prat were a little too much for a man; they would have been all right for a girl, you understand . . ."

"Do you know him, then?" she exclaimed in surprise.

"No, no, but it's easy to guess from the way you talk about him. You'll meet a young fellow of an altogether different sort, see if you don't. Strong and gentle—that's the important thing. Sometimes ugliness adds to the attraction."

"I can't believe that!" she said.

"You don't have to believe me. You won't see what others find ugly in him, or indifferent, or commonplace. Sometimes even something frightening can be attractive . . ."

"You're joking!"

". . . something a little frightening, not too much. Didn't Monsieur de Prat ever take you in his arms? Oh, don't be frightened, I mean just playfully, in fun? No? Nor anyone? Some day a boy will take you in his arms . . ."

He was talking, lowering his voice a little, saying things he didn't know he knew how to say. The first time . . . the way it comes over you, you don't know exactly why; there you are, you wouldn't break away for anything in the world, and strange ideas come to you. You don't understand why this young man is so slow in what he's doing, why he strokes your hair, his eyes, you would like something else— What? Who knows?

The girl remained sitting, motionless, like a hypnotized bird. She no longer said anything. She was holding her breath. Was it really fear that she felt? The mist of gold under the bonnet, the smoky light of the candle which turned the adorable freshness of the cheek to gold—it was a primitive contrast which spoke more to the senses than to the art of the painter.

Suddenly, bang bang bang. What was that racket coming from below? The spell was completely broken. Someone, below, was knocking on the ceiling. A voice was shouting, "Hey there, you turtledoves, everyone should get his turn! I'm starving down here!"

And Denise leapt to her feet: "*Mon Dieu,* I'd forgotten that gentleman!"

It was the officer who had slept in the storeroom. He had been on the point of intercepting Théodore's dinner as it went by, and had let it get past him only on the promise that he should be served immediately.

No wonder he was impatient!

When he had washed and dressed, and, grimacing over his swollen feet, had again put on the boots Denise had cleaned as she had brushed his clothes, Théodore went downstairs. He wanted to find out where the Musketeers' quarters were and whether they were leaving or what. On his way, he found the Durand ladies busy setting up a kind of cot in the shop by way of a bed for the downstairs guest whom they could not decently allow to sleep again on the cases in the storeroom. They were putting him up right in the grocery shop now. Denise was making up this improvised bed, while her mother, a woman who looked old though she was probably not yet fifty, and whose bony face contrasted strangely with her heavy figure, was making conversation with Arthur d'H—— who had apparently charmed them both by his good humor, and that naughty-boy look he had about him—curly black hair, like little springs, and bubbling with mischief. The Grenadier might have been considered well built had he not been a little too long in the body. But he was so full of life, so ready to laugh, that no one thought of noticing the rather coarse details of his physique. "Ah, me," he said to Géricault after they had introduced themselves to each other. "Tonight I'm sleeping here! Anyone can run after the King who wants to. Go and find out what's happening if you want to, my friend, but I advise you to do the same."

Beauvais by lanternlight was a strange sight to someone who had passed through it only in the morning and on the point of collapsing with fatigue. Going in the opposite direction, Théodore at first lost his way among the narrow streets. There were people everywhere in spite of the weather, which relented only occasionally. All of them—dismounted horsemen, servants, children, shopkeepers, priests, citizens and their wives, peasants, prostitutes, beggars . . . a surprising number of beggars— All of them jostled, talked, hailed one another, in an incomprehensible agitation. In these narrow streets, most of the houses were of wood, or were half-timbered, with gables, painted pictures here and there, niches with saints, poets. By no means all of the streets were paved, and those that were not were nothing but puddles and thick mud. These, though, were preferable to others paved with uneven stones from the river on which the unwary passer-by twisted his ankles, and where he was bound, sooner or later, to put his foot into the central water-filled gutter, which carried away refuse tossed into it and slops that could be seen flying unceremoniously out of the houses. When he at last found his way back to a large square which he recognized, Théodore felt more at ease. Here, surrounded by lopsided shanties, by old, narrow, gabled wooden houses, no two of them alike, by lighted shops which left the center of the square in darkness, stood the large structure he was looking for. Built in the style of the previous century, without any relationship to the medieval scene, it had a great flat frontage of fine stone, with a balustrade on top which caught the last glimmer of daylight, and Greek-style pilasters with capitals adorned with garlands.

There were officers on the steps, messengers alighting from their horses, a coming and going which left no doubt that this was an active headquarters. It was the town hall and here were housed the more or less reconstituted offices of the Royal Household. Théodore made inquiries and learned that M. de Lauriston's Musketeers, those at least who had reached Beauvais, were in barracks to the southwest of the town:

"There, you follow the rue Saint-Jean, or rather, no, so that you won't get lost, turn there, straight ahead. You'll see the theatre. By the way, something you might enjoy there at the theatre tonight . . . let me see. Yes, of course, they're giving *Les Héritiers Michau*. You've seen it already? Too bad! Oh, I agree, it's rather a warmed-over dish, but Mme. Borsary is quite delightful! What was I saying? Yes, you pass the theatre, and go on to the boulevards —where the old ramparts have been torn down to make a promenade. In my opinion it's too bad—monuments of military art—but you know the people around here, they prefer trees along the Thérain. They'll put up benches where you can go and sit with them, smoke a pipe and read the newspaper.

"Anyway, you turn to the left, cross a street, and there are the barracks. You can't miss them. Did you follow me? So, to the left, as you leave the square, a little to one side, the rue du Théâtre on your right, the boulevards to the left, the second block. . . . No, no, it's only natural, Lieutenant."

All this only to be told at the barracks that there would definitely be no movement that evening or during the night, that at best the troops might be mustered and regrouped sometime in the course of the day on Tuesday, that nothing was known as to the time of departure, nor as to destination, but while awaiting orders, the officers billeted in town should assemble at the barracks at six o'clock—that is to say, at sunrise.

Instead of returning by the way he had come, Géricault went round the barracks whose approaches were congested with vans and wagons of every description. Their drivers looked exhausted, the horses pitiful. He wandered through the dark streets at random, and chanced upon a district whose wretchedness was overwhelming. The houses were squalid and dirty, with washing hanging from the few low, narrow windows. Inside, through the open doorways, the ragged inmates could be seen, crowded on top of one another, the children sickly, the women faded before their time. The whole scene wallowed in refuse. An almost intolerable stench hung over the area. These were weavers and drapers, dyers and tanners, leather dressers—the workers, most of them unemployed, who sent their old people, their infirm and their children to stretch out their hands to passers-by in the streets and squares at the center of town. Lights were scarce here. People went to bed early to save oil or candle. Théodore was trying to find his way—the town was not very large, but had been laid out haphazard; and the darkness was complete once he got into the poor streets—when by chance he fell in with a group of Musketeers who had provided themselves with torches and were in search of a wineshop where they could drink. All of them were young and carefree and, overjoyed at having encountered one of their own comrades, they slapped him on the shoulder and would not hear of his not going along with them.

Their carefreeness, it turned out, was wholly show—their remarks made this clear, once they were sitting in front of a drink. Like Géricault, they were broken with fatigue despite whatever naps they had snatched during the afternoon. Their backs were sore, one of them was suffering from boils on his buttocks, another had had to throw away his boots and was wearing slippers. Yet the worst of the matter was not all this, but the uncertainty of the morrow. Were they going to have to ride again, and if so, whither, and for what? Where was the King? Were they being taken to England? Rumor had it that they were going to embark at Calais or Boulogne, were bound for La Vendée, where the Chouans had risen in arms—ah, that was more like it—but it wasn't certain. What kind of deals were going on in Paris? It was said that Macdonald was waging a big battle before Melun. My eye! Macdonald had decamped like the rest of them, if he hadn't gone over to Buonaparte!

Their main worry was the report they had heard here and there that the rebel troops, detachments of which had been met on the roads, had re-formed at Saint-Denis and were setting out in pursuit of them. Or else the Light Infantry of the Guard, Lion's men, those of the Lefebvre-Desnouettes mutiny, were marching to bar their way. Both, perhaps. . . . What resistance could the Royal Household offer, scattered and weary as the men were? How could they fight? They must hope that the others knew nothing of their situation and would concern themselves first with disposing their units in accordance with the rules of strategy, thereby losing a day, a day and a half—the time the Household troops would need to assemble, for their cannon, their supplies to arrive. Because all these young men were at least as much concerned about their baggage as about their own skins. Where were their pursuers? Nobody knew. Perhaps somewhere around Beaumont, or else they were trying to outflank them to the west and cut them off from the sea. It was rumored too that they had outdistanced them, reaching Amiens by way of Creil, to separate the King from his Household troops and link up with the insurgents in the North. In short, no one knew anything, and the best thing was to go and get some sleep while that was possible. Especially as they still . . . But the horses!

These Musketeers had not abandoned their mounts on the road, as had many of the Guards or Grenadiers. But the beasts had reached Beauvais on their knees. The horses must be rested, first of all! And what came after must be left to the grace of God! All afternoon carts, carriages of all sorts, anything that could be found, had been requisitioned or bought to carry the sick, the injured, the wounded. It was said that all the Household's money was going into this, and into supplies of hay that were to be taken along, no one knowing what lay ahead. Whole garrisons, it was said, had gone over to the other side and were burning the hay so that the royal troops would find none when they turned up. And what about their pay? They hadn't reached that point yet; each of them had his small portion of treasure, and they'd live off the country long enough to join up with the Russians and the Prussians who were in Belgium. . . .

This suddenly put Théodore into a cold sweat: the Prussians, the Prussians—he had forgotten them. And also his horse, poor Trick, left with the postmaster in the Picardy suburb. He would go and pay Trick a visit. He tossed his share of the reckoning on the table, and took leave of the Musketeers.

"It is the total irresponsibility of the nobility, in particular its neglect of the estimable prejudices of the days of chivalry, which has caused it to lose its dignity and standing, and led to the frightful misfortunes it has been our lot to witness. The false grandeur of the eighteenth century. . . ."

The smell of smoke blended with a kind of perfume with which the Duke periodically drenched himself. It was the only luxury Emmanuel de Richelieu permitted himself, save for the gloves which were a mania with him, and which he had made to measure. During the hours they had been chatting together, Marmont had watched him with amusement as from time to time he reached for a big flask and poured some of its contents on his hands, his hair—at times opening his shirt and rubbing his chest with it, moistening his armpits, a scented toilet water with which he had loaded his saddlebows on setting out, as another might have done with rum.

"We have lost," Richelieu was saying, "that simplicity of manner our ancestors possessed. A perverse philosophy has turned the very persons who should have been the guardians of religion away from it. The only way to bring a misguided people back to its ancient virtues is to restore the Faith, and its ministers, to a splendor and majesty that must compel respect. But what laws, no matter how wise or severe, could guarantee us against a return of these deplorable ways, unless the nobility sets an example by its zeal and its morality? I hear distinguished gentlemen accuse the common people—a rabble, it's true, whose uprising was made possible by the license that prevailed—of all the crimes of this abominable revolution. But don't they realize that those who meant to undermine royalty had no scruples at first about spreading among the ignorant, among the dregs of the big cities, these philosophic principles which caused the downfall of the monarchy? The nobility had to be assailed first and was, in fact, assailed first. It was the nobility, neglecting purity of religion, which left its lands, came to Court to lead that life of depravity preached by the new philosophy, and thus, by the spectacle of its own corruption, prepared the days to which our youth was the appalled but impotent witness."

This abstract style came quite natural to the Duke. It was not his usual style, but when the conversation took on a certain breadth, and especially when the governor of New Russia—normally deprived in his provinces of anyone to whom he could talk who appreciated the beauties of the French language, or forced there to use Russian, which he was far from being able to handle with the same ease—found himself with a compatriot who was more curious to listen to a man of singular reputation and experience than eager to expound his personal views: then M. de Richelieu was more than inclined to let himself be borne along by language which in its rhythm was closer to the written than the spoken word. This, the language he used in his reports to his august master, had done a good deal to enhance his prestige with the Emperor Alexander. He had acquired this faculty for noble expression from his preceptor M. l'Abbé Labdan, a great admirer of Fénelon, whom that worthy ecclesiastic considered to be the necessary antidote to the prose of Jean-Jacques Rousseau, a prose whose very beauty seemed to him to have a corrupting influence.

And so it had become the usual thing to compare the work of the Duc de Richelieu on the banks of the Black Sea to the kingdom of Idoménée, as it is pictured in *Télémaque*. Marmont had often heard this special eloquence praised. Yet he could not help detecting in it something stiff and formal which perhaps marked the distance between the life that he himself had led—the problems he had had to resolve, always without time for reflection, in Spain, and even in Illyria where he had fleetingly assumed functions rather similar to those of Emmanuel de Richelieu in New Russia, and since then even more so on the battlefields of Europe, in the race of the armies, in the wake of an insatiable Emperor—between his life and Richelieu's proconsular existence on the borders of Islam and of Asia, where both time and his powers were limitless, where he was the absolute master of an immense land, an arbiter among hostile and primitive peoples, having to account for his acts and deeds only to a distant sovereign whose confidence he enjoyed, devoting himself to building, and not to leaving behind him a trail of death and destruction wherever he went. . . .

Marmont, following the Duke's speech even though absorbed in his own thoughts, smiled to himself: his thoughts had unconsciously taken on the rhythm and the manner imposed upon them by the other's speech, the balanced cadence of his sentences. The Marshal was quite aware of his tendency to succumb to influences. Perhaps he had never felt it so markedly as with Bonaparte, and this above all was what he could not forgive his former master. Yet, although it always vexed him to recognize, as at present with Richelieu, this kind of intellectual dependence, it was by this very fact that he gauged the prestige, the force of the other's personality, so different from what he had known in the King's entourage. And even in the Emperor's. . . .

The word *Emperor* had intruded itself quite naturally in the sequence of his thoughts, but suddenly he became aware of it, and it unnerved him.

Richelieu had reached the point where he was expounding with considerable vigor and a kind of recrudescence of passion the almost wholly perfidious role that scholars and scientists of the third estate—whom he considered the nobility's cruelest enemies—had played in relation to the nobility, when the servants came in bringing the light meal the Duke had asked to have served in his room. He was frugal in his eating habits, and of this Marmont wholly approved. He, too, was not well suited to the abundant meals of the Tuileries and the gluttony of the Bourbons. Moreover, since the Duchesse de Massa had left the prefecture, politeness did not require them to appear for a formal meal. As for Marmont, he had received a report from the Beauvais military headquarters about the contingents which had already arrived there, and he could wait till the morning muster to gauge how long it would take to assemble the Royal Household and then set the time for departure.

They had talked all day, and none of the subjects they had discussed had been exhausted or even thoroughly explored. At this precarious moment of history, when the very cause that brought them together seemed to offer no future for either of them even though they went out of their way to affirm the contrary, these two men felt themselves circling in a dark realm in which—who knows? —a word might suddenly reveal an unforeseen path. Richelieu, assuredly, spoke only for himself, and he expected nothing from the Marshal except perhaps the stimulus of a presence that can lead a man to say what he might not hit upon alone.

Marmont, for his part, was looking to this tall, lean man with the swarthy complexion to shed some kind of light that would make life tolerable for him. Because, deep down, he did not find it tolerable today. Perhaps he had only appeared to take the step that had separated him from his past: he was still the slave of all kinds of ideas—ideas which had been current in the world in which he had lived since he had reached manhood. He found himself both shocked by certain affirmations of the Duke's, and at the same time already gauging the distance he would have to negotiate in order to concur in those ideas, the ideas of the world he had chosen. As for example, when Richelieu held education to be responsible for the misfortunes of the country and condemned what Marmont had always heard spoken of as *the enlightenment*.

"The Third Estate's baseness in the revolution," Richelieu was saying, and he looked before him as though this third estate were there in its entirety before a tribunal, and he the prosecutor at its trial. "The Third Estate's baseness has sufficiently demonstrated that it was madness to allow it access both to riches and to knowledge, since it could make use of them only to subvert the State. The third order must be kept in blessed ignorance, its ambitions must be confined to achieving an honest well-being so that it will not make too great demands upon the nobility and take advantage of it by its skill in affairs, or its knowledge. We must have done with this false religion of progress. . . ."

As he listened, Marmont accepted this point of view, wanted to share it. He saw clearly that, through failure to accept it, the destiny he had traced out for himself led down a blind alley. But at the same time deep within himself he felt a resistance, perhaps out of pure habit, set up by all those prejudices he had acquired without ever having examined them, simply because he had bathed in them as in the open air, and seeing them suddenly so formally denied . . .

"I should like to add, Monsieur le Maréchal," Richelieu continued, putting perfume behind his ears and on the nape of his neck, "that one of the great faults of the monarchy has been to permit, and at times even to encourage, the nobility to indulge in the promiscuity of the third order. Or worse. . . . Excuse me—one should never introduce personal considerations into the discussion of ideas, but in what I am about to say I should be unable to prevent your establishing a link between my words and your life, which is not the main point, believe me."

What in the world was he driving at? Marmont felt a shiver run through him. He did not care to have any allusion made to what had been haunting him lately.

"But you have suffered enough, I know, in your private life from an order of relationships which had become natural: and even King Louis XVI had preceded Buonaparte along this path, by authorizing, if not advising, misalliances. . . ."

Ah, it was only that—Marmont breathed more freely. If it was only a quesiton of Mlle. Perregaux!

"A monarch governs by the very weight he gives to prejudices; and what prejudice is more indispensable than that of birth to maintain the nobility in its rank, and the third estate in a condition of respectful modesty in which it does not dream of aspiring to equal those whom their proved ancestry makes unequal at least in that? It is the unrestrained accumulation of wealth by the people, who obtain an advantage over the nobility through trade, and the lucrative posts that the State distributes without regard to birth, on the pretext of remunerating talent, which have given rise to this perverse ambition whose effects we are now witnessing. The imprudent freedom to accumulate wealth has almost irresistibly brought with it those lamentable alliances between impoverished nobles and the ambitious middle-class. I am not unaware of the tragedies to which these ways have led, and you understand me, I know. . . ."

So, it was not only the Duchesse de Raguse. At the time of his marriage, Marmont had had to obtain forgiveness for his aristocratic origins rather than to claim them. His father before him, for that matter, had taken a young lady from the world of finance to wife. And the daughter of Perregaux the banker had married one of Bonaparte's generals, not the provincial petty nobleman whose coat-of-arms was worth no more than an *assignat*.* Today, on the contrary, the Duc de Richelieu was speaking to a man of his own caste whose youthful errors he charitably overlooked. After all, there had been adventurers in the camp of the Princes; adventurers who today were in the service of some king or other, like that Nassau who had been in command at Ismaila when Richelieu distinguished himself; that lover of Catherine the Second's, who had been a Spanish general and a German colonel before becoming a Russian admiral and a Polish prince, the son of a Frenchwoman and a Dutchman— He had even been in the service of France. How could Richelieu, who had spent his life in the Russian army, fail to understand those other adventurers who had placed their swords at the service of the Republic and the Empire, but after all of France? How could he fail to understand the *chivalrous* appeal which noble youth, cut off from its elders and from a fleeing monarch, could find in a military career that opened so readily before it in armies in which a man could become a general before the age of thirty?

"I do not blame anyone," the Duke was saying, "for having or for not having emigrated. I myself left France with the consent of the King and the Constituent Assembly—though neither, to be sure, proved grateful, since I thereby lost my ancestral possessions, and even the return of the Bourbons has not changed this. Louis XVIII has not given me back one square inch of land, and the statues, my pictures, my family's collections, are in the Louvre by the law of the Usurper, and remain there by that of the new monarchy. Were it not for the poverty in which my sisters de Jumilhac and de Montcalm must live, I should have no shadow of regret. One is bound to consider a certain number of facts as established if one wishes to see domestic peace maintained under the intelligent power of the King. I ask for nothing, and I can go on living on the pittance that comes to me from Odessa. And if France must undergo another period of infamies, I can always return to the service of the Emperor Alexander.

* Form of paper money issued in 1790 by the Constituent Assembly against the security of lands forfeited to the State. By 1796 they had become virtually valueless.

"All this is simply to tell you that I do not share the judgment of too many members of the nobility who dream only of revenge, and who after all bear their share of responsibility in the treasons of a Ney, however worthless he may be. You have seen how the Princesse de la Moskowa was treated at the Tuileries? Don't you think such a title must gall the lips of a man who has served the Russian dynasty as I have? Yet if we had played a little less at humiliating Mme. Ney, at reducing her to tears on her return from the receptions at the Palace, perhaps her husband would have behaved differently now. You will find these words and those I spoke a few moments ago rather contradictory: it is one thing to safeguard the future of the nobility by reforming its ways, and quite another to abstain from a blind severity regarding mistakes committed in the past— A severity which could only have the effect of consolidating alliances which are contrary to the Monarchy's interests. The nobility is like Buridan's ass: unable to decide between the mown hay offered it, and the limpid water that does not fatten it. Yet why does it not look to building its own fortune? This would spare it from bastardizing itself. Note that I don't consider this leveling down to be the worst thing. There is a good deal of stupidity in those I was speaking of a moment ago who think they can make everything good by regilding their escutcheon, and saying *I won't get my hands dirty!* Take for example one of His Majesty's companions on the road ahead of us. I meant M. le Duc d'Havret, whom I have known since childhood. He's an excellent man—who can deny it? But look what his father was—the Marshal, whose name, like mine, was Emmanuel. Ah, there was a *grand seigneur!* The Croy d'Havrets are people of the north, and the Marshal, who was a prince of the Holy Roman Empire and served in Bohemia and Bavaria, was one of the victors of Fontenoy, and set up the defense of Boulogne, Dunkirk, in fact the entire coast. . . .

"But it is neither this, nor the part he played in the sieges of Antwerp and Maastricht, nor his heroism at Ramillies and Lawfeld that I regard as his true claim to greatness. Do you know that it is because of him that the Anzin Company, despite prejudices, timidities, and red tape, has been set up on the Scarpe and the Escaut, and that this company has brought into being the treasure of coal by virtue of which France can feel itself independent of Hainaut, whence it had formerly to import its fuel? Four thousand workers, six hundred horses, thirty-seven mine shafts, twelve fire pumps—more than one hundred thousand pounds every year to the sick, the widows and orphans. All this area was vegetating in middle-class hands until Emmanuel de Croy, with his feudal rights over the lands of Condé and Bruay, brought into operation a new form of association, from which he generously did not exclude people of the third estate—the joint-stock company of which he was the director. Thus was the old seigniorial property transformed, while the initiative of the third estate was limited. In 1794 I saw the Marshal's work with my own eyes; it was during that unsuccessful campaign of the Austrian army, which it was my fortune to follow, at the sieges of Dunkirk, Valenciennes, Condé. I had never visited any mines; it was hard for me to imagine what was implied in the way of investments, the machines, the perpetual accidents. We camped in the very place where that other battle was being waged, because the working of mines is also a war. In the Allied camp there were people who wanted to destroy those installations, con-nected as they were with the operators of the Charleroi mines. The republicans' return prevented this, which was of course fortunate for the French economy. I don't know whether a statue will be erected someday to Emmanuel de Croy for his industrial intelligence as well as for his boldness in maintaining the position of the nobility.

"But look at his son. He is a prime example of the aristocracy that has left its province for Versailles. He was about thirty years old when the Marshal died. He had not been involved in his father's affairs; he was a colonel in that Flanders regiment the Revolution was to hand over to Macdonald. He represented the nobles of Amiens at the States-General, went to Coblenz, and was sent to Madrid by the Princes as ambassador of a government in exile. I shall not reproach him for having attempted to have his name struck off the list of *émigrés*; I have done as much myself. For other reasons, to be sure—my sisters . . . But imagine his having been willing to accept a small income at the beginning of the Empire, by way of compensation for Emmanuel's whole vast creation! That's the extent of his ambition. The mines passed entirely into middle-class hands, and the infinitely shrewder Cambacérès, together with Perier, a Grenoble banker, replaced the Croy d'Havrets. Thus the nobility defaults, through failure to understand the new world and how it could reign. That is what our poor King is carrying along with him in his carriages: so you understand why rather than gamble on this, I place my hope in the armies of Russia or of Prussia."

Marmont could not refrain from thinking that the mineowners of

Hainaut might perhaps still have friends in those armies, to the detriment of Marshal de Croy's work. But was it not necessary to choose between the foreigner and Napoleon, who would work on the common people, the half-pay soldiers, and would reopen the era of proscriptions, of firing squads in the ditches of Vincennes? He shuddered at the thought, and the mines of Anzin ceased to weigh in his scale. Besides, Alexander was generous, and Richelieu had his ear. Perhaps that young Stempkovski, whom the Duke had dispatched ahead, was already carrying an appeal to the Emperor of Russia for aid to the Bourbons. There was no need to choose; the choice had already been made. And Marmont looked at Richelieu.

In this candlelit Gothic chamber in Beauvais on a rainy evening, it was funny to imagine the sun, the dust and the winds of the Black Sea—that heartbreaking district capital which had grown up around the fortress of Hadji-Bey, and which had existed for just twenty years, where Richelieu had had streets laid out, trees planted, a theatre built. And in that jumble of Germans and Tartars, Circassian prisoners, Russian landowners moving from the interior with their flocks of serfs, attracted by the right to distill and the freedom to sell alcohol—a right of which the Czar's administrators were constantly seeking to deprive them—and by the profits to be derived from goods in transit on which Richelieu strove to prevent the central power from imposing a duty which he had gone to infinite pains to have exempted—in that world, threatened by incursions of the Caucasian princes, Turkish invasions, the *feljäger* bearing catastrophic imperial ukases, the rivalries of the governors, plague and merchants' intrigues, it seemed that Richelieu, drenched with perfume, neglecting his own comfort, his curly hair turning white too young, had had no other idea than to build and create gardens. He mixed stories of cruel war, of towns set aflame, of rape and pillage, with a sort of spectacular opera composed wholly of brilliant balls, masquerades, and country excursions; and his lyrical flights reached their peak when he spoke of the villa that had sprung from the desert at the touch of his magic wand, a villa with acacias, elms and Italian poplars nestling among gently sloping hills which yesterday had been nothing but sand, where a kind of temple with columns and a thatched cottage, replica of the one in the Petit Trianon gardens, were lost to sight among shady paths that climbed the hill capriciously.

This villa he had at first bequeathed to young Rochechouart, but since Léon had returned to France and had, somewhat abruptly, left the service of the Emperor of Russia, the Duke had decided to leave it to his aide-de-camp, Ivan Alexandrovich Stempkovski, nephew of Cobley, the English general who commanded the troops at Odessa. All of which was further enlivened by anecdotes about a journey taken by Mme. Narichkin, Alexander's inamorata, and the parties given in her honor; by a description of the plague of 1812, of shattering scenes in a village where they had had to burn the sick in their houses without having made sure they were dead. In short, the listener was struck alternately by a kind of levity in the relating of stories full of human drama, and by something suddenly revealed in a casual phrase; and he discovered that this seemingly futile personage was endowed with a breadth of vision, a kind of administrative genius, an unexpected spirit of abnegation. A human heart, in a word, beat beneath the courtly dress.

"All this," Richelieu went on, "is unfortunately at the mercy of an imperial misunderstanding, of a favorite in Petersburg. The Emperor is a man of superior intelligence, but his vigilance can be circumvented. What misunderstandings the outbursts of a Prince Peter Dolgoruki, for example, have created between him and his most faithful servants! And then, too, the machinery of the Russian state is vast and ponderous, it is impossible to imagine to what extent the very people who operate it can find themselves powerless before it. If I were to tell you—"

An aide-de-camp brought in some papers for the Marshal to sign.

The Duke had narrowed his nearsighted eyes: as he did not see well in the semidarkness, he thought he recognized Fabvier and said, "Good evening, Colonel, did you have a rest?" To relieve his officer's embarrassment, Marmont quickly explained: this was not Fabvier but a very young ensign. Richelieu apologized, saying that there was no harm done, because Colonel Fabvier was a fine fellow for whom he would not mind being mistaken by the ladies . . . and one or two remarks about this lad, so well developed for his age, as though he had been speaking about a horse in its presence. The blushing ensign murmured something as he pushed papers in front of the Marshal. While Marmont was studying them, Richelieu began to laugh softly.

"You see," he said, "how official papers and red tape never fail to claim their due. You have an army of barely three thousand men, scattered over ten leagues, who have dropped with fatigue wherever they happened to be—and you still have to countersign the certificate of flight and disorder."

And when they were alone he asked, "Was it like that too in the army of . . ." He found it awkward, with Marmont, to use the words he ordinarily used, but the Marshal understood him and nodded his head.

"It was the same. You must know that, Monseigneur, you who have exercised command. War is office work first and foremost—and blood is no sparer of ink. I remember at Salamanca . . ."

He told his story, and it was a curious one, but he realized that Richelieu was not listening to him. Where had his thoughts strayed? The silence that prevailed for a moment after Marmont had come to the end of the anecdote—a surprising silence after this long gossip—shed no light on the abrupt reverie into which the former governor of Odessa had sunk. The Marshal respected it, until the other, again seizing the flask on the table, once more poured some scented water on his hands.

"I believe," Marmont said, "that I interrupted you with my Spanish recollections. What were you saying?"

Richelieu trembled, like someone surprised in his sleep, and looked about him. "I was saying—" Then suddenly he went on in a vein that bore no relation to his last words:

"It is time, high time, to have done with the spirit of adventure. To have done with adventure. Order . . . order is what France needs. Let the Murats return to their stables! And those of us who roamed the world from Gibraltar to Samarkand in search of an excitement that turned us away from common problems, bent on a purely personal lark, must return to the abandoned road, to the path of honor. . . . It is time . . ."

He spoke almost in a whisper, as if to himself. Suddenly he raised his voice, and as though he had only just begun to talk to Marmont, he added, "What were you telling me, Monsieur le Maréchal? You have a property at Châtillon, and you have been thinking about developing it with a view to launching a new industry. . . . That is very interesting: tell me about it."

The relations between the nobility and the Third Estate are not always those that M. le Duc de Richelieu had in mind when speaking of their dangers. If Théodore, whose passion for horses detained him in the stable to ensure that everything had been done for his Trick, had returned to his quarters a little sooner, he could have convinced himself of this with his own eyes. And the author will surely be reproached for not having hastened Géricault's return to the Durand grocery shop—even at the expense of this young man's character and his solicitude for his horse—in order that, on opening the shop door, he might have witnessed a spectacle which is described in detail in all contemporary novels. But the author, it must be said, feels an aversion to doing so; and while it is much more difficult, in the middle of the twentieth century, to describe a city destroyed by war than a La Rochejacquelein Grenadier raping a sixteen-year-old girl in a grocery shop on the improvised bed that a blind mother herself had helped make up for him, or on the floor where, as the child struggled, they both rolled—because this has not greatly changed in one hundred and forty-odd years—well, no! even though the novel should lose its unity of mood, seem to interrupt its progress, and remain incomplete at this point, the reader is not going to be able to mark the work here by turning down the corner of the page to pass it on to a lady of his acquaintance so that she can immediately find the passage for which it is worth skipping everything that goes before, and perhaps all that follows too. The conversation between Denise and Théodore has been sufficient to suggest the effect the Musketeer's words might have had in that ingenuous head and the sequence of thoughts that had led up to the apparent triumph of Arthur d'H——, to whom Théodore had given no thought. Poor Denise! She wanted to go on a long journey and the overnight guest in the grocery shop both attracted and terrified her. It is true that she might have blamed Théodore for having aroused her curiosity as to that unknown and wonderful pleasure of which he had spoken, that other kind of Italy. But such was her youth, and such her education, that she did not know that a man does not content himself with taking a girl like her in his arms. That is all.

And now she had gone off in the rain and the night, crazed—where was she going?—not daring to appear before her mother. An author with a better sense of drama would have seen to it that Théodore, on returning, should meet her either at a street corner or as she came out of the grocery shop. But life arranges things otherwise, and besides, even if their paths had crossed, the darkness would have prevented them from recognizing each other. In Beauvais there was no municipal lighting to help. What was to become of Denise does not belong to this story. Suffice it to say that by morning she had not come home. Had she thrown herself into the Thérain? The river is too shallow and inconvenient for despair; and desperate young girls were not allowed up the towers of Saint-Pierre at night. Melodrama must therefore be ruled out.

When Théodore passed through the grocery shop, he did not even notice the prevailing disorder, since there was no light. He climbed the ladder to his attic with the least possible noise, so as not to waken the Grenadier, who had fallen fast asleep on his cot with a sense of duty accomplished. Théodore would never know anything of what had happened, since at dawn he would pass through the already empty shop to report for the Musketeers' roll call at barracks. He had no wish to awaken his hosts, and Arthur d'H——, who had risen earlier, had had even less wish to do so.

The reader here might be surprised at the fact that the author, who has not hesitated to give historic names to the characters in his novel, should limit himself to referring to this episodic character by an initial, and he is entitled to some explanation on the subject. Arthur or otherwise, M. d'H—— will remain M. d'H——, even though his name, rather obscure at the time, could have been written out in full: but the fact is that the family—his offspring, and those of his brothers and several cousins—has proliferated, and while the author is under no obligation to take its numerous present-day representatives into account, he has nevertheless thought of them. As a matter of fact, M. d'H—— hardly belongs in this novel, through which he passes merely to do a wrong. But perhaps a few words about his family's history may not be out of place here, precisely because it is totally outside this story.

The family of H—— (I have changed the initial) belongs to the petty nobility but is of ancient lineage. A marriage linked it under Louis XV to a gentleman of the Chamber, another under Louis XVI to a tax official. The father of our second lieutenant retired to his property in Normandy during the Terror, and his son, born in 1790, was at the moment when we meet him about the same age as Théodore Géricault. He had served the Empire, and one of his brothers had married the daughter of a great banker. As for him, he received his baptism of fire before Leipzig in 1813, and in 1814 he quite naturally passed over to the Bourbons, at the same time as the general under whom he was serving, M. de Beurnonville, who was an old friend of his father's and had known him as a child when he lived in the château of H—— in 1797 as inspector of the armies of the coast. Having joined the La Rochejaquelein Grenadiers under the first Restoration, he was, after the break-up of the Royal

Household, among those who took service in Bonaparte's army during the Hundred Days. He was quickly pardoned for this, and from 1816 served in the Royal army, was married very decently to the daughter of a man who had been an army contractor during the war in Spain, and became a marquis under Charles X.

However, during the events of 1830, he remembered in time that his former chief, Marshal de Beurnonville, at the end of the Empire had made him enter the Grand Lodge—that of both the Marshal and of Macdonald, as well as of Joséphine de Beauharnais. And of Fouché. He can in fact be recognized in the painting at Versailles representing the welcome given to Louis-Philippe d'Orléans by Alexandre de Laborde, and several other insurgents of 1830, before the town hall of Paris. A deputy of the moderates for Seine-Inférieure during the July Monarchy, the Marquis d'H—— commanded one of the sections of the National Guard that helped General de Cavaignac to repress the insurrection of June 1848, and the Empire made him a senator. He welcomed the Prussians marching on Rouen to his château (he was then eighty years old), reminding them with considerable dignity of the excellent relations which his family had enjoyed with their predecessors of 1814, and asking them for news of his cousin, the Duchesse de M——, lady-in-waiting to Queen Augusta, from whom he had been cut off since the beginning of hostilities.

He passed away under the presidency of Jules Grévy, fortified by the rites of the Church. He was ninety-four years old. As we see, the life of Arthur d'H—— was one of those long lives without major incidents, which can be quickly told and in which the events are those of contemporary history rather than of the personage. Arthur no longer belongs to the period of noble adventurers, he is the link between the old aristocracy and the new which, without wholly conforming to the views of Emmanuel de Richelieu in the matter of alliances, seems nevertheless in the end to have understood what constituted the practical basis of the founder of Odessa's thinking as to the necessity for its members not to abandon the modern sources of wealth to others. Thus it is that social transformations work themselves out somewhat differently from what is initially imagined by the great prophetic spirits who see them always in a somewhat Utopian light, to which reality gives a correcting touch.

The family of H—— has in fact grown considerably, has extended the network of its alliances, so that in our day it has representatives both in the army of the Republic and in nearly all the country's major industries. There are H——s who have recently had to leave Morocco where they had settled, others who have emigrated to the United States as a result of deplorable events that have again divided those people of France who enjoy a certain standing. But on the whole, the family flourishes, especially because, in accordance with the tradition that it has observed since the eighteenth century and which our marquis had been careful not to allow to die out, reasonable marriages have enabled it at all periods to correct political disasters and the vicissitudes of fortune. The H——s, it must be said, were perfectly cut out for this, and almost all of them have kept the physique of that full-blooded second lieutenant—somewhat short perhaps, but robustly healthy—whom we met in Beauvais one March evening in 1815. They have good teeth, stiff, curly hair, a predilection for horseback riding and all violent sports, they can be recognized in miniatures, daguerreotypes and recent photographs, possessing characteristics which would make it possible to establish their pedigree without official papers. I speak of them as of a family of dogs, but there is something of this about them, and it makes them good sons-in-law for big industrialists and international financiers.

There are H——s in the Jockey Club, at the Pomme-de-Terre, and one of them, although he has written nothing, has even been elected to the Académie Française.

It is only in recent times that a certain degeneracy has appeared here and there. In particular when, at the beginning of the twentieth century, a marquis whose mother, it must be said, was half Jewish, had the romantic idea of marrying a little above what was reasonable and ran off with a young person allied to a reigning family who had but little means. This undoubtedly explains what became of their son. For if in specialized works the names of several H——s are to be found marked with the symbol that means *fallen on the field of honor* —some in the Free French Forces, others in the anti-Bolshevik Legion—there is for this son, who did not serve in the army, only the simple mention that he died in the Dachau concentration camp in Germany. The family is no prouder of him than of Ulbricht d'H——, who put himself a little too much forward during the same period and had to expatriate himself to Argentina, where he is a banker.

Well, had I given the La Rochejaquelein Grenadier his name, I should have been afraid that the members of this great family, several of whom are permanently in the councils of our variable governments, in diplomacy, and in the steel and chemical industries, might be pained to see one of their ancestors or of their uncles (for there is still a nephew of Arthur's, a M. d'H———, whom I met during the war in Flanders, when he had gone back into the service at sixty-five and was then councilor of the French state and for some reason or other condemned to national indignity, and who therefore is today seventy-eight or nine, and was as a child dandled on the knees of the old Marquis)—to see one of their ancestors, as I was saying, in a somewhat unflattering posture from the point of view of morality in action; and they might on this account forbid their spouses, sisters, daughters and nieces to read this novel which, considering their great number, would reduce its circulation dangerously. But I should have been even more afraid that this memory, which can be judged in various lights, might on the contrary be for several of them the source of a virile pride that I should have deplored, and which, all things considered, it would have been painful to me to encourage, with reference to the physical qualities and the energy of their lineage. If the incident of March 20, 1815, on the Grande-Rue Saint-Martin in Beauvais is not featured in the family archives, I am not going to be the one to introduce it.

For this reason I have limited myself to a letter for the name, and to a wholly panoramic view of the story of the Grenadier and his family: the entire affair thus remains in such a state of uncertainty and generality that too many of our contemporaries might recognize their own family therein and derive vanity therefrom to enable a single one to be altogether sure that his is really the one involved, or to find therein a hereditary justification for his own excesses.

For man is not an animal.

VIII

Spring

NO ONE had had much sleep at the prefecture. Between eleven o'clock and midnight Macdonald had brought his daughter home, and from him Marmont had obtained confirmation of the army's treason. Before the Maréchal-Duc de Tarente could set off again toward Abbeville, where he expected to join His Majesty, fresh news from the capital had reached Beauvais with an aide-de-camp of General Grundler's, the former commander of the Seine, whom Clarke had taken with him as secretary-general to the War Ministry when he had replaced Soult. Throughout the day Paris had witnessed unbelievable things, defections, the tricolor everywhere, and Napoleon was expected from one moment to the next. In a letter which the aide-de-camp brought to Macdonald, Grundler complained of being without news of his minister. His chief no longer appeared at the ministry, he had sent an officer to the rue Royale, to Clarke's residence. No Clarke. What did that mean? Clarke, who had been preferred to Soult as being more reliable— Had he gone over to the other side? No, he was simply nowhere to be found . . . vanished. Grundler's aide-de-camp had met the Law School volunteers on the road; these poor youngsters looked exhausted, and their officers did not conceal their fears: the thing was that they were marching surrounded by rebel troops, which they had just barely avoided in Saint-Denis. The behavior of the Bonapartists, for that matter, was rather peculiar. For the moment, they hardly seemed to

229

want to clash with the loyal troops that were leaving the capital. Grundler was asking for orders. Yes, and by the time he received them, what would he do with them?

And then, about four in the morning, the sub-prefect had been awakened. It was General Hulot who had arrived with Macdonald's carriage, which had been repaired, bearing the news brought to Beaumont by Bonaparte's agents. Massa had hastily led him to Marmont, to whom he gave a succinct account of the entry into the Tuileries. The Emperor had taken up residence in the Louvre again at about nine in the evening. The mailbag was full of heartbreaking news.

All night it had blown great guns. The wind swept down the chimneys and sheets of rain beat against the shutters. Tragic weather. At moments it was like vans thundering on the cobblestones, then the voice would swell and swell, like nature's protest against what was happening. Sleep . . . how could anyone sleep in such a din? Each sudden lull in the wind created an even more unnerving silence during which a man waited for the return of the tornadoes. But such silences were never of long duration.

At last dawn paled in the windows. In the low mists spring was beginning in Beauvais. Patrols could be heard in the street, voices with the strangeness that they assume at this hour of solitude.

The wind had dropped. It was no longer raining. Rays of sunlight timidly pierced the clouds.

Already dispatch riders were bringing orders. The Guard, relieved at the gates of the barracks and the buildings given over to the Royal Household, was passing through the town. The workers at the factories which began their day at six o'clock—not one minute of daylight must be lost of the days which lasted only twelve hours at this season—looked at the soldiers washing at the fountains in the wind and shrugged their shoulders. What were all those people thinking? Hard to imagine.

And shortly after six o'clock the Princes, having left Noailles before daylight, descended like a whirlwind on the prefecture, with the vanguard of their troops, Damas's Light Horse, under the command of César de Chastellux, and Grammont's Lifeguards, under the command of Tony de Reiset. At the improvised war council, the situation of the troops in Beauvais as set forth by Marshal Marmont had flabbergasted the Comte d'Artois; and despite the illusions to which the Duc de Berry was still clinging, Monsieur, who knew perfectly well how long it would take for the train they still had behind them to assemble, and the state the soldiers were in, could not conceal his consternation. Where was the King? Had he changed plans? Was he going to Dieppe to board ship? Entrench himself in Dunkirk? Or was Lille still his objective? Who could say? If they could only join him, by cutting across through Amiens so as to spare the men unnecessary fatigue—but was the road to Amiens free? What was the real state of mind of the Picardy troops? They decided to send a a scout in that direction, and M. de Reiset was assigned to pick an intelligent Lifeguard—there must be such a one—who would be able to get back in the course of the day to make his report. How far was it from Beauvais to Amiens? Fifteen leagues. With a good horse, it was possible to get there easily in six hours. Give the horseman some gold, have him buy a fresh mount in Amiens for his return. He'll be here before nightfall. M. de Reiset left.

Of course it was absurd—six hours for fifteen leagues one way, the time needed to survey a big city, the detours that might be necessary because of the presence of rebel troops (otherwise, why were they sending the scout?), and six hours to come back, when it was already half past six in the morning, and it would be dark, or nearly so, at seven in the evening. No one pointed this out to the Comte d'Artois— Did he himself really think he was accomplishing anything by sending a Lifeguard alone to M. de Lameth's? The decision seemed to have been dictated by nervousness rather than military wisdom. Monsieur might even have already made up his mind not to wait for this horseman, but to head for the coast in any event.

The truth of the matter was that the Comte d'Artois, who in Paris had been so set against crossing over to England, now saw no other hope—at least if the road to Amiens was closed to them—than to embark at Dieppe with as much of the Royal Household as they could take aboard. Obviously they could not do this without His Majesty's consent. But His Majesty, as always—well, when they needed him he just wasn't there! Meanwhile it would be folly not to avail themselves of what they had in the way of a war treasury; the most urgent and immediate was to buy, regardless of the price, all available horses and carriages in order to be able to remount the horsemen and transport infantrymen incapable of further marches like that of the previous day.

In the barracks where the Gray Musketeers were assembled, the order for the purchase of horses had reached the company commander, M. de Lauriston, just before eight o'clock. Which was quite fast, since in less than an hour it had had to be recopied three times in triplicate, each time with a new signature, on its way from the prefecture to the barracks, from Marshal Marmont to Captain Lieutenant de Lauriston. A group of twenty Musketeers, commanded by Lieutenant d'Houdetot, left barracks at about eight fifteen to go and take possession of a sizable herd of horses reported to be a short distance from Beauvais. Géricault was among their number. It was cold and windy but the rain had stopped, and bursts of sunlight came through a penetrating fine mist. The horsemen rode without a word through the northwest suburbs, having left the road to Calais to their right, taking a paved road where a signpost indicated the direction of Rouen. Théodore caressed his animal's neck with his hand. So, good old Trick, did you sleep well at that postmaster's? How were his oats? A horse is strong. Trick did not seem to remember yesterday's long trip. . . .

Beyond the last houses on the outskirts of town, the river divided into branches separated by islets of reeds. The earth—bald patches of chalk with scattered clumps of grass—impeded the indolent water, which barely flowed. The valley of the Thérain with its scattered buildings stretched out among bare trees, cut by ditches, by drainage channels. The marshes, where reclamation had begun a hundred years before, were drained partly by the hand of man, partly by natural canals; they were putting forth their first March shoots, a tender green beneath the dead straw of winter. In the bend of one of these the village of Saint-Just rose to sight.

Here they came to a halt amid a crowd of dirty, wretched children, who gathered round them like flies, and a wineshop keeper offered to guide the Musketeers toward the meadows where the horses were grazing. They accordingly proceeded at a walk, following this man who limped, turning northward to the foot of a steep hill which abruptly changed the whole character of the landscape. Up there a village was perched, with a church which looked abandoned, gray and blind. A poor road led up to it, and Theodore experienced an urge to climb up there, to expend his strength and also to shake himself free of the long boredom of the flatlands. But this was out of the question. The horses were on their right, in those meadows. They could see them from a distance.

Those who were guarding them had seen the Musketeers coming, too, and when they understood what was happening over there, the Musketeers had to break into a trot, leaving the wineshop keeper of Saint-Just behind. The three mounted peasants with the herd of some hundred horses had suddenly begun to round them up, to stir them into motion, pressing them with whips and shouts. At the prodding of their herders, who wore wide-brimmed hats and ragged mud-colored clothes, the herd surged back upon itself, heads tossing, bodies rearing, flanks colliding, in a near-stampede, and abruptly the gray, brown and black mass broke and fled headlong. The men guarding the horses had obviously realized what the arrival of this party of soldiers meant, and with a primitive instinct they were fleeing, driving the horses before them as though they had any chance whatsoever of avoiding the requisition in this way.

They were galloping across the field now, the horses' hoofs making a wet sound in the soaked earth. The Musketeers broke into two files and flanked the fleeing herd on either side. The shouted curses of the herders, the threats of the cavalrymen, rang back and forth. One of the surrounded peasants, a fair-haired stalwart with a mustache that fell over his lips and blue eyes which had a hunted look, stopped his mount dead. Théodore had seized the animal's bridle. The peasant, covered with patches and darns, was beside himself with fear. He motioned to the others with his hand, a sign of impotence, of surrender. He shouted incomprehensible things to them. What do these people talk? From a distance the others could be seen to hesitate, then they seemed to realize the uselessness of their resistance. The Musketeers nearest to them had drawn their saddlebow pistols.

Théodore no longer looked at anything but the shiny damp coats of the horses. There were colts that were too young which they would have to leave. Almost all of them were obviously riding horses, although some of them had the heaviness of draught animals.

The peasants had regained their composure. Houdetot had just told them that they would be paid for the animals. Yet what could it matter to them? They did not own the horses. They were only the farm hands to a kind of big bandit, half peasant, half petty nobleman, for whom everyone now had to wait. The rain had begun again, a light rain like seeds falling in spurts.

Bon Dieu, fancy having to get soaked in order to bargain with that Picard horse dealer! He was both obsequious and arrogant. He wore a kind of cape and high boots, and spoke almost in French, correcting himself when he fell into too strong a patois. But he said "un guevo" for "un cheval." He was of course willing to sell to His Majesty's soldiers; he was a good royalist. He had been afraid they were rebels, with all the rumors flying round. And besides, that confounded Corsican had taken all their *guevos,* just to let them die in Russia, so now . . . "If it's just a few you're wanting. I guess

I can't say no . . ." He fell back into an incomprehensible patois and waved his stick in the air. He proceeded to pick out those he would not sell, ordering them to be separated from the others. They were obviously the best animals and he was trying to unload his old nags on the Musketeers. They had to use hard words, produce gold, threaten. And what about that one? And that one? It could have gone on endlessly. "All right, what about that one, the black one, why won't you let us have it? It's a well set-up beast."

"Captain," the man said—he had hesitated over the rank, "he's a stallion, 'n I need 'im for a stud. 'E won't do you no good—'e's vicious. 'E'll never let you ride 'im."

"That's what you think!" Houdetot shouted. "We'll show you!"

He turned in his saddle and seemed to be looking for someone. Suddenly he caught sight of Géricault: "Musketeer, show this horse dealer that that horse can be ridden!" He pointed to the horse. Théodore jumped down from Trick, and walked toward the animal. It snorted and reared.

The man sneered and rubbed his boots with his stick. "Jest you wait and see." It took two men to bridle the animal.

Géricault, having tossed his cloak on the ground and seized him by the mane, jumped onto the horse's back. He motioned to the helper to let go of the bridle. The horse broke away, leaped, and set off at a gallop. The rider, using his back muscles, confined himself to keeping his seat. He had caught the reins, and he lifted his wrists, trying to bring the animal to a walk. As the herd backed away, the black horse shook itself, bucked, refusing the rider; but Théodore stuck, squeezing his mount with his powerful legs. The horse swung around, reared, tossed, and reared again. Abruptly it darted forward like an arrow, and horse and rider could be seen tossing and struggling in the drenched meadow. And then suddenly coming back. Théodore was sitting back smiling, holding the animal solely with his legs, his arms dangling, having dropped the reins through sheer bravado. The horse lowered his head, showing a white star on his forehead. When he turned, a white stocking was visible on his right hind foot. It was what the Spaniards call an *arzel,* and one of the Musketeers, who had fought in the peninsula, said that it was a horse that was not to be trusted. Houdetot frowned. He shouted to Théodore, "The reins, man! What kind of a circus is this? We're not at Franconi's!" Then to the horse dealer, "You see!"

"All right," said the other, "if 'e's willing! But I warn you, 'e's vicious, 'e's like as not to break yer back, that *guevo!*"

They made a deal for seventy horses. That many fewer for Napoleon! Forming the animals in a column they brought them back to Beauvais.

The town was unrecognizable. And not only because the weather had lifted, and the sky was a bright blue. The Royal Household was assembling, and the companies that had spent the night in Noailles with the Princes had arrived to join those that had preceded them. The place swarmed with men, horses, carriages. M. de Mortemart's artillery pieces were in front of Saint-Pierre, and the big square looked like some kind of fair. The rest of the morning was spent wrangling over the horses among the Lifeguards, Light Horse, Grenadiers, Gendarmes and Musketeers. Officers ransacked the shops, buying everything they could lay their hands on in the way of boots to replace their own, which had been sacrificed. Alas, there were no longer any to be found. They were quarreling over who should get a pair of felt shoes.

In the midst of this extraordinary disorder, which grew with the arrival of all sorts of ramshackle vehicles—carts, canvas-covered wagons, old patched-up mail coaches, berlins whose doors wouldn't shut, charabancs—a museum of provincial horrors among the columns of horses that suddenly came into view, with the remount officers running after them, demanding them for their men, shouting indignantly that the Lifeguards were getting everything: "*Loutre Dieu!* we're made of the same stuff, and the Grenadiers have a right to ride like the rest!"—suddenly Théodore caught sight of Marc-Antoine. D'Aubigny was carrying on like a man obsessed, his freckled face furious under his bearskin, dragging a saddle on his arm and yelling unbelievable obscenities. Théodore laughed to himself, thinking of the Vauban mansion, of Monsieur his father, and Marc-Antoine's fine manners with the ladies at Frascati's, and he hailed his friend. Marc-Antoine looked at him blankly, then recognized him and said, "Ah, you've managed to hang on to your Trick; you're lucky!"

Because *his* horse, that marvelous jumper on which he used to ride from the Porte des Martyrs to Versailles in a single stretch and with which Théodore on Trick was barely able to keep up—yes, *his* horse: he had had to abandon it on the road, between Beaumont and Noailles, yes—abandon it! And the big tears in the Grenadier's eyes made him snivel. At first Théodore was tempted to laugh at him, but he changed his mind when the other said to him, "*You've* never killed a horse, your horse—you understand, *your own* horse!" It had been a superb chestnut, an English thoroughbred.

It had fallen in the mud on the road, broken a leg—finished! But when you have to take your pistol and put it against an animal which looks at you with trusting eyes—

"Listen," Théodore said, struck by a sudden idea, "I have a horse for you, a magnificent animal! Nobody wants it; they're afraid of it. They say it's an arzel."

It had occurred to him that the black horse he had mastered in the meadow beyond Saint-Just would be perfect for his friend. To begin with, Marc-Antoine was like himself, he liked to ride stallions. And then, there was a world of difference between that black spitfire and the animal d'Aubigny had had to kill by his own hand. Which was all to the good, because then he wouldn't be reminded of his old mount. They found the stallion without difficulty, and Houdetot let the Grenadier have it, although it had been bought for La Grange's Musketeers. Léon de Rochechouart, to whom it had been proposed, had refused it. An arzel? Was Houdetot out of his mind? The superstition was widespread throughout Spain and Portugal. Marc-Antoine was delighted and smiled, forgetting his recent grief. They managed to get a bit and bridle on the black devil, and a saddle on its back, and its new master pranced before the terrified onlookers, just the way he was in the 1812 painting. Théodore watched Marc-Antoine ride off with an affection verging on tenderness. Ah, *there* was a horseman!

As Théodore was watching Marc-Antoine prancing on the Place de l'Hôtel de Ville in Beauvais, and could not help thinking of the back shop on the Boulevard Montmartre where the young Vicomte d'Aubigny had come and posed for the body of his "Chasseur" in the autumn of 1812—at about noon on March 21, 1815, Robert Dieudonné, his model for the head of that same "Chasseur," and now a lieutenant in the 1st cavalry regiment, was in Paris with his squadron, no longer on a dappled gray horse as in the painting, but on a red bay, on the sunny square inside the Louvre where the Emperor was reviewing the regiment which but a short time since had belonged to the King's cavalry.

The sun was shining on this city not yet dried by the last gusts of early morning. The green and red cavalrymen on black and white saddles with red shabracks, the horses pawing the ground, faced the Arc de Triomphe du Carrousel and the Tuileries. A crowd of Parisians filled the far end of the square where Labédoyère's regiment was encamped after having arrived by forced marches; and the windows of the buildings that congested it were full of people. Lieutenant Robert Dieudonné watched the Emperor move down the line. Tanned by the sunshine of the Isle of Elba, he appeared smaller than of old as he sat on his white horse—perhaps because he had put on weight. The tricolors fluttered on the Pavillon de l'Horloge, a band was playing, as it had the day before, *Où peut-on être mieux qu'au sein de sa famille?* And tattered clouds like gesticulating arms were sailing above the Louvre.

The colonel, who had just saluted the Emperor, turned on his dark chestnut to direct the maneuver. He was a new colonel: the old one had been relieved of his duties that morning, and Adjutant Le Bourry, the successor he had named, had in his turn been relieved at the beginning of the review by the Emperor who had replaced him by Exelmans's aide-de-camp. Baron Simonneau did not feel quite at home with the four squadrons under his command for the first time—*Column forward, march!*—and noticed that the squad leaders, probably stirred by the solemnity of this review, so unlike any other, failed to keep their eyes on the seams of the coat of the leader ahead of them, as regulations required. *Form close column, at a trot, march!* It must be said, too, that it had been a long time since he had been in command of this maneuver. Previously he had had no regiment, and as aide-de-camp to Exelmans he had shared his fate. What an extraordinary thing! Here he was, colonel of this 1st Light Cavalry Regiment into which, exactly seventeen years ago this morning, on March 21 in '98, he had come as a simple horseman. *On the third squadron . . .*

The sun was drying the damp uniforms, making the metal strappings and the sabers gleam; and it was being said—there hadn't been time to go and see—that over there, in the garden, the famous horse chestnut tree was in bloom in honor of the King of Rome. The new colonel was immensely pleased at the remembrance of how excruciatingly funny his predecessor, the pitiful Saint-Chamans, had looked on the road yesterday when Exelmans sent him to speed up the march of the light cavalry; Napoleon was awaiting it in Villejuif to escort his carriage. He was a truly worried man; for twenty-four hours his officers had been driving him crazy. It had taken him all night to make up his mind to leave his regiment. Simonneau had been told that Saint-Chamans, as a first gesture to mark the irrevocable character of his resolution, had sent for one of his captains and instructed him to sell his horses. An officer who had fought in all the wars of the Empire! What had possessed

him to sell his horses, just when Napoleon was returning? Simonneau
himself would gladly have bought his predecessor's dappled bay—
but it would have caused talk; not to mention the price. Besides, that
dappled bay had too fine a build. He was better off with his
chestnut: although it was on the heavy side, it had a lot of stamina.
Perhaps the new colonel didn't have the old one's air of distinction,
but, with his powerful Hérault accent, he far outdid him in solidity
and breadth, as his horse did his predecessor's.

The 1st Light Cavalry and the 6th, together with three regiments
of Dragoons, formed the 1st division of the 2nd Cavalry Corps,
which the Emperor, upon his arrival at the Louvre the night before,
had placed under the command of General Exelmans. The Emperor
had given Exelmans the order to set out in pursuit of the Royal
Household immediately after the review. They would not return
to the Panthémont Barracks where the regiment had spent the night.
Their vehicles and supplies had gone on ahead; they would catch
up with them at Saint-Denis. While the column re-formed in
marching order along the Seine, before the Tuileries garden, Colonel-
Baron Simonneau saw Quartermaster Grenier approaching. Grenier
was the regimental treasurer; he had been introduced to him a short
while ago—that is, Adjutant Nourry, invested with the command by
his predecessor, had introduced him just before the review, concerning a pressing matter to which Simonneau at that moment had
not been disposed to pay attention. After the review, he had said.
So the quartermaster, on his horse which was of a kind the Baron
did not think much of—it also was of too slight a build for a
cavalry officer; solid animals were needed, for war wasn't the Bois
de Boulogne—Quartermaster Grenier had approached and was
saluting. "I haven't time to listen to your accounts, my good fellow.
We're heading for Amiens. What? What's so urgent? M. de Saint-
Chamans? What are you talking about, what about M. de Saint-
Chamans? Colonel de Saint-Chamans had given reasons of health
for staying behind in Paris."

That was just it. The quartermaster had in his possession a note
from M. de Saint-Chamans . . . "What? A note? What do you
mean, a note?" "Well, you see, last night, after the regiment had
been assigned to guard His Majesty the Emperor on his return
to the Tuileries, the colonel . . ." Well, for heaven's sake, my good
fellow, explain yourself! On an order from General Exelmans, the
quartermaster had had two francs given out to each of the men
upon their arrival at barracks on the rue de Grenelle—which was a

wise precaution with horsemen who had eaten and drunk nothing for a good many hours, and who might otherwise, considering the circumstances and the excitement of the evening, have done a bit, well, a bit of pillaging in the shops of the district . . .

This quartermaster fellow was exasperating. As it was an order, it had had to be carried out: so what was the problem? Well, there had been no money in the regimental till, and Colonel de Saint-Chamans had advanced it out of his own pocket. . . . Advanced what? Forty sous? Well, there were four hundred and fifty horsemen which made a good nine hundred francs. And so the colonel, that is M. de Saint-Chamans, had that morning—

Simonneau burst out laughing. The resigning officer putting in a claim for nine hundred francs! Let him apply to Marshal Davout! It was up to the Minister of War to decide whether he should be given money or sent to the guardhouse for deserting his post on the return of His Majesty the Emperor. *Bon Dieu!*

It was extraordinary to see the sun when no one had thought it would ever come back! The pleasant mildness of spring was taking hold of Paris, and at every turn people were shouting *Vive l'Empereur!*, saluting the green and red cavalrymen wearing the tricolored cockade whose mounts made a sharp rattle of iron horseshoes on the dry pavement.

The quartermaster was galloping toward Saint-Denis where he should have been already with the quartermaster corps that had gone ahead. He was preceding the regiment, bearing the new colonel's instructions for the setting up of advance quarters. There, at divisional headquarters, he would find marching orders in plain language, names of places in code.

In the column, at the level of the 3rd squadron which was under Major Lanthonnet's command, Lieutenant Robert Dieudonné, with his Norman face and drooping, stiff mustache, rode like a man moving in his sleep at the head of his company, which was without a captain, Bouexic de Guichen having resigned the day before. Was it not odd that those same cavalrymen who had nearly rebelled when Soult had sent them to Béthune only a few months ago were now leaving Paris without a murmur? Not a comment. They knew they were going in pursuit of the fleeing Princes. Not one, even among the Parisians, had asked to go home. They all had a kind of great laughter within them. They felt themselves masters of the world. What did Paris matter? Everything was beginning afresh, that was it, everything was beginning afresh with the spring. Who knew? They were going to reconquer Europe—and above all, have done with those confounded aristocrats.

The last two days—since that long wait on the Place Louis-XV when Colonel de Saint-Chamans had had to yield to Captains Riquet and Bouvard—that was when everything had started. After that, they were no longer the same—Arnavon, Schmalz, Rochette, Delahaye, Rostant, Saint-Yon, Chaiqueraud or Dole, lieutenants and second lieutenants for whom rank no longer signified anything. *Bon sang,* those hours in Corbeil and Essonnes! In the small villages on the right bank where the companies were spread out, all evening, all night, they had waited for news—Arnavon, Schmalz, Delahaye, Rostant. In that confounded rain, with the wind blowing a gale. Without saying anything, they kept their eyes on the colonel and his friends, Squadron Commander de Fontenu, Major de Mayronnet, Major Le Nourry, Captain du Bouexic de Guichen—not to mention the cousin, Louis de Saint-Chamans, who, with his relative, had come from the 7th Cavalry Regiment—a second lieutenant in 1812, a prisoner like Robert himself and the doctor at Leipzig in 1813, and by 1814, through patronage, adjutant of this regiment, while Dieudonné, at the end of these three years, was still a lieutenant. All those people were in a dither. It was plain as the nose on your face. And on the road, here and there, those conferences with colonels they met, Marquis So-and-so, Count What's-his-name— How they had laughed about it—Rostant, Saint-Yon, Arnavon, Schmalz.

Monday morning—the weather had improved somewhat, and there was only an occasional downpour—when they came, Arnavon, as it happened, and shortly afterwards Schmalz, Rochette, Dieudonné— when they came and told him, told Saint-Chamans, the colonel, since Louis, the adjutant, has no sense of humor, that the King had skedaddled and that the Princes had followed him, by way of the road to Calais, well . . .

"Come, come!" the colonel had said. He had a round chin, an average nose, an average mouth, and those innocent blue eyes—and Arnavon, afterwards, you should have seen him, he gloated, the bastard, he gloated. Whereupon the sun had made its appearance, like a convalescent still huddled in his muffler. When the colonel called them together, it had been because the order to turn toward Saint-Denis had just arrived. Saint-Denis was on the road to Calais. They had seen this Cuirassier who had brought the letter from Lieutenant General Girardin. He had shown up at the stroke of seven-thirty and they had taken him to the colonel—not Arnavon, but Schmalz—to try to pump him. The poor fellow was in a state and convinced that the officer knew he should have arrived in the course of the night, or even the evening before— He had somehow lost his way between Villejuif and Essonnes. Not that the road was so complicated, but it happens when a man is alone, in the dark, the rain and the mud. He had a hunted look, that Cuirassier; he must have stopped somewhere, slept or something, so dirty no one would want to touch him even with tongs. They weren't in the habit of eavesdropping, but at the roadside, in front of the house where the colonel was still in undress, they drew close in case there might be fireworks—Delahaye, Schmalz, Arnavon, Rostant—in short, the gang. There had been no fireworks. The colonel had gone out with his letter. Round chin, average mouth. And he had mustered all his men—it was no longer raining—including Garnier the quartermaster and Gobard-Desmarets the standard bearer. In a loud voice, Captain Bouvard announced that the Paris garrison had left the capital to go and join the Emperor. The colonel went no, no with his hand, and when all sorts of people, Captains Riquet, Percy, Girardt, and of course Arnavon, Delahaye, Rochette, Rostand, Schmalz, began to shout that they must set out for Fontainebleau, he gave the order to mount and assemble at the Corbeil bridge.

This was not altogether a refusal: from the bridge it was possible to go to Fontainebleau or to Saint-Denis. After that the colonel, with his round chin, had gone in the morning sun in quest of information to that general who the day before had delivered a little speech for their benefit on the Place Louis-XV. He was, it seemed, an Austrian—fought against us at Essling, and entered French service only in 1811. The colonel could be seen coming back on the road. With a crony of the same type. From a distance they could be seen bewailing their lot. We were on the Corbeil bridge, and we liked it there. Arnavon, Schmalz and *tutti quanti*. Unhappily, next to the bridge was a wineshop which was being overrun. By second-class cavalrymen, of course. You should have seen the sky-blue eyes of Saint-Chamans (Alfred-Armand-Robert). And that ever-so-large mouth! Especially as there were civilians from Paris paying for drinks, and people were bawling *Vive l'Empereur* wherever you turned. The colonel didn't hear these things, with his little ears jammed between the gorget and the curls. He looked good, though, on his horse, right out in the middle of the bridge, spick and span as in garrison, officers all around him, asking the comman-

ders of the companies if their men would follow the orders to
march to Saint-Denis by way of Villeneuve-Saint-Georges.

You would not have expected them to say no: but no one should
ask things like that in such a small anguished voice and with such
terrified sky-blue eyes. Behind the colonel's back—an average back,
you understand—officers were brandishing their sabers and looking
as if they were ready to swallow you, standing in their stirrups, their
arses lifted off their shabracks—all of them, Brille, Brachy, David,
Rochette, Irouard, Senarmont, Riquet, Bouvard, and Schmalz of
course, and Arnavon. . . . The colonel looked around and noticed
with terror that hardly anyone was still wearing the white cockade.

But the sun was not quite what it is this morning. It was, as I
said, convalescent. The fine weather, the really fine weather, was
holding out for the return of Père la Violette. In the end—today,
that is—we should be going to Saint-Denis, and without any fuss!
But yesterday—

Yesterday, no question of it. They cried: *Vive l'Empereur! À
Fontainebleau!* Saint-Chamans was a bit surprised. But determined
not to hear the first cry, because if he noticed it the thing would
become too serious. He said that they had misunderstood the
direction: nothing had been said about Fontainebleau, the order was
for Saint-Denis by way of Villeneuve-Saint-Georges.

He turned to Lieutenant Colonel Deluit and instructed him to
get hold of a guide to Villeneuve-Saint-Georges. At which everyone,
everyone—except perhaps Fontenu, Le Nourry, Bouexic de Guichen
and Cousin Louis—had begun to roar: *À Fontainebleau! À Fontainebleau!,* thus showing a good deal of tact, since they were no longer
shouting *Vive l'Empereur!* Everything was very friendly; the officers
had surrounded the colonel, were talking to him as though he
were an overgrown boy, pulling his horse by the bridle. It made a
tight group of superior officers. All of them, Arnavon, Schmalz,
Bouvard, Riguet, Saint-Yon, Delahaye, Rochette, Chaiqueraud—
and Alfred-Armand-Robert in the middle, with his average nose,
average as they come.

Captain du Bouexic de Guichen was the only one really to give
us the slip: what they had whispered into each other's ears, he and
the colonel, was their affair, but Bouexic had left as though he—his
horse, that is—were on fire. Afterwards, Saint-Chamans said that
M. de Guichen had solemnly handed him his resignation, since
General de Girardin's orders were not being followed. Thus is history

written. Then Lieutenant Dieudonné found himself in charge of the 2nd company of the 3rd squadron.

At last the trumpets had sounded, and it was all very theatrical. The horses crossed the bridge—not that way! Hey, there, not that way! But that was precisely the way we were turning, no use pretending we had made a mistake and taken the road to Fontaine-bleau for the road to Villeneuve-Saint-Georges. With or without a guide. We had trotted a league when we ran into the 4th Cavalry Regiment coming toward us. Monsieur's Light Cavalry, jonquil-colored collar and facings—very elegant on the green uniform. We wanted to tell them the news—Arnavon, Schmalz, Rochette, I mean—since they seemed to be turning their backs on the show. It was not nice to let comrades go the wrong way without telling them. But the colonel began to beg, to groan, and he turned his average head from Arnavon to Schmalz, and from Bouvard to Saint-Yon, as if we had all been colonels. "Don't urge them to desert!" he kept saying, and we took pity on the poor man. After all, the others could see for themselves. Their colonel had come and ridden a little distance with Saint-Chamans; it was an exhibition of exquisite politeness. I couldn't hear what they were saying, but it must have been about something else. We saluted him when he turned back to join his own cavalrymen. You might have thought we were in the *grand siècle* of Louis XIV, all sabers bared, and he went off very pleased with us. It wasn't five minutes later that we fell in with a General Something-or-Other in a scarlet uniform with gold braid and white leather equipment, and accompanied by the colonel of the 1st Lancers. Saint-Chamans led them out of earshot and spoke to them. He must have spilled everything, because the others let out *oh's* and *ah's,* and they all separated as at a family funeral.

Thereupon it was like Sister Anne in the tale of Bluebeard: there were yellow and green horsemen passing. They could be seen from afar, and now there was already dust. And as they passed us what were they throwing down? Papers. Some of the men stopped to pick them up.

Talk about being thirsty! And hungry! I didn't notice the name of that little village where the colonel sent us to quench our thirst. As for him, he had pushed on farther: after all, if he wanted to slip away! But it wasn't that. We found out later. In the distance we did see regiments moving toward Paris, Hussars, Dragoons, Lancers— we didn't know what they were. The men surrounded us, asked questions, and we just acted very important. Was Fontainebleau still a long way off? The funny thing was that the papers the horsemen on the road had thrown to us, making for Paris as they were, were proclamations signed *L'Empereur et Roi: Napoléon Ier*. Everybody was grabbing them, and although I wasn't able to read them, they seemed to me to be decrees, the first legal measures, the order to seize any Bourbon, a list of suspects in which Marmont figured.

If they were going to Paris, perhaps we were wrong to insist on going to Fontainebleau? Where was the colonel? Had he made off? Who could tell? Whereupon—we had been resting for a good hour and treating one another to drinks, and chickens and ducks all over the streets of the village, the peasants were very gay—a carter arrived shouting something we didn't understand. Just imagine, on the highway over there, a quarter league away, the Emperor, yes the Emperor, was reviewing two infantry regiments that had come from Paris to meet him. What about us, then? To horse, to horse! Ah, we didn't wait to be asked twice! The men, the officers, pell-mell. . . . Shortly before reaching the road we decided —after all, a minimum of decorum—we put some order into the ranks. But when we arrived there was no one about. Napoleon had left in his coach, and there was Saint-Chamans, all alone, looking lugubrious and scratching his round chin.

No more talk of Fontainebleau. We were heading for Paris. As though we had obeyed Girardin. Saint-Chamans was making the best of it. He kept us down to a walk, and was constantly shouting "Halt!"—no one knew why. It seemed that we were to quarter in Ris-Orangis. Deluit and Cousin Louis went on ahead with the quartermaster corps. Why were we being kept standing there? We set out again, and it was now that Baron Simonneau made his appearance. We were nearing Ris. What had come over our poor average nose? With that southern accent, right out of the wine-growing regions. So now! We had to put spurs to our horses. The Emperor . . .

No use going into detail! Here we were arriving at Saint-Denis in bright sunlight with Colonel Simonneau. People were carrying bunches of violets. They acclaimed us. Middle-class people, workers. We formed a division with Dragoons and other cavalry. There they were in the tree-lined square in front of the barracks. The cavalry was Berry's regiment, green coat with sky-blue collar and facings, and the Dragoons in brass helmets with black horsehair plumes, the short jacket of green cloth, the flat yellow buttons, white trousers under the boots, the collars, facings, lapels and lappets varying according to the regiments. We marked time for three quarters of an hour before starting. We were in pursuit of the Princes and their whole red and white rabble; we were off to chase the noblemen through Picardy and Flanders. Tallyho, tallyho! Ah, things were certainly reversed.

We had joined the Emperor at Villejuif at nightfall. In every open window were lighted candles; it was like a great festival. There wasn't much time to see *him,* for he was all but surrounded by generals. Had they sprung up from the pavement or what? People cried *"Vive l'Empereur!"* He got into a kind of mail coach, the same unlikely rattletrap in which he had traveled this far, and the 1st cavalry was cut in two, two squadrons ahead of the carriage, two behind, with Robert Dieudonné among these. We galloped. There were riders on white horses at the doors of the Imperial carriage. When we reached the Barrière de l'Enfer, the place was full of people crying *"Vive l'Empereur!"* and *"À bas les nobles!"* which must have pleased Messieurs de Fontenu, de Meyronnet, de Juigné, not to mention the two Saint-Chamans cousins. But all the rest of us were commoners, and we laughed. Now that he had come back, there was no more need for dukes and barons; our Emperor would be the people's Emperor.

There could be no doubt, judging from the enthusiasm shown when we passed through an industrial town. It was on the poorest that the Emperor could rely. The only thing that mattered to the others, as we saw in 1814, was their money—even those who had got that money through him along with everything else, their houses, their titles, their decorations. Besides, the new Empire would need the support of people who were ready to sacrifice everything. People who have nothing die more readily. And then, too, even in the army there were plenty of officers and soldiers for whom Napoleon, in contrast to the Bourbons, was first of all the champion of the Republic. . . . Ah, if only he were to say, if the Little Shaver were suddenly to say that he, the Emperor, was proclaiming the Republic! If he would unite around himself all those who had not benefited by our victories—Carnot, the Abbé Grégoire, Levasseur, those of whom no one ever spoke, but in whom the people believed. . . .

"Strange nobody is following us: are we alone on this road?" Robert had made the remark aloud, and cavalryman Langlet informed him that not long after Saint-Denis the Dragoons had turned off on the road to Calais. The division was probably making a pincer movement on the rear of the Royal Household.

For all I know, things may deteriorate farther on: but here on the Ecouen plateau the sun has plenty of space, scattered peasants in the fields are burning dry grass or spreading manure with forks, and here we are all of us passing along the road, Arnavon, Schmalz, Delahaye, Rostant—in short, the gang! We don't feel fatigue, and we'll still be galloping at nightfall. Last night we bedded down at half past ten, we had come along the new boulevards, the Invalides, the Pont Louis-XV to the Tuileries. Napoleon entered through the gate of the Pavillon de Flore, through a delirious crowd, but I saw none of it because we were behind the first two squadrons, facing the Palace as if to guard the Emperor against an army. There were cannon pointed at the gates. . . .

As he proceeded in the direction of Creil, Robert Dieudonné dreamed about all this. He was riding with his eyes open, but his head was full of the sleep of glory. Already the sun was growing dim, and there were heavy clouds.

Captain Bouvard, going back to the 2nd squadron behind Dieudonné's company from the head of the column where the staff was, had just told Robert that they wouldn't be sleeping in Clermont tonight as planned: an order had just come to accelerate the movement of the troops. In these villages the people were patriotic. They remembered the Cossacks, not so long ago! In Luzarches, or wherever it was they halted, the girls came out and brought them drinks. The men leaned down from their horses, tossed them some rather free remarks, and the girls blushed without dropping their eyes. How nice it would have been to spend the night with them! Robert was given to quick romances. In Chantilly the workers in the porcelain and lace factories, M. Richard-Lenoir's cotton spinners and cloth printers—or at least those who were left after last year's crash—came to cheer them, and the quarrymen gathered round them as they were leaving the town. They passed through the woods without paying much attention to the fact that the sky had become overcast. It was a country of trees and water, and so they reached the heights that overlook the Oise. Then there was a first downpour, and they did not stop. They crossed the river, passed through Nogent, climbed a slope. Not quite a league farther on the order came from ahead: *Halt!* It was funny, the way it was ricocheted, picked up by the men in the rear; and the column stopped. Ah, the cavalry, when it was well disciplined, a unit that maneuvered as it was supposed to—well, it gave a man a feeling of pride, a kind of physical pleasure!

They were at a crossroads, at the foot of a hill; a small road with a signpost on the left pointing in the direction of Mouy crossed the highway. On the right, it traversed a plain as far as a slope, on which a small town was built in terraces amid tilled fields and fine trees, perhaps less than a quarter of a league away. Dieudonné had alighted from his horse. The relay post was a small square building with three windows, the middle one of which on the first floor formed a picturesque arch beneath the inscription LODGING FOR MAN AND BEAST; there was a café on the ground floor, and here the lieutenant learned that this place was called Rentigny, and that the small town over there was Liancourt.

Just then the order arrived to make for Liancourt, because this was no weather to remain on the highway. There they would find a park, a château, and fodder. Accordingly they remounted and followed the road leading to the town, passing through a kind of garden of planted fields, with fruit trees, where peasants straightened up in their patches of land to watch the cavalrymen go by. Dieudonné was not a little astonished to observe a vineyard on the slope ahead, as though the very climate here had not been that of Picardy.

After having crossed a brook, which they were told was called the Béronelle, the convoy halted before the entrance to a park that opened on the right; huge shady trees—at least sixty feet tall and well spaced so that the air circulated under the bare branches—separated the cultivated meadows from the well-proportioned buildings which, seen at close range, appeared rather neglected.

The outbuildings of a château which had been destroyed, they consisted of two wings between which was a fine courtyard, edged at the far end and on the left by buildings used as living quarters, and toward the park on the third side by a kind of long gallery with a balustrade. This at least was what remained of it. It had been restored by the present M. de La Rochefoucault on his return from emigration, after the château itself had been completely destroyed in the Revolution. The main body was Louis XIII, in fine stone, the slate roofs decorated with round gable windows. The gallery seemed more recent.

The storm broke as they were dismounting. But it was obvious that it would not last, for blue sky showed in the southwest.

People came out to meet the cavalrymen. The first one Dieudonné asked where he could water his horses. The man, a fair-haired, clean-shaven, tidy craftsman with side whiskers and bright eyes, answered him with a strong English accent. Most of the people, once they realized who the newcomers were, disappeared again inside the buildings. Except for a heavy-set fellow who looked like a servant, or just a cut above. There was no way of knowing whether or not M. de La Rochefoucault was in the smart-looking residence which could be seen a short distance away, in the park to the right, near the ruins. He seemed to feel no need to show himself. The welcome was distinctly cool.

The squall was dying down. Many cavalrymen had taken shelter under the trees; others had found refuge in the courtyard. Robert Dieudonné, on foot, ventured a little distance into the park where gardeners were burning dead branches and dry leaves at the foot of the big trees. In the fading light, there was a fascination about the long line of crackling flames and trailing smoke which seemed to ignore the downpour.

Seen from here, the side gallery of the outbuildings still had an air of great distinction about it. Low, broad windows alternated with taller rounded apertures which had been walled up. From the rooms on this ground floor came a strange sound. The cavalrymen had gone up to the windows, Dieudonné with them.

Who was peering at them like that from behind the panes? In the already dark rooms a swarm of children had crowded round the windows. Pale urchins with big, sad, serious eyes. What was this? A school or a home? Harsh voices were heard, and all returned to their places. The noise, which had stopped, now began again, a kind of clicking of machinery. This La Rochefoucault was apparently a great philanthropist who gave, as they say, *gave* work to five hundred poor children. This was a spinning mill, where a few specialists brought over from England had built improved rooms— two children and one man could do the work of a dozen adults, and the children were paid ten to twelve sous a day, a grown man thirty to forty. As this was being explained, Schmalz began to joke about philanthropy; but the chap who was doing the explaining, the bald, heavy-set one, a kind of majordomo, became angry and went red in the face: because M. de La Rochefoucault was a benefactor who did more than this! In agriculture, he was a scientist, as progressive as you would find, and thanks to him everything had been transformed, the countryside had become a veritable paradise, and there was nothing that didn't grow. Rape, flax, hops, hemp, all kinds of vegetables, fruit trees . . .

"Vines," said Dieudonné politely. Yes, even vines—and all this gave work to the people who were aware of what they owed to M. de la Rochefoucault. And if the children were allowed to run loose, they would only turn into rogues and go wrong! It was a good thing they worked thirteen, even fourteen hours when the days were long—that would help them to develop into real men. Perhaps *Messieurs les officiers* did not know—or they would undoubtedly have more respect for the master of the house, who had not waited for the Revolution to do good but had given these buildings over to lodging and training children of needy soldiers at his own expense—perhaps they did not know that it was this same M. de La Rochefoucault who had been the first, after his return from England, to introduce Dr. Jenner's method of combating smallpox into France in 1800. Not to mention that until 1806 this had been an arts and crafts school, established by that great man. The school had now been moved to Châlons. It was easy enough to judge people . . . The old man was trying to preach them a sermon . . .

"How about you, do you like philanthropists?" asked Schmalz, and Arnavon began to whistle softly.

They had profited by the halt to care for the horses, water them, give them oats. The oats had been a little short, but that was because the stables of a La Rochefoucault were not of a size to take care of a squadron. Besides, the men were ravenous; they would have been glad to have a meal here, but the kitchens had gone on ahead. The rain had stopped, and the children, boys and girls, were coming out, running in all directions. Some could be no more than seven, or else their growth had been stunted; the oldest were certainly under fourteen. They jostled one another as they peered at the horses and the horsemen. They were dressed in rags, all pieced and patched, most of them in linsey-woolsey of nondescript color. They spoke among themselves in low voices. They must have been told that these soldiers were in pursuit of the King of France. A priest assembled them, made them line up to go out on the road. In what was now complete darkness, the long line of fire danced through the park, swayed to right and left by the winds, casting a red glow on the tree trunks. There was no light in the living quarters of the house.

To Saint-Just-en-Chaussée? But, damn it, it's already dark, and it's at least ten leagues to Saint-Just! Well? We'll be there sometime after ten, and then we'll have something to eat, so . . . Go and talk to the men, see how they feel about it. The way the men of the 2nd company of the 3rd squadron felt about this was quite clear—*merde mes fesses!* and that was about all. To saddle, to saddle! Clermont, Fitzjames . . . They gave the impression they would willingly ride to the end of the world, even in this fine drizzle which had begun again on the chalky ground beyond Clermont. And Lieutenant Robert Dieudonné felt proud of them, both of commanding them and of being one of them. Not for anything in the world would he have shown them his fatigue. He knew this feeling: it was the brotherhood of arms, which made a man feel not only that to fall behind when the others were keeping pace was something he would be ashamed of, but that it would actually be a betrayal.

He knew perfectly well that the men liked him. In the first place because with the flattened carrot-red curls that fell over his forehead, the stiff blond mustache notching his upper lip, his skin reddened by the open air, his Norman hulk, at home on horseback or herding cattle, he looked as if he belonged to the same breed as they. In the night he was just another horseman, recognizing ahead of him or beside him, by their way of carrying their shoulders, by their size, by any number of familiar details, all these familiar outlines with which his own blended on the flat, receding road with its black trees and its scattered villages. Dufour, Léger, Lenglet, Painvin, Bottu, Lambert, as well as Arnavon, Schmalz, Rostant, Dela-haye. . . . What had they in common, officers and men, that gave Robert the feeling of belonging to this marching column as the water of the sea belongs to the wave? Odd: he had never wondered about this before. For him it had never been a problem, of the sort that had undoubtedly arisen yesterday for Saint-Chamans, for Bouexic de Guichen, Meyronnet, Fontenu.

It was self-evident, the result of his whole life history: the countryside in which he had roamed as a child before his parents went to settle in Rouen, where he played in the schoolyard with the Géricault boy and others and in the fields, in the big meadows along the Seine where they mounted the young horses that were very much like them. . . . His uncle, who had lost a leg in Flanders, and used to tell stories—of the treachery of Dumouriez, of the intervention of the army commissaries, of Levasseur whom he had known well. And when his father had been arrested in the Germinal rising against the Convention and deported to Cayenne . . . until the day when the conscript of 1808 had anticipated the call—

So many things had created in him that strength of body and of soul, tempered the man he had at last become, the warrior, the horseman. . . .

He was like the others and yet different from them—from Arnavon, Rostant, Schmalz, and in an obscure way closer to Lenglet, Bottu, Léger, Painvin. And what had become of Géricault, who suddently sprang to his mind? Good old Théodore, whom he had found again in Paris, who had done his portrait in 1812: if you could call it a portrait—just the face, the mustache—when a Dieudonné was given the torso and thighs of a Baron or Vicomte d'Aubigny, whoever that dandy might be. Dear Théodore! With him things were sometimes complicated. He was crazy about horses: yet, no matter what Robert said to him, he had refused to enlist in the cavalry. He would have made a hell of a good cavalryman! Well, once the Emperor was back, chances were he would have plenty of orders for equestrian portraits. A new government is always a boon to painters!

IX

Appointment in Poix

IT COULD not have been more than a quarter past three when Bernard jumped down from the seat of his wagon in the Grande-Rue Saint-Martin in Beauvais. He took off his tall hat for a moment and looked about him. What he saw in the mist-suffused sunlight was the usual scene of the arrival of the Paris mail coach.

He paced back and forth in front of the post house—a youngish man of thirty, rather good-looking, with close-cropped brown hair and that air about him of a man who was idling deliberately, not waiting for someone. His manner was slightly comical, like the attempts at elegance betrayed by his dress which was rather poor but unmistakably inspired by newspaper advice on fashion, such as that a man could take a chance on wearing knitted trousers—gray, vicuña-pink or autumn-leaf in color—if he had a well-developed thigh and a slender knee, but that these colors go only with black boots. The young man wore gray, having apparently hesitated, in view of his occupation, to entrust himself to pink—a bit scandalous in the skin-tight fit worn in Paris. He had a black coat of English cut with a velvet collar, buttoned high, and a white cravat. There was something not quite spick and span about the whole outfit, something even a bit worn and frayed, beneath the tall gray velour hat. On his arm he carried a coat: he would probably look more at home in that as he presently climbed back into his wagon, which he had left at a little distance before jumping down from the seat—a black vanlike vehicle with a green canvas tilt for the driver, harnessed to two white percherons. But there was something odd, all the same, a kind of contradiction between this character with his careful, though somewhat shabby, clothes, and the team of which he was apparently the driver. A queer coachman for a delivery wagon!

The old man who had stepped down from the mail coach had at once realized that this was the unknown man with whom he had an appointment. He took deliberate delight in letting him wait a few moments and hesitate between himself and two or three other passengers. Then he went over to him and recited the ludicrous sentence he had been told to say upon approaching the one who would be waiting for him. Why are such unnatural passwords always chosen? The young man gave a start and looked at the traveler with his tired brown bag, his long bottle-green double-breasted frock coat, his soft top boots, and a felt hat which, with his long, graying hair falling onto a frayed velvet collar, made him look a little like good old Benjamin Franklin in the familiar pictures of him.

"So it's you, monsieur!" the young man murmured, and there could be no mistaking the tone of his voice. He had recognized the traveler. This affected the old man rather disagreeably; he had not believed himself to be so well known. Especially to the younger generation. "In the present circumstances, citizen," he said, with an attenuated Provençal accent, "please remember that I am M. Joubert, buyer of knitwear for MM. Calleville of the rue du Caire, Paris. I assume you have a good memory."

There was no reason to tarry, the deceptively fine weather was not to be trusted, and the young man helped M. Joubert up onto the seat of the wagon which was sheltered by the canvas tilt. He himself, after having spread a leather-edged cover on his passenger's knees and donned a heavy box coat which had lost its color through wear, went round to the other side of the vehicle and climbed up beside his guest, having first made sure with his hand that his two big pistols were in their place under the seat. He picked up the reins and from his thick, pale lips came a sound that made the use of the whip unnecessary.

"I must apologize, monsieur, for the discomfort of this equipage," he said as they were leaving the town. He had a certain Picard hesitancy in the nasal vowels, and spoke in a deep, rough voice. "It's the kind of vehicle I need in my occupation. I use it to carry the yarn spun at Abbeville which I distribute in the villages where the home-weaving is done; and then I pick up the cloth to be dyed in Beauvais. At the moment we are traveling empty."

"Ah, I see," said the old man in a moralizing tone, "you are contributing, citizen, to the exploitation of the people in the countryside, and to their use against the interests of the town weavers."

He had shown a certain insistence in repeating the word "citizen." His companion reddened a little, and this time said, "Citizen, I am only a carrier, and I earn my pittance by working for M. Grandin, of Elbeuf, who bought the Abbeville mill from MM. Van Robais. I am not a merchant-manufacturer. It is the things I have seen in my trade that have molded my convictions and led to my coming to meet you at Beauvais today." He was obviously doing his best to avoid the Picard accent, though it crept into certain words. "But I have no call to defend myself before you. You come from Paris, and you will understand that I'm burning with curiosity. What is happening there?"

What M. Joubert knew was very similar to what the prefect and Marshal Marmont had learned that morning, although he told it in a different tone. A rather critical tone which might have shocked a partisan of the Emperor's if he had not known that the man was anything but a monarchist. There was only one additional item of information in his account, and where could the traveler have learned it? It was that Napoleon had sent for Carnot, but that the interview would not take place until this evening. The Emperor probably wanted the support of the man known throughout the country for having organized victory against the foreign armies during the Revolution. On his side, M. Joubert also asked questions: about the look of things at Beauvais, the streets with the disorder of the Royal Household, the carriages of every kind, the piled-up baggage, the curious, the beggars, the unemployed workers. And he inquired about the state of mind of the population. Was it known whether the royal troops were going to establish themselves here or on the Somme? Because there was this danger, at least so they feared in Paris—and M. Joubert emphasized the *they* as he had the *citizen* a moment ago—that the establishment of a front by Marmont would mean that the Bourbons had received assurance of foreign support, and if the Kaiserlicks and the Cossacks should again overrun Paris. . . .

The dyers of the Thérain were hardly likely to have been in a position to inform the cloth merchant's carrier as to Louis XVIII's strategic intentions. He had simply delivered his merchandise and then betaken himself to his appointment, having seen little more than M. Joubert could have glimpsed from the coach. But even if there were no foreign armies, they were in danger of being overtaken by the Light Horse or the Grenadiers, and they must hurry to reach Poix ahead of them.

"Poix?" the Parisian exclaimed. "Is that the place that has been chosen? But then we shall obviously be in the path of the troops! That's not wise."

Well, that was true, but when the thing had been planned no one had expected that the King would be taking the road to Calais. New arrangements could not be made at the last minute; there were too many people to notify.

"Too many people? But how many of us will there be?"

The young man shrugged his shoulders. He could not say precisely, but that was what he had gathered from the conversation he had had with a *friend* (he stressed the word). Inasmuch as they wanted to make contact with all layers of society, and in particular with the poorest—

"Listen, Bernard," M. Joubert said.

The young man gave a start and looked at the man beside him. So he knew his real name? Discretion was decidedly a one-way affair. But then, had he not recognized M. Joubert too? Of course it was not the same thing.

"Listen, Bernard," said M. Joubert, "I am not unaware of the personal reasons you may have for spending the evening in Poix, but all the same . . ."

Taken aback, Bernard was unable to answer. To begin with, he had had nothing to do with the choice of place, but if he had said so M. Joubert would not have believed him, since he *knew*. And what M. Joubert *knew* was something about which he could not speak either. Who could have told him? It would do no good to deny it. All he could do was to avoid letting the words be spoken, because in that way Bernard could seem to have agreed with something else.

"And consequently," M. Joubert added, "you have arranged to put me up at the forge: is that right?"

So there could be no mistake. "You must know, citizen," Bernard said, urging his horses on, "that Müller the blacksmith is a reliable man."

"So they say," Joubert murmured, and he fell into a deep silence.

Whether or not it was the fresh air, Bernard's cheeks had taken on a deep red hue. The secret was not his alone. There was something painful about the fact that this old man should share it, no matter how great the respect Bernard bore him. Of course, it was a mistake to confuse these things—but where, I ask you, could the traveler be more safely lodged in Poix than at the forge? And abruptly he thought of Sophie, remembered Sophie's face, and everything else vanished from his mind.

The road might not be bad in ordinary weather, but with the recent rains the surface layer of pebbles had been washed away in many places and the wheels rolled on the foundation stones, flints of the kind found here in the fields, where the peasants spent half their lives picking rocks out of the *cauchin,* as they called this clayey soil, and piling them into those little reddish-brown pyramids that dotted the fields. And then, too, on a wagon seat you felt the jolts. Especially when you were traveling empty. The old man was wincing, and when he removed his hat to wipe his brow Bernard saw that he had become completely bald on top since the familiar portraits of him. Still with that characteristic brusqueness of expression, M. Joubert turned toward his driver and said, "You see, young man, I knew your father well."

Only the memory of his father could blot out Sophie's image. Just at this moment, a party of horsemen trotted past the wagon, and Bernard tightened the reins in order to draw his horses to the side of the road. It was the vanguard of the Musketeers on their gray horses, and Bernard watched them pass with a kind of shame. M. Joubert was surely right. Then the young man heard within himself the echo of the words that had just been spoken. "My father?" he said, and as always at the thought of his father he experienced that mingling of anger and tenderness. The old man had obviously said that, had intended to say that, to blot out the previous reference to the forge, to Müller.

"You are very like your father, Bernard. Anyone who knew him would recognize you as his son. It was a great blow to me that we were unable to save him." He sighed, let a little time pass and continued. "Men like him . . . Unfortunately, he put too much faith in military means, in conspiracies within the army. It is a folly that many are guilty of, you see, and I myself was not exempt from it for a time. We have lived so long under a military regime. Essentially, we see things as Napoleon wanted us to see them." A silence. Then, "But you—you who go about the countryside with your spun wool, who know the secrets of the poorest, who are linked to them in their hardships, in the misery in which the children and the women live . . . tell me: do you believe it is possible to unite the countryside and the towns? That, you know, is the problem in France. France is still a country of peasants, and in the towns the workers look upon the peasant as a competitor. They rebel, but against the machines. They fight, but among themselves." A silence. "What will the peasants do with Bonaparte back in power?"

Words are like the gravel on the road, they scatter. Underneath could be sensed the hard stone, the deep anxiety. Bernard did not reply. Why answer? M. Joubert knew better than he.

"You understand," said M. Joubert, "we must not let ourselves be deceived by appearances either: perhaps Napoleon will get the upper hand, come to an understanding with the Czar. Or else within three months we shall be invaded and France will be crushed. Unfortunately, it is not for us to choose between the two. But that is the military aspect of the question, the outer aspect. Victories, defeats, deafen and blind us. The history of the last quarter century, since the Bastille, is not a succession of battles—at least not *merely* a succession of battles. During these twenty-five years there have been a good many other struggles to which the world pays little attention and which won't be taught in the schools for a long time. Another revolution. You're right on top of it, and you don't see it. It's the rise of industry, all relationships changed, not only by the laws, the acts of violence, but by the machines, by the multiplication of the machines. And it has only begun. You see, when one army is beaten by another army, the emblem is changed, the uniform is modified, but it's still a uniform, still an emblem. Nothing resembles a general so much as another general. Why, one day last year I saw Prince von Schwarzenberg in a theatre—you wouldn't have had to change much to make a Brune or a Ney of him! You can turn the cannon around: fear simply changes direction, the men remain what they were before. But the machines . . . How many mule-jennies have you in the department of the Somme? And it's not only cloth and cotton, there is coal, coke, steam. People don't realize what's happening in the mines and the forges. The thing about machines is that they change relationships among men, and thus the men themselves. Men to whom we should perhaps have paid more attention. To command the future it will no longer be enough to wield armies. All calculations may founder before the unexpected transformation caused by a small, soulless machine. Do you really believe that it was on the battlefields that Napoleon was beaten? He was beaten by the industrial crisis of 1811, by unemployment, by the chaotic condition of the labor market." He suddenly realized that he had asked Bernard a question and not given him a chance to reply. Yes, what about the towns and the countryside?

It was difficult to say. A lot of things can be contained in a small question, and even a long answer can touch only on details. What aspect of the subject should he tackle? How, Bernard asked himself, could he express what he vaguely felt, especially since his mind was full of what M. Joubert had just said?

"Well," he began, "in my trade . . . Wherever I go on my rounds, from Abbeville to Amiens and Beauvais, what do I find? The village weavers, those who work on machines supplied to them, or the spinners who use the hand- or foot-driven spinning wheel, the carders, grouped together or not, whether they go through a dealer or deal directly with the factory, are beyond the jurisdiction of the town. Their village has a mayor. And what does the mayor want? He wants to make them pay for a license, as if they were tradesmen. Imagine, citizen, those poor people, for whom neither their age nor their sex is a protection, divided between labor on the land and industrial slavery, working until eleven at night and getting up before dawn . . . tradesmen! Owning neither the machine without which they cannot work nor the material they turn out. You should see the way they live, families crowded between walls of straw, earth and wood, under a thatched roof that the least spark sets ablaze, with beaten earth for a floor, the dampness, the waste water that doesn't drain away, puddles lying against the house, the liquid manure, no windows so as to retain the warmth along with the stench and the smoke of the peat fire . . . tradesmen! And because I represent the manufacturers they look to me to save them, they ask me to defend them against the commune! And do you know on what they base their hopes—what they consider the magic key? The *livret,* citizen, the infernal register which the city workers consider their yoke, that abominable invention of the Empire which completes their enslavement to the factory and which, alas, consummates what the Revolution brought them. That's why it's so difficult to make them realize that the Republic and even Napoleon are less their enemies than are the Bourbons! What is chains to some seems like liberation to others. The mayors have no register for them and say they know nothing about factory legislation. So you see it's all but hopeless to make them see eye to eye, to give them a common goal. And it's another story again with the locksmiths of the Vimeu, the serge makers of Grandvilliers or of Crèvecoeur, the flax spinners of Gamaches, the pottery makers of Vron—glassworkers, cabinetmakers, carpenters, stonecutters, hatmakers, dyers, cutlers, harnessmakers, and how many others?—all the trade-guild corporations divided among themselves and despising the others."

The old man was looking at Bernard. He was thinking that unfortunately the problem was even more complicated than that, and then involuntarily he noticed that his companion could be considered a handsome man. How well he understood Sophie! He remembered her as a child when, after *Prairial* (May 20, 1795)—more fortunate than Romme, Durcy, Soubrany, Goujon—he had had to go into hiding in the home of a friend of Gracchus Babeuf, between Abbeville and Amiens—in this province of Picardy which had been de-Christianized by poverty, and was the traditional country of peasant revolts. The fairhaired child he had dandled on his knees and who called him *m'n oncque*— Suddenly the image vanished, because the name of Romme had passed through his mind a moment before— Romme, the friend of his youth, whom nobody in this ungrateful country remembered twenty years later. He would have been sixty-five today. And he would have been off to Auvergne or elsewhere, as he himself was now in Picardy, he would have been in some rattle-trap like this, chatting with another Bernard. Twenty years pass quickly, and yet it's a long time. What must little Sophie look like, after twenty years? Would she even remember *s'n oncque?* Had she ever spoken about him even to her handsome Bernard?

They met stolid peasants with their horses, returning from their plowing. A small hand plow lay abandoned in a field. Elsewhere they were harrowing.

Bernard went on talking. About prison labor and the weavers whom the manufacturers found in the hospitals and were able to get to work for low wages. About the workhouse, on the outskirts of Amiens, in which, among vagabonds and the insane, were convicts unfit to work in the galleys, women who had been pilloried, and all kinds of people serving sentences imposed by the departmental courts. These workhouses were cramped crowded buildings enclosing eight narrow courts. In some courts the moans and screams of lunatics were heard almost continually. The men and the women had separate quarters and distinct workrooms, each equipped with three dozen spinning wheels. The possibility of installing mule-jennies was being studied, but there was a lack of space. The inmates were supposedly paid a worker's wage, but the establishment withheld certain amounts and the work was calculated by the piece, so that it was hard to say exactly what their wages were. There were several looms, of an antiquated type dating back to the previous century. The prisoners, the beggars and the insane had to pay for the tools out of their wages.

"Imagine that hell, with the cries of the demented, the noise of the spinning wheels and the clatter of the looms filling the air from early dawn to nightfall, with no other horizon than the chapel which separates the men's workroom from the women's! Prayer and vegetable gruel . . . What are the chances of uniting these people to the peasants and the factory workers? I've heard a manufacturer say he would like to see the work of the asylums extended to the galley slaves. He even pushed philanthropy to the point of opposing the death sentence, because it deprives him of weavers."

Was the old man listening? The regular trot of the heavy draught horses, the jolts of the road, his dreams of the past, combined to give his face a statuelike expression, making his already substantial nose look enormous. When at last he spoke, what he said had nothing to do with the workhouse.

"Tell me, Bernard," he said, "did your father ever talk to you about Romme? I mean Gilbert. Because there was Charles, his brother, the one who had made a study of the tides, and who survived. But Gilbert . . . At home I still have that strange book he published in the year III (1795), the *Annuaire du cultivateur pour la troisième année de la république.* In the first edition, which was printed in the author's absence, the printer inadvertently omitted the whole month of Prairial (May)—as though it ought not to appear in the work of a man who was to forfeit his life in that very month."

"Is it certain he's dead?" Bernard asked. "There are people who say that after he stabbed himself, and before he could be carried to the scaffold, he managed to escape, and he's supposed to have been seen on the 18th Brumaire in Saint-Cloud summoning the people to rise up against the *coup d'état.*"

"Alas," said M. Joubert, "those are tales people console themselves with. In his book, the day that happens to be today, the first day of Germinal, bears the name of a flower, the cowslip, instead of a saint, and I remember the comment that accompanies this word, in Romme's calendar: *its leaves can be eaten cooked; its flowers flavor wine, and its roots beer: sheep eat the plant.* When I lived in this region with Sophie's father, and you were just the age of the children who are put to the looms to help the weaver, I remembered those lines, and I used to go with the flock which he had so laboriously developed by crossing a Spanish merino with Picardy sheep—and I have seen the sheep browsing on cowslips in the woods. . . . Romme could not have lied."

"You lived with Sophie's father?" Bernard exclaimed. "In Saint-Riquier?"

"Yes, my son, in Saint-Riquier. Where your father and hers did more than people realize for the country's independence, by their studies on reproduction among sheep stock at a time when it was a national obligation to break away from the English trade. Do you know I was sent there by another patriot, whose views paralleled theirs? He had discovered the origin of the wretchedness of the landless peasants from the papers of the landed proprietors of Picardy, and proposed to feed the increasing flocks by creating artificial meadows on the principle of rotation of crops, which was unknown at the time."

"Babeuf!" Bernard said, and the other nodded. Then both fell silent, letting their thoughts drift back to that past which was at once so close and so distant. They were united in this common reverie, spanning the forty years of age which separated them, the young wool-carrier and the old member of the National Convention, both feeling, perhaps in a different way, how deeply things were linked together—the cloth industry, and the wool-bearing animals, and the meadows, and the patriots who had seen so far ahead and so accurately where France's interests lay.

The light of day was already fading and the sun, a veiled disk on the left, seemed to leap as it followed them behind the shreds of mist which at times entirely concealed it. The road passed through villages, climbed the ridges of plateaux, with the Petit-Thérain valley running alongside it, on the twilight side, below. There were still peasants in the red-tinged fields, stooping to pick up the stones and pile them.

And M. Joubert continued, as though he were talking to himself: "Despite all the crimes he can be held to account for, despite the recall of the *émigrés,* and everything that in the end contributed to his downfall, it must be recognized that in this field it was Napoleon who carried our old dream forward. Of course it was his blockade policy . . . but he understood, he protected the cloth industry and had the Spanish rams brought in, encouraged the men who were transforming the land and developing the livestock, encouraged the inventors of machines, facilitated the immigration of English workers. Still, we were right to conspire against him, against war and tyranny. Your father and Babeuf, too, had been against Robespierre at first, against the Terror. . . . And then, when the men of Thermidor put an end to the Terror, he came out and fought for the Constitution of '93, *for* the work of Robespierre. And we today . . . The man who overthrows the Bourbons is no longer the same Bonaparte. And what we are going to ask the people—"

"You're not planning to do that!" exclaimed Bernard.

"Yes, my son. Like Babeuf . . ."

"But Robespierre was dead then! He was nothing more than a banner! Bonaparte is alive."

"He's alive, and therefore more useful than a dead man. He has the army. An army shorn of its aristocrats. We must make it the army of the people, unite the people and the army. . . . Don't look at me like that, I'm not mad. Do you know that a week ago, in Vienna, the Allies proclaimed the deposition of Napoleon and solemnly outlawed him? The news reached Paris at the same time as the Little Shaver. Do you understand what that means? It's '92 all over again, the country in danger, foreign armies threatening our frontiers. Now, as then, victory depends on the people—either it's a people's war, or it's treason. Don't you see that the Revolution is beginning again? We're taking it up where Maximilien Robespierre left it, with the experience of all these years."

"So," Bernard said, "that's what you're going to tell them tonight?"

They fell silent. Rain had begun to fall on the canvas tilt. Bernard's head was on fire, and his feet were cold. What was this old man saying? That Napoleon was the successor of Romme and of Babeuf! He knew perfectly well that M. Joubert and Babeuf had by no means seen eye to eye. At the time, they had formed one of those alliances dictated by expediency. They differed completely on an essential question, that of property. M. Joubert was apparently aware of the weight that the name Babeuf carried in Picardy. And before this young man whose father . . . But where did the people's interest lie? This was the slogan of the "organization": to join the people. The people . . . And when he thought of *the people,* images became jumbled in Bernard's mind, images of wretchedness in the Picardy countryside, the hospitals where overworked men and women died like flies, the beggars at the entrance to the villages, the peat workers on their flatboats along the Somme, and in the towns those strange sects fighting one another. . . .

M. Joubert's voice suddenly grew intimate, tender. "And tell me, my son, tell me: Sophie . . . has she grown up to be very pretty?"

Bernard trembled. He just realized, on hearing this name mentioned for the second time so naturally that he had not noticed it a while ago, that M. Joubert had named Sophie in passing without actually speaking about her. The old man repeated, "Is she very pretty?"

"Yes," said Bernard. "She is, citizen, she really is."

Two black-and-white cows were penned behind a makeshift wire fence to the right of the road. The land in the distance, with its bald chalk patches, showed little difference between the pale grass and the tan furrows. They were nearing Grandvilliers.

Military information is at times transmitted in strange ways and with a speed that is difficult to explain. It was on Monday night, almost immediately upon his arrival at the Tuileries, that the Emperor had decided to place Exelmans in charge of the 1st division of the 2nd corps, and it was only after the review at the Carrousel, which was concluded at about twelve-thirty midday on Tuesday, that this division, which was to pursue the Royal Household, could begin to carry out its assignment. Nevertheless, at four o'clock in the afternoon the news reached Beauvais, seventeen leagues away. Who had brought it? The Law School volunteers. In a state of complete exhaustion, having marched since the night before last, they were reporting at the post composed of Grammont's Lifeguards and the Gardes-de-la-Porte. Three or four of these youngsters were brought before the Comte de Reiset. The count asked their names and listened to them with that air of condescension he liked to assume. It was they who claimed that Exelmans's horsemen were in hot pursuit, knowing what these horsemen themselves did not know, and this at a time when Simonneau's light cavalry could have traveled no farther than to Chantilly, while Colonel de Faudoas's horsemen had not yet reached Beaumont. Was this a piece of information that had been transmitted by some postillion or mail coach traveler; or was it a sheer invention born of fear in the minds of these youngsters in headlong flight and collapsing with fatigue, suggested by the already legendary character that Exelmans, the cavalry inspector, had become after the recent incident in which he had been involved and which had stirred all Paris? This was hard to believe, since Exelmans's horsemen were in fact pursuing the Royal Household. Yet it was not without plausibility.

In this fleeing semblance of an army, there were names that could thus send minds spinning dizzily—and not only those of the Law School students in their outlandish costumes. Marshal Ney, Labédoyère, Lefebvre-Desnouettes, Exelmans, names in which rebellion took body and shape. When the Musketeers whom Théodore had met last night tried to imagine danger, they thought first of all of the proximity of the troops of Lefebvre-Desnouettes. But one of them had quite naturally spoken the name of Exelmans, not as a certainty but as a likelihood. It was in the air. Like the "plot" which was accepted as an indubitable fact. All the King's followers were absolutely convinced that the return from the Isle of Elba had been engineered from beginning to end in Paris, in Queen Hortense's drawing room, and that the conspirators were known by name. And all this had not mushroomed overnight, but had been going on for months. Except for Ney, whose action had been a terrible surprise, were they not those who were heading the insurgents, or who were at the Emperor's very side—Queen Hortense at the window of the Tuileries, Charles de Flahaut on horseback before the gate, Fouché in the antechamber? Actually, all or nearly all of these had been caught unawares by the landing at Antibes. What many of them had been seeking was not Napoleon's return, but a certain liberalization of the regime, or the transfer of the throne to the Orléans family, and they were a hundred leagues from any thought of an adventure which had appalled them from the first moment, an adventure which they felt had no chance of succeeding—and which had horrified them all the more since they knew that they themselves would be marked out for repression. In a few days everything had changed, and now some even boasted of having schemed and contrived to bring about the subversion. Did the Emperor believe them? At least he pretended to.

To return to Beauvais, these boys, talkative as one is in a state of utter exhaustion, had talked their heads off to the first officers they had run into, and not only to Tony de Reiset. Everyone, feeling sorry for them and at the same time stirred by the devotion of these youths who were forced by nothing—no oath, not even their calling—to embrace madly a lost cause, everyone welcomed them, gave them food and drink, made much of them; and they chattered on, adding further to the military disorder of the town. They told of their defense of the Marne at the bridge of Saint-Maur which no one had attacked and where they had planted the gold-fringed white flag, a gift to the Law School battalion from the ladies who had served as hostages for the late King Louis XVI—so that they might have been so many Epaminondases escaped from Thermopylae.

Actually, they had escaped only by a kind of capitulation, the soldiers who had gone over to Bonaparte having taken pity on these children and their panoplies. To hear them, their flight from Vincennes to Saint-Denis, over the dirt roads so as to avoid untoward encounters, had been epoch-making. And when, at the approach to this town, they had been sighted by a regiment of Light Horse which had left the highway to descend on them, they had lined up along a wall to the cry of *Vive le Roi!,* ready to die to the last man and unable to retreat, not trusting themselves. They told the whole story without realizing that the generosity of their assailants—who, on seeing with whom they had to deal, had let them go on their way—somewhat modified the character of their epoch-making adventure. And the same was true of their loyalty to the flag they had received from the lady hostages. A good many of them indeed had, at the instigation of their officers, turned around and gone home, long before reaching Saint-Denis, so as not to abandon Papa and Mama and their studies—and to preserve for the France of tomorrow lawyers and jurists devoted to the monarchy and to religion. But those who had pursued their way with bleeding feet, their backs still aching from the pavingstones of Saint-Brice on which they had rested for a couple of hours, were entering Beauvais with the terrified fanaticism engendered by this night, the anguish of which was metamorphosed in their talk into heroism, accompanied by the specters they had met, the illusions and the terrors of that calamitous road strewn with stragglers, dead horses, abandoned weapons, lamentable ruins of royalty.

No one had touched these truant students even though, unlike their comrades who had accompanied the Royal Household, they were not dressed up à la Henri IV but had been fitted out on Sunday night at Vincennes with infantry uniforms—knitted trousers, greatcoat, shako with white plume, pack—and a gun which they did not know how to handle. But all through the night they had met black horsemen moving toward Paris, and they were absolutely convinced that these were Lancers, an extraordinary number of Lancers, who had gone over to the Usurper. These Lancers had passed them in silence, without any attempt to find out who these northbound troops might be, a phantasmagoria of gliding shadows outlined against the moonless sky—the sinister sound of the horses' hoofs, the procession of lances, like a long nightmare. Where all these lancers were coming from on the night of March 20th, when for days and days the garrisons to the north of the Oise had already converged on the capital at the orders of the royal general staff, was something no one had puzzled his head about. And so it is with all the phantoms that haunt the minds of peoples whose gods are collapsing.

But at Beauvais, what all this added up to was that the Imperial cavalry had been sent in pursuit of the Royal Household, that Exelmans in person would be at the gates of the city at any moment, and that he would have to be met, under the worst conditions, in this disorder, by these soldiers who were no soldiers, most of the units scattered, men who were overwrought, youngsters, old men who had come back into the service, the Princes caught in a trap, and the King, heaven knew where, abandoned! In no time at all, panic gripped the civil population: was there going to be fighting in Beauvais, then? That would be no laughing matter. The men of Exelmans's cavalry were formidable soldiers who had slept and bled on all the battlefields of Europe, veterans of the Revolution and survivors of the crossing of the Beresina, half-pay soldiers who hated the Royal Household, furiously determined to settle accounts once and for all with those who had driven them out of the army— It would be a massacre, with the city as battlefield. Even now the best families were piling into their carriages, and in the streets those whom M. de Massa called the "uncontrollable elements" were growing aggressive. Women were weeping; there was an incomprehensible coming and going of patrols; decisions were being made by the various companies without any co-ordination among themselves. Everyone was expecting catastrophe.

Who had brought the news to the Comte d'Artois? Had it not reached Monseigneur first? No matter. What is certain is that no one doubted Exelmans's imminent arrival at the gates of the city, and no one checked either the origin of this rumor or its substance. The Princes accepted it as a military datum and made their decisions accordingly. Orders flew in all directions. The Musketeers, more manageable than the other companies, were sent on along the road to Calais as scouts, ahead of the bulk of the Household, and Grammont's Lifeguards, commanded by Tony de Reiset, made up the rear guard, forming a protective shield around the unmounted men, all the stragglers who could still be picked up, the carts hastily crammed with equipment, exhausted men, the wounded and the sick. Some thirty wagons rounded up since the morning were loaded with volunteers, and the white flag of the lady hostages—for which they ran a good chance of dying sitting. To say nothing of the fact that the owners of the said wagons were driving them themselves and it had been necessary to promise to pay them the hire fee at every stage —otherwise they were going straight home. Ah, the sublime devotion of the French to the Crown was no longer met at every step!

Amidst all this, had His Highness the Comte d'Artois forgotten the Lifeguard who had been sent to Amiens that very morning to find out whether the road was safe in that direction? This was the question the Duc de Richelieu asked Colonel Fabvier when they met in the courtyard of the prefecture. The colonel, who had just left Marshal Marmont, looked at Richelieu and could not help asking him what uniform he was wearing—a question which, at any other time, would have verged on insolence. Emmanuel de Richelieu did not take it so, and replied that it was the uniform of a general in the Russian army, his clothes having been so drenched he had had to change them. Was he actually already thinking of leaving France then, or did he think Alexander's troops, billeted in Belgium, would cross the frontier?—but Fabvier did not ask this.

"But you have not answered me, Colonel," observed Richelieu.

As far as Marmont's aide-de-camp knew, Monsieur had decided not to wait for the scout who had been sent to Amiens. Had anyone, for that matter, ever seriously contemplated waiting for him? If Exelmans's men did reach Beauvais, he would only have to take to the little side roads and could catch up with the Household at Poix or Grandvilliers. And surely they weren't going to jeopardize the safety of the troops, as well as that of the Princes, just to wait for a Lifeguard! Whether it had been a good idea to send him to Amiens or not was a question that should have been considered in the morning. What did he mean, Poix or Grandvilliers? How far was it from Beauvais to Grandvilliers? A little more than seven leagues, and eleven to Poix. Not much of a start! True, but was there any choice? They had to sleep somewhere, and the troops were unable to exert themselves further. They could only hope that Exelmans would not be in too much of a hurry. Especially as the plan was to put the Princes up at Grandvilliers, since Poix had no really suitable quarters for them. They would therefore be with the rear guard, the unmounted horsemen, and the most exhausted men, with M. de Damas's company and Grammont's, and Mortemart's artillery. The most alert troops were to spend the night at Poix in order to establish contact with His Majesty—of whom there was still no news—by morning. As a matter of fact, even before the arrival of the volunteers, Monsieur had given way to the impatience he had exhibited since morning, and at half past three had sent some fifty Musketeers ahead. It was these men who had overtaken the cart carrying Bernard and M. Joubert.

It had actually required less than an hour to make the decisions, give the orders, and effect the departure of the leading group, which included the bulk of the Gray Musketeers. Théodore had looked at the clock on Saint-Pierre. It was exactly five. Eleven leagues to negotiate. At a good trot they should reach Poix between eight and nine. The marching orders for the bulk of the troops accompanying the Princes were given for six o'clock, and they had some four leagues less to go; but with foot troops who would require a good six hours, the movement would not be completed before about midnight. The sick were already being lifted into the carriages, and Théodore saw the law students waiting their turn. They were highly excited, obviously not quite used to their uniforms, which had not been made for them, and as he passed this agitated gathering Géricault felt himself gripped by both pity and irritation. These lads of all sizes exhibited the kind of emaciation characteristic of overgrown adolescents. Their rumpled hair, their way of dragging their weapons, a lack of discipline due to ignorance more than to anything else, combined to create an impression of pathetic immaturity. They assumed a bantering air—but in their eyes was a questioning look.

After all, they were no younger than Moncorps, who was riding just ahead of Géricault, his musket by his side: he had the same spareness of build, the same look of a young god led astray. But though he was of approximately the same age as most of the volunteers, his shoulders were better padded. It was this especially that struck Théodore: tall or short, of all shapes, the whole pack of students, none of whom had shaved—some had a light blond down by way of beard, others a kind of dark smear—the whole hotchpotch of youths from all parts of France had drooping shoulders. In this they differed strikingly from most of the horsemen who surrounded him—these had been developed by horseback riding, hunting, war—so that they seemed to belong to a different race. The men of the Royal Household, dissimilar in so many respects, had on the whole a certain unity of stature and of build. And the out-of-placeness among them of these newcomers who talked feverishly to the soldiers as to their elders, sitting on their packs whose straps had bruised them, some plainly showing the effects of the exhaustion of the past two days, mud-spattered, rumpled, some sleeping on the shoulder of the man next to them, others unable to keep still, the look they had of human merchandise collected by none-too-particular horse dealers, impressed Théodore as a kind of idiocy and injustice. Why must these young fools be dragged into an adventure which was none of their concern? They had become involved in a settling of accounts in which they absurdly regarded themselves as knights-errant of honor and of loyalty, whereas the issue was merely between officers of family and officers who had risen from the ranks, between the hierarchy of the Empire and that of the Monarchy.

It occurred to him that others could in turn reproach *him* for having become involved in a scrap which was no concern of his. At the thought he shrugged his shoulders. He was no longer a boy. What he was doing he was doing without illusion; he was not defending a white flag donated by lady hostages, he was pursuing his destiny without attributing to his actions the character of a crusade; he knew that he was enrolled by mere chance in one gang against another gang. His honor had nothing to do with the fleurs-de-lis, with a white rag fringed with gold, but was conditioned simply by the shame of changing camps.

The Musketeers formed into a column. Captain Lieutenant de Lauriston, coming from the front, passed with drawn sword, followed by several officers. The daylight, fading under the gray sky, flamed up from below toward the west, in the direction of Rouen, into great orange-hued streaks. As they were leaving the city they could see, circling above the trees, a flock of crows which seemed to be surveying the riders as though a meal were being prepared for them. Then there was a great smack of wind, and the rain.

Louis Müller, of Ottrott-le-Haut in Alsace, had been seven years old when his father was accidentally killed by a cart loaded with stones which had collapsed on him. His mother, having her hands full with five children, had apprenticed him to an uncle who was a smith in Ottrott-le-Bas, and at ten, being remarkably well built for his age, he could handle the big bellows and hold the horses' feet, and was even able to wield the sledge hammer to forge iron. At thirteen he had gone to industrial Klingenthal, half a league from his village in the valley of the Lames, since by then his uncle had a son of an age to replace him. He had learned something about all the trades practiced there; he had been made a member of the Enfants de Maître Jacques, and he had been on the point of setting out on his Tour de France when the Revolution broke out. His tour was now ruled out, the *compagnons*—journeymen—were scattered; and at Klingenthal bells were being melted down to extract the copper, and the forges were turning out saber blades for the cavalry, bayonets for the Republic. But Louis missed the horses he had grown so fond of at his uncle's. When a state of national peril was proclaimed, he was nineteen, and he joined the Hussars as a volunteer. Flanders, the Netherlands, Italy, Egypt, Austria . . . His dream had come true, since he had been made the regimental blacksmith, which did not prevent his being wounded ten times and coming down several times with fever.

On his return to France, while stationed at a regimental depot on the Somme, he had been badly kicked by a vicious animal and left with a stiff knee. War was a thing of the past for him! He had been treated at Abbeville, and one winter evening in 1810 chance had led him to Poix, where out of pure nostalgia he had found his way to the local smithy and had begged to be allowed to shoe a broken-down horse which had just been brought in. He had done the job so well that the smith—who, because his boy helper had just been called up, was left with only an apprentice named Firmin—had begged the lame ex-soldier to stay and work for him. Müller was too old to be simply a boy helper, but the smith was a tired man and full of grief, for he had lost a son in the Imperial navy, and a daughter from consumption. He drank more than was good for him, and he found Louis a good drinking companion, who cheerfully consumed an amount of what he indiscriminately called *schnapps,* speaking French with the accent of the region he came from, but using the language of the camps.

The blacksmith had got into trouble for having hired his own helper, which is forbidden by the trade-guild, and the forge had already been blacklisted when in the nick of time Louis remembered that he had been initiated into the Compagnons du Devoir at Klingenthal, which he was able to prove although his papers were not up to date. The war, his service with the army, made his case a special one. Everything was eventually straightened out; but during the lengthy negotiations through an exchange of letters with Klingenthal, the blacksmith's wife ran away with a good-for-nothing cartwright. It was learned shortly afterwards that she had perished in a fire which had burned down a village near Amiens. That was in January 1812.

The blacksmith drank more and more. He could not forget his wife's elopement; and some days later he was found hanging from a rafter with a letter stuck in his buttonhole in which he begged the

Emperor's forgiveness for having put an end to his days and bequeathed all his property, his forge and his house, which was of goodly size, to his journeyman Louis Müller, of Ottrott.

Louis found himself suddenly at odds with the Compagnons du Devoir, not because of any irregularity in the way he had just become a master, but because the master smiths in this region, as almost everywhere else, who had joined the Devoir only at the end of the previous century, had committed some grave breach of the rules of the trade-guild and had been disavowed by the other trades and expelled from the Devoir.

Louis, who was now going on thirty-eight, had a strength which neither illness, alcohol nor shell fragments had been able to destroy. Those arms of his, when he swung his hammer and struck the anvil, were something to marvel at. At that time the disaffection generated by the perpetual wars was spreading in Picardy, and Müller shared it all the more vehemently as he was no longer able to take part directly in the fighting. Very soon after arriving at Poix he had got to know all the republicans in the town and its vicinity. And in no time at all his forge had become famous, because on the whole road from Paris to Calais there was not a blacksmith who was his equal at handling difficult or malformed horses. Such things get around, reputations seem almost to be carried by the wind. Louis Müller was extraordinarily skillful at driving nails into even the most misshapen shoes.

When the master had died and Louis had come into his inheritance, he had made Firmin his journeyman, in spite of his youth, and without paying any attention to the rules of the guild. Firmin had been beaten mercilessly by the *compagnons,* who had broken his nose and marred his looks for life. But Louis had gone to La Mère—the landlady who "mothered" the itinerant members of the trade-guild—and had flung fifty francs on her counter, pleaded his case, and said he wanted his helper left alone. The money had its effect as a proof of good faith, and Müller did have a case. But he was warned to beware of Firmin, who had violated his oath in staying with him. Today, they said to Louis, he is betraying us for you, but tomorrow he will betray you. Müller shrugged his shoulders. There was no lack of work, he needed an apprentice, and his neighbors gave him their son. But he still lacked a wife.

He found her in a girl of eighteen from Saint-Riquier who was visiting Poix for Easter that year and staying with a girl-cousin of hers. This cousin's elder brother had been in the habit of visiting the forge often during the lifetime of the former master blacksmith, and used to talk politics while Müller was shoeing a horse.

Lame though he was, Louis was not backward when it came to the girls. This one was so young and so fair (she reminded him of the girls at home) that he completely lost his head over her and committed a blunder. Sophie yielded to him, having never before had a man take her in his arms, and they had to get married. It so happened that this alliance with a republican family drew the blacksmith even further into politics. The cousin was not the only one with convictions. Sophie was the daughter of a sheep breeder who had played a role in the days of the Convention. Napoleon was getting deeper and deeper into Russia, and imagination was running riot in these circles: there was talk of changing the course of events, especially since Malet's conspiracy had suddenly revealed the fragility of the regime; and meanwhile the disastrous bulletins from the Grand Army were being read with consternation.

A child—a boy—was born in the first days of 1813. Now the palavers in the forge had given way to an actual conspiracy: an organization was formed in Picardy whose ramifications reached even to the capital. Old traditions were revived, and those who headed the conspiracy, men of various backgrounds who had escaped the meshes of the police during twenty years of unsuccessful plotting, realized the necessity of uniting the varied elements of strength among the people. This was no easy task and required any number of secret meetings. Agents went from hamlet to hamlet on a variety of pretexts. And Müller, at the suggestion of his father-in-law in Saint-Riquier, was put into contact with a young carrier named Bernard whose job fitted him for liaison work since it enabled him, without arousing suspicion, to come and go from Abbeville with consignments of yarn for Van Robais. He was a spirited lad, and he had recently lost his father, who had been implicated in a military conspiracy in Pas-de-Calais. This young man fell into the habit of spending the night at Poix, in the big house where Müller lived with his family, his journeyman Firmin, the lad with the broken nose who was now going on eighteen, and the servant-girl he had hired, to the great scandal of the neighborhood, since he considered Sophie—who was less than half his age—too delicate to do all the work entailed in running the house, cooking and taking care of their child. The house was so big that even when Bernard was staying with them there was still a large empty bedroom under the rafters, next to Firmin's.

The "organization" had great confidence in Bernard, whose father had been the public prosecutor for the commune in his village in Robespierre's time and had afterwards been mixed up in all the conspiracies in the name of liberty. But he had unfortunately been denounced for his association with a Cambrai regiment—*provocateurs* always managed to insinuate themselves in all military affairs—and a link was seen between this and Malet's conspiracy: with the result that the hapless man had been shot in the ditches of the citadel of Arras. But this did not keep his son from having eyes, and a heart. The inevitable had therefore happened: the agitation he felt every time he saw Sophie, about whom he used to think interminably during his long trips all over Picardy, had not escaped the notice of this child-woman for whom Müller had been hardly more than a moment of madness. She began to wait for the irregular visitor, to grow nervous when he stayed away from Poix longer than usual. She did not know she was doing wrong; she simply enjoyed his visits, so she thought, as she would have enjoyed seeing her girl-cousin, for example.

This was a time when, throughout Flanders and Artois, deserters were terrorizing the inhabitants by raids upon the villages from their hideouts in the woods and marshes. These extended to Picardy, and when a whole series of armed attacks against travelers occurred in the region, Sophie began to tremble for the carrier. So often and so well did she voice her opinion that Bernard ought to be in a position to defend himself, that in the end her husband made him a gift of the two saddlebow pistols which he had brought back from the Hussars. How Sophie had polished them before the young man carried them away!

To keep people from gossiping, Müller decided that they would say Bernard was a cousin of his wife's, since actually the village he came from was not far from Saint-Riquier. From then on they spoke of the "cousin"—the cousin was coming, the cousin was late. . . . The net result of this was that the neighborhood, far from charitably inclined, had not the slightest doubt as to Mme. Müller's imaginary transgression, for everyone knows what to think of that kind of cousin.

But it was a long time before Bernard dared to bare his heart to Sophie. He was on the point of doing so when the invasion came with its cruel days, during which to speak of love seemed like sacrilege. It was only when the foreign troops had withdrawn that he had found the courage. He regarded himself as a monster because of the conspiratorial ties between her husband and himself, and because he was welcomed here out of respect for the memory of his father, whom he virtually worshiped. Sophie, thunderstruck, realized at his first words that she had been doing wrong for a long time, and indeed how could it be otherwise? It was the first time she had had leisure to dream about a man, and this one was young and handsome and his full lips seemed perpetually to invite the kiss which she could not give him. Their sin lay wholly in furtive conversations which she would abruptly break off, making Bernard swear that he would never speak to her again. For that matter, they were hardly ever alone, and always felt themselves watched. More by Firmin, the lad with the broken nose, who was quite smitten himself with the mistress, than by Müller.

Their secret stared everyone in the face, and people imagined more than there was from seeing the way they looked at each other. Only Louis Müller noticed nothing. Eventually, however, the *friend* from whom Bernard received the messages he carried here and there got wind of the gossip. His initial reaction was one of anger, and he had been tempted to give the overgallant carrier a dressing down; but he restrained himself. He was of a rather Machiavellian turn of mind, and after due reflection his republican morality had given way to the consideration that an amorous adventure would be a convincing alibi for his go-between.

On March 21, 1815, the Van Robais wagon rolled into Poix at twilight, half an hour or so after the group of Musketeers that was preparing billets for the Royal Household. A quartermaster who had come to the blacksmith's home to make note of the rooms had driven Sophie to distraction, especially as Bernard had arrived unexpectedly immediately afterwards with that old gentleman whom she had not recognized. What did you say? The young man whispered the name in her ear.

"Jean-François?" she repeated. She was saucer-eyed: she must have forgotten *s'n oncque*. He tried to calm her. Everything would work out! If the Reds found the beds occupied, they would have to sleep somewhere else. And what about my dinner? Her husband reassured her. "We're in no hurry: I still have a *guevo* for a carter from Saint-Romain." "It's just that I need more than an hour to prepare my blood sausage . . ." "Black pudding? Ah, Madame is setting out a great spread!" "It's in honor of our guests." "Well, let's say we sup at eight. Is that all right?"

Louis and Firmin had gone back to work, the carter holding the horse's hoof. Louis didn't know what got into Firmin: there were days when he seemed incapable of doing the least thing, dropped everything, and he wondered why he had ever taken on such a bungler. As clumsy with his hands as a cow with its tail! Müller let out one of those enormous Alsatian oaths that came back to him when things were really bad and the Picard words no longer sufficed. What the hell is the use of having arms if you can't use a hammer with them? With one thing and another, things had got a little late. They had not put any more charcoal in the forge, and the fire was dying down when that soldier appeared on the doorstep, his horse dragging one foot, and another mounted cavalryman behind him.

X

The Night in the Thicket

LUCKY for Théodore that it had happened as he was coming
into Poix. He had noticed it immediately, with the first pavingstones. Trick had suddenly begun to limp. Moncorps, seeing Géricault
dismount in the rain and the mud, had turned around. "What's
wrong?" he called. It took no time to locate the trouble: a lost
shoe. Lucky, because if they had had to travel several leagues like
that Trick would have been useless. Fortunately it was less than two
hundred paces to the smithy. And the officer of the post had told
Géricault that there happened to be two rooms at the smith's,
and he would billet him and Moncorps there.

But the smith did not see it that way. Certainly, he would shoe
the horse, and to oblige he would be willing to do it this very
evening. "Just let me have my supper. I have some friends staying
with me, and my wife's made black pudding. Putting you up is
another matter. The two beds happen to be occupied by our
visitors."

Moncorps began to shout to prove himself a man, and to act like
a Musketeer. The blacksmith looked at him with amusement, as one
who would only have to raise his fist. Théodore used the gentle
approach, explaining that he would have to leave his horse here, if
that was possible, and that of course his companion and himself
were tired. This all took place in the diminishing light of the
forge, of big dying coals which had dropped to the ground, and

there was that young fellow with the broken nose who was sweeping up the dung dropped by the carter's horse. Géricault saw all this, as well as the hanging bellows with the chain and the handle, the hearth with its hood, the anvil with the hammers, the tongs, the whole display of tools which reminded him of the smith at the gates of Rouen for whom he had once painted a sign. But during this exchange, what struck Théodore even more than the mustachioed Alsatian Titan, who had preserved from his days as a Hussar the habit of wearing his hair long and gathered in a queue, though he no longer powdered it, his leather apron right against his skin, shirtless, his shoulders and his enormous bare arms, his hairy armpits: a formidable creature, with one stiff leg, his face marked by all the winds of Europe, and the sweat—what struck him even more than this giant was the tall, swarthy fellow with the broken nose, remarkably hirsute for his age, who kept going round sweeping, tidying up, peering slyly at the King's officers out of the corner of his eye, a wild Donatello figure with the face of a Michelangelo.

Knowing perfectly well that the Vulcan did not give a tinker's damn, Théodore repeated, "We're exhausted . . ." with that patient air which was often interpreted as gentleness or politeness, but which was much closer to stubbornness. Unexpectedly the youth spoke up.

"I could sleep downstairs in the big room, master," he said with oafish obsequiousness and a smile that made Müller feel like landing him one. He spoke in the heavy Picard dialect, almost incomprehensible to the two Musketeers. "If my bed is too small for two, they can put the pallet on the floor. It don't make no difference to me, it's good and warm in the big room. Can't put people out in this weather!"

Unused though he was to the Picard speech, Théodore sensed both cunning and effrontery in the young fellow's words. The blacksmith looked like a soldier of the Empire, and perhaps his journeyman was a royalist since he seemed so anxious to give shelter to the Musketeers. In any event the Titan grunted and swore in a language even more incomprehensible. Whereupon the smith himself tied Trick and Moncorps's horse to a post and sent the boy with the broken nose to the stable—so there *was* a stable, then?—to fetch some oats, and while the boy was on his way he explained that he had a horse in his barn, and the water was here in the forge: their mounts could rest while they had dinner. He would take the gentlemen and convince them that the house was full.

He and Firmin tied the nosebags to the horses' heads, and the blacksmith pushed Firmin with a tap that might be friendly or punishing. The boy's lip curled into an involuntary sneer. Vulcan had removed his leather apron, baring his knotty and hairy torso which he wiped with a rag and covered with a shirt which he took off a nail it had been hanging on, next to a jacket which he also took, but kept on his arm. Then all four went to the house—it had stopped raining—where three people were waiting for them round a table in a low-ceilinged room lighted by a stub of candle at each end of the table and a big wood and peat fire burning in the hearth under the stock-pot. The room smelled of smoke.

At the sight of the soldiers a tousle-headed young man had stood up. As though to be on his guard, or rather—no, out of respect for the uniform. Their entrance had caught him unawares, as he was leaning over a cradle in which a child of perhaps two was sleeping, and his hand on the edge was not far from that of a young woman, presumably the mother, who was rocking the cradle from where she was sitting on the bench behind the table. Looking even more like Vulcan here than at the forge, the blacksmith squeezed the back of the woman's neck in passing with a proprietary gesture, and Théodore saw the candle flame dance on the young man's face like a grimace of displeasure. The light which shone on the woman in her white jumper gave a golden glint to the hair that fell from under her bonnet. She was a slip of a girl, on whose figure child-bearing had barely left a trace of fullness. She lifted her shoulders in a show of submission, but her anxious gaze seemed to seek forgiveness for this conjugal intimacy from the young man who was on his feet.

Géricault immediately saw this, sizing up the whole situation—as an outsider often can. And he looked away, at the servant-girl squatting before the enormous hearth with its disproportionate hood, stirring the soup in the pot with a long spoon and tossing an occasional lump of peat on the fire. The young woman paid attention, or seemed to pay attention, only to the workbasket full of colored wool yarn at her feet, the young man saw only her, and the servant-girl only the fire. Following the gaze of the limping Vulcan to the back of the room, Théodore could guess from every glint as it caught a copper surface, a piece of earthenware, a face, a movement, the whole picture, the ingrown situation, the potential drama. What is said, and what is concealed—who could paint that? There was no longer a Le Nain in France, and the candidates for the Prix de Rome, taking Vulcan as their cue, would all reduce this scene to an idyll, to an ancient drama, à la David. But this wife, who might be unfaithful, was no Venus, not even a Flemish goddess, a Rubens; barely, in fact, suitable as a subject for a painting.

Vulcan was explaining to the gentlemen that as they could see for themselves, with his wife and himself, the servant girl, Firmin, this young man from Abbeville (their cousin)—and Monsieur who had come from Paris to buy knitted goods . . . Théodore, who had only glanced at him, now turned his attention to the figure sitting at the end of the bench at the other side of the hearth—an old man, bald, with a fringe of hair falling on his velvet collar. When Moncorps repeated the proposal the journeyman had made in the smithy, Vulcan merely shrugged his shoulders, and the young man and woman were obviously of the same mind. At this point the bald gentleman spoke up in a slight southern singsong which startled Théodore amid the Picard voices, like a Provençal echo of Carle Vernet, his old teacher.

"Why, certainly," he said, "certainly. We can't turn away two officers of the Royal Household in this rain—without their even having had a bite to eat. Don't you agree, Sophie?"

This was said with a kind of insistence that was like an order. The three men exchanged glances in which questions and answers passed back and forth. The young man obviously did not agree, but before his guest's insistence the master of the house made a gesture which could mean, You must have your reasons. And Sophie immediately put in, "I'll see what I can do. But the gentlemen will understand that it will be pot luck." The young man, looking annoyed, went round the table, sat down with his back to the fire, and downed the tall glass of pale beer almost at a gulp.

Sophie told the servant-girl to help the gentlemen with the things they had with them: their portmanteaux which they had unstrapped from their saddles, their sabers and their muskets. While they dropped their drenched coats and removed their surcoats and cuirasses, Müller went over to the old man. The point was, M. Joubert explained in a whisper, to avoid any kind of incident by refusing lodging to these Musketeers: they were obviously dead tired and would sleep like logs without bothering them. To do otherwise would be to run the risk of attracting attention to the house—and how would they then be able to leave it presently, if their movements were watched?

Bernard regarded their guests' red coats, the showy uniforms of these runaways, with disgust and anger. So, he was going to have to sit down to table with them. Moncorps's saber fell, making a noise that startled the child in its cradle. The smith picked it up and examined it attentively, drawing it from its sheath. "Ah," he said, "times are certainly changing. In what service are you, gentlemen? In my time I've forged blades for Light Horse, Grenadiers, Artillerymen, Dragoons, Hussars. This one is new to me." He flung saber and sheath on a chest with a certain contempt.

"But my dear Müller," M. Joubert said in the most natural tone of voice, "can't you see that these gentlemen are Musketeers? All you have to do is look at their muskets!"

"In my day," said the smith, "there were neither muskets nor Musketeers. At Klingenthal we forged the weapons with which the frontiers were defended."

Had Moncorps been alone, things might have degenerated into unpleasantness. But Théodore, sitting next to the mistress of the house, acknowledged the filling of his beer glass with a bow, and began calmly to question the blacksmith as to the differences between cavalry blades. The master of the house was sitting with his back to the fire, his huge bulk outlined against its glow, and while the servant-girl placed the soup on the table and everyone began to help himself, he proceeded, as though this were a game the rules of which were familiar to all, to deliver a long technical dissertation on the smith's art of making cavalry blades from the moment when the tilter brings him the bloom drawn to the right dimensions up to the point when they are handed over to be tempered and sharpened —the firing, the chamfering, the welding. . . . He was still expounding the complicated processes, in smith's language which Théodore found hard to follow, when the blood sausage was brought on.

The black pudding was in truth marvelous, especially after a long day's ride in the rain; but neither Moncorps nor Géricault was able to put away anything like the quantities that seemed natural to the Picards, even to the young carrier, whom love had not robbed of his appetite. Théodore caught a glint of amusement in old M. Joubert's eyes as he witnessed this gluttony, and the glances of the two Parisians met for a moment in mute agreement.

Müller had by now reached the point where he was describing the shaping of the blades—how the blade of the Dragoons' or Carabiniers' saber has no curve, unlike that of the Light Horse's, and especially the Hussar's, which is the most curved of all.

It came to Théodore suddenly that the smith was not an inveterate chatterbox, but an artful man who was covering a difficult situation. A silent sneer on the face of the broken-nosed journeyman confirmed this. As did the questions—obviously disingenuous, like, "And what do you call a chamfer die?" Or, "How many white heats does it take to forge the tang?"—that M. Joubert was asking, and which enabled Müller to begin again afresh. Moncorps was saucer-eyed—he was undoubtedly struggling to keep himself awake; but Théodore, pretending an interest which actually had a different object, was wondering if he was being taken for an idiot, or what in the world it was that they were trying to hide from him.

As he was keeping an eye on the Donatello with the broken nose, he suddenly realized what was probably the key to the enigma. Firmin was merely feigning an interest in the curve of cavalry blades—his eyes were busy elsewhere. He was casting furtive glances from his mistress to the man who went by the name of Bernard, and an onlooker did not have to be very smart to divine the reason for this sly surveillance. As the journeyman could not imagine that the Musketeer had seen through him, he even allowed a kind of murderous gleam to come into his eyes once when the lovers smiled innocently at one another. Théodore was startled, to the point of losing the thread of what was being said about the so-called Montmorency blades which were used only by the 2nd Line Regiment of Light Horse. Or at least that had been true about 1792. Thus, in this dwelling in a small town of Picardy, while the destiny of France was passing by with the King's cavalry, at this moment when everything was once more tossed into the balance—good, evil, the meaning of life, the nature of loyalty to country—here, quite apart from all this, a drama was unfolding, a drama of youth and jealousy in which the smith, his wife, Bernard and Firmin had their parts—and what part did the traveler with the plump neck and gray hair play? But there could be no doubt of it: this deluge of words was a screen to an approaching crisis ripening in the minds of each of its participants.

The cheese was commonplace, but the bread was fresh. Which caused the master of the house to interrupt his discourse and observe to his wife that this was folly, for people ate more than when it was good and dry. Whereupon Bernard winked an eye and recited, *"Eine jone fème—Du bos vert—Du pain ter—C'est la ruination— d'eine moëson."* * At this everyone burst out laughing. Apparently it was a household joke, and Théodore must therefore have been wrong in judging Müller to be avaricious.

The servant-girl had prepared the big room next to Firmin's, which meant moving M. Bernard who would take the journeyman's. Moncorps had given up trying to save face and, after asking Théodore to take care of his horse, he was shown upstairs. Müller assured the young lieutenant that he had nothing to worry about: his horse would be put in the stable. He would do it himself while Firmin went to stir up the fire in the forge. As Géricault rose to join him in the smithy the fellow curtly told him that he would not be needed, that he could stay where he was or go to bed. But Théodore paid no heed. His presence in the company of the lady and her gallant would obviously have appeased the journeyman's jealousy, but being instinctively on the side of mutually requited love, he had no wish to play this role.

Trick greeted him with a gentle whinny and edged toward him, turning his black muzzle and intelligent, anxious eyes on his master. Théodore patted his neck affectionately. He had earlier relieved the animal of his load; the roan-gray coat had dried in the warmth of the forge and was slick and shiny again. Firmin, who was working on the bellows of the forge, shouted something— "Maybe it would be a good idea . . ."—followed by something completely lost in the Picard speech and the roar of the bellows. Théodore cupped his ear with his hand and came closer, and the boy, eying him slyly, raising his voice and speaking slowly as simple people do with strangers, tried to explain that it would be a good idea for him to call Bernard and have him serve as stable-boy.

Behind them the voice of the master, who was returning from the stable, rose angrily. "Leave Bernard alone, you scoundrel! After he's run all over the countryside for three days. The lieutenant must be up to holding his nag's hoof. What do you say?"

This last was addressed to Théodore, who acquiesced. Müller had removed his coat and was pulling off his shirt. Géricault gazed at him admiringly. What a model he would make! He was handsomer than Cadamour. The blacksmith passed his head through

* A young woman—green wood—fresh bread—are the ruination—of a house.

the neck-loop of the leather apron, which made him bend his back so that one could see the side muscles attached to the ribs, fantastically distinct and articulated, like claws of flesh, in the shadows and the lights coming from the forge. This back, massive as a tree trunk, made the journeyman, well set up though he was as he pulled the chains of the bellows handle, look like a gnome by comparison. Trick rested his sad head against his master's shoulder.

The journeyman was sweating profusely, and the master took one of the chains from him to work the bellows faster and bring the iron resting on the coals above the small trough to a red heat. From time to time Firmin used a sprinkler to toss water from the big stone trough next to the forge onto the fire in order to keep the coal from burning too fast, and Müller lifted the charcoal with his right hand, using a perforated shovel so that the water flowed into the small trough, while his left arm continued to manipulate the bellows whose counterweight rose and fell with a groan.

Théodore was taking in every detail of the scene as if he wanted to engrave it all on his memory—the hearth raised on its iron feet, the hood that created the draft, the fire, the iron turning red-hot, the double movement of the bellows, and the two men, the instruments standing within their reach against the forge, the sprinkler, the coal shovel, the right-angle poker with which Müller stirred the coals the moment Firmin sprinkled them. Trick stood motionless beside his master. Did he know that all this concerned him? Yes, certainly.

And now, holding the shoe-turning hammer in his right hand, the smith with his left seized the red-hot iron with a large pair of tongs, and with a vast gesture swung it like a nocturnal sun to the anvil, while the journeyman picked up a long hammer, came forward and began to strike the iron with it. The shoe-turning hammer and the journeyman's long hammer began to beat alternately, the repeated noise filling the forge. Théodore stared for all he was worth, completely absorbed by the sound and the force of the blows. He watched the iron flatten and take shape, followed every detail of this victory of man over the incandescent metal, the alternate hammering, the gradual bending, the form becoming defined. Suddenly the journeyman's long hammer was withdrawn, and the blacksmith alone turned the iron with his tongs on the anvil, rounding it with the hammer. There was absolute precision in the combined movements, the two arms working unerringly, the enormous left wrist squeezing the tongs, the right fist coming down with the hammer on the beak of the anvil; and the iron, becoming round and gradually forming a ridge on its inner curve, swelled like flesh at each blow of the hammer on its outer edge. Then, letting go of the tongs and seizing the mallet-shaped chisel, the smith proceeded to cut away what had to be removed, placing the chisel firmly on the iron to be cut—still beating with the hammer, without missing a blow. The journeyman passed him the punch to make the holes in the shoe, and the chisel rolled to the ground: the eight holes were formed, four blows to the right, four to the left; on both sides near the calkin, the toe of the shoe, leaving the ends free. They were still only sockets, and the shoe when turned around showed eight bumps. Eight blows of the punch completed the puncture from the other side.

"I'm making small holes," Müller shouted, for the customer's benefit, as though he understood why. Théodore only knew that big holes are punched when the nails are close to the inner edge of the shoe, small ones near the outer edge. He had seen the blacksmith study Trick's hoof closely a while ago.

Silence had returned. Müller was tying to his waist two leather pockets into which he put four or five small tools, a small hammer, short tongs, some twisted object, nails, a rasp. Théodore could not make them all out. What was surprising was the almost blinding speed with which the choice of the objects was made, and the co-ordination of the movements, not a single breath being lost so that the operation was performed at white heat. Now it was his turn. He brought Trick and lifted his hind leg.

"Not that way!" the blacksmith shouted impatiently. And Firmin muttered something from under his broken nose to the effect that they should have called Bernard. But he came over to Théodore and put the horse's foot in his hand: "There, like that, the fetlock against your thigh, pass your hand over the hock." Géricault was able to follow his movements rather than that confounded Picard patois which came out entirely through the nose.

It hurt Théodore as though it had been his own flesh when he saw the bare sole of the foot after Müller had scraped off the mud; and when he trimmed the edges of the hoof and the frog with the paring knife, it was not Trick but he who shuddered. "There, he's fixed!" said the blacksmith, and taking the shoe that Firmin handed him, he tried it on. "Not too bad. Have you got a good hold on him, Lieutenant?"

Suddenly Théodore felt that the relationship between himself and this somber giant had changed. He was no longer the gruff, suspicious fellow who had treated him as an intruder. And when Müller had driven into the hoof, close to the heel, two nails, long, slender and with big heads, one on the right and one on the left, with the hammer that he had pulled from his left pocket, there was even a friendly glint in his eye as he said, "You can let it down now, Lieutenant, so we can see if it fits."

Théodore let Trick's foot down gently, and as it touched the ground the smith tipped his head sideways and looked at the foot from all sides with the air of a tailor giving a fitting. There was nothing to modify, it seemed to fit. Then Théodore had to pick the foot up again, and, remembering his lesson, he rested the fetlock against his thigh and passed one arm over the hock. Müller drove the nails in, the points coming through the wall of the hoof, cut off the points, trimmed away the part of the hoof that extended beyond the shoe, then proceeded to clinch the nails where they had been cut off.

As Trick moved slightly, Théodore pressed the foot harder and murmured, "Come, come! Look how handsome you are, Trick!"

"Let his foot down," said Müller, and he took his rasp and filed the ends of the nails on the wall of the hoof. Then there was a moment of silence, then the blacksmith proceeded to give advice. Ordinarily a horse should not travel the day after it has been shod, but of course there was no helping it; the lieutenant would ride his mount tomorrow. . . . "Don't worry if he limps. There's no reason he should. It's just that the day after a horse has been shod, he often gets an idea in his head: he pretends—that's it, he pretends. He gets over it the second day. Avoid overworking him if you can. How far are you going—Abbeville or Amiens? If it's to Abbeville that wouldn't be too bad; the road that way isn't too hard—not too soft either, because the first day a foot that sinks gets tired."

Théodore watched the journeyman pick up the tools, pincers, hammer, hoof-knife, the unused nails, the shoe-turning hammer, the chisel, and put everything away in its place. He watched him come and go, scatter the coals on the hearth of the forge, sweep up the hoof parings, mute, like a mindless mechanism. And then suddenly in the glow of the fire, as Firmin was taking down his master's garments from the nail, Géricault perceived on the journey-man's face the ravages of a passion which disfigured it to the point that it invested the bashed-in, ungainly face with grandeur.

There, thought the painter, the way he looks now is how he should be drawn! And he reflected that an Othello of nineteen is something rather extraordinary.

Géricault could not get to sleep. Not that the pallet on the floor was too hard for him: but after leaving the forge and climbing up into the attic where young Moncorps, nose squashed against a kind of bolster, had not even stirred when he had come in, he had only partially undressed, keeping his boots on and his saber within reach. There was something vaguely disquieting about this house, and he experienced a feeling of uneasiness which was magnified by the fact that he had not seen the premises in broad daylight, that he was not familiar with the layout, had no idea what was on the floor below, and so on. Through the dormer window that looked out on the sky there was a suggestion of faraway moonlight which left the house in darkness but shone down on the roofs and on the valley below.

Now Sophie blended in Théodore's head with the young girl at Beauvais who had brought him his meal: the same halo of blond hair beneath the bonnet, the same expression of mingled fear and ingenuousness, perhaps a little fuller of breast. He tried not to let his imagination dwell on her. There is something yielding and supple about very young women which tempts a man's strength; he immediately imagines his arms clasped about that frailness. Especially as another memory came and joined these two fair-skinned girls, a shape more animated, more rebellious, but susceptible of the same abandon. Théodore again visualized the gateway on the rue des Martyrs, the assembled children, Trick held by the porter, and that body against him, conscious only of being held, letting itself go limp for a moment—Caroline, who had vanished all too soon. He tried to separate the three images but, with a certain sense of guilt, kept confusing them; managed for a moment to distinguish one from the other, as though he had drawn aside branches in search of a face, only to discover a different one. He found this betrayal of Caroline surprisingly pleasurable; lingered over it, toyed with a curl, the touch of an arm; then suddenly, despairingly plunged into a forgetfulness that left him alone, without her, without Caroline. Only a suggestion of a bit of blond straw still floated on the night air.

There were noises in the house. Light, brief, smothered noises. Sufficient though to disturb a young and easily alerted man inclined to interpretations least conducive to repose. Where did that light cough come from which was not even a cough, but a hoarse expelling of breath, the rasping of a throat? There were creaks, which were like a spark of light in the silence. Once or twice, far off, through the open window, muffled voices made the desert of the night more palpable. There was the vast stillness ever on the point of bursting, yet persisting; then a movement of Théodore's body would make the pallet crunch, and he would freeze at a new sound. He reopened his eyes to stare into the darkness.

The awakened sleeper again visualized the scenes at the forge and the evening meal. Quite separately. Passing from one to the other, to return to the first. His special attention, having attached itself to one thing rather than to another, had retained little more than arrangements of lights, oppositions of shadows and of faces, as though he were trying to reconstruct the scenes, the meaning of the attitudes, the presences. But what haunted him most was not a certain pictorial atmosphere, as he had at first tried to convince himself—perhaps to deceive himself, to hide from himself what was absorbing his thoughts. No, he was haunted by the glances he had seen exchanged, or rather the import of those glances. Between the various figures in the scene. That old man—what was he doing here?—or that jealous youngster, or . . . But it all converged on the same soft whiteness, which stirred in the depth of the night. And there was no way to avoid imagining her, the woman Sophie, the linen bonnet and the white jumper removed, her breasts still swollen from nursing the child she had had by that uncouth man. No way to avoid imagining them together at this moment, below, in an unknown room, from which perhaps came that furtive panting. . . .

That other whiteness of the flesh, that submission to man, the natural gesture that does not dream of a refusal, woman. Abruptly, and with amazing precision, Théodore remembered what had come over him the very first time he had seen a woman give herself, reveal herself to him as a woman, open herself to him. . . . Avidly he listened to the silence, heard his own heartbeats, and he would have liked to push away the enormous shadow of that inevitable Vulcan, whose weight he imagined on that whiteness. And suddenly, through the skylight, like the flight of a bird, the high clear chant of a clock on the church. How many strokes? Théodore had not started to count from the beginning—eleven or twelve? No, this was nonsense. He must sleep. If he could. Théodore turned over.

He stretched. He believed himself capable of a good many things. But not of sleeping. What if he should get up and go to the window, smoke his pipe, try to see the moonlit landscape yonder? . . . anything.

What was it now? The sound had stopped, but it was unmistakable, it couldn't be dismissed or denied. Besides, it was repeated. Where did it come from? From the landing, from the stairs? Théodore turned over and there, under the door, undeniably, was a streak of light. Someone behind the door holding his breath, a floorboard creaking beneath a foot. Théodore felt about in the dark with his hand. He could not find his saber—ah, yes. Instinctively he withdrew his hand and pretended to be asleep: he had seen the door open slowly, slowly . . . and the light climbed from the floor upwards, defined a man's form, a hand holding a candlestick. Through his lashes he recognized Bernard. Dressed. His face lighted thus from below made his features look different, the thickness of his lips, the tangle of his hair. It was difficult to grasp the expression on that inverted face; but there was no mistaking the horse pistol that came suddenly into view in his right hand. Motionless, taut, ready to leap, Théodore gauged his chances. He was at a disadvantage, all he could do would be to grasp the intruder by the feet—what else? The candle lit up a kind of smile that accentuated the shadows beneath the eyes, and then, with the same slowness, the door resumed its course in reverse, the intruder was nothing more than a vague outline that gradually contracted, darkness encroached, the door shut, the light was again no more than a streak on the floor. The steps receded. The sound of them diminished as they apparently descended the stairs, one at a time. Then a pause. The candle must have been blown out. Then the wood contracted beneath a sound felt rather than heard, down and down. In the dark, the hand had again found the saber, felt the cold of the naked blade, caressed it.

Below, did he hear whispers? How otherwise explain sounds that were no longer those of creaking objects, of things touched? Yes, there had been an answer, a little sharper than the question. Assuming that it was an answer, and that there had been a question. What was going on? Where was that fellow Bernard going, holding a pistol in his fist? Was it for protection or was he bent on murder? And with whom was he exchanging whispers? The servant-girl or the old man? The ear now perceived the imperceivable. They were descending the stairs. To kill the young fellow with the broken nose? All the possible variations of the drama, like combinations of cards, ran through his mind. What if it were a general plot against the husband? Vulcan caught in his sleep . . . *Mon Dieu,* they had gone out, that was the outside door that just squeaked. Théodore had risen to his feet, saber in hand: he went to the dormer window and leaned out. Outside everything was fantastically calm, moonlight broken by black and silver clouds. But the edge of the roof prevented him from seeing the street below. Steps could be heard vanishing, and the brightness of the moon cut with great blue and white streaks the unknown landscape, the countryside nearby, the hills. Suddenly, without having seen or heard anything, Théodore felt a presence behind him, a human danger, and turned around with the saber half raised. *"Sh!"* said the voice, and a hand seized his wrist.

He did not struggle long for he quickly recognized Firmin, who was right up against him, talking his incomprehensible language. He shook him off. "What do you want?" The swarthy fellow pulled him by the sleeve, his finger to his lips, and they were out on the landing, lit by a candle placed on a step so that it had been invisible from the attic. The whispered conversation was not easy, in the first place because the journeyman kept motioning with his hand for Théodore to talk more softly, and also because of his speech, which was all hisses and nasal twang and words that Théodore could not make out. Obviously he was anxious not to wake Moncorps, so as not to have to confide in him. He told the lieutenant to get himself ready, to take his weapons, to follow him. "What do you mean, my weapons?" He could see himself going downstairs with his musket! The saber would do. But what was it all about? And the other kept shaking his paw, *ssshhh!* With the greatest difficulty Géricault made out the name of the King in all his gibberish. *El roué, el roué . . .* Well, what about him? What the hell had *el roué* to do with all this?

Firmin wanted to show him something—about Bernard; and as this name crossed his lips it was impossible, even in what was barely a whisper, not to detect the hatred. What about Bernard? And the gentleman from Paris. Ah, that was it! The journeyman wanted him to trail the two men who had left the house, he wanted Théodore to see what they were up to. At this time of night? "And all this because of the King, my lad? Are you trying to pull my leg? A lot you care about the King! What are you trying to make me believe?" Géricault had seized Firmin by the wrist. The boy swore he was telling the truth, shushing all the while and shaking his ugly broken nose from which the words seemed to proceed.

"Don't think I don't know what you're up to," Théodore whispered into his ear. "I saw you at the table, the way you looked at your mistress! Jealous, eh? You needn't go to the trouble of inventing all that business about the King."

And he picked up the candle and raised it to get a better look at the liar's face. Even by the poor, flickering light of the candle stub it was obvious that the young fellow was suffering the tortures of the damned, that he was ravaged by passion, or perhaps by fear of the Musketeer, or even more likely by the fear of awakening the master and the mistress downstairs. He suddenly dropped his vain protests, realized that the King's interest was not an argument to make the officer follow him downstairs, and capitulated, gave up: yes, it was because he hated Bernard that he was begging *Monsieur l'Officier* to follow him.

"Why should I go and spy on the lad? I've no reason to do that!"

Despair and fury registered on the journeyman's face, he clung to the Musketeer's sleeve, and suddenly, inexplicably, Théodore was won over, convinced by the hideousness of that face. He thought to himself, What was I saying? Othello? This is Iago. Yes, Iago!

And so he went down the stairs with Iago, treading cautiously in the footsteps of the boy who was familiar with every inch of the way, and who sheltered the light of the candle with his hand as he crossed the second-floor landing. There they had to pass through a hall before reaching the steps leading down to the ground floor, which he had seen earlier in the light of the flames from the hearth. Despite the embers, the big room was full of noisemaking obstacles. "You'll never find them, they're a long way off," he murmured, to which Firmin replied, "They won't get away. I know where they be!"

The air outside was unexpectedly balmy, full of all kinds of mysterious and invisible things. They were in the shadow cast by the hill, with the moonlit valley and the moist earth over there in the distance, the manure piles here before the doors between the brick houses with their thatch or slate roofs, and Géricault was following his agile guide whose eyes saw in the dark like a cat's. Suddenly Firmin touched his arm, and the two flattened themselves in the shadow of a house behind a projecting wall. Two Musketeers were going down the narrow street, one of them bearing a torch: a patrol. Why should Théodore hide from his own men? But the journeyman put a restraining hand on his arm. They were approaching, talking as they came. One of the men was saying, "Do you believe that story of theirs about the dying man?" "Why not?" said the other. "People go on dying. Just because the King's taking to his heels and we along with him, is no reason . . ." "You believe those people were out to fetch the parish priest, at this time of night?"

By the time the other answered he was out of earshot; the patrol had passed, the darkness returned. Without a word, Firmin started walking again. They climbed a brick-paved slope between two rows of houses and came out on a level with the roofs on their left. A high stone wall rose above them on their right. Théodore had ceased to ask questions. They climbed above the village, the roofs at their feet, the moon suddenly before them, its light flooding over them. To the left it filled the wells of the small courtyards behind the houses. As they came upon the church from below, there was a terrace on their right between the old walls, and a flight of steps which they proceeded to climb. It was too early yet for matins, and turning up here at such an hour seemed almost criminal. A tall gray church which was quite unlike common churches, a pale fortress, a Jacob's ladder to the lunar world. It looked as if it were about to tumble down on them as they passed in front of it—then still more steps. Firmin pushed a small gate, and they were in the cemetery.

The journeyman knew his way among the tombs, and slipped toward the back between the tombstones and the railings. Above them the clouds passed in great frayed masses; the wind had risen. The moon vanished, although its light could still be seen in scattered patches in the valley below. A strange whiteness seemed to hang over the far end of the cemetery, and at last the reappearing moon revealed the ruins of ancient fortifications. His companion drew him to the right, along the wall, signing to him to indicate that they must move cautiously. They circled a kind of rotunda, reached a point where the stones had fallen away, making a breach in the wall. Here Firmin stopped, stepped across and turned around to extend his hand to the Musketeer. A piece of rubble rolled beneath his foot and Théodore could feel his guide's terror. What was all this mystery? They had some trouble in getting through, scaling the wall in order to avoid the ordinary path lower down. Then they made their way through a confusion of branches and creepers in

thickets strangely crisscrossed by little paths, lanes that suddenly
divided as though they were in a well-laid-out park. But they had
to be careful not to make the twigs snap in the underbrush which
seemed to be a tangle of ivy and brambles. The ground sloped
upwards, the trees were taller—what were they? Oaks? No, small
elms, dogwood—broomsticks still with their black winter hair; perhaps a plantation gone wild.

Before them, where the lanes seemed to converge beneath the
trees, there was a light, a dim light, in a large clearing. Firmin's hand
was more eloquent than his lips. His fingers said: careful, we've
reached it, that's where they are, they mustn't hear us. And he drew
the Musketeer to one side onto a path that led downward. Stop—
over here. They were now below the level of the open space, where,
by the light of torches stuck in the ground, people could be seen under
the pines. Without a word they clambered up a kind of ridge and were
now close enough to see the men's feet, their boots, the bottoms of
their coats. At this point Firmin stopped and put his mouth to Théodore's ear. He was leaving him now, he whispered, because if *he*
were to be found here . . . And with a noiseless leap he vanished
into the thickets. Théodore had instinctively reached out his arm to
restrain him. But he could hardly run after him or call him. The
gathering of the conspirators—for what else could it be?—was too
near at hand, and the informer had escaped.

Géricault drew as close as the bushes would allow, being careful
to keep under cover. Even from here his view was far from perfect.
It was like looking up from a ditch into the circle with its fantastic
lighting. Beneath the slanting trunks of the tall trees at least a dozen
men were already in a heated discussion, their words pitted against
one another, like their shadows and their gestures. Some were meticu-
lously dressed, others were virtually in rags. Were they bandits or
what? Théodore pulled some branches aside and saw that the clearing
was a kind of crossroads, the junction of five lanes similar to the
one he had followed, and these men, who formed groups that he
could not make out clearly, had no doubt come by separate ways.

There is perhaps nothing that is initially so disconcerting as to
arrive at the theatre a little late, with no idea of what the play is
about, so that everything—the relations between the characters, the
place where the action unfolds, the time—must be reconstructed on
the basis of a word, an attitude, a comparison. But in the theatre
there are conventions that enable the latecomer to figure things out
by analogy. The show that Théodore was witnessing, as though he

had been in the orchestra pit, belonged to no genre known to him; it introduced him to a world the King's Musketeer had never suspected, in which the established relations were unknown to him, and every word uttered assumed a knowledge acquired neither in the schools nor in the ateliers of painters. Added to this were the weirdness of the landscape, the smoky light, the consciousness of danger, the fear of revealing his presence and the impossibility of getting close enough to obtain a clear view of the faces, the angle from which he was looking, the strangeness of the feelings expressed, an unknown vocabulary in which the Picard dialect was by no means the main obstacle.

A more careful count indicated that there were some fifteen men gathered here who seemed to have converged from the points of the star to meet at its illuminated center. Some came forward into the full light, others remained somewhat in the background. There were perhaps more than appeared at first sight—twenty or even more— judging from the snapping of branches and the swishing sounds of bushes.

At first Géricault had difficulty untangling all the impressions that crowded in on him, understanding that this was not an accidental encounter of adversaries who were now sizing one another up, but an organized meeting which seemed by common consent to be presided over by the old man who claimed to be a buyer of knitted goods from Paris and whose face, here in the light which accentuated the double chin, had assumed a solemn character as he stood, hat in hand, indicating with his finger those upon whom he called to speak. There were words that were lost, others that rose like gusts of wind. It was clear that there was disagreement among several of these men who were making lurching movements toward one another which others restrained. They were people from all walks of life, some wearing middle-class coats with town hats, others apparently soldiers in civilian clothes, some tradesmen or men of law; and men whose dress showed the infinite variations assumed by the raiment of the poor with something about them of the field and the workshop, visored caps, shapeless felt hats, tasseled bonnets, smocks—the mason's plaster-spattered jacket next to the dyer's leather apron, a shepherd's or coachman's greatcoat, a priest's cassock, what looked like a day laborer in a vest and shirt sleeves, a jacket on his arm and his feet in wooden shoes.

And who were these people? Weavers probably, some wearing a kind of woolen material about their shoulders, others the kind of rags that might be seen on scarecrows in the fields. And there was a big fellow in tall boots who, Théodore gathered, spoke in the name of the river people who were without work for months on end, the ones who transported peat on flatboats to Abbeville or cargoes of brick or stone on the barges that plied the canals. Who would give them more to eat—Bonaparte or fat Louis? The little scrawny chap with a bell-crowned top hat, a jabot and a cape, waved his arms indignantly: "That's the trouble with you! All you think about is filling your belly!" But he was out of order, and Monsieur Joubert told him so with a certain formality: a lawyer ought to have known better than to interrupt another speaker. The people were entitled— Whereupon the lawyer again lost his self-control: "The people! In Arras the people are waiting for the Emperor!" The bargeman's reply was in the Picard dialect and incomprehensible to Théodore, but several men burst out laughing and slapped their thighs. The lawyer from Arras must have understood, judging by the furious expression on his face. Suddenly the discussion took another turn, and a deep but indistinct voice spoke words that did not reach Géricault.

"Got to have the know-how," someone close to the Musketeer shouted. He was a mere outline against the light, and Théodore could not tell what he looked like. "How'd you find work if all the peasants were weavers?"

It was clearly no easy task to maintain order in the discussion. Then M. Joubert called on a man who seemed ageless, thin, worn like the earth against which he had matched himself all his life. He was all bone and sinew, and he was perhaps the most wretchedly clad among those present.

"The King and Napoleon," he said, and he had a melancholy, raucous voice, "they're both just waiting to kick you in the ass. . . ."

Bernard obviously knew him. He was standing next to him, and when the fellow said things that not even the people from Arras or Béthune could make out, he helped him, translating into French for M. Joubert's benefit. He was a day laborer from Ponthieu, so poor that at forty-three—what? he was only forty-three?—he was still unmarried. He had had no time to become a weaver, he had neither wife nor child to give to the spinning mills, but with either Napoleon or *el roué* he knew one thing very well: it was those who owned the land who squeezed the people, and twenty, twenty-three years ago people used to league together in his village, when the fine gentlemen, the lawyers from Amiens or Arras, used to come and tell them they were going to divide the land, give it to this, that or the other one. . . . "We knew that the minute you owned a bit of land, well, you needed this and you needed that, and suppose you were sick? Who is going to pay for the seed? One thing leads to another, you get into debt, and the big fellows make you work on the land. . . . The land should have been left undivided; it ought to belong to everybody, and then nobody could take it away from you."

The lawyer from Arras attempted to explain that this was a backward point of view, that the Revolution and the Empire, it so happened . . . But it was not his turn to speak. It was the turn of a flax spinner, a big excited fellow who kept correcting himself after almost every sentence. He was for Napoleon, but on one condition, which was that the people's associations—the *sociétés populaires*— be revived. They would never get anywhere if they had to listen to the peasants, the weavers, the masons, the lawyers, the postmasters, the day laborers, while all of them had their say. But the main thing was to get rid of the nobility, the nobles had to be got rid of. . . . "And who the hell brought them back," cried a furious voice, "if not your Emperor?" But the spinner continued: Napoleon's return, you had only to look—and his hand pointed in the direction of Poix— meant the flight of the aristocrats, only the people couldn't trust anybody except themselves, so that by uniting the way they used to, in associations, to keep an eye on what was happening, to make themselves heard, condemn abuses . . .

Most of those who were listening were too young to know exactly what the people's associations had been, and they interrupted the spinner to ask him questions. What were those associations for? Who belonged to them? And the spinner spoke of the associations in his small town, where the carpenters, the justice of the peace, the day laborers, a wineshop keeper, the sheep and calf dealers, the schoolmaster, the miller, the ceiling plasterers, a thatcher, the surveyor, the cooper, the cartwright, two tailors, the glazier, the smiths, farmers and their journeymen, the stonecutter, the masons, the shoemaker, used to meet with the gendarmes, former priests, stocking makers, the salt depot inspector, forest rangers, the innkeeper, a brewer, the registrar's clerk, hatmakers, wigmakers . . . This was greeted with bursts of laughter: everybody, in other words! No, not everybody—the patriots! But while the lawyer from Arras, who called these associations "clubs," seemed to be of one mind with the flax spinner, the word *patriot* seemed for the majority to have lost something of its value in the past twenty years or more. Or at least to have changed its meaning, because two or three among the most poorly clad exclaimed that they did not give a tinker's damn about patriots; what they wanted to know was were they forever going to be bound to the masters with that infernal *livret,* treated like vagabonds if they left the factory without having paid their debts, most of which were the money advanced by the master, to the last sou. And one of them shouted, "Napoleon means bread at thirty sous, as in 1812!" At this point a gray-mustached man in a long frock coat, leaning on a cane, could be seen coming forward into the light, and M. Joubert called for silence. "Citizens," he said excitedly, and his voice was hoarse. He coughed. "Citizens . . ."

He was a man of about fifty-five, a former officer of the Republic, one of those who had risen from the ranks. A cavalryman in the Queen's Regiment, then a soldier in the 45th Line Regiment in 1786. He had been twenty-nine at the time of the storming of the Bastille. He was a sergeant major when he had married in '92 . . .

Someone shouted, "He's giving us his whole life history!" M. Joubert silenced the murmurs with a motion of his hand, and invited the soldier to continue.

"When my eldest daughter was born, in '93, I wasn't on hand. For seven years I was in all the campaigns of the Republic, from Fleurus to Wetzler, where I won my captain's bands—in the 2nd Infantry Line Regiment . . . in the army of Sambre-et-Meuse and in La Vendée under Lazare Hoche. Like him, we, his officers, would always have refused to act as a police force, and we would have strangled anyone among us who would have raised his hand against the government. My wife had left Béthune, where her family comes from, to join me in Westphalia, and there she gave birth to a son in 1797. Like Hoche, who had died in Wetzler in a way that's never been made clear, we all considered the young general of the army of Italy to be a republican, and our hearts glowed with his victories . . ."

A part of this speech did not reach Géricault, because just in front of him several men had put their heads together and were jabbering in the Picard dialect, drowning the voice of the speaker in a confused murmur. At a call to order they separated and fell silent.

"Brumaire," the orator continued, "was an indescribable blow—a sudden challenge to liberty. The army voted in those days; and I voted against the Consulate. Up to then everything was clear. You didn't have to wonder who was a patriot. When I married Aldegonde, in Béthune, the enemy was almost upon us. My father-in-law Machu was a friend of Joseph Lebon and of Darthé. The people who today repudiate what they then believed heap the responsibility for what has happened in the country on these men. I knew Darthé. *There* was a patriot! He stabbed himself to death before the court of justice that condemned him. That was when I was in Westphalia . . . at the time Frédéric was born."

The good man was telling his story without any regard for chronology; they had reached a point two years later, why was he going back? In short, this republican, even while he disapproved of Bonaparte, had remained in the army until Napoleon had had himself crowned Emperor; and then, again, he had voted against the Empire, and he had had to leave the army, with his major's insignia. He had gone into trade: he had to support his family, after all, and they had had still another son in 1805. An opportunity had offered, and he had gone and settled in Italy—in French Italy, the department of Marengo, the name of which recalled the young Bonaparte, the dreams dating back to before his betrayal. In Alessandria-della-Paglia. At first everything had gone well. He had handled supplies for the army. Then, after the depression of 1811 . . . Anyway he had been engulfed in the general calamity, he had lost the army as a customer . . . bankruptcy . . . It was at the time when bread was at thirty sous that he had brought his family back to Béthune, his wife's native town, and the country seemed to confirm his own ruin, the adventure into which the Emperor had dragged France.

"Citizens, bread at thirty sous in 1812 was a terrible hardship for the people. But in 1813 when we saw the soldiers returning from Russia, when the news from Germany confirmed the complete military reversal, when I met old comrades from the wars of Liberty who brought us the certainty of the defeat, the renewed threat of the foreigner on our frontier . . ."

"Well," someone shouted, "I suppose you went and volunteered?"

And he shook his head. "Worse," he said. "My son was sixteen at the time of Leipzig—I gave him to the Emperor! He went into the 2nd Line Infantry Regiment which I had abandoned rather than serve the Bonaparte who had betrayed the Republic. He was a sergeant at seventeen when the Allies crossed our frontiers. He behaved like a hero at Besançon where he fought hand-to-hand with the Hungarian Grenadiers. But with France betrayed, how could he remain in the army? He took leave in the autumn, and he was with us in Béthune on a six-month furlough when the rumor of the Emperor's return reached us. He left us last Sunday. He must have reached Paris in time to see Napoleon at the Tuileries. He did not hesitate, and I feel as he does: Napoleon returns, we must take up arms again. *I'm*

telling you this, I who for ten years of my life refused to bear arms
when they were not the people's arms! Mind you, I'm not against
the people's associations which the journeyman here spoke of a while
ago, but what can people's associations do, citizens, without arms?
Napoleon returns. He will be what the people make him. If only the
people are armed—"

At this there was a fine uproar. Arms, arms! To fight again! And
against whom? The English, the Germans, the Russians! Someone
shouted, "The people don't want to fight, they want to eat!" Many of
these people were mistrustful of soldiers; they expressed it in a variety
of ways. It was obvious that they had had enough of perpetual wars.

Squatting uncomfortably behind his shrub, Théodore could make
neither head nor tail of the chaotic debate. He dropped one knee to
the ground, and caused a slight noise of crackling twigs. He froze. His
hand had clutched some large fresh leaves close to the ground—soft,
cool, and he could feel some flowers between his fingers at their
center: what could they be? Primroses, probably. He could imagine
them, mauve, with yellow hearts. He pressed them, kneaded them,
and suddenly something stung him: nettles so early in the season!
nasty things . . . He could hear less than half of what was being
said, and he had to make an effort to reconstruct a lot of what he
caught since the Picard words and the many technical expressions
threw him off.

But the extraordinary thing was that a deep, inexplicable change was
going on in Théodore himself, a change which the words spoken, the
strength of the arguments, the working out of an idea, hardly justified.
It was as though shadows were gliding within him, a simple unconscious trend. He was unaware of it at first and merely let himself be
carried along. But presently he realized that he *was* being carried
along, though without yet making any judgment about this fact. It was
like this at the theatre, and he was at the theatre—you witnessed a
drama or a comedy, you had not chosen the ingredients, you were
caught up in the author's design, he led you without your knowing
where. Perhaps it was because you had paid for your seat, but you
accepted things as they were presented to you in order to be able to
continue to follow the play, even though you had your own ideas, and
in real life would perhaps be on the side of the miser against the
prodigals, of the prosaic family against the mad lovers. Here, in order
to follow the *plot,* Théodore had to make up his mind one way or the
other, his sympathy had to go out to this set of actors as against those

others. And the odd thing was that this King's Musketeer, this Don Quixote of the world of yesterday—a world which today was in headlong flight—as he listened to these clashing arguments, seemed to be taking Napoleon's side as though his anxiety were that these nobodies, these wretches, this priest, these middle-class citizens, these day laborers, might not understand the new role the Emperor was going to assume. He was afraid the play might not have the ending he wished, like those members of the audience in the gallery who are carried away to the point of shouting to the hero on the stage that the traitor is behind him, who are grief-stricken by a queen's refusal of proffered love, who would change the course of history so that Titus could marry Berenice. . . .

No, Napoleon did not inevitably stand for war, but he would assuredly shatter the absurd universe to which this red uniform tied him—and this uniform alone, which he could tear from his skin at any moment, the uniform hated by these nobodies as well as by Caroline. In any event the Emperor's return meant the reversal of fatality, of the order of the men in power; it meant the beginning of a different life which trembled here among these men, wretched with a wretchedness he had never really seen or suspected, a swarming of destinies deprived of hope. Where did they live, what were their women like, what monstrous prices did they pay for the bread of which they spoke with an anxiety so novel to Théodore? And he was afraid that these unfortunates might not understand the chance that was offered them, that they might let their opportunity escape. Suddenly he felt himself overwhelmed by this notion that he was at the theatre, that his sympathies were due to the lighting, to the author's skill, to the actors' playing, and like a child he feared that the enchantment would end, that presently, when the curtain fell, he would find himself again face to face with his old ideas, his old beliefs, that it would be as though neither the play nor that extraordinary emotion created by a gesture, a speech, the nobility of a phrase, had ever existed. He was afraid it would all prove to have been only theatre. He wanted desperately to continue to believe, to be a part of this fantastic universe lighted by low torches beneath tall twisted pines, above a fortress and a cemetery, in the bend of a valley in Picardy, while the Princes, the Lifeguards and the Musketeers slept down there in darkness and fatigue like thoughtless brutes unconscious of the real drama, and the horses in the stables, the barns, and the sheds stirred gently on their bedding, weary and resigned to tomorrow's road.

Mon Dieu, I am again about to do something that is against the rules. But how can I resist? I know that the author is not supposed to step into the picture, and even less to commit the anachronism of making references to his own life. Yet there is nothing to be done about it, the temptation is too strong. Besides which this recollection —I can't help it—comes to me from a dark corner of my memory upon seeing Théodore Géricault watching the conspirators of Poix. It is a story I have never told, not even at the time it happened. The trouble is, it's hardly a story, just a picture, a fleeting sensation.

I was twenty-two, or even less, since it happened in the spring or at the end of the winter of 1919, near Saarbruck. There had been strikes in the mines around there, and the men of my infantry battalion were mounting guard. Some officers who came to look things over had taken me along one evening, into the hills—it must have been in the direction of Voelklingen, if I remember rightly. I can visualize the entrance to the coal mines, the pit, the cage, the winding-gear. It was already dark. I knew the men on guard at the post. I had seen them when they had come for their medical examination— I had treated one of them for pneumonia. Soldiers and officers alike were heedless young lads, and they had had enough of the war which was being further dragged out by the occupation in this dreary country. It was rather cold—the same kind of cold as on the night on the outskirts of Poix. We talked about everything in a devil-may-care way, and the essential thing in life was to say cherry-blue or currant-green instead of red; fanfare instead of music. But I could see that this very breeziness concealed an anxiety. Whereupon we were called out. "We" is a manner of speaking. The night crew was refusing to go down into the pit. Those who had just come up had noticed something or other in the levels, something to do with the timbering, or seepage. Anyway, these men were at the pithead, those who had just come up covered with the blackness of the depths, the others ready, dressed, their arms crossed; and the overmen were shouting, the German engineer was trying, or at least pretending to try, to arrange things, the French military were threatening, the men with their guns ready, some thirty of them.

What was I doing there? I had very little idea of what it was all about. I had never seen a mine, even in France. The workers . . . I had not given much thought to them up to that time. These were speaking among themselves, their deputy was giving aggressive answers to the captain who was questioning him (the captain I also knew; we used to play bridge together), and a second lieutenant whispered to me, "Look, Doctor, look at those damned Huns." I could make out nothing of what was being said. To begin with, the miner spoke a German which was not the German I had learned at school, nor even that of the young ladies of Saarbruck. And then the interpreter who translated for the captain summarized three minutes of anger, of short sentences following one upon the other, between those wolf's teeth in the dark face under the helmet, with a simple: "He says it's dangerous." The captain was toying with his cane, tapping his boots with it, very bored. (General Brissot-Desmaillet, who was in command of Saarbruck headquarters and who had read Nietzsche, used to say, "When you call on the ladies, never forget your cane!") He was not a bad man. He didn't want trouble. But after all! Were we the victors, or weren't we? France needs coal. That's all I want to know.

I won't go into details.

There, pressed one against another with almost no space between their shoulders, arms bare, were those flesh and blood men, that angry wall, the eyes, the words flung out; at any moment this might take a nasty turn if our men were to fire. Because there was no arguing; I was on one side, not on the other. No choice. That was when I felt within myself, like a panic, what must have come over the Musketeer Théodore Géricault in the thicket behind the Poix cemetery. That was when I suddenly felt within myself that those menacing strangers, those Huns, that *they* were the ones who were in the right, that it was they whose resistance expressed everything great and noble in man. And we, then? We!

That night nothing extraordinary, nothing terrible, happened. The men did not go down into the pit. No issue was made of it for this once. Much ado about nothing, the young second lieutenant said to me when we went back, showing me the photograph of a young girl at Bischwiller, in Alsace, through which we had passed before coming into the Saar basin. With a fur collar and cuffs, holding a little cat against her cheek. If we give in to them this way, they won't respect us. Who do you mean? Oh, the miners? I went back to my quarters where I read, I remember, *Der Golem,* a contemporary German novel which had been recommended to me at the best bookshop in Saarbruck. And then I gave it no further thought. There was nothing to think about. Nothing to tell.

It's strange. Later, much later, I had the impression that that night had weighed heavily in my destiny. Perhaps I gave no sign of it. Such was the romanticism of the young people we were then. We

couldn't show it. Just consider: it was at the time when a copy of
Dada 3 had reached me by mail from Zürich, the very thing to make
the intelligence officer look upon you kindly; in it was a poem I
had written, cut to size, a hundred verses, which ended with . . . No,
it wasn't that one, it was another, written in that Saarbruck suburb,
Burbach, next to the steel plant . . . which concluded with the
lines

> *La beauté la seule vertu*
> *Qui tende encore ses mains pures . . .**

But what has all this to do with our story? With all this, I have
lost the thread of that colloquy in March 1815, a portion of the
things said, and I return to it even more bewildered than Théodore
Géricault, the King's Musketeer.

Someone—it might have been the flax spinner—had just mentioned
France on a note of pathos, brandishing the threat of a new invasion,
the country again in danger; and a farmer from a village near Abbeville called Saucourt had begun to speak of the Prussians and of the
hundreds of rations that private citizens had had to supply to the
occupying forces—all charged to the community—not to mention
officers' and soldiers' rations . . . and the draught horses. Who was
going to reimburse them for all that? Then came a great roar of
laughter from a mason who bluntly retorted that as far as he was
concerned, no one could take his horses or his oats away from him
since all he owned was his trowel, and besides he had debts, just like
the commune of Saucourt. "So much the worse for the landowners!
What you haven't got, no one can take away from you."

M. Joubert tried to explain that this was a shortsighted way of
looking at things. Because the Prussians' debts to the small landowners would in the end have to be paid by the commune; that is to
say, by everyone, the day laborer, the mason. But the other merely
replied that he didn't see why, and that the commune was quite wrong.
Where he came from, the debts from the invasion and the sums levied
by Napoleon in the last days had doubled the taxes of the commune,
to the King's benefit: there was no difference between them, they were
all nothing but robbers. But as far as he was concerned, he didn't
believe you could solve anything, armies or no armies, with people's

* Beauty the only virtue
  That still holds out its pure hands . . .

associations in which judges, landowners and masters rubbed shoulders with starvelings. What the masons needed were masons' associations. And a locksmith from Vimeu loudly agreed with him, speaking against politics, which is a business for fine gentlemen. It was obvious that others agreed with these two.

The lawyer from Arras said that this was contrary, not to the laws of the Empire but to the Republican Constitution itself. The Republic is for freedom to work, it forbids combinations of journeymen as of masters. He spoke in flowery language and freedom rolled in his mouth like a pebble on the beach during a storm. Here everyone put in his word: they had just touched on what was the open wound for most of these men, although for opposite reasons. Théodore lost his bearings completely. He had no idea what the *livret* they were talking about was, nor the conciliation boards, nor the employment bureaux. Nor why the lawyer shouted so loudly that those benevolent societies, those friendly societies that were being proposed as a substitute for the clubs, were merely a hypocritical means of circumventing the law. Nor exactly what was meant by a combination, a word that kept recurring and seemed to represent the major accusation against the rebellious workers.

One almost had the impression that the word hurt their mouths, that this accusation made them sick. All of them claimed the right to combine. Here the spinner was against the lawyer. And this was where the row between them began. And they snubbed Bernard when he tried to reconcile them: they knew him, he was carrier for Grandin, the new master-merchant of Les Rames. Why should weavers put any trust in him? In January, Grandin had laid siege to a house in which several of them were meeting— How had he found out? Someone had informed on them. There had not even been a combination in this instance, but there were four or five of them together, all weavers, and that had been enough for the masters and the police. They had been arrested as a precaution, on the grounds of intention to combine. Two of them had spent five days in prison, one was still behind bars and was going to be sent back to the department he came from. "We'll see if the Little Shaver's return makes any difference! Governments come and go, but manufacturers remain; for combination, even the intention to combine, you come under the surveillance of the police, of the prefecture—two years, three years, five years— even if meanwhile the Prussians or the marquises take over. Also, you can't just up and get a different job: because on the *livret* they reckon your pay without giving you a chance to argue. Whatever the master puts down that he owes you or you owe him, the advances, there's no way of proving he's cheating!"

"But after all," exclaimed the lawyer from Arras, "relations between master and journeyman must be based on good faith! Besides, by law the master is taken at his word for the amount of the wages, payment for the year gone by and the reckoning for the current year."

" 'E's taken at 'is word?" one of the weavers from Abbeville shouted. "And me, am I taken at my word when I say 'e robs me?"

It was at this moment that the thing came into Théodore's mind: a deep, throbbing thing, like a blow, a wound. This squabble among men who were yet sufficiently close to one another to have come together, or at least to assemble, in this dangerous night meeting in the hope they must have had that some good, some action at least, might come from it; this squabble—first of all, it struck him as merely something accidental, like his joining the Royal Household. Each of these men had only made his limitations felt. Each one said not quite what he should have said had the play been well constructed. Even those verbal challenges, that refusal to trust one another, seemed to express a will on the part of all to find something in common—they did not know what, but certainly a truth infinitely precious to each, which until then all had felt to be lacking.

He was perhaps wrong, but it did not seem to him that any of them was fully assured of his own truth, of what he had brought with him in his heart of hearts this night to offer to the others. All of them marked by life, by diverse lives, slaves of what they had been, seeking the natural issue, the next step, the logical conclusion of their experience, of their subjection, of their fatigues, of their misfortunes. The end of a long wretchedness. And, for the first time in his life, Théodore found himself face to face with the implacable nakedness of men, the necessity of their destinies, before men who gave him the feeling of being in a leaking ship where nothing mattered any longer except the unending struggle to plug the cracks in the ship, where there was no longer beauty or grandeur or virtue, save in this sacrifice of the heart, of the spirit and of the body.

For the first time Théodore found himself confronted by something not himself. He did not understand one word in three that these people were speaking, and as yet he felt hardly anything except his uselessness before them: what ought he to do to help them? What could he do for them? How could he even join his strength, his breath, his soul to their fever? They were the others. Here for the first time he had seen *the others:* and that was the laceration, the physical pain, *the others.* There were no others in the barrack room of the Panthémont Quarters, at Frascati's or in this fleeing pack, any more than to the animals in a wood other animals are the others. In this society to which he belonged at school, in the studio, among Musketeers, there were only differences in uniform, in the cut of the coat, in the manner of wearing one's hair. Here the difference between men, as men, as flesh-and-blood beings, as well as the resemblance among these men, derived from data which until now Géricault had never considered—from tragic data. That was it: he had just entered the world of tragedy.

He had just entered it—or rather he remained on the threshold, too committed to retreat yet a stranger to this world, in his inability to take that step forward that would throw him into the furnace. He was there, present yet absent. He could not join this gathering, and if he were discovered, how could they see him as anything but a criminal, a spy, a despised creature? He was possessed by an over-whelming fear, not of the castigation that would descend on him, not of being killed—for they would kill him, that was certain, and he would not blame them: no, but by the fear of a quite different, in-tolerable suffering, of a doubt impossible to dissipate, of the error of which he would be the object and the victim before he could say to these men what was in him, something he had not known to be there, but which was there, for good, for good: that he was one of them.

In Voelklingen, *I* was afraid they would kill them, *the others,* in front of me, in my name, without my having been able to tell them what I had not even told myself. . . .

Could Théodore really understand these men in their disagree-ments? There were those who spoke of the nation, who appealed to patriotism. And there were those—like himself when he had agreed to his father's paying a man to go and die in his stead—who were not carried away by the idea of sacrifice, who wanted to live. They spoke of *eating.* How could he have understood them, knowing noth-ing either of their existence or of their ideas; for he did not know that those who asked only to eat were ready to die rather than betray their brothers' secrets, on account of some baroque oath which was their poetry—sworn in a factory somewhere in Lille or Rouen. Théo-dore knew nothing of the Compagnons du Devoir or of the under-

ground societies to which several members of this assembly undoubtedly belonged. He had no idea how much diplomacy had been
required of the organization's "revolutionary agents" just to bring
them here—because the instructions from Paris were to win over the
compagnons—the journeymen. He knew nothing, he would never
know anything of the moral code of these men whose law it was to
punish crime and honor virtue; nothing of the rivalries between the
guilds, their brawls. . . .

Tonight those who had come did not speak their strange language,
did not use their chosen names taken from towns and flowers, did not
even attempt to recognize one another. In this assembly to which they
had come as witnesses, as observers, no one would convince them of
anything; it would require a century and three revolutions to convince
them of anything. No one, not even the man from Paris who now
began to speak, this M. Joubert to whom Théodore listened from
where he was crouching just behind the speaker. M. Joubert's
gestures, the movements of the arm holding his hat, were outlined
above the eavesdropper against the light from the torches.

M. Joubert's speech was nothing more than what he had said yesterday in a rambling way to his young driver as he traveled in the
Van Robais cart between Beauvais and Poix. Tonight he said it in a
more ordered way, that was all. And rediscovering ancient, somewhat
old-fashioned words, with references to Graeco-Roman antiquity. It
was a little above the heads of some of these people, but essentially
these were words that Géricault could understand, even though the
Davidian aspect of the vocabulary annoyed him a little—words
which he grasped and on the whole respected. They were the phrases
he was expecting; he recognized in them the conversations of his
uncle the regicide, and the echo of what little Dieudonné as a child
used to tell him about his father in the deep grass along the banks of
the Seine where the horses ran untethered and the wild wind made big
white waves. For Théodore it was not a matter of whether M. Joubert
was right in every detail. What Théodore heard above all in this
speech, in this time of perpetual about-turns, was the voice of an
enduring loyalty. That, for him, was where honor lay, even when
loyalty was directed toward things in which a man did not believe.
And M. Joubert had spoken of Darthé, as had the man from Béthune
a while ago, and of Babeuf whose convictions were forged between
Abbeville and Amiens, among the poorest of these men, or their
like; of Bernard's father, put to death by a firing squad at Arras.

Théodore shuddered: all kinds of vague ideas took shape within

him, and the recent memory of that last Sunday morning on the
Grenelle drillground, where Generals Malet and Lahorie had fallen
. . . the Chinese Baths . . . the crowd in that Palais-Royal café.
These were not faraway matters, business disposed of which Papa
Géricault thought about by his fireside with a retrospective little shudder. They existed, they spread, they were reasons of living men whom
he might meet, who had their own lives, who had gone through the
Directory, the Consulate, the Empire, with fixed certainties, consistent
ideas; who did not possess a house on the rue de la Victoire or the
rue Saint-Honoré, lands to cling to, decorations or titles. . . . And
here one of them was affirming that Napoleon—the Napoleon who
was returning, putting the nobles, the Princes, the King to flight—was
no longer the same, was no longer the gilded Napoleon, the distribu-
tor of benefices, but another—"If we wish it, if we know how to go
about it, if we back him, and if we are united in this."

"Who do you mean, *we?*" a voice shouted, and the speaker was
taken off his guard. Because the one who had shouted was not a
weaver from Abbeville, or the good fellow from Amiens, or the day
laborer from Ponthieu, but Bernard, young Bernard, in his English-
cut coat, the son of the man who had been executed in Arras. Again
there was an uproar, and now Géricault refused to hear anything, to
know anything further. He had heard the words which were for him
the essential ones. What did it matter to him how all this would end,
whether these men would separate as strangers, or whether common
resolutions would be reached, what practical measures would result
from this meeting? He did not want to know because this did not
concern him, and he would then have felt as though he were spying
—he who tomorrow was going to follow the mad course of the fleeing
King.

He must leave, take advantage of the noise of the dispute to get up
slowly, slip away, return to the thick of the wood, the fortress, the
cemetery. His heart was pounding. He did not want to be seen, to be
caught now. Each rustle of leaf and branch behind him, the uncertainty, everything sharpened his senses to a frenzy of awareness. "Am
I afraid? No, it's not that. It's not fear. I just don't want to be
caught. Because of what I believe, which they would be unable to
believe that I believe. I must be careful. For their sake, as well as my
own. It is they I am protecting. It is what I believe, which they also
believe . . ."

His saber impeded him, he had to hold it to prevent it from knocking against a tree, a shrub. Find his way in this checker-board of

moonlight and shadow, no longer lighted by the distant fires of the torches. Once out of the thicket, which way to go? He had come from that direction, he seemed to remember: turn to the left . . . It was suddenly colder. A pebble underfoot slid away, made a noise. He stopped, listened, then made his way cautiously through the ruins . . . on the white edge of the fortified wall. He had misjudged, he should have taken the next path. He could have jumped from here—the distance was less than nine feet—but he might have raised the alarm. He followed the wall deeper into the thicket—branches, thorns, dead brambles. Only when he reached the cemetery did he feel that he was safe. He took a deep breath, looked at the tombstones, the High Mass of the church, passed through the gate, went down the first steps.

Suddenly, on the stairway, a shadow, a whispered voice, a man across his path. He whipped out his saber. The other leaped back. "Don't strike! . . . It's me—Firmin!" Théodore dropped his weapon, and when the boy came close, his ugly broken face stretched forward in the moonlight, he could see the gleam in his eyes, the curve of his shoulders; he seized him with his left hand, squeezing the thick of the arm. Beneath his strong fingers he could feel the serpent-quivering of the muscles betraying Firmin's anxiety as he dragged him along. "Not a word, come along." They turned onto the terrace at the foot of the great medieval wall, and before them, above the parapet, they could see the shining slate roofs, could measure the courtyards like shadow daggers between the houses. They went down the steps, the road, reached the houses, passed below the level of the roofs, descended into the dark narrow street.

Then Firmin, who had so far been docile in the grasp of the fist that held him, abruptly shook himself loose like a man who was about to take to his heels. But instead he came and pressed himself against the Musketeer, mumbling his Picard gibberish, his mouth against his ear. Théodore pushed him away roughly; there was something indescribably revolting about the contact—an impudence— "What are you saying? Talk louder, more distinctly." And this time he understood. "Must go fetch the guard." Then he seized him even more roughly, and although it was like touching a snake, he dragged the informer with him toward the blacksmith's house.

But the boy tried to break loose; he spoke in a low voice, saying things that Théodore did not need to understand in order to grasp their import. It was clear that he had not taken the Musketeer up there just to treat him to a show. He wanted Théodore to fetch the guard, call out the soldiers, surround the woods with sabers and muskets, seize the conspirators, the traitors to the King, Bernard. . . . In the lower streets the moon now flowed from above between the houses, a milk of silence in which everything seemed immense and beautiful, even to a large abandoned cart with its big wheels, even to the manure piles in front of the doorways. A bell sounded in the church tower.

Suddenly, without a word, Théodore pushed Firmin before him, flung him to one side into the shadow of a barn, out of the moonlight, and there, backing him against the wall, he struck him twice with his fist full in his dirty face. The other screamed, with a choked cry, "Murderer!" Before Théodore had time to digest this, the young savage had flung himself upon him with all his might, shoulders hunched, head down, aiming for the stomach, his arm poised to strike. But his blow missed, and for a brief moment the two men reeled from its impact.

The Musketeer had instinctively reached for his saber, but the touch of the metal caused him to interrupt the movement of pulling the blade from its sheath. He had turned around, waiting for the second attack, which did not come because Théodore had kicked his assailant in the chest and sent him rolling. Firmin, beside himself with rage, did not give himself time to recover his balance and pull himself together before again flinging himself upon the adversary who had over him the advantage of science. But this time Théodore saw the glint of steel in the madman's hand, the glint of something that might be the smith's fleshing knife. He parried with his right arm and let fly with his left fist. So French boxing doesn't satisfy you, my lad; well, here's a sample of English boxing. And now, gripped in his turn by a kind of sullen fury, he proceeded to belabor Firmin, who parried with his elbows, hit out again and again with his armed fist, whirled round and came back for more. And then suddenly, the Musketeer's fist having struck him on the chin, the boy went limp and rolled on his back.

He lay motionless. Théodore, having inflicted the drubbing, felt an immediate relief, and at the same time a touch of anxiety. He bent over the fallen figure, being careful to keep the pointed sheath of his saber between them— Having a saber at your side is deucedly inconvenient when you're boxing, because that bit of scum was not beyond resorting to foul play. But he saw that the hand had opened, and the knife had rolled out of his reach and was lying in a pool of moonlight. Théodore picked up the tool and whistled. A fine coward's weapon. He leaned over the now moaning Firmin. "Come on, get up, you've had your lesson. Get up, I tell you, it's time to go back, do you hear?"

The boy turned his head and tried to brace himself, sitting against the wall. He had obviously had all he could take. Théodore seized him under the arms, lifted him, steadied him against the barn wall. He saw the ugly face, and something wet on the boy's lip, blood . . . Théodore had slipped the knife into his trousers pocket; he could feel it through the cloth. He laughed softly. "Come on now, take hold of yourself like a man." Firmin groaned again, his head sagged on his shoulder, and he lifted one hand to his mouth and tried to see what was dripping from it. "All right, you're bleeding, my lad! It won't kill you. Come on, here we go." He had taken Firmin's left arm and passed it over his shoulder, around his neck, and now he half dragged, half carried the limp body. Firmin went along passively, tried to hold himself erect, and leaned on the man who had beaten him with the confidence that strength inspires in a brute. "Thanks!" he said, sniffing blood and tears, then broke into soft sobs. In this fashion they reached the blacksmith's door.

"Now then, no noise! How would you explain all this to your Sophie, eh? You idiot!" And once in the big room, he threw Firmin like a bundle onto the couch the little traitor had made for himself by the hearth.

Firmin dropped upon it, and in the last glow of the fire his shoulders could be seen shaking with despair and shame, his fists against his lip and aching jaw. "Listen to what I tell you, you young rascal, and remember it: if you move away from here before morning, I'll slit your guts open and I'll cut off your ears so close that they'll be no bigger than your nose. Do you hear me, you ape?"

Théodore climbed the stairs softly; Firmin's smothered sobs were still audible in the depths of the night. Then, by the time he reached the hall on the second floor, he no longer heard them. In the garret Moncorps was sleeping blissfully, and neither the creaking of the door nor his comrade's muffled step disturbed his trusting sleep. Géricault sat down in the dark on his pallet, listening for a long time to the deep, deceptive peace, trying to guess from shadows of sound the reality of the bodies that breathed in the silent house. He drew from his pocket the knife with which the smith had trimmed Trick's hoof and put it on the floor. It shone. He looked at it. Looked at it long. Long. His fists were aching yet content, as though they could measure the thrashing they had given by the pain they felt.

The drawn saber was close beside him, and he touched it from time to time. The moon now shone down through the dormer window on the waking dreamer. And he—he felt like a forest full of murmurs, of unknown words, of speech that suddenly had a ringing sound. Nothing was as it had been before. The world . . . so much richer and more terrible than he had known . . . the world full of turns and lights, the precipices, life— Life, he repeated to himself—and everything seemed both to be contained in that little drunken word, and to overflow from it, with the images of this night, a night so different, and the white light pouring on the roofs; and downstairs, that human, abject thing, sobbing dumbly, swallowing its mucus.

Sleep suddenly seized Géricault by the shoulders and turned him over like a child on the pallet, through which he no longer felt the floor.

He did not hear the front door or the step of the two men returning. Their whispered conversation on the first-floor landing. Bernard repairing to his room. He did not hear him pacing up and down like a lion in a cage, there in the next room, unable to make up his mind to go to bed. He did not hear his sighs. He did not interpret the sound of clothes dropped on a chair. He did not hear the returning silence.

He knew nothing of what was going on downstairs. Nor outside. He did not see the moonlit splendor fade, did not see the black clouds scudding, did not hear the rain begin again, tapping on the roof with a thousand insistent little forefingers. He did not awake when the innocently dreaming Moncorps turned over and cried out like Tom Thumb surprised in his sleep in the deep woods by the Ogre. He did not hear the clock strike the hour. And strike again.

Nor, any more than earlier, when the door had opened behind him and the forge hand had approached him in the dark, did he now hear the thing occur again—Firmin's footsteps entering the black garret, coming close, surprised at no longer finding the light of the moon, hesitating between the bed and the pallet, between the two sleepers.

It was no longer the fleshing blade that he clenched in his hand, but a knife, the knife used to cut a hog's throat. He knew how to kill a hog; he had learned that on his father's farm in the country. He knew the creature's panic, he had sometimes held it with both arms, seizing the head by the ears, while his older brother lifted the blade: and his own ears still rang with the animal's horrible cry as it met its fate. All that blood sausage, that tripe inside convulsed with fear. . . . He pressed the knife, a strong knife which did not bend when you plunged it in, a short wooden handle, thick and round: with such a knife you could be sure of your blow. But you had to see where you struck. If you tried to slit the arteries of the throat, the man might awaken, struggle in his blood. It was easier to kill a hog than a man.

To kill a man you must strike him to the heart. With a man the heart was the center of everything. That thing that beat, that went mad in the presence of women. Deep down, Firmin was not sure that man thought with his head. He felt obscurely that it was in his heart that man's follies and great decisions took shape. It was from the heart that a man bled most, from the heart which bled within the body, emptying inside the man, and in the shirt, in the naked torso was left a frightful mouth that scarcely showed, but from which ran a tiny trickle. He had already seen a man killed in this way, last year, a Prussian lured into a trap. It had taken three of them to hold him. A magnificent specimen of a man.

Only you must see where the heart beats, find the place to strike, so as not to break the blade on the bones of the rib case, so as to pass through the bars to reach the heart, man's weak spot. In the drafty attic a shivering Firmin found himself covered with sweat. He was standing as if by a miracle between two sleepers, between the two from whom to choose his victim. He put his left hand on his mouth, as if to prevent himself from crying out.

On the bed, the smaller figure turned over. Again! "He's not the one I'm after, but if I stab the other, while I have my knife in him, buried deep, holding tight, while I twist it so as to do more damage, if he wakes up with the pain, if he yells, or struggles, the other will hear it, will jump on me from behind and I won't be able to free my blade from his ribs. So, even if I turn around—and I'm certainly stronger than he, strong enough to smother him in my arms, bite him in the throat, gouge out his eyes . . . the blood flowing over me everywhere—I'm done for, because of the racket, the screams, the whole house waking up, Bernard kicking the door down and coming in with his pistols, the people downstairs . . . And Sophie, Sophie . . . I'm nothing but a murderer, they'll put me to death on the public square in Amiens.

"Why didn't I go to my room instead, go after the other one, Bernard? He's the one I hate, not this King's soldier. The knife was really for him, to split open that body that yearns for Sophie's. But no, I had to come here where there are two of them. If I began with the younger, I'd be in the same fix. Kill the two of them so quickly they wouldn't have time to wake up, that would be the thing. . . ."

He knew perfectly well, Firmin did, why he had come here and not to Bernard's room. Because hate was something you had to feed, you carried it with you, you got drunk on it, you swallowed it and rolled it around in your belly, you lived with your hate; nothing was terrible enough to satiate it. Cutting a heart open was an innocent game; you wanted something that lasted, that hurt for a long time, that hurt horribly. Hatred was nothing. But shame, rage, *shame.* It was shame which had brought him here into the attic on a night so black that he could not see where to strike. What if he missed? You could remain in the dark for hours above a sleeping man, holding your knife in the air. You could hear his breathing. You had to be guided by that. You were obsessed by the horrible fear of missing your aim.

But how could you allow this man to continue to live? His regular breathing was in itself an intolerable challenge. How could you allow this man to be alive tomorrow when day broke, how could you allow him to wake up when you now held him at your mercy in the dark— this man who had beaten you, knocked you down, this man who had seen you sob with pain and humiliation, who had taken the liberty of picking you up afterwards, of holding you like a big brother, of dragging you, with a kind of contemptuous tenderness: how could you let him live, how could you live yourself, always being beaten by others, by this one as well as by the Compagnons du Devoir, marked in the face—this time he had lost a tooth—threatened, trembling before the promised punishment. "I'll cut off your ears, do you hear me, you ape? . . . so close that they'll be no bigger than your nose . . ." To kill. Nothing could wipe away those words except killing. Like a hog. "Let him bleed. And let him scream, too! Why not! After all, I don't give a damn! They'll catch me, they'll kill me, but I shall have heard him scream, with pain, with fright, with terror, dying and not wanting to die. . . . After that, come what may." The hand must press the small round handle of the upraised knife, and in the night seek and find the place, the place of the heart . . . But you couldn't see anything, you mustn't miss, the sleeping form (how he was sleeping!), the air whistled in his nose and his throat, the dog must have his mouth half open, his breathing was labored, he even sighed . . . You must be sure of your blow. Strike, for God's sake strike, you coward! Don't you realize you're trying to find excuses not to strike?

Théodore did not feel this murderous presence. He did not see the madman's eyes upon him, that left hand tempted to touch his naked body surreptitiously through the opening of the shirt, those fingers that longed to feel, count the ribs, find the mortal spot. Théodore slept, and he dreamed. Perhaps he was dreaming all this, because what likelihood was there of Firmin's having been able to enter here without being heard, of his having been able to remain there so long to dream his bloodthirsty dream, and why indeed, if he were out to kill, had he not gone to the other side of the landing, to kill his rival? The reasons that he gave himself or that were attributed to him, even before the question was raised, were nightmare reasons, and had no basis in reality. Like this whole night, in fact, which defied common sense, this whole adventure in the moonlight, the cemetery and the thicket, the un-likely meeting of men invented out of whole cloth, speaking a language never heard, in the light of fantastic torches. Why should they have met there, on a windy height, at night? Come, come, it was preposterous.

None of this had happened. Perhaps it was no more than a dream of Théodore's, of a Théodore who had not even left his pallet when he presumably heard two men leave the house, who had split in two in a dream, at the point where for the first time the Picard Iago materialized in the garret, in defiance of all probability. He had not seen the adventure of the cemetery, he had not beaten the forge hand, he had no blood on his hands, he was sleeping, that was all, he was sleeping.

And had he even dreamed all this? It was not a forge hand with a broken nose, oozing sweat, humiliated in the depths of his soul. It was not . . . but now that I think of it, it was not Théodore, the sleeping Théodore lying there, dead tired, too exhausted to dream, who dreamed, who had dreamt all this. Perhaps it was someone else, perhaps it was not even Théodore's dream, but someone else's—whose? Well, young Moncorps's for example. It was a schoolboy's dream. He had learned to dream like that at the Hixe boarding school where he had been with his classmate Alfred. Those boys had their heads stuffed with literature. All this was Moncorps's mad dream, and had its source in his reading of the novels of Mrs. Radcliffe, or something of that kind. The house was quiet, the room was empty, Bernard was sleeping beneath a big red eiderdown, and below the blacksmith was clutching Sophie in his powerful arms, both carried away into a world forever

forbidden to us . . . and downstairs, near the hearth, Firmin who
had not come upstairs, who did *not* hold a knife—there was the
knife, for that matter, there in the drawer—who had cried himself
to sleep and dreamed (for he also was dreaming) that he was
strong, that he was tall, that he was happy, that he was loved, and
that he had a nose.

Unless . . . Why, of course, that's it, it's myself. *I* am the
dreamer. My head has nodded several times, I have finally dozed
off on the page of the manuscript, my disheveled hair getting tangled
in the blue ink of the words. I am asleep. With my cheek on the
paper, my left arm hanging along the table leg. My right arm folded,
my hand clutching the fountain pen whose point has broken, making
a hole in the page, beneath the weight of my forehead falling against
my wrist. I am asleep. I am dreaming. All this is my own dream.
Of course. Because, as a matter of fact, all this has to do not with
Théodore's life, but with mine. Don't you recognize it? Nothing of
this could have occurred in 1815, don't you see? The sources are
obvious. My life is my life. Not only Voelklingen in 1919, not only
that. My whole life. The experience of my whole life. The way
I have of roaming the world, discovering strange crafts in their
every detail, how a horse is shod, how a sword is forged, or the
taxi drivers of 1934 who found their way into one of my novels
dressed as taxi drivers of 1911, or Kabyle motorcar washers in a
Passy garage, and the miners of Lens and of Carvin in the detail of
their underground lives, while the war unfolds among the spoil
banks, the French retreat. . . . Political unions. . . . This people
disunited, divided, the poorest not knowing which way to turn,
acting against their manifest interest. The lack of an ideology. The
time it will take for all this to work itself out, or to seem to work
itself out. . . . You remember your enthusiasm on September 27,
1935, at the meeting at which the unity of the labor movement
was decided upon?

And then—it all has to be begun over again. Always. The
tide comes and sweeps away the sandcastles. Twenty years . . .
What is in my mind when I write, speaking of Bernard: *the son of the
man who was executed at Arras?* Oh, the recurrence of all things,
salvos, bodies in ditches! The despair of this entire time . . . will
it even be in my lifetime? Ah, it is not that I cling so to life, but to
die before seeing the thing on its rails, the departure, the engine
picking up speed! I tell you that Géricault was interested only in
horses, and in chiaroscuro, in opposites. So you see that I am the

one who is dreaming, in the middle of the twentieth century, from disillusionment to disillusionment, this blood being shed is not . . . Did Napoleon have to put republicans to death? This blood being shed, my comrades. And so many obvious things challenged again and again. Mistakes have been made, mistakes will be made again. Men will fly at one another's throats, strike their own people, their own flesh. Where is the place of the heart? Where is the place to stab? Because there is hate, but also shame. Ah, I am mixing everything up, but it is I who am dreaming, in the middle of the century, amid this divided people, and not young Moncorps or . . .

The proof. I have the proof. The story about the place of the heart. That story about the knife held poised in the night, and the murderer who in defiance of all probability hesitates for hours on end before striking, looking for the place where the knife will make only a tiny prick, to kill with certainty, just a big drop of black blood next to it, within the breast, the minimum of evidence for the maximum of effectiveness. . . . You can read and reread all the Radcliffe novels, shake them, leaf through the pages, send all their phantoms tumbling out, right side, wrong side, you won't find it in any of the volumes secretly passed under the desk to young Moncorps by his little classmate, Vigny, during the study periods at the Hixe boarding school. But *I* know where that story comes from—don't you? From an English novel, to be sure, but one that will not be written for thirty years, forty years. I don't remember exactly and I don't give a damn. You can look it up in a dictionary, and of course the important thing is that neither Firmin nor Géricault nor Moncorps could have read *Martin Chuzzlewit* thirty or forty years before Dickens wrote it—whereas I have known it since I was a child. Every night my mother would read Dickens to me to put me to sleep, the red-covered Hachette collection which sold at twenty sous; and not once but a thousand times, after going to sleep, I have visualized the scene, the man who has come into the room and who for such a long time seeks the place of the heart. . . . Here I have been dreaming for some four hundred pages, nothing of all this has existed, or rather all this *does* exist for me, along with the railways, the radio, radar, and there is no longer any smithy on the road from Paris to Calais, but only oil stations, and big tractors, red like the volumes of Dickens and blood, in the fields of March, while the smoldering turf-sods turn black and smoke along the roadbanks.

XI

On the Roads

THE interminable night had ended at last. Wednesday was about to dawn in Poix amid a steady downpour. The Black and the Gray Musketeers were waking up.

That night during which the King had finally decided to take the shortest road from Abbeville to Lille, as Macdonald had begged him to do since the morning, instead of sticking to his original intention of following the coast by way of Calais and Dunkirk as though in that way he could have jumped into a boat at any point if ever Exelmans's horsemen should appear. Another reason was that the royal treasure, the Crown diamonds, had preceded him along this road, transported by M. Hué in a carriage covered with a big black mourning cloth so the people mistook it for a hearse removing the remains of Louis XVI and Marie-Antoinette and bared their heads as it passed. And Louis XVIII had perhaps not altogether abandoned the project of going to England, fought so vigorously by Monsieur, his brother, who that very night, tossing ceaselessly in his bed at Grandvilliers, was in the process of convincing himself that the best course, after all, would be to embark at Dieppe, or else at Le Tréport, and in his head was composing a hundred variations of a letter to Louis le Désiré which would convince him of this.

At Lille, at about nine in the evening, Louis-Philippe d'Orléans returned with Marshal Mortier, Duc de Trévise, from Valenciennes where they had reviewed the troops, both of them worried about having left the regiments at Lille without supervision for so long. Only on Tuesday morning, through a dispatch emanating from Buonaparte's men, had they learned the news of the royal flight, and they had made a great effort to hide it from everyone as they had left for Valenciennes. But things get around, and they were both greatly put out at not having received even a word from His Majesty. Where was he? The essential thing was to try to keep the knowledge of what was happening from the soldiers and the people. They would lock all the gates of Lille to prevent the Usurper's emissaries from slipping in! The trouble was that this would hinder the peasants from coming to town for the Wednesday market. They decided to open the gates in rotation, as their police force was insufficient to enable them to keep a check on more than one gate at a time. Whereupon, who should turn up, just about an hour after her brother, but Mademoiselle, sister of the Duc d'Orléans, bearing news of Paris's latest throes. The brother and sister were busy talking when a courier was announced: he was the bearer of a letter from Blacas, dated at Abbeville, informing Louis-Philippe that His Majesty was in Abbeville and would wait for his Household to regroup before making any decision as to future movements.

This was exactly the hour when, at the theatre in Lille, again, as for the past three nights, the final song of *Joconde, ou les coureurs d'aventures,* by Messrs. Scribe and Isouard—a rousing song that calls for a "crusade to fight the Infidels"—was received by a standing house, in a state of indescribable enthusiasm, to cries of *Vive le Roi!* and *Chassons les ennemis!* From which the Duc d'Orléans, whose "observer" had reported this to him, could only gather that the officers of the garrison were not theatregoers, because their state of mind was causing him a great deal of worry. It was true that when the Duke had attended the same show on Sunday night, just at the time when his royal cousin was lighting out from Paris, he had heard the clamorous *Vive Orléans!* with his own ears, and observed that these shouts came from men in uniform. This had given him matter for reflection as to what he might do in case Louis XVIII should take ship for England, and he should find himself, with the armies of Flanders and Picardy, the only representative of the dynasty in a position to resist the Usurper. . . . It seemed to him that, once again, he had only to extend his hand to touch the Crown. Would his whole life pass thus, holding out this temptation, this mirage, before him? But he must let nothing of this show; make no false step, no premature gesture. His fear of betraying himself was even stronger than his thirst for power. Ah, how long must he dissemble? Meanwhile, before going to bed, he discussed with Mortier the measures to be taken on the morrow: a review of the garrison was imperative. They would have to talk to these people, appeal to their patriotism.

The first effect of the security measures at the gates of the city was to deny admission to Bourrienne, whom Louis XVIII had appointed police prefect of Paris on March 13th. He had left on Monday morning, not caring to wait for Napoleon who in Cannes had put him on his list of proscribed persons. All the gates were locked and he was forced to find lodging at this late hour in a suburb. And without having too clear an idea as to who was holding Lille. Was it the King, who must be here by now, or Bonapartist soldiers from whom he had everything to fear? Or the Duc d'Orléans, who was quite capable of playing his own game? To think that he had come posthaste, that he had driven in the mail coach through towns full of songs and tricolor flags, constantly fearing recognition, all this just to wind up in a wretched room without even a fire, where his night was completely wasted!

But at Abbeville things were going very differently from what M. de Blacas's letter might have led its recipient to anticipate. Could it be the arrival at full gallop that evening of a messenger who echoed rumors concerning the progress of the Imperial horsemen—could it be this that induced the sovereign to listen at last to Marshal Macdonald? Perhaps the cries of *Vive l'Empereur!* uttered by soldiers in the town may also have influenced his decision. A post of cuirassiers there professed detestable opinions. In short, no one knew anything until the last minute, and M. de Verville, the sub-prefect, was full of admiration for His Majesty, for the calm he displayed when, upon being pressed to hasten his departure (in particular by Berthier, who kept walking about with Mme. Visconti's casket under his arm, and was beside himself since Macdonald had whispered to him a few hurried words explaining what had happened at the inn on the rue Compoise at Saint-Denis), he made the sole concession of allowing dinner to be served one hour earlier at the Hôtel de la Sous-préfecture, where he had been staying since the previous day surrounded by the ceremonial of the Tuileries, at least to the extent to which it could be observed with the means available at Abbeville. And what a dinner! A royal trencherman! As the seven courses of the menu succeeded one another, and the monarch told one spicy story after another, those present might have thought themselves at Versailles!

To such a point that in order to put Macdonald at ease rather than for any other reason, the Marshal had been sent on ahead as a scout—there being, in fact, no one else, neither guards nor messengers. There were the ten horsemen—but how could they take even one from their number to serve as dispatch rider without weakening the escort of the royal carriages? A Marshal of France must be good for something. General Hulot was to accompany him: that made virtually a vanguard. The rest would join them. Berthier was growing nervous. He had hoped to question Macdonald further after dinner. They would join them. . . . Easier said than done.

"We shall join them soon enough. Just let me relax and taste this . . . is it Chambertin, or what?" "Oh, His Majesty has hit the bull's-eye! Chambertin it is." "Wait . . . what date? 1811, perhaps? No, a little greener than that . . . I'll wager it's 1813!" The sub-prefect could not get over this. Macdonald's carriage, after changing horses at Hesdin—or rather, no: for M. de Verville had felt it his duty to say, coughing a little as he did so, that the state of mind in that town was detestable, and the royal escort consequently avoided it, making direct for the suburb of Marconne, at the top of the ridge, and the inn of a Sieur Couronné whose very name compelled him to loyalty, and who, upon being notified by Macdonald, had sent to the Saint-Leu post to fetch relay animals for the six carriages. But Berthier had not yet managed to speak to Macdonald, who had had to ride on ahead as dispatch rider immediately upon the arrival of the royal train. From there, accordingly, they made for Saint-Pol.

The King, in his six-horse berlin, reached the town in bright moonlight with two footmen on the seat in Court uniform, as in Paris. Poor chaps! They were not very warm, sitting there with their arms crossed. (This was no longer one of those breakneck rides round the capital that Father Elisée had recommended to His Majesty as helpful for his rheumatism!) And the five carriages followed, with ten men in all as escort, Father Elisée beside the driver in the last one, among the servants. Here too the horses were changed at the other end of town, at the Béthune gate where Macdonald had stopped, so that the attention of the notables had already been aroused. The King was persuaded to enter the nearest house to rest. It was a miserable district where they spun linen and made stockings on looms, and there was a lime kiln, and pottery factories, its population all being craftsmen. His Majesty had to be helped down from the carriage and almost carried. He was taken into a stone-floored room level with the road and cluttered with household utensils. It was the poorly heated home of a widow who lived alone. The old woman was half awake, half dressed, and terrified, wonder-struck: the King in her house! It was the great adventure of her life, happening without warning, without her being in any way prepared for it. She was going to lose all its benefits.

She looked about her, trying to think of something to do that would be in keeping with the event. Some gentlemen in bright uniforms were busy settling the sovereign in her only armchair, and she looked about for what was most beautiful in this room that reeked of cold smoke from a stove where at this hour the peat fire was no longer burning. And she saw her pride and comfort, the large, faded, fringed curtain, all threadbare and heavy, which protected the room against the draft from the window. Recklessly she pulled it down, tearing it from the top, and spread it out under the sovereign's feet like a carpet, having heard him say, "Oh, my feet, my feet . . ." For at Abbeville it had been discovered that His Majesty's portmanteau, everything by way of wardrobe that had been hastily packed, had been stolen during a halt, and—well, never mind the shirts; but what was serious was that the royal slippers had disappeared and no shoemaker in town had had any that would fit those enormous deformed feet.

In spite of the hour, and the remoteness of the spot, there were still people who would have importuned the monarch if a guard had not been posted at the door. A guard! Well, that was a manner of speaking—there were no soldiers to mount it; the entire escort did not suffice to guard the convoy, ahead, to the rear, and in the direction of town; by way of sentinels they had to fall back on what lay to hand, that is to say Berthier, chewing his nails and casting occasional glances in the direction of the precious casket which he had reluctantly placed on the widow's chest of drawers, and Blacas himself, both with their naked swords to their shoulders: which was a rather amusing sight. Berthier was in despair at having to do picket duty: he had again been unable to talk with Macdonald. And the expression on the face of M. Godeau d'Entraigues when he came running to pay his respects to the royal traveler and recognized in the two ill-assorted comic-opera guards who had crossed their swords before him to prevent the sub-prefect of Saint-Pol from entering the hovel—recognized in the plump swarthy figure and the tall beanpole with the red nose the Prince de Wagram and the secretary of the Royal Household!

Blacas, to help keep himself awake, could worry over his collection of medals: it had, to be sure, been sent off far in advance in the direction of England, but he had no more news of it than of his young wife— Oh, as far as she was concerned there was nothing to worry about! She knew England, spoke the language perfectly . . . As for Berthier—Macdonald's hurried words at Abbeville about his meeting with Mme. Visconti at Saint-Denis, and the "slight mishap to her health" that had forced her to retrace her steps toward the capital, were enough to rob him of sleep. He should never have left . . . never have left . . . Would he ever see again Grosbois and his mansion on the Capucines? If only he could have brought the Gérard portrait of Giuseppa with him! Giuseppa . . . if only it wasn't serious!

It was five o'clock, even earlier, when the royal train, with the good Saint-Pol horses, stopped to relay once again on the main square of Béthune. It was not yet raining as it had been at Poix and the post was in a hotel opposite the belfry which occupies the center of the square, but which at that time had houses around it, and shops, built for the most part during the previous hundred years despite remonstrances by the authorities. And that week almost the whole space between these buildings and the houses surrounding the square was cluttered up with booths and tents, because there was a fair—not the big October fair which took over the whole town, but a fair confined to the main square, where for two or three days it occupied the market area and itinerant vendors offered their wares. The gendarmes were guarding all this against thieves who might sneak in and pilfer, and also against thieves suspected of hiding inside the fair itself. You never knew with those gipsies . . . That is to say, the gendarmes were both snoozing at the postmaster's in the Hôtel du Nord . . . and they woke up at the arrival of the carriages which had stopped at the corner of the rue Grosse-Tête. But they did not at once realize with whom they had to deal.

The horses were being unharnessed; it was still quite dark, and the sound of all the coming and going had awakened the bearherd in the little rickety house on wheels in which, in order to keep warm, he was sleeping naked between his two muzzled beasts. He looked out through his back window at the ostlers, with their torches, unharnessing the horses and leading them away. The first person to become aware of what was happening was an old woman with a black hood, Sister Félicité, a former religious of the Hôpital Saint-Jean, who by episcopal permission had taken up lay duties during the Revolution. What was she doing here at such an hour? But you are forgetting that this was Holy Week, she might have been watching over the Holy Sacrament at the Saint-Vaast Church, and now be returning home. She was in fact leaving home, and was on her way to *day mass,* as these matins were called. Egged on by curiosity, she drew close to look at the big puffy nobleman sticking his nose out of the window of his berlin coach, as a passing torch lighted up his face, and suddenly she recognized the King—not from his portraits, but from having seen him in the flesh, in 1814, at Calais, where she had happened to be at the time of the return from England, having gone there to nurse a niece of hers through her lying-in. The King! Sweet Jesus, what did it mean? She could not help drawing close, and the royal gaze fell upon her. She stammered, "Your Majesty . . ." and Louis XVIII abruptly remembered Varennes and his late brother recognized thus at a relay post during his flight. With a vague movement of his head he nodded a greeting to the old woman who resembled Death.

Emboldened by this movement, Sister Félicité came to the door, bowed and exclaimed with anguish, "Sire, to what do we owe your honorable visit? Has some misfortune occurred?"

It is the job of kings to know how to lie. Le Désiré, lifting his heavy eyelids and turning his afflicted back ever so slightly, made a limp gesture with his hand, to reassure her, and said, "Do not worry, all will be well."

These were words that she could not have kept to herself, and at this time of day with whom could she share them? Sister Félicité entered the Hôtel du Nord and there met Mme. Brassart, wife of the iron merchant, in a dressing gown and hair curlers, who, having opened the shutters upon hearing all the bustle in the square, had come out for news. And Sister Félicité, thinking she was speaking softly, repeated in a piercing voice, "All will be well, all will be well!" which caused one of the gendarmes slumbering on the bench to look up. "The King!" she went on, and Mme. Brassart, when she understood, turned a deep crimson.

"The King! The King among us! But what shall we do? Take him something hot?"

An excellent idea! Sister Félicité advised chocolate, and Mme. Brassart ran home, explaining to her husband, who had been one of the cartload sent from Béthune to be guillotined in Thermidor (July 1794), and had owed his life only to the fall of Robespierre: "The King, Riquet! The King!"

But the gendarme who had heard Sister Félicité had rushed out to inform Lieutenant Huet, his chief. This was how the royal presence began to be bruited about, and in no time at all people began to come out of the houses, to run up and pay their respects to the sovereign. First of all, his house being on the square, came M. Delalleau, the mayor, who as he emerged from his doorway, still getting into his coat and slipping on his sash, cried *"Vive le Roi! Vive le Roi!"* so that no one could doubt he had been the first to do so. And then there came forth from the tents not only the bearherd with his animals, but a flock of gipsies, a giant and three dwarfs, the clairvoyant, the tight-rope walker in pink tights, the weight lifter who was usually seen only in the scantiest of apparel but was the only one completely dressed at this hour; and these were followed by all sorts of people coming from the houses with their women in the morning chill, all or nearly all in undress or only half clothed, in shirt sleeves or wrappers, one boot on and the other carried in the hand, or struggling to button themselves as they went. There was Major Vermines (and Madame, whose head was covered with curl papers), who was in command of the district but had no soldiers with him because the garrison was recalcitrant, and who, knowing where its feelings lay, had not even alerted it. Lieutenant Huet, of the 20th Legion of the Royal Gendarmerie, the Pas-de-Calais company, had allowed himself to be preceded by the mayor; the Comte de Maulde, because it had taken him time to collect his men, who numbered five including the two gendarmes on guard, so that he was the only one to have his troop here. Captain of Engineers Bellonet, for example, who followed them, had been reduced to a single orderly who had disappeared, sleeping somewhere with a Béthune wench of ill repute. And if the truth must be told, Adjutant de Boiron d'Aguières, in charge of levying royal volunteers, happened not to be at Béthune that night: he had gone to Lalloeu (that town having made a poor showing) to raise recruits among former deserters from the wars of the Empire and among followers of Fruchart, the self-styled Louis XVII, who, before he became an official personage, had been the leader of the monarchist gang that had terrorized the region.

While he had received the Comte de Maulde and the other military with a coolness that Blacas made even more conspicuous by his way of treating people, Louis XVIII gratefully drank Mme. Brassart's chocolate. "The good people!" he murmured. This lady had told him the story of the last tumbrel as she stirred a lump of sugar into the piping-hot beverage. You could understand that a man like Henri Brassart, who had seen the guillotine at such close range, would be devoted to His Majesty. So much so, in fact, that forty days from now he was to enter the municipality under appointment by the Emperor. But the chocolate was hot and well sweetened. "The good people!" the King repeated. As for Berthier, he was not reassured: the mountebanks on the square made him hug his casket all the tighter. And he had as yet managed to exchange only a few words with the Duc de Tarente upon his arrival. Just enough to plunge him into despair. . . .

But immediately behind the higher officers, whose presence emphasized the hostility of the common soldiers, there was a rush of officials: all the magistrates of the lower court had come in a body as well as the deputy public prosecutor and the registrar. Among these His Majesty was struck by only one name, that of one of his judges, M. Décrépitude: he had it repeated three times and despite his fatigue, it made him laugh till the tears came. And the six solicitors to the said court. And the justice of the peace. Then the tax assessors and collectors, all in disarray, in rags, the registrar of mortgages who had forgotten to comb his hair and looked as if he had just been caught *in flagrante delicto.* The whole lot of them rigged out in haste, flanked by an assortment of ladies and damsels accompanied by infants in the arms of nurses still in dressing jackets, for His Majesty to bless, or at least for them to have something to remember.

This early dawn ceremony before the door of the royal carriage was not lacking in comic appeal, and the King took it all in with mingled tenderness and disdain, letting his gaze roam over the still mist-shrouded square. The famous belfry rose in the center above the three-story houses leaning up against it, with their double rows of attics contrived in the slates of their steep roofs in violation of edicts issued by the municipal magistrates—the famous belfry stood out above the city like an enormous gray gendarme scrutinizing the imperfectly dispelled darkness; and from beneath its pyramidal hat the carillon began suddenly to peal forth with its thirty-six small bells, *ting-a-ling-a-ling.* . . . The song rang out above the square filled with the boards and booths of the fair and struck against the surrounding buildings, which were in fact scarcely higher than the houses clinging to the belfry but looked tall because they were all narrow and pressed together tight, tight, with their exaggeratedly steep Flemish-style roofs, their cutout ornamental fronts, and their stone chimneys, in twos and threes, like lookouts for a battle of birds in the sky, a forest of lookouts.

But the absurdity of this improvised court was brought to its peak by a latecomer in slippers, a puny fifty-year-old who had managed to don only one leg of his trousers and was trying to slip on the other as he ran, all his clothes hastily tossed on one over the other—a jersey, a shirt, a vest—without his having taken the time to button anything, his coat under his arm, a feathered hat on his head, holding his cravat in one hand and his sword in the other, unable to decide whether first to attach his sword to his belt or tie his cravat around his neck —a question of precedence—so that, having come into the presence of His Majesty, he was unable to uncover himself since he had no free hand. He was M. Duplaquet, sub-prefect of Béthune—a post he had held through every regime since the Consulate; he was saved only by the arrival of the fresh team, and limped off with one leg bare, or nearly so, dropping his sword, picking it up only to lose his cravat, convinced that through his clumsiness he had ruined his career forever. A nasty urchin of ten, who had come out with his mother to see what was going on, offered to hold his trousers so that he could slip them on. But the sub-prefect declined this offer because he had just recognized the lady, who was the mother of another son who was well known to the police: the harebrained fellow had taken it into his head to enlist in the infantry at the age of sixteen, had been wounded at Besançon the previous year, was suspected of republicanism, had been discharged on half-pay with the rank of sergeant, and had come back to Béthune apparently in order to plot with the garrison.

After having made himself ridiculous before the King, whose carriage was starting off in the direction of Lille, all the sub-prefect would have needed was to compromise himself further by slipping on his trousers with the help of that whippersnapper. It took less than that for a report to put you down as a suspect! M. le Sous-Préfet knew this from experience. What he did not know was that the father of these two lads, a former officer, had attended a clandestine meeting at Poix that same night. . . .

Dawn . . . the members of the *Confrérie des Charitables* on their way to matins contemplated it with stupor, as did the crowd on the square and in the rue Grosse-Tête and in the direction of Saint-Vaast. Dawn began to turn moist, to soften; it was not so cold as yesterday, was not really cold even; it was obviously going to rain again.

And over there, at Grandvilliers and at Poix, it was already raining on the Royal Household and the Princes. Over there, everyone thought the King was still at Abbeville, for there had been no report of his departure. It seemed that His Majesty was unfamiliar with the use of messengers, or at least considered it totally unnecessary to dispatch any to the Household, which had such difficulty in following him, or to the Princes, for whom he had no concern whatever. At Grandvilliers the Princes were holding a council, drafting the letter that the Comte d'Artois had ruminated in his sleep, announcing to the King that, all things considered, the Household, in its present state of disorder, scattered over a dozen leagues, exhausted, winded, crippled, burdened with sick and wounded, having to limit its pace to that of infantry, had no other possible choice than to embark at Dieppe, and that Dieppe itself was far enough away, all things considered; that the King could make his way there from Abbeville, and thus reach England with at least a military escort instead of like a poor beggar abandoned by God and men. Already the bulk of the Lifeguards were on the road, and when the council ended, M. de Reiset's Guards and M. de Damas's Light Horse in turn got into motion, closing the convoy that had formed behind the Comte d'Artois in his carriage and Monseigneur le Duc de Berry, with Marmont and his suite, on horseback; and the rain fell on Monseigneur in his light gray oilskin cloak with its black collar, as he came and went, backwards and forwards. César de Chastellux, saluting him with his sword, noticed the big motionless tears at their ancestral post in the Prince's eyes: Charles-Ferdinand was thinking with terror that they would never let his Virginie enter England, and that while he would see his two beloved daughters, he would also see Mrs. Brown again—Mrs. Brown, whom he couldn't abide, but whom the Prince Regent regarded as his wife in the eyes of God. The hypocrisy of these Protestants! Mrs. Brown, of course, was English.

And to the rear, on the road, men on foot, jolting carts too heavily loaded for their horses, M. de Mortemart's artillery constantly getting stuck in the mud, stretched out in an initial disorder, feet dragging, halting at every league. . . . Everywhere the same subdued rain-washed light prevailed over the bumpy, muddy roads. Tuesday had not been too bad, but Wednesday began inauspiciously, making up for yesterday although it was milder. A real Holy Week Wednesday, with the sky going into anticipated mourning, and bunches of box-wood stuck on the calvaries at the crossroads.

At Poix, Lauriston's and La Grange's Musketeers were waiting for the bulk of the Household before they in turn got into motion. They had risen before dawn, and the order had come to remain with arms grounded until the Princes arrived. A carriage had preceded them, a tilbury suitable for a ride around a lake! Léon de Rochechouart's curiosity was aroused: who was the eccentric in that black tilbury with yellow wheels, his legs wrapped in a green and blue rug? His aide-de-camp, Montpezat, had recognized him: it was General Ricard. He was bearing the Comte d'Artois's letter to His Majesty, and was on his way to Abbeville where he expected still to find the King. The same Ricard who in 1809 had been the accomplice of Soult when he made his bid for the throne of Portugal. He had changed horses at Poix, for he had to make all speed, and he had just had time to confirm the orders to the two captain-lieutenants of Musketeers. He also confirmed that M. de Castries had left Grandvilliers at the same time as himself, dispatched by Monsieur by way of Aumale to Dieppe, to round up all the vessels he could find. What did that mean? Were they changing direction? In any event, they would have at least an hour and a half with nothing to do; the horsemen were surrounded by field kitchens distributing a hot beverage which it would be an exaggeration to call coffee.

The Comte de Rochechouart, whose carriage bearing his effects and those of the Duc de Richelieu had remained, like the Duke himself, with the Princes' column, looked enviously at the barouche belonging to M. de Rastignac, his distant relative and comrade in the Black Musketeers. It was a barouche of elongated shape, and brand-new, its newness obvious even after the ordeal of this journey, the coachman having just given it a thorough washing: a fine green barouche with brass fittings and black wheels, the very last word in stylishness, just look at the inside: entirely lined in green morocco leather, it was like a fine binding, a beautiful valise. And M. de Rastignac's baggage was in the same style. It would be more agreeable to travel in a carriage, but that was ruled out: the example came from above, and must be conformed to. In this lamentable flight it was something, at least, to have such a pretty toy following along behind. "My dear fellow," said Rastignac, "do you think that we're really going to cross over to England? They'll never let me take my barouche aboard."

"Bah!" retorted Rochechouart, "a lot can happen between now and then. If the King takes to the sea, M. de Richelieu intends to continue by road to join his master, the Emperor of Russia . . . and M. de Stempkovski, of course, our dear Vanya. Personally, you know, I would just as soon cross into the Low Countries; the cooking is better."

And Géricault, looking at this small town which he had hardly seen except at night, decided that, despite the rain, he wanted to take advantage of the occasion to check something that was very much on his mind. Leaving Moncorps to take care of Trick, he climbed the hill to the church, which now appeared much closer, and on beyond the small houses with their inner courts, and up the stone steps that led to the terrace on the right of the church. He followed the path that he must have dreamed he had followed; he had no longer a clear recollection of what had happened, and he tried to untangle what was real from his dreams. Where did the imaginings of the night begin? He felt the need to find the traces, if any existed, of the spectacle that revived in his mind with the steps he was repeating. He pushed open the gate to the cemetery, followed the wall of the fort, circled the rotunda, and saw the crumbled wall. . . . He climbed over it, a stone breaking loose under his foot, and he was in the brushwood; he came to a path between masses of shrubs interlaced with old brambles, the ground carpeted with ivy: so it was no dream—here were the lanes that wound and converged beneath the big twisted pines.

He had reached the spot. The ground showed obvious traces of having been trampled recently, of a score or more of men having stood and shuffled there. A burned-out torch, almost wholly consumed, near where the man from the rue du Caire had stood, confirmed his confused memories. A few steps back the slope dropped abruptly into the thicket, forming a bank of clay that still bore the imprint of a body, the trace of the eavesdropper among the broken twigs. So this was the spot, and Théodore shut his eyes the better to reconstruct the situation, to remember. What he tried to recapture was the vanished words. He had difficulty in recalling them; they came back at random, crossed and tangled. He no longer remembered who had said what, and he reconstructed the scene as though it were a text in an unknown language—he could assemble the characters but the words were meaningless. The church clock struck seven. Under the shrubbery bloomed primulas and, beneath last year's straw, scattered green clusters of nettles. Now he had reached the very center of the circle. Here, where the tracks converged under the tall pines, the curve of the hill dipping down into the valley half hidden by low-hanging mist could be seen in one direction while the opposite view directly overlooked the road to Calais where it climbed upwards to the right from Poix.

Everything was clear. There was no point in lingering. Géricault headed down one of the tracks branching out from the circle, the one that ran below the cemetery, circling it in the direction of the church. Everything, he concluded, must have happened. It was not an hallucination.

A trumpet call rang out below. He must hurry, for it was the boots and saddles. And suddenly he regretted not having seen Sophie again this morning: she had still been asleep when he left. Firmin had vanished: as for him . . . It was odd, but what the Musketeer now craved more than anything else was to talk to Bernard. About what? About politics, or love? About both, perhaps. . . . It was raining, there was a feeling of spring. The trees, like tousled urchins with their mop of fine bare branches, softly laid their heads on a tender gray sky, above fields blond with old straw and young tillage.

As a matter of fact, they were not leaving. The Princes had arrived, but it seemed that the Household was having difficulty in keeping up with them. Even if the three leagues that separated Poix from Grandvilliers had been negotiated at infantry pace, the bulk of the troops should have arrived by eight, or a quarter past. . . . The Musketeers, who had drawn to the side of the road to let the Comte d'Artois and Monseigneur pass, remained in that position; their horses were restless and pawed the ground. An hour wasted . . . an hour and a quarter. Théodore had seen a black wagon drawn by white horses pass by in the direction of Abbeville, and thought he recognized Bernard on the seat under the green canvas tilt. So the last chance had slipped by him to no avail. How stupid!

But what did he expect to gain from a conversation with this ladykiller? And he thought, Go on fetching yarn for the village weavers, my lad, spin your plot as you go, and dream about your Sophie! We belong to two different worlds, our paths will never cross again.

There were the La Rochejaquelein Grenadiers. Lifeguards on foot, escorted by a company on horseback, or at least as much of a company as it had been possible to mount. You could see, without asking any questions, why it had taken these people more than three hours to traverse three leagues. The situation was deteriorating from one day to the next as the horses became exhausted, and more and more horsemen were marching on foot, leading their horses by the bridle. And then the military convoy had got mixed up with all kinds of odds and ends of carriages—some carrying the sick, the wounded, the old men in uniform, the boys let out from school; but it had also been unexpectedly reinforced by some hundreds of civilian barouches and coaches heavily laden with women traveling with their servants, their dogs and their children; and on the road there were continual accidents—ladies becoming indisposed, officer friends of theirs getting in with them. There were valets walking, each holding two or three animals, while their masters rode in the carriages; and the train of the Lifeguards, the Light Horse, the Gendarmes of the King's Guard,

the Gardes-de-la-Porte, the Swiss Guards—more than twenty carriages for the Swiss Guards alone! *et cetera*—observed no discipline;
the drivers tried to get close to their masters, having no idea whether
they were ahead or behind, in the vanguard with the Princes or
straggling far to the rear. Those who were on foot kept stopping in
despair over the rain. As they passed through the villages, half the
travelers needed something or other: they noticed a shoemaker's shop
and woke the man up, made him open his door so that they could
try on all his boots, his shoes. Or the unreasoning craving to take
shelter. Others who had set out without eating anything cleaned out
the *estaminets,* asked at private houses if there were no cold meats
available, or at least some bread that was not too stale.

It was easy to understand why the Comte d'Artois had resolved
to cross the sea: from Abbeville, where they were supposed to catch
up with the King, the sudden movement in the direction of Dieppe
might disconcert the pursuers, and thus afford time to embark.

So in the end it was a little after nine o'clock before this enormous
mob at last got under way, leaving Poix by the road that climbed the
hill, circling the cemetery above the valley, and emerging suddenly
from among the trees into a quite different landscape, an immense
bare plateau stretching as far as the eye could reach. Moving at a
trot was now out of the question: the Household must be massed, they
had to wait for the people on foot in order to flank them, and now
they proceeded despairingly at a walking pace in this monotonous
landscape, in the rain, in the mud. . . .

It was enough to drive you mad to mark time like this on a road,
to get yourself drenched, with a horse already tired from the preceding days. And as he had been warned might happen, Théodore felt
Trick falter from time to time; it was all very well to know that it
was just pretense and that every precaution had been taken, the foot
smeared with clay, but it made him nervous all the same. In the end,
in the course of the halts, the things people said began to make an
impression. It was all very well not to let yourself be carried away by
the general hysteria. It was all very well. . . .

It was on the second day that everyone talked as if he had seen
them, had seen Exelmans's horsemen. To be sure, no one had seen
them. But since the start they had begun saying they were right on
their heels, what with the slowness of the march, the halts and now
the rain in their eyes—a torrential rain—it must begin to be true;
and people turned around, lifted themselves in their stirrups, to look

behind. What was coming? . . . nothing, or rather, yes: everything
. . . that is to say the vast obstruction of the road, the piecemeal
column, the mixed-up carriages, the complaining men on foot, the
Household as far as the eye could reach. . . . "If they are on our
heels, we must have long heels, so we have no way of knowing."

With Captain-Lieutenant de La Grange's authorization, M. de
Rochechouart trotted from front to rear as best he could, escorted by
the faithful Montpezat, in order to join the Duc de Richelieu; or at
least that was the pretext he had given. Having seen M. de Rastignac's
barouche, he was especially anxious to know whether his own cabriolet was following. Along with the Duke's portmanteau, it carried Léon
de Rochechouart's entire fortune: eight thousand francs in gold in a
traveling case and a change of clothes, a Court suit. His servant was
inside to guard it; but Léon was not too sure of Bertin his coachman,
whom he knew but slightly, having hired him only recently, and after
all, in this monumental disorder the riffraff was not beyond temptation.

He passed through the crowd of Grammont's Guards, a congestion
of carts and masters' carriages—no cabriolet in sight. There was M. de
Reiset struggling— A man, Léon reflected, better able to cope with
women than with a regimental train. This took him back to the end
of 1813, at Baden, where they had had such great fun after the battle
of Leipzig. He just couldn't resist telling Montpezat how he had met
some German ladies who had known Tony de Reiset at Potsdam in
1807. They had not forgotten him in six years and they spoke of him
behind their fans, giving details that French ladies rarely divulge, but
which were very complimentary to Tony.

"Where are you going, Monsieur de Rochechouart?" asked César
de Chastellux as he passed, leaning from his horse which had stopped
flank to flank with that of the Comte de Damas in response to a saber
salute in their direction.

The Black Musketeer stopped and came to pay his respects to
M. de Damas and his son-in-law. There was no denying it, the Light
Horse amid all this maintained a better appearance than the others.
Léon said as much, in flattering terms, to Comte Charles and his
adjutant commander. From them he learned one of the reasons for
the great uncertainty that had prevailed that morning at the Princes'
headquarters. The Lifeguard who had been sent from Beauvais to
Amiens the previous day had reached Grandvilliers during the night.
From Amiens he brought back merely the news that the garrison had
adopted the tricolor cockade; but Exelmans's much-talked-of horsemen had not made an appearance, at least not up to the evening when

he had left the prefecture of the Somme, where the prefect, M. Alexandre de Lameth, had received him very oddly, without its being at all clear to which side he really leaned. But when he had reached Beauvais three hours after the Household's departure, Imperial mounted orderlies were already there preparing billets for a regiment of light infantry. The Lifeguard brought a message from M. de Massa for Marshal Marmont, and another for Macdonald, from his daughter. The prefect of Beauvais confirmed the imminent arrival of the Imperial troops and referred to a statement by the Allied sovereigns made in Vienna more than a week previously, but he did not supply the text, so a lot of good it did them! But the charming Nancy's husband announced that the telegraph, which the King had given orders to dismantle, was again working like a charm, and that a message from the Tuileries announced the departure of forty thousand stalwarts under Exelmans's command, on the heels of the King and his Household.

Forty thousand men! More than eight times their own number! So in any event, the story about Exelmans was no figment of the imagination. After that, whoever wanted to could cast stones at Monsieur for having suddenly espoused the project he had so vigorously fought, and having decided to lead the faithful troops across the Channel.

"But see here, my dear fellow, are you really looking for the Duc de Richelieu in that direction?" said Charles de Damas with a faint laugh. "He has gone ahead with His Highness. By carriage: I think he's really had enough of the horse, and Father Elisée's treatments have not been very effective. . . . Back there, to the rear, you won't find anything but vehicles, the tag end, ladies frightened by the prospect of the return of the Mamelukes!"

It was becoming difficult to continue on his way. Léon de Rochechouart, straightening in his saddle so as to make the most of his small stature, privately and somewhat regretfully abandoning the hope of finding his cabriolet, which was surely caught somewhere in the tag end in question, saluted the captain-lieutenant of the Light Horse again, motioned to Montpezat, and turned his horse around in the direction of the head of the convoy. What a damned nuisance, having to overtake the whole column. . . . England! The prospect certainly didn't appeal to him. He would just as soon have accompanied Richelieu. After all, the Czar would forgive his having left him a bit hastily for the service of His Majesty Louis XVIII. Yet who could tell? Alexander was vindictive. And if they had to make for the northern border, they ought to make a decision, the Duke and he, at Abbeville. Anyway, it would be out of the question to embark five thousand men at Dieppe: where would they find the boats? Here the crush was so great that he had willy-nilly to leave the road, climb the bank and take to the drenched fields.

It was hardly more than five leagues from Poix to Airaines, a distance a horseman could usually cover in two hours at most, even going at a walk part of the time. But at the rate at which they were now moving, with the repeated halts, and the emissaries constantly being sent from the rear to the front and from the front to the rear with orders for which they had to wait so as to be able to transmit them to the command, with the mud and the rain, the increasingly heavy rain, the thicker and thicker mud, it would take them at best three hours—that is to say, the advance guard, for the rest were dragging their feet, and there were gaps in the convoy. As a matter of fact, the Princes sat down to table at the relay inn, and the companies' meal was organized in some of the barns of Airaines, in the outbuilding of a factory which made canvas for ships' sails, and another which made sacks. It was here that the contents of M. de Massa's message to Marmont was bruited about because, mysteriously, no secret could be kept more than two or three hours, and because from the commander-in-chief to the kitchen brigade, from the general staff to the stableboys, there seemed to be a kind of osmosis: it was not indiscretion, it was a physical phenomenon about which nothing could be done.

Théodore, who had gone to the blacksmith's to have a fresh application of clay put on Trick's hoof, was among the last to hear these rumors, and he gave no credence to them. Forty thousand men? The figure, at least, appeared exaggerated. . . . At which point, what should he see before an *estaminet* but the black van with the green canvas tilt and the white horses, glimpsed earlier at Poix—yes, there was no mistaking it. And inside, at the counter, Bernard leaning on his elbows drinking cider and talking and gesticulating to the serving-maid. Instinctively Géricault went in. And now he felt a little foolish. How could he approach the man? Especially as the fellow was quite obviously drunk.

What, for that matter, did Théodore expect from the Abbeville carrier? What could such an impossible conversation bring him? He could not hope for confidences, he could not elicit them. As long as he wore the livery of the monarchy on his back, he would encounter only hostility or guile. He could not take a short cut—say he had been present at the meeting in the thicket, and tell how deeply he had been stirred by the words he had heard. Nor could he tell Bernard the unlikely story that he, the Musketeer, had been ready to place his hopes in the returning Emperor up to the moment when Bernard's voice had brought him back to himself, had taught him that harsh lesson (*"Whom do you mean, 'we'?"*), so that it was to him, to Bernard, that Géricault was now turning to ask the questions that had been tormenting him for several days, pressing on him more and more during the flight of the Royal Household, in this spectacle of disorder, of the collapse of a world.

Yes, he was a witness of the royal Passion in this Holy Week without having any faith in the mission of the Sons of Saint Louis. Yes, changing cockades, for him, did not mean changing ideals but simply changing illusions. And the sudden pulling up short of the reins (*"Whom do you mean, 'we'?"*) by that disheveled young man in the threadbare coat which betrayed his hopeless aspiration toward provincial elegance, had shaken Théodore more than all the rest. Yes— who were we?

He hesitated to answer his own question, to put faces to that *we,* the faces of the wretchedness he had glimpsed. Setting aside the fact that he was a Royal Musketeer, had he any kind of right to include himself in that *we?* He suffered from a feeling of being a stranger to this little personal pronoun, to what it might embrace. He even felt a certain humility before this *we*—he was ready to ask, to beg to be included in it. Not in the crowd that cries *Vive le Roi!* one day only to bedeck itself with violets the next; not in the rush of half-pay soldiers, the scramble of those who considered themselves frustrated, the hunt for jobs. But in that immense nameless mass which ultimately pays with its blood, its life, its labor for the struggle of the powerful. Would they accept him? Had he even the shadow of a claim to be considered? If only he had had confidence in his art, if he could have invoked that. But how do the destitute feel about a painter?

He who would now always be suspected because of this uniform that he had worn, because of the share he had had in the royal flight —and what were people saying? Dieppe, England . . . Could he leave this country, his country? The odd thing was that all of a sudden, in these Picardy plateaux, in this monotonous, empty landscape in which nothing was either beautiful or appealing, the word *country,* like the word *we,* clutched him by the throat, rose in his gorge. It was here in the rain, in this universe of poverty, that at every step he felt heavier, more attached to this earth. He could not leave: this was

being borne in upon him. But then . . . it was as though the relations
between him and other men—those who were not fleeing on foot or
on horseback, those who did not carry the standards of the exodus
(how he could laugh now at the *Quo ruit et lethum!*), those for whom
the question of taking the boat or crossing to the Low Countries did
not arise—as though the relations between him and others had completely changed, and he could no longer live among them in the usual
way; he would have to account to them, and bring an end to all that
frivolity, the hours spent at the tailor's for a uniform, the parades in
the Bois, at Versailles, Frascati . . . And had he even the right to
become again the painter he had for the past six months refused to be?
Even this was in question. Could he still live at home, outside what
was happening? He was thinking all this, raising these question marks
with a kind of childish fear in which he could not make out what he
himself wanted to be henceforth. Was he afraid of this change in life,
or was he burning to take his place in it? Both, undoubtedly. He saw
the future as an extraordinary conflagration. He said to himself, too,
that that conflagration would be the beauty the future held in store,
and that what he feared above all was that he would not be ready to
understand it. Was man equal to history? He remembered the café
owner on the rue d'Argenteuil, the vacant-eyed substitute, his father.
What had this to do with the thoughts that were rending him, in the
din of this Airaines *estaminet* crowded with horsemen who had come
in for a drink; and at the counter that fellow Bernard who laughed
sneeringly and talked in a loud voice, waved his arms and avidly
swallowed yet another glass. *Ugh,* he was abominably drunk! At this
time of day, and at such a moment. A fine lover, upon my word, and
a hell of a conspirator.

Although it might have been love or the upsetting nature of what
was happening which was making him drink, which had overcome
him to the point of causing him thus to lose his dignity . . . Anyway, there was no way of talking to this man who was no longer himself. He would leave.

A group of Grenadiers in their bearskins was passing the doorway
as Théodore unhitched Trick from the iron ring where he had left the
animal. Géricault looked to see whether Marc-Antoine was among
them. No. What were they talking about? They were a rather sorry-
looking lot in their washed-out uniforms, several of them ill-shaven
—they had already begun to let themselves go; their voices rose and
fell by turns like those of hunted men who suddenly remember that
they must not act as though they knew it. Exelmans's name sounded

on their lips with a noise of broken glass. Exelmans . . . It was becoming an obsession; no one spoke of Napoleon, only of Exelmans. The name had been spoken with an affectation of detachment that could deceive no one.

The panic which Exelmans's name conveyed everywhere in the long-drawn-out column of the Royal Household, its echelons, its stragglers, as well as the stupefying rapidity with which the general staff's measures and intentions became known to all, were, of course, perfectly explicable phenomena. It so happened that upon leaving Grandvilliers the commanders of the rear guard, informed of the news brought by the couriers and being responsible for the safety of this magma in which it was impossible to distinguish the troopers from the mob of fugitives, the civilians and the private baggage of these gentlemen officers of the Household, had had the idea of making use of the alarming news to accelerate the pace of the stragglers. In all wars, in every exodus, there comes a moment when, after all classic army methods have failed, a leader resorts to psychology in order to cope with the fatigue of the soldiers. And psychology, which is often a dangerous weapon in the hands of novelists, is something that the military handle as a child does a gun.

Casimir de Mortemart's artillery was with the rear guard—and this did not simplify the movements—especially since if it were ever to come into play it could only be by firing to the rear. But since at this stage the companies of Light Horse under M. de Damas constituted the Prince's escort, everything in the rear echelon came under the command of M. de Reiset; and he, as we know, was, in the absence of his chief (who was with the sovereign), in charge of the Lifeguards of de Grammont's company. The La Rochejaquelein Grenadiers preceded them, as though to open the way. Tony de Reiset was an accomplished gentleman who divided his life between the battlefield and affairs of the heart. He had a tendency to behave with his troops as with women, to obtain whose favors it was no sin to lie a little. He had accordingly sent for three or four young men of his company whom he knew because one of them was a relative and the others were sons of old comrades; and having made them swear on the royal fleur-de-lis not to betray the source of their information, he instructed them to circulate among the men bringing up the rear of the Household and among the jumble of carriages, spreading the rumor that Exelmans and his horsemen were approaching on the heels of the convoy at full gallop, even that files of Imperial horsemen had been sighted on parallel roads, keeping out of sight but ready to intervene when the attack was launched from the rear. And finally, that the Usurper, who was notorious for his ruses, had sent out soldiers by mail coach dressed in civilian clothes with their uniforms in a sack; soldiers who were meant to come forth at the psychological moment to give the impression that villages were already occupied when the loyal troops reached them. The youngsters were not forbidden to embroider on these stories and they went to it with a will, both out of contempt for the stragglers and that panic-stricken crowd following in carriages, and in a spirit of fun, carried away by imagination, the example coming from on high, prevarication assuming the aspect of devotion to the royal cause.

"And above all, don't forget to say we are changing direction and being routed toward Dieppe"—so that fear should be accompanied by its corrective, the next goal, and the hope of the end of the nightmare: embarkation. "What do you mean, Dieppe? In that case we should have taken the road to Aumale!" "No, not at all: we have to pass through Abbeville where His Majesty is waiting, and from there, once regrouped, we shall march west in perfect order, thus creating confusion among our pursuers who expect us to do battle along the Somme."

It will be realized that in these conditions no decisions of the high command were secret any longer. Moreover, the young horsemen— moving up the line of the convoy, meeting the women's exclamations of terror, the despair of those who were still marching through habit, men who limped, overtaxed feverish children, old men who had given up trying to pass for urchins—found themselves inventing beyond the realm of plausibility in order to correct the depressing effect caused by their remarks, which were originally intended only to act as a whip to the calves of all these people. They invented ambushes discovered at the last moment, shots, minor skirmishes in which Musketeers and Grenadiers had come upon men of Exelmans's forces and taken them prisoner. "Ask the Grenadiers . . . they're just ahead of us." From this to mentioning information proffered by these prisoners as to what was happening in the country, on the recapture of Grenoble and Lyons by loyal troops, on the great success that Monseigneur le Duc d'Angoulême was enjoying in the southwest, where the entire area had risen up against Buonaparte, and even that the Duke was marching on the capital where he would effect a junction with the army of La Vendée, was but a single and easily negotiated step. Meanwhile they jolly well had Exelmans's cavalry and Dragoons both behind them and on the side roads and in the thickets. "Come on, my lads, a little courage! It's not so far from here to Abbeville where His Majesty is waiting for you to distribute crosses, stripes, and posts."

The prospect of promotion was of course one of those ideas thought up by professional soldiers, but it had no effect, or rather an opposite effect, on the occasional soldiers—the Law School volunteers, for instance, for the dear children who were still trying to march despite their exhaustion—I mean those who had not been loaded into carriages by the time they reached Beauvais, who had not given up since Beauvais—these found both an insult and a cause of even deeper depression in the idea of a reward dangled before their noses like a carrot to keep them moving forward.

At the halt at Airaines five of them had reached the limit of their endurance: one, tall, slim and very pale, another dark and small with a voice like a girl's, a third with blond curly hair who unfortunately had a tic of the lip, and two others, nondescript, on the verge of tears. For the sake of setting an example they had doggedly continued on foot this far and had refused to climb into the carts with their comrades. But here, when they saw the black van with the little green canvas top above the seat and its two white Percherons at the door to an *estaminet,* they stopped, went into a huddle, and decided to enter the dram shop where the carter must be.

A funny sort of a carter who had set his tall cylindrical hat on the counter, a kind of dandy who might have spent the night in the fields, his clothes all rumpled, rather threadbare if examined closely, his hair mussed, and his large lips trembling and pale. A drink or two too many, it would seem. A funny look in the eye, in any case. And the girl who was serving him was laughing in a rather forced fashion at the things he said, for there was nothing funny about the stream of words that poured from his lips. There were people sitting about, some military, some peasants.

When the volunteers asked Bernard if he wouldn't take them in his van, he stared at them—at the dark-haired young fellow who had spoken with his young lady's voice, at the pale spindleshanks, at the curly-headed one you felt sorry for, and the two without anything in particular about them, except that one of them limped—and he was seized with one of those laughing fits that won't let go of you, that make your belly ache and bring idiotic tears to your eyes. Give them a lift! That was a good one, and he tried to explain to them that his horses, Philidor and Nepomucene, had also had as much as they could take. But they kept insisting. They were a bunch of whining

young fools, fed up with a pretense of heroism, who mixed up the
rain and fatigue with honor and the flag of the lady-hostages, in short
everything to make Bernard slap his thighs. Which were well developed, with shapely knees: that was why he wore tight-fitting breeches
in the Paris fashion.

"Go ahead," he said, "have one on me. All of you!"

"But will you take us?"

"Drink, drink, we'll see about that later."

He, Bernard, carry Law School volunteers! He could imagine nothing more stupid or nauseating! But they were mere lads who could
no longer even keep on their feet. They looked as if they still had ink
spots on their fingers. They must be fools to quit Law School to go
traipsing in the wake of the horsemen of a skedaddling king! It beat
everything! "Left your mamma, your girl friends? For what? Mud,
rain, rain and mud, over endless roads, a country with neither trees
nor mountains to distract you . . . public monuments few and far
between, and of little interest . . . people who are rather glum and,
between you and me, pretty wretched, pretty wretched. And the King
somewhere up ahead . . . if he is up ahead! After all, who's seen
him? Not you, certainly!" How fatheaded could people be? "And
from what they say, Exelmans's cavalry's on your tail, eh? Ah, those
fellows—they're not like the King! We've seen *them,* they're the only
one we *have* seen, the only ones we see. Can't you feel them hot on
your tails, my pets?"

"Could it be, monsieur," asked the tall pale one in dead earnest,
"that you have gone over to Buonaparte?"

"Ah, that's a good one. Come, let me treat you to a drink! To
Bou-o-na-par-te! You're an odd one, all right, I like you. . . . Me,
go over to Buonaparte? You haven't looked at me . . . why, my
little altar boy, the whole country has gone over to Buonaparte! You
don't believe it? Where are your eyes, my lambs? The whole country!
Just because you've seen a few big citizens and officials in the towns
who are still gambling on the Monarchy and hoping to make connec-
tions that will advance them in their career— But go and talk to the
people all around, just take a few steps right or left, to the farms, the
villages. The entire peasantry is ready to replant trees of Liberty or at
least to cry *Vive l'Empereur!* You don't believe me? You're just
simple-minded! You're in enemy territory, you're heading north
where all the garrisons have adopted the tricolor and trampled on the
fleur-de-lis and the whole caboodle. You're caught like rats, my children, like rats, with the cat at your tail and rat traps in front of you!"

They were pitiful to see, they spoke of the Throne and the Altar and the Princes, and of all the noble ideas they had acquired from their lady mothers and the priests' school whence they all came, except the curly one who had got into this by chance. "But all this aside, monsieur, will you take us or won't you? We can't even stand any longer, and it's raining so hard!"

Bernard leaned back and half closed his eyes. He was wonderfully drunk. It was the kind of deep intoxication that still allows you to walk, although you know in your own mind that you will suddenly reel from one wall to the other. The kind of drunkenness that makes you feel giant-sized, your head ready to burst through the ceiling; you could beat up everybody, there are no limits to your strength except that you no longer know exactly how to use it. Too bad. He looked at the five imbeciles, of whom he could have made one mouthful, there, just one mouthful. He was beginning to feel sorry for them. The curly one had a cute little face, and the other with his canary-bird voice, but it was the tall scoundrel who was the most likable.

The white horses were before the door, the van was empty. The *estaminet* was in an uproar! All this was unbelievable—what was he doing there? Last night . . . Bernard no longer remembered what had happened last night very clearly. Perhaps it had all been a dream: the tall pine trees, the torches, M. Joubert—Jean-François Ricord, who went by the name of M. Joubert and represented MM. Calleville of the rue du Caire, in Paris. "I suppose you have a good memory?" Ah, ah! It was rather funny. And all those faces in the night, the locksmith from Le Vimeu, the flax spinner, the officer from Béthune . . . and here he was drinking with the King's volunteers in this wine-shop. "Your health, boys!" He raised his glass of cider, a bitter cider into which they put dogwood seeds, a fine cider, in the white light it looked like piss, didn't it now?

But all this was stage setting. All this was a mask. It hid something he didn't want to think about, something within him that stirred but which he repressed, a recent memory, a pain in the fog of his head, in the cage of his chest where the mad heart beat. A word conveyed by a glance, a small cold hand that slipped in and withdrew, the word Good-by . . . But nothing—not the din of the place, nor the remarks of these scatterbrains, nor the cider, nor his effort to think of other things—nothing, nothing could efface that dancing image from his eyes, the moment of parting, and his ears still rang with the words whispered furtively, yet distinctly . . . *Good-by, Bernard, this time it is really good-by!* If words had a meaning—but words had no meaning; why had she chosen those words? Oh, Sophie, Sophie, my Sophie . . . You may well say *my,* you dolt, when you are alone and she belongs to another. You can refuse to believe. She said it, *it is really good-by.* And we can no longer see each other, what we're doing is wrong, we must stop it, where will this lead us, I can no longer lie, I love my husband, yes, yes I do, I love my husband . . . in a different way perhaps . . . but he's my husband. So what, so what? All right, but what use is it to say that it's monstrous? It does no good. . . .

"Monsieur," said the curly one, "I beg you . . . we beg you . . ."

Bernard's laughter had a clear ring, like the money he threw on the counter.

So they piled into the wagon, and Bernard took the beanpole alongside him on the seat: he looked so poorly, a little fresh air would do him good. The rain would sober Bernard himself.

"Yes, Nature, go into mourning! Your son, your friend, your lover, is approaching his end!"

There was a certain love of ostentation in Bernard which drink perhaps accentuated, but it was ostentation for his own benefit, to prove at least to himself his superiority to the world that surrounded him. And he had uttered the words with a kind of dark joy, the box coat flung over his shoulders, having climbed up on the seat and taken the reins in his hand, while the lanky boy sat down next to him.

Bernard was prey to an idea. What could have happened in the course of that night at Poix to cause Sophie to take leave of him in this way? And Bernard suddenly convinced himself that she loved her husband, that her husband in the course of that night . . . That was the worst. He could resign himself to never seeing her again, but not to the thought that she was happy with someone else, and his imagination conjured up vivid, intolerable visions of that happiness.

He suddenly became conscious of the fact that his companion had been talking volubly for some moments without his noticing it. The student was treating the carter to his life story, which was funny enough: and the carter had not heard a single word of it. However, the life of a twenty-year-old lad in his second year at Law School who aspired to a magistrate's office at Chartres or Nogent didn't amount to much. But the thing was that he had a girl-cousin . . . Like everyone else, eh?

Sophie. Never to see Sophie again. In this world in which one got rid of the Bourbons only to fall back on Bonaparte. Why was he, a poor fellow employed by Van Robais, traveling through the Picardy countryside in every kind of weather, with the spectacle of poverty, and the despair of seeing no way out, despair over these people who were incapable of uniting, of understanding their own interest, ready to fall into any hands, to heed the speeches of clever men, disloyal to their dead, led by the first comer into ventures which were foredoomed to failure? Whom could he trust? Not even that former member of the National Convention, that companion of Babeuf's . . . not even himself.

"You can't imagine, monsieur, how beautiful she is."

All at once Bernard burst out laughing. He could hear himself the day before, in this same place, on the seat of the van, uttering almost the same words to M. Joubert, and it struck him as ludicrous. He asked quite seriously: "Do you think that you can really aspire to the magistracy, young man . . . and kill yourself for your girl-cousin?"

The other was startled: he had said nothing about killing himself, but he was deeply humiliated by the irony of the question, and he replied, most stupidly, "Does that appear incompatible to you?"

To which Bernard made no answer, and whipped up his horses. Then after a silence he said, as though speaking to himself: "If Exelmans's Light Cavalry has occupied the banks of the Somme, access to Abbeville will be prohibited to idiots carrying royal volunteers in their wagons, my dear and worthy young man, and I shall lose my position with the estimable M. Grandin d'Elbeuf, who is the present owner of the factory of Les Rames . . . and sufficiently flexible politically to worm his way into the good graces of the new power at my expense."

"You think," asked the dear and worthy young man, "that Exelmans's Light Cavalry really is on the Somme?"

"You heard what those people in the wineshop at Airaines were saying? You didn't? You did? So, then. You've got yourself into a fine mess, just as I have."

"But, then, why did you take us?"

"Why? Because I'm beyond life's little worries. Because it was the stupidest thing I could possibly do. To play myself a trick, just like that. To give myself a new slant. To have you talk to me about your girl-cousin . . . She's pretty as a picture, eh, your cousin? And she's never yet said *adieu* to you?"

The student made a gesture with his hand as though shooing away a fly. He felt uncomfortable. He wasn't going to argue with this bantering carter. "You think," he said, "that Exelmans's Cavalry—"

"I don't think, I know."

Sheer meanness. But how funny, this enamored youth of twenty who so grossly forgot all about his loved one when fear entered into the picture. He just invited you to string him along. Panic. "I know," repeated Bernard.

How did he know? After all, he had not seen them, and you know me, I'm sort of like Saint Thomas. Saint Thomas? Well, you take what you can get in the way of an ideal. But just wait, I'll let you touch the wound in my side presently, you'll be able to put your whole hand in it. . . .

"Of course," said Bernard, "of course I've seen them."

Seen? Really seen? And where? What a greenhorn the apprentice notary was. Why did they make a boy like that so tall? It would never do him any good, it was just waste of matter. Bernard could feel him tremble: "Are you cold?" he asked slyly. And the other, "Thank you, I have a knitted shirt underneath." The imbecile! Fellows like that, you felt like giving them such a drubbing that it would make them shit in their pants.

"Come, now," said the student, "since His Majesty is at Abbeville!"

"That's just it. The fact is I'm very worried about His Majesty's fate . . . and about the fate of Abbeville where I'm going and which is perhaps being put to fire and sword at this very moment!"

"But where have you come from, monsieur? How do you know?"

In this world everything was falsehood. Love, liberty, the people. Ah, Sophie, Sophie. Am I less capable of lying than others? And of enjoying my lies? Their King is at Abbeville? Or elsewhere . . . "Where have I come from, you ask where have I come from, young fellow? General Exelmans's troops have reached Amiens, thus flanking the movement of the King's Cavalry by way of Creil, and while the regiments pursuing you by way of Beauvais have undoubtedly reached Poix by now, those which have been deploying along the Somme since yesterday in order to prevent a crossing are getting ready to make a flanking attack on you by way of the crossroads from Picquigny to Airaines, and at the junction of this road with the valley, somewhere about Pont-Rémy—once they have closed the circle behind you by their junction with the others on the road from Poix to Amiens—"

"What, what? I don't understand you. I can't follow you, I haven't any maps. But we must warn our comrades, we must . . . But how do you know all this? How do you know?"

"You asked where I'd come from: I've just come from Picquigny by
the road that leads to Airaines where you met me. Picquigny is the
Light Cavalry's center of operations. I was there delivering yarn to
some weavers, and I chanced to hear Napoleon's officers in an inn
shouting at the top of their lungs as they were explaining how things
stood. I won't tell you what they said about His Majesty's fate,
because after all they're quite capable of taking their desires for
realities."

The beanpole was desperate, but he needed a lesson in geography:
this was not easy to give when a man was handling two draught
horses and couldn't make a sketch. The Somme valley stretched approximately east and west from Amiens to Abbeville, and the distance between the two towns was not much more than eleven leagues.
Picquigny was about four leagues from Amiens, Pont-Rémy nine.
The road from Paris to Calais on which they were traveling bisected
the valley at Pont-Rémy, and was only eight leagues from it at Poix
and four leagues at Airaines. It was at most two leagues from Pont-
Rémy to Abbeville. "Do you follow me, young man?" The Amiens–
Poix–Pont-Rémy triangle was roughly an isosceles triangle of which
the base was eight leagues and the sides nine leagues each. They were
traveling on the west side. Exelmans occupied the entire east side
and the base, and was coming up on their rear. . . . It still wasn't
quite clear? But bon Dieu, what in hell did they teach them at school?

"Monsieur," said Spindleshanks, who was sucking in his cheeks
and fidgeting on the bones of his meager buttocks, "I think I understand. So you saw them? At Picquigny? We must warn . . .
warn . . ."

And he proceeded to shake the canvas of the wagon, trying to
attract the attention of the others. But they, sheltered within against
the rain which showed no sign of stopping, resting their feet, and
again carried away by their youth, were singing songs that were
certainly not hymns, and were quite out of place on a Wednesday of
Holy Week. The beanpole was beside himself. He seized Bernard
by the arm, begged him to stop, but the other would not listen, to
hell with the command, with Marshal Marmont, the Princes. He
had to get to Abbeville, even if it meant leaving his volunteers in a
ditch when their presence became compromising. . . .

At last they reached the top of the hill from which the road led
down to Pont-Rémy. Here the valley of the Somme spread out before
them in the rain, broad and dotted with bare trees and the first
green-gold touches of the willows. They were driving past the knoll

of Caesar's camp which commanded the countryside to their left, when the whole convoy came to a standstill and there was nothing for it but to stop the horses. The beanpole flung himself from the seat; horsemen—Lifeguards—were blocking the road. The student joined his comrades behind, and Bernard's heart warmed to their cries and their hurried words. The volunteers had jumped down from the wagon and were waving their arms in animated discussion as to what they should do. Now they'll spread a little more panic, reflected Bernard, and the thought filled him with delight. He slipped his hand under the seat to make sure the two saddle pistols, his faithful companions, were still there. He watched the volunteers running along the road. One of them, the curly one, had shouted to him that they would be back: as though it had been necessary to reassure Bernard who could not have lived without them! Run along, my little chicks. He saw them talking to a horseman who leaned forward, listened, had the words repeated, and pointed with his finger to a mounted figure a little distance away. The swarm was whirling.

Was there any good reason why he should wait for those gentlemen? . . . All was falsehood. For what had his father given his life? In order that those very ones who were his comrades might put their own hand in the executioner's. Perhaps I'm wrong, but I can't take it. They'll tell me I have no understanding of the general interest. Perhaps. Perhaps. I can't take it, that's all. For years I've been working for the "organization." Blindly. And what if this was my mistake? But what can be done about it? The best that I had to give . . . I can't stand seeing people living like animals, worked and sweated, and then sent to the slaughterhouse, the knacker's yard. There was that in my life—my loyalty to the "organization." . . . I said to myself, my father will not have died in vain. . . .

The white horses shied on the road. Over there troops were pulling back.

Idiot. You felt guilty about looking at the wife of one of your own people. Your own people . . . Who are yours, Father? Who are mine? Now there'll be a fine confusion between the soldiers made thirsty by one year of the monarchy, and the King's men who will switch sides with all possible speed necessary in order to keep their lands, their châteaux, their businesses. Peek-a-boo, the blue ribbons will be abandoned for the red. Ah, I've no wish to go through all that again. It nauseates me. Everything is falsehood even to the fear that seizes these people in their guts: just look at them. . . . Even fear, which is so real, is a lie. Yet there is a real fear, the fear that keeps me from thinking what I am thinking, from facing . . . The fear that puts all these words that speak of other things into my head . . . They are afraid, they and I.

Bernard's inventions had indeed dropped into the right soil at the right moment. And the volunteers, who had only to open their mouths wherever they went to be believed, so deeply had panic taken root among the troops, had been passed from hand to hand, the beanpole in the van, up to the command echelon at the bottom of the hill where Tony de Reiset, the Comte de Damas, and César de Chastellux were waiting on horseback to learn the reason for the delay. The Princes had passed five minutes before, and they were afraid of being cut off from them. Louis de la Rochejaquelein was at Pont-Rémy with his Grenadiers, who could be seen in the rear from here with their bearskins . . . but anyway!

M. de Reiset recognized the beanpole as being one of the young volunteers who had been brought to him upon their arrival at Beauvais and who had made the best of impressions upon him. This fellow, this tall, slim fellow, had even been presented to him, and he was annoyed with himself for not remembering his name, because it would have made such a good impression if he had, by chance, remembered it, so that he could have said to him, "Well, my dear So-and-so, what is it?" A trick that was always extremely effective: Napoleon, with his devil's memory, was a past master at it, the blackguard! What was this all about? When, talking all at once, the volunteers had told their story, leaving it to Spindleshanks to dot the *i*'s, Tony de Reiset pulled in the reins and turned toward M. de Damas, who had not heard clearly and had to have the gist of it repeated.

Oh, the gist was simple and clear. They must catch up with the Princes immediately in order to keep them from falling into a trap. The Somme could no longer be crossed, they could at best try to slip over to Abbeville along the left bank, if Exelmans had not already reached it, and the valley from Amiens to Pont-Rémy . . . "What do you know about this?" asked Charles de Damas. "The information sounds reliable, but after all . . . We ought at least to send someone to check it." Tony, for one, firmly believed it: the rumors he had invented and spread a while ago were miraculously confirmed, and Reiset, who had at first thought of himself simply as a profound psychologist, now appeared in his own eyes a strategist of genius.

The greater part of the Royal Household was here before them, massed at the entrance to Pont-Rémy. The order was given to the companies to go into the fields and pile arms. In this rain? Believe me, heaven's rain is better than men's. In any event there was no time to be lost in sending out dispatch riders. Dispatch riders? A lot of good dispatch riders would do! A detachment . . . a sizable detachment. César de Chastellux proposed sending all the Light Horse—he would head them—into the valley of the Somme to delay the bulk of Exelmans's horsemen and keep the command informed by messenger.

Charles de Damas did not see it this way. It seemed too risky. Perhaps, too, he did not want to be separated from his son-in-law. Was it the Light Horse's duty to guard the Princes? He proposed— and, coming from him, a proposal was tantamount to a command— that they send only some fifty horsemen, and preferably not the Light Horse. A highly mobile group which could pass for an advance party and which would make it look as though the Household was changing its direction and making for Amiens. Once the enemy was alerted, such an advance party could more easily disengage and beat a quick retreat. To offer battle was out of the question, for there would be a risk that they would be broken through, and the momentum of the enemy cavalry hastened in the direction of Abbeville; that was to say, of His Majesty's headquarters. Whom to choose? Were not the Grenadiers immediately at hand?

Thus it was that Marc-Antoine d'Aubigny was given command of this flanking detachment, with orders to make contact and then immediately to break it.

Whereupon Charles de Damas remarked that there might be a point to questioning that carrier from Les Rames who had given the information to the young Law School volunteers—who had again proved their intelligence and their loyalty to the Throne. There was no difficulty about finding them; but the carrier had remained at the top of the hill and it proved necessary to climb it again because of the extraordinary congestion on the road.

A Guards aide-de-camp accompanied the volunteers. "There he is!" cried one of these. The officer looked up and saw the black wagon with its two big white horses completely surrounded by a dense crowd which further complicated the flow of traffic. What was it? What had happened?

The beanpole elbowed his way through the crowd. People flung uncomplimentary remarks at him as he jostled them aside, but he had come to within a few feet of the team when he saw the tall hat which had rolled into the road. On the seat, under the green top, the driver's body had toppled over and was jammed against the partition behind, but where the head should have been—was that still a head?—only a gory mass remained. A large pistol had dropped beside the corpse, another hung at the end of the dangling left arm, the reins were being held by one of Mortemart's artillerymen, the white horses were whinnying.

Bernard no longer had a face. He had fired one of the saddle pistols, *from which she had wiped the dust,* into his own mouth, and, wonderful to relate, had not missed his aim. Because there is one thing in the world that is not a lie and with which a man does not toy. And this truth was signed with a shattered head on the brain- and blood-spattered canvas. People were screaming "A doctor! a doctor!" What for? Everything now was clear as death. No need for a man of the craft to explain the obvious with new lies.

Someone, a man from thereabouts, in a big gray smock, had seized the white horses by their bridles, and upon a ringing, sinister *Ho!* the black wagon began to move into the crowd which drew back. The volunteers and the aide-de-camp followed. With the movement the dead man up under the cover fell sideways. This caused a long shudder to pass through the spectators and a pause, a hesitation on the part of the man who was pulling the horses. Then he bent his shoulders and continued on his way. People shouted questions at him from the side of the road. He answered in his Picard dialect, "It's a man who gave way to despair. . . ."

There was nothing for it but to take this piece of evidence to the commander of de Grammont's company. For how could one doubt the word of a dead man? Now Bernard's information was *proved.*

Ahead, led by Lieutenant d'Aubigny on his arzel horse, the fifty Grenadiers were entering Pont-Rémy in single file, at a trot. From his horse, Tony de Reiset, who had watched them leave, could still see them as they turned right and vanished from sight. He remained for a long moment with his eyes fixed on the point where they had turned, seeing unseeingly the landscape which opened on the valley, with the château of Pont-Rémy among the trees on its island in the Somme.

The order came from the Princes to resume the march along the left bank toward Abbeville, but before entering the town the Lifeguards were to mass in battle formation. M. de Reiset communicated the written note to the Comte de Damas. They looked at one another.

"Good God, what about the King?" said Tony.

Charles de Damas made an evasive gesture. It meant: they wouldn't dare—and: well, after all!—and also: the King doesn't die. The thought even passed through his mind that Monseigneur le Duc d'Angoulême was safe in the Southwest where the people were monarchist, and that Madame Royale would be a magnificent Queen of France, like a picture of grief, with those eyes of hers still haunted by the horror, the tragedy of the Temple. After the Comte d'Artois, to be sure; if some misfortune should have befallen the Comte d'Artois . . . Which heaven forbid!

XII

The Valley of the Somme

THE entire valley had been submerged in fog since morning. The fires lighted at irregular intervals the evening before had smoked for a long time until in the end the rain had got the better of most of them. Here and there lingering wisps of smoke blended with the mist. The peat workers had been too precipitate in their anticipation of spring: they would still have to wait before burning the heaps of earthy peat, the waste from what had been extracted from the bogs the year before, low-grade peat, not good enough to make briquettes, which lay scattered about on the common lands. When the weather permitted, they burned their heaps from which, in late March, little yellowish plumes would rise everywhere among the trees and rushes; later the peasants came and carted away the white ash, spreading it over the meadows and the fields where the late wheat grew, for it was a good fertilizer.

But rain does not prevent the cutting of peat. Indeed, what else is there to do for those who divide their time between the marshes and work in the fields? For Eloy Caron, peat digger, who occasionally hired himself out for the heavy work of the Commune, there was no choice at this season, even though most people waited for Easter; for him, an unbeliever, there was no point in waiting for Christ to be resurrected before beginning to work. On the first day of spring he picked up his large peat spade and made for the strip of ground at the edge of the bog where he had already dug out with the sharp edge of his spade the stack of turf clods used to warm the house. He took thirteen-year-old Jean-Baptiste with him as his helper: the boy was taking his mother's place now that she was pregnant again. Other peat cutters like himself could be seen through the fog on their way to their patches. But where Eloy had his, near the shelter of reeds he had built last month, it was peaceful and isolated. Eloy did not like company.

He lived, in fact, with his family in that out-of-the-way part of the marshes of the Somme between Long and Longpré-les-Corps-Saints, on land belonging to the commune of Longpré-les-Corps-Saints— which, like a number of the poorest people in the area, he insisted on calling Longpré-sans-arbe, as it had been renamed by the erstwhile Republic. His house was the most distant, the farthest outpost in this desert of water and rushes, a low thatched building, windowless for greater warmth, ventilated only through the door, its mud walls braced by whitewashed beams, on a foundation of heavy boards coated with tar. There he lived with Catherine, who at thirty-five was already old, deformed, colorless, having had thirteen children in nineteen years, of whom six were dead, while the oldest boy had run away with the gipsies. They had one cow and a few chickens, three sons and three daughters. And the father, the old man, plied the trade of beggar. Around them, as far as the eye could reach, stretched the bogs, the drenched earth bristling with rushes, weeds rising between the young trees from beneath the sheets of water—white poplar, ash, elm—among which the copsewood had barely begun to sprout after the wholesale timbering, repeated every year for the last twenty years, during which people had flocked here to fell the trees on the common lands and the nationalized estates which their former owners were powerless to protect. And it would take perhaps a hundred years for the landscape to forget the mania to fell the trees that had taken possession of people in those days of famine. If, in the course of those hundred years, no new revolution or war were to sweep over the land . . .

Beyond Longpré the eye was arrested by the high embankment that descended almost perpendicularly into the valley; on the other side, on the right bank of the river, the land climbed more gently, in a more friendly way—but that was a far distant country.

Eloy's country was this strip of submerged meadow, bristling with poplars, cut by canals, by meres; beyond, where the channels of water were lost to sight only some thousand yards away, he no longer felt at home. The Somme passed in the distance there, in the broadest stretch of the valley, and curved away less than half a league from the slope of its left bank, but it was like another region. Eloy's country was this long stretch of mire and wretchedness between Amiens and Abbeville, where a man had to fight landowners, tradesmen, the Commune's crop watchers, the ambition of all those cheats who tried one after the other to take possession of pieces of bog by putting up illicit enclosures, the calamities of the seasons, the requisitions of the towns, the passage of the military. . . . Eloy's country was this mist and these low-hanging wisps of smoke, where a man went in rags with no sweet thing in his life except for the milk from the lean and wheezing cow which grazed on soaked grasses and swamp flowers in the flooded pastures. They had managed to make just a bit of a garden in which green beans did not grow as well as the small tight cabbages found all along the course of the Somme. But it was Eloy's country, as peat was his bread and butter, as Catherine was his wife; and he had never even thought of leaving them. This was his country and this was his life. Here he had grown up, seen the seasons pass, had exhausted his strength, suffered cold and hunger; here he had entrenched himself with Catherine; here, year after year, he had heard her scream in childbirth. His hair had begun to turn white before he was forty. But he had been fortunate enough to avoid conscription, whereas his brothers had been killed, one fighting for the Republic, another for the Empire; as for the deserter, the one he liked best and after whom he had named this son of his here, Jean-Baptiste, he had simply vanished.

His feet on his *line,* as the board fastened with pegs to the edge of the peat bog was called thereabouts, Eloy had been at work with his son for several hours, working his peat spade under fifteen to eighteen feet of water. It was heavy work. He pressed the twenty-foot-long handle with all his might, then pulled back to break the clod loose, brought the spade up hand over fist and swung it, dripping, to the bank. Jean-Baptiste carted the peat away in a wheelbarrow and stacked it latticewise, so that the air could circulate among the chunks and dry them.

Jean-Baptiste had to hurry and sweat to keep up with his father, for he knew that if he lagged behind he would be beaten on head and shoulders with the handle of the spade. And that hurt.

The rain was falling steadily now, drenching the peat workers, making boards and ground alike slippery underfoot. Starlings fluttered about them, and when Jean-Baptiste moved away they alighted in a flock on the damp peat clods to look for earthworms.

Old Caron—Jean-Baptiste's grandfather—before illness had deformed him and when he still had the muscles for it, used to ply this trade, as his son Eloy was doing that day. But for a good long while now he had been forced to live on public charity. The village priest, the one who had come back at the time of the Consulate, had indeed tried to shame Eloy: "So your father holds out his hand to people, and gives you the sous he collects?" As if Eloy gave a damn. Since he could no longer work, the old man might just as well live on everybody's charity as on *his*. As a matter of fact, he might have listened to the *other* priest, the one who had sworn to uphold the Constitution, and whom he remembered as a decent fellow who didn't mind a glass of wine now and then. But this one—"I can tell you he won't get rich on extreme-unctioning me! He's always sermonizing!"—and where had he been when they were hungry, when there was no bread, and two of Eloy's children, the tiny ones, had died for want of milk? You should hear him, now that a big showy cross had again been erected by the roadside, agreeing with the fine gentlemen who had crawled out from their hiding places that the peat workers, the dayworkers thereabouts, were all good-for-nothings because they didn't come when they were called—to kill themselves at their toil for a few sols; and that they lived like thieves because their poor cow, all skin and bone, grazed on a piece of ground that did not belong to them; and asking for the abolition of the common lands, to keep the workers from being so lazy. . . . That cow! It kept them from sleeping, it was discussed in all the deliberations of the municipalities. Because of the cow the farmers, as they called those who lived by the work of others, were obliged to call upon strangers to do the plowing and harvesting. Especially as the cows of the peat workers and the small peasants had to go to the common marshes, since they had no fields where they could graze, thus further deteriorating the pasturelands in which their masters, without needing any authorization, dug more and more holes so that the country looked like a gutted cemetery with its black empty pits. It was enough to make a man think all the dead had set out for hell without waiting for the Last Judgment.

All this passed through Eloy Caron's head as he wrenched his spade loose from the bottom, and the arguments of the rich made him sneer and rage. He mumbled to himself; then shouted *"Han!"*

when the weight detached itself from the mud. Jean-Baptiste glanced at him anxiously, wondering what in the world was wrong with the old man, and already felt on his shoulders the blows he would certainly get soon.

Eloy was reviewing, one after another, all the grievances that filled his life when he happened to glance at his son and was struck speechless. Jean-Baptiste had dropped the handles of his barrow and stood there, openmouthed, his face turned in the direction of Longpré. Just look at that! Eloy exploded to himself. Wiggling his nose like that, and those lazy arms of his! Then he burst out: "You just wait! *I'll* wallop you!" The lad did not reply but raised his arm, pointing to something on the road over there.

A detachment of horsemen, with bearskins, coming up the valley at a trot, had suddenly stopped in their tracks, nose to nose with another group wearing uniforms of green and red who could be seen among the trees coming from Amiens.

And suddenly a shot rang out.

Colonel-Baron Simonneau had insisted on giving his orders to Lieutenant Dieudonné in person. The regiment had reached Amiens at about ten in the morning, after a trot of fourteen leagues in five hours, and had been greeted by the garrison and the tricolor. The town looked like an immense fair, for the news from Paris had been made public here, and, despite the rain, the crowd, the girls, the soldiers, were transforming this day into a holiday to which the authorities gave every encouragement. It was extraordinary to see how many itinerant musicians had turned up in all the *estaminets,* all the inns. There was dancing everywhere; improvised orchestras perched on tables serving as platforms; all the tunes of the Empire rang out in a medley, every pretext served to raise a clamor for *La Marseillaise.* Simonneau's Light Cavalry had been given shelter in sheds on the western outskirts of town, near the Promenade de la Hotoye which was still so appallingly denuded—unrecognizable to those who had seen it twenty-five years before as had, for instance, Doctor Denoix in his childhood—with all the immemorial giants felled and replaced by those small trees planted under the Empire. And Arnavon, Schmalz, Rochette, had gone to roam the banks of the Somme—there was no holding those fellows back—where market gardeners had their small flooded plots. The men were making their toilet because earlier it had been rather hurried—they had set out from Saint-Just-en-Chaussée at five o'clock, and if, as rumor had it, they were staying in Amiens this evening, they could hope for leave, and then . . .

The kitchens having been set up, the 2nd company of the 3rd squadron had eaten their soup and tended their horses which were tied to the trees. Dieudonné had lit his pipe. There was no denying that he swore when he was summoned by the colonel. It was always his company which was called out on duty, because it had no captain and everything was heaped onto a lieutenant's back! Nothing had changed, then; things were still the same as they had been with Saint-Chamans? But once orders had been received . . . After all, captain or no captain, they were showing confidence in him. And in his men. "I know that we can count on your company for anything," Simonneau had said. Probably just a way of buying you. But it did buy you. Saint-Chamans did not act that way: he snapped out orders over the top of his gorget, and that was that.

The assignment was to proceed along the valley of the Somme as far as the approaches to Abbeville, or at least until contact was made with the royalist troops. In any event, the company would probably be unable to get beyond Pont-Rémy, so that the horses would not be required to do more than eight leagues. Because it was quite unlikely that the detachments of the Royal Household would pursue them when they fell back. And they were to stick as closely as possible to the adversary. The object of the maneuver was to make Marmont feel the presence of the Imperial troops, to accelerate his march, to narrow the area around him, to create an atmosphere of insecurity, of doubt as to whether the intention was to choose a place of battle at a more distant point, a kind of trap which would close on the Reds, or else—and this was more likely—merely to give him this impression in order to force him to leave France as quickly as possible with a part of his men, thus creating conditions favorable to the desertion and the rallying of the others. The country must cease to regard Louis XVIII as its legitimate sovereign: the Comte de Lille must be thrown back upon the Allied lines, thus becoming once again the pretender in exile. All the same, in the messages that were being distributed with a good deal of noisy publicity by telegraph as well as by messengers sent galloping in all directions, it was mentioned that orders had been given to seize the King and all Bourbons wherever they might be found. And a dozen other persons among whose names Robert read those of Marmont and Bourrienne. But nowhere was anything said about attacking the Royal Household.

Simonneau made a point of emphasizing this. Because a premature battle might precipitate foreign intervention, and the Emperor needed time to reorganize the State and the army.

Should it prove necessary, a dispatch rider would carry the lieutenant's report to Amiens. Was all that clear? "You are not obliged to get there at breakneck speed. You will stop at Picquigny, to discover if the crossroad from Picquigny to Airaines is occupied. Then you will proceed at leisure to Pont-Rémy, and nothing foolhardy, you understand? Show yourselves: that's all. Perhaps all you need do is assemble at Longpré and send a few horsemen toward Pont-Rémy with orders to join you as soon as contact is made, you understand? I leave it to your judgment . . . you're an intelligent officer. I've seen your record, it's a disgrace that you still haven't the third band! Another column will form on the right bank of the Somme, and if you need to, you can effect a junction. This evening we are moving on Doullens."

They had set out about noon. At this season the Somme Valley had barely begun to turn green. The road on the left bank, at the foot of the embankment, was out of sight of the river for an hour and a half. The villages they passed through were hardly more than clusters of houses at road junctions. From the slopes of the hill, branches of undergrowth, like gray, knotty arms, held out festoons of creepers above carpets of dead leaves. Nature was like a dusty old lady who no longer paid much attention to herself, but who nevertheless still gave evidence, despite her withered, shrunken appearance, of how beautiful she must have been when she had soft glistening hair. Full-grown timber trees, piercing this gray tangle, lifted unbelievable quantities of balls of yellow and russet mistletoe to the rain-washed sky in the black embroidery of their boughs.

The company marched, Dieudonné at its head, followed by the chosen horsemen who had been given him, some ten of them, carrying lances but actually belonging to no company, so that the lieutenant knew nothing about them. In general he was opposed to this system which introduced distinctions between horsemen, in weapons as in choice, and broke the combat unit, interfering with the solidarity of the men. Beyond Dreuille they perceived the river through the rain. It flowed rather lazily between the tall poplars and the already green pasturelands, gutted here and there by the black holes of the peat bogs. It was rather hot on this early afternoon despite the persisting rain—not above seventy degrees probably, but by contrast with the day before, Robert found the warmth oppressive. In Ailly, in Breilly, the people were on their doorsteps watching the cavalrymen, and there were cries of *Vive l'Empereur!* Beyond Breilly the Somme veered away toward the hills beyond its right bank, leaving between it and the road a long stretch of marshes and a thin scattering of trees. Dieudonné had begun to think that it was all very well to inspire confidence, and that the colonel should indeed treat him to explanations that went beyond elementary strategy. But what was *he* doing with *his* men? He was simply asking them to obey, he explained nothing to them. Well, when they got to Picquigny, where they would make a halt, he would have to . . .

When they got there it was not yet one o'clock. Robert had been expecting to find a town, and it was hardly more than a village of some twelve hundred souls and at most three hundred hearths. Here the welcome was altogether enthusiastic, with flags which had been kept hidden under the Bourbons now sticking out of the windows. The inhabitants, very poor on the whole, living on peat and on weaving for the Amiens or Abbeville manufacturers, insisted on treating the Emperor's horsemen to drinks. No, they had seen no one, they knew nothing about the Royal Household. The shopkeeper wouldn't allow the lieutenant to pay for the tobacco he wanted to buy for his pipe. Some people came in from La Chaussée-Tirancourt, on the other bank of the Somme. They had seen the Imperial Light Cavalrymen coming from Amiens on their way to Flixecourt. Enthusiasm is a fine thing, but at the moment Dieudonné was not interested in small talk. He assembled his men and made them climb a rather bad road up to the terraces of the château, which was a ruin of the kind that appealed to M. de Chateaubriand or to English poets, but not to this Light Cavalry lieutenant who had little use for things that had been destroyed. From here there was a splendid prospect of the valley, cut up by pools and bristling with white poplars, spotted by brown peat stacks, and the pitch-black peat trenches which seemed to be awaiting the victims of an impending massacre; and everywhere in the fields and pastures little smoking mounds, despite the rain. What interested Robert, though, was not the valley, but the endless plateau behind them, above the ruined towers and walls—deserted, denuded, spotted with white chalk, where the seedlings had hardly anywhere begun to pierce through the earth. A poor road, the crossroad from Airaines, furrowed it obliquely and disappeared in a ditch as it led down to Picquigny. In the distance Robert perceived a vehicle coming toward them. They waited for it. It was a wagoner who was bringing hempseed oil and sacks from Airaines; he had seen the

King's men, and he confirmed the fact that the Lifeguards and the Reds were moving along the Calais road toward Abbeville. There was nothing particularly eloquent about this Picard with a week-old beard and a big whip, but when he came to describe the disorder and confusion of the retreating forces he revealed unexpected resources of language.*

It was on the terrace of the château of Picquigny that Lieutenant Dieudonné made his little speech to his men who formed a circle on horseback around him. Perhaps he did not tell them everything Simonneau had confided to him, but the essentials at least, so that they would not be mere blind executants. He addressed himself particularly to the lancers, because these famous elite horsemen did not know him, and he wanted to awaken in them a spirit of responsibility and solidarity. Now was that clear? The orders were to make contact, to show themselves. Give the impression that the whole Imperial Cavalry was present, was about to descend on the Royalists . . . but not to attack, indeed to refuse combat, to break away, and yet remain close . . . as though they were simply surveying the Royal Household's movements, its flight, as though they were encircling it . . . creating a feeling of insecurity in the minds of the runaways; but no ill-considered gesture; they must wait for orders, there was to be no shooting on any pretext.

They resumed their course along this poorly repaired semblance of a road on which they had traveled from Amiens. The rain was coming down more heavily now and the ground was dreadfully soaked. The horses' hoofs sank in the mud. Beyond Picquigny the landscape hardly changed: still on the left that embankment covered by trees with balls of mistletoe, the same network of old creepers, but for a time the Somme followed the road on the right between the poplar trees, its marshes on the right bank; then the river turned aside.

In Croy, the old château of the dukes—those very ones who now had a fine house near Lille and had initiated the Anzin Mining Company—was by now hardly more than a memory. The Revolution, in all these villages where the peasants had periodically set fire to the châteaux since the Jacquerie of 1358, had done no more than complete the work of the centuries. In Hangest, in Condé-Folie, no trace was to be found of the baronial mansions dating from the time when all this was foreign land, enclaves of the Holy Roman Empire be-

---

* ". . . *eine bande ed' guerdins à caricouillette, eine bataclan de holaqueux enraqués, imbarnaqués dins l'ordière* . . ." (a gang of straddling scoundrels, a kit and boodle of broken-down lackeys mired in the rut . . .)

longing to the King of Hungary. Now the hills swerved away to the left, flattening out in the distance, the valley broadened with its pools, its marshes, its sparser trees, the river lost to sight over there about half a league away. It was half past two when they reached Longpré.

From here too a crossroad led to Airaines. That is to say that from Longpré the Calais road the Royal Household was following was less than two leagues distant. Odd, thought Robert: the colonel had called his attention to the Picquigny branch road, and not to this one. As a security measure he would leave two men here with orders to inform him if military elements should appear on the road to Airaines. Anyway, it was less than a league and a half from Longpré to Pont-Rémy. They continued on, still in the same formation, the lancers at the head in columns of three. The wooded embankment again overhung the road, they were passing through a region of meres with the Somme lost somewhere beyond. Dieudonné was daydreaming. Practical-minded though he was, he was also a dreamer. His mind was roving back over the past, he was thinking of Rouen, of his father, of Théodore and his companions. It was strange these days how everything kept bringing him back to Théodore, to the picture the painter had made of him, and how angry he had been at being given the torso and thighs of that insolent aristocrat. . . . He had been unable to stomach the Vicomte's levity, talking about the people. It had caused a fine squabble.

At a turn in the road, suddenly before them, less than two hundred yards away, a number of horsemen wearing bearskins appeared, advancing in single file. Halt! The Light Horse, behind the lancers, massed as the order was transmitted. And over there across the marshes, at a fork where one road dipped down toward the Somme, with a few houses clustered at the crossing, the others, as though it were a game, seemed to obey the same command. But then they hurriedly formed a long line which extended beyond the road to Abbeville on the crossroad—some ten men, the others forming behind, and a horseman advanced alone toward them. What was this, in heaven's name, the battle of Fontenoy? * Robert spurred his horse forward to meet the other. After all, they were not Kaiserlicks! And as he came up to him Robert Dieudonné, com-

---

* Fontenoy, a town in Belgium, the site of a famous battle between the French and the English, in 1745, in which each side, out of courtesy, invited the other to fire first. The British fired the first volley, which took a frightful toll, but the French won the day.

manding the 2nd company of the 3rd squadron in the 1st regiment of Imperial Light Horse, suddenly saw before him the man of his reverie—the man with whom he had quarreled so bitterly in a back shop on the big boulevards where Géricault had painted his canvas of 1812—Marc-Antoine, Vicomte d'Aubigny, lieutenant of the La Rochejaquelein Grenadiers, who saluted with a saber and shouted in a loud voice, *"Messieurs, vive le Roi!"*

The shot had been fired immediately after the shouts of *Vive l'Empereur!* that had risen in answer to Marc-Antoine d'Aubigny. The Grenadiers had never, up to this point, come face to face with what they called treason. They sat frozen, their fingers on the triggers of their pistols, before horsemen who three days before, on the Place Louis-XV, had still carried the proud name of the King's Light Horse. At this unimaginable outburst one of them, a very young man who had been in the army only three months, had been unable to resist: his finger had contracted. The bullet had hit no one, and the quiver that had passed through the Light Horse was that of thoroughly disciplined men whose nerves had been steeled by ten to twenty years of combat. But Lieutenant d'Aubigny, caught by surprise, his sense of fairness wounded, had abruptly turned around in his saddle to see who was guilty. And just as abruptly his horse had reared, leaping and bucking in an erratic and violent dance, perhaps seizing a moment of revenge, and it dashed away, leaping over the edge of the road and carrying its rider off into the fields. Marc-Antoine had lost his balance, and in the twisted position in which he had been caught by surprise, let go of the reins. His saddle, perhaps badly girthed, had slipped to one side, and as he tried in vain to draw himself back into position by the sheer strength of his Herculean legs, the saber he still held in his fist could be seen flashing in the grass.

This was the scene that Eloy Caron and his son had witnessed from afar. They stood there, on the edge of the bog, gaping at the fantastic leaps of the arzel horse and the vain efforts of the horseman to right himself. Into the rushes dashed the diabolical black beast, stamping and snorting, skirting the pool. Instinctively Dieudonné had set out in pursuit of the runaway horse, followed by two Grenadiers. The arzel horse, swinging its rider—one foot in the air, the other leg bent under his mount's belly, unable to get free of the stirrups—raced down the narrow strip below the level of the road, whence with savage speed it reached a spot planted with white poplars, against which Marc-Antoine's head and shoulders were knocked a dozen times. Then suddenly the big man, bumped and battered against the tree trunks, was convulsed in a monstrous cry, all at once let go the saber which he had until then inexplicably held tight in his fist, and was dragged along, limp and inanimate, by the runaway animal which whinnied triumphantly.

Eloy, leaning on his peat spade, and Jean-Baptiste by his abandoned wheelbarrow, saw this tornado descend upon them and did not stir. The pursuing horsemen, who were getting stuck among the rushes, one of them sinking into the pool up to the horse's belly, were yelling something that the peat workers did not understand. They saw that the dragged man was covered with blood and at last grasped that the Light Horse officer behind him was shouting, "Stop him, for God's sake!" Eloy reflected that the water would do the work better than he could, and besides it was none of his business, but, the boy having flung himself stupidly in front of the horse, his father ran after him to protect him, swinging the peat spade to bar the runaway animal's path. The sideways leap that this caused the beast to take to avoid the formidable long pole threw its unconscious burden free and, relieved of the hated horseman, the arzel made off and proceeded to wade into the peat and the rushes, calm now, and splashing noisily some twenty feet away, turning the white star of its black forehead toward its stationary pursuers.

Robert Dieudonné alighted and bent down over the moaning, mud-smeared, bloody horseman. But when he tried to lift him by the shoulders Marc-Antoine opened his eyes, which had become dark and absent, turned them toward him, and suddenly shrieked, an inhuman, superhuman shriek. The immense broken athlete's body fell back into the arms of Robert, who was overcome with anguish. It was he who had occasioned this, without knowing how or where, whether in this wounded head or that obviously broken leg which formed a right angle above the boot. He laid his burden back on the wet grass and the soaked ground. He kneeled down and passed his hand over the soiled brow; the eyes stared at him now, fixed, horrified, as though they were looking at death itself. Robert bent down and spoke gently to the wounded man. "Don't be afraid . . . don't you recognize me? I'm Théodore's friend." But it was useless, for the fear in those pupils was not of the enemy, of the soldier, but of something they saw within. The eyelids fluttered and closed.

The two Grenadiers arrived, having left their horses on the edge of the road with Jean-Baptiste. One of them was the young man who had fired the shot which had occasioned all this mischief. He was a tall, fair, curly-haired youngster with a tiny head set on a solid man's neck out of all proportion to what it was carrying. Completely forgetting that he was speaking to the officer on whom he had just fired, his eyes full of tears, trembling at his responsibility in the incident, he questioned the Light Horse lieutenant: "He will live, won't he, Lieutenant?" And Robert, shrugging his shoulders and without looking at him, replied, "How do I know?" while he tried gently, maternally, to stretch out the big body whose head moved back and forth while from the mouth now came a kind of muffled song, the diminished groan of suffering.

The injured man could not be left here. Immobilizing the leg, the four of them, with Eloy Caron, tried to carry him to the rush shelter where the peat worker had made room by taking out the tools. Here at least he would be sheltered from the rain. But what they held in their arms was no longer a man; once again that terrifying cry issued forth which seemed to emanate from the entire flesh, from the entire skeleton broken in several places, for it appeared that handling the trunk also caused screams of pain, perhaps there was a rib broken . . . By the time they were under the roof of rushes, in the shadow where it was hard to see, where they stumbled into the tools that Eloy had not had time to remove, the pain had assumed a rhythmic character, and the unconscious man who was no longer Marc-Antoine d'Aubigny, Lieutenant of Grenadiers, but a suffering, animal thing reduced to that broken, whistling noise which seemed to be the death agony; the man under whom a straw mat had been slipped commanded the respect of his four carriers by the very excess of his pain: they were aghast at the spectacle. Eloy was the first to leave, saying something to the effect that at least here the officer would not be rained upon. Robert Dieudonné got up again. All this had happened in almost no time, but it seemed hours to him. He said, "We can't leave him here indefinitely." And one of the Light-Horsemen commented, "But we can't carry him anywhere, Lieutenant, it would kill him."

The rain had redoubled on the pool, the pastures, the poplars, the peat. The arzel horse, having extricated itself from the mud into which it had started to sink, emerged among the reeds and whinnied its victory. Dragging the loosened saddle, it approached the edge of the road peacefully, paying no attention to Jean-Baptiste as though it was bent on telling its story to its two brother-slaves.

Over there, at the Catelet crossing, where Light Cavalry and Light

Horse remained facing each other, Robert's second lieutenant, who felt the responsibility of command, had taken his place in the lead, between the two troops, and a horseman of the other side—about whom it is of only the most minor importance to mention that he was the same Arthur d'H—— whom we met at Beauvais—had done as much to replace Marc-Antoine. There they remained, face to face, on their mounts. There was no need to say anything to one another, to come to any kind of understanding. Both sides, motionless, quite naturally accepted the idea of a kind of truce, and all looked away, down the road in the direction of the pool, where little more could be made out than the horses held near the edge of the embankment by a young peasant. In this pelting rain time seemed no less long to the waiting horsemen than to Robert Dieudonné leaning over the moaning Marc-Antoine.

Robert was overcome by a kind of stupor. Because at the very moment when all this had unexpectedly occurred, his imagination had been engaged by the violent scene that had occurred between himself and the pain-racked man lying here on the ground, almost three years before in the back shop on the boulevard where Géricault was working. Robert was not superstitious, or tempted by comparisons, nor was he in the habit of giving supernatural explanations to coincidences. But this time his matter-of-factness was disconcerted, he no longer knew what to do, and it seemed to him that it was himself whom he saw there unconscious, his own body which had fallen from Géricault's horse. Ah, what childishness! He braced himself, looked at the two Grenadiers and at the man of the marshes, the rain outside, the grass and the peat, and 'said, without being quite sure of himself, like an officer who has no orders but gives them nonetheless, "We ought to get a doctor." Then he thought, He must be cold, poor fellow! He unfastened his cavalry cloak, spread it gently over the injured man, covering his legs . . . and was suddenly appalled at the thought that the cloth might weigh on the fracture.

By a strange phenomenon the Grenadiers, mere lads, had both quite naturally come to consider this officer who had gone over to the service of the Ogre as their superior, and his words to them were an order. They saluted and went back to their mounts, which Jean-Baptiste was holding. The lieutenant's horse stood beside the hummock of rushes, by a post to which Eloy had tied it without being asked. Robert called them back: to him, too, they were no longer King's men but soldiers at his disposal. He told them to inform

Second Lieutenant Legay that he was to assume command in his absence, and to inform the officer in charge of the Grenadiers that, as far as he was concerned, he would remain at Lieutenant d'Aubigny's side until the doctor arrived. In addition, he requested that both officers should withdraw their respective troops, so as to avoid contacts and incidents. Not for a moment did the abnormal character of these double orders cross his mind, or those of the two country youths. Thus at this crossroads beside the Somme marshes, at about three o'clock in the afternoon on this Wednesday, March 22, 1815, Lieutenant Robert Dieudonné, of the 1st Imperial Regiment of Light Horse, temporarily placed under a single command the two divided segments of the French army which had been sent out to reconnoiter each other, with mutual orders not to fight, merely to make contact and then break away.

Pain sometimes prevails over the sense of being. Why have these tormentors moved him? His leg has suddenly spoken louder than his head. Stars of fire. It takes hold of your whole body, rises to your throat, the cry comes from your belly and escapes through the broken ribs. An enormous shadow hovers over everything. His open eyes see nothing but this presence.

Where am I? and am I? There is a sea of lead in my skull, black lead, its level wavers; and at times when it tips too far to one side in the kaleidoscope, left or right, depending on whether the boat rises or falls on a wave, there is a kind of sinister light in which a world is revealed—is it reality or dream? I don't know . . . Ah, Mamma, Mamma! It tears and it burns . . . a gray, misty, dark world streaked with wind and rain. Where am I? There must be water close by, and the earth is drenched with it, and the air; that is why it is dark in broad daylight. In the kaleidoscope, above the suns against a black background, among the purple plumes, the red streaks, those vague drifting planets, there is a still, pale area in which a face leans down: who is it? A man I've seen somewhere . . . a familiar face . . . And thoughts float about which I do not seem to perceive clearly, to put together, the words end to end . . .

All right. Who has shaken the kaleidoscope? Wheels, serpentines, sufferings, *aïe,* ah, it's too much, it goes right through, ah hell, Mamma, hell . . .

I see nothing but my night. I am alive; since I am in pain, I am alive. But what is living? It is having two legs and being able to stand on them. Have I still got legs? I have at least one leg, since it is like a scramble of nettles, of stars . . . What right have they to be carrying me? The bastards! Put me down, put me down, you bastards . . . They can't hear me, since I can only scream. Everything that I think becomes a formless scream; can anyone understand what fire says? My leg is a log, and my poor head, my goddamned head. Mamma!

It must be a dream, with these haunting smells, this twilight, the rain. My poor head rolls, and the lead moves, the boat, the night . . . The real world is the world you dream about, all kinds of changing scenes, silhouettes, childhood, big gardens, fields, woods, my dog Médor, who was black in broad daylight, like the light here where there is no longer anything but pea-soup suns behind the eyelids.

What are they talking about? I wish I could hear the words, that the words were words to me, words which could be strung like rings on a piece of rope . . . Ah, this rope that they twist around my leg, it cuts me, it flays me, it works into my flesh . . . There is no rope, there is no leg, no words, a simple murmur, a man's voice. What does he want of me? Don't let him touch me, for God's sake, don't let him touch me! I won't allow him to touch me.

There's something hard under my back. I was on horseback. Why have they made me lie down? Why do they keep me lying down? I rebel, I get up, that is, I want to get up. But the orders I give this body have no effect, except pain; the cry rises in me like an untuned flute. I am no longer anything but bones, badly put together bones, soulless bones; a scream.

I was on horseback. Where was that? In what free space, what springtime, the wind on my chest and arms, my strength, my body confident in itself, master of my muscles, my head full of stories, ideas, between yesterday and tomorrow, things to do, the taste of wine on my lips, and a woman in my arms: who is she, that woman I left behind, that soft, moaning, happy thing, that naked necklace tied to my neck, ah you have hurt me, hurt me terribly, unknown woman, whore, whore . . . do be careful of my leg, whore!

Again a flood of stars, spirals. Night invades all. I hear this man speak.

"My God, do you think he's going to die?"

Ah, it would be laughable if I could understand. My eyes roll in my wounded head. Sounds no longer have sense. What can it matter to him, to that man, that enemy, if someone is or is not going to die? To live is something I can understand: it's suffering. But to die, what is to die? It can't be. You don't die. Absence is a funny thing—your own absence. I fall. Motionless. With a fall that cannot be stopped, since I don't move. I. What is that—I? This man talking, *You think he is going to die?* How difficult it is to wake up in a nightmare! And I want to wake up. With all my might. Impossible. Because I *am* awake. Ah, there it goes again, the boat lists, the lead, the night . . .

Someone has put something on my forehead. Cool. But not enough. Not cool enough. Something damp. Who is taking this liberty with my forehead? Again. Perhaps it is perspiration. Oh, the pain. Will it never end? The shadows speak to one another, nod their heads. I should be afraid if that were possible. If anything were possible. A while ago I was afraid. Mamma! oh damn, damn, Mamma!

One shadow calls the other *Doctor*. That's odd. You don't say Doctor to a horse. Who is a horse? Who is a doctor? I have been lying here motionless for years. "Doctor, will he live?" That isn't what he was saying a while ago, the last word was different. But there is no way of finding it again, it must have fallen, rolled away on the floor, under the bed, and it is too dark to find it. One dark calls the other dark . . . Doctor! And perhaps Doctor means long sentences, a kind of telescoped saying. The man on the left says Doctor to that specter standing on two feet, dressed in black. But for the matter, everything is black. Even the smell that fills this place.

"He mustn't be moved for the present. Not until we know whether he has a fractured skull."

What is this gibberish? It makes no sense. For the present. Be moved for the present . . . A spasmodic noise comes from the motionless thing, a short and a long breath, short and long, which falls short and slowly rises again; words won't help, or the odd question: "You wouldn't have two boards to set his leg?"

Dreaming is like becoming accustomed to the dark. Here something bright can be discerned, but everything is blurred. There must be a roof, since the rain no longer falls on us. Or at least only at a slant, when there is a gust of wind, and the big rushes outside bend on the water. If it was a cabin there would be walls all around. It isn't a cabin but it is a roof. With black things piled up against it, from which comes that acrid smell, a dirty, suffocating smell. A smell of rotting things. Somewhere, far back in memory. Memory? That's a word which must mean something resembling the moon in the water. Memory? I had a memory, like a hand, or legs. Where have I put my memory? My child, some day you will lose your head, come here and let me fix your cravat . . . It has something to do with . . . there, I've lost the word . . . the mem, the mem, the memory. *Nom de Dieu, foutu nom de Dieu!* Oh, my leg, my leg! Leave my leg alone, you sons of bitches, leave my leg alone! It bites, it burns, it scrapes, it breaks, look out . . . I'm afraid . . . I can't . . .

"That way the leg is immobilized. Between these two pieces of board. Bind it tight, Lieutenant . . . good and tight. Don't be afraid of making a tight knot."

At last, at last, the stretcher had arrived. With infinite precautions, the two Grenadiers and Robert Dieudonné placed the wounded man, the makeshift splint on his broken leg, on the stretched webbing, and the stretcher was carried out of the rush shelter, into the warm and penetrating rain, beneath the vast canopy of clouds swinging on the tops of the still-leafless white poplars dancing in the wind. "Cover him." His cloak had been pulled up over his face, as if he were a corpse.

As if he were a corpse. It was strange, what could penetrate into that closed world, that brain. As if he were a corpse . . . no one had said *as if he were a corpse*. Was it something someone had thought, or was it Marc-Antoine? . . . Suddenly he did not want to die. I am young, I feel my heart against these aching ribs, my strength. I want to live. You don't die at twenty-five, not people like me. There will be the sun, the great sun outside, with its long gold claws on meadows so green they are yellow. The long shadows of the trees on the meadows in the morning, a pool of running water, the frightened pigeons with a great tumult of wings, and I on the pavement, still alone, in the courtyard. It is so early, you can hear a horse lashing out in the stable. The pigeons, now reassured, bold, coming to see if there is a bit of bread or bran, plump, heavy, ungainly, with tiny heads and red eyes, gray, violet, white: they peck here and there in the carnation beds, at an earthworm . . . There will be mornings and evenings. The comb of sunlight through the ash trees and the beeches, the low shrubs overgrown with vines and wild flowers, that fragrance, what is that fragrance? Oh, at least once, and after that I'm willing to die, once more the month of May in that royal fragrance of the hawthorns! The big white hawthorns, like ermine. The barely open mauve blossoms, in the pale green of the reeds, with their black heads . . . the already rank undergrowth where the boot again marks a path . . . A big park blending into an indiscreet wilderness of birds and shy things that run away. The earth passes through a new puberty, bares its body, on which the first ants scurry.

"Set the stretcher down," said the doctor. "Here, no, here . . . gently, gently!"

The eyes opened under the slipping cloak, the forehead was exposed to the rain, the dark pupils rolled, streaks of blood showed in the turned-up whites. People crowded round, there was a babble of children's voices. Then the movement was resumed, the stretcher was lifted, carried into what must be a house, with no light except what came in through the door, a kind of thick darkness, an armpit of darkness, with sharp odors, smoke that made Dieudonné, the doctor, cough . . . A smell of stagnant urine, a woman who called out from a kind of bed at the far end, "What is it?" An infant crying.

"You're not going to leave him here?" one of the stretcher bearers asked anxiously—the very lad who had carelessly fired at the Light Horse lieutenant a while ago.

"And where do you expect me to leave him? There isn't a roof between here and Longpré, and it would kill him to carry him that far."

The doctor knelt beside the injured man, he must undress him, at least partially . . . to see what was wrong with his body. At the far end of this smoke-filled lair the sound of a quarrel could be heard, the man and the woman, in that incomprehensible language which always seemed to be blowing its nose.

"He ought to be taken to the hospital, but it's two and a half leagues to Abbeville. It would be madness, on a cart."

It was the doctor's voice. The injured man felt it roaming over him, like fingers. And again the Grenadier:

"It would be horrible to die here."

"Don't you think, my young friend," said the doctor, "that it's even worse to live here?"

Again the pain, the frantic shiver, the reeling of the head, the thick veil that sank, sank . . . had they all stopped talking? Only the pain, only the pounding of the pain, was audible to him.

The gray veil . . . where have I seen this gray veil fall over things before? A morning in October. Late October. The Grenelle drill ground. The wall of the Farmers-General. Only it was not I, but they. Before the trees. We had escorted them on horseback. There was that same fine drizzle. Paris there in the background. A short distance away, people, drawn by curiosity perhaps, or friends of theirs. Malet shouted to them: "Remember the twenty-third of October!" I knew Lahorie; I had met him at Mme. Hugo's. He turned his head in my direction. Had he recognized me? Even if he had seen me, with all he had to think of in the short time he had before he died, he would not have recognized me. That young man seen in passing at his mistress's, the summer before . . . The firing squad had been formed. Infantrymen, fortunately. Not us. *We* were guarding the approaches. On our horses. Those men who were going to die. Some of them in one way, others in another. Most of them tried to find words. With luck, they would be remembered, would at least survive in that way. Others stood with heads bowed, one was weeping. But at least they themselves gave the order to fire. The salvo caused my horse to rear. Remarkable how afraid animals are of guns . . .

Suddenly, there, where it hurts, hurts so atrociously in my head, my leg seems to have gone to sleep, the star that separates its branches is pale as an October morning, white on black, on the black forehead of the arzel horse . . . I wish I could smoke, perhaps smoking would fix everything.

"What is he saying? Did you hear, Doctor?"

The doctor had not heard.

I saw the officer approach General de Lahorie for the *coup de grâce*. What a strange expression! He was still moving. He had turned his eyes toward the officer. "He looked at me!" this soldier said as he passed Marc-Antoine in returning to the ranks. The *coup de grâce*.

Marc-Antoine knows very well, now, what the *coup de grâce* means. No, no. Then it was a general who had been shot, he was on the ground, he still moved, an officer approached, the gun, the shot— after all it was more humane. But the other time he, Marc-Antoine, had seen the eye turned toward him, the horse's eye. The animal on the ground, its leg broken, dragging itself, whinnying. The eye. The blaze turned toward him, the beautiful horse's head, gentle, *his* horse. The *coup de grâce*.

What the death of a general does not explain, you can grasp by killing a horse. Your own horse. A horse's eye is immense. Immense and bulging. Shiny. A kind of onyx. A large smooth stone. It shines, unreproaching, trusting. And I? I too have a broken leg, useless, immovable, the Abbeville hospital is too far away: are they going to kill me?

"Please understand, Cavalier, and tell your comrades. You can leave without shame or regret. Your lieutenant must remain here, and we shall not consider him as a prisoner but as wounded. We ourselves shall not remain here. The doctor will look after . . ."

The voices and the men had moved away. And consciousness. Except for the pain which was still there, seated in the head. The leg was cold, absent. Suddenly, though, a sentence from the door: "Doctor, I leave him to you, as though I were leaving my own body." Who said that? The lieutenant? If I am his body, why does he leave? He abandons me. My head abandons me! Ah, if it could be true, that bitch of a head! It is calmer, relatively. The smoke in the room. The paleness in the doorway. There is movement. Curious children. An old man's voice yelling after them. The flies scatter.

There is nothing but time ahead of me. Endless time.

What is this war, anyway? Against whom are we fighting, and for what? It seems to me it was only a military parade. There were a lot of people. Not only the army. People, women. Where were they all going? Where were we going? I can no longer remember. It seems to me that it had been going on for several days. Why does one parade several days in succession? Where did I sleep last night? It's strange, I've forgotten everything. In any event, it must have been some sort of a pleasure trip. There were youngsters on foot. Crowded carriages . . .

He no longer had much idea what he was doing there. Yet little by little the clouds were dispersing. He was beginning to see the room he was in, the children who had ceased to pay any attention to him, the old man sitting next to the stretcher, looking at him. And then it began to come back to him. The King . . . He had forgotten the King. Remembering the King's existence gave him a whopping headache. Then suddenly it was as if he were going to sleep: he felt his head wobble—no, he must resist, stay awake at all costs. The King. He had totally forgotten him. They had been following the King. But what did that mean? Was the King running away? Was a king who ran away still a king? And they who were running away with him, were they still themselves? It was terrible the way everything kept turning around. What were these people going to think of him—that old man, those children?

The old man was leaning on a cane. With both hands, his chin resting on them. He was dirty. Like everyone here. A little dirtier perhaps. Because there was water outside, the water of the marshes. But in this house they were not going to form a human chain to bring it in. These people didn't spend much time washing, but let the peat and mud dry on their faces. Try as he would, he couldn't keep his eyes open. It would happen. It was happening. He was falling, falling again . . .

While the injured man fainted or went to sleep—who could say which?—the grandfather, leaning on his stick, in his tatters, for rags are the beggar's work clothes, looked at the young man who had lost consciousness and shrugged his old shoulders. He wondered if the injured man had any money on him, where he kept it, and how he could get hold of it without being seen by those dirty brats who would go and squeal to their mother that Pépé was robbing the officer of his sous. Not that he had any moral scruples but he would have to share, and sharing was not his strong point. With the end of his stick he surreptitiously lifted the cloak spread over the recumbent figure. The other groaned. The old man stopped and looked around slyly. With this weather his day had been wasted: no use begging for alms in the rain. And already on Sunday . . . especially as his son took all he had, and at the *estaminet* they refused to give him beer on credit.

Where did he hide his money? Gold, most likely. In his pockets, his belt? The belt was unfastened, as well as the top of the trousers, the doctor had done that . . . The beggar wondered if, by chance, the doctor had stolen the officer's gold without being seen when the opportunity offered. Then he dismissed the thought. How could he have got such an idea into his head? A doctor steal! That would be enough to make you lose faith in everything. The old man bent forward, tried the weight of the belt. Upon this contact through the shirt, the wounded man opened an eye. He saw.

He saw, not as in his delirium a while back. A bristly face bent over him, the beard reaching to just below the eyes, white and dirty, full of black streaks and yellow spots, the eyes foxy, avid, with an infinity of little lines in the crow's feet, the brow furrowed with wrinkles under the unspeakable wide-brimmed hat. He felt the hand on him like an insult, the old hand exploring, hesitant and awkward. The horror it aroused in him made him forget that he was riveted there, paralyzed, unable to command his limbs. And suddenly, he also saw his own hand lifted up as though to push the old man aside, his hand, not obeying him but anticipating him, feeble, impotent, but nevertheless frightening the man leaning over him, making him withdraw a little, stopping his searching. He must say something. Could thoughts cross his lips? What Marc-Antoine had in him stopped in his throat, rattled there, made a brutish noise, broke loose: "Drink . . ." The old man straightened, moved away terrified, his stick fell down. "Drink," said the injured man, and it was not what he had wanted to say, but having said it he felt a mad thirst, a desiccation not only of his mouth but of his whole body, and his head rolled to one side. God, was he going to lose consciousness again?

The pain stopped it, held, concentrated the attention of his poor head.

Suddenly there was a great stir, an incomprehensible agitation in the room, a rending of the smoke that filled it. The snotty-faced children were swept aside; a shadow in ragged skirts, a mass of shapeless stuff, had alighted between the doorway where the light was and the eye. A woman's raucous, weary voice—there was no telling what she was saying—one of the cuffed brats was sniveling, lifting his elbow too late. And the woman was on the old man like an avalanche of justice and of punishment; he raised his stick, she screamed, the stick came down, swerved aside.

She was apparently a very big and very old woman, with a torn dark dress under which could be seen an undergarment which was black with filth where it hung down below the skirt in front. Her bodice which was open down the front revealed the uplifted mass of her breasts over the shapeless, enormous belly. She might be thought to be pregnant if it were possible at her age. The ravaged sweat-covered face, unwashed for a week, frighteningly ugly, the straggling hair, strands of which fell over one temple, a mess of filthy white-streaked old straw.

She screamed at the disgusting old man who wanted to rob the officer, "You son of a bitch!" And if he had had that money he would just have drunk it up. And raising his cane to strike a woman, and she about to give birth from one minute to the next. Foul obscenities rolled in her mouth, she panted a little, leaned forward, spreading her thighs because of that huge belly, bracing her hands on her bent knees.

Now that Marc-Antoine observed her at close hand in the rain-drenched light, he saw that she was not an old woman. She was worn-out, ravaged, but not old. She panted as she looked at him. With an animal's lack of discretion. Interest flashed into her eyes. She passed her hand over the injured man's forehead where a fly was buzzing. A filthy deformed hand. Her pale lips trembled. As though in spite of herself she murmured, "A handsome lad . . ." and this was more frightening to Marc-Antoine than the old man just now, so unequivocal was her expression. He moaned again—"Drink!"—and suddenly the woman stirred, gathered herself up, exclaimed: "There you are, all of you, like flies, and nobody gives this handsome man anything to drink!" There was a general scattering in the course of which the old man with the beard vanished, arms intermingled, something was passed from hand to hand, and suddenly at his lips Marc-Antoine felt the bowl, something wet, he opened his lips, sucked . . . a strange insipid brew, neither beer nor cider, a thickened water, and the woman said to him, "Drink, drink . . ." and incomprehensible words. Then lifted the back of his head a little. Oh, that hurt. But he must drink . . . when suddenly, in the middle of a loud scream, the bowl escaped from the hand holding it to the patient's lips and fell, the liquid spilling over his neck, his shirt, his chest. What was happening?

The woman was convulsed, flung herself back with her hands on her belly. She shrieked into her hair which had tumbled down over her face, her shoulders shaking, her breasts quivering. She went off into the dark with her children, screaming in their turn, stumbling against her legs. She vanished to the back of the room, and Marc-Antoine, who couldn't turn his head, nevertheless could imagine the sordid bed on which the mass collapsed. What was it? His eyes questioned the old man who had come back, to pick up his stick which had fallen next to the stretcher.

"The labor pains," said the old man, with that wise look children of nature have.

But things had calmed down. These were only the first pains—she would be brought to bed later. The oldest of the children stirred the fire again, for daylight was fading. A wretched smoky flame began to light up the picture . . . And suddenly Marc-Antoine knew that he was going to live.

XIII

The Seeds of the Future

I T WAS exactly six o'clock when M. de Siméon, the prefect of Lille, arrived for dinner at His Majesty's. That is to say, at the residence of the mayor of the city, M. de Brigode, where the King was lodged with his escort. The Hôtel de Brigode, generally called the Hôtel d'Avelin, was a large and very fine mansion at the very northern end of Lille, which was perhaps why it had been chosen, in the light of the garrison's state of mind, so that His Majesty could make a dash for Dunkirk without having to pass through the town again. He had been put under the protection of Captain Vanackère who commanded a troop composed of Grenadiers, of whom they were not very sure, and of militia gunners on whose sentiments it was reasonably safe to rely. There had already been trouble between Grenadiers and gunners, so it had been reported to the prefect, and it looked as though they were spoiling for a fight. The Maréchal-Duc de Trévise was just informing the King of this state of things. Present were Berthier, Beurnonville, Macdonald—all the generals, the ministers who had come rushing to Lille—Jaucourt, Bourrienne, the Abbé Louis, the Abbé de Montesquiou, the whole escort, M. de Blacas, the Prince de Poix, the Duc de Duras, the Duc de Croy, the Duc de Grammont, the Prince de Condé, the Duc d'Orléans, some fifty guests, as well as M. de Brigode of course, various town notables, and Father Elisée's cassock.

Through the window of the big drawing room, they could see the guard in the court, but His Majesty had moved to the back of the room, speaking with Marshal Mortier, and was looking out at the gardens on that side, where the buds of some very early shrubs were already opening in the warm afternoon rain. The King called this to the attention of the Marshal, who had no more idea than he had what shrubs they were and said they would have to ask M. de Brigode.

In the group where M. de Grammont and the Prince de Poix were commenting in very severe terms on the odd behavior the garrison had exhibited upon the King's arrival, there was a show both of anxiety and of anger. And I don't know who—an aide-de-camp, I think— exclaimed so loudly that everyone heard it: "Since these gentlemen are looking so sour, all we need do is send a courier to Tournai, have the drawbridge lowered, and introduce twenty English battalions into Lille to knock some sense into them!"

The King, who, like everyone else, had heard this, turned around. And his questioning glance attached itself to Mortier. The Marshal murmured: "Rash fellow! You may do such things, but you don't talk about them."

They moved to the table, and despite the sumptuousness of the linen, silver, crystal and porcelain, and the elegance of the staff of servants, it was apparent from the dark looks of most of the guests that the talk of the groups who had just fallen silent had been far from encouraging. M. le Duc d'Orléans was at His Majesty's right, and the conversation between them was by no means animated.

Was His Majesty purposely speaking almost exclusively with the man sitting on his left, who was the master of the house? He was saying things to him in a low voice, the purport of which the Duc d'Orléans was unable to judge. In truth Louis XVIII was in a curious frame of mind: he had put up a good appearance throughout the journey, but his nerves were at last beginning to give way. And then there was the rheumatism. He had just undergone a treatment at Father Elisée's hands, and it had been of no great avail. He felt like a hunted man: in the haste of departure, he had slyly outdistanced his brother and his handsome nephew, leaving the Household in the hands of the Ultra-Royalists, so as to compromise the Artois faction in the disorder of the flight, and so as later to appear to have had no part in possible incidents. Perhaps he would not have been altogether displeased if his brother were to fall into Buonaparte's hands: for a year the intrigues in the Pavillon de Marsan had been interfering with his sleep. Everyone was after his crown. That impatient brother of his, his sons, as well as this cousin to his right. Everything got found out. They were all plotting. Fouché was in the service of the Orléans faction. Vitrolles was acting as Charles's police agent. If Buonaparte had not come back, one or another group would have tried to overthrow Louis, that was obvious. Should he not take advantage of the present convulsion to prepare the future—his return with the Allies—and to compromise all the pretenders? And to think that it had been he who had been the first to extend a hand to the young Louis-Philippe when he came and threw himself at his feet, fresh from the armies of the Republic, after the Dumouriez affair! At the time, Louis had been looking for a counterweight to his brother's maneuvers. . . .

The King was thinking about all this, speaking of other things, of the enthusiastic welcome the people had given him as he passed through the country. Suddenly he made a grimace. His kidneys! Oh, that Father Elisée! Never had he been of any real use to him except that time at Hartwell when he obtained M. de Charette's letter against the Comte d'Artois for him, a weapon which had perhaps been forged by the English secret service, but was occasionally useful to bring his brother to order. . . . It was a letter he could publish at any moment, accusing Monsieur of having, through cowardice, been responsible for the defeat of the Chouans. All at once, he heard the Prince de Condé at the other end of the table saying something curious. He asked him to repeat it. M. le Prince de Condé, who had arrived during the afternoon and seemed to have had little idea of the garrison's state of mind, had chosen this moment to make a remark that at first caused general consternation, then produced a fit of laughter which was difficult to hide.

"If we remain here tomorrow," said the Prince in a loud voice, "does His Majesty plan, since it is Holy Thursday, to practice the washing of the feet of the poor, as usual, and in what church?"

The hubbub of the covers and the dishes, the private conversations, afforded a momentary diversion, but the Prince who thought he had not been heard, being deaf himself, and having reached the age when corpulence and the satisfaction of rank take the place of wit, repeated in an even louder voice, trying to make himself heard above the din: "In what church does His Majesty plan to wash the feet of the poor tomorrow?" Only the recollection that he was the unfortunate grandfather of the Duc d'Enghien, and the head of the former army of the emigration, prevented them from laughing in his face.

M. de Brigode, who was better informed as to the state of things than the prefect, whispered into the prefect's ear that the Grenadiers' knapsacks had been searched, and had been found to contain the eagle and the cockade. "Bah!" said one of the men sitting nearby, "I've seen some in town already wearing them on their shakos!"

The garrison's mood was in truth worrisome. Since morning the signs had been unmistakable: while it was true that the people in the markets, the humble folk, the peasants from the countryside, had cried *Vive le Roi!* upon Louis XVIII's arrival in the streets of the town a little after noon, the troops massed to meet him and escort him had shown a reserve that boded no good. And all afternoon the agitation of the military had been noticeable. His Majesty was upset because the Duc d'Orléans and Mortier had brought the garrison back to Lille: the regiments had been sent to the Camp de Péronne, and the fact that they had been given orders to come back placed the King in a false position, since he was told that the garrison would rebel if the Household were to come and join it. He was therefore obliged to be the prisoner of the rebellious spirits here, while the only loyal troops had to be kept away: orders had been sent to Monsieur to gather the Household at Béthune. And in addition, all the volunteer companies which had been formed by the good people in these parts had been sent off toward Paris, including those enthusiasts who had come to M. de Brigode in the theatre itself and asked for weapons just a week ago, while *Joconde* was being performed, not to mention Captain Porrel's gunners, and at their head two of M. le Duc de Berry's honor guards on horseback; M. de Formigier and Charles Fievet, son of M. Fievet who was just over there. . . . That was the next day, Thursday. Friday it had been the turn of a second company, with two pieces of artillery, under the command of Captain Costenoble. And now there was no more artillery, the National Guard was so weak that it could not even handle routine duties, and if the Royal Household were to arrive, it would find facing it at least seven thousand men, thoroughly rested, armed, and hostile.

M. de Siméon knew all this. And the attachment that he felt for the royal family made him wish the King to blazes. He was, it should be mentioned, a man of subtle mind who wrote a little, and in these last days . . .

His Majesty made everyone laugh by telling the story of M. Duplaquet, the sub-prefect of Béthune, who had been unable to get into his trousers. They were trying to talk about anything rather than the present situation. They were saying that tonight, too, the theatre would be full and the marks of devotion to the sovereign that were repeated at each performance of *La Partie de Chasse* would surely be observed again. At this M. de Siméon was unable to refrain from coughing, and M. de Bourrienne, who was looking at him, understood quite clearly what was in the prefect's mind in respect to the spontaneity of these demonstrations. The Minister of Police had been present at the King's arrival, mingling with the crowd, and he had acquired some idea as to how things stood. Still, as the Maréchal Prince de Wagram seemed to see only the black side of things, and his remarks were causing His Majesty to raise his eyebrows, Bourrienne, who was an experienced courtier, having served a valuable apprenticeship with Napoleon, hastened to say in a loud voice to Berthier that the news received from Vienna and his personal information led him to prophesy that the sovereigns of Europe would not tolerate Buonaparte's insolence and that by the end of June His Majesty would again be sleeping in the Tuileries.

These words made quite a sensation, and everyone stopped talking and looked toward His Majesty, who did not seem to take too seriously what he probably assumed to be a piece of social flattery; and the questions he asked showed with what feeble assurance he contemplated the future. But then, probably on noticing that his words were being greeted by a look of consternation all round, and darkening the expression on Berthier's face even more, Louis XVIII said a few flattering words to Bourrienne, which were undoubtedly meant to dissemble his real feelings.

The chandeliers had been lighted even though it was still broad daylight, but inside the house, so narrow was the street in which it stood, the light was insufficient for a royal meal. M. de Brigode's wines were excellent, and the meat at his table much superior to what they had had at M. de Verville's. The dinner should of course have been planned to include ladies, which would have made it gayer. But it would have meant too many people. Look at the face Berthier is making! My dear fellow, it's really unseemly to show one's feeling like that! Jaucourt, who was sitting next to Bourrienne, asked him if he knew what had become of Mme. Visconti . . . a mention made by Macdonald . . . No, the Minister of Police knew nothing, he had left the capital with other fish to fry. But just look at Berthier: there he sits chewing his nails . . . that's all he can do when he isn't fucking his Italian woman. . . .

The Comte de Jaucourt always used colorful language. He conformed to the Versailles tradition. Bourrienne, for his part, had known the Prince de Wagram a long time. He was not to be fooled: deep down in Berthier's heart there was also an unrequited love for Napoleon. And at this table, at this moment, Berthier was not only chewing his nails, he was torn between the honor of belonging to the King's entourage and the desire to go and dance attendance on the Emperor. . . .

Yes, Berthier continued to chew his nails. Father Elisée, who sat two places away from Jaucourt, leaned over toward the Count and, wrinkling his ugly sweating nose, said to him in that would-be subdued voice of his, "Monsieur le Prince de Condé's suggestion in connection with Holy Thursday deserves more attention than it received . . . but I would suggest that this time the poor whose feet are to be washed might be the Marshals . . ." This delicate joke fortunately did not get beyond the minister. But it was true that Mortier and Macdonald looked no less sinister than Berthier. The Abbé de Montesquiou, who sat opposite Jaucourt, must be thinking of the same thing he was, for he said, "Changes in a political regime are always difficult moments for a Marshal of France. No, thank you, red wine does not agree with me, even when it is as excellent as this Bordeaux . . . From what Château does it get its name, Father—you who are an expert in these things?"

Father Elisée flushed. They knew perfectly well that this was not his strong point: His Majesty had twitted him about it more than once when he had mistaken a Beaune for a something-or-the-other. Then suddenly attention was drawn to an aide-de-camp who had just leaned forward next to the King after saluting him, to announce what was undoubtedly important news, for Louis XVIII drew back, letting his napkin drop from the table, and said hurriedly, "Send him in." Everyone suddenly had the feeling that the scene was changing, passing from dinner table comedy to the drama of the world outside.

It was General Ricard whom we saw early in the morning passing through Poix in a black tilbury with yellow wheels, his legs wrapped in a green-and-blue rug. He was the bearer of a letter from Monsieur to the King whom he had expected to find at Abbeville. He had had to travel fast, from relay to relay, in order to reach Lille at about seven in the evening. The King settled him next to himself, making room for him at his left next to M. de Brigode, and from this point on turning his back to his cousin d'Orléans, to whom he did not speak again until they left the table. Louis-Philippe appeared deeply humiliated and was forced to fall back on the Maréchal-Duc de Trévise who sat opposite him.

The King had listened to Ricard's brief account—the state of the Household which was to spend that night at Abbeville where Monsieur had hoped to find the King, his own journey by way of Saint-Pol and Béthune . . . The general was saying that Monsieur would leave Abbeville for Dieppe with his men, who were quite incapable of going farther. There he would wait for the King—"Do give me the letter," said Louis XVIII with a look of impatience. And he plunged into it without paying much attention to the end of Ricard's story. All eyes were turned toward the sovereign. He looked very much absorbed. When he had finished the letter, he went back to the beginning and seemed to reread it more carefully. They knew that His Majesty had had a fit of pain in the afternoon, and he sighed, which must be because of his poor feet.

His Majesty quickly realized—especially as Grammont spoke in a loud voice, being a little deaf—that their words were being overheard, and that the news was spreading round the table, particularly that they must abandon all hope of seeing the Royal Household, which had become unserviceable and was embarking at Dieppe. And there were voices that said, "After all, why not call in the English and the Prussians? They'll make short work of that rabble!" Louis XVIII glanced in the direction of these blunderers: there were people from Lille present who were probably loyal to his person, but capable of indiscretion. He did not notice that Mortier, on hearing this careless remark, had assumed a black expression and was biting his upper lip so that it all but completely disappeared.

"Surely you speak some other language besides French, General?" the King, turning to his left, asked General Ricard.

"I speak Italian, Sir," said the General. "Italian it is, then," said Louis XVIII. His Majesty was polyglot. Louis-Philippe understood Italian, but the King was speaking too low to his left-hand neighbor for him to follow the conversation. The Duc d'Orléans had only one concern: to get rid of the King. Suppose His Majesty remained in this town indefinitely and the garrison should rebel: it would surely be claimed that it was a plot hatched by the Duke. As a matter of fact, the King was quite disposed to leave Lille, where he did not feel safe. Before dinner he had decided to leave at midnight for Dunkirk. To inspect the frontier, he claimed. . . . All right, let him get away with that bit of hypocrisy: but if ever he got the idea that he wanted to come back! . . . Macdonald would have preferred him to leave only the next day after the review that had been announced: he clung to the idea that a night departure had all the earmarks of flight. Louis-Philippe was preparing a whole arsenal of arguments . . . It was also necessary to counteract the effect of a piece of news brought by M. de Siméon, according to which the road to Dunkirk was likely to be

quite unsafe around Cassel. Because in Cassel there was General
Vandamme, who had not forgiven the King for having exiled him
from Paris last September, twenty-four hours after his return from
Siberia . . . The news had struck His Majesty. And it was true that
Vandamme enjoyed the backing of the people of Cassel, his birth-
place, where in 1792, at the time when the country was in danger—
Louis-Philippe remembered it well—he had levied the volunteer company of Light Infantry of Mont Cassel. How to reassure Louis on this
point?

When they left the table, the King called together the three Marshals, his cousin d'Orléans, and M. de Blacas d'Aulps of course, to
hear General Ricard. Everyone had risen and the group went into
the bedroom that the King had been given in the Hôtel de Brigode.
Macdonald brusque as usual, Mortier with a smaller and tighter mouth
than ever. The Prince de Wagram's agitation was noticeable, and it
did not pass unperceived. Berthier had felt fidgety all through the
meal, and since General Ricard's arrival he had been beside himself.

"Couldn't he stop chewing his nails, for heaven's sake?" Jaucourt
said to Bourrienne. He certainly was chewing his nails furiously that
evening.

Berthier . . . Berthier . . . After all, what does anyone know
about him, about what is going on inside him, about the reasons he
has for chewing his nails? Everyone ridicules him. He is small—so
what? If he were tall, what difference would that make? He has a
paunch—he isn't the only one to have one at his age. No, people
snigger because he is in love, and they haven't waited until he was
sixty-three to do that. In the army of Egypt, for example, the other
generals used to joke about it with their subordinates. Those loyal to
Napoleon did not forgive him 1814, and the King's entourage, the
nobility, did not forgive him his origins. Oh, I do not claim to be
objective, but still . . . The military despise him because he is not
a man of the battlefields. But would there have been Napoleon without Berthier? Without the nights spent growing pale over papers and
maps, without Berthier's enormous administrative work, would there
have been a Grand Army—without him, without his knowledge of
everything from gaiter buttons to cannon—without him to prepare
the stages, organize both the rear and the front? The Emperor knew
what he was doing, and at Wagram it was neither Lauriston leading
the decisive charge with a hundred pieces of artillery, nor Macdonald,
made a Marshal in the morning, whom he had named Prince de

Wagram, but Berthier. This Berthier, hungry for property, who himself inserted the name of his mistress's son in a list of nominations to the Legion of Honor—even though it is not true that, as General-Baron Gourgaud claimed, on the morrow of Marengo he wrote down Captain Sopransy's name five times in his report in order to have him credited with this victory—but who certainly brought back pillaged treasures from Italy . . . Yes, all this perhaps . . . And they say he considered it quite normal to pass from one sovereign to another like the furniture in the Tuileries.

But what is unfair is to look at a man of that time either with the eyes of his contemporaries or with the eyes of today, the eyes of another morality. He should be looked at not only as Léon de Rochechouart or Exelmans saw him, as Seignobos or Malet were to see him, but as he saw himself. And he should be judged not only in the light of that week in which we meet him, not even only in the light of his past, but also in the light of that last, finishing touch that the future, his brief future, will give to his picture. That is the whole difficulty, it is what makes me dissatisfied with everything that I am telling, and not only concerning Berthier, but also all the actors in the tragicomedy of this Holy Week, dissatisfied with the fact that we see them here only within the limits of that week and without the illumination of their further destiny, of what they will become.

Not only Berthier. All of them. They should all be seen with their future.

Take, for instance, well—just a name tossed into these pages, a character barely glimpsed, not really met: the Duc de La Rochefoucault-Liancourt. What did those officers of the 1st Light Cavalry Regiment who momentarily took shelter on his property on Tuesday evening get to know about him? And was it up to me to take sides between their feeling, in the face of those children who worked twelve and more hours a day for twelve sous, and the admiration and esteem that one of his subordinates felt for this Duke? A philanthropist, you understand, and we know what to think of philanthropy. Nowadays. With a century and a half of experience. And all the superiority we assume in judging paternalism, after *Les Mystères de Paris* or *Les Misérables,* the estimable Mme. Boucicaut and Marshal Pétain . . . Yet who was right, at that time, that fellow before the commons of Liancourt, or those young horsemen, the Arnavons, the Schmalzes, as prompt to judge that aristocrat as is almost anybody in our own time?

The point is not only that it was this Duke who introduced Jenner's vaccination into France, or that he could have lived quite differently, without putting those children to work at mule-jennies, that he could have lived like others of his rank, of his family, of his class, instead of in a seven-foot-high cell in those communal rooms, giving everything, except his library housed in the ruins of the château, for the development of new industries, their equipment, the training of young workers—but also that this master—for after all he was a master— was to become the promoter in France of a new form of workers' association which he himself was to create, the first mutual benefit society: this being in order to circumvent the law forbidding any combination of workers; that it was this Duke who was to provide the workers with the model for the organizations by virtue of which, less than fifteen years later, in Lyons, they were to be the first in the world to take up arms for their class. And it was because of this that, having been elected as deputy of the Oise, a deputy of the Center, not a liberal, a republican, to the Chamber of Louis XVIII, the Duc de La Rochefoucault-Liancourt soon found himself forced to retire to his lands; and the day of his funeral the people, who knew him, accompanied him as later Paris was to accompany Béranger, and the King's Gendarmes charged the procession, dispersing it, and the coffin was knocked to the ground out of the arms of the workers who were carrying it.

At times, even in this obvious light, the immediate future nevertheless may give to other men an aspect different from what we have been able to glimpse in the course of a halt of the Royal Household. Duke for duke, this time take a Richelieu. Another one who is regarded as suspect by everyone. The Ultra-Royalists had no liking for him, he was not a true *émigré,* not a man of Condé's army. The Bonapartists and the republicans saw in him only what he was—a reactionary, an aristocrat. Well, yes, he was an aristocrat and a reactionary, the servant of a foreign Emperor, an enemy of education for the people, anything you like. If I should take it into my head to defend this aristocrat, this reactionary, perhaps I need only refer to his past, to his role in New Russia, where this Frenchman transformed newborn Odessa which has never forgotten him, where he was the bearer of progress and the auxiliary of French trade, helping to create on the Black Sea outlets for Mediterranean ports, for Marseilles. But this would be next to nothing, it would be forgetting the future, what he became when finally Louis XVIII turned a deaf ear to his ministers and his favorites, and appealed to him; and Richelieu, over the opposition of the English, the Prussians and the Emperor of Austria, relying solely on Czar Alexander's confidence in him which he had won over all the years, was able through him to bring about the evacuation of French territory by foreign troops. Yes, the Duc de Richelieu's tirades to that traitor Marmont in the prefecture of Beauvais, the attention he bestowed upon his person, spraying himself with perfume, and perhaps also what is somewhat suspect in the too great austerity of his ways in respect to women—all that is undeniable. But who can forget that throughout this century in which the new consciousness was being born, Richelieu was to be regarded—by Jules Michelet, a child of the time, and by all those who breathed with relief when the last Uhlan, the last Cossack, the last Croat, and the last Horse Guard left France—as his country's Liberator?

There are in France, to my knowledge, but two works on this singular man—a monograph written in the late nineteenth century, and a book dating from the same period on his role at the congress of Aix-La-Chapelle. No French university professor has had the idea of saying to a student who has asked for a subject for a thesis: Why don't you take Emmanuel-Armand de Richelieu? He's a curious fellow, and little has been written about him. I shall perhaps be blamed, as I am blamed for having defended Barrés or Claudel, for these few parenthetical lines in favor of the Duke with the dark complexion and the curly hair. But I must confess that it would have disturbed my sleep not to have written them.

Don't worry, though, I won't go so far as to try to rehabilitate Marmont, the Duc de Raguse, in your eyes. Even though he perhaps does not altogether deserve the suspicion of treason that has become attached to his name.* Is he in fact much more contemptible than a Soult or a Clarke? It is a matter of taste. For the material facts, for the *Ragusade* of 1814, are we to believe Napoleon disembarking at Cannes as he revives the bloody accusation, or that firsthand witness, Colonel-Baron Charles Fabvier, our old acquaintance? The colonel thought it his duty to take pen in hand to defend his former chief, but while he certainly did not consider him to have been involved in the military aspect of the betrayal—in Souham's retreat at Essonnes —even though he may be right in this, it is not the whole story . . .

* Marshal Marmont, Napoleon's former aide-de-camp and one of his most trusted generals, took upon himself in April 1814 a political role which has been stigmatized as treasonable. Paris had capitulated to the Allies, and Czar Alexander was ready to accept Napoleon's abdication in favor of his son, Napoleon II, when Marmont, with the connivance of General Schwarzenberg, the Austrian commander-in-chief, withdrew his corps of 20,000 men to Essonnes, out of the possible theatre of operations, and concluded a secret convention with the enemy. This put Napoleon in a position of such military inferiority that he was obliged to abdicate unconditionally.

for the day before, in the conversations with the Austrians, Marmont had already committed treason. But I have no strong feelings about Marmont. On the other hand, I *do* care about Fabvier.

I have written this book, and my initial purpose in writing it was to combat comparisons between periods that are not comparable. Nothing is so absurd as to judge, to explain the past on the basis of the present. Nothing is more false or more dangerous. I don't know how what I am writing here will be read, but, whatever my wishes in the matter, I cannot prevent the reader from indulging in that game of which I disapprove. For example there are those—and I am quite aware of them—who on the basis of the very efforts I am making to put the men of the time back into their setting, and not to let myself judge them arbitrarily, on what we have learned to consider a betrayal, whether of Napoleon or of Louis XVIII, will draw conclusions and apply them to our time, will see in these men some excuse or other for those who can be considered only as traitors to France in the time of the Lightning War, on the eve of the atomic era. Well, no—there is no common measure between a Fabvier and . . . these people—I was about to mention a name, but I refuse to choose, I cannot, even negatively, insult a hero of the Napoleonic wars and of the war of Greek Independence by comparing him to *that*. But it is necessary to go further. A soldier of the year 1815 is not a soldier of 1940, even if the landscape and the disorder of a retreat are similar —because the contradictions of the one are not the contradictions of the other—because the meaning of words has changed from one period to the other—because in 1815, for example, it was still considered normal to cut off a condemned man's hand with an ax before executing him—because there was at that time no counterweight to the idea of nation—because a patriot would not have dreamed that, for example, he had duties toward a people who were not his own— because the word *humanity* was devoid of meaning—because a war was a crime only if it were lost, etc. It is precisely with a Fabvier who went over from the Imperial to the monarchist ranks, only to conspire subsequently against the King, that we see the whole combination of conceptions of the time vacillate in the direction of present-day ideas that were to assume shape, value and scope only much later, when they became incorporated into a system, an ideology, when they lost their empirical character and became principles. But this is because they ceased to be the fumblings of one man and became incarnated in human masses, to be identified with new men, new makers of history, who were the opposite of the adventurers of that time. Thus Fabvier.

Should this character have appeared in this book only to bring a few messages from Marmont to the King, or to the Household waiting to be reviewed on the Champ-de-Mars, for a meeting at the Carrousel and a dream in a garret in the prefecture of Beauvais? Even now I can imagine the criticism that will be made: it may be leveled at Fabvier or at others, but let us assume that it is directed at Fabvier. The author will be taken to task for his clumsiness in placing minor characters in the foreground, in unnecessary scenes, and what was the necessity of entering into the private life of this young colonel, torn between Marie-des-Anges and Marie-des-Démons? Don't expect me here to defend a book from which it would be necessary to remove every page, every sentence, indeed every word of every sentence, if I were to listen to that kind of remark. But it is true that this character, a minor one for the reader, is a major character for the author, one whom the said author blames himself, on the contrary, for having allowed to remain in the background, in the wings, throughout the book. For while Berthier's passion for Mme. Visconti invites a smile, what better could the author of a love story ask in the way of a hero than Charles Fabvier who, if memory serves me, saw Maria-de-los-Angeles, the Duchesse de Frioul, for the first time about 1805 when she had just married Duroc, his friend, and who from that time on loved this "perfect woman" with a hopeless love that Duroc's death in 1813 seemed to make forever sacrilegious, and there was all the whole fantastic and adventurous life of nineteen years between that death and the day when the Duchesse de Frioul consented to become the wife of this man who had loved her from afar for twenty-seven years. . . .

It is that life of which I have felt the lack here to illuminate this incidental character. Does this officer of the Empire who considered it his duty to remain in the army of France under a returned King and, because he had sworn loyalty to him, to accompany this King in his flight to the frontier—does this officer remain the same if we know what became of him later? If we see him, having refused to leave France but refraining from taking up service again in the army of the Hundred Days—if we see him on the morrow of Waterloo uniting with a few men near the frontier to harry the invader, instead of adding his voice to the monstrous chorus that regarded his country's defeat as a stroke of good fortune—a *franc-tireur* against the

foreigner who was bringing back Louis XVIII to whom he had once
been faithful? . . . And there he is in Lorraine, as the invasion armies
pass, shooting at a Prussian convoy from behind an embankment.
Will he remain the same, this Charles Fabvier, after 1817 in Lyons,
where he sides against General Donnadieu who was imposing the
orders of the Ultra-Royalists? Will he remain the same for you when
the logic of History has pushed him to conspire against the very King
whom he would not abandon in 1815, and he is forced, because of
his involvement in a succession of plots, to leave his country whose
frontiers he had refused to cross in 1815? When, side by side with
that young man of Béthune whose father had attended the meeting
above the cemetery in Poix, you see him in 1823 on the Spanish
frontier, on the bridge of Behobie, leaping up before some French
soldiers to ask them to turn back, not to invade the Spanish Republic
and to adopt the tricolor? Will he remain the same for you when, like
Byron, he has become a hero of the Greek people's war of independence? When, having returned under an assumed name in July,
1830, he wields a gun shoulder to shoulder with the Paris workers
during the Trois Glorieuses? * Ah, perhaps then you will forgive
Maria-de-los-Angeles, widowed for nineteen years, for yielding at last,
for betraying the memory of Duroc for this man who was then fifty,
who could so easily have lived like everyone else, like Tony de Reiset,
the young Rastignac, or Marshal Marmont, with the cross of Saint-
Louis, property and a royal revenue, or who, like a Léon de Rochechouart or the young d'H——, could have married the daughter of
an army contractor.

Men and women are not only bearers of their past, the heirs of a
world, accountable for a series of acts; they are also the seeds of the
future. The novelist is not merely a judge who asks them to account
for what *was;* he is also one of them, a being eager to know what
will be, who passionately interrogates these individual destinies in
search of a distant great answer. There is no criminal so black that
he does not seek in himself a slumbering light. There is no fate fixed
in advance, or seemingly so, in which I do not hope to see arise a
contradiction of its very data. Even if this were history—and I swear
to you that for my part I have reached Flanders with the Royal Household without knowing whether Louis XVIII would really leave French
soil or what would become of Napoleon, and the name of Waterloo
was nothing more to me than a few letters on a map, the future again

---

* The three days (July 28, 29, 30, of 1830) of the insurrection in the Paris
streets that overthrew Charles X.

was at stake—I should cast the dice once more without knowing what spots would turn up.

As in the case of Berthier. As in the case of the unhappy Berthier at Lille who chews his nails, who is yellow, and heavy, no taller than my boot, with a paunch, with joints that creak, aches and pains, his heart at moments pounding madly. Ten times that day he has written a letter, ten times he has torn it up. It would obviously be simpler to write nothing, to run back to Paris, or, at the last moment, to say: No, I won't leave French soil. . . . Only there is Marie-Elisabeth, Marie-Elisabeth and the children, over there, in Bavaria. If only he had not sent them there! They are in Bamberg, damn it. He could go and fetch them, bring them back . . . Will he be allowed to bring them back? His father-in-law—probably. But the Emperor of Austria. He will have to write an eleventh letter. With all the horror, the humiliation. God knows how Napoleon would take it! By whom to send it? By Mortier, if Mortier stayed . . .

Everything is jumbled in Alexandre's head. France, the shame of becoming an *émigré*. What this word has meant to him all his life. And the wrench of leaving his properties. He loves Gros-Bois, he loves Chambord, his Hôtel des Capucines. That, after all, is his life. Men, after a certain age, are like dogs; they attach themselves to houses. And Berthier tries with all the strength of his mind to put aside his major anguish: Giuseppa. . . .

The few words spoken by Macdonald, that accident at Saint-Denis. He knows what it is, there was that attack last year, what the doctor had told him—and even if Mme. Visconti gets over it, it is nevertheless another step toward death. There is one thing that frightens him more than anything in the world, and that is a world in which he would be alone, a world in which there would no longer be a Giuseppa. He is quite able to leave her, no longer to see her—he is used to that—all those wars. And then, it is no longer as in the days of the Egyptian campaign, there is no longer, at his age, that physical slavery, that obsession of sex, that daily madness. But if he were never to see her again, if he alone of the two of them were to survive the agonizing break with the whole past. Oh, a man may lose his father, his mother: the pain he feels relates only to his childhood! But Giuseppa . . . If Giuseppa were dead, everything that has been would have disappeared, the only being who knows what he is going to say almost before he has said it, who always understands him because she knows all the little things, and the big ones, and that which is bitter, and that which intoxicates him. *Mon Dieu, mon Dieu,*

I should not want to survive. He feels a pain in his heart—how grateful he is to this heart for pounding like this! Perhaps this heart will kill him before he learns . . . But no, I'm an idiot. It was nothing, an indisposition. How well she got over last year's attack! She looked better afterwards than she had before. That face, so young, so smooth: for a moment the madness of long ago comes over him, the haunting visions . . .

Oh, I know, an old man harking back on the adventures of the bed, who throws too much light on what is supposed to be left in the dark, who thinks with a precision that can so easily become ignoble not only of what was his own youth and that of this woman, but also of the long lechery of life, in which the wonder of the first years is transformed into experience, into virtuosity, into complicity. How revolting to eyes other than his own! Because this is not an ideal love, a high-minded devotion of the kind songs will be written about, but love, you understand, true love—the love that lives by desire and its fulfillment, the Phoenix that is born again of its fatigue, love, marvelous physical love, which shrinks before nothing, and awakens again covered with sweat to consume itself in its strength and its imagination. And even here at Lille, even in this extremity of unhappiness, this aged man, halfway between his wife and his mistress, on the remote edge of this country whose standard he has helped to carry afar for a quarter of a century, with all his faculties, and—why not say so?—his genius . . . in this confusion of the soul, the agitation of his heart, and the uneasiness that comes over him, the rheumatisms . . . torn, overwhelmed . . . how can he have become what he is, be here, with this fleeing gouty king, these wigs, this bankrupt gang, he, he Berthier, Prince de Wagram et de Neufchâtel . . . how? Even now, if he turns his back upon his unhappiness and his shame, he forgets them, because of that sun that is not the sun of Austerlitz, that sun of Giuseppa in his arms, Giuseppa wriggling and begging for quarter, seized again by the frenzy of the senses and flung, at his mercy, at his mercy, into the rumpled sheets—a massacre of the bedchamber, and this pain he has in his arm, undoubtedly from having rested on it too long in a bad position with the woman's weight and his own . . . Let them laugh at him if they want to, let them laugh till they burst—how could he forget the unforgettable?

Poor, poor Berthier . . . naïve lover, after so many years still resembling the young man who had just discovered himself capable of making a woman cry out, still resembling those lads who come away from a bedchamber marveling at themselves and at life, and who may be seen in the deserted streets of a moon-drenched town dancing and singing all alone! And unable to keep things secret, to shut the door, to prevent himself from being taken by surprise . . . He has lived surrounded by ironical peeping Toms. What he regarded as his secret treasure had always been exposed to all eyes. How people have made fun of him! And they have never stopped. For example, they still roar over that story of the stolen letters. Even today, even at Lille, this Lille of despair. You should have heard Father Elisée just now, with all the indecency of his greasy lips, his hands accustomed to every chore, miming as much as telling about the affair. Inventing a little, too, although that is not the point. To Jaucourt and Bourrienne, in one of the Hôtel de Brigode salons full of candles already burned far down, one gone out and merely smoking. The affair of the stolen letters. Mark you, it's no novelty to anyone. It has always been known. You can imagine . . . all those letters, from the armies, since the time of the Republic, decorated with little drawings, with breath-taking details, the faltering language of a lover making an ass of himself, and the crudest details, the refinements of a soldier's imagination which even war cannot repress . . . all this was pretty well known, what with military censorship, police censorship—you can well imagine!

But when the thing exploded in Portugal— What do you mean, in Portugal? Berthier was never in Portugal. Don't interrupt me. In Portugal. And this time it was no longer the open secret of police censorship which passes things on to headquarters, to the men of the Directoire, to the entourage of the First Consul, no: it became public, they were passed from hand to hand, mentioned in the newspapers . . . Oh, to be sure, those letters could not possibly be reproduced! Their nature . . . It was the English who had thought that up. A lot of stupid things are said about the English. But there is one thing for which they must be given credit. In the matter of organizing espionage they cannot be equaled. And I know what I'm talking about. Pitt's and Cobourg's agents, as the sans-culotte imbeciles used to say— Well, just take what happened at Quiberon . . . But let's stick to Portugal. In point of fact, of course, it was not in Portugal that those letters had been stolen, but quite simply in Paris, on the Quai Voltaire, at the ex-embassy of the Cisalpine Republic. Mme. Visconti changed her lady's maid quite often; she lost her temper easily, would give a servant the sack for a spot on a gorget, a lost handkerchief . . .

And untidy on top of it all, never locking anything up, and also too confiding, inclined to tell her servingmaids things which concerned only the Marshal. . . .

"In short! I was in London when this stupefying correspondence reached there, and as I was paid the honor of being consulted on French affairs . . . ye gods! All the strumpets of Leicester Square came to me to get me to show them those letters. There were details in them—details! For at least six months it was all the fashion among the wantons of London to make love à la Berthier . . . How is it done? Come, messieurs, surely you are not going to ask *me,* with my robe, my ministry? Well, if you insist . . ." And the three heads drew close, Jaucourt very eighteenth century, Bourrienne professional in attitude, the Father between them . . . "But the stroke of genius of the English was to hang fire . . . I don't know, five, six years. One fine day, when Soult was in Lisbon, and quite disposed to have his hand forced by the good Portuguese people who were itching to have him for King: lo and behold, from the English ships blockading the coasts there came to land . . . but I'll bet you can't imagine how! . . . in bottles, which the sea rolled onto the beaches . . . copies by the hundred of the correspondence between the lovely Giuseppa and her little Sandro. Peasants, fishermen, picked them up . . . carried them to the local police who did not have sufficient knowledge of French to understand certain technical words . . . tried to obtain the information from dictionaries . . . in vain. My dear Bourrienne, your people would have had more flair, I imagine, and would immediately have found out what they wanted from the harlots who must have learned the whole vocabulary of unprintable words from the Imperial soldiery . . . In the end, the stuff fell into the hands of a double agent who took it to the French command. When it was understood what it was all about, you can imagine the uproar; but they soon discovered that they no longer controlled the secret: for the bottles rolled right up on the sands of the Tagus—they were found, here one day, there the next; it was the talk of Portugal. I don't know how great a role it actually played in lowering the esteem in which the French were held in the Lusitanian Republic, but it appears that when Buonaparte learned of it, he flew into a rage that threatened to smash all the Sèvres porcelain in Compiègne . . . and did Berthier get an earful!"

Poor Berthier . . . but the fact that he was laughed at does not prevent his having received a citation of a kind not vouchsafed to the most famous military men. It is but a note added by a certain Stendhal to his little book *De l'Amour,* in which he wrote:

> . . . they say that old age, by modifying our organs, makes us incapable of loving; for my part I do not believe it. Your mistress having become your intimate friend, gives you other pleasures, the pleasures of old age. Love is a flower which, having been a rose at morn, in the season of flowers, is transformed at eventide, when roses are no longer in season, into a delicious fruit.

Here Stendhal had penned in the margin of the manuscript: *For me. Amours du Prince de Wagram.** A note which he struck out, for he had this delicacy: because in 1822, when *De l'Amour* appeared, Mme. Visconti was still alive.

And now that neither Alexandre nor Giuseppa is among the living, it is Stendhal's sentiment which prevails over all gossip. This beautiful story, which continued in the setting sun, of Giuseppa Visconti and the Prince de Wagram who loved each other. The rest will be nothing more than the dirtiness of men which the Atlantic can well roll endlessly onto the beaches of Portugal or elsewhere, along with the debris from the great depths, the pierced shells, the seaweed and the flotsam of distant shipwrecks. The future will remember only the lovers' long fidelity, their perseverance in love, without concerning itself with those little betrayals between them which are without importance—Mme. Visconti who on one occasion went to bed with Elleviou the singer, who, as everyone knew, did not care for women, as well as with others in passing—including Macdonald—any more than it will be astonished at how they managed things when the Emperor put a young Bavarian princess into his Minister of War's bed—and could the naïve Berthier suspect, when he wrote to Mme. Visconti from Moscow to tell her in the most graphic terms how anxious he was to get back to his young wife, that his letter would be intercepted in the forests of White Russia by the partisans who were harrying the Grand Army, and that one day, in the twentieth century, it would be published, together with all the mail thus seized—including several missives by a certain Henri Beyle, better known by the name of Stendhal? Dust, dust . . . Time launders people's linen, the filth does not survive, the great wind of History passes and purifies, and it is as though the windows

---

* Thus in the original (translator's note).

and doors of their dwellings had stood open to all the drafts for a
century and more, and now all that is to be seen is the curtain
ripped by gusts of wind, swept outside, still waving vaguely, like a
human hand in farewell. Of all this nothing will remain but the
music—the divine, the profound music of love.

That is the distant future, ours. But Berthier's future, his immediate future, it is he after all who forces us to revise everything,
even though his name be listed in the Dictionary of Weathervanes
with those of the officials who had their feet in the camps of both
the Empire and the Monarchy, of the painters who added fleurs-de-lis
to a banner in a painting of the Revolution, of the writers who
substituted the Duc de Berry for the Little Shaver in an ode . . .
Approximately two months. In order to understand Berthier, we
need the blinding light of those two months.

He moves toward his destiny like a miser, with his casket containing Giuseppa's jewels. That evening at Lille, that last evening
in France, once alone in the room he has been given in the Hôtel de
Brigode, he has opened this casket, and spread out the pearls and
the precious stones on the bed. In his stumpy, hairy, swollen hand
he holds this wealth, he pours out the diamonds. The feeble light
of a candle plays among them as do his fingers. If we limited ourselves to this picture, what would we think the Marshal was calculating, weighing? In truth, they are mere pebbles to him, pebbles of a
sea that has ebbed away, together with all his past life. In truth, what
are the jewels to him, if they no longer caress a neck, shoulders, if
they do not rest between the curves of the swelling breasts, what are
those bracelets which no longer slide up from the wrist to the forearm, an incredibly white forearm for such a dark woman? Yes, all
this is for sale, so that they can live by it—he, Marie-Elisabeth and
the children. It is so natural that Giuseppa should help them; for
that matter he has left her that piece of paper in exchange—an
annuity. He may disappear, die; Mme. Visconti will have enough to
live on.

How strange it seems today that a man fleeing his country in
the midst of a great political upheaval should have been able to
settle upon his mistress an income from his abandoned property
which would be paid her by a banker, quite regularly, for the rest
of her life—and she was to go on living, I believe, for another twenty
years. In this world that we have perfected, such things are no
longer possible. A Berthier would no longer have anything but
what he carried with him, and the lands, houses, bank account he

left behind him would be confiscated. His old mistress would give Italian lessons in order to live, assuming that she were able to find pupils who were not afraid of being compromised. Or she would do housework. She would certainly not receive a check from MM. Laffitte and Perregaux every month.

At least he does not have that worry tonight, the Prince de Wagram. He only wonders what Giuseppa would put round her lovely swollen neck to go to the theatre. She has, to be sure, kept her corals, which are of little value, the big baroque brooch which has a siren lying on a kind of palm, the long pale pink chain with a green-gold clasp, but . . . The foolish creature! she has even given me her sapphires, though I told her to keep them . . . And Berthier, with the tip of his podgy ring finger, lifts the ring with the nearly black stone, of that deep blue that water among rocks sometimes takes on. . . .

There are all the diamonds: the necklace of small flat rectangles in four rows, the long ear pendants, the two bracelets like cuffs of crosspieces, the pair of brooches, and the semidiadem formed of flowers on branches of diamonds. The sapphires of the Principality of Neufchâtel: everyone had recognized them; it was just after the Emperor had granted the principality as an appanage to his Minister of War; and the first time she had put all that on to go to the *opéra* . . . Giuseppa wore, I remember, her big sleeveless ermine cloak, lined with navy-blue silk embroidered with white bees. All Paris had turned around to look at her, and M. Visconti, beside her, impassive, was examining the boxes with his mother-of-pearl and gilt opera glasses for a sweetheart of his own.

All his life was here, in these outspread stones. Those he had given her in Rome in the first days, the gifts from Milan, the return from Egypt . . . There were rings that were battles, neck chains that were peace treaties. There were also alcoves, mad nights, hotel rooms and the beds of palaces—when Mme. Visconti had worn nothing but those brilliants or these burning topazes. For she knew Sandro's heart. There was the solitaire he had brought her on the eve of his marriage to Marie-Elisabeth. She had given back everything, and Alexandre even discovered two or three jewels in this jumble of sparkles that he did not remember having given her: the jealousy this kindled in him was like a deep wound. Who? Many a time on official evenings at the theatre he had caught her smiling behind her fan at a passing man. With that air of complicity that responds to a courtesy too ceremonious to be innocent. . . .

When he thought that she could have been in the arms of other men, he suffered so terribly that he felt like sinking his thumbs into his eyes, like slitting a wrist or worse. . . . Oh, it was no use now torturing himself over what may have been. The violence of their quarrels. The outbursts of anger. And then the reconciliations . . . on the occasion of a public meeting, at somebody's house . . . at an old friend's . . . at a soirée, with all those people about, the mad desire to run away, to be alone with her once again—to be.

All the precious stones were strewn over the rumpled bed where the Prince de Wagram had intended to rest while waiting for midnight, the departure hour set by His Majesty. He had half undressed, and was in a state of disorder in which sleep had caught him, when the door he had omitted to lock opened and Antoine entered the room.

The postilion, who also served as his valet, showed no surprise at this odd sight, and he left his master the time to recover from a dream in which Marie-Elisabeth had just caught him with one of her ladies-in-waiting on the staircase of the Hôtel des Capucines, and Giuseppa was scolding him in the name of conjugal fidelity. And it was only when the Marshal had collected his wits and said, "Is that you, Antoine?" that the postilion gave a slight cough and said, *"Votre Altesse Sérénissime . . ."* Because Antoine could never accustom himself to not addressing his master thus, though it was nearly a year since the Principality of Neufchâtel had had to be returned to the House of Austria.

"What is it?" Berthier grumbled, and as he sat up the sapphire necklace slipped to the floor. Antoine noticed nothing. It was half past twelve, and His Majesty had changed his mind, they were not leaving. His Most Serene Highness could undress and sleep in peace. "What? We're not leaving?" They were not leaving, that was the fact. The King of France was exasperating beyond endurance. Could he really not remain of the same mind for half an hour!

And now that he has carefully put away—Antoine having vanished —all this jewelry in its cases, and the cases in the casket tucked under the bolster, the key hanging from his neck on a little gold chain, Berthier, the light extinguished, has turned over several times before going to sleep, but I can no longer see his face, I can no longer scrutinize through his features the dreams that have invaded him. I remain in this darkened bedroom alone with the sleeper's future.

I have never set foot in Bamberg. This little Bavarian town is for me but an opera set. Idyllic Germany. With trees and music, and moral axioms embroidered on cushions. Here the sun has torn away the mists of Picardy and Flanders, the year has made a great step forward toward the bliss of fulfillment, the lilac blossoms have wilted and dropped, drives in the country have the lightness of the sky and the leaves, and there are a thousand different reasons for singing and laughing. May comes to an end with bare arms, the open air, people sitting on the doorsteps of houses, and military parades, cool dresses. . . . It is balmy, warmer than normal for the season, people begin to seek the shade. And even beggars could be lovers. But there still are cold nights. . . .

I have never set foot in Bamberg. Yet when Berthier returned from that drive with his father-in-law, Duke Wilhelm of Bavaria, who had insisted on showing him the improvements recently made on the castle of Seehof, near Memmelsdorf—a charming baroque building with stone steps, adorned with statues in the park and orangeries on which it prided itself—the Marshal found his wife reading and he asked her what the book was. And it was one which had appeared the previous year, a *Don Juan,* written by that young man whom the Duke had introduced them to that evening last week when there had been music at the palace, and who was stage manager at the theatre—Mr. Hoffmann. So that I find myself caught between several Bambergs, that of my imagination, and the one where Ernst Theodor Amadeus Hoffmann lived, a Bamberg lightly touched by the wing of the fantastic. The court of Duke Wilhelm is henceforth that of the prince who is seen in *Lebensansichten des Keters Mürr* (1821), and that theatre on the square—opposite the narrow two-story house, with a mansard roof and an attic for the dreams of the Cat, where Hoffmann lived—is Hoffmann's, the setting of his dreams. Berthier went there from time to time with the Princesse de Wagram and the Duchess of Bavaria, his mother-in-law, a woman who was very fond of music. . . .

I have never set foot in Bamberg, and I am caught between the idyll of Goethe's Germany, the city of Hoffmann, and that modern Herculaneum that Elsa* has seen and which she describes in her novel, *L'Inspecteur des Ruines,* where the ridiculous swastika cross and the gutted furniture of the Third Reich are found in the destroyed villas. I am caught between these three Germanies and the real

* Elsa Triolet, the author's wife.

Bamberg of the tourists, built on the isle of Regnitz between the two arms of the Main, Bamberg with its Kapuziner Strasse and its school, the Fishery and Little Venice, the canal, the romantic park, the Theresien Hain, where the memory of the Mad King hovers, and on the left bank opposite the island above the Rathaus, when you have passed the two bridges, the Domberg, at the top of which, on Karolinenplatz, stand the old cathedral and the ancient episcopal palace, the two embodying the whole Middle Ages and the Renaissance of Franconia; and across from them the new palace with its severe columns, a gloomy and monotonously regular structure brightened only by its east wing, where the Berthiers had come to live, which overlooks the slope leading down to the Rathaus. And what more do I need to know?

The Prince de Wagram does not go about much in the town, although Bavaria was for a long time, unlike the rest of Germany, Napoleon's ally. The Prince de Wagram drives outside Bamberg through idyllic Germany, through the villages, up there to Altenburg, reached by an avenue of lime trees, or to Rothof where there were such beautiful cherry trees, or into the Michelsberger Wald . . . The Prince de Wagram, absent, his eyes on the peaceful landscape but seeing nothing of it, chewing his nails, thinking of other things, of a woman who no longer has any sapphires, of a world from which he was excluded, of Chambord and of the gentle Loire . . . At times, if he ventures into the country on foot with his faithful Antoine, the chief of police of Bamberg follows him at a distance, discreetly, or on days when that high personage has other fish to fry, one of his faithful officers. His heart is not very good, but Doctor Ziegler when called in swears it was nothing.

Holy Week is far away. . . .

How did Napoleon take the letter that Berthier finally confided to the Maréchal-Duc de Trévise on Thursday morning? Was it actually transmitted to him? Alexandre was perpetually haunted by the thought that he had not written what he should have written. It was his form of remorse. A remorse which sprang less from his conduct upon the return of the Bourbons than from that letter. Yet it was indeed remorse, shame. At times he felt sweat oozing from his pores. He looked about him, wondering if people were aware of what he was thinking. The people who surrounded him. Of course not. They saw nothing. It would not be well to show what he was thinking. To anyone. Not even to Marie-Elisabeth. What he thought, in particular, *about* Marie-Elisabeth. For it was an odd mixture: of pity and annoyance. Before, he had not looked at her with those critical eyes. There had even been times when he thought her pretty. In a certain sense. Now, although he knew that they had both had a hand in it, Giuseppa as well as his wife, distance tended to make him idealize Mme. Visconti, and to put the responsibility for things on the Princesse de Wagram. It was she who had pushed him into breaking with Napoleon; she wanted her place at the court of Louis XVIII. Of course Berthier had let himself be persuaded, and how hastily, even, he had accepted the conclusions they had both reached. It was this hastiness that was held against him: look at Macdonald, no fuss was made about *him* because he had rallied to the Princes a week later. Yet when a man had perceived his destiny, when he knew that he was going to make the jump, was it not better to make it right away? That was what he had told himself a year earlier. But 1815 was different from 1814. All this, anyway, estranged him from his young wife, who was wholly absorbed in the children. And in the gossip at the Bavarian court. Although she was quite agreeable to returning to Gros-Bois, to resuming the games of whist with Mme. Visconti. *Her* reasons were not her husband's, that was all. What conversation was possible between them? If he had spoken to her of France, she would have turned big empty eyes on him.

Then there were the jewels. They were sleeping, in the casket, at the bottom of a small locked cupboard in their room, the key to which he carried on his person. Marie-Elisabeth must have noticed the disappearance of the key, but she had said nothing about it. Besides, before her husband's return, she had not used this small cupboard. What was she thinking, seeing it locked, the key removed? Perhaps nothing at all. Perhaps that he was keeping State papers in it. She was rather discreet by nature. As for him, it was strange, but it embarrassed him to show these jewels to Marie-Elisabeth, even though she knew them, having seen them on Giuseppa a hundred times. He had not yet told her that he had this resource, since the money he had brought with him had sufficed up to the present. How would he go about it when he had to tell her? He was afraid his wife might suddenly want to wear the diamond *rivière* or the sapphire necklace. That would have been very disagreeable to him. Very disagreeable. Especially since these jewels constituted his independence. Precisely by remaining secret.

Duke Wilhelm, his father-in-law, was a very understanding man who got along beautifully with his son-in-law. He had been glad of Berthier's arrival. He was going to be able to try on him that defense he had learned to the attack which the Prince de Wagram liked to use in chess. And then there were his grandchildren, three of them now, whom he would have liked to keep. At least the boy, the eldest, who was five. Make a little Bavarian of him, teach him choral singing, to ride a horse, to handle a sword. But if the young couple—he called Alexandre and his daughter "the young couple"—wanted to return to Paris, he for one was not going to put anything in their way: you never got anywhere by going against people's wishes, that was all he had learned from life, and from his brother the King of Bavaria, Max I Josef. But the Comte de Montgelas, who was Max I Josef's minister, had not dared to take the responsibility upon himself, and had asked Vienna's opinion. And unfortunately Vienna, that is to say His Imperial Majesty, Cousin Franz, did not take the same view. Nor did the Allies, in session at the Congress. Franz, it seemed, held the Prince de Wagram in such high esteem for his military qualities that he was afraid if he were to let him go, even with all the promises in the world, he might foolishly be handing over to Buonaparte the organizer of an Austrian defeat. He had accordingly given orders to refuse Alexandre the *laissez-passer* which Berthier had requested for himself and his family. And upon the orders of Max I Josef, the chief of police of Bamberg, from the protector he had been up to that time, became the Prince's jailer. He was at his wit's end, was constantly on duty at his prefecture, ready to jump on his horse. He made life intolerable for everyone, postmasters, carriers, by draconian regulations; and every stranger at the city's gates was a suspect, searched, questioned, locked up. . . .

Especially as it had been found out through an agent that the Marshal had tried to obtain fifty thousand francs at a usurer's, on jewels that he had.

The season was a fine one, and the house was full of flowers that Marie-Elisabeth herself arranged in the vases, the ladies-in-waiting having no more taste than the maids, she said, in the matter of bouquets. She was very eager to return to Paris or to Chambord with Alexandre, even if it meant that the Marshal would have to maintain an attitude of reserve, and that life would be somewhat humdrum. But for heaven's sake, why did he go around putting on such a ghastly face? Bamberg was rather boring, but tolerable for two or three months. The palace wing that they had been given . . .

It was the east wing of the ducal palace. It formed the corner of Karolinenplatz, opposite the cathedral, and looked down over the whole slope extending to the Main. From the top of this less than a century and a half old building, with its three stories, not counting the slated mansard roofs, the view embraced the tiled roofs of the old town. And to the south and west, behind the cathedral, it was possible to make out the green countryside, the background of hills in the direction of Altenburg and the Michelsberger Wald. There was a garden behind, extending to the Residenzstrasse, and this was fine for the children. For people who had come with a simple carriage and a few trunks, it was in fact a little disproportionate to be living in such quarters. A series of halls and salons communicated with the main part of the palace, and here they were with a small German staff, Antoine, and Mlle. Gallien.

Mlle. Gallien was the children's French maid who had come with Marie-Elisabeth. She also took care of Mme. la Princesse's linen to occupy her hands and her mind while she supervised the little ones or when they were asleep. She said that the great disadvantage of the palace was having constantly to go up and down stairs. Especially for her, as the children had been settled on the second floor, a second floor which was actually a third story on that side because of the dimensions of the rooms on the ground floor and the slope of the hill. It was a corner room which on one side overlooked the square, and on the other the approach to it, from the lower end of Karolinenstrasse, at the point where there was a maximum of air and sunshine from early morning on. Excellent for the children! And one additional story did not seem to worry Alexandre who, short-winded though he was because of his heart, would climb up to their room on the slightest pretext. To such a point that Marie-Elisabeth had had something of a suspicion of his having intentions regarding Mlle. Gallien: but it must be admitted that this was unlikely. After all, he was a good father. There is nothing like children late in life to change a man.

To be sure, he did not like beer, which weighed on his stomach, but Papa, full as always of attentions toward his son-in-law, had had basketfuls of bottles of Rhine wine and of Tokay brought to them. The Prince de Wagram certainly had a very poor command of German but, at least in the family, everyone always conversed in French in his presence. Why was he going around with that face?

No. There was absolutely no point in talking of France to Marie-Elisabeth. She would think it was nostalgia. To be sure, it was nostalgia too. And there was Gros-Bois, with the dogs they had left there, hunting dogs that Alexandre loved. It would be pointless. She would not understand. They did not speak the same language.

Why did the Marshal refuse to see people? I'm not saying that the local nobility was very scintillating, but at least they helped to pass the time. Here, with so many rooms that they didn't know what to do with them, strings of salons, they nevertheless were not at liberty to have separate bedrooms, as they had had recently in Paris. It would have seemed incorrect in Bavaria. An immense bedroom on the first story, with windows on both sides, overlooked the garden on one side, the city on the other: I have always loved rooms like that, with the daylight passing right through; the only thing that was the least disagreeable was the proximity of the cathedral. Bells chimed the hours. The Bambergers were very proud of their bells: in particular of a couple which they called Heinrich and Kunigunde in memory of the Emperor Henry II and his spouse, whose recumbent figures in stone, sculptured by Tilman Riemanschneider, sleep right in the center of the cathedral. When Heinrich and Kunigunde got going, it woke up the people in the palace. And in the night, when she was wakened in this way, Marie-Elisabeth would see her husband sitting up in bed and looking toward the open window, sometimes in the direction of the garden, sometimes in that of the city. He did not answer when she spoke to him in a low voice. He would tremble. She did not know whether it was the bells or this trembling that must have wakened her.

Once, toward evening, as she was going up to the children's room she heard Alexandre's voice. He was speaking to Mlle. Gallien. Although it was unlike her, she stopped behind the door. He was saying: "You are from Tournus, Mademoiselle Gallien? How strange! I remember Tournus very well. A good part of the town was once a fortified abbey, isn't that right? I stopped there on my way back from Italy . . . How strange!" Marie-Elisabeth opened the door abruptly: Mlle. Gallien, at the back of the room, was changing the baby's diapers; the other two children were already in bed. Mlle. Gallien was paying no attention to the Marshal, who was standing in front of the open window a great way from her, in the light of the setting sun. Both his hands were on the handrail, and he was flexing his knees as though he were doing exercises. "How strange!" he repeated, and turning around saw his wife and said to her in the most natural way: "Mademoiselle Gallien is from Tournus: imagine." This meant absolutely nothing to the Princesse de Wagram, who was hearing Tournus mentioned for the first time in her life. Alexandre, above her shoulder, pointed his thumb, for his wife's benefit, in the direction of the firmament which was orange streaked with mauve, and said, "You really have violent colors here, in your sky."

Truth to tell, the French were rather frowned upon in Bamberg because of the time when they had been there and had repressed outbursts of patriotism. Antoine, the postilion, had completely given up going to the beer houses where young people used to clink stone mugs with cries of *Hoch!* and expressed themselves in very explicit terms on His Most Serene Highness. They had not forgiven the Marshal for having had five young men of the Tugendbund shot in 1813. With this sentiment was linked a certain opposition to the Bavarian royal family which so short a time ago had been France's ally—an opposition, it appeared, secretly kept simmering by agents of the King of Prussia. Two or three times there had been cries and fists shaken in front of the palace. The Bavarian constables had dispersed what could hardly be called a crowd. . . . In spite of all this, preparations for war against France were going forward with great enthusiasm among the young people; no one had any doubt as to the outcome of the fighting, and people everywhere drank to revenge, to the end of Napoleon who had made a kingdom of Bavaria and a king of Max I Josef, the brother of Duke Wilhelm.

The Marshal would have known nothing of all this if it had not been for Antoine—who obviously did not tell everything. But in the morning, when he came to shave the master, Marie-Elisabeth no longer being present, they had a good moment together. As he bent over His Most Serene Highness's cheek, which was stretched over the silver spoon he had slipped inside his master's mouth, Antoine, with the tip of his tongue between his teeth, would stop talking . . . Then when he went to put more soap on the shaving brush he used to sing; he couldn't help it, songs of his province—he was from Berry and had the accent of the region—and Alexandre, who had at one time been greatly irritated by this, now noticed what a fine voice Antoine had, a true, rich voice; and he even looked forward each day to this moment of shaving because of it. Suddenly he was no longer among strangers. . . .

Between games of chess, Berthier used to hold lengthy conversations with his father-in-law. There was no great difference in age between them. The Duke of Bavaria was a tactful man, and he understood his son-in-law's feelings, his anxiety concerning his country. He used to give him a version of the news that would not wound him too deeply. He was interested in the fact that Alexandre, in his youth, had known personally several famous chess players at the Café de la Régence. Without mentioning your Napoleon who, they say, can hold his own against professionals. . . . And what about this gambit, were you expecting it? All this took place in a charming small rococo room on the garden side. But even there they were not out of reach of Heinrich and Kunigunde.

At the end of April, Berthier had resigned himself to sending his family back to Gros-Bois; and this time the Comte de Montgelas had not thought it necessary to consult Vienna, since the Marshal was staying in Bamberg. Marie-Elisabeth, with Mlle. Gallien and the children, had accordingly taken the berlin and were on their way to France via Switzerland when, at Stockach, General the Prince of Hohenzollern had had the carriage stopped because it had not got the visa of the headquarters of the Allied armies. His wife's return had shown the Marshal the strength of his cage. He had written to Uncle Max, the King of Bavaria. In vain. His health was indifferent: in writing to His Majesty Louis XVIII, at Ghent, he had, with all respect, alleged this as a reason for informing His Majesty that he must no longer count on his services. . . . His Majesty happened to have been counting on Berthier to command the small army corps wherewith the Monarchy meant to represent France at the side of the Allies whose troops were beginning to mass in Belgium. There was going to be war. War against France. A second time, in a deferential letter, Berthier refused his services to Louis XVIII.

On May 29, the Comte Barclay de Tolly, commander-in-chief of the Russian troops, had settled at the castle of Seehof, as though Duke Wilhelm's remodeling of this charming dwelling had been intended for him. And with him the army corps of General von Sacken, which occupied Bamberg and its vicinity. There were feasts in their honor. At Hoffmann's theatre, the Prince de Wagram met General von Sacken in the ducal box, while a composition by the director of the theatre was being played. A very pleasant conversation ensued, in the course of which the Russian general had no trouble convincing Berthier of the certainty of success of the Allied plans. They would be in Paris in a month at the latest, and the Marshal would be able to return home, go back to his properties, his hunting. The following day he was seized with an unaccountable fit of choking. Doctor Ziegler, who was sent for again, said it was nothing. Mere nerves.

Mere nerves, probably, the need Berthier seemed to feel that week to speak with von Sacken on various pretexts. The following Wednesday he learned from the lips of this general that the Cuirassiers of the Russian Imperial Guard would parade in town next day at about noon. Everybody in town was speaking of it; at the palace it was the subject of conversation at dinner. As for Marie-Elisabeth, she was well aware of the fact that there was something wrong with her husband, and when they were in their room she tried to speak to him about their forthcoming return to Paris. He did not reply. She said, "I shall be happy to see Giuseppa again. I'm worried about her health." He said nothing and they went to bed.

All night Marie-Elisabeth had felt Alexandre turning over and over in the bed. She would have liked to talk to him, and then she couldn't, she was dead tired. And what could she say to him? He took everything the wrong way these days. Anything she said to him in an effort to make things right just made them worse. The other evening, as he was undressing, she had again noticed those two keys round his neck, one rather long, the other tiny, hanging from a chain he had worn constantly since he had arrived in Bamberg, and she who never asked her husband questions, less through fear of indiscretion than from strength of character—she wasn't one to ask questions—the Princesse de Wagram had suddenly said, "What are those keys you have there, *mon ami?*" Actually, she didn't care. Besides, she knew: the long one was the key to the locked cupboard, so she had really had no reason to ask. It was simply to talk, to break an unbearable silence, to turn Alexandre's thoughts into a new channel. He was so somber, so obviously tormented. Well! What an unfortunate idea! "Why do you ask me that today? I always carry them, and you've seen these keys many times. . . . You're spying on me. As a matter of fact, I'm well aware of it. I can't go up to the children's room without hearing your footsteps on the stairs!" And so on. But he had not answered her question.

That morning, then, the Cuirassiers of the Russian Imperial Guards, about to set out for Belgium against the French, were to parade in Bamberg, and spirits were considerably agitated by what Marie-Elisabeth called the "German fever." She herself had to go out, but she had been advised not to let her husband leave the palace. In the morning, he had several times gone up into the children's room with a telescope, for from there it was possible to see the Russian troops maneuvering far out in the countryside. She was afraid he would take her advice amiss, and yet when she told him that it would be preferable, today, if he did not go into town, he did not explode, did not exclaim that he was being treated like a little boy, that it was unendurable. He said nothing at all. He looked gloomy and downcast. "Besides, in this fine weather, *mon ami,* you have the garden. . . ." She should not have said that, and she bit her lip. But on the other hand, no. Alexandre was very sweet this morning. A little sad perhaps, but very sweet.

He had the garden. Nothing more. He spent a part of the morning in the garden as he had been told to do. Through the windows, Antoine looked out at His Most Serene Highness. The master was in the garden, that was really all one could say about him. Then the children, the two older ones, that is, had gone down. Mlle. Gallien, who had work to do in the house, had taken them, exchanged a few words with the Marshal, made a curtsey and come in again. What game were those tots playing? The smaller one was running after her brother and could not catch him. Then she was distracted by a butterfly. The boy called out something and she began to cry. His Most Serene Highness undoubtedly had his mind on other things. Because instead of consoling the little girl and scolding the boy, as might have been expected, Berthier suddenly headed for the steps like a man who had just been struck by an idea. There he hesitated for a moment, then hurriedly stepped indoors. The bells of the cathedral were ringing at full peal, but they could not drown the sound of military fanfares that could be heard approaching. It must be the Russian regiment making its entry into Bamberg.

In the bedroom on the first floor, the window looking out on the garden was wide open, and through it came fresh, wonderful fragrances. The Marshal unclasped his collar and drew out the gold chain that he carried about his neck, pulled it around with its two keys and with some difficulty, using his fingernail, opened the rather complicated lock. He got the casket out of the cupboard and placed it on the bed. The room had just been done, and the bedspread, so smoothly spread out, rumpled under the weight. Alexandre had placed the small key in the lock of the casket, and it was sheer nervousness, this desire that had come over him to look at the jewels *once again.* But the bells outside, the brasses and the drums, stopped him, and he changed his mind, left everything—the casket, the keys, the chain—on the bedspread, and went abruptly to the window on the street side, putting his foot on the sill, as on a step, to try to see the parading troops which were coming out onto the square and were still hidden from him by the corner.

That was how Mlle. Gallien surprised him, one foot lifted, and no doubt he felt foolish, since he put his foot back on the floor. Mlle. Gallien was bringing back Mme. la Princesse's underwear which she had gone over after it had been laundered, replacing a little mother-of-pearl button here, resewing a silk ribbon there. She had not expected to find the Marshal in his room and she stammered some excuse, although the linen she was carrying on her arm should have made that unnecessary. Berthier looked at her. She was no longer very young, had never been particularly pretty, but he thought of the little girl she had been in that old town on the banks of the Saône, where the Hungarians had come in the ninth century with Saint Stephen . . . Why should he remember that just now? The martial music had become deafening. "You can't see anything from here," he said. "I wanted to see that famous regiment pass. . . ."

Mlle. Gallien had put the linen down on the bed next to the casket. She was somewhat astonished. The Marshal knew perfectly well that to get a view of the countryside, the road from the Seehof to Bamberg, it was necessary to go up to the third story. Had he not gone up there a little earlier with his telescope? Nevertheless she answered, "If Your Excellency went up to the children's room . . . From the corner window up there you can see everything." And he looked as if he were obeying her, crossing the room, telling her to hurry up and get the children ready because the carriage was waiting for them below to take them riding. "Go down into the garden, Mademoiselle Gallien . . . the children are there." This surprised her, too, for there was nothing that needed to be done to make them ready except to put their gloves on. Whereupon the Prince de Wagram did something wholly unexpected: he took Mlle. Gallien's hand and kissed it in passing. Heinrich and Kunigunde outside were ringing for all they were worth.

Mlle. Gallien had not got over her astonishment before Berthier had gone, and she remained, holding in her other hand the hand which His Excellency's lips had just pressed, without understanding—not really upset, perhaps, but astonished, very astonished. It had made her forget the Princess's linen and why she was there. She went out onto the landing. Up there, the door to the children's room must have remained open, and it made a fearful draft. As Mlle. Gallien was going up to shut it, and the bells had suddenly stopped ringing, she heard deep sighs, heart-rending man's sobs. And the Marshal's voice saying distinctly: "My poor country!" She stopped, afraid of committing an indiscretion. Then there was a sound like that of a falling chair hitting the floor, and at that point she hurried up to the children's room.

Little Elisabeth was asleep in her cradle, her thumb in her mouth. The other two were still in the garden. But the room was empty. I mean that the Marshal was not there, or was no longer there. An armchair had been hoisted up on the little platform in front of the window, and the telescope was on the floor next to it. Through the open casement, from the outside, came the clamor of the onlookers, the blare of fanfares, and the din of Heinrich and Kunigunde which had begun to ring out again.

When the body of the Marshal, whose head had been smashed on the pavement, was brought back along the front of the house, everyone quite naturally thought that he must have suffered a spell of dizziness. Antoine wept, and kept repeating that this morning while he was shaving him, His Most Serene Highness had seemed so gay, so happy! It was only when Marie-Elisabeth, on her return, asked Mlle. Gallien about that casket on the bed, next to the linen, that they both understood what had happened. And suddenly, the Princess took the maid in her arms and wept softly with her, and she whispered into her ear that no one must ever know.

All her life, Mlle. Gallien was to hear sounding in her ears the sighs that had escaped from the children's room in which there was no longer anyone when she entered. Twenty times they came to question her about those last minutes. Especially after that stupid rumor of assassination spread through the town: it was, they said, German patriots who—four or five of them while the Imperial Guard was parading—had broken into the palace and defenestrated Marshal Berthier in order to avenge the martyrs of the Tugenbund. How, where, without anyone's seeing them . . . but the rumor was so persistent that in order to dispel it, it had been necessary to authorize one investigation after another. The idea of suicide was naturally looked into. But would a father choose his children's room from which to jump out of the window? And in the end they came back to the first version: a spell of dizziness—everyone knew that the Marshal had terrible poundings of the heart; and the autopsy had shown that his stomach was in a bad state, which causes vertigo.

All her life Mlle. Gallien would hear those heavy sighs, and that voice saying *My poor country!* No one knew why, but she formed the habit of constantly caressing the back of her right hand with her left whenever people spoke to her of certain things. Nor why she wept when, in the spring, there were drafts in the house.

It was a little after seven in the morning when Antoine entered the room, bringing hot water and the shaving dish, and opened the curtains on a rainy sky. Berthier did not wake easily and had a hard time disentangling himself from the extraordinary dreams that filled his slumber, especially toward its end. Outside there was an unholy racket made by the banging shutters.

"What a confounded wind, Your Most Serene Highness," Antoine said, turning around. "Anyone would think all the roofs of Lille were going to tumble on the passers-by. Hasn't Your Most Serene Highness been disturbed by the din?"

Berthier sat up in the bed and passed his hand through his hair. As it came down, the Marshal's hand stopped to feel the chain on his neck from which hung one small key—not two.

"It seems we are remaining in Lille, Your Most Serene Highness, although we have been told nothing as yet. But, since I learned from the servants that His Majesty had just called Monseigneur le Duc d'Orléans and Monsieur le Duc de Trévise to his room, I thought it well to awaken your Most Serene Highness."

And a little later as Antoine, having slipped the silver spoon inside His Highness's mouth, was singing a tune from his home province as he passed the razor upward in order to remove the excess soap, the Marshal made an impatient movement that resulted in his receiving a small cut.

"Idiot!" he cried. "You've cut me and we have no alum stone! I've told you a hundred times not to sing when you're shaving me. Those songs of yours get on my nerves!"

XIV

A Day of High Wind

H OLY THURSDAY of 1815 began amid the anger and justice of heaven. A cyclone swept down from Dieppe, where M. de Castries was vainly assembling useless ships, spread over Saint-Valéry with its screaming sea gulls, and Abbeville from which the Royal Household had set out before dawn, across the valley of the Somme and past the little clay and thatch house where Marc-Antoine was regaining consciousness as Eloy Caron got up to go and fetch the midwife, all the way to the frontier which a somber horseman had just crossed. The rider's tattered military coat and the strange old torn leather topcoat showing dirty wool through its holes, betrayed a prisoner returning from Russia. All the trees were bending to the point of breaking, the roofs could be heard creaking, there were whirls of leaves and broken branches, the clouds seemed to be torn in holes like the horseman's *tulup* (sheepskin coat)—but they did not allow the sun to come through. Nervous animals stampeded across the fields seeking shelter. Old women prostrated themselves in the churches, pulling their black shawls tight over their shoulders.

At Lille, M. de Blacas d'Aulps was busy seizing *Le Moniteur*, which gave notice of the composition of the Imperial government. At the stagecoach stop errand boys ran off, carrying packages of other newspapers which no one had thought of seizing, and under the porches passers-by were already opening them and exclaiming: Fouché, Caulaincourt, Carnot! A poster was hastily printed: the declaration of the Powers in Vienna—ten days old, but the text had just reached Lille. Doors slammed, shutters banged. The wind reigned in lordly fashion over the follies of men, knocking down fences in the villages, blowing hay off haycarts, scattering heaps of grass. Over toward Montreuil the alarm bell mingled with the flames: an entire village was going up in smoke, and the wind twisted the fire, tossed it right and left from dwelling to dwelling, while people rushed from their beds in all the disorder of early morning. At a notary's in Doullens where he had set up his office, Colonel Simonneau listened to Lieutenant Dieudonné's report. "Couldn't you shut the door behind you?" The draft flung bills of sale, deeds and registry documents to the four corners.

The horseman who had crossed the frontier near Armentières entered a small inn; he was benumbed with cold and was regarded with suspicion: what was this beggar with his colorless coat, shiny in spots, dirty and torn, with wisps of wool coming through from the inside? They refused to serve him until he showed his money. An ageless man—ravaged, his weather-beaten face further darkened by a week-old beard in which white and black were mingled. He was returning home. He was returning home at a time when others were leaving. He had no idea what was happening, he didn't understand. As he passed through the Belgian villages, people had said all sorts of things. For him, Captain Simon Richard, anything was possible, and nothing really mattered. Last year, it had been months before he had heard of Napoleon's fall. Now they were saying the Emperor was back, and the King was somewhere in flight. Simon had not asked for details. He was intent only on making the little money he had last, getting a cup of good hot soup and some bread. This tall, sad, ragged man, on this discarded plow horse which he had bought by the sweat of his brow back in Prussia and which he rode as though it were a thoroughbred without noticing the way people looked at him along the country roads, had walked on foot from the far ends of Europe, making his way toward the only destiny still open to him —his people's house on the Somme where, long ago, as a child, he had learned fencing from Céleste de Durfort, his elder by seven years, from whom he had turned away so savagely in that pile of half-dead men at Vilna. . . . And who could tell whether, coming like this without any other papers than those of a certain Simon Richard, the peasants would recognize their young *seigneur,* the Olivier who used to play with them in the days before the Revolution. What had become of his companions of that time? Men like himself, now, at the end of a long life—because at thirty-six a man was at the end of his life if he had lived through these particular thirty-six years.

When Olivier had left the world—the Emperor's Court, Compiègne, and everything that he refused to think about—ten years ago, a little more than ten years ago, he had been a high official of the Empire at the age of twenty-six. A man became a general at thirty in those days . . . but *he* had entered the army as a man might enter a religious order, under this name of Simon Richard, a simple infantry soldier, with his knapsack and his pipe. As a man might enter a religious order. There were lucky people who believed in God. They flung themselves into an order, shaved their heads, dressed in rough homespun. Olivier would so much have liked to believe in God. He had even tried to convince himself that he did believe in Him. But he had only to look into a mirror to burst out laughing! So there was the army. In the lowest rank. The humiliation of discipline. Left to himself, he would never have been anything but this simple soldier on whom vexations were heaped. Unfortunately, at every stage he had encountered men who sensed something out of the ordinary in him. Corporal . . . sergeant . . . And as he courted danger, his temerity in those mad wars had a hundred times been taken for courage, his longing to die had been hailed as heroism, and he—that is to say, Simon Richard—had, in 1810, been made an officer, a second lieutenant in the Light Cavalry. And it was as a captain of Hussars that he had fallen into the hands of the Russians, at Vilna, after eight years of that life.

He had been recognized twice. In Spain, by his younger brother who had chanced upon him—and Philippe was already a colonel. In Vilna, by Céleste. Twice he had escaped, had been able to plunge back into anonymity. The second time it had been easy. He had been a prisoner. He had been taken away with a convoy to the confines of Asia. Had worked at building roads. Under the knout. In that country of mud and snow where nothing was edible, where forced labor aged you by twenty years in two. And there he had had a woman with him, a poor serf, whom he had taken at first like an animal. Because a man is a man, and there was nothing to be done about it. Then, lo and behold—gradually, as the veil of language between them fell, this Dusya had become a human being, a presence, a miracle. He did not love her, he did not pretend to. Was he still able to love? But he respected her. Yes. He respected her, this soldier's wench, living among the huts on the Inchon. She had got used to him and had, curiously, begun to be faithful to him. Faithful! There are words that are ironical as a whip. As rain and as the torment into which he had plunged back. It was Dusya who, before he left, had given him this *tulup* that he was wearing, so that he might survive the winter. It was too warm for the season now, but when a man had nothing else to wear . . .

At about ten o'clock in the morning, Simon Richard reached Lille. It was still blowing a gale.

The traveler looked at the extraordinary panorama, the first French city he had reached after years of exile. Except for the color of things, from here—that is to say from the road before the Porte de la Magdeleine, this long flat town bristling with churches and monuments above the odd system of redoubts and bastions that bordered it along the ramparts mirrored in the water of the moats all round—this town might have been taken for a city in Tuscany. To the right, Simon saw the parish church of La Magdeleine with its dome and its Italianate buildings, the tall grain store with its roof tiled in a two-color checkwork; farther on, the Saint-André district and its church; but on his left the masses of Saint Pierre and the tall square tower of Saint Catherine had the Flemish severity. To the west, the city stretched into the distance, visible all the way to the Porte de Fives. The striking feature of this landscape was the glacis of the ramparts, laid out like a Greek key pattern in stone before the walls of Vauban's fortifications. The countryside reached right up to the city—uniform, flat, cut by roads running to the gates, with its plowed fields whose furrows, stretching in every direction, gave the whole the appearance of a great stretch of corduroy patches. There was a sentinel on top of the walls, and the Porte de la Magdeleine was shut. Simon shouted to the sentinel and tried to reason with him. But his only response was a movement of the gun that seemed to mean, *Be on your way!* What was he to do? Why couldn't he enter Lille? Fortunately for him, a peasant coming along the road with his donkey cart explained to him that the gates were opened in rotation, and that the sentinel's gesture indicated the right gate for the time of day, over to the east.

Simon proceeded by the side of the peasant, who was far from talkative and told him only that the King was in the town, which explained these police measures. The King? What was he doing here? They could not pass through the Porte de Gand, and had to continue on along the little roads which cut across the fields in loops and detours until they at length reached the Porte Saint-Maurice which was open. The peasant passed through straightaway—he was apparently known. But when it came to Simon, his gear—that curious cap on his head—made him suspect to the sentinels. While they were looking at his papers he had dismounted, and the wind whirled an unfolded newspaper up to him. He picked it up and read the news without much interest. Except for the item about Comte Lazare Carnot's being named Minister of the Interior. Well, he thought, so now he's a Count. . . . His papers were returned to him.

The storm passed through the flames of the burning village, across the deserted countryside, the roads choked with men, horses and carriages. Across Doullens and across Béthune, across Saint-Pol and Hesdin. Everything movable flew off and went rolling about—skirts, tiles, bushes. Every poorly stopped hole in the dwellings was visited by this inquisition of the wind, every fissure of human life, every secret of the soul, every recess of the mind. It blew across the universe as though this were to be the end of it. The men marching north could hardly think of anything except this violent blast that roared about them, enveloped them, deafened them, made them stumble as they walked. All the problems they bore within them had been rolled away by this all-enveloping wave. Emperor, King, Country—the words were wrenched loose from them. It was as if the wind carried them through a country about which they knew nothing, amid a people who were strange to them, mysterious, incomprehensible, who behind windows watched them pass their houses; barred and bolted they hardly knew against whom—whether against nature or against them. An army . . . Were they still an army? An army must be someone's army. They were no longer the army of the people they were abandoning. They were no longer defending anything, were merely defending themselves against the wind, the wind occupied them, twisted in them as in the well of a staircase. Since dawn. Since before dawn.

Since before dawn, Tony de Reiset, who had written incoherently to his wife from Beauvais asking her to send him all the gold she could get hold of, had been in low spirits, cursing himself for his stupidity. Where would that gold go? How could it reach him? And Amélie would have deprived herself on his account . . . the children . . . They had been marking time on the road after leaving Abbeville, letting the re-formed companies go by. The Grammont Guards were still assigned to cover the rear guard. In the early dawn they had had to witness the passage of those monstrous equipages, those amorphous throngs, that hotchpotch of civilians and military, the servants with the horses, the vehicles of the Messieurs, all shaken by the wind, whipped by the rain, with unaccountable stops, questions asked, the anguish of these people, their eyes wide in panic; and if any horsemen passed at a gallop, spattering them with mud, thinking they must be Exelmans's men.

To the fatigue of three days and four nights had now been added fear, and it was growing, creating panic, making eyes gape and hearts pound. As they journeyed through this forest, someone had suddenly said it was the forest of Crécy, and the word circulated among the Guards until the shadow of the Hundred Years' War weighed on them like a phantom. They were passing the sites of ancient massacres, of famous defeats, and it was as though they were marching on bones in broken armor, the great corpses of the royal past, the ancestors of these Grenadiers and Musketeers, the mercenaries and the Princes, everything that constituted the immense shadow of the gouty fleeing King somewhere up there in front, no one knew where. Tony de Reiset could not remember a comparable squall since . . . since . . . It was at the time when Kléber had been in love with his sister, and his own heart beat wildly with visions of glory. Nor had he ever had this sense of fatigue, of exhaustion, since that month of August 1804 when he had traversed eighty-five leagues in thirty-six hours to go from Soissons to Plombières to warn Blanche of the calamity that had occurred—the anonymous letter revealing their love to her husband, who had abruptly left Paris and spoken of killing her. . . . They had encroached on the black, plowed fields so that the convoy, once again brought to a stop by carriage accidents, could reorganize. They wallowed in the black, soft, sticky mud, sinking into it, the horses left along the embankments. The men were pale, suffering from the cold that people feel when the weather has begun to turn warm; some of them swore, stamped their feet in vain.

And close by, the man who owed his unhappiness to Tony, Comte Olivier, who had become simply Simon Richard, passed through Lille with its streets full of people, officers and soldiers, women and old men—a market place in which fantastic stories and rumors circulated, to be greeted with shouts and causing crowds to form. The wind had not died down, but it had got the better of the rain, at least for the moment. Simon mingled with a throng where heated words were being exchanged. But he had difficulty understanding what was said, and he questioned the people nearest to him. The Royal Household was supposedly marching on Lille with Monsieur, three thousand men according to some, five according to others; the King had summoned them to welcome the foreign troops which were at the frontiers. The Duc d'Orléans had lied; he had sworn to the troops that the King would never call upon the foreigner—that was only two days ago. (And to prove it, yesterday there had been an officer of the Prince of Orange at the city's gates.) And the peasants who had just been to the Porte de Béthune said that the Duc de Berry was arriving with two thousand Swiss, and that he was barely a couple of leagues from Lille. . . . Simon stopped, questioned those whose eyes turned toward him, fascinated by his ungainly appearance. What a predicament! To have come from the steppes of Kirghiz to Lille, in Flanders, to find these soldiers rioting, speaking of cutting the throats of the King's Guards if they dared to enter the gates. . . . The streets were in a wild uproar. Men were tearing the white cockade from one another and donning the tricolor. Their uniforms had not changed with the return of the Bourbons. The Cuirassiers still had the helmet with its black horse tail and the black fur on the vizor, and the red plume, the epaulets scarlet like the lappets on the green coat with pink pipings and the silver buttons with the eagles, the shoulder strap and the white gauntlets.

As though nothing had happened. Simon Richard had toyed with the idea of making himself known, of volunteering for service. But to whom should he turn? To those who were ready to welcome Napoleon, or to those who were fleeing from him? Which adventure should he choose? To return to the Imperial army would be to resume the place in the world that he had run away from; to follow the King would mean fleeing from this country which it had taken him months to reach on foot and on horseback, working on farms, interrupting his journey for weeks on end in order to earn enough money for the road. Everything appeared equally vain to him. Even the word *slaughter* spoken by a furious officer of the 12th Cuirassiers barely revived in him for a moment those ideas of vengeance that at times woke him up at night. But did he still hate the man who, out of boredom, had stolen his wife from him eleven, twelve years ago, and then abandoned her? That vain and fatuous Tony. That insignificant creature. The great love he had professed for Blanche! Seven months, and then he had asked for the hand of a little provincial chit, daughter of a chatelaine of the region, at whom he had been casting his eyes for a year or more! Even his face was probably no longer recognizable.

All the cackle of a district market, the stalls loaded with vegetables and fruit, the early produce— It was not the big Wednesday market held on the Grand'Place. The dealers were crying their wares from beneath soaked canvas awnings, some of which, swept up and carried away by a gust of wind, threatened to create panic among the peasants. He passed through all this, a captain in rags and worn shoes, looking for an unpretentious inn within his means, for his horse even more than for himself. . . . This heavy red beast which was for the moment his sole companion, his major worry. He had had to work a long time in order to acquire him, everything that he had possessed had gone into him. It had been in the heart of Prussia. He had been walking for months and months, all the way from that straggling village of Siberian shacks which he had left in mid-July. How farsighted and tender Dusya had been! What would he have done without his *tulup?* It had seemed funny then in the burning sun of the taiga. He had walked, walked. Broken, needing his strength, sleeping in barns. In the summer it had been easy to find work . . . but when autumn came, and with it the snow . . . Why had he not stayed at Petropavlovsk, like that soldier of Condé's army who had gone there with M. de Vioménil at the end of the century, had married there and with his children lived there on the work of others? No. Not that, any more than the rest. He could not become a settler on the marches of Asia. Why leave? But why remain? And at every step that same question. He might have stayed in Poland, or in Germany. Simply sat down on the ground to die. . . .

He regarded the money in his pocket and the inn before him. This one was as good as any other. Was it within his means? He could put up his horse here anyway. Perhaps they could tell him where he could find work. *He* did not need a bed: perhaps they would let him sleep on the ground, in the stable, or the barn. . . .

Apparently they took pity on him. He asked where he could go to find work.

He could try in the market place. Sometimes the peasants needed help. If the barrowmen didn't chase him away—they did not like strangers! He would just as soon have stayed and slept on the straw. But he had to earn a living. "If I hear of anything through the customers . . ." said a tall, thin woman who seemed to do everything around there. So he went off down the street to earn his living. His living! To live or to die! It was like leaving or staying. He knew very well that he would live as he walked. Was it cowardice? There were times when he felt it was. But to kill himself meant attributing such importance to this life. He had not killed himself in 1804, either. He lived as he walked. It was always the next step that led nowhere.

For the moment, here he was on the central square of Lille. It was crowded with people: soldiers, civilians, formed groups. The Hôtel de la Grand'Garde, with its double staircase, connected by a balcony on the first story, was the headquarters of the Cuirassiers and of the Duc de Trévise's staff.

It was to kill time that Simon read the freshly put-up poster. A tall *hallebreda,* as they say in Picardy, standing behind him sneered: "*You* believe all that?" Simon turned around and looked at him. He might be a coachman. No, he was one of those men who pulled the two-wheeled sedans called *vinaigrettes;* his was there next to him, resting on its shafts. If I believe it? In order to believe it, it would be necessary to read more than the words. Let's see. And Simon forced himself to reread the text that he had glanced through mechanically: *The Powers signatory to the Treaty of Paris, met in congress in Vienna, informed of the escape of Napoleon Buonaparte and of his entry into France by force of arms, owe it to their own dignity and to the interest of the social order* . . . and so forth, and what then?

The big *hallebreda* pointed to the poster: "That isn't going to prevent him from sleeping at the Louvre!" Probably not. And he went on: "Besides, their poster is all lies! It's meant to frighten us!" Simon shrugged his shoulders. You never knew. The other was getting angry. "What? You, in your dirty rags, you're for the Princes? for that flea-ridden fat man who's going to get us all shot by the Prussians?" This made Simon laugh. Was he for the Princes? Who was flea-ridden? He walked off without replying. And what was that fellow muttering now, harnessed once more to his vinaigrette like the good Christian horse he was? *That Buonaparte had placed himself beyond the pale of civil and social relations, and that, as an enemy of the world and a disturber of the peace, he had become an object of public obloquy* . . . et cetera. But if that poster truly meant anything, it meant war. If that happened he might perhaps have to go back into the service. In spite of the fatigue, the immense moral fatigue. Armies would again assemble here and there. There would be fanfares, parades, farewells. Then the plodding from town to town. The long convoys of supplies and arms. There would be the games with the map, placing the units here and there. Small rectangles with a St. Andrew's cross in them. Until the cannon spoke. And they would speak. . . .

Simon was overcome with an infinite lassitude. There was a church in front of him. He would gladly have entered it. Because in a church you could sit down. But he had to look for work, and at this time of the day there were jobs to be had carrying loads in the markets.

What startled Théodore now was the remarks of his companions in flight. Young Moncorps's ingenuousness, for example. And he was not the only one on the Saint-Pol road. It was as though these souls no longer responded to anything but fatigue, aches, rain and wind, hunger (when do we halt? when are we going to eat?), and as though all this had nothing to do with the rest, with the questions they were asking themselves before leaving, with those that the news gave rise to. After all, was it possible that three thousand men could share the mentality of the Law School volunteers, accepting as sound the ready-made ideas, the purely decorative commonplaces of the monarchy? Was it possible that these three thousand men could have covered some fifty leagues since Paris amid this spectacle of disorder, of the hesitations of the Princes, without plans, or, worse, changing plans at every step, plagued with doubts, surrounded by real and imaginary specters, not knowing whether the enemy was behind or in front, if the people of their own country were friends or foes, waking up at night at the slightest noise as though someone were coming to kill them in the dark . . . Was it possible? They told one another hunting stories, talked about garrison balls, held discussions on their coats of arms, on family alliances, their lands, uniforms, horses. What did this enormous futility conceal? Because it was impossible to believe in it. Thoughts must be running through their minds parallel to their words, thoughts their words tried to hide. Like Géricault himself, who of course would tell *them* nothing of what haunted *him*. So unsure was he of himself. Continuing to advance on horseback in a direction where there was nothing for him to find. But dominated by the memories of that night at Poix, by the discovery of an unsuspected world before which he could only measure his ignorance. To whom among these men could he speak about the people? The question was like a shrug of the shoulders.

Nothing any longer appeared the same to him. Every wretched house, every man in the fields, every farm hand, every headdress, every petticoat that stole away at the soldiers' approach—they were to him as though he were touching with his finger an unknown, yet discovered, reality. He no longer looked on passers-by, on a crowd, as such; every human being assumed a meaning, a life of his own. He thought with something akin to anger of those painters who in

their landscapes would leave to any nobody the painting of the little
figures with which they would strew them conventionally. The slightest outline of a human form conveyed to him the substance of a
being. A being of flesh and blood like himself. How was it that this
simple idea had not come to him sooner? He had of course known
it in the abstract. If the question had been asked him, he would have
said that the water carrier and the marquis had a body made of the
same matter, that their blood was no different and was shed by the
same means. And a thousand things in this vein. But even so. He
had not known it, really known it. It had been like a lesson learned,
repeated by rote. He had never wondered how people obtained what
they ate, or indeed what they ate. For since they were alive, Théodore
naturally assumed that they ate, and he knew of course that their
work paid for their food. But it was without really grasping it, as
when a person said that the earth was round, and how many leagues
there were between Europe and America. Now, behold, he saw every
man, every woman, through new eyes, measuring richness and poverty
by their garb, seeing how some were pinched, how extravagant others
were. How, I ask you, could he have spoken of this to Moncorps?
And of the fact that comfort was like a varnish that made men and
women, in a sense, resemble one another; that it was the worn coat,
the darn, or the emaciation due to poor food which made man reach
out to man—the shoes worn too long, even ignorance, those eyes
for which so many things were new, those ears that had difficulty
with words they heard used. How could he have spoken of this to
Moncorps? Why, take Moncorps, for example. No stupider than
another, really. Just a little wet behind the ears.

Yet what were they all thinking of? It was not in Théodore's
character to despise his fellow men. Thus he imagined that even the
emptiest, the most limited, of his companions were like himself, that
behind their eyes, in their heads, there was something more than
what they said. He very much wanted to respect his fellow men.
Because they certainly were fellow men. As those people living in
wretchedness were his fellow men. The truth of the matter was that
he had a very great need to reaffirm this to himself, to such a degree
that he said it aloud: "They are my fellow men!"

"What?" asked Moncorps, not sure that he had heard aright. They
had paused on the road, for Casimir de Mortemart's guns had once
again got stuck in the mud ahead of them, and were being pulled
out by the horses; men were shouting.

"Nothing," replied Théodore. "I was dreaming."

The wind which had died down a little was rising again. The capes of their cloaks had blown up over the heads of some of the riders, the tails of their helmets were tossed about oddly, stood up straight . . . No, there was nothing about these Grenadiers with their bearskins, these helmets or cocked-hatted Musketeers, to suggest birds of prey, as at the Panthémont Barracks at dawn on Palm Sunday. The wind scattered, ruffled them like a flock of starlings. In a nearby field stood old fruit trees, neglected, unpruned; they had the postures of puppets when the puppet master's hand has been withdrawn.

Théodore was dreaming, that was true. He was dreaming. To respect his fellow men. Nothing was so horrible as to search for base motives to explain the behavior of others. Undoubtedly there were people who were base. Yet it was better to be mistaken about them than to attribute their motives to others just because they did not think as he did. For example, when he had been listening to the conspirators of Poix, he might have put them down as full of envy, intriguers, men consumed by ambition, or even regarded the wretched demand for bread as an insult to lofty ideas. . . . And now, was he not also in danger of explaining this fidelity to a fleeing monarch as the expression of personal interest? Certainly there was an element of that in some. But, for example, there were men among them loyal to His Majesty Louis XVIII—perhaps those who could be seen passing in drenched cloaks, astride horses no longer sure-footed—who sincerely believed that in defending the King they were defending religion. And, unbeliever though he was, Théodore tried to imagine what went on in the minds of people who believed in God—not through faulty reasoning, or ignorance, or self-interest, but for good reasons, the highest, the worthiest. Fundamentally, while he did not share the Christian faith, he thought that the great ideas of Christianity, a certain *goodness,* the earthly essential of its morality, were things that were close to him, things he could not reject or despise. He would gladly share a Christian ideal, without the religion. Whether there were a God or not. He was even responsive to the beauty of the myths of the Roman religion, provided they remained myths. He could not espouse that levity, so frequent among Voltairians, which shocked him in Horace Vernet, for example, and was directed not at religion itself, but at the things of religion, because, for those who believed, those *things* were not mummeries but the incarnation of ideas which were worthy of respect.

He had no liking for priests, but before a priest, even though he might be a sort of caricature, he would think, not of priests in general but of that particular man, who had become a priest and who for this reason must have believed deeply in the priesthood, in devotion, in the sacrifice of self. Every time a priest had disappointed him, revealing a petty soul, or unworthy thoughts, his resentment had been directed at that particular priest, not at the others. He even considered a certain religiosity among some youths, young Vigny for one, as a mark of nobleness of mind. It would not have occurred to him to offend Moncorps by any remark pertaining to this realm, even though it was odd, at the halt in Hesdin, to see this little fellow rushing off to church. After nine leagues on horseback . . . Holy Thursday, you understand . . . The Last Supper for Théodore was a subject for a picture which had often been treated by the masters. It interested him from the point of view of composition, and perhaps until today he had never thought about the meaning of that great banquet, where Judas sits among the Apostles: *A little while, and ye shall not see me: and again, in a little while, and ye shall see me.* . . . The absurd idea of Louis XVIII as Christ revolted him. Against this fleeing king. This was a measure of the fact that his conception of Christ was a noble one which bore no relation to his beliefs.

How this would have surprised his uncle, the regicide! *He* was rather theophilanthropic—he was against all representations of the divinity. How could he expect a painter to agree with that? Although Théodore had no propensity to represent Christ and all the rest of it and preferred to paint men as they were, soldiers for example, with their naïve eyes, their simple idea of life. Or carters, beggars. At the same time, he distinctly felt that those people must bear a closer resemblance to saints than did middle-class citizens and princes. Which implied in him, in the last analysis, a respect for saints, the acceptance of the notion of saintliness. He was discovering it, as he was also discovering that feeling that he had for the people. They were twin plants that were growing in him at the same time, the one illuminated by the other.

He had no general conception of the world, and he was even quite disposed to brag that he could get along perfectly without one. But perhaps, from one stop to the next on this monotonous and muddy road, in the long spells of marking time while waiting for the unmounted men to catch up with them, a vision of things—new, embryonic—was forming in him. Comparing the poor and the saints was perhaps a first step, an attempt to systematize. . . . And Théodore remembered the speech he had delivered to young Thierry at the Palais-Royal on the subject of Caravaggio, but this time applying to himself the things he had said. Essentially, there was nothing new: it was Caravaggio's way of seeing things that he, Théodore, had up to now considered solely from the aesthetic point of view—the hatred of artificial composition, of draperies, of columns, of prettiness in general, the sheen of velvet or silk as a painting process, as a way of distributing the high lights. But now he suddenly understood that to Caravaggio this was a quite different matter: it was human—transcribed, to be sure, by means of painting, but human first of all, an affirmation of *the others,* as it had been revealed to him that night at Poix. The law of contrasts was indeed the secret of art—but of what contrasts? And the opposition of light and shadow was a means, not an end. . . .

All this came pell-mell. And as a counterpoint he was aware of his horse's anxiety. After five days, Trick was showing signs of exhaustion from the demands that had been made on him. And the animal too was a kind of saint. Géricault remembered the story that Marc-Antoine had told him at Beauvais the day before yesterday of how his horse had died. But this brought back to him what he had discovered at Abbeville from the lips of that Grenadier who had been with him, apparently, Arthur d'H——: about his friend's having been injured, a fall from a horse, from the very horse Théodore had found for him . . . the arzel, more of a devil than a saint: the veteran of Spain was right, those animals were treacherous. What had become of Aubigny? Left somewhere on the Somme, between life and death. In a clash with Exelmans's cavalry. At times he would say to himself that Marc-Antoine and he had nothing essentially in common except their love of horses, and that he liked him only as a model, for his physique. Always he came back to the same thing. Beauty. Art coming first. Yet now the painter found himself no longer thinking of Aubigny merely as a dummy. A man was not just a subject. Not even that arrogant vicomte, who seemed to have no life other than the physical. A man. Something that breaks. That bleeds. That moans. The soul showed through the break. To speak of a man, to paint him, was it not necessary first to be able to show that he was susceptible to pain?

A horse too. From time to time, despite the mud, Théodore dismounted and walked a bit, holding Trick by the bridle. He talked to him, telling him things he himself found astonishing. There was something terribly innocent about a horse.

About a man too. Houdetot, for example, that brute. At the Hesdin halt, where the Conche, swollen by the rains, rushed with murky violence through the town, pressed between the houses that dipped straight into it, he had seen in Houdetot's eyes that wild look spent horses have. And they were far from the end of their tribulations this day. It was not yet ten o'clock. As they got farther away from Paris, from the well-ordered world, from the private mansions, drawing rooms, ladies, cafés—life, in short!—all these officers who there had been like tailor's dummies, faultlessly dressed, straight of posture, the embodiment of the conventional idea of a gentleman, became more human, with all their fatigue, their anxiety, their bewilderment. This perhaps was why it was still impossible for Géricault to do what he had an almost irresistible urge to do: go and sit down on the roadside embankment, let the convoys, the companies pass; then retrace his steps, stopping at the farms, returning to the natural order of days and things, toward Paris, work, women, art . . . Impossible. Even more than at the departure, at the Carrousel. At every moment more impossible. To desert— He feared neither the word nor the thing: but it depended on what he was deserting, and yet as he felt himself more and more distant from his companions-at-arms, ready to condemn them socially, to the same degree he felt growing in himself a feeling of solidarity toward them which had nothing to do with the army, the King, oaths of loyalty—a human feeling that made it impossible to abandon, not this cavalry corps, this company to which he was bound by a kind of obligation at which he could easily have snapped his fingers, but these men, to whom he owed nothing, whom he might at any moment begin to regard with hostility, these men on whom nevertheless misfortune weighed a little more heavily, physically and morally, at each step. . . .

Yes, Houdetot. Why did Houdetot single Théodore out for such special attention? Because of that cousin of Houdetot's who wrote verses. And in that big stupid head painting and poetry were one and the same thing. In Hesdin, then, he had shown Musketeer Théodore Géricault a special confidence by slipping him a newspaper which he had brought secretly from Abbeville. *Le Moniteur.* The item of interest was the list of Napoleon's ministers. But also a decree that accorded to Lazare Carnot the title of Count, by reason of his defense of Antwerp in 1814.

Théodore found this picturesque, and nothing more. The importance of the thing escaped him. Anything he could have said about it would have had to do with Carnot's personality, and how this new Minister of the Interior—and why of the Interior? it was incomprehensible— was considered by others. But he could not explain to Houdetot what he had heard at Poix, how M. Joubert spoke of Carnot. . . .

"You don't see? My dear fellow, it's as plain as the nose on your face: the two decrees bear the same date. Napoleon, at the same time as he takes this regicide into his government, has made a point of elevating him to the nobility of the Empire."

"So? I don't see . . ."

"You're just a babe in arms. Why were we so afraid of Bonaparte's return? We expected the populace to rise up and engage in wholesale revenge. It offered to support him. But he wanted none of those voices, my dear fellow. Napoleon refuses to be the Emperor of the rabble. . . ."

A strange attitude for this lieutenant of the Royal Musketeers to take! He had been the Emperor's page, and no doubt, in the way things were going, he saw a ray of hope for the aristocracy in general, and personally a possibility of going over . . . After all, if the Emperor . . .

But Géricault was less concerned with the childish calculations of a man of Houdetot's stamp than with what had just made his nerves tingle as he heard the officer's words: *Napoleon refuses to be the Emperor of the rabble.* . . . What that meant for those poor people of the other night, for the one whose father had been shot, for that weaver, for that day laborer, for the others . . . for the hope they bore within themselves—still contradictory, but like a great sun in which they wanted only to believe. Géricault remembered his own feeling, there among the thickets: how he had been afraid these people would allow what he considered their opportunity to pass by, by not trusting the Emperor—not that he, Théodore, was in any way for Napoleon, but because it had seemed logical to him, natural. To get rid of the aristocrats . . . that was their common idea, the one thing that united those men otherwise so completely divided by traditions, beliefs; those men who were elated at the flight of the counts and the marquises. And then the Emperor, their Emperor, was returning; and the first act of his new reign was to write on the brow of the man in whom the people believed: *You shall be a Count!* Ah, Houdetot and Théodore were somewhat out of adjustment; there was little chance of their understanding each other. So much the worse.

It was as they were coming into Saint-Pol that this same Houdetot came down the column and said to Géricault, in passing, "You know who they say lives here? The Monster's sister!"

He might have been speaking of one of the Bonaparte princesses, but no. The Monster was Robespierre. Whether Charlotte lived at Saint-Pol or not did not greatly concern Théodore. But Saint-Pol was one of the regions where the memory of the Terror was still vivid. Houdetot would have liked to see the Monster's sister. He spoke of her as of an animal in a zoological garden. Or a local curiosity. But the chances were that she was hiding, living under an assumed name. Or more likely, it was just hearsay. Because could you see this woman living among families who still bore the wounds of Maximilien's crimes!

This was something in which Théodore had not the slightest interest. All he sought at Saint-Pol was a good stable, and a bundle of hay on which he could sleep next to Trick. Even if only for an hour. Because the bulk of the troops, which were still expected, would be quartered here for the night but they, the elite horsemen, as Houdetot said, once they got their second wind, would be put back into the saddle at about two, two-thirty: they would sleep at Béthune. Well, what of it? Less than eight leagues!

All right. But that would make how many today? Twenty, twenty-one. They were getting used to these long stages, after all. Eleven, twelve hours on the road . . . The King's Gendarmes were with them at this halt. The Comte Étienne de Durfort had come and saluted M. de Lauriston. Moncorps had found his friend Alfred. Young Vigny looked rather overcome with fatigue, but he was trying not to show it. Sad because they would surely miss Holy Thursday vesperal mass at Béthune.

He was right enough. Because on leaving Saint-Pol, Alfred was left lagging behind. A lost shoe. So, while the others were trotting toward Béthune, he was left alone in the rear, proceeding at a walk. He sang to keep up his spirits. What was the name of that village, where he wasted so much time getting his mount reshod? The road, after that, was far from gay. It was raining. Alfred kept on singing. An air from *Joconde*. . . . Even though he put his horse at a trot, he knew perfectly well that he would have to spend the night somewhere along the road. The vesperal mass was out of the question. It was at this point that he began to dream about a fine moral subject: the ease of abnegation. . . .

From time to time he turned around, and he thought he saw piercing through the distance behind him the tricolored flames of Bonaparte's Lancers: which was perfectly absurd since, with the exception of Raguse's company, which was ahead with the Musketeers and the Gendarmes, all the Lifeguards and the La Rochejaquelein Grenadiers were on the road, straggling from Abbeville to Saint-Pol. And Exel-

mans's horsemen were advancing on Béthune by a quite different road.
But Alfred de Vigny did not lack imagination.

The King had, to be sure, given orders to dismantle the telegraph,
at Lille as elsewhere. But the Duc d'Orléans was anxious to get the
news, and the signals continued to be received at the top of the tower
of Saint Catherine's where in 1793 the Republic had had the first air
telegraph installed. The dispatches were kept secret. They reached
the field commander, M. le Maréchal-Duc de Trévise, and Mortier
transmitted them to Louis-Philippe. Those, at least, which he thought
it well to pass on.

There were people who were struck above all by the inclusion of
Carnot in Buonaparte's new government. Others were mesmerized by
Fouché. Bassano, Caulaincourt, Mollien, Cambacérès, Davout—
there was nothing surprising about any of these. But Carnot at the
Interior, and Fouché at police headquarters! Louis-Philippe was
torn between two feelings: the burning desire to see the King well out
of the way and the urge to get in touch with Fouché. Once again, the
police was in the hands of the Orléans group, and he was itching to
discuss all this with Macdonald and Beurnonville, that is to say with
Freemason dignitaries who might perhaps advise him. Should he leave
the country, follow the King? Or remain and try to make his peace
with Napoleon? It would be difficult. The best, obviously, would be
to withdraw, to fall back on some position away from the elder
branch: leave it to that branch to compromise itself by appealing to
the Allies to attack France. But where? There was only England where
the Duchess was already waiting for him.

Yet in spite of the ties of Freemasonry, in which the Orléans group
was powerful, Louis-Philippe was afraid to reveal himself too clearly
before the Marshals. A man became a Mason for various reasons;
many members of the military had joined the Freemasons at the time
of Brumaire, and the First Consul relied a great deal on this order
upon which he had conferred important privileges. But there was no
lack of generals who became Masons more in order to know a city's
state of mind or not to lose sight of hotheads who might be thinking
about using the Lodges for some subversion or other. The fact that
Macdonald and Beurnonville were Worshipful Masters was no guarantee. The thing was to remain a candidate for the throne, but not to
show it, not to show his eagerness . . . That was a fine disappointment he had had this morning when he had been summoned to the

King's quarters with Mortier. But that Louis XVIII, at about eight in the morning, should have decided to remain at Lille was probably no more final than his having decided at midnight to leave it, only to change his mind half an hour later. The atmosphere of the streets and squares, the threat of insubordination among the troops when it had been believed that the Duc de Berry was entering the town, could not fail to upset the King's plans. And in fact, at about noon, the three Marshals and the Duc d'Orléans, called to the Hôtel de Brigode, heard from the monarch's lips that the departure of the royal escort was set for three o'clock in the afternoon. Louis XVIII did not say whither they were bound. Louis-Philippe had to ask the question before the King confessed that he was resigning himself to leaving France. Why not Dunkirk, as he had planned up till now? He feared he might be cut off on the way by Exelmans's men or by insurgent troops, and he brought in, as he had the previous night, the argument about General Vandamme's presence in Cassel. "And then too," he added, "I can still reach Dunkirk from beyond the frontier as well as from inside it, if I deem it expedient. . . ." In short, Ostend was the next stage.

It was here that the click occurred. One is always surprised on shutting a box by that little noise which indicates that the lock has engaged. That was the noise created by Macdonald's brief speech in response to Louis XVIII, telling him that he had been faithful to him to the end, as he had been in 1814 to Napoleon, but that he begged not to be made to cross a frontier that His Majesty would surely be crossing again within three months. Jacques-Étienne would await the sovereign's return on his property of Courcelles. It cannot be said that this pleased Louis XVIII: His Majesty's vexation was plainly visible on his face. But was he in a position to show it? In any event it was better to believe that he was leaving an accomplice here in France. . . .

Louis-Philippe was looking at his royal cousin: what he in turn was going to say depended on the King's answer to the Duc de Tarente, for he did not intend to take any risks. But the click had occurred.

"Monsieur le Maréchal," said Louis XVIII, with the same good-natured smile he had summoned up while signing the Charter, "I have always had great respect for the frankness with which you express yourself, and as far as I am concerned loyalty is the outstanding trait in your character. What better proof could we give of our confidence than by authorizing you to remain on the soil of the Kingdom?"

And he turned with a questioning look in the direction of Mortier. The Maréchal-Duc de Trévise, with his heavy chin and his small thin mouth beneath the long nose, a true soldier, with a fine figure and nothing of the dandy about him, gave what amounted to the army's reply. He began at the point where Macdonald had left off. He had decided to retire to his properties. He was handing the King his resignation, but was asking for orders concerning the exercise of his command after His Majesty's departure.

This time Louis XVIII barely blinked. There was about this monarch a mental agility as surprising as the versatility of his resolution. So that was how things stood? Well, he would play the game. The main thing was that Mortier's actions should not pass as insubordination. One did not need to be extraordinarily astute in order to imagine what they would be: the best course was to back him in advance, and later be able to affirm that the Marshal had acted thusly on his orders. After all, he had to prepare the ground for his return. In this sense the historians who regard Louis XVIII as a great king do not lack justification.

"If the circumstances," he said, "*oblige* you"—and His Majesty in emphasizing this word accompanied it by a smile—"to pin a cockade on your hat, do so; but you will always keep mine in your heart and you will wear it again when the occasion arises, I am certain."

It is to be observed that Louis XVIII seemed to be interested only in the behavior of the Marshals. That of Berthier was so obviously equivocal that for a moment the King thought of asking him: "And you, Monsieur le Prince, are you also leaving us?" But essentially this was unimportant. It was better not to seem to think that the defection of two Marshals necessarily implied that of the third. If Berthier were going to leave him, well, they would find out later. The King therefore let him chew his nails, and was preparing to bring the interview to a close. He had not once looked in his cousin's direction. The displeasure he felt toward Louis-Philippe was manifest: he was angry with him for having introduced into Lille a garrison that the Duke should have left at the Péronne Camp, and thereby making the city unreliable. Also for having inconsiderately assured the people of Lille in his name of his resolve in no event to summon foreign armies to his aid. What did he know about it?

It was therefore the Duc d'Orléans who decided, in violation of all etiquette, to address the King. "And what of me, Your Majesty? What does Your Majesty wish me to do?"

The anxiety and humility of the tone did not deceive Louis XVIII.

This time he was the one to make the lock click. The King turned to the Duc d'Orléans and said to him with a royal insolence that he manifested only toward him, or toward his brother Charles: "My word, you can do whatever you please!"

None of the three Marshals, each of them too much concerned with himself, was able to seize the full impact of this little sentence which disposed of the future of the Orléans group. They took no interest in the answer in which Louis-Philippe stated that he would remain at Lille as long as he could hope to serve His Majesty's cause there, and that if he saw this was impossible, he would go and join his wife in England.

And not the King, Mortier thought, suddenly realizing that the Duke would be remaining on his hands. No, that was too much! He would have none of that . . . he would see to it. But what was wrong with Berthier? He was edging up to Macdonald.

Giuseppa's lover was in fact trying to talk to Jacques-Étienne, and he did so as soon as they were in the adjoining salon. He wanted Macdonald to make it known in Paris . . . (In Paris? To whom, in Paris? Jacques-Étienne looked at him in astonishment.) In other words, he wanted Macdonald to make it known in Paris that Berthier did not intend to emigrate . . . his command as captain-lieutenant of the Guards forced him to escort His Majesty—I mean the King— but he would hand in his resignation as soon as he was in the Low Countries, and he would go and fetch his wife and his children who were at Bamberg, and bring them back to France. The message was obviously for Giuseppa. Madame Visconti needed to be re-assured. *Mon Dieu,* I hope her health . . .

Then Berthier hesitated. He looked to see if anyone could over-hear him, then added very hurriedly, and a blush came to his cheeks, "I suppose it will not be difficult for you to make this known also to M. Perregaux, your son-in-law? I should like M. Perregaux to be informed . . . He is my banker, you know."

Macdonald smiled. He was quite aware of the fact that his second daughter Adèle's husband and M. Laffitte, his associate, would have the Emperor's ear. Berthier was not so stupid as he seemed.

They would accordingly leave at about three o'clock. That is to say, the King, Berthier, accompanied as far as to the frontier by Mortier, and a detachment of the 12th regiment of Cuirassiers, if a sufficient number of white cockades were still to be found, and the suite—ministers, dukes and princes, generals, and Father Elisée—

"Poor Beurnonville," said Mortier to Louis-Philippe, "he has no choice: he is on the Emperor's proscribed list."

It was the first time that the Duc de Trévise had said *the Emperor*. Louis-Philippe took note without seeming to, and he said to Mortier, as though he were thinking out loud, "Beurnonville . . . Wait a bit . . . Why couldn't you suggest to him that he write to Bassano? But naturally he will think of it himself: they were prisoners together in Austria. I remember, when we had had him arrested, Dumouriez and I . . . and the two of them together were exchanged for Mme. Royale. . . . The Directoire. . . . Such things are never altogether forgotten. *The Emperor* would listen to Bassano, his minister."

Mortier was startled to hear the Duc d'Orléans in his turn say *the Emperor*. And he thought to himself, there's *one* thing on which *I* am going to call the tune! He was not going to leave it to anyone else to proclaim the Emperor at Lille. Nor, whatever happened, was he going to allow the foreign armies to enter. And Louis-Philippe might want to play one or the other card. Mortier knew him from the time of Dumouriez's army.

Simon Richard had been roaming through Lille since morning. He had had plenty of time to admire the architecture of the houses, the love shown here for baroque decoration, with sculptured pilasters, caryatids, a whole confectionery of stone, in which faces blended with ornamental motifs, coupled cupids on the pediments, shells, winged cherubs . . . He was particularly struck by the character of the narrow bays which formed the inordinately tall façades. The great variety of style, the fancifulness of the ornamentation, only accentuated a common spirit which seemed to have animated the builders for at least two centuries. But there was some mockery in the captain's observations on the subject of architecture. At the market he had been turned away everywhere because of the licensed barrowmen with their badges. The only work he had been able to find had been after the hour of a lunch he had not had, because at that time all the badge-bearing barrowmen were busy; he was hired to help carry unsold grain from the Place Saint-Martin to that big storehouse near the Porte Saint-André, whose imposing structure he had noticed above the ramparts upon his arrival. This was the usual practice, in order to avoid cornering and speculation in grain. But for a back-breaking porterage job the peasant who had employed him had given him four sous and a piece of *blanzé*—bread made from the flour as it comes out of the mill and not exactly of the best quality.

As he was returning from the storehouse, loitering along the streets, he came upon a great gathering of people. In the middle there was a train of carriages, the first of which, a berlin drawn by six horses, was holding up the whole convoy because it had a broken trace which was being repaired on the spot. The crowd seemed extremely worried. The King's name was heard flying about, on a note of alarm. It was in fact Louis XVIII who was leaving the town, and the people in his suite were being asked where he was going and whether he would return. When no answers were forthcoming, public anxiety was increased.

Simon did not share this anxiety. What difference could it make to him whether His Majesty were headed for Dunkirk or Ostend? He calmly ate his *blanzé* bread, making it last, and wandered off in a direction opposite to that of the convoy, which was being escorted by Cuirassiers on their heavy chargers. He crossed a canal, followed a long straight street which was all but empty at this time of day, and turned to his left. The wind and the rain continued. He felt frightfully tired, took out his four sous three or four times from his pocket and swore, calling his grain merchant all the foul names he had learned in Spain, in Austria, in Russia; then, looking up, he saw a square tower which he remembered having noticed from afar that morning. Mechanically he circled the houses that separated him from the entrance to this church, its narrow semicircular chevet pressed between its aisles, its stone scaling. It was Saint Catherine's, on the tower of which the visual signaling was installed. This time the exhaustion that he felt was too great for him to resist the sanctuary's appeal. He entered it through the small side door, wondering whether he would be made to pay for his seat.

Saint Catherine's is not a very beautiful church. Although it is very old, it had been rebuilt in the sixteenth century and patched up a century later. The only remarkable thing about it, apart from its dark wooden vaults supported by enormous beams, is the great painting before which Simon stopped. The painting was poorly lighted, but he recognized a Rubens. He smiled to himself, thinking of his appearance: an odd-looking art lover. He had preserved the love of such things from a youth which today appeared impossibly remote. On the Inchon no one spoke of painting. Yet on the Inchon they would have understood the meaning of that muscular executioner whose powerful paw already rested on the condemned woman. But he must not let himself be stirred to pity, or take her for Blanche in a beautiful white silk robe, about to die. . . .

When he had had his fill of contemplating the "Martyrdom of Saint Catherine," suddenly preferring that tall, narrow painting next to it, the Christ with His hands bound, the prisoner against a black background who was being pulled out of the darkness by a half-naked jailer, he passed into the great nave and sat down beside a pillar, letting himself be carried away by the organ which was playing a kind of deep lament. There were tiny flames in hanging red glasses in the half-darkness. The violet-draped central altar, above which flew two worldly-looking angels with a mere suggestion of wings, was surrounded by candles whose uneven flames danced before Simon's eyes. Against his pillar, chewing his last mouthful of bread, he felt his eyes shut, weariness slipped into and filled his whole body. He had opened his sheepskin coat because of the heat of the afternoon and the sweat from his labors almost suffocated him.

Through half-closed eyes he saw shadowlike women prostrating themselves on the prayer stools, and one, tiny and emaciated, who out of humility preferred to kneel directly on the cold black slabs; children in surplices in the choir, aged men telling their beads, their voices in prayer making a low murmur. The organ was weeping. Simon—or rather, it was Olivier whose memory was faulty—said to himself with astonishment: But I thought the organs were silent on Holy Thursday! And all this, like the "Martyrdom of Saint Catherine," brought his youth back to him. Who would have recognized this rag-clad man as the child Céleste de Durfort had taught to use a sword? He recalled those happy times, and others when he used to escape with the village urchins and they trapped birds; the valley of the Somme, where they played at war in the marshes, hiding among the tall rushes, borrowing the flatboats of the peatworkers in the bogs. And he was a little peasant like the others; he had become friendly with Jean-Baptiste Caron, the son of a peatworker, and his big brother Eloy whom he used sometimes to go and help gather peat. And in the autumn the wild ducks would pass above their heads. It was astonishing to think that those happy times were the days people spoke of with such horror.

The truth of the matter was that Olivier and his family had lived through the Revolution very peaceably, despite the great name they bore and the lands that had been taken from them. He had left France only when his father was appointed ambassador to Russia; and when Louis XVI had sent his father to Rome, he had remained at Longpré, where his uncle came to visit him in his parents' absence. It was undoubtedly that free-thinking uncle who was responsible for his having lost the faith his mother had first instilled in him. But from his earliest years he had considered the love of letters as the mark of superior men. Everyone in his family wrote—the grandfather his memoirs, the uncle light, epistolary novels, the father works of history and plays. They had refused to emigrate, and they actually came close to paying for this with their heads: they had become suspect in the year I of the Republic (1793) and were sent to prison—fortunately rather late—and in the end this produced nothing more than a tale written by the uncle which appeared in the year III. Up to the time of the Consulate,* Olivier's family had lived on the books that his father wrote, and the vaudeville-larded comedies, the operas that he had arranged to have performed. Olivier was then twenty. He had left Longpré and his playmates, and he had entered the École Polytechnique with a brilliant record. When he returned to the Somme, he was appalled to learn that his comrade Jean-Baptiste had disappeared—having been taken as a conscript, he had become a deserter. He had never been seen again. What had become of him? It was incomprehensible. As a result, Eloy had grown uncommunicative and melancholy.

For Olivier, life was so simple: he did not have the military vocation of Philippe, his young brother, who had put himself under Macdonald's orders in the year VIII. Olivier, of course, wrote on the sly, but especially, yielding to the craze for things English, he translated novels by Miss Edgeworth, *Letters on Botany* . . . All this was enough to dazzle his Cousin Blanche, whom he married the year that he recast into literary form the lectures on chemistry given by his professors at the Polytechnique. And for his wedding his father, who had become a confidant of the First Consul, had had him appointed sub-prefect at Soissons. What an easy, pleasant life—and was he not himself a charming, well-brought-up, cultivated young man, resembling that free-thinking uncle who was still, in his fifties, the darling of the ladies? Why should his life have been different? And I have before my eyes a biographical dictionary published twenty years after the day when Olivier in rags listened to the plaintive organ in Saint Catherine's. It is said there that he appears *to have been interested*

---

* The government established as a sequel to Napoleon's *coup d'état* on November 9, 1799, which lasted until May 18, 1804, when he was proclaimed Emperor. At first a triumvirate, composed of Bonaparte, Siéyès, and Ducos, and then of Bonaparte, Cambacérès, and Lebrun, the Consulate in 1801 became a one-man government with Bonaparte invested as Consul for life.

only in literature, and that he died in 1818, on August 16. Everything, in fact, that constituted his real life, the tragic and violent life that tore him from his home, drove him under an assumed name on to the battlefields of Europe, landed him in the prisons of Russia, in Siberia, like the Christ by Philippe de Champaigne in Saint Catherine's Church, goes counter to the rules, and it has, with natural delicacy, been forgotten, as have Blanche's indiscretions; nothing has survived except his literary works and two dates, his birth, his death. And even of his death, nothing is said. . . .

And while Olivier was dozing off, lulled by the organ and by memories, old at thirty-six under all the weight of unhappiness and of the superhuman fatigues of war, of captivity and of his return, he was caught up again by the uncertain image of a velvet-eyed young woman, of a child-woman rather than by Rubens' Saint Catherine of the Martyrdom, derived from an English portrait, with that whiteness of the skin that seemed the reason for her given name, and the blood close under the cheeks which flushed at a mere nothing, and which a mere nothing restored to their natural whiteness—that frail perfection which the first experiences of motherhood transformed into a femininity that made her amorous husband tremble merely to take Blanche's hand. . . . God, may the executioner spare her in her white silk dress!

Ah, let us not speak of Blanche . . . It so happens that with this man too the light of the near future gives me the true color of this human adventure. He died, says this dictionary, on August 16, 1818, at the age of about forty years. . . . Does a man die at that age, with a body tempered by trials and adversity? His heart, which I hear beating, was that of a soldier, regular, perfectly normal, he could live out of doors, he had no ailment other than that secret wound of memory. And on August 16, 1818 . . . Why, then, did he die that summer—a summer warm and plump as the arm of a pretty girl? I visualize the scene: somewhere in the valley of the Somme, in one of those channels through which Eloy Caron's boat passes. Eloy helped by his son Jean-Baptiste, leaning over the flat edge and using his peat spade to bring the body up. Olivier had disappeared for the second time, had not been seen since the day before . . . and the day before that he had been seen in church for the Assumption. That had seemed odd, for him. His family was inquiring after him among the country people all about. . . . And Eloy, in spite of the time that had passed and the not too serious nature of childhood friendships, after thirty years when one of those friends is

a *grand seigneur,* the other a poor peatworker, Eloy, immediately
convinced that there had been a calamity, had begun to look for this
M. Olivier, the young Count, as he was still called even though his
hair was peppered with white. For anyone to take his own life was
for Eloy a mad, incomprehensible thing. But wasn't Olivier a little
mad? So, then, the peatworker had a vague feeling as to what must
have happened, and he had headed his flatboat in the direction of
that channel where once before, about 1790, a girl had yielded to
despair because of a child she had been unable to get rid of, and the
young Count, at the time, had been so struck by it— So much so
that last week he was still talking to Eloy about it: *You remember
that girl a fellow from La Chaussée-Tirancourt got with child? How
she was fished out of the water over there, how enormous she was?
There were grasses in her hair.* Now Eloy Caron was shouting to
Jean-Baptiste, "Ho, give me a hand, can't you!" And the boat had
come near capsizing when the body was hoisted up because the
whole weight was on one side.

Thus life was to end for Olivier, who had brought back from
Siberia that black mood which became the talk of Longpré. Black
as the background in Philippe de Champaigne's painting. And ideas
that were not those of his rank. It had taken three years for this
hypochondria to lead to its natural end. Three years, in the course
of which two visits by a blond woman, in her silk dresses, with her
two children, already thinking beings, had done nothing but aggra-
vate the blackness of his meditations. Three years, in the course of
which the memories of Siberia had ceased little by little to be those
of Hell and aroused in him a nostalgia for the only human things that,
in his hypochondria, he remembered in his whole life. Dusya . . .
he remembered her, not for those nights in bed with her, but because she was one of the few unquestionably good beings he had
met there—obscure people, superstitious, ignorant, coarse of manner.
And also men, deported like himself, Russians, who used to meet
behind their guards' backs and talk about life, the future, the tyranny
to be overthrown . . . Vague and grandiose ideas had passed from
them to Olivier—to Simon Richard—hopes that were like sorrows.
He had brought these dreams back from Siberia to France, in secret,
and he could talk of them to no one. To no one. They would have
laughed in his face. What semblance of possibility was there in all
that? Everything had fallen back into place, the world went on as it
always had, with some on top, others underneath. Even Eloy would
have shaken his head and looked at the young Count pityingly if

the other had told him what was being said over there, on the Inchon, in the taiga.

There was no hope that things would change. Society was well and solidly based on its foundation of lies. Blanche was bringing up her children, thank God, in accordance with the precepts of religion and the rules of society. In Paris she inspired both pity and respect. She gazed at you from the center of the painting with a look that pierced your heart. The fool, the executioner, was the man who one day had left her through one of those impulses that nothing could excuse . . . and the fine position he had enjoyed. That was fourteen years ago exactly; it was precisely on August 16, 1804, that Olivier had disappeared. Then, too, the region had been combed, as it was thought he might have come here, and Eloy Caron had sounded the lanes of water, the channels, with his great peat spade. Why did they persist in the idea that he might have drowned himself? The rumor had gone round that he had been found, not in the marshes of the Somme but near Paris, in a pond in the forest of Meudon. M. Philippe, his brother, and their father had hastened there. They had been shown a drowned man who bore no resemblance to Olivier. . . . That was the last day of August, 1804. The father clung to every kind of hope: in the first days of September he had called the attention of the police to a house where a noise could be heard at night "as though someone were being kept prisoner there," he said. He was hopeful that his son had been abducted and was being kept locked up. It was near La Celle Saint-Cloud, and Fouché's men had surrounded the house in the dark: but when they broke in, it turned out to be a bakery, and the noise that of the journeyman kneading the dough. The vanished man was also thought to have been seen at Plombières on September 14: this rumor was based on Blanche's presence there with the Empress in August, but as she had left a month before, the story made no sense. For nearly two years every corpse was taken to be his. The police called the family every time they found a drowned body they could not identify.

Why did the family persist in believing that he must have drowned himself? Now it seemed that his long-anticipated destiny had been at last fulfilled. And Olivier lay in Eloy's boat, and young Jean-Baptiste, stunned, was looking at the drowned man . . . drowned forever.

A man brought low by fatigue, asleep in a church on Holy Thursday, can resemble a drowned man, especially in the false light produced by red glass and its green shadows. He can resemble a Christ being led away with his hands tied. He was not concerned with the sacrifice *in Cena Domini* which was being prepared in Saint Catherine's Church, where M. Descombes, the parish priest, who had returned from exile when Napoleon was made Emperor, busied himself in the sacristy, the door to which was ajar beside the side altar to the right, while up in the tower a messenger from M. le Maréchal Mortier, Duc de Trévise, explained to the signalman the telegram he was to write so that the Marshal, by showing it to M. le Duc d'Orléans, could get Louis-Philippe to agree to leave the city without delay. . . . All this, the service of God as well as the service of man, was remote from this man drowned in sleep on the rush-bottomed chair, his head thrown back, his face contracted, his eyes lost in the depths.

What filled this artificial night, this seated dream, was precisely what Simon refused to dream of when awake. He had passed through the forbidden door; he was in Armida's garden . . . Armida, Catherine, what was her name? This dream was not meant for a church; it was sacrilegious in character, but what could Olivier do, what can I do about it? She was lying on the floor, on her side, one leg stretched out, the other bent, completely naked in her lovely black hair which she flung back with a motion of her young shoulders. She had taken off her beautiful silk dress, her body had the bloom of adolescence, and she leaned back on her frail arms watching the man approach, her small breasts pointing toward him. Her magnificent teeth in the pale mouth seemed to have been made for smiles and for appeal. It was easy to read in her eyes what she was expecting—Blanche, or Catherine, what did you say her name was? —in her eyes, beneath the high arches of the brows lifted toward the man, with the confidence of desire . . . Where was this? At Soissons or in Paris, in a room of silk and velvet, with a thick-pile carpet . . . Who in the world taught you this abandon, little girl, can it possibly be I? Soft quivering child flesh, made by its youth both chaste and provocative. Was it possible that some day you might be like this for another, with your crazy little head beneath the weight of the long unbound hair tumbling down like a curtain over your childish breasts? How you lifted yourself up toward me, on the support of your disingenuously round arms. You have bitten your lips to bring the blood to them, you open them; they make a little round O which calls to me . . . God of heaven, why can't I extend my hand and touch you? I remember that soft firmness beneath my fingers, and how you used to fling your arms round my neck, you feared not being close enough to me, you clung to me, your legs . . . your legs . . . And then that way you had of suddenly escaping, of turning away: where did you learn that science of desire, yours and mine? Even women who make a profession of it have not mastered that curious art, as you had, from the first moment. . . .

Meanwhile, it was nearly five o'clock in the evening, and in Saint Catherine's everything was being prepared for the evening mass. The deacon had laid the three linen cloths on the altar, and the corporal cloth on which rested the ciborium with the hosts to be consecrated, covered with the white silk veil of Holy Thursday, with a ribbon sewn in the middle to make it secure before the procession. The tabernacle—the golden door, on which Moses twisted his arms before the Burning Bush, was not visible—was open and remained empty as required for this solemn mass which represents the Last Supper. The ministrants today, round the celebrant, were not only the customary children, but several priests and clerics who were grown men. In the sacristy, deacons and subdeacons had donned the albs of white linen that fell to their heels and tied the cingulum about their waists. Over the alb, the deacons wore the white, short, wide-sleeved dalmatic, reaching to below the knees. The subdeacons were entitled only to the tunic. There was haste and a buzz of whispers in the sacristy because M. le Curé Destombes, in the violet chasuble which signifies the mortification of the flesh, was showing signs of great impatience: "Well," he said to one of the subdeacons, "have you found them?" They did not have twelve —the poor from the almshouse who had been ordered had scattered over the city, probably drawn by curiosity to see the King. M. Destombes murmured that there was another King whom Christians should be far more eager to see—the One hanging above the faithful from a keystone in the center of the great nave, crucified against the void— But this still did not give them their twelve.

The procession had already formed, the celebrant and the ministers bearing their book of canticles and circling round the church, to advance from the back of the great nave toward the altar. All carried the maniple on the left arm. From a distance, M. Destombes saw the Poor whom they had managed to find being pushed in the direction of the twelve seats placed in two facing rows of six right in the middle of the choir. But one seat remained empty. As the procession reached the altar, while the entrance antiphon rose and he was saying the first prayers at the foot of the altar, M. Destombes caught sight of a man in the nave, by the last pillar before the choir, to his left—a man wearing strange rags, asleep on his chair, his mouth opened. He whispered a few words to one of the servers, who bowed and turned back upon his steps.

M. Destombes, having donned the stole, mounted to the altar and bowed, kissed it, then picked up the censer and perfumed the altar with it.

Simon Richard had not heard the Introitus, but he awoke during the singing of the *Kyrie eleison*. A priest in a surplice was shaking him, and it came to him that sleeping here and in this way must be considered out of place and he tried to apologize. But that was not the point. He must take his place. What place? The bells had begun to ring full peal, the organ was playing the *Gloria*. Simon had no idea what all this was about, but he followed the subdeacon, who settled him on the twelfth chair, in the midst of the Poor. He looked at the people next to him, old men wearing almshouse garb, like hunted, aged animals, one with a dripping nose, another with a face twisted by paralysis. . . . What did they want of him? Why had they put him with these people?

Suddenly the bells and the organ were silent, with that great silence, the silence of the Passion, which they would break only with the Pascal vigil. And the voice of the celebrant rose:

Deus, a quo et Judas reatus sui poenam, et confessionis suae latro praemium sumpsit . . .

Lord, how far away Olivier's Latin was! Yet this beginning of the prayer made him think of the Judas of his life—Tony de Reiset, who had destroyed his happiness: had God punished him for his crime? And was he himself the penitent thief on the way of the cross of existence, he who had deserved recompense for his faith? He did not understand the part he was being made to play in this holy comedy, he did not hear the Epistle of Saint Paul to the Corinthians. He was suddenly filled with hatred. A hatred forgotten, ancient, and ever alive . . . and what was the Gregorian chant saying?

Christus factus est pro nobis obediens usque ad mortem . . .

A hatred which reduced to unimportance everything that was happening, the undoubted mistake of which he was the object. What was the priest saying? What was this Gospel, in which Olivier again seized the name of Judas Iscariot, son of Simon . . .

Dicit ei Petrus . . . : "Non lavabis mihi pedes in aeternum."

Respondit ei Jesus: "Si non lavere te, non habebis partum meum."
Dicit ei Simon Petrus . . .

And Simon Richard had a hard time following Simon Peter's story. Suddenly, when the celebrant and his ministers came solemnly down from the altar into the choir and advanced toward the Poor, of whom Simon was the twelfth, he understood what was happening, and he wanted to protest, like Simon Peter: "Thou shalt never wash my feet." But what could he do? On a table next to the Poor the deacons had placed the washbasins and the vessels of water. The celebrant and the holy ministrants had put aside the maniple, the celebrant had removed his chasuble, they knelt before the Poor and unfastened their shoes. . . . Then Simon experienced the deepest shame of his life. Incapable of getting up and running away, averse equally to scandal and to blasphemy, he simply measured the infinite depths of falsehood, the abyss into which he had fallen. . . .

In the silence of the organs rose the Gregorian chants, the strange femininity of the voices of young boys.

Postquam surrexit Dominus a cena, misit aquam in pelvim . . .

The deacon who was washing Simon's feet could not help murmuring that it was the tradition in the almshouse to send only poor people who had first been cleaned. And Simon Richard looked at his naked, dirty feet, and said very fast and in a low voice, "I beg you to forgive me, Father . . ."

Ubi caritas et amor, Deus ibi est . . .

The song swelled, sustained by the entire schola and the faithful who filled the church, while the kneeling priests finished their task. And the celebrant rose to his feet, washed his hands and wiped them without a word. Then all again took the maniple and placed it on their left arms. The celebrant had resumed his violet chasuble, the procession re-formed, returned to the altar.

The Poor now put on their wretched shoes again. Simon felt the flush on his brow and cheeks, while over there the *Pater noster* was being recited softly. Then the response rose, ringing out:

> *Domine, exaudi orationem meum . . .*
> *Et clamor meus ad te veniat . . .*

Suddenly Simon could stand it no longer, and got up, moving toward the back of the church. A shudder went through the church, the faithful seemed as though struck by lightning, deacons turned around, the beadle approached the recalcitrant Poor Man to make him go back to his seat where he should have stayed and listened to the Psalms, then after Communion waited for the procession of the faithful to the Holy Table until the ciborium was put back on the corporal cloth and purified by the celebrant . . . and everything that followed after that so long as the servers had not put down the maniple, and the celebrant had not removed his violet chasuble to don a white cope. And even then the role of the Poor was not ended. For they had to take their place, to the accompaniment of the hymn *Pange, lingua* . . . in the procession that would deposit the holy species in the ciborium covered by the veil of Holy Thursday, with the censers, in a chosen chapel; and all the altars were stripped of their ornaments, with the exception of the High Altar which remained alone and empty, in the silence of the Passion, while everyone entered the sacristy. There the Poor were at last sent back to the almshouse with good words and clean feet.

Simon, having pushed the beadle aside, found himself in the street, and he felt nothing except a ferocious hunger against which the overpowering odor of the swung incense had been quite ineffective.

It was six in the evening, but the bells no longer said so.

At this moment the humiliated man remembered Soissons, where he had been sub-prefect, and where, in the prison, there were verses written on the wall of a cell which he had taken the trouble, at the time, to decipher with his twenty-four-year-old eyes:

> *Las! Je suis prins de douleur*
> *Mourir mieulx me vaudrait*
> *Que souffrir telles empreintes . . .* *

What had they done to the prisoner, which he called marks? For the moment Olivier repeated to himself the verses of the inscription and wondered, having suffered what he had suffered, if it would not have been better for him to die. He was to ask himself this for another three long years and five months, or almost.

When Simon appeared at the inn, the sentimental drudge who had given the poor prisoner from Russia a kind reception (*And you know, there's one like you, he's just come back too, and he's taken command of a group of volunteers who have set out for Paris . . . I wonder what the poor young people are going to do now!*) literally flung herself on him: she had been waiting for him so that she could

---

* Alas! I am full of grief—Better were it for me to die—than to suffer such marks . . .

tell him . . . a pottery dealer, one of his two horses had had an accident . . . so, to haul the merchandise twelve and a half leagues from here, if your horse can be harnessed . . . *hein?* All right, why not? It was in a southwesterly direction, the way he was going, and this would give him a good two meals at least. But you've got to leave right away, my poor man, and there goes your night. Fortunately he had slept in the church.

Louis-Philippe had stayed within the limits of the fortifications, as had Mortier, who had left to Macdonald the responsibility of accompanying His Majesty as far as the frontier post, with his escort of Cuirassiers, the carriages that carried the ministers, the notabilities of his suite, and Father Elisée. It was only later in the evening, at about six o'clock, when Marshal Macdonald had returned, that the Duc d'Orléans went to the headquarters at the Grand'Garde to discuss the situation with the Marshals and the general officers who were at Lille. As a matter of fact, these had already been convened by Mortier, and their minds were made up. Mortier had already put before them the choice between loyalty to King and loyalty to Country. There was no doubt that, with the King gone, nothing would stop the garrison from rallying to the Emperor.

It was at this point that the Duc de Trévise produced before Louis-Philippe's eyes the document that had been carefully prepared at Saint Catherine's on his instructions. It was a dispatch in which Marshal Davout, the War Minister, ordered the arrest of the King and the Bourbons who were at Lille. Mortier, even while he told the Duke that he had nothing to fear and begged him to remain in the city as though he had no knowledge of the dispatch, was careful to give him details that increased its plausibility. For example, that it had been transmitted from fifteen leagues away. It required no great mental effort to understand that this meant from Arras. And in order to strengthen the effect of this news, the Marshal added that he had had confirmation of the dispatch, since shortly after His Majesty's departure he had been visited by one of Davout's aides-de-camp, whom he had had arrested when the other had shown him his orders— which were to arrest the King, and, more precisely this time, the Duc d'Orléans in person. But while he had shown the dispatch, Mortier did not propose to fetch the aide-de-camp from his prison and question him in Louis-Philippe's presence.

The Duke, after all, only wanted to be convinced that he should flee. His wife was in England . . . He took merely the time needed to write the essential official letters—to Marshal Mortier and to the commands of the Lille region—to release them from their oath, and advise them diplomatically to place themselves at the service of the Usurper. He was careful to draft them in such terms that they themselves would assume all responsibility and that these letters could in no eventuality be turned against their signer. He had, further, to make arrangements concerning the men of his household, some of whom were to remain, others to follow . . . which was the way the Orléans group always operated. In any event, he would be unable to leave with Mademoiselle, his sister, before quite late in the night.

While Louis-Philippe overwhelmed him with thanks and spoke of his loyalty, of which this was not the first proof he had had, the Maréchal-Duc de Trévise lowered his eyes and pursed his lips.

"Monseigneur is too kind," said Mortier, and he looked up, showing candid eyes. "You are wrong to regard as virtue what is but the natural disposition of my character."

He was one of those men who can utter such statements without experiencing any need to smile. In his youth he had been intended for trade. As a dutiful son he would certainly have followed the path traced out for him by his father, and carried on the moleskin business his father had founded, had it not been that with the Revolution the profession of arms had become tempting. He knew how to lie about a dispatch received, as about the quality of a cloth. But that night, at Lille, he did not know that twenty years later the man he was going to so much trouble to send packing would watch him die, by a blow intended for his master. It was the morning of one fourteenth of July, before King Louis-Philippe's departure for the review that was to be held on the Boulevard du Temple. As there was a rumor that there was to be an attempt upon His Majesty's life, Mortier, his War Minister, said, with that same voice, that same air of modesty and devotion that he had used at Lille, those same honest eyes: "I'm a big man, I shall cover the King with my body." It so happened that when Fieschi's infernal machine was flung from a window in front of the Jardin Turc, felling fifty men and I don't know how many horses, the fragment that might have struck Louis-Philippe pierced the heart of Mortier, Duc de Trévise. He was big, he had covered the King with his body . . . His eyes remained wide open, with that expression of insufferable honesty. A green moleskin cloth was spread over him, like those made in Monsieur his father's factory at Cateau-Cambrésis. . . .

It so happened that on that same Holy Thursday, Davout had

written from Paris to General Exelmans that if the King were still at Lille when his horsemen reached it, he should be allowed to go to Belgium with the Princes and those who might want to follow him. And in this same letter he also said: *I know positively that Marshal Mortier is very well disposed and that he is only awaiting the appearance of the Imperial army to declare himself.*

Nothing could be truer. Mortier was impatiently awaiting Napoleon's soldiers. And while Louis-Philippe was writing the letters whereby he gave a free hand to those who were militarily responsible to him, the Duc de Trévise, in his offices at the Grand'Garde, was composing his report to His Majesty the Emperor, stopping occasionally, with his tight little mouth, pen suspended in mid-air and eyes full of honesty. The report would demonstrate that it was his firmness and the sound measures he had taken that had preserved the Emperor's good city of Lille for him: for the Princes' plan had been to bring the Royal Household here; but the Marshal's and the garrison's patriotism, their determination to allow no troops to enter Lille that did not accept the Emperor's authority— He stopped: he had just remembered that remark at table the day before, at M. de Brigode's, those Ultra-Royalists who were ready to call the English and the Prussians to Lille. A shudder ran through him. Yet he had better not mention that.

Macdonald, as he had come to take leave of Monseigneur the Duc d'Orléans—for he wanted to go to bed, having slept not more than five hours the previous night, which was very little for him—had remembered to inquire whether His Majesty had sent a message to Monsieur to inform him that he was leaving Lille. Louis-Philippe himself had not thought to ask, and the King, of course, as throughout their trip, had neglected to inform the Princes: this was with him a consistent line of conduct. The Duke begged the Marshal to draft a letter for Monsieur himself, and they decided to send it in two copies by way of Béthune and of Arras—the Household might have followed either route. Whereupon the Marshal went off to bed in the Hôtel de Brigode, now quite empty and melancholy. Mortier had asked him to remain at Lille with him next day, inviting him to lunch and to dinner. And Macdonald was looking forward to this halt in his life, to this intermezzo, he thought to himself, and hummed a little air from Mozart. Mortier and he would talk things over, tomorrow, at leisure. How should they act? Jacques-Étienne congratulated himself on being with such a good friend in such delicate circumstances. Meanwhile he fell immediately to sleep.

During all this, every soldier of the garrison had adopted the tri-color cockade, and there was dancing in the streets despite the wind that whipped the flames of the torches and sometimes put them out. All the wineshops had remained open, and to hell with regulations. And in the cellar of the Quatre-Marteaux, on the square opposite the theatre, there was a great consumption of *couques-baques,* which are buckwheat pancakes, and beer was drunk by the bottleful.

On the Grand'Place, in front of Mortier's headquarters, firecrack-ers were being set off. The noise drew the Marshal to the window; and when he realized what it was all about he smiled and murmured, "And to think that this very morning those people were shouting *Vive le Roi!"*

If the wind of Holy Thursday had defeated the rain from Lille to Béthune, the same was not true in the region this side of Saint-Pol. M. de La Grange's Black Musketeers had remained in that town where they had been joined at nightfall by Guards belonging to Grammont's, Wagram's and Noailles's companies, in great confusion, with the Swiss Guards and the artillery. The La Rochejaquelein Grenadiers, Lauris-ton's Musketeers, the Gendarmes, had pushed on to Béthune. The Princes were putting up for the night at Saint-Pol, attended by M. de Damas's Light Horse; and by Raguse's company, with Marmont, the only one that was in marching formation. They seemed to have lost M. de Croy's Scottish company, that famous elite company, and that of the Duc de Luxembourg, tied up somewhere near Hesdin prob-ably, at best.

Actually, the train of the Household that evening stretched from well beyond Hesdin as far as Béthune, under the persistent downpour, in the yellow mud, the ruts in which the heterogeneous vehicles got stuck, stopping entire units. Apart from Raguse's company, almost all the Guards were dispersed, and the Devil himself could not have unscrambled them. This whole mass limped along, stopped without orders, at its own whim. Fatigue, the dreary sky, accidents, blocks on the road, had made of these three thousand men a spaced-out mob which was no longer an army. Nearly two thousand ill, crippled deserters had fallen by the wayside. Isolated individuals were look-ing for their companies, got tired of looking, and decided to sleep in a barn, a village, under an abandoned carriage. The bulk of the men on foot, that evening, had not yet reached Saint-Pol. They were haunted by the presence of Exelmans's men. These were invisible, but present, all the way from Abbeville, from the moment when a party of Grenadiers had clashed with the Imperial Light Cavalry. They might be those just behind, but perhaps those were only stragglers from the Household. In this anxiety, groups of horsemen, carriages, ventured into crossroads, lengthening their journey unnecessarily, believing themselves thus less exposed to raids by the Imperials. Axles were constantly breaking. Carts loaded with young and old, moving at the walking pace of such nags as it had been possible to find, suddenly blocked a dirt road which one traveler thought he was the only person to have taken. People fed themselves as best they could, and for the latecomers bread became scarce, and they were lucky indeed if they found a bit of cheese to go with it, and some thick heavy beer.

The villages were becoming hostile. They were, for that matter, few and far between in this region. The earth of the drenched fields, the interminable road, the bare trees, the drowned sky, composed the setting for what all of them now looked upon as an incomprehensible flight. Soldiers who no longer had even the hope of fighting were no longer soldiers, but fugitives. The volunteers had stopped at Saint-Pol for lack of horses to replace the wretched, harassed animals that held back rather than pulled their wagons. The people of Saint-Pol were still talking about the honor His Majesty had done them by relaying at the gate to their town, and such was the credulity of the citizens that no one believed the King would leave French soil. What idea did they have in their narrow heads as to what was going to become of Louis XVIII, of the Princes, and of that disordered expedition which, after all, they were witnessing with their own eyes? None, to tell the truth. Sovereigns and generals disposed of armies, they crossed these plains—at times for battle, at times on simple military marches. Then time passed and news arrived of a victory or a defeat; foreign armies in turn marched along the roads, quartered in the towns. . . . Who consulted the inhabitants? And what did it all mean?

But at Saint-Pol, the people who had property preserved a terrified memory of the Terror, of Joseph le Bon*: and so to them the King seemed their safeguard, and for them to accept the idea that the King was fleeing would mean that they too must consider their own fate. So they trembled and looked in another direction. For that matter, no one south of Lille, whether at Saint-Pol or Béthune, knew that that very afternoon Louis XVIII had crossed the frontier at Menin. Nor that the Comte d'Artois's nerves were about to give way.

* A member of the Revolutionary Convention, born in Arras, 1765; executed 1795; notorious for his ruthlessness.

Théodore had stopped here, at Béthune, in a state of utter exhaustion. It was almost night; they had passed through a region of marshes and the suburb of Saint-Pry with its big priory. They fell upon a town bristling with fortifications, whose triangular lunettes with the gates and the counterguards between them still preserved the medieval character, although all this was pure Vauban because of the tall mass of the half-ruined château. The part of the town where six thousand persons lived looked very small, and from it rose the great belfry and the church of Saint-Vaast. The complex system of the waters partially surrounding the town, with those two bridges they had just crossed, was difficult to make out. Suddenly one felt oneself a prisoner of the houses. The poorly paved streets bordered with stalls, most of which were shut at this hour, were far from inviting in the dingy light cast by the few oil lamps, despite the white flags hoisted at the windows in the wet wind. Small courtyards, in which washing was hung out to dry, opened on to the streets; and from these came a smell of slopwater, stagnating everywhere. The poorest part of the population turned out with their rag-clad, half-naked children, drawn by the entry of the cavalry. All these people were apathetic, and it was only when they reached the junction of the rue des Treilles and the rue Grosse-Tête that cries and acclamations, shouts of *Vive le Roi!* began to be heard from the windows.

"Do you think we've missed mass?" Moncorps asked.

Théodore shrugged his shoulders. By way of mass, he needed a good bed. Where were they going to lodge? Here again it was every man for himself. The horsemen came to a halt on the Grand'Place, in front of the belfry rising from the houses that surrounded it, and dispersed. There was more room here than on the night when His Majesty had halted, because the circus people had struck camp, and there was no longer a market. According to what people said, Imperial troops were at the approaches to the town. However that might be, the Comte de Maulde, who was in command of the area—he who had resented the decidedly cool reception he had received from his old friend Blacas the other morning—had ordered that the gates be closed, and, exhausted though they were, the Gendarmes and the Grenadiers had to furnish pickets to circulate along the ramparts and set up posts at the counterguards. Théodore was thankful to have escaped this fatigue duty. He took Trick by the bridle, and had set off in search of a house with a stable or a barn when suddenly he stopped in astonishment.

Before him a man in civilian clothes but of military bearing, leaning on a cane, was holding by the hand a scamp of about ten who must have been guilty of some mischief, and was scolding the child. Théodore was sure he recognized him by his voice. He was the major of that night at Poix, with his gray mustache and his long frock coat, who was for arming the people, whose son had enlisted. . . . Géricault yielded to an absurd impulse: perhaps he was thinking that this retired officer must have a place where he could put up his mount, but rather— No, it was because he was at a point in his life when he had to talk to a man like him.

"Mon commandant . . ." he began, and immediately realized into what a hopeless situation he had got himself. Well, all he could do now was make the jump.

The man had stopped and turned around. The sight of the Musketeer's uniform had certainly had the same effect on him as on Caroline Lallemand, for he pulled the youngster by the arm and was about to walk away, mumbling something in his mustache and wrinkling his brow, when Théodore said the one thing that could stop him: "Major, I must talk to you. Don't judge me by my uniform. I need your help in deciding what to do with myself."

The major stopped again, hesitated, and looked at the Musketeer. "To me?" he said. "Why do you want to talk to *me,* young man? I don't know you."

"But I know you," said Géricault, "and I don't think an old comrade of Lazare Hoche can refuse me the benefit of his advice this evening."

"Oh!" the other exclaimed, "and how do you happen to know me, monsieur?"

"From the other night, *mon commandant.* In the wood, above the cemetery, at Poix . . ."

The old officer gave a start, then looked around, thought a moment, and suddenly said, "All right, come with me. We can talk more comfortably at home."

He lived nearby, close to where the Musketeers had entered the town, in a funny little alley which formed a kind of horseshoe round what looked like a big shed built over the foundations of Saint Nicholas's Chapel. It was called la rue Serrée (the narrow street) and well deserved its name. "You can put your horse just across the way," the major explained. "Monsieur Tocquenne, the blacksmith, owns that big building you see, and employs some hundred workers. He's an obliging fellow. We'll ask him; he lives at the other end of the street, next to the Chambre des Charitables. . . . It won't be too far to take water to your beast; we've a good cistern—and with these rains! You shall have my son's bed. He left us on Sunday, and you look as if you have more need of a bed than conversation."

In addition to Jean, this ten-year-old son, and the one who had left for Paris, the major had a twenty-two-year-old daughter, like a Rubens; her name was Catherine, but she bore a greater resemblance to her mother than to the Saint: both of them wore their blond hair in flat, smooth bandeaux; both were small, with good figures, though not exactly pretty. While these ladies were busy preparing the guest room and the dinner, the major led the way into what he called his study, a rather poorly furnished low-ceilinged room filled with shelves of books, among which Théodore noticed the works of Jean-Jacques Rousseau. From it a door opened on a large room which, since the windows were shuttered, Théodore did not immediately recognize as a pottery shop with an entrance on the rue Grosse-Tête. The major explained: "Aldegonde—that's to say, my wife—runs this small business. One must live. She gets pottery from Lillers, where it's made, as well as from Aire: those painted plates . . . But tell me, by what miracle does it happen that a King's Musketeer is a member of the 'organization'?"

"I owe you the truth," Théodore said, feeling himself blushing. "I am not a member of what you call the 'organization,' but don't be angry, please, *mon commandant*. Let me tell you my story. . . ."

Outside, gusts of wind could be heard, banging the doors.

XV

Good Friday

THE rain had left for Rome with the church bells. The day of the
Passion rose dimly under a moisture-laden sky, a dawn which
seemed blurred by all the tears of the Garden of Olives. But the men
wallowing in the partially paved towns, or on the roads—which were
very poorly graveled here on the confines of Artois and Flanders—
did not trust this lull in the downpour. Now that it was no longer
raining, the mud on their feet was like an insult. It was the time of
day when Saint-Pol was just half-opening some of its shutters. In
the *estaminets,* beginning the day's business by candlelight, workers
from the tanneries and the breweries were hastily swallowing a cup
of chicory so as not to lose a minute of the daylight. Between the two
arms of the dirty, muddy Ternoise, the Church of the White Friars, the
largest here since the parish church had been destroyed under the
Directory, was full of people telling their beads, in the great under-
tow of prayer, before the bare altar which was without a cross, without candelabra, without cloths. The Duc de Berry in his gray oilskin
cloak was pacing the square, flanked by his faithful La Ferronays,
and by his dear friend the Comte de Nantouillet, impatiently waiting
for his father to be ready. He returned the salute given him by César
de Chastellux, whose horsemen were lined up on either side of the
inn, ready for departure.

Monsieur, as he was being shaved in his room—it was not yet daylight—let his mind drift in a dangerous reverie. The reports he had
received of occasional contacts here and there with rebel troops, the

451

obsession with Exelmans, the growing reserve shown by the people as the Household entered the towns, all this was still as nothing compared to the King's silence. The Comte d'Artois could not help piecing together the odd features of his brother's conduct in the past week; that is to say, since that session of Parliament at which Louis had sworn to die rather than leave Paris, and at which he himself, carried away by the mood of the moment, had suddenly bound himself and his sons by oath to remain loyal to the King and to the Constitutional Charter. He would never forget Louis's glance, his contemptuous smile. Everything had begun at that moment . . . and the suspicions. Then there had been that horrible scene. M. de Charette . . . Ah, Charles knew it by heart—the accursed letter that His Majesty used to fling in his face on special occasions! A letter dating back to November, 1795, when Charette had learned of Monsieur's departure from the Isle of Yeu, his abandoning the Vendéens to their wretched fate and returning to England.

It came back to him, word for word, in the lather the servant was brushing on his face, so that it was impossible to tell whether Charles was red or pale: *Sire, Your brother's cowardice has been our undoing. In landing on the coast it was in his power either to lose all or to win all. His return to England has decided our fate: before long, I shall have no choice but to perish vainly in your service.* . . . No, it was not possible: Charette could not have written that! It was an English forgery, those unspeakable English. . . . He would rather die than go back to live among those people! But why had the King again brought up the name of François Charette de la Contrie just at the moment of departure? What scheme was His Majesty brewing? What plan had he in his august head? To get rid of the younger branch? When he made Madame Royale marry the Duc d'Angoulême, Louis had deliberately snuffed out the future on that side since he knew perfectly well that she could have no children by him. As for Berry, the King—that is, the King and his police—were behind all the campaigns intended to compromise him. Who else could have spread through Paris the legend of the marriage with Mrs. Brown, who was not even a Catholic, so as to prevent Charles-Ferdinand from becoming the hope of the dynasty? What was the gout-ridden King up to? And now this flight, this surrender . . . The Princes flung to Exelmans as bait, to cover Louis's retreat. . . . No, my brother, *we shall not perish vainly in your service—not we!* They must rejoin the King immediately, thwart his designs. . . .

Monsieur, his son and Marmont met in a very restricted war council.

The Marshal was completely at a loss. The vanguard of the household was at Béthune. There was no choice: they must go there, join it, and from there make for Lille by way of La Bassée—that was the normal route, as was clear from a glance at the map. In violation of common sense, the Comte d'Artois kept insisting that the shortest way to get to Lille was by way of Pernés, Lillers, Robecq, Merville, Estaires, Armentières. . . . But those were tiny roads, making a big detour; the men are tired. The Duc de Berry was chiefly worried over what would become of their people at Béthune. That was something Monsieur cared nothing about. He replied to his son that they would send the whole train to Béthune—the men on foot, the volunteers, those who had arrived late in the night, like the Scottish company, the bulk of the baggage. . . . But they, together with Raguse's company, La Grange's Musketeers, Grammont's, de Noailles's and Wagram's Guards—and, of course, Damas's Light Horse which were like their own guard—would make for Lille, behind the screen of this maneuver, by the west, so that if His Majesty were to leave the city for Dunkirk, as several had suggested in Paris before the departure, you remember? . . . They could join him on the way. . . .

"Why," asked Marmont, "should His Majesty leave Lille? It's the only stronghold in which he can entrench himself and hold out until the Allies' arrival." The idea occurred to him, although he did not formulate it aloud, that Monsieur wanted to reach Armentières because of its proximity to the frontier, and not at all in order to get to Lille. But then he remembered the baggage: the Comte d'Artois would not have sent it to Béthune if he had intended to slip out of the country. . . . In any event, even if it was stupid from a military point of view, Monsieur, in His Majesty's absence, was the Monarchy. His wishes amounted to orders. There was nothing to do but comply.

The Duc de Berry meanwhile was looking at the map: but if Estaires was where they wanted to go, the road through Béthune was shorter; from there they could make a beeline for Estaires, along the Canal de la Lawe. In other words, through Lestrem. Ah, that child would never understand anything! It would have to be explained to him.

The whole problem, for the Comte d'Artois, was one of safety. They must avoid the places where there might be rebel garrisons, and the roads where such troops might be in movement. "What places," asked the Duc de Berry, "between here and Lille? What are you talking about, Father?"

Monsieur ignored the questions. Passing through Pernés, through

Merville, meant crossing regions which were deeply attached to the Monarchy. Did not Charles-Ferdinand remember the fiery tales he himself had told his father on his return from his tour of the north last August? He had been full of heroic stories of the revolt of Pernes in '93 then: had they not shouted *Vive le Roi!* and *Mort aux Patriotes!* at the very height of the Terror? Monsieur very carefully avoided recalling the name of this insurrection which had broken out in the course of a patronal feast, because it embarrassed him to utter the words *Petite Vendée;* and he went on quickly to talk of Merville. There too they would be in a citadel of the Monarchy— again omitting to mention that Merville was but one of the centers of the rising of La Vendée du Nord, which he preferred to call "le Pays de Lalloeu" (thus naming the part for the whole)—in the days when Buonaparte had been sinking ever deeper into the Russian snows. And at supper yesterday evening, in this very spot at Saint-Pol, had they not again heard the story of that wonderful Merville youth, Louis Fruchard, whom they called Louis XVII because he was the seventeenth son of his family, and who had seized the subprefecture of Saint-Pol, with a cockade of white paper bearing his nickname pinned to his hat, wearing a wagoner's blue overall with yellow paper epaulets pinned on his shoulders? Merville was, in fact, the capital of the rising. Fruchard had had nearly twenty thousand armed men in the two departments, and in February 1814 they had been supported by a detachment of Cossacks and Hussars from the Czar's Army, under the command of Colonel-Baron de Geismar. . . .

"Look at the map, my son, and you, Monsieur le Maréchal. . . . You will see that for nearly nine leagues there is not a village whose name does not figure on the glorious roll of honor of the monarchist insurrections. It is as though we were entering a great forest of loyalty. It is, in fact, a country of forests."

"And marshes!" grumbled the Duc de Berry.

In conclusion, the Comte d'Artois said plainly that during this time the least mobile but the most sizable part of the Household, extending over roads that would cover their march toward Lille to the south, would constitute a shield and a decoy, if need be, for Exelmans's soldiers.

Marmont looked at him. Was Monsieur ready to abandon the main part of his troops, and *even the baggage,* in order to ensure his own safety? Perhaps this was of no concern to him, with his carriage in which he lugged along those mysterious small casks. . . . Marmont had not said a word, but the Comte d'Artois read his thoughts. "Monsieur le Maréchal," he said somewhat haughtily and with great dignity, "a Bourbon must think first of all of the future. And, whatever the sacrifices involved, the heartbreak caused by certain things, must first and foremost preserve the dynasty." Saying which, he placed his hand on the shoulder of his son, of that son who begat children as easily as one breathes.

The assembly at Saint-Pol was accordingly broken into two columns. The one that set out for Béthune inherited M. de Mortemart's cannon, which were ill adapted to rapid movement or to the roads the other was to follow. The Béthune-La Bassée road was the only paved one in this region. And besides, they might be of use at Béthune if it should become necessary to sustain a siege. But the movements were in fact kept secret, and the unit commanders believed that it was simply a matter of employing two roads to hasten the march, and that the two columns would eventually converge on Béthune, the one passing through Lillers and there making a right turn in the direction of that town.

This was what M. de Mortemart, who with his guns was accordingly in the column making for Béthune, had told his cousin Léon de Rochechouart, who was in the Lillers column among La Grange's Musketeers. Only a few moments later, in the street, M. de Rochechouart met the Marquis de Toustain, the Wagram Guard with whom he had arrived at Beauvais by carriage and whom he had known since his earliest youth in Portugal. As he happened to be assigned to follow the same itinerary as the Black Musketeers, M. de Rochechouart was committing no indiscretion in repeating to him what he considered to be true; namely, that they were making for Béthune by way of Lillers. But the name of Lillers struck the Marquis. Lillers. Balthazard. Balthazard was his brother-in-law de Chermont, Mme. de Toustain's brother. It was to Lillers, among his wife's family, that Balthazard had chosen to retire. The idea occurred to him to outdistance the column and drop in on the family and give them a hug, and he persuaded a friend of his, M. de Montbrun, a lieutenant with the Swiss Guards, who was traveling in a small swift carriage—a cabriolet with a wonderful horse that he had been fortunate enough to find at Abbeville—to accompany him to Lillers, convinced that Lillers was on the shortest route to Béthune, having no map to make him realize the absurdity of that bit of information spread by Léon de Rochechouart. By setting out immediately with that trotter they could gain an hour on Monsieur and rejoin the troop as it passed.

The assembling of the Guards and Musketeers, in fact, already
gave them half an hour's start, and even though the road was drenched
it was not yet half past seven by the time the cabriolet delivered them
at Lillers. Balthazard was not at home and was presumed to be at
Lille, and Mme. de Chermont, whom they had got out of bed, was
worried by rumors brought back from there this very morning by a
potter who had returned in the night with his vehicle, rumors already
repeated to her by her servants. What? The Lille garrison had revolted, had donned the tricolor? And what about His Majesty, then?
The Comte de Montbrun felt that this was very serious and, leaving
Toustain to his family effusions, went off to get further information.
The potter could not be found; he must have gone to bed after a
night on the road, having lugged his merchandise in a wagon for
twelve and a half leagues. But it appeared that he had reached Lillers
in the company of a carter who at the moment must be wetting his
whistle in an *estaminet* at the lower end of the Place de la Mairie.

During this time, that part of the Household which accompanied
the Princes and Marmont was traveling along the road from Saint-
Pol to Lillers by way of Pernes. The region, to which MM. de Toustain and Montbrun, completely absorbed in conversation in their
carriage, had paid little attention, was quite different from that which
they had traversed on Thursday. The road, lined with trees, full of
ups and downs, passed through wooded country sprinkled with
thatched houses that bore little resemblance to those they had seen
in Picardy. In this part of Artois, which borders Flanders, there was
none of the stagnant waters, the disorder, the dirt, which had so distressed Monsieur the previous days. Here the doors of the whitewashed peasant dwellings opened on to interiors reminiscent of Dutch
paintings, so clean and polished were the kitchens, so shining and well
kept the furniture and the tiled floors. The hamlets nestled in clumps
of trees—which was all very fine, save that there was no sign of the
famous monarchist loyalty which had caused the Comte d'Artois to
choose this route. The inhabitants had not been forewarned of the
passage of the loyal troops, and nowhere were white flags to be seen.
The peasants were already in the fields. Pernes, where blood had been
shed for the King, was but a big village whose center, surrounded by
its white houses, was composed of a great meadow where sheep were
grazing, and this was about all of it that they saw. The Duc de Berry,
with that nervousness which characterized him, came and went along
the column; but today he had abandoned the Little Corporal manner
and spoke to no one. The white cloaks of the Guards made him think

of the Pernes sheep. His father had at last succeeded in communicating to him a feeling of insecurity, from which he had been miraculously free until now, even though it prevailed among nearly all the troops. And what would it have been if they had heard the conversations that the Comte d'Artois was having with Armand de Polignac and François d'Escars in his heavy four-wheeled green carriage, marked with the royal coat-of-arms!

It took them barely two and a half hours to cover the six leagues that separate Saint-Pol from Lillers, but here they had to treat themselves to a good halt. The town, in the middle of a plain dotted with large clumps of trees like those surrounding the Chermont dwelling, was disposed around two great squares linked by a short narrow street. On the first, which was the fair ground, there was a rather attractive-looking inn where Marmont invited Monsieur to enjoy a rest. But someone, I don't know who, had told the Prince that at the far end of the second square there was a chapel dedicated to Our Lady of Sorrows which was claimed to be miraculous. Having expressed the desire to go and pray there, as was fitting on Good Friday, Monsieur left his equipage in charge of the Light Horse Guard and headed for the sanctuary. The anxiety that gnawed him had awakened his religious feelings. Ever since Mme. de Pollastro's death in England, Charles had exhibited great piety. But the thought of Exelmans's horsemen had magnified his morning fervor. All right, let him pray, if he wants to pray, thought Marmont: and he entered the inn where he ordered fried eggs and bacon. *"L'Venderdi Chaint?"* exclaimed the servingmaid. The Marshal retorted that the Pope dispenses the military from fasting in the course of a campaign and smiled at the girl, who was handsomely buxom, the way he liked them.

Monseigneur the Duc de Berry had accompanied his father to the chapel, but he did not enter it. His eye was caught by a curious brick and white stone house just opposite, whose sculptured wooden gable formed the angle of the street; its ground floor was occupied by an *estaminet,* and this gave the Duke a great thirst for beer. There was something about it that reminded him of the public houses in London, where he had spent a good deal of his time as a youth when the throne had been something distant and altogether hypothetical to him. "Shall we go and have a drink?" he said to La Ferronays, who was distressed by this vulgarity, but who made it a principle to gainsay Monseigneur only on extreme occasions. There was no preventing the Prince from mingling with the riffraff.

The temple of Our Lady of Sorrows was tiny, but it retained the ostentation of the previous century of royalty. Upon entering it, the Comte d'Artois was struck by the shadow of a kind of vestibule, separated from the bright chapel where some ten men and women were praying on their knees by a solid wooden screen to which old women and beggars were clinging. It suddenly seemed to him that he had no right to pass this barrier, that, not having gone to confession, he was not sufficiently pure to cross this separation between darkness and divine light. How would he celebrate his Easter this year? And where? He mingled with the poor and seized the great wooden bars with his hands, bowing his forehead against them. Over there on the other side, a priest kneeling before the altar was reading an indistinct text, to which the faithful responded. This was not a mass: on Good Friday mass is in the afternoon. Monsieur could not hear the words of the prayers. He was not able to see clearly the large paintings on the side walls: to the left, he thought he made out a very strange Descent from the Cross, but his eyesight was decidedly failing.

He sought in his memory everything that the teaching of long ago had left there of that day of the Passion and of the Death of Our Lord. And he remembered that it was customary on that day to read a passage from one of the minor prophets—who was it? Hosea, I think, where it said: *O Ephraim, what shall I do unto thee? O Judah, what shall I do unto thee? for your goodness is as a morning cloud, and as the early dew it goeth away. Therefore have I hewed them by the prophets; I have slain them by the words of my mouth. . . .* And he moaned. And he pressed his brow harder against the wooden pillar, and he did not notice that the wretches were drawing away from him, were backing into the vestibule as though it would have been criminal for them to remain there, around this Seigneur, even though they did not know he was brother of the King of France. And as far as that went, the brother of the King of France was now nothing more than a fugitive.

And he moaned again. "My God, my God, forgive us if our goodness has been but the early dew: yet have we not restored Your altars, have we not replaced statues in the empty niches at the street corners, in the abandoned chapels by the roads? Now You are giving the ungodly the advantage over us. Recalling to chastise us the one who dared abduct the Priest from Rome. . . . And on this day of Your crucifixion, do You not see that we too are crucified? My God, forgive me, here I am reproaching You while the cross is being raised, and I hear the hammer and the nails. . . ." And he repeated in a low voice the first words of the Passion according to Saint John:

When Jesus had spoken these words, He went forth with His disciples over the brook Cedron, where was a garden, into which He entered, and His disciples. . . . And Judas also, which betrayed Him, knew the place. And he thought with fearful anguish of Exelmans's horsemen. Did they also know the place? Where was the Cedron, and where would the sons of France cross it? "My God, my God, forgive me for comparing what is not comparable, what it is a sacrilege to compare."

The Black Musketeers and the Lifeguards, with their horses, were gathered on the two squares, forming an encampment of vastly greater dimensions than the fairs that were customary there. They brought water for their animals, which was quite simple at Lillers, a town full of springs in which almost every house had its well. The people were proud of this and spoke contemptuously of Béthune where they drank water from tanks. . . . That done, they left one comrade to take care of ten mounts and the other nine spread out, going to the inn, to the *estaminets,* to the private houses into which the inhabitants were inviting them, offering them food. Yes, the people here had a certain weakness for the Royal Household: they had evil memories of the time when the Emperor had actually had the town occupied by his soldiers because of the bad spirit of the region, in which almost all the youths had been recalcitrant.

So it happened that the wineshop across from Notre Dame de la Miséricorde was full of Guards and Musketeers when Monseigneur the Duc de Berry entered with his two companions. He had been recognized, and the people stepped aside respectfully to make room for them. Except for a very excited Swiss Guard, whose back was turned and who was talking with gestures to a person with a mustache, dirty and unshaven, wearing a Russian-type cap with drooping earflaps, and a torn sheepskin coat which covered a kind of blouse and exhibited strands of grimy wool through slits in the leather that was shiny with wear.

Monseigneur was about to give the rude young man a dressing down when he recognized him to be someone he knew. It was M. de Montbrun, a man of his own age who had been his guest at hunts on several occasions, on account of a girl-cousin of his who had a rather pretty face.

"What the devil are you doing here, Montbrun?" he exclaimed, "and in what company!" For really, the man he was talking to must be either a beggar or a bandit. And M. de Montbrun, saluting Monseigneur, hastened to explain the nature of his conversation. This fellow—and the "fellow" gave a rather aggressive smile; he did not seem to realize in whose presence he was—had just come from Lille with a wagonload of pottery, and he was saying that the garrison there had rebelled, had hoisted the tricolor, and the people were following its example. . . .

Berry flew into a temper and flung himself on the man, shaking him by his leather coat and shouting, "You lie in your throat, you churl!" The churl shook him off disdainfully, while Montbrun anxiously explained to him who Monseigneur was. This did not seem to impress the man greatly, but it did deter him from what might have been a violent physical reaction. He looked the Prince straight in the eye and said in a voice hoarse with fatigue and lack of sleep, "I have, Monseigneur, merely answered the questions asked me by this gentleman who seems to be a friend of yours."

What impudence! Nantouillet came forward. This man must be apprehended, questioned, made to explain who he was. The Guards who surrounded them came closer, threateningly. "Let him be!" said Berry, waving the others away. "I'll question him myself." He turned toward the troublemaker. "Come now, my good fellow, who are you, to begin with? And what confidence can we have in what you say?"

The man in the sheepskin coat, who had folded his arms, now unfolded them. "I don't ask for your confidence, Monseigneur," he replied, "and you may believe me or not, as you please. The garrison there is wearing the tricolor, and there are perhaps ten thousand men in the city who become quite furious when they speak of the possible entry of the Household into Lille. I heard a Cuirassier officer say in the street that if the Guards dared show themselves at the gates, they would be allowed to enter only to have their throats cut."

His haughtiness of manner, and the educated character of his speech which contrasted so sharply with his garb, caused the Duc de Berry to change his mind. Still with a certain majesty, but in a softened tone, he said, "I do you the honor, monsieur, of asking your name . . . and where you come from."

A rather indefinable expression came over the man's face. "My name, Monseigneur, would probably mean nothing to you. Where I come from, on the other hand . . . I come from the fortress of Petropavlovsk, in Siberia." The Duc de Berry was about to exclaim that he must therefore be one of Buonaparte's brigands when a new-comer, in defiance of all etiquette, shouted, "Petropavlovsk!" on a note of surprise that caused everyone to turn and look at him.

It was the Marquis de Toustain, who was looking for Montbrun, having heard the King's horsemen arrive. The name of this distant fortress evoked in him memories of the past when he had been exiled there, together with his uncle, M. de Vioménil, by Czar Paul the First in the last days of the previous century. This he hastily explained to Monseigneur by way of excuse. And suddenly this became a kind of confirmation of the stranger's story. If this Petropavlovsk existed, if M. de Toustain could testify to a reality so remote, of a Petropavlovsk where Marshal de Vioménil had been in 1798, then the words of this bizarre character must be considered in a quite different light, and it might be necessary to take what he said with some seriousness. Should he not be taken before Monsieur? Certainly he must not be allowed to speak of such grave matters before the troops.

"Gentlemen?" said the Duc de Berry on a note of interrogation, and he paused, his big head turned in its collar between the hunched shoulders as if in search of someone. "Who is in command here, gentlemen?" And seeing the green rosette worn by most of those who surrounded him, he added, "You are Garmont's Guards; where is your commander, gentlemen?"

A movement over by the door, as though someone were being fetched who was only a few paces away, seemed immediately to bring back the officer requested who had literally come running in from the street. He had been found on the doorstep of the chapel where he had been waiting for Monsieur, who was still plunged in his reveries.

"Ah, it's you, Reiset?" said Monseigneur. "Have this man brought to the inn, so my father . . ."

A flicker of astonishment animated the face of the man in the sheepskin coat, then immediately vanished as he began to move toward the door. "I shall go there, Monseigneur," he said with a respect which his flashing eyes belied, "without need of anyone to show me the way. It is the inn on the other square?"

The people moved aside to let him pass. Berry simply called to him, as though to give him permission: "You have forgotten to answer me: your name?"

"I am Captain Simon Richard," said the man, "of the second Hussar regiment. But I beg you, M. de Reiset, if I understood your name correctly, to refrain from touching me . . . I loathe that kind of promiscuity." And he violently thrust away the hand that Tony had placed on his shoulder.

Left to themselves at the inn after listening to the returned prisoner-of-war, Monsieur, his son, and Marshal Marmont looked at one another anxiously. The testimony was unimpeachable, the details were too precise to have been invented, and the man himself of a caliber not to be judged by his clothes. What were they to do? Continue on the road to Lille at the risk of running into a party of rebel soldiers outnumbering the less than fifteen hundred men they had left of the Household? It would be best to fall back on Béthune, so that they could at least give orders to those they could not take with them. And then there was the baggage, the carriages, the horses. As a matter of fact, Monsieur carried his own treasure with him in those small casks that cluttered up his carriage. For *he* traveled in a carriage. Only now and then would he have a horse brought to break the monotony of the journey, and to show himself to the troops. At Béthune, in any event, they would soon find out how things stood. There would perhaps be a message from His Majesty? *Hmm,* Monsieur was doubtful of that. But anyway, how far were they from Béthune? A little more than three leagues. . . . On horseback they could reach it by ten o'clock. This would give them time to think. A small vanguard might perhaps be sent to Lille . . . or they could appear with Mortemart's artillery. And if by chance the King were still there?

That Captain Richard believed him to have left. But this was based on words overheard in the street. He had not seen him, really seen him, seen him with his own eyes pass through the postern gate and leave the town. He had been told . . . people who had come from there . . . perhaps they were mistaking their desires for realities, or had the King simply gone for a ride? You're being stupid, my son. The King go for a ride in such conditions! But then perhaps he had gone to visit another garrison—with the secret desire of finding support against those Cuirassiers. . . . Between ourselves, I don't understand Mortier! Isn't he able to impose discipline on the troops under his command, or what? However, *if* His Majesty had left . . . where would he have gone from Lille? You said yourself this morning, Monsieur le Maréchal, that there was no better place to await the Allied armies. It was that captain who claimed that Louis XVIII had left. He had been quite unable to say *whither* His Majesty was bound; the man may have been mistaken . . . In any event, no one must be told anything. No reason would be given for the counterorder— Too bad that the designation of the stages between here and Lille had just gone out to the various units along with the marching orders. Pah! they would change their direction, that was all, and if anyone thought it strange . . . Besides, on leaving Saint-Pol they had very wisely let it be understood that they were going to join Lauriston and La Rochejaquelein at Béthune. . . . The remarks of the Guards who had been in the *estaminet* just now would carry little weight. And what had they really understood, heard, or simply believed? Ah, I have an idea. And what an idea! All they had to do was summon M. de Reiset on some pretext or other, and tell him casually, without too much insistence on secrecy, that this change of direction was the result of a message received from the King—it was very plausible, they hadn't heard from him for so long—whereby His Majesty expressed his desire that the Household should not march directly to Lille . . . That was it, his desire . . . if it was His Majesty . . . All right, they would discuss His Majesty's orders, which was better than if they were to discuss Monsieur's, because who was in command here? "Why, you, Monsieur le Maréchal. In my name, but it's you."

So then they had to get their people together. "Monsieur le Maréchal, go ahead and give your orders. . . ." Very good. The Comte d'Artois settled himself in his green berlin. Armand de Polignac prevented the small cask which had fallen from the seat from rolling out, and propped it next to him. François d'Escars sat opposite them.

When the man with the sheepskin coat saw the horsemen in the saddle, he smiled and murmured something between his teeth. Then he went off to find the potter in whose shed Le Rouge was resting. Captain Simon Richard was now absolutely sure of himself. He could return to the valley of the Somme. And even become Comte Olivier again. For he had looked Brigadier General Antoine de Reiset in the face, he had even felt Tony's hand on his shoulder and he had not trembled, he had not experienced the urge to leap on him, to kill him. . . .

Now everything was possible.

But Blanche . . . I wonder: can she have changed as he has, have become heavy and pasty? How old is Blanche now? She had been eighteen in 1802. Was it possible? Already thirty-one? A mature woman. And since he had seen Tony, with his double chin, the crow's feet . . . He would certainly look upon Blanche as a stranger. Thirty-one years . . . Women are old at that age in Kamchatka.

I say nothing about the children. Have I ever known them?

"I have listened to you carefully," Théodore said to the major, who was his host. "Since last night you have told me everything I needed to know to understand what I heard at Poix. Yet I'm no further ahead, and I find it impossible to decide one way or another."

They had been walking through the town and had paused in this officers' café at the foot of the belfry, in one of the houses leaning up against it. Before them was the spectacle of the Grand'Place, where Swiss Guards, Lifeguards and Gendarmes were encamped. The Musketeers had done sentry duty this morning on the ramparts and at the gates. Two cannon surrounded by Grenadiers were in front of the city hall. The townspeople and the carriages that had been abandoned here, the gates of Béthune being closed, added to the general confusion. Not to mention the long carts brought all the way from Beauvais, in which volunteers who had just arrived were sleeping on straw, and the lamentable effect of the white flags, discolored by rain, at the windows on the square. Since half past eight that morning men on foot had begun to arrive from Saint-Pol, entering Béthune only after long negotiations at the gates. The children of Béthune ran alongside the convoys, as though this were just a big celebration, skipping or playing leapfrog to the cry of *Falico-faliboulette!*

"If my only choice was between Napoleon and Louis XVIII," the Musketeer went on, "perhaps the mere fact that one of them is a fugitive and the other has the army behind him might influence my decision. But I am aware that there is a third choice: and the idiocy is that you who have convinced me of it are unable to convince me that this or that can favor this third choice, if I should feel impelled to adopt it. The trouble is you cannot answer one question, the very one that brute Houdetot put to me: why did the Emperor have to inflict the title of Count on Carnot when he called him to the ministry?"

The major shrugged his shoulders and went on smoking his pipe. What did that matter? You either did or didn't have confidence in Carnot, a republican who had never gone back on his ideals. The alliance of the army and the people was guaranteed by his presence at the Emperor's side, that was the important thing.

"Houdetot says that in doing that Napoleon refused to be the Emperor of the rabble. He sees the thing with all the bias of his caste. But I . . . I understand you perfectly well on one point: the only way France can resist the nobility and the Allies, the conspirators and the foreign armies, is by arming the people. Will Napoleon do it? Don't you see that he in turn is going to give France another Charter; he will call it a Constitution—and then what? Life and the round of festivities will go on as before in the mansions of the rich. The people will go on starving to death. If the army is victorious it will be used to intimidate the people. If it is beaten by the foreigner, it will be in for hard times, that's all. One day shouting *Vive le Roi!,* the next *Vive l'Empereur!,* and then beginning all over again. What is there for me in all that? I shall undoubtedly go back to Monsieur my father's if I'm given a chance. I'll go back to painting. That is my work. I am not a baker or a carter or a blacksmith. Do I prefer to paint under the Emperor, who wants to be portrayed without anyone to overshadow him on canvases that Baron Denon censors . . . or under King Louis, who gives prizes for good exercises to the glory of Henry IV or religious subjects consistent with the interests of royalty? Will nothing change in our lifetime? Can we help in any way? Or are we in Augean stables which no one, not even Hercules, can do anything to cleanse?"

The major said it was necessary for a man to believe he could change the world. The Revolution . . . everything they had seen . . . Of course things did not move in a straight line, there were reverses, setbacks. But . . .

"The Revolution . . . perhaps! How can I judge it? All I know of it is what I have heard. Yes, our fathers"—and here Théodore felt himself flushing, thinking of his own father—"anyway, I'm sure men of your age believed in a real world upheaval. All the great and generous ideas . . . leading up to what? To that blood bath. To those crimes. No, don't interrupt me! Everything they tell can't be just lies. Even if Robespierre was right. And I have an uncle who voted for the King's death; he has never tried to convince me. Crime begets crime, and the one that corrects the first is none the less a crime. Besides, what is the blood the Jacobins shed compared with that the Emperor has caused to be spilled? Listen, I don't give a damn about the Duc d'Enghien—that's not the point; but Napoleon. You will tell me that royalty was based on a patent crime against the people. And what about the Emperor? What did the people want? Why did they grow weary, why did they let themselves be frustrated? By way of rest, they got twenty years of war, and a police such as the world had never known. To be sure, events are irreversible, and on ascending the throne Bonaparte created this police, which I admit is necessary, but it overwhelms us, spreads its tentacles everywhere, controls, provokes. It is liberty which brings the police into being. For the purpose of defending and limiting it. Now Napoleon returns. But his return is not his triumph, nor that of the people, it is Fouché's."

He was speaking mechanically. His eyes were following the vast bazaar of uniforms, helmets and bearskins, coats childishly gilded, braided, trimmed, all the vanity of the epaulets, the accoutering of men as of circus horses, gold tassels, shoulder knots, plumes. All the tinsel by which he had himself been seduced.

"No," said the major with sudden fury, "Fouché is not the police, but *a* police—that of a group. And I don't know what political considerations place it under Carnot's orders today. But if anyone is the winner today, who can deny that it is the army? We see it even here, where M. de Maulde has had to consign troops to the citadel while the Whites and the Reds camp in the city, because . . . You saw those officers with tricolor cockades crossing the square in a carriage, without anyone's daring to stop them!"

"The tricolor cockade or the white," Théodore exclaimed, "that's the only choice you offer me! If the Imperial colors today mean the army rather than the police, don't you see it is only because the army is not the people's army but the force that serves to uphold the government, the instrument by which General Bonaparte governs? Yes, the guillotine has disappeared from the squares, but youth has been whipped into line, sent all over Europe to act as a police, and war pure and simple has been preferred to civil war. That is the only choice I am given, one pretext or another to shed blood—disorder or war, no other prospect! Lord, will it always be so? I can't look at a man without thinking of him as dead and bloody. Whether he belongs to one group or the other . . . Watch the way his mouth twists, his eyes turn up, his color darkens, pales. Ah, I shall be with the victims! It is not life that gives beauty its colors, but pain, the calm of death!"

The major shrugged his shoulders. They were alike, these artists! Beauty, beauty . . . That was not a point of view. Death— I ask you! They mixed everything up, reveled in contradictions. They were like Buridan's ass. "Listen, do you know the story of Buridan's ass, who like you hesitated between a measure of oats and a bucketful of water . . . equally attracted, and as a consequence unable to move? You know that Buridan was from Béthune."

Géricault sensed a note of contempt in the other's voice. His problem was in fact not that of Buridan: he felt himself repelled equally by the Empire and by royalty, that was all. "The ass, in this context," the major went on—and Théodore wondered if he had read his mind—"doesn't hesitate between the traditional throne and the Imperial throne, don't you understand? But between emigration and France."

France! That was perhaps the only word that could shake the Musketeer who had nothing of the soldier about him but the clothing—a painter torn from his canvases, from himself. He had lived among men for whom France ceased to be herself when a man left her, when the King abandoned his country. And suddenly he remembered the deserters of the Carrousel, those provincial squires who had not been able to bring themselves to follow the King to the frontier. So they had been right?

"There is no path for me to follow in this century," Géricault said, speaking again, and he seemed to be looking somewhere beyond the streets at things that were invisible from here. "Later, perhaps—when men have settled quarrels which don't excite me. Later . . . I'm going to paint, that's all. But what? That's the mystery. This people, perhaps, which has no place in the shadow of those whose glory it is to kill, to kill them. I shall give the people their place in my paintings. I shall paint them as they are, without hope, their strength wasted, their beauty squandered."

He was inventing this as he spoke. But after all, isn't thought always improvisation? "I should like to tell stories. With colors and shadows. Stories. To drown this noise of chains in our prison. Stories worthy of us, stories of new calamities. And then, I know: my canvases will be looked at, will be discussed, there will be a stir in the newspapers and the reviews for a certain time. After which, eyes will have changed, and painting too. I shall no longer be understood. People will speak of nothing but my *manner,* they will no longer hear what I was saying, what I shall have said. Faces change, feelings pass, giving way to others. David paints for eternity. I should have liked to be the painter of that which changes, of the captured moment. Look at Béthune on a Good Friday—no one will ever paint that. Some day painters will become wise. They will be able to content themselves with a bowl of fruit. I shall be dead before then. *Dieu de Dieu,* I shall be dead before then . . ."

"I don't understand you," said the major. "If I were you, I should go to the old-clothes dealer on the rue du Rivage and buy a civilian outfit."

Just as he was saying this a great clamor was heard, and people came running, and the horses that were hitched together turned their

heads and whinnied, and drums began to beat, drums that were trying to stir into motion dead-tired men and horses; and from the rue
Saint-Vaast, M. de Damas's Light Horse could be seen coming out
onto the square, with General Marmont and the Duc de Berry, followed by M. de la Grange's Black Musketeers, and behind them a
crowd of white cloaks, the Guards . . . Monsieur's barouche,
Guards, and carriages, more carriages, yellow, green, black . . .
with the baggage of these gentlemen, and their valets looking important.

The Princes were arriving from Lillers by the road passing through
Chocques. Another three and a half leagues. But it was not so much
the distance as the fear. The fear felt by the Princes who knew or
could guess. The fear felt by those who did not know and who were
disturbed by these changes in itinerary, these about-faces. The fear
of Exelmans and the Imperials. And then on returning to Béthune,
suddenly they had before them the disorder and the lassitude, their
own image as in a mirror, with the Household corps already dispersed, capable neither of defending themselves nor of fleeing. In
this town, within its walls, its gates shut by order, the counterguards,
the sentinels on the crests of the ramparts, the posts on the advanced fortifications. What was there to say about the road they
had traveled? After Lillers, for a while it ran through woods and
across pastures. Nearer to Béthune the earth became chalky, and
ahead was the panorama of the town, with Saint-Vaast, the citadel,
the belfry. It could be clearly seen that the town was perched on a
rock, with its irregular walls, its fortifications. To the right, and over
there to the north, were small woods with dropped stitches in the
fabric of the landscape between them and hills in the distance. A
plain already green . . . What was César de Chastellux dreaming
of? His horse carried him, he shut his eyes. He visualized Charles
de Labédoyère. Our uncle, too, had brought us up on Jean-Jacques
Rousseau. But the finest words do not justify disloyalty.

Ah, let us shut our eyes also. I lift my weary hand to my head,
I press my eyelids, one after the other. Now the future takes shape
in this waking half-sleep. No longer the future of a man this time.
And don't pester me with your brother-in-law, M. de Chastellux, I
have no idea what Labédoyère looks like. I know only that he will
be stood up before a firing squad. And it will be as though you
yourself were being executed. No, not *your* future. No, the future of
this landscape on which I have just shut my eyes.

In that future—which is our present—what has happened to the landscape? What is the meaning of this upheaval of nature? Whether I turn in one direction or another—toward Marle and Bruay-en-Artois to the south, or farther toward the east, Noeux, and that whole region which I can visualize; or on the other side of Gomeham to Oblighem, Vendin, Annezin—I see the plain lifted up in black mounds, strangely tipped at their tops by an oblique arm, and on some of them a greenness has already begun to spread. Everywhere incomprehensible buildings, with geometric, lunar forms, and tiny dwellings of men, of dark brick, all alike, a long boredom of poor red and black houses, nothing that recalls former times, not even the churches—everything has been so often destroyed, so often rebuilt at the lowest cost—just a place to sleep between one day's work and another, despite the tiny baroque gardens, the lean-to sheds and the dumps of refuse, and against the houses a row of flowers, poles for sweet peas to climb, on the walls large inscriptions in color boasting the merits of a leather jacket, a wine, mineral waters. . . . You have seen ants, driven away by fire, reassembling, rebuilding their anthill? Patiently carrying their eggs, dragging enormous twigs?

Here black dominates. It gets into the eyes, under the nails, into the pores of the skin, it impregnates the lungs. It makes those gigantic mounds of dust called spoil-heaps. The black that rises from the earth, the greasy mud of the coal, something like a breath of darkness which is exhaled by pale mouths and pigments the mucous membranes, the hands, the roads, the dreams of childhood and the decrepitude of premature old age. There is nothing, nothing left of the past. The domesticated waters form loops, the canals carry long flatboats, where blackness sits in meditation. Nothing is left of the past. Men's problems are no longer the same. Except for fatigue and hunger. They write big scandalous letters on the walls, with chalk or white paint: about one of them who has refused to fight under the command of a German general, against the deputies, against one war and in favor of that distant war, and the last posters call a general to power, or proclaim the union of three arrows, of a hammer and a sickle. . . . Everything seems to come from that discovery in the bowels of the earth, the coal that has invaded the countryside. Even those enormous grasshoppers on wheels, those red vehicles, those horseless trucks, whose size is on the scale of a measureless undertaking. The future. Has it chosen between Louis XVIII and Napoleon? Who reigns over this chaos after the deluge? The people? To whom do those hills of darkness belong? Those complicated machines?

A hundred, a hundred and forty and some years have passed. Nothing is recognizable any longer. The relations between men, their souls, their lives, the landscape—these have changed. Even what seemed eternal. That which is changeless can be painted. There are painters of that. Of what lives and what dies. Of despair and anger. Yet there is also something that cannot be painted. Change. Both in the belly of the earth, and in people's heads.

César de Chastellux reopened his eyes on what was. The countryside. A flat agrarian region, patches of woodland, their trees still bare, underbrush, and the first shoots in the green fields.

And before him Béthune, a big gray artichoke with some of its leaves torn off. César turned around, and looked in the distance to see if Exelmans's horsemen were coming. Like everyone else, he had this greater anguish of not seeing them come, when he knew for certain they were there, somewhere, ready to fling themselves upon the Household, preparing heaven knew what diabolical operation. But behind him, César saw only the King's horsemen, lagging, exhausted, anxious, the white cloaks, the helmets, the red dolmans. The plain. Flat as a man's hand, except for those denuded woods. Why should he expect it to be otherwise? The plain. With no black, triangular hills, topped by an oblique arm . . . What are you saying? The March plain, already green, spotted with chalk. As it had always been, as it would always be.

And, on approaching the town, they saw on the road a kind of charabanc, as for a marriage, with a red and beige striped canvas top, a festooned baldachin. Full to bursting, noisy, joyous. Uniforms. On the seat, on the running boards, and the whole crew on the benches, between the benches, standing. All of them were officers. The coachman, who was a lieutenant, whipped the four horses pulling the vehicle. What was the matter with them? Were they drunk? When the King's horsemen drew closer they saw that all the officers in the charabanc were wearing the tricolor, and they drove past the stupefied column with a noise of laughter and little bells, and great shouts of *Vive l'Empereur!* Where were they going? Who could tell?

Monseigneur le Duc de Berry, who was on the point of flinging his horse in their direction, stopped at a word from La Ferronays. It was true: they did not know what they had before them or behind. What was happening at Béthune? And who could tell: were these people joining Exelmans, or what? Shame. Big tears once again rose to the eyes of the Prince in whose veins was the whole future of the Bourbons.

The Princes and their troop were arriving from the Porte d'Aire, by the Marché-au-Fil; they crossed the Grand'Place to the lugubrious sound of the drums, the carriages following over the crude, uneven pavingstones, defeat and anguish written on the faces of the horsemen, horses and men crushed with fatigue. There was no need for words. The mingled crowd and the soldiers, the volunteers on foot, the Guards in the freedom of their long halt, the Grenadiers on duty before the town hall, the customers suddenly standing up in the cafés —everyone understood that this was the hour of a great disaster. But what exactly was happening? Where was Marshal Marmont leading his men? Was he not going to stop, had he not come here to assemble the divided Household, the scattered units, to reconstitute the train of the loyal troops so that they could proceed toward Lille, toward the King?

Instead they were moving like a convoy that passes through a town and is not setting up quarters. What did this mean? The question was not only in the minds of the military and civilian throng along the street, at the windows, in the cafés: it was lodged like a terror in the convoy itself, these horsemen marking time, massed in the narrow streets, passing through the anxious crowd; these horsemen who had traveled almost ten leagues since dawn, had inexplicably changed their route, veered their march to this town of Béthune which they had thought to be their objective, and who apparently were being dragged beyond, toward Lille where the garrison had rebelled. For on leaving the square, the head of the column had taken the rue Grosse-Tête and was turning into the rue d'Arras. . . .

Captain-Lieutenant de Lauriston was at the town hall with the sub-prefect, the mayor and M. de Maulde. Through the window he witnessed this spectacle and could make neither head nor tail of it. But look, they must tell Monsieur and the Marshal: they didn't know. They had not seen the Duc de Trévise's message! M. Duplaquet, the sub-prefect, dashed downstairs, taking the steps two at a time, with various officials at his heels. They ran, forced their way through the crowd and rushed between the horses' legs, catching up with the Comte d'Artois's carriage, which had already reached the rue d'Arras, across from the rue Serrée. M. Duplaquet could be seen removing his hat, and Monsieur making a sign with his hand to the coachman through the carriage door. The brakes ground, the wheels scraped on the pavingstones. What was the matter? Ahead, they were still marching. The horses behind bumped into one another's hindquarters, not responding quickly enough in their mechanical movement to the horsemen pulling on the reins. Monsieur had called a Light-Horseman, who ran down the narrow street in which he had barely room to pass between the wall and the column, in order to inform the head of the column, Monseigneur the Duc de Berry. . . . What was the matter? Monsieur's carriage could not turn around. François d'Escars jumped out of it. Armand de Polignac immediately followed him and held out his hand to the Comte d'Artois, who stepped down and put his plumed two-pointed hat on his head.

Brief orders, horses pulling back, several horsemen jumping down from their mounts . . . The Princes, and M. de La Grange, the Marshal, a whole group of generals whom it was difficult to recognize, along with M. Duplaquet and his companions who gesticulated and bowed and scraped, returned to the square, to the steps before the town hall, where M. de Lauriston welcomed them.

César de Chastellux had gathered a detachment of Light Horse before the town hall, and the Grenadiers had moved off, saluting with their sabers. What was going on inside? The inexplicable thing was this last-minute order, according to which they were not stopping at Béthune. A dispatch rider had been sent to the area commander with a message from Marmont. César could make nothing of it. And his father-in-law was in no position to inform him. M. de Damas was ill, he had been put into a carriage far to the rear and knew nothing. To a yellow coupé containing the trunks of the commander of the Light Horse and his son-in-law, the treasurer of the company, Deschamps had brought the portfolio containing his accounts, which had been casually tossed on top of the basket that held the silverware. César looked at the Grand'Place, which was even more tightly packed as the column surged back. He saw his cousin Louis de la Rochejaquelein pass, summoned to the town hall for consultation. He saw all the disorder and all the confusion, but his eyes became veiled with mist. He thought of Exelmans's soldiers who were apparently skulking around them, who would envelope the town if they did not get out at once. What would they encounter on the road to Lille? Garrisons were on the march everywhere. Who was giving the orders? Who?

And then, suddenly, all he saw before him was the image of that handsome devil, Charles de Labédoyère, whom he thought he had won over to the royal cause. Labédoyère triumphant, with that handsomeness of manner and appearance, that haughtiness of speech, smiling . . . Labédoyère, who would be shot when autumn came. And what if Labédoyère were among their pursuers? What if they were to meet face to face?

"Let's not stay here," the major said to Théodore. "Come to my place. We can reach the shop before the troops move on again. You'll be within reach of your horse, if need be."

From the rue Grosse-Tête, through the pottery shop, they went into the rue Serrée. Géricault wanted to make sure that Trick needed nothing. But here too Guards had poured back, M. Tocquenne's yard was full of horses, and the horsemen had dismounted, the workers at the forge were pouring out drinks for them. They were Guards of Noailles's company, with the blue braid, and all these people, delighted over a respite, laughed and fraternized. Oats had been brought to Trick as well as to the newcomers. They were drinking the King's health in the verjuice of the region. Théodore looked around to see who they were, and there were Béthune workers as well as the Guardsmen.

"Aren't you drinking, comrade?"

A tall lad with curly chestnut-brown hair and a pointed nose was holding a glass out to Géricault. They introduced themselves to one another. The Guardsman's name meant nothing to the painter: another petty country squire who had added some extra syllables to his name. He was from the Mâconnais and possessed an infectious gaiety, which was odd at such a time. But he knew Géricault's name. "Are you related to the painter?" he asked, and Théodore blushed and turned his eyes away as he said in a half-whisper that it was himself. "Ah!" said the Guard. "Monsieur, let us then drink to art, in this bastion of industry, among these worthy fellows who understand nothing about it! Do you know the painting of M. le Comte de Forbin? Apart from the beauty of Madame de Marcellus, his daughter, he is guilty of landscapes which in their way are reminiscent of Claude Gelée le Lorrain. He is a friend of my family's—but I am especially grateful to him for what is Italian in his painting. Ah, Italy, monsieur, you will never be wholly a painter until you have been there! You have never been to Italy? Let us clink glasses to the wonders beyond the Alps, to what awaits you there, in Italy!"

Suddenly the name of this Guardsman came back to Théodore's consciousness; he was not altogether sure that he was not mistaken, but the stress on the word Italy seemed to remind him of something:

"Your name is M. de Prat, if I heard correctly? Excuse my asking you to repeat it."

"That's right," said the other. "Alphonse de Prat de Lamartine, Monsieur Géricault. But you have not answered me: will you go to Italy some day?" And after a moment's reflection: "Have you by chance, monsieur, read any of my verses?"

"Not exactly," said Théodore. "But I have heard them recited. A girl . . ."

"Ah? True, my verses often please young ladies."

Théodore was by no means certain that it was his verses.

The war council held in the big assembly room of the town hall was not, this time, a small staff meeting, but rather a gathering of all the commanders around Monsieur, Monseigneur le Duc de Berry and the Marshal. Lauriston and La Grange were there, as well as the Duc de Mortemart, Louis de La Rochejaquelein, Étienne de Durfort, the Comte de Vergennes who commanded the Gardes-de-la-Porte and Colonel Druault who was in command of the volunteers, M. de Maulde and the civil authorities, MM. Delalleau and Duplaquet, the Marquis de Baynast. No one had called this chance meeting, in which the greatest confusion prevailed. Monsieur sent to fetch Charles de Damas, who had thought it best to remain in his coupé on the square, because he had a fever. But he came to add his voice to this conductorless concert.

The point had been reached where it was no longer possible, in face of the news of His Majesty's departure, to conceal the Household's real situation from the company commanders. Yes, Louis had left France without waiting for them. Without even informing them. Yet if they, too, left, it would be impossible to conceal this news from those who remained here; but it must not become known to the lower echelon of those who were to accompany the Princes.

What was that? *Who* was going to remain? M. de Lauriston and M. de La Grange both spoke at once. Were they abandoning the troops? No, no, the Marshal reassured them. It was obvious that in order to ensure the Princes' safety as far as the frontier, a large contingent of the cavalry, those who were best mounted, must escort Monsieur and Monseigneur, and there . . . well, they would see who was willing to go farther and who wanted to stay behind. This was all a question of what was in the treasury. They would not be in a position to maintain three thousand armed men in Belgium. Once the coffers were empty . . .

But by what route were they to leave? The road to Lille through La Bassée was the best, since it was paved; yet Monsieur was afraid of meeting a corps of the garrison on the way. They must avoid the neighborhood of all fortresses. Henceforth, the army meant Buonaparte.

Monseigneur the Duc de Berry again brought up the itinerary he had proposed that morning at Saint-Pol: to follow the Lawe River, by way of Lestrem and La Gorgue, and reach the region between Bailleul and Armentières where there were few frontier posts. They were at this point when they heard a muffled clamor outside, and M. de Damas, who had gone to the window, said that something resembling a panic was occurring on the square. The men were dashing to their horses, assembling at their officers' command, drawing their sabers, and suddenly there were cries: "To arms! To arms!" While the generals were discussing this among themselves, M. de Maulde was sent to see what it was all about, and Colonel Druault went down with him, much concerned about his law students.

They were met on the staircase by a Light-Horseman who asked them where the Princes were and, rushing into the council room, recognized the Duc de Berry and cried, "Monseigneur, we are lost! Exelmans's troops are storming the town!"

Then, in a great din, everyone and Monsieur crying, "My horse, my horse!"—all the commanders together with the Marshal, Monseigneur and Duplaquet the sub-prefect, the mayor and his assistants, all rushed down the stairs, frantically buckling on belts, adjusting swords, donning helmets. Outside, the disorder was further augmented by the continuing arrival from Saint-Pol of stragglers of the column—the unmounted men of various formations, Guardsmen, Swiss Guards, isolated individuals, heterogeneous groups—who, entering by way of the Porte de Saint-Pry, surged into the square through the rue Grosse-Tête and the rue du Pot-d'Étain, so that it was virtually impossible to get the troops back into formation; and Monseigneur had all the trouble in the world, first in finding his own and his father's mounts, then in assembling Grenadiers and Light Horse. Followed by volunteers and Swiss Guards on foot, all marched in the direction of the Porte du Rivage where Lancers were said to have just appeared and demanded admittance to the city. Citizens had harnessed themselves to two of Mortemart's guns and took it upon themselves to drag them to the ramparts in order to fire on the assailants.

It is not a great distance from the Grand'Place to the Porte du

Rivage, through the dirty street congested by butchers' stalls, bones scattered over the ground, pools of stagnating blood from the slaughtered animals. The troop passed down its length on horseback and reached the gate, which Monseigneur ordered opened to let him pass.

There were none of Exelmans's soldiers here, any more than there were elsewhere. These were two squadrons of the 3rd regiment of Lancers. They had passed through Béthune on March 21st, coming from Aire where they were garrisoned; at that time they were continuing the movement toward Paris which the King had ordered the week before. But, on reaching Arras, they had learned of His Majesty's flight and, under the command of General Teste, had rallied to the tricolor. This morning, on their way back to their garrison, they had appeared at the Porte d'Arras which they had found shut, and had parleyed in vain for admittance to Béthune. A spirited exchange of words at this gate had started the panic that had swept through the town. Their colonel had said something totally uncalled for, and in a strong military vein, such as "If you don't open, I'll take the town by storm!" After which he had ordered his men to take the road that circles the ramparts between the Porte d'Arras and the Porte du Rivage, and had disposed his men in formation on the meadow called le Marché-aux-Chevaux which slopes down from the gate to the canal. There was no reason for the incident to have occurred; the Lancers would have gone off by way of the drill ground and the suburb of Catorive, since in order to get back to Aire they had to follow the road that begins at the Porte Neuve. But the arrival of the Duc de Berry and Monsieur, with their imposing guard, prevented this movement. When the Porte du Rivage opened, the Lancer colonel in turn believed himself to be under attack.

It must be understood that at this moment Monsieur and his son considered the massing of the Lancers precisely at the Porte du Rivage, through which they must pass if they decided to follow the Estaires upstream past Lestrem, to be a strategic maneuver. Whence their haste to run and defend the exit toward the frontier, which they were quite ready to believe—by heaven knows what process of divination—the Lancers were preparing to block. Noailles's Guards, hurriedly remounted, came running behind the Princes, and one of them, being improperly harnessed, still under the effect of the verjuice drunk at Tocquenne the blacksmith's, got himself tangled up in his weapons, so that a pistol went off. Pressed rump to rump, the horses quivered, especially as Monsieur, in front of them, wearing a plumed two-pointed hat, had nearly been thrown, and his horse started to gallop. The Comte d'Artois, who had had no intention of getting to the head of the column, decided to pretend he had done it on purpose, and urged his horse forward almost right in front of the Lancers massed on the Marché-aux-Chevaux. François d'Escars spurred his own mount to catch up with Monsieur. The Marshal and Monseigneur could not remain behind, and La Rochejaquelein's Grenadiers had no choice as to whether or not to follow the Princes, because of the Guards who were descending upon them from behind shouting, *Vive le Roi!* To which the Lancers naturally responded: *Vive l'Empereur!*

They looked very menacing, the two squadrons on their horses in the market meadow, under the bare branches of the trees, even though they were not more than five hundred strong. The Princes' escort had actually stopped between the gate proper, which was rather low and wide, the only gate of Béthune in the old style, and the outer gate which was flanked by two stone pilasters each surmounted by a sphere. The Duc de Berry advanced, with La Ferronays, Nantouillet and a few Light Horse, a dozen men, Monsieur and Marmont remaining behind.

Monseigneur looked at the Lancers with their gilt helmets, their sleeves and green trousers with yellow braid, and their blue breastplates striped with white leather, their white gauntlets, their sheepskin saddles. They had the tricolor pennon on their lances, and their sabers knocked against the flanks of their horses which they pressed between their black boots. The Duc de Berry trembled with rage: it was a regiment that he himself had visited and harangued. As he came up to the colonel, whom he knew, the nobility of his bearing was unfortunately somewhat compromised by a Grenadier who had taken it into his head that he was in danger, and who turned around toward the town behind him shouting, *To the rescue of the Prince!* Upon which the two cannon which the citizens had dragged to the ramparts hove into view and were pointed at the rebel troop, while the cavalry coming out of the town massed around Monseigneur who, instead of the twelve to fifteen horsemen he had expected to follow him, suddenly found himself surrounded by a swarm of men and horses, of all arms—the entire garrison was coming out, and there were Guards of Raguse's company, and Musketeers arriving from the Porte d'Arras, the infantry following them, and behind them the royal volunteers and the Swiss Guards, so that the Lancers found themselves almost enveloped, except on the drill-ground side, as though it had been intended to leave them the freedom to retreat in the direction of the Porte d'Aire.

Horsemen and foot soldiers of the Household now numbered nearly a thousand on this narrow space. The inexperienced volunteers who were coming up thought there were at least four thousand of them. It was in the midst of all this hubbub that Monseigneur, seeing the Cross of Saint-Louis on one of the squadron chiefs, went straight up to him, shouting, "By whose order have you left your quarters?"

The sequel is variously told. Actually, no one except the horsemen who were close to the Prince heard the actual words, of which nearly all historians have related only as much as was reported to them by the royal volunteers who, being at some considerable distance, heard none of them. The fact remains that a Lancer was seen to emerge from the ranks, waving his lance, and shouting: *"Vive l'Empereur!"* The Duc de Berry answered him, bellowing, his face so crimson that one might have thought he was having an apoplectic fit: "Get back into the ranks, you bastard, or I'll run you through with my saber!" There are people who claim that at this moment a Lancer captain recognized an intimate friend of his among the La Rochejaquelein Grenadiers, and spoke some very fine words: they might kill him, but he would not strike a Frenchman. . . . At least that was what was heard by César de Chastellux, who was thinking of Labédoyère. All this is very confused, like the fact that Monseigneur had stuck his naked sword against the chest of a Lancer corporal who had nevertheless shouted *Vive l'Empereur!* . . . and at all events the threats of the first moment were forgotten, and the Duke called on the colonel to have his men withdraw. Which proved more effective than the shouts of a moment before. While the colonel assembled his men and ordered them to withdraw toward the drill ground, Monseigneur, quite uselessly, called after the Lancers *Vive le Roi!;* the only effect of which was that when at a certain distance the Lancers repeated the cry *Vive l'Empereur!*

There was nothing for it but to turn back into the town.

For a number of reasons the Princes found it impossible to depart earlier than about four in the afternoon. First of all there was the extreme confusion that prevailed everywhere, the general ignorance as to whether the Lancers had really withdrawn or not, whether they were alone or constituted an advance guard, whether other troops were going to appear at the gates. But above all, the men of the Household were at the limit of their nervous and physical endurance; they had to have time to get their bearings, to eat, to reassemble. Apart from all this, Marmont was not certain of the route to be followed, of the men to be chosen for the escort. And then Monsieur had disappeared. Where was he? There was great agitation in the town hall, but M. de Polignac allayed everyone's fears: the Comte d'Artois was at Saint-Vaast; he was at confession.

"Fortunately," the Duc de Berry said to La Ferronays, "we are in a town where the entire population is for us. I could see that last year; and just look at the white flags at the windows."

The truth was that a number of white flags had already disappeared, and in many homes the women were busy sewing red and blue on them. The sky was very dark. Rain was to be expected again, and the Guards looked at the clouds and at their cloaks which had hardly dried. Were they going to have to sustain a siege in this town or leave it, and if so, for where? Where was the King? Oddly enough, in this respect the secret, though it was shared by nearly thirty persons, was kept—sufficiently so for Tony de Reiset, for example, to believe that His Majesty was waiting for them at Lille. Orders had been passed on to him which he found incomprehensible. Choose the best horsemen . . . Were they then abandoning those they had come here to fetch? In each company the same tune was heard. The commands rang out, horses were moved, men were counted. Should they give up the rooms they had found on arriving this morning, each for himself as usual? No one knew what to say to the householders, all those good people who were wondering whether to put sheets on the beds or not . . . Or not. Everywhere those two little words conveyed the general anxiety.

Were the carriages going to follow, or not? Were they to leave everything, or choose which of their things to carry with them? Guards, Gendarmes, Musketeers, Grenadiers, rushed to the train of private carriages—either to their own or to that of a comrade to whom a precious bit of baggage had been entrusted. They could be seen in the streets, laden down beyond reason; if they really were leaving, they couldn't possibly take all of it with them! There were conversations with householders who were being asked to keep this box, that valise, this case, as a precious trust.

And then they learned that they were staying in Béthune. What? Not leaving? Yes, they were leaving—but not all of them. Well, *were* they leaving or not?

The anxiety and the dispersal were such that, except for a mounted detachment of Raguse's company in front of the town hall and the pickets on guard at the town gates, there was no longer anything resembling regular units, only a vast conglomeration of companies, a jumble of arms, in addition to which most of the unmounted men had transformed the Grand'Place into a kind of forum in which groups formed, discussed, broke up to join others. Orators stood surrounded by Grenadiers whose black bearskins would gravitate toward one another and by Gendarmes and Guards: a hotchpotch that was military only in the matter of dress. The civilians took little part in this, but nevertheless, and even now, at a decisive moment like this, white cloaks or red dolmans were seen to vanish into doorways or down alleys behind a petticoat. But most, truth to tell, had their minds on other things. The rumors going round were being commented on, here in low frightened voices, there with indignant shouts. It was the younger ones especially who made themselves heard. They went to question their elders, paying little attention to rank, and often the ages were reversed, and all, or nearly all, contemplated the thought of not following the Princes as an unmitigated disaster. If they had to die one way or the other, they preferred to die with them— But was it even a question of dying? They avoided thinking about a shame which was a good deal worse than death.

A restless Théodore had been unable to stay with his host. He had exchanged a few words with M. de Prat who, a small package under his arm, was off to go on guard duty at the Porte d'Arras. On the Grand'Place he looked for the Musketeers, but those he spoke to were no better informed than he as to their immediate fate. He found Moncorps deep in conversation with some volunteers—one a kind of beanpole, another a small dark chap with a girlish voice, a third a curly-mopped youth with a facial tic. These youngsters had only one fear, which was that anyone should have any doubts as to their loyalty to the royal family. They spoke excitedly of the scene that had occurred at the Porte du Rivage. Their admiration for Monseigneur le Duc de Berry's behavior was boundless. They still believed in the possibility of a sudden resurgence of loyalty which would see France rising as one to defend her Princes. They could not accept the thought of crossing the frontier, abandoning the country to the Ogre; but they were ready to do so if necessary. . . . "You too?" Géricault asked Moncorps. And Moncorps dropped his eyes. Théodore moved away.

Heedless of the crowd, jostled, walking at random, pushed against a gun battery by the passage of a group of horsemen who shouted to the crowd to make way for them, stopped suddenly by Swiss Guards involved in a quarrel with some Grenadiers who had mimicked their accent, buffeted right and left under the belfry, trying to reach the other end of the square and the Hôtel du Nord, where he thought he had glimpsed M. de Lauriston on horseback, he wondered once again what he had come here for. If, in the absence of something to live for, he could at least have found something in this scramble to die for! That energy to be spent, which perhaps is youth, and which he had heretofore been able to use only in his mad rides, filled him as never before to overflowing, to the bursting point, unendurably. At least something to die for. . . . What bitterness he felt when he thought of how he had foolishly refused to take his place in those wars in which men at least had fought! To have become a soldier at last—only to run away.

What was the meaning of this whole expedition? Except for a few raw youths who fell for every hoax, and whose loyalty to the Bourbons satisfied them as an ideal, what was in the minds of the rest of them, the immense majority, and their chiefs, Napoleon's turncoats and the *émigrés* who were again taking the road to exile? They were thinking of the few thousand francs they had been able to bring with them, of the case containing their dress trousers and their toilet kit which they had perched up on a carriage. It was pathetic to hear them. To see the fear on their faces. Fear of what, good God? Of being attacked, surrounded, besieged . . . and after that? Wasn't that war, and hadn't they chosen it as a calling? From Paris to Béthune, all they had had to do was to flee. They had not seen even the shadow of a gun, the mustache of a rifleman. Yet they were afraid. Of being wounded, of falling in the mud, of not having a roof to sleep under, of unequal combat, of the sword that strikes and the bullet that pierces—they were afraid to die. And they had found nothing more for which to die than had Théodore.

A column of horsemen had assembled on the square, and suddenly Théodore heard cries ring out all round him. *They're leaving, they're leaving!* It was true. Lifeguards and Musketeers. What am I doing here? Géricault asked himself, and he tried to reach the point where the horses were tied to find out from someone what, who and how. Within him he felt that stupid and inveterate sense of duty, that fear of not doing what ought to be done, which was inexplicable at such a time, especially in the light of the thoughts that haunted him.

It was the Princes' escort, headed by Marmont. But although, with the officers' spare mounts, it was composed of two thousand horses, it had only a little more than fifteen hundred horsemen. And of these not more than three hundred were Musketeers, both the Blacks and the Grays, under the sole command of M. de Lauriston, followed by the bulk of the Lifeguards. Around Monsieur's carriage, a green berlin with the royal coat-of-arms, was a group of Light Horse under César de Chastellux. M. de Damas's yellow coupé followed immediately behind. The Duc de Berry, in his Light Horse uniform with his gray oilskin cloak which made him visible from afar, was already advancing over the uneven paving of the rue du Rivage between the butchers' stalls. Then came some Grenadiers round another yellow berlin marked with fleurs-de-lis. Two barouches, six or seven wagons and two carts loaded with baggage. Artillery caissons but no cannon. More carriages. Guards brought up the rear. What? Was that all? It was not possible! The rest were going to be assembled, they would be leaving later, to cover the Princes' retreat. . . . The departure of the column had been the prelude to an immense general flight: the Grand'Place was emptying, everyone ran to his lodging, to his horse, to his company's office when there was one; and on the square there remained only those who were asleep in their vehicles, the traveling kitchens, bewildered infantrymen, the cannon.

With Monsieur's approval, Marmont had put Captain-Lieutenant de La Grange in command of the troops abandoned at Béthune, making Lieutenant-General Comte de Montmorin commander of the fortress, with Mortemart's cannon, the infantry, and a good part of the cavalry. The men who escorted the Princes had left town by the Porte du Rivage where the Imperial Lancers had been massed earlier in the day. Once they were past the postern, scouts were sent ahead; they crossed the Marché-aux-Chevaux, advanced in the direction of the canal, crossed it, made a reconnaissance, satisfied themselves that there were no troops in sight in any direction and returned to join the column which had formed in marching order on the Marché-aux-Chevaux.

The road, which more or less followed the Lawe, first passed through a small woods that presently hid the town from view. But by this time the character of the country had completely changed. First of all the road itself had no paving or fill; it led across a kind of marl in which the water stagnated, and within half a league after leaving Béthune the carriages began to have difficulties that forced the men to dismount to help the coachmen extricate them from the mud. The edges of the road were difficult to determine after the rains of the last days, the ground was so soaked that it was impossible to see the big stones against which the horses stumbled. At turnings when a road led off into the fields, the riders lost their way and suddenly found themselves on a horse knee-deep in mud, and they themselves got stuck when they dismounted.

The surrounding fields were in large part flooded. But where they were above water they were very green, and divided into great rectangles by ditches full of water along which willows grew near isolated farms. An even greater complication arose from the fact that the water courses that ran through the entire plain between the Lys and the Lawe, all the way from Locon, surrounded the fields and came and collected in the roadside ditches, so that the least swerve caused carriages or horses to fall into water up to the middle of the wheel or the chest. Stone steps some twelve inches apart, which formed a walk for pedestrians between the streams and the road, added further to the danger. One heavily overloaded wagon capsized, and a great fuss was made by the owners when their baggage had to be abandoned save for a few pieces which could be piled onto another wagon. The farther they advanced, the more impassable the road became. The horses had difficulty in pulling the vehicles. The horsemen halted to give their mounts a breathing spell whenever they came upon some relatively dry and solid ground.

The result of all this was that the convoy quickly broke up into sections, some troops outdistancing others, the carriages bringing up the rear. The Princes were accompanied by all the commanders of units which had been assigned to join the column with the bulk of their strength. Captain-Lieutenant de Lauriston with the Black and Gray Musketeers, and MM. de Villiers-Lafaye, de Reiset, de Fournel, de Léautaud, the Baron Lascours, the Baron Fabvier with the crack elements of the Lifeguard companies. M. de Damas was in his carriage, as was Lieutenant-General de Bordesoulle who had come to Béthune to rejoin the Household after having escaped from Stenay where his troops had rebelled. M. de Bergennes, M. de Mortemart and Étienne de Durfort had made room for the Duc de Richelieu in the other large royal berlin. Louis de la Rochejaquelein rode beside his cousin, Chastellux.

This was loyalty's last rampart. But men and beasts were exhausted by their uninterrupted exertions since Paris. And it had begun to rain again, a fine drizzle which brought on darkness well before nightfall. Moreover, they had been up and moving for more than twelve hours, and because of the general uncertainty no one had rested at Béthune. A sudden closing of the gates had separated the Marquis de Fougère from his Law School volunteers, who had tried to follow the column but had found themselves shut in behind the last carriages, and he was relating his misadventure to Léon de Rochechouart, who was in the van with the Musketeers behind M. de Lauriston, both of whom were escorting the Duc de Berry, more taciturn than usual. They had reached La Gorgue, near Estaires, where the Lawe meets the Lys, a point which marks the beginning of the Lalloeu region that the Comte d'Artois was always talking about. But the Comte, whose whole escort stretched out in staggered formation a good league ahead of him, had stopped even before reaching Lestrem, a distance of two and a quarter leagues from Béthune, which with great difficulty had been negotiated in a little over two hours. Monsieur's berlin had got stuck in the mud: while it was being extricated there was nothing for it but to get out. Might as well rest here. Where were they?

It was La Fosse, a hamlet of Lestrem. The houses and the ruined church were to the right, beside the Lawe. Monsieur's carriage had one wheel in the ditch, at the crossroads, but the local priest, alarmed by all this traffic as he was working in his garden at the close of day, had come to the road, and it was he who advised MM. François d'Escars and Armand de Polignac, who had got out of the berlin, to take the Comte d'Artois some hundred yards down the road to the big building that could be seen there on the left. It was the finest farm in the region and M. Joye, the farmer, was a hospitable man and loyal to the Monarchy.

Here they were really under water. The big stream had overflowed, the ditches were filled right up to the level of the road. The Comte d'Artois, in his loose cloak, with his two-pointed hat whose plumes seemed never to have been white, was carrying a small cask in his arms as if it were a baby. His two companions were doing the same. The reason was that the berlin was in a bad way, and Monsieur had no inclination to leave his gold on the highway with two or three artillery caissons.

The farm was called the Ferme des Ifs, because of the row of yew trees planted along the northern bank of the wide water course. It rose above this lowland like a kind of fortress, with a defensive gate, flanked by two towers, which led by means of a drawbridge to a space framed by broad, deep ditches. Beyond the gate was a meadow bordered by poplar trees; the farm was to the right, past another ditch, a large whitewashed stone building with a thatched roof. And behind, a barn taller than the house. The horses were brought here and the men of the escort found bedding. Inside, the height of the barn was startling, like that of a church, for the pillars were made of whole tree trunks transformed into columns. The beams were enormous. Here the farm implements and equipment were kept, and there were horses and a supply of hay.

Daylight was fading. With a respect that bordered on stupor, the farmer and his sons welcomed these great personages, at first not quite grasping who they were and what they were doing on these bad roads. The farmhouse's largest room, from which a stone staircase rose to the bedrooms, was meant to serve dinner to forty harvesters or more. The bearded peasants, with their women and their children, stood there, tall and strong, robust like pillars of an abundant life, finding sources of wealth even in the unruly waters of this desolate country. They were the *seigneurs,* and these Counts, these Dukes, these Princes, were descending upon them like exhausted gipsies, or a company of traveling actors who have lost their way between two performances in distant villages and continue to bear the names they assume when playing noble tragedies. At a word from the farmer, one of the sons lit a fire in the huge fireplace. It was very damp that evening. Cold, even.

How long were they going to stay? M. Joye, in his eagerness, had tried to relieve the Comte d'Artois of the heavy-looking cask he was carrying clutched beneath his cloak. "Let it be!" said Monsieur. "On this Good Friday evening we must continue to bear our own crosses. . . ." And he let himself drop on the stone steps of the staircase, leaning on the cask. The fire illumined the scene more brightly than the candles.

"But," said the farmer, "Your Highness"—he was not too sure whether he should say Highness or Excellency—"will have something to eat with us . . . if he wishes. Marie, prepare the big bed for His Highness!"

"Do nothing of the kind, madame," said the Comte d'Artois, and he looked as if he had truly reached the limits of his endurance. "I want no room, nor bed. I shall remain here."

"But Your Highness," said the man, "the stone is hard!"

"The stone is hard," Charles replied, on a grand note of fallen majesty. "That is all a fugitive like myself needs henceforth!"

And he would not be budged. Even to eat. He had to be served separately on the steps, his arm embracing the cask as though he were afraid of thieves. The room was so high-ceilinged and so deep that the candles licked at shadows everywhere. Like a fawn-colored carpet, the light from the fireplace stretched to the foot of the stairs. The half-dozen fine gentlemen who were the Joye family's guests this evening were drenched to the bone, and had taken off their boots and put their cloaks to dry. They spoke words that became comprehensible only when they began to inquire as to the condition of the roads beyond Estaires. Where were they going? Here Monsieur abandoned the dissimulation that he still displayed toward his whole escort and asked which was the point closest to the frontier. When he had been told that it was at Seau, opposite Nieuwkerke, it meant nothing to him. But once it had been explained that Nieuwkerke was the Flemish name of Neuve-Église, this meant more. "Are you quite sure, Your Highness, that a bed . . ." Monsieur repeated that he was a fugitive, and that the stone of the staircase sufficed for a fugitive.

This insistence made such an impression on the farmers that the phrase has been transmitted right up to the present day to the farmers who occupy the Ifs, which is no longer lined by yews, and where the farm has been rebuilt in another square section marked off by streams although one of the great beams of the barn can still be seen. And on stopping there the author of this book has heard it repeated that the Comte d'Artois said: "I am a fugitive, a fugitive . . ." Three wars have destroyed and redestroyed the farm, but the echo of that voice still sounds there, refusing a bed and claiming the right of a fugitive to sleep on stone.

M. de Polignac had stretched out on a wooden bench: not being a son of France, he was not entitled to stone. M. d'Escars was content to lie on the floor, his head on a sack of flour. At the door, two Light-Horsemen mounted guard. The casks had been rolled under the vast harvesters' table, the children had gone up to bed with the daughters-in-law and the grandmother, and the candles were snuffed out except one, which was placed behind a pillar so as not to prevent Monsieur from going to sleep. And M. de Damas, who had remained seated by the table like a schoolboy who does his lessons while everyone sleeps, dozed off on his elbows. For a long time those gentlemen who were not yet asleep heard the Comte d'Artois sigh as he leaned on his cask. The name of Jesus even came to his lips. . . . Then, however uncomfortably they were settled, not daring to ask for more when the King's brother demanded stone for himself, all eyes shut, one or two snores could be heard. . . .

And in his dream Monsieur pushed away his brother, who wanted to take his cask from him, and spoke to him about M. de Charette. Then Charles, struggling on a flooded road which, however, mounted to Golgotha, said, "No, no, never will I follow you to England! I shall not cross the Cedron, because on the other side there is Judas." And Judas, unmistakably, had the face of Father Elisée, who was saying: "Charles . . ." (what familiarity!) "Charles, give me your cask; if you don't give me your cask . . ." Charles knew perfectly well that he had owed enormous sums to that vile Torlachon ever since Quiberon, but he would not give him his gold, and Elisée Torlachon was holding up a menacing finger, saying: "When you get to England, Charles, remember this: Messieurs Lloyd and Drummond, to whom you still owe thirty thousand pounds sterling from the follies of your youth, will have you sued and thrown into prison for debt! You know that only I can arrange this . . . and that if you don't give me your gold I shall tell everything. And not only what pertains to money, Charles! For there are sins you did not confess to the priest this afternoon in Saint-Vaast—nor to any confessor previously. And you will be damned, Charles, for having dissimulated your faults before the Penitential Tribunal!"

Charles pressed the cask full of gold to his chest, and he murmured: "Never, never will I go to England . . . Rather die . . . Never will I cross the Cedron. Get thee behind me, Judas Iscariot, not from me can you demand your thirty pieces of silver! Forger, forger! It was you who wrote that damned Charette letter, it was you who gave it to the English! Never, never will I go to that accursed country. Get thee behind me, Torlachon, get thee behind me!"

But in the night at La Fosse, in the commune of Lestrem, above the stone staircase where the two-pointed, white-plumed hat rolled, a lunar landscape floated which no one saw or could recognize, a city composed of three hills connected by hanging causeways; a city inhabited by violent winds, where the view was limited by hills; the sea seemed to be there though it could not be seen. What was that palace set on an old street guarded by soldiers wearing the black fur busby, with a knot of ribbons and three plumes falling over the shoulder, coat of scarlet cloth, kilts of red-striped green woolen over bare knees, and red-and-white plaid stockings, the sporran at the belt, the silver-buckled shoes? Here hovers the shade of Mary Stuart, here Riccio her lover was murdered before her eyes. . . .

That is where you will go and end your days, Charles, Comte d'Artois, dreaming on your cask of gold—here you will end your days, in this palace of Holyrood, in Scotland. For in France you will no longer have even the hard stone of the staircase in the Ferme des Ifs, near Lestrem, to sleep on—soft as it still is to the fugitive.

It was not raining in Béthune, where all the windows were lighted, when Marshal Macdonald arrived in the pitch-dark at about eight in the evening. He was in the same carriage that had been repaired at Beaumont, but the horses he had been given on leaving Lille—those that happened to be available with the extraordinary comings-and-goings of those days—were not very sturdy, so that he had wanted to change them at La Bassée after traveling six leagues. But there were no horses in La Bassée, and he had had no choice but to rest. He had chosen this route instead of the road through Arras, thinking that he could reach Paris via Amiens without running into the military congestion in which everyone might not look with indulgence upon a Marshal still wearing the royal uniform.

At the inn, Jacques-Étienne ordered a light meal. Soup, and some vegetables—he didn't trust the fish. Yet he had had no lunch, and perhaps those terrible headaches he was having were due to fasting, although he had had a long sleep. No wine or beer, however. He could not get over the trick Mortier had played on him. Mortier, with whom he was to have spent the day, the friend whom he had been congratulating himself on having. Well, when Macdonald had sent word excusing himself for being late for lunch—just enough to give himself time to dress, as he had slept late—Mortier had canceled the meal. Already the Empire had been proclaimed, the troops had adopted the tricolor; and on telegraphic information from Paris the command had been put into the hands of Drouet d'Erlon, who had emerged from a hiding place where he had taken refuge early in March, after Lefebvre-Desnouettes's rising which he had supported. Mortier was leaving for Paris momentarily, summoned by Marshal Davout, the new War Minister. Well, things had certainly been done quickly! And I who was so happy at the prospect of spending a day with dear Édouard . . . Between ourselves, this was certainly the first time Macdonald had called Mortier Édouard, even to himself. There was too much vinegar in the salad. He summoned the waitress and asked her to make another, without any dressing—he would make his own dressing. When he thought about it—last January Exelmans had left his enforced residence and had been tried before the military tribunal of the Sixth Division; that is to say of Lille: Mortier had scandalously acquitted him then, hadn't he? And he had made no effort to put his hands on Drouet d'Erlon, with whom he had so promptly come to an arrangement this very morning.

But at this moment, in the adjoining room—for at the inn at La Bassée people ate in several communicating rooms—he suddenly heard his own name spoken by a young voice. He leaned over, saw a lad—a quite presentable stranger—who was toying with some letters, showing them to the person on the other side of his table. Jacques-Étienne was overcome by curiosity, he looked closer, recognized the letter that he himself had written Monsieur the previous day before retiring to advise him of the King's departure. And the young man's table companion laughed very loud and began to sing:

> "Bon voyage, Monsieur Dumollet!
> A Saint-Malo débarquez sans naufrage . . .
> Bon voyage, Monsieur Dumollet!
> Et revenez si le pays vous plaît . . ." *

Macdonald went in and made himself known, to bring these people to a sense of elementary decency. Who was the messenger entrusted with those two letters which should have been posted by the two routes at the same time, the one through Armentières and this one, in order to reach Monsieur, en route?

The young man blushed, but apparently felt no guilt. The dispatch commissary for the Royal Household, the one who had brought the dispatch Monsieur had sent from Beauvais to His Majesty, and who had been entrusted with the two messages, should have delivered one of them to this young man and taken the other himself by the second route. But it so happened that he had friends in Marchiennes—that is to say, less than six leagues from Lille, but in another direction—so he had got rid of both letters. . . . But you, young man, what are you doing? You received those letters before midnight, and you've got no farther than La Bassée. "I was told," the young man retorted with apparent good faith, "that I would meet the Household on the way . . . and then I arrived here, exhausted, and I had to sleep."

So Monsieur was still ignorant of the King's departure. Macdonald

---

* Godspeed, Godspeed, Monsieur Dumollet!
  May you land without mishap at Saint-Malo . . .
  Godspeed, Godspeed, Monsieur Dumollet!
  And if you're pleased, come back and say hallo . . .

retrieved the letters, and went off to his carriage in a rather bad humor. It took only an hour to reach Béthune, but it was not so easy to get into the town. It was like a besieged fort, although no troops were to be seen at the foot of or at the approaches to its walls. He had to parley endlessly at the Porte d'Arras, to which the road from Lille as well as the one from Arras leads. At the counterguard there were blue-rosetted Noailles Guards who would not listen to reason. Fortunately, an officer with them recognized the Marshal and told him that Monsieur had left with three hundred men upon the receipt of news from Lille. What news? By whom? Since the letters were there in his pocket!

But the truth was that when he reached the town hall, where he went straight upstairs to the town-commandant, General de Montmorin, he found an assembly of the officers who had remained in Béthune under M. de La Grange's orders. Apart from himself, they were brigadier generals and colonels, the Household commanders having all left with Monsieur. They felt themselves on the whole to be little known to their troops. They hesitated to apply the orders that had been left with them to assemble the troops on the Grand'-Place and tell them that His Majesty, on crossing into Belgium, would be unable to maintain them all, so that they were kindly requested to return to their several homes. These officers were highly embarrassed; they were not absolutely certain of the King's departure; they were afraid the companies might cry treason. . . .

Among these officers was M. le Général Dessoles, chief of staff and commander of the Paris National Guard, who had just reached Béthune, on his way to Lille to join the King in his capacity of Minister of State. He took Macdonald aside and got him to confirm what he knew of the King's departure. Had he really crossed into Belgium? That changed everything. General Dessoles had no intention of leaving his country. "You yourself, Monsieur le Maréchal, seem to be retracing your steps." There was between them at least one bond: their mutual love of music. Dessoles gave concerts at his home which were much talked about, in which Cherubini and the Vicomte Marin did not disdain to take part.

Well, there was nothing for it but to call the troops together on the square and let them know their fate. The Marshal was categorical; he told M. de La Grange this must be done, and it was therefore necessary to comply. In any event, nothing was final so long as the cavalry had not returned; no one here was qualified to carry out the formal disbanding. You, *mon général,* perhaps? . . . Why I, rather than you, Colonel? Macdonald watched them toss the responsibility back and forth like a ball. The road to Amiens passes through Doullens where he had been told at Lille—by Mortier—that Exelmans had his general headquarters. Oh well, they would see! Will you travel with me, Dessoles? But were they going to be able to leave Béthune? Because even though there had been no sign of Exelmans's horsemen at the Porte d'Arras, everyone in town assured him that the fortress was besieged, and that it would be madness to venture on the road to Doullens. . . . It was the road through Saint-Pol which led across the marshes and was reached through the suburb of Saint-Pry—if any of the gates were blocked, that one certainly was! They were told of the afternoon's incident involving the Duc de Berry at the Porte du Rivage. The town was surrounded—at some distance perhaps, but surrounded.

Dessoles accordingly climbed into Jacques-Étienne's carriage. He had witnessed Napoleon's entry into Paris—on the sly to be sure— and he was full of stories. Good. At the Porte de Saint-Pry, after the exit difficulties had been overcome, they found themselves on an absolutely empty road. The people at Béthune must be dreaming about Exelmans. They both laughed over the imaginary siege.

Never would Théodore forget the sight of the Grand'Place at Béthune in the torchlight, with the congestion of carriages, artillery pieces, the entire space filled by nearly fifteen hundred men, most of them youngsters all but mad with anxiety and impatience, among whom rumors were already circulating about some of their chiefs. Names were mentioned, at first only tentatively and circumspectly, but for one who whispered them there were ten who shouted them. Who? Well, M. de La Grange was there to do the dirty work and M. de Lauriston had gone off with the Princes. . . . They were only rumors. But at this tragic hour, the open windows, most of them lighted, from which citizens and their wives followed what was going on outside, the cafés illuminated with low lamps, the inadequate street lamps blotted out by the hand torches, the lanterns lighted in the unharnessed carriages by coachmen standing on the seats—everything shone with a false brilliance under the heavy sky into which the belfry rose. At this tragic hour, these young people were beginning to understand that they had been lied to for several days, that they were being led to unknown ends, were being abandoned to a destiny which they loathed. Naturally they were inclined to judge those who commanded them, to wonder about the thoughts of their chiefs, remembering their origins; and at this hour, Buonaparte's former officers were all suspect to them. They remembered what La Grange was, what Lauriston was, what the Marshals were. Weren't they going to return to their former master? And the word treason was on every tongue.

They were there in mingled groups; they had gathered from every corner of town, where drums had passed calling to arms. Some had come late and hadn't heard, so that everything had to be repeated to them, and in a rage they tossed their helmets, their shakos, their bearskins to the ground and began to weep like children. The guard posts had delegated a man to come back and keep them posted.

Suddenly Théodore, who by this time was almost ready to heed his host's advice and had a while ago taken a walk down the Rue du Rivage, where the butchers were clearing up their stalls, to see what the shop of that famous secondhand clothes dealer looked like—it was apparently doing a thriving business—suddenly Théodore felt his heart give way at the thought of leaving. He was shaken by the contagious force of this public despair, by these sudden explosions of anger, by the obvious violence of the feelings which must have been burning, concealed under the ashes. Was it possible? These futile lads, sons of good families whose Papas had bought them their officers' commissions, these youngsters who couldn't do anything but bray and drink, whom he thought he knew, were nonetheless rent by despair and the fear of dishonor, and must therefore have been possessed by loyalty and faith—by faith in things they did not understand perhaps, but by faith, by loyalty . . .

"No, no!" shouted a Grenadier, and no one needed to ask him what this outraged negation meant. A number of King's Gendarmes, a solid mass of them, had drawn their sabers and lifted them in the light of the torches. Even those pitiful volunteers who had worn out their shoes and bound their legs in canvas— Look at that tall fellow there, the expression on his face . . . And the Swiss, what was wrong with those Swiss, why were they beating their chests, shaking hands with everybody?

Where was Moncorps? Where was Houdetot? And young Vigny? In this crush that contracted, slackened, dispersed in the fantastic light where tied horses suddenly reared, he made his way through the crowd. A Lifeguard had been wounded and was being carried away. He was unable to recognize anyone, to locate an acquaintance. Especially as they were not grouped by arms since they came running from all directions. There were Grenadiers in front of the town hall; on the balcony was that new general whom nobody knew, surrounded

by miscellaneous officers, wearing all the uniforms of the Household.
. . . What was the name of the one who had just spoken? Lieutenant-
General de Montmorin. "Where does *he* come from? Is he in your
outfit?" "Hell, no."

And Théodore was dumbfounded by what he heard, because except
for the vocabulary it was extraordinarily similar to what he had heard
that night at Poix, from altogether different lips. They too spoke of
la patrie, they too spoke of peace. And women came out of the houses
and went up to these sobbing children and took them in their arms
and wept with them. They had believed they had the strength and
the numbers, they had believed right was on their side, the country
behind them. And here they were being delivered over, it was quite
clear, delivered over to that phantom army by which they had felt
themselves surrounded for days, followed, spied upon, which was
there, but which they could not see, of which they had seen only those
Lancers earlier, traitors to their King, still wearing decorations received from the hands of Monseigneur the Duc de Berry. . . . They
had been brought into Béthune in complete ignorance, they had
thought it was the next stage, and then it turned out to be the trap,
perhaps long prepared—the trap that had closed on them. They were
prisoners! What good were these weapons in their hands? these cannon
which they had been dragging all the way from Paris, and which had
not fired a single shot? And on whom, indeed, could they have fired?
There was no enemy, there was only a vast conspiracy into which they
had been drawn by unworthy chiefs, and they, the unfortunates, the
imbeciles, who had believed in everything, in the flag, in the fleur-de-
lis, in the dynasty . . .

"What's the matter?" cried a Light-Horseman to the volunteer who
was talking. "Don't you believe in them any more?"

No one heard the reply. It was like a dance of specters; they
changed places, seemed to salute one another, met and turned back.
There were more and more groups; the men pushed one another in
order to hear what a comrade in the center was saying; they leaned
on one another and there were cries: *"We must fight! We won't
surrender!"*

Yes, how could they believe what they had just heard? *The King,
forced to leave Lille, unable to count on the loyalty of the troops that
form the garrison of this fortress, regretfully finds himself obliged to
leave France.* . . . When those words fell from the balcony not everybody heard them, and many who did thought they had misheard. It
had to be repeated. That general whom nobody knew: *The King,*

forced to leave Lille . . . and the whole story flew from mouth to mouth . . . *and is withdrawing to Belgium.* When had it happened? There were people who said two days before, others just yesterday. Meanwhile it had been kept from them. They blamed the only general officer they knew, La Grange. The Princes had left with their escort, when all of them, all of them, wanted to accompany them. *The King thanks all those who have remained loyal to him, urges them to return to their homes, and there await better days.* What did that mean to most of these men? To those who had spent their whole lives in the service of this king who had abandoned them, who had known emigration, the humiliation of serving under foreign officers, who had crossed Europe, from country to country, wherever the Usurper still left a little room for them, on the fringes of the armies and the campaigns. Their homes! Return to their homes! And the mockery was not less for these youngsters who had taken up arms, believing, as their elders had believed in Condé's armies or in those of Napoleon, that they were embarking upon an epic adventure, upon a life that would envelop them in its excitement. *The King instructs the general officers to disband the Corps which may not enter armed into a foreign country.* . . . Unbelievable! It wasn't possible! It was not the King who had said this; where were the papers written with his own hand? What proof had they that they were not being fooled? It was an invention of La Grange's! He was discarding their standards! He was throwing away loyal hearts!

Never had Théodore heard anything like it. So it was not true that those heads were empty, it was not true that nothing made those hearts beat. They believed, these Musketeers, these Guards, these Grenadiers, they believed profoundly in this king, at the very moment when he abandoned them. It was a heart-rending scene, like that of a man who comes home and finds the house empty, his wife gone . . . and says with his heart bursting in his chest: "But she had no reason to leave me!"

The officers questioned, when they could be pinned down, interpreted the royal communication which, as far as could be understood, had been transmitted by Monsieur. Had not M. de Montmorin added that nothing was to be done until the cavalry had returned? The cavalry, or at least as much of it as had followed the Princes. For a good part of the cavalry was still here. Why this irresolution? If the King's orders . . . But that was it, they were not orders: the King had released them from their oath, and now they were free either to return to their homes, or to follow the King abroad. Who had said that? And wasn't it under the pressure of opinion, the fear of appearing to be in league with the La Granges and the Lauristons, who were becoming symbols of Buonapartist treason? Now groups began to crystallize here and there round a man who proved to be an orator. The men, even the youngest ones, ordinary Guardsmen with no regard for rank, interrupted him, asked him his name. "And who are you?" It was the Vicomte Riquet de Caramon or the Marquis Dubocage, it was the Comte de Saint-Morys or Baron Paultre de Lamothe . . . It was M. de Mondore or M. Labbé de Chamgrand. The men shouted: "Did you ever serve under Buonaparte?" They protested. There was applause for those who had belonged to the Princes' army. This was how Théodore learned the name of the lad he had noticed several times since Beauvais, and who was to be seen everywhere, a volunteer, lean and lanky, with long arms like a windmill, and what a talker! He was the one who had ridden between Poix and Abbeville in the wagon of that carrier who had blown his brains out.

At the foot of the belfry, a group of perhaps two hundred had gathered momentarily, and Théodore joined them. They were not all youngsters, for here were also older men, civilians attracted by the vehement words, coachmen who had stepped down from their carriages with their whips, children who had refused to go to bed. But most of them were of an age with the one who was speaking, who was perhaps eighteen. Ah, it was easy to see that he was preparing himself to be a barrister; what a gift of gab! Actually, he was well aware that opinion was in his favor, and he gestured wildly to supplement the fire of his words. But to be quite fair, he spoke well. In his words you could hear the sound of flags rippling in the wind and he held his gun in his hand. "The Princes," he said, "could not order us into exile with them. See with what grandeur they release us from our oath! But what do they truly expect of us? Can the French heart accept surrender? It is up to us to accept the sacrifice, the misfortune of exile. Let us be equal, I say let us be equal to the destiny that awaits us—bitter yet great, severe and difficult!" Here someone who had not heard his name the first time he had been asked interrupted him by shouting, "What is your name, comrade, you who talk so well?" The orator stopped, filled with a sense of injustice, since he had already given his name once, and repeated: "Royer-Collard—Paul, law student, I am the son of the doctor. . . ."

The name was a passport, not because of his doctor father, but because of his uncle, the great Royer-Collard, who had been the

King's counselor in exile. Théodore looked at the orator, and at those eager young faces turned toward him. He was being applauded, but there were also Guardsmen, Musketeers, who spoke among themselves in low voices, nudging one another. A small group seemed to want to push forward a tall well-built horseman whom Géricault could not see clearly, and only from behind. He was trying to ward them off, protesting. When he appeared in the middle of the circle, in the light of a torch raised to his face by a King's Gendarme, Théodore recognized him with surprise, and from the first words, the audience— those at least who heard him—seemed captivated. The others, those farther away, cried: "Louder! Louder! We can't hear." Then M. de Prat got up on the axle of a caisson wheel, next to an artillery piece, and he began his speech over again with all the fire that belongs to a youth of twenty-five, and that strong desire to be liked which could be felt in him—and which was rarely disappointed. "My name is Lamartine, and I was born at Mâcon, of a family that has never left this country, believing as it does in the rights of our land, as our ancestors believed in the right of the throne. . . ." Apart from his rich, deep voice, a certain awkwardness, due no doubt to the fact that he was speaking in public for the first time, gave a special charm to his speech. Looking at him and listening to him in this night light, Théodore had to admit to himself that M. de Prat was indeed handsome, and he could understand why little Denise had wanted to go and sit on his bed to hear him talk of Italy.

The young orator said a good many things about the life of those provincial nobles from whom he had sprung. Scorning the corruption of the Court, they were on the one hand enemies of the crimes of the Revolution, and on the other hand *constant and moderate supporters of its principles* . . . Here voices rose, and some fanatics tried to interrupt him. "Let him speak," someone shouted. He went on:

"To my father's and my brother's way of thinking, Coblenz was a folly and a fault. They preferred the role of victims of the Revolution to the role of auxiliaries of their country's enemies. I was brought up on those ideas: they have flowed in my veins. Politics is in my blood!"

They preferred the role of victims. . . . After that phrase, Théodore heard little else. It was a way with him to be struck by certain things. This young man was thinking aloud. And there it had come out. What he was saying was true. Géricault had known such nobles to whom their country was dearer than their race, and who had had to pay dearly for having remained in France, and yet did not complain. But what was that Noailles Guardsman saying now? That the

cause of Liberty and that of the Bourbons were linked. That was
going a bit far. Ah yes! The Charter. *"We owe our strength to the fact
that we are associated, heart and soul, with the republicans and with
the liberals. We are animated by the same hatred of Bonaparte . . ."*
It suddenly seemed to Théodore that this was a continuation of the
scene in the thicket above Poix. But now it was a monarchist, an odd
kind of monarchist, who had risen to speak, who said that if republicans and royalists together would use the weapons of opinion to
oppose Bonaparte, his reign would be short-lived. Unite the French
against tyranny . . . *"Don't you understand that, willing as they are
today to ally themselves with us on the ground of constitutional
liberties and a restoration of '89, they would separate from us
violently if they saw us on foreign soil under a flag which was not
that of our country's independence?"*

There passed over this youthful gathering a breath of wonder, a
thrill which had its source in the fact that they had never before heard
such language from anyone. Most of them, like him, were not *émigrés,*
but children who had been raised in those dilapidated châteaux, those
run-down properties where parents who had refused to flee had long
hidden them in childhood. And then the young Lamartine expressed
the fear that one step more, beyond this boundary of loyalty and
honor, *would denationalize them*—he uttered this verb in detached
syllables—*and leave them with nothing but regrets, perhaps, some
day, remorse* . . . *"To emigrate,"* he said, *"is to recognize defeat on
the ground where we must fight."* And the more reasons he gave these
young men to return to their families, to get back to their mothers,
their sky, their sweethearts, the closer they felt drawn to him who was
speaking. Fight? They had only to be present in France, to make use
of freedom of opinion and speech. And when he said, *"I shall not cross
the frontier,"* it could be felt that these were the words they had been
waiting for, and that he had won.

This group was divided between two contrary resolves; but those
who still wanted to join the King on foreign soil were few in number,
most of them volunteers like the preceding speaker. Seven or eight
of the men surrounding him waved their arms and walked off. Théodore wanted to talk to M. de Prat de Lamartine, but that young man
had jumped down from his caisson and was so tightly surrounded that
Théodore gave up trying to reach him. He would go and visit him
later at M. Tocquenne the blacksmith's, to ask him two or three
questions. It was the political side of the speech that interested the
painter, and he was also struck by the fact that this member of the

petty nobility should speak of republicans as he did. The Grand'Place was filled with groups like this one, they formed and dissolved, there was applause, whistling, even people who got into tussles. Unexpectedly, Théodore noticed beside him a boy of about ten who was looking at him with the admiring and critical seriousness children sometimes exhibit before their elders. It was little Jean, his host's younger son. Géricault spoke to him gently, and Jean replied that his mother had sent him to say that he had not had dinner and that they had been waiting for him, that it was never too late to sit down to table. Théodore took him by the hand and they left the lights and the speeches, and turned down the rue Grosse-Tête, but the pottery shop was closed and they had to go round the corner and enter through the dark, narrow alley.

"We were waiting for you," the major said severely. They went and sat down to table.

But when, after the meal, Théodore dropped in at the blacksmith's at the other end of the alley, M. de Prat de Lamartine was not there. He had gone back with his friend, M. de Vaugelas, to do guard duty at the Porte d'Arras.

XVI

Tomorrow Easter

I AM *poured out like water, and all my bones are out of joint* . . .
This phrase from the Psalm they had sung in Saint-Vaast while
he was confessing his sins pursues the Comte d'Artois in his dreams.
*My strength is dried up like a potsherd and my tongue cleaveth to my
jaw* . . . Where is he? He is sleeping on the hard stone. *For dogs
have compassed me; the assembly of the wicked have inclosed me*
. . . The gold, the gold is all that remains to him of grandeur and of
glory, and he has placed his cheek on the little cask . . . *They observe me and contemplate me. They divide my garments among
themselves, they draw lots for my tunic* . . . There is nothing so
terrible as fear when you sleep. There is fear, and fear in dreams, the
fear of being naked, the fear of falling, the fear of murderers: where
does it come from? From the falsehood that is in us, the things unsaid,
but also from what I possess, what can be snatched from me, a fear
of thieves. . . . These atrocious efforts to awaken, for he knows he
is asleep, at least to prove to himself that he is asleep. If I awaken,
I must have been asleep. The effort is like a fall. I don't see my
entire life pass before me, but my whole dream, what was it like?
Fear, pulling back, seizes me, drags me back through that shuddering,
that breath of the unknown. I cannot die, since I am asleep . . . Am
I asleep? And if this were dying . . . *Deliver my soul, oh Lord, from
the sword, my life from the dog's paw!*

Sounds of steps, people talking in low voices, a coming and going, the candle relit or brought out from behind the pillar—he was not sure. He heard the murmur of the men waking up at the table where they had fallen asleep, a bench was pushed back, feet dragged, there was a groan.

Yes, a farm at La Fosse, in the commune of Lestrem. The room in which forty *Augusters* dined at harvest time. Enormous, with its shadows reaching all the way up to the faraway ceiling, its beams; and on the stone staircase Charles threw back his cloak, noted that the cask was still there, got up, made sure his clothes were buttoned, stepped forward. "What's the matter? What time is it?"

It was one o'clock in the morning. God was dead. Saturday was beginning, the long Saturday when nothing takes place except death. What was that messenger saying, breathless from having traveled all the way from Béthune to this station of the cross in less than one hour? But of course: it was only two and a half leagues. And now the trivial things resumed their place. There was a damp atmosphere of wet cloth and thick breathing, the odor of man and the odor of wool.

The messenger was a young Guardsman with a turned-up nose. He had removed his helmet and was mopping his forehead, having let his gun fall against the table where a jug was asleep next to a cob of bread. He was wearing the green edging of Grammont's company. Who could tell? Perhaps he was a spy in disguise. He had the heavy accent of Burgundy. Or a traitor— Perhaps he is the one who is going to betray me! He had sworn the oath composed by the Prince de Poix: *You swear to serve the King faithfully, and if anything contrary to the interest of his service comes to your knowledge to inform your captain and the captain on duty, to accept pay, wages or emoluments from no foreign Prince but only from His Majesty . . .* He was panting, seemed to have about him the steam of the horse left at the gate.

Armand de Polignac questioned him and he answered: "I was at the Porte-Neuve post, under M. de Toustain, of our company, with men of various corps. The new general who is in command of the fortress had put three hundred men at each gate, and there are four through which it is possible to pass otherwise than on foot, which makes twelve hundred men on guard. We were covered by the Swiss Guards who occupied the lunette. The two artillery pieces on the rampart were also manned. About midnight the lunette signaled to us that horsemen were approaching the Porte-Neuve. We cried *Who goes there?* and a dozen men came forward to parley. It was one of the Usurper's generals. He had come from Hazebrouck with I don't know what troop, and he wanted to enter Béthune. We shouted to him to go on his way. He insisted, he made threats. He wanted our cannon, he could make good use of them. 'If it's a fight you're looking for,' we shouted, 'we have three thousand men in the fortress, and the people are on our side!' Three thousand was twice our numbers, but it's a good idea to impress the adversary. He hesitated a little, said there was no occasion to fight since there was no longer a King in France, but only an Emperor. We told him again to go on his way. Then he said that if we were counting on the Princes, we might as well know that another part of the Hazebrouck garrison was in pursuit of them and would in all probability be waiting for them at night in the vicinity of Estaires. That is my message. M. de Toustain said to me, 'Take your horse, my lad, get hold of Monsieur de Reiset who is with the Princes and let him know.' Where can I find M. de Reiset?"

That the message had been delivered, and that there was no further reason to look for M. de Reiset, were points on which it was impossible to convince a Lifeguard who had sworn to inform his captain if he heard of anything that was contrary to the King's service.

Monsieur gave orders for him to be taken, not to M. de Reiset, but to Marshal Marmont at Estaires. But before letting him leave, he asked him one question: "The Porte-Neuve—that's the gate also called the Porte d'Aire, isn't it? All right. And you were able to leave without any difficulty, you didn't fall in with rebel horsemen?" The young man had not gone out through the Port-Neuve, precisely because he had feared just this. He had been sent out through the Porte du Rivage, from which the road led to Estaires. "And you saw nothing? No one?" Nothing. No one. An odd kind of besieged fortress, which a man could leave as he pleased without ever running into the besiegers! But why was the Hazebrouck garrison moving on Béthune if Exelmans's horsemen were already investing the city?

The Comte d'Artois had no means of knowing that the general who had appeared at midnight at the Porte-Neuve was that same General Vandamme whom the King had relegated to his estates at Cassel, and whose name had been sufficient to dissuade His Majesty from taking the road from Lille to Dunkirk because it passes through Cassel. He had no means of knowing that, upon the announcement of Napoleon's arrival in Paris, Vandamme had left his country house whose gardens extend over a whole flank of Mount Cassel, from which can be seen the sea, Belgium and thirty-two townships, Béthune and Estaires as well as Ostend and Lille, Calais and Saint-Omer. Nor that he had taken command of the Hazebrouck garrison on Thursday, and on

Friday received the telegraphic order to report at Doullens to place himself at Exelmans's disposal. Nor that all the rest was his own invention, and that having been unable to enter Béthune, he had circumvented the town and continued straight to Saint-Pol by night without giving any further thought to the Household or the Princes.

Meanwhile, at Lestrem, at La Gorgue, at Estaires, the rumor of Exelmans's imminent arrival at the head of a column of cavalry spread like wildfire. The guards on duty went from door to door rousing the officers from their beds, drums beat the call to arms, it was raining, the men were still dressing as they came out on the street, horses galloped in all directions, shadows were challenged in the dark, the men stumbled upon one group or another, Guard commanders would find themselves with the Grenadiers, and Grenadier commanders with the Musketeers.

The hardest job was to get the carriages in motion again, and from La Fosse, where Monsieur was in the rear, to the small sprawling town of Estaires where Marmont was, the confusion was already very considerable. It was now necessary to explain to everyone what was happening, all the things that had been concealed from them. The task fell to Monseigneur the Duc de Berry. The men were gathered on the square of Estaires in the rain, before the belfry whose bells, being civil ones, do not leave for Rome every year from Thursday to Sunday, and continue to chime the hours and half hours with a mechanical chime which covered the Duke's voice, stringing out its notes in a tune that was not immediately recognized, but the words of which suddenly came to the orator's mind: *Bon voyage, Monsieur Dumollet!— À Saint-Malo, débarquez sans naufrage* . . . like an atrocious mockery. Monseigneur said they had just received, just now received, by a dispatch rider, a message from the King, who had had to leave Lille and France, and the rallying point was Ypres: they were going to cross the frontier. Those who wanted to follow the King could do so, but the men in charge of the units remaining at Béthune should return, together with those who preferred not to leave the national soil, in order to effect the disbanding of the troops.

So they were no longer bound for Lille but for Bailleul, or at least for an unnamed point between Bailleul and Armentières. Definitely in a northeasterly direction. Since the frontier was to be crossed at the nearest point, they would follow as straight a line as possible. . . . But here, in truth, was where the difficulty began.

If they had had trouble in reaching this region in the twilight, now that they had crossed the Lys it was much worse going in the pitch-

black night under those heavy clouds and in the downpour. A guide
had shown where a road began, turning off the main street of Estaires
and leaving the road to Armentières on the right. But at once they
found themselves in that region of marshes and peat bogs which was
reputed to be impassable for two-thirds of the year; and marking
time every two to three hundred yards to allow the convoy to reassemble wasn't going to help them discover where to go when there
was a fork in the road, and there were plenty of forks. Here the roads
cut across one another in every direction— They called them streets.
It was like a big unbuilt town, and you lost your way, especially as
whoever had laid out these roads seemed to have taken a delight in
making them as twisted as he could; and at every turn you wondered,
Do we go straight, does this lead into a field? And suddenly you were
in the rushes, in a stream, get yourself out of there, *nom de Dieu!*
Because here the fields and the water were marked off in great
rectangles, and for the carriages especially it was great fun. . . .
And speaking of going straight ahead—don't you think we're going
back in the direction we came from? Damned if our leaders know
any more about it than we do! Who was that who spoke? Oh, I beg
your pardon, Monsieur le Maréchal. . . . If there were a house,
we could ask our way. Yes, but there is none. Buildings are few and
far between. And, speaking of which, the way to where? Bailleul? No,
Steenwerk. . . . At Estaires they told us that to get to Steenwerk,
you go to the right, then you take the left via Le Petit Mortier, or Le
Doulieu; you were bound to come out on the same road. Via Le
Doulieu it was a little longer, but anyway— All right, all right, only
it wasn't just once that they had the choice of going right or left, every
road couldn't lead to Le Petit Mortier or Le Doulieu. *À Saint-Malo,
débarquez sans naufrage.* . . . In the daytime, people on foot could,
if they were able to jump from stone to stone, follow the stepping
places that edged the roads. But horsemen, at night . . .

Fabvier marched at Marmont's side. He suddenly spoke in a voice
that the Marshal no longer recognized, and Marmont was at first
tempted to pull his horse away. But immediately he recognized his
aide-de-camp by the nature of his words. Fabvier said to him, "Why
don't we go back and shut ourselves up in Béthune? We can sustain
a siege there, even a long one. It's obvious that Bonaparte is afraid
of a battle that would pit Frenchman against Frenchman and might
serve as a pretext for foreign intervention."

"The question does not arise," said Marmont. "We are crossing
into the Low Countries. The King is already there."

There was a silence, broken by oaths. A carriage had just capsized. Whose carriage? The horses were stopping. Come, this is none of our business, we are at the head; let's move on. The head of what? We don't know if anybody is following us. If they've lost their way at a turn, all the rest will follow in their footsteps. . . .

"Monsieur le Maréchal," Fabvier said, and his voice was full of anxiety, "in Paris you accepted my plan for fortifying the Louvre. The King would have none of it, so much the worse. Now he is at Ypres or somewhere. That is a matter between history and him. But don't you understand that for Napoleon, the essential thing is the fiction that the country has called him back, that he has met no resistance? If we resist, if blood is shed . . ."

Marmont did not reply. He turned up the collar of his cavalry cloak; there was a wind that nipped his ears.

"It was almost warm this afternoon, and now how cold the weather has turned with nightfall."

Fabvier was in despair. Why have a Household, why assemble and arm young men, if they were not going to fight? Either they were right, or they were wrong. If they were right, they should fight to prove it.

"Perhaps," he went on, "Béthune is not the ideal place. I mean its situation, too close to Lille and Arras, because otherwise with its Vauban walls . . . Perhaps we could fall back directly on Hesdin, which is farther from the frontier and would be less of a temptation for the Allies. . . ."

"I don't understand you," said Marmont. "What worries you is the proximity of the Allied armies? And not Exelmans's soldiers?"

"Monsieur le Maréchal," Fabvier explained, "an untimely intervention on the part of the Allies would have the effect of consolidating Bonaparte's alliances, and it would throw us into the foreign camp."

Marmont gave a nervous little laugh. Fabvier could not see the expression on his face. But Hesdin was not likely to have any more appeal to him than Béthune. As far as he was concerned, he could not afford to linger in a country in which the Emperor was master. From the moment when he had landed at Cannes, Bonaparte had expressed himself clearly as far as Marmont was concerned: a wall and twelve bullets. But if the Marshal crossed the frontier and joined the King, was that reason for the others? *Mon Dieu,* how the road twists! Well, look at this, we're in the water, we're sinking, what is it? Peat? Back, back! All you hear is *plop, plop, plop.* And what's wrong with this horse? Is he lying down or what?

They had to wait. Wait for the others.

Who were the others? Perhaps *they* were the others. Presently they would be at Armentières, or at Estaires at worst. If it was true that Exelmans's or Vandamme's men were advancing on them from Haze-brouck and knew they were at Estaires . . . "Halt! Who goes there? Ah, it's you, Lauriston." "Monsieur le Maréchal, His Highness the Comte d'Artois has had to leave his berlin; it went off the road into a ditch from which they have been unable to extricate it." "Upon my word! And what about his casks?" "He has distributed them to Guardsmen, and now they are in God's hands!" "Well, you take it lightly. That's our war chest. I for one was opposed to sending the Crown jewels to England. Can you see us in Belgium, reduced to beggary? Who's that horseman behind you? Excuse me, Monsieur le Duc, I hadn't recognized you in the dark, a fiasco, a real fiasco . . ." M. le Duc de Richelieu was on horseback; where was his carriage? "Oh, you know, it isn't my carriage, it's de Rochechouart's cabriolet. I don't know where he is—I thought he was up in front with you."

I have no idea where Léon de Rochechouart was, and as for the cabriolet . . .

They stopped. They started again. They stopped once more. People spoke among themselves. There was a rumor to the effect that their cannon, well, their cannon had been sent to Armentières and hadn't been able to get any farther. What? Armentières? They hadn't even reached Armentières. . . . No, no, by another road. Then just go and try to explain that from Béthune it would have been necessary to make a detour through Lille. Nobody thought of the simplest answer —namely, that they were traveling without cannon. And besides, of what use were cannon? But then, why all those caissons?

Léon de Rochechouart's cabriolet was on the road behind some Grenadiers. And what was in front of the Grenadiers you'd have had to be pretty smart to tell. But they were certainly forging ahead. There was also a barouche and a wagon. The wagon, nobody knew why, was being driven by a man of the region, a civilian. You couldn't understand a word he was jabbering. And for a man of the region, he certainly didn't seem to know where he was going. In the wagon there were trunks and three men. In the cabriolet carrying the Duc de Richelieu's things, and Rochechouart's portmanteau, Léon's valet was tightly squeezed; each jolt made him stretch out his arms to keep one thing or another from falling over, which made the coachman laugh heartily. The coachman was a new man, but after five days and five nights of travel—or was it five nights and four days?—people begin to know one another. . . . He, too, spoke a funny language, but not like the wagon driver. He was a Parisian, Bertin by name, with an argot, you would have had to be from Belleville to understand—anyway, certain words. M. de Rouchechouart's valet, who was the son of a servant at Versailles and accustomed to using the most refined language, was horrified by all this argot. This Bertin fellow had a tattoo on his arm which he didn't like people to see. As the valet had come upon him washing at Abbeville, thus discovering that the blue snake which wound round his left arm had its head on his right breast, the coachman—or as he himself said, *le cochemard*—had pretended to believe that there were unmentionable reasons for the other's curiosity; and from that moment, he teased his companion, who was made quite uncomfortable, because perhaps after all there might be something in what he was saying. Tonight the coachman was in a foul mood and he began a discussion with his companion on the question of the Emperor. This word on a coachman's lips in such circumstances! "You aimin' to wear your ass out all your life? You fancy bein' a flunky? Listen to me. . . ."

A man was a proper gentleman, or he wasn't. It was a real disaster for a gentleman to find himself in these marshes at night, responsible for M. le Comte's beautiful enamel kit, and next to such a creature. And it was therefore like a boon from heaven when they ran into that Lifeguard who turned up on foot during a halt, jumping from stone to stone, carrying a big package in his arms. He explained that he had had to abandon his horse, which had sunk in the mire, and asked permission to join them and make a threesome. The coachman swore. There was no room. The valet, in his carefully modulated voice, insisted that they could manage by squeezing. "All right, climb in," Bertin cried. "Monsieur's a good egg, but be careful! He's a queer one!"

Time passed slowly in the rain. They had left Estaires, it might have been about two in the morning—or four. Suddenly they found themselves nose to nose with a detachment of horsemen. Halt! Who goes there? They were Musketeers—either one or other group must have lost its way—but how did they happen to meet? And which way did they go now?

In Béthune, at the gateposts, on the ramparts, or in the lodgings to which they had scattered, the men of the Household slept poorly or not at all. There were not more than four hundred men in billets, once the guard detachments had been assigned. Théodore had had a long conversation with his hosts, in which a Captain de Bellonet, commanding the engineer corps at Béthune—an engineer from the Polytechnique whose ideas ran along the same lines as the major's— had joined. He had won the cross of the Legion of Honor at Wagram, at nineteen. And as Théodore repeated what he had been thinking in the course of the day, that he had not even found anything to die for in the King's expedition, the captain had looked at him in astonishment, and said suddenly, in an aggressive way: "Having nothing to die for, monsieur, is having something to live for." Which our horseman found very striking, but not convincing. The taciturn young daughter of the house seemed to have taken to Théodore. At about midnight little Jean, who had insisted on staying up and was all ears, had been sent to bed by his mother—he couldn't keep his eyes open. "Ah, Jean-Jean," the major said, "it's time to go to *schlaf*." This was a word the Prussians had brought last year when they had been at Béthune from mid-April to mid-May with General von Jurgas. The only good reminder of their passage. A relative of M. de Bellonet's, who had refused to provide bedding for their horses in the stable of an inn on the rue d'Arras, had been chased through the whole town by the Prussian soldiers with drawn swords, until death ensued. No one wanted to see anything like that happen again in Béthune, you may be sure. But meanwhile it is time for us to *schlaf* too, my friends!

Schlaf was out of the question. In Fred's room—the room of the son who had left for Paris—Géricault had an oil lamp with a green opaline shade, but with no oil in it, and a candle in a candlestick to see by. He sat down on the edge of the bed, a big four-poster bed of light yellow German oak with a festooned valance and green serge curtains. It was all the girl had told him as she showed him the room. This Catherine was a strange girl. Not pretty, but strange: "It's our Uncle Machu's bed, which he left to Fred. Uncle was one of the priests who took the oath to uphold the constitution. Life was made impossible for him." Yes, it was really a country priest's bed, and Catherine had explained how it happened to be there, as though the Musketeer might have wondered about it. She had looked to make sure there was water in the big-bellied pitcher on the night table. They were always afraid of being short of water in this town.

Suppose, Théodore said to himself, suppose I had taken this girl's hands and kissed her. It's an idiotic supposition. I had no desire to, and besides, because of the major . . . Of course the supposition was idiotic, but perhaps it meant that if he had taken Catherine's hands, and it had led to something, he would then have had something to live for. It was not true that having nothing to die for was sufficient to give you something to live for. Where did that engineer learn to reason like that? At the Polytechnique?

The truth was that a while ago, when we suddenly found ourselves alone, I mean without our chiefs who had followed the Comte d'Artois, when all at once, without having consulted one another, we understood that our fate was in our own hands, and we began to discuss democratically . . . democratically . . . what course to take, something in our lives had changed. We ceased to be men whose decisions are made for them, who have only to execute, who go where they are told to go. Almost instinctively it reminded me of the meeting at Poix! Perhaps that's what freedom is, and perhaps a life in which freedom reigns is worth living. Perhaps. The young Royer-Collard—his idea was to obey. What upset him was that in order to be able to continue to obey the same chiefs, he would be obliged, today or tomorrow, to *disobey them*. A soldier does not think, does not judge, does not decide. Or else he is a rebel. I myself feel an irresistible urge to be a rebel, and none at all, in the last analysis, to be a soldier. That captain-engineer— He's a soldier, after all, and when he insists that I must at all costs have something to live for, does it occur to him that if I live, if I continue to live, it will be in order to be a rebel? In other words, the negation of *his* morality? And Théodore reflected at the same time that rebellion in life is a little like contrast in painting. But contrast of what with what? Rebellion against whom?

He had taken off his shoes, he was slipping off his socks without stooping by rubbing one foot against the other. It gave him extraordinary pleasure to feel the air on his bare feet. What did this Fred look like, this youth into whose bed Théodore was going to sneak like a thief, the priest uncle's bed? He was eighteen, and had already fought, and he knew what he wanted, he was marching toward a future that he visualized, he meant to play his part in the birth of that future—to change the world. He was a soldier and a rebel. But there was the rub. How to reconcile the two things. To be the soldier neither of a king nor of a general, but of an idea. Perhaps that was what freedom was. . . . A fine subject for a *Prix de Rome!* Was that what a *prêtre constituant* was, too—a priest and a rebel? What had Uncle Machu looked like when he slept here behind the green bed curtains? Was he the one who had married the major to his Aldegonde? At that time people didn't necessarily get married by way of the church. . . . It seemed that Fred looked like his mother, and therefore like his sister. But I really should be thinking about going to *schlaf*. . . . I thought the major looked tired, tonight. And if I had taken Caroline Lallemand's hand, everything would have been different, and I should never have left. . . .

In the entire town and at the guard posts it was the same—nobody could make up his mind, even for a moment, to go to sleep. They would be a fine-looking lot tomorrow. Today, in other words. And they consulted together in twos, in groups, aloud, in whispers. Was it possible the King intended this? What to do? Wait for the cavalry's return? And then it would be too late. Yet they must guard the town, deny access to the enemy, be ready to fight at the gates, on the walls, in the streets and alleys if need be. It would be glorious to be buried beneath Béthune. . . .

Is your mind wandering? Be buried! Have you had a look at the people round here? As for the comrades— You saw that Lifeguard, Paul, the one who spoke after you did? What's the blue edging? Luxembourg?—No, Noailles, I think—he had them all with him . . . to serve the King in France by good words. Soldiers—can you call them soldiers?

And others made a small bundle of things that they could take with them. Others . . .

Nevertheless, if the old-clothes dealer on the rue du Rivage was doing such good business, it was because quite a few of these youngsters already . . . even before hearing the King's message . . . But—had they become deserters? Take it any way you like, now the orders were to desert.

Day was dawning, still with that fine drizzle like a tulle handkerchief. They had wandered over three leagues since three in the morning, losing their way, finding it again, stopping with the anguish of not knowing who was coming and of finding that no one came. Four hours of going round in circles in the marshes, the peat, and the mud. There were people doing strange things, walking with pistol in hand, who might have fired on you for a mere nothing. Still, when the sky began to pale, it was a relief. The question was where they could really sleep.

"Come now, don't be discouraged: anyway, Steenwerk here is not even a league from the frontier. We'll sleep in Belgium. All we want. In Belgium . . . Is Belgium so close? And are you planning to cross into Belgium then?" One of the men talking trudged along leading two horses by the bridle. "They don't mount them so as not to tire them. They're a general's horses. And your feet are not a general's feet, that's why you're on them, eh? We've come this far, after all, we're not going to let go at the last minute. . . ."

The cavalry was being assembled, but nearly all the carriages were missing—broken axles, most of them stuck in the mud; others were unaccounted for. Everyone had mud at least halfway up his thighs; some were covered with it from head to foot. Those who, like Léon de Rochechouart, had crossed the Beresina, spoke of it, made comparisons. Rastignac was saying, "I can't understand why my coachman doesn't come. Haven't you seen a green barouche?" Most of the caissons seemed to have fallen into the rushes or the streams. "There are dismounted horsemen—all right, you, what of it?" "The frontier is too close. You'd do better to stay here, try to sneak over to Armentières." "Where the hell is Armentières?"

Monsieur was on horseback on the outskirts of the village. With Armand de Polignac and François d'Escars by his side. How old was he really? That morning he was an old man. M. de Damas no longer spoke of his fever, which did not mean that he was over it. The Marshal was almost the only one whose carriage had come through. Who in the world was in that incredibly mud-spattered berlin? Marmont had made a check: his company's chest was still there. But he could not act differently from Monsieur, and although he would have welcomed a little more sleep, he must remain on horseback—people had their eyes on him. M. de Richelieu questioned Léon de Rochechouart: what about that cabriolet? "We must hope it will catch up with us, either here or at—what is the name of the next town?—La Crèche." "At La Crèche, then. Montpezat!" "Yes, *mon général?*" "Do go and see if the cabriolet is not somewhere back there." "Very good, sir."

What did I say this rain was like? An ox's breath, a spray of misfortune. It was not the heavy rain of the last days. It was a different kind of wretchedness. It touched your skin, to a point at which you couldn't stand it. Ah yes, flies—water flies. And if they had to return with the same horses, cross the marshes again? Then they had better not wait until the evening. Why no, since they were going to Belgium! Belgium was the secret word of hope. Meanwhile, the rain was like a thousand fly-feet. The road was no longer so bad, except that it had never been meant for cavalry, the King's horsemen, the stamping of horses in close formation. And besides, it was slippery, they were moving in a kind of mustard. They stopped again.

Those were Luxembourg Guards who had tried to catch up at a trot. Who was the officer commanding them? A fine idiot he must be.

There was the road over there. Halt! Again? The cavalry would not venture out on the road parallel to the frontier without a reconnaissance to make sure there was no danger. But some Lifeguards had already crossed and were camping in that meadow over there. That didn't matter. The reconnaissance set forth, and they waited in the rain for it to return. The local people, up at dawn, had come out to see the cavalry, but for the moment the cavalry was marking time. Léon de Rochechouart was keeping M. de Richelieu company. Montpezat had returned, having found nothing. The mud-streaked berlin was open, General de Bordessoulle stepped down from it to stretch his legs. Fabvier had left Marmont and set out for a farm a short distance away. Hogs could be seen in the courtyard, the children had gone out on the road to look at the soldiers at close range—then they had grown bored. It was raining, a fine drizzle that was not annoying. It was only after a while that you noticed it was going right through you. There were sicknesses like that. The children were no longer paying attention to the troops. They played among themselves, impervious to everything else. Even to the rain. They formed a circle and sang, some ten of them, a big girl and small fry. They sang:

> *"C'était le Roi de Sardaigne,*
> *Le vrai Roi des Bons Enfants,*
> *Qui s'était mis dans la tête*
> *De détrôner le Sultan . . ."* *

And listening to the words, Fabvier felt a catch in his throat. And there was a small girl who looked like the child of Marie-des-Anges, a little plump, like her. After the verse, the children stopped going around and clapped hands:

> *Et ran, plan, plan, gard', gard', garde!*
> *Et ran, plan, plan, garde en avant!* †

It was a very dry rain, as when you spat between tight lips. Ptt! ptt, ptt! The circle had begun to go round again.

* There was a King of Sardinia—The true King of Good Children—Who had made up his mind—To dethrone the Sultan . . .

† Tam-ta-ta-tam, guard, guard, guard
Tam-ta-ta-tam, Guard, forward!

Il se fit faire une armée
De quatre-vingts paysans
Et pour toute artillerie,
Quatre canons de fer blanc . . . *

The children stopped and struck their palms to mark the time:

Et ran, plan, plan, gard', gard', garde!
Et ran, plan, plan, garde en avant!

And again they began going around, shaking their heads, their hair, as if to shake away the cobweb of the rain:

Un âne chargé de raves
Pour nourrir le régiment . . . †

Fabvier stopped listening to the round. He breathed the morning. A faint smell of wet smoke. *Et ran, plan, plan . . .* A recollection going back to before the flood, when it was fine and warm, near Pont-à-Mousson. Then the children were himself. And the grown-ups could do what they liked about making the Revolution, fighting, dying . . . rounds were rounds, children were kings.

Ils virent une rivière
Qu'ils prirent pour l'Océan;
Une infinité de mouches
Qu'ils prirent pour des géants . . . ‡

Et ran, plan, plan, gard', gard', garde! . . .

The rain was like an infinity of flies, the rain had invaded life. Where was Marie-des-Anges? Where was Pont-à-Mousson?

Quand ils furent dans la prairie:
"Mon Dieu! que le monde est grand!"
Ils se dirent: "Voici l'enn'mi,
Vite, vite, allons-nous en!" §

* He had himself an army made—Of four-times-twenty peasants—
And all the artillery that he had—Was four tin cannon.
† A donkey with a load of rapeseed
To feed the regiment . . .
‡ They saw a river—Which they took for the Ocean;
An infinity of flies—Which they took for giants . . .
§ When they were in the meadow:
"My God! how big the world is!"
They said to themselves: "Here is the enemy,
Quick, quick, let us run!"

And here the rain began to fall very hard, and the children, at the end of the refrain, took to their heels, running in all directions, crying, *"Allons-nous en!"* while over there, at the entrance to the village, the trumpet was calling the scattered horsemen. They were leaving. Peasants in the freshly cleared ground crossed their arms on the handles of their spades. The children were no longer to be seen. The horsemen cut obliquely toward the northeast, from which direction the rain was coming, pouring down on the white cloaks, the helmets, the tails, the bearskins. Over there a line of trees could be seen: it was probably the road; the terrain sloped down gently toward it, and on the other side, over there, those hills, probably Belgium. *Mon Dieu! que le monde est grand!*

It was eight in the morning when Monsieur with his plumed two-pointed hat, the Duc de Berry in his gray oilskin cloak, and Marshal Marmont in his big white cloak with its black stand-up collar, came out on the highway from Lille to Dunkirk, five quarter-leagues south of Bailleul, from the La Crèche road, to be precise, with some fifteen hundred horsemen behind them, despite the number who had dropped behind on the way. After Monseigneur the Duc de Berry's little speech at Estaires, several had made a declaration to the effect that they were returning to their firesides, not wishing to cross over to foreign territory, and there had been deserters and panic mongers who under cover of the dark fled toward Armentières or Fleurbaix—not to mention the handful of bad characters who, tempted by the casks of gold that had been entrusted to them, had sneaked off: common thieves. . . . But there were no artillery caissons, and nearly all the carriages had met with accidents or got stuck in the mud.

They were found later, those carriages—three coaches, two of them with coats-of-arms, four small transport carts, four draught horses with their team harnesses, a great number of broken artillery caissons. They contained baggage, silverware and money; seventeen platters, three dozen dishes, fourteen dish covers for the table service, all of silver and with the King's coat-of-arms. Plus four saddles, two of them postilion saddles, two sabers, a sword, two helmets, a pair of pistols and various toilet articles, stable and kitchen utensils. And, I nearly forgot, a squadron horse with complete equipage, which a Light-Horseman, M. de Cognart, had handed over spontaneously at the Estaires town hall. And shabracks, horse blankets. A hat with white plumes. A gold and silver sword belt. Three pairs of boots. Four more saddles. Fifty halters. Ten snaffles. Twenty stable surcingles. Two saddle covers. A worn portmanteau, emptied. Six small canvas cases, empty. . . . No cabriolet.

The Princes and Marmont hardly did more than cross the highway; that is to say, they swung back perhaps four hundred yards in the direction of Armentières on the paved road; then with their cavalry they passed down the bank, on the Belgian side, into the valley which is the actual frontier. And there, spotting the only sizable farm around, the Comte d'Artois said they must halt to tidy themselves up a bit and shave, so as not to appear abroad looking as they did. Then, while the Princes and those of their companions who were to follow them were doing this—everyone dismounted, the horsemen and the horses surrounded the farm—some of them went in, occupying the vast enclosed courtyard, a big paved square with a manure pile and chickens, at the far end the buildings that served as living quarters, and along the other three sides, iron-doored stalls where the hogs, the cows and the horses were kept, with urine running everywhere. The peasants, who had come running with pitchforks, had become most polite before this vast deployment, and now everything was humming like a hive within these tile-roofed stone walls. But why am I trying to describe them? It's all done, I enter and I recognize the place.

On the night of May 26, 1940, after having driven through a flaming Armentières, assailed by a suffocating heat and with burning twigs and sparks flying in through the window, our little group belonging to the 3rd D.L.M. had landed here. A plane that had bombed the buildings had been brought down not far from the farm. I have described this somewhere, why do it over again?

> . . . It's an odd kind of farm with a square courtyard entirely surrounded by buildings. In the dining room men from various branches of the service, the administration, the kitchens, yawn, try to play cards and chat with the stretcher bearers, the nurses. To these men who can see the frontier through the window with their own eyes, the news of the Belgians' surrender has something of the character of a sudden shipwreck. The ship had been thought to be as solid as land, and here suddenly it begins to leak in every seam. In the courtyard were all the cars that we had left, the drivers dozing inside. We could see smoke, fires, in every direction. The sister-in-law of the farm's mistress had come from Hazebrouck to visit her, and there she was, unable to return home since the Germans had overrun the area between her village and here; and then, when the two women

found out about the Belgians, they both knew their husbands were mobilized in Belgium, or at least they imagined that they were in Belgium. They kept going round and round in the house, moaning. We'll never see them again. This is the end. The Boches are coming. Let them kill us, what does it matter! There's nothing left to live for. . . .

This is what I wrote in that novel of twenty years ago, that novel which, like my life, is still unfinished. But in life a scene occurred at this extreme point of France where, in 1815, Charles d'Artois shaved in order to arrive fresh at Ypres. Where, in 1940, we were waiting for the English to withdraw, so as to have a free road to the sea—a scene occurred which I have not described. You remember, *mon lieutenant?* You had hated me for a long time, and you thought the moment had come. You went and talked to those women, you had your back turned to me. But I could see their expression of horror piercing through the sense of panic. Their eyes were saying, "Who? Which one?" And with your chin you pointed over your shoulder at me. You had told them my name, which was not so famous as you had hoped, you had explained to them who was responsible for this war, for this disaster, you had told them what party I belonged to . . . And they had flung themselves on me, with their children and their fingernails; one of them, poor woman, had picked up a knife. You had reckoned without the soldiers, my soldiers who defended me. What became of you after that? You became a militiaman under the Occupation, I believe. I heard about you later. It was of no great interest to me. But the novel here said something else:

This dance of death had unleashed the men who were present. Jean de Moncey heard these soldiers, his companions, with stupefaction. He had never known what they thought . . . Now the insulting words swept over all of them like a wave. All of a sudden. How many of them suddenly proved to be defeatists? They were suddenly full of a black bitterness. They hated their officers. They spoke a language that had never been heard, except perhaps in bad dreams. To die—to die for what? The name of France abruptly set three or four of them raving. Oh no, enough, enough! We've heard that one before.

Alain was deathly pale. Almost in a whisper he said to Moncey: "That's the terrible thing, you see . . ." Jean thought so too. A soldier can be beaten, strategically . . . He can be cut off from his own forces, pursued, hunted . . . he can fall, fall physically. But this defeat which sank into the mists like a knife. This defeat which became their flesh and their thought. Was it really the end?

Oh place of confusion, station where the calvaries cross and contradict one another, place of abasement, point of metamorphosis of souls, open wound at the country's extremity . . . There is no comparison between these two sarabands, the quest for the sea by the remnants of the army of 1940, the Princes' flight on the eve of Easter in 1815. It was in both instances a day when the gods died, that is all. What were these young men—not so different from those I was commanding in 1940—thinking about, with their fine drenched uniforms, their exhausted horses, and all their great illusions at half-mast? The same farm, the same livestock, the fields around . . . The peaceful setting belied only by the architecture of the farm that hunched its back against centuries-old invasions, with no windows looking outwards, compact and yet unaccustomed to the thunder of war. The small valley with its scattered trees, the frontier under-brush, and over there on the hills, a foreign road, the smoke from an invisible house—Belgium.

The Guards who had been put on duty on the edge of the road brought in a man who had lost his way, who was beside himself, trembling, stammering, in rags. He asked to see General de Roche-chouart. Léon came out of the farm with Montpezat. In the muddy road in which they wallowed, a rag, a poor being beyond horror, flung himself on his master, kissed his hands, said words that did not hang together. It was the valet. *They beat me, threw me to the ground, they tried to drown me, threw rocks at me* . . . "What in the world, what happened? And what about the cabriolet, my cabrio-let? Where have you left it? And Bertin—where is Bertin?"

The name sent the unfortunate man into a frenzy. "Bertin. The *cochemard!* Ah, ah, the *cochemard!*" "What are you talking about? Are you drunk?" Drunk with what? Drunk from exhaustion, perhaps, from fever. . . . If he had been rolled in the muck he could not have looked worse. Because the horrible thing—the theft, what happened last night, the chase across the marshes, the falls in the peat holes, the whiplashes that had cut his back and his face—all that was as nothing compared to the humiliation, the degradation of a man who had his dignity—only a servant, if you will, but his servant's dignity. . . . They first tried to make him their accomplice. "But whom are you talking about?" "Well, the *cochemard* and that Guardsman I was foolish enough to allow to climb into the cabriolet."

"How is that possible? After all, all the Gentlemen of the Household are of good family—officers—and then this one . . ." "The loot he was carrying . . . When they began going through the baggage I protested. They cuffed me. If you knew the words they used! Monsieur le Comte's kit, that beautiful enamel kit . . . Monsieur le Duc's things . . . The money . . ."

What could be done about it? He had been robbed, he had been robbed. But on this rainy morning—a small rain of the comb or rake type that scratched you slantwise and looked like gravel falling in the puddles on the road—there was something irresistibly comical about this poor, pitiful valet, as there always was for Léon de Rochechouart about a man going to pieces, whether here, or in distant Kirghiz or Portugal. He took hold of himself: he must control his impulses. To laugh, at a moment like this, would appear incomprehensible. And also too cruel. . . . I who was talking about the Beresina a while ago. Here I am, no further ahead than I was then, without a sou—just the clothes I'm wearing, the knife in my pocket—but, three gold pieces, I'm lucky at that! All that is left of the five hundred francs I brought with me. . . . And my two horses. But what a face my good uncle is going to make. The funny thing was that Armand-Emmanuel de Richelieu, in his uniform of a Russian general, was fleeced as completely as Rochechouart, and having lost both his portmanteaux had also lost the very possibility of resuming the appearance of a Frenchman.

Nor was M. de Rastignac to see again the green barouche of which he had been so proud, with those stunning accessories of matching morocco leather. It was probably the one that turned up at Lille, in very bad condition, all broken down, the leather torn away, without baggage, without a drag chain, windows broken, lanterns gone. Nor M. de Damas his yellow coupé. And there he was on his horse, between Monsieur and François d'Escars, leaving the farm for the farewell to the troops. He was shaking with fever, he saw everything through a fog. What did César de Chastellux say? The carriage, the baggage . . . Oh, in this disaster, this or that more or less! All he was sorry to have lost, but really sorry, was the miniature of his grandson which he had had in a box lined with blue velvet, the portrait of Georges de Labédoyère, little Jojo, whose absence would make exile all the more cruel to him. And also, it must be said, an English silver watch with an alarm, which was so handy . . . anyway, a souvenir!

The Light-Horsemen, who had followed the chief into the courtyard of the farm, formed the escort at whose head the Princes and Marmont marched. On this great, green, wet field, the Lifeguards who were impatiently waiting, weary and bewildered by the marches and the countermarches of the last days and the last night; the Musketeers and the Grenadiers reassembled for the first time in a long while, seemed to be anxiously awaiting a verdict already known but which they still obstinately hoped might be revised.

The group formed by the Princes, the Marshal, MM. de Damas, de Polignac, d'Escars, and the Duc de Richelieu in his foreign uniform, advanced. Behind them were M. de Vergennes, M. de Mortemart, César de Chastellux, Lauriston. The troops were lined up in front of them with the officers who had been put in charge of the guard companies, their commanders having one and all, with the exception of Marmont, left with His Majesty. The rain had stopped; the air was a little warmer. The weather was gray and muggy, hopeless. *Mon Dieu,* how long the wait had been for this frightful moment. It was eight o'clock when they had come onto the paved road. It was now eleven. What had they been doing in there for three hours? It couldn't have taken that long to shave. It was said they had been holding a long conference. What for? Everything seemed clear, they had come here to cross over into Belgium . . . not all, of course. But did it take so long to decide whom they were taking and whom they were leaving? Every man looked at the man next to him and wondered which way he would go. They were almost like children—and, indeed, most of them were still children. They were afraid of being abandoned, they looked toward France with terror, because God knew what awaited them there. But also a distressing warmth rose to their foreheads when they thought they were about to take the decisive step, to make the break, to cross to foreign soil. The fears were equal. The chances unknown. Monsieur had spurred his horse forward. He raised his sword, he saluted the loyal troops. . . .

To address nearly two hundred horsemen out in the open was neither simple nor easy. Especially with an aged, broken voice. The weariness of prolonged insomnia. No one had observed that before beginning to speak, the Comte d'Artois had secretly made the sign of the cross. He had put his hand to his pocket to touch the mother-of-pearl rosary which the Holy Father had sent him from Rome with his benediction. And then he had saluted with his sword.

The words at first came clearly, perhaps carried by the wind. It was a brief farewell speech, a speech of gratitude which suddenly did not reach beyond the first rows. Monsieur was visibly unable to overcome his emotion. He was taking leave of the troops, who could not cross the frontier armed. They already knew the refrain. "And with what could we pay for your keep? We are going to join the King. You, with the officers we are instructing to lead you, will return to Béthune, to rejoin your comrades. . . ."

Here everything became lost, the voice dropped, the wind had veered, the words flew away to Belgium, toward the road on the hill, the distant wisps of smoke. A kind of mortal cold descended upon every horseman. Something within them fell apart. They were no longer listening. They were facing their destiny as those Princes were theirs. In a shipwreck in which there was only one lifeboat, and the rest drifted off on the mastless raft. . . .

What—was that all? Yes, that was all for them. The commanders were summoned to the entrance of the farm, to which the Princes had returned. They had seen Monseigneur's gray oilskin cloak whirl round. Those who were close enough had seen Anne d'Autriche's tears in Charles-Ferdinand's eyes one last time. In the courtyard, the real farewells began, the personal farewells. And Captain-Lieutenant de Lauriston begged to be allowed to accompany the Princes to the King. Was he being candid? He already knew that the duty of disbanding the Household devolved upon him, that he was to join La Grange at Béthune. It was the duty of all those who commanded a company to stay behind. If later on they wanted to join . . . M. de Lauriston would be in command of the Household until its dispersal. No, Monsieur could no longer control himself. He was wracked with sobs. This country which they were leaving, of which only a little strip of earth remained, only a little strip of phrases between the Princes and emigration. . . . Outside, the last escort was being formed. Three hundred Lifeguards and Musketeers under Colonel Fabvier who would thus accompany Marmont to the end. They would go as far as Neuve-Église, the first town on the other side. And, there again, they would separate; those who wanted to would escort the sons of France to Ypres, into exile . . . Richelieu, Bordessoulle, Marmont, Beurnonville, La Ferronays, Nantouillet, François d'Escars, Armand de Polignac, Rochechouart. . . .

Three hundred Guards and Musketeers—the last army. And M. de

Lauriston had left for Nieppe, three-quarters of a league from the farm, where the assembly for Béthune would be called. And the men could rest until morning. Regain their strength. Let this long, sinister day pass, this day on which God had died, and France had neither King nor Princes. Tomorrow, who knows? perhaps the sun would shine. It would be Easter Sunday, the bells would ring again, they would turn toward France with a large question in their eyes. Three hundred Guards and Musketeers had gone as far as Neuve-Église. Two hundred had come back. Only one hundred horsemen and two carriages that had been saved accompanied the Princes as they set foot on foreign soil. At Nieppe, the company commanders paid a visit to the new commander, M. de Law de Lauriston. But already there had been defections, horsemen had been seen leaving the farm and heading at a trot in the direction of Bailleul. No one was going to run after them, nor after those who, upon reaching Nieppe, decided to continue on to Lille.

So it was, even in the Royal Household. Some would make their submission. A little hurriedly. They would don the tricolor. But it was a small minority. Perhaps . . .

A little before noon, seven exhausted men reached Bailleul. They asked for lodging and were sent to the town hall. There they said they wanted a safe-conduct because they wished to resume service under the actual government. The seven were Guardsmen of Grammont's company, those who wore the green edging. And a little later, some Grenadiers and Musketeers turned up at Armentières, at Erquinghem. At Nieppe even, while the Household was still there, Light-Horsemen went and declared themselves at the town hall. It was of course true that Marshal Marmont and M. de Vergennes had been alone in distributing the company chests to the men of their commands—Raguse's Guards and the Garde-de-la-Porte respectively. As a result of which they could wait at least a month without soliciting employment in the Imperial armies. Eight hundred francs a head. That was the price of this little extension of loyalty. . . .

And at Lille, during all this, Bertin the *cochemard,* with his companion, sought out the usurers in order to dispose of the collection of silverware contained in an enamel case in their possession. But apart from this they had a neat little sum to share, eight thousand francs in gold louis—enough to have a good spree. After that they would see.

They had buried the cask before entering the town: there was nothing else to do. It would have attracted attention to them, and there would always be time to go and fetch it. They kept watching each other furtively, with murder in their eyes.

Ever the gray sky over Béthune. The lull in the rain had lasted since morning. Many Guardsmen, Grenadiers and Musketeers were still asleep, having spent the night in interminable passionate discussions. Yet it was two in the afternoon. Those who got up at this untoward hour to pick up the thread of life where they had left it were caught up again in the fever of the garrison. Now no one any longer doubted that he had been betrayed: neither those who still wanted to run away and join the King in Belgium, nor those who had already made up their minds to turn back, to throw up the game. The word *treason* justified both groups. Even the Princes were not spared. How could the Duc de Berry have abandoned them? And as for Monsieur, they spoke of another Quiberon. . . . There were secret meetings, people stopped talking when someone approached, it was difficult to relieve the posts since everyone was on guard. On the ramparts the patrols strained their eyes looking for Exelmans's horsemen in the marshes, in the woods, on the roads. Up there they met between one gate and the next and began to talk, forgetting the service and the danger in order to comment on what they had learned in the course of the morning. M. de La Grange had informed the troops that laying down their arms would be the condition on which they would be given their freedom. Because the town was shut, locked, and bolted. How had they dared? "I told you La Grange is a traitor! Proposing we should buy the right to return home by letting ourselves be disarmed!" The disbanding operations had in fact begun in the companies' offices, where those in the greatest hurry had gone and registered, where their passports were made out. But all the same, they weren't getting away that quickly! No. They must wait for the cavalry. When would it be back? Tonight, probably. Nothing would be official without first receiving the signature of the commanders of the companies. Tomorrow, perhaps.

The path covered by the patrol rounds was extremely complicated; the advance posts forming a lunette extended like big thorns from the mass of the walls. Seated against the cannon, Swiss Guards scrutinized the horizon, perhaps with the idea of risking a shot out of sheer boredom. The way back down into the town was by small staircases and vaulted passages. Here was the rue du Rivage with its butchers, its refuse, its stench of blood and rotting meat. Théodore came upon Moncorps in front of the old-clothes dealer's, handling a carter's outfit, corduroy trousers, dimity jacket, big felt hat; and when the youngster saw his elder, his face turned every color. Almost in a whisper, he said to Géricault, "At the point we've come to . . ." The anxiety in his eyes! Whereupon the youngster, avoiding conversation, abandoning the garments, suddenly walked off. A perfectly presentable outfit, as a matter of fact, and not too dirty. Théodore measured the trousers against himself: not his size, but anyway . . . He'd see about it later.

On the citadel side lay the Petite Esplanade where executions were held. That was where Louis-Auguste Paternel and Isidore Leprêtre, of the village of Prédefin, had been shot at the end of January, 1814. Heading a party of peasants, they had killed a sharpshooter of the young Imperial Guard in a wineshop at Nédon. And the punishment was carried out in the presence of their relatives—fathers and mothers, brothers and sisters—and before a mute crowd. It was a holy spot to those who were devoted body and soul to the King. And it was where seven volunteers had now chosen to assemble. Among them were Paul Royer-Collard, the beanpole, Alexandre Guillemin, the curly one. . . . Save the flag! That was their first idea. But in order to make their escape they must wait for dark and take advantage of someone's entering town, when a drawbridge would be lowered at the Porte-Neuve or the Porte du Rivage.

Géricault slowly returned through the Grand'Place, a melancholy nomads' camp where other volunteers were still slumbering, lying under carts, behind the wheels. Cooks, quartermasters' assistants, administrative personnel, roamed about listlessly and yawned. And more Swiss Guards, full of *Gottverdom!* And there was one who said something to the effect that if he had known, he would not have cut off his mustache just to please the King. Water peddlers passed with their barrel on a wheelbarrow. But it was a bad day. No one had the heart to wash himself.

"I saw you," Catherine said when he returned to the pottery shop. "But why didn't you tell me, Monsieur Théodore? I would have been glad to offer you one of Fred's suits rather than have you go to the old-clothes dealer's where you get castoffs that have dragged around God knows where. . . . But my brother is small, compared with you! His jacket wouldn't even button on you!" There was admiration in her voice before this handsome man, *bien diableux,* as they say there—a devil of a fellow. But the words also served to conceal her thoughts. Théodore could tell. Something was preying on the girl's mind. "What's wrong, mademoiselle? Your mind isn't on what you're saying."

She was flustered at having been found out. "Oh, it's nothing. But Father isn't well . . . He said we were not to tell you."

"But I must talk to him . . ."

"I don't know if you can," she said. "Certainly not for long; it would tire him."

Events pass over a country, the impression grows that individual life is suspended, that nothing can happen out of the blue like this; and then it *does* happen. It was possible that the major had overtaxed himself recently. The truth of the matter was that even before going to Poix he had not been feeling very well. But he had refused to pay any attention to the way he felt. He would not have missed that meeting for anything in the world. He had come back from Poix, by way of Doullens, and Saint-Pol. On horseback. And he was no longer used to such trips. What exactly was his complaint? The doctor had just left, he had prescribed medicines, herbal teas.

To know a man, you have to see him in his bed. The major, surrounded by pillows, lifted himself up, leaned on one elbow. But he was an old man! To begin with, without a collar there was the looseness of his skin. . . . In the feeble light that came from the window, the room was full of shadows. On the round bedside table, like a mahogany pillar, stood a cup with a greenish-yellow infusion, a spoon with a trace of white powder. "A letter has come from Fred," the sick man said with a poor attempt at a smile. "I've chosen a good time to be out of sorts, haven't I? The youngster has gone back into the service."

What? Letters were arriving from Paris? By what road? By mailcoach, of course. And this morning they had let . . . They? Exelmans's men? The major gave an odd smile. "Exelmans's men? There are no Exelmans's men. That's all talk. No, I mean that the guard at the Porte d'Arras let the mailcoach through! Because actually it is you who are besieging us, you know."

The old man turned in his rumpled sheets. "Don't excite yourself!" his wife Aldegonde called from the adjoining room. She must have seen him in the swing-mirror, all that remained of their Italian splendor. "Don't excite yourself, Frédéric. The doctor said—"

He coughed and wrinkled his nose. "If you listen to those quacks . . ."

Then he spoke of his son.

Théodore listened to him, thinking of his own father. How full of fears M. Géricault was for him—of horses, the temperature, women, comrades, illness, drink—a hen-father! And how proud this father was of *his* offspring—a daredevil, a scamp, afraid of nothing, though not very big of stature and rather sickly. From the time he went to school he used to fight with any bully twice his size, coming home with an ear all bloody and dangling, so that it had to be sewn on. . . . "Imagine, at sixteen and a half he got into a fight with those Hungarians . . . at Besançon. But I'm driveling, I've already told you the story three times. He's a patriot, I assure you. You couldn't have kept him at Béthune when the news of the landing came. . . . He had to be in it. You see, not all youths today are like those youngsters who ran away. There are youths and youths . . . lads like Fred. People talk about the Soldiers of the Year Two—well, yes: what about the Soldiers of the Year Two? We had every reason for enthusiasm, the people in arms, the King in prison, the new ideas. But what about the youngsters of today, who seemed to be without hope, without a horizon, and then look! What they must have in them to make them jump into the battle where it's hottest and thickest! They certainly don't catch their fire and flame from what is happening now, from the world we've made for them. It must come from within, from here." And he struck his chest with his closed fist. Then he went off into a fit of coughing, and he stopped talking to get back his breath. "Am I tiring you?" asked Théodore. And he, "That's all right. I'm never tired when it comes to talking about my youngster, believe me. Children like him—that's what the future is made of."

And Géricault asked if Fred . . . "I say Fred, as though I knew him!" . . . if Fred was enthusiastic about Napoleon? Because this was something that gnawed at him, the fact that young people—his own generation, and even younger ones—could get all worked up over that man who was coming back. Youth . . . Or could it just as well have been someone else? Or was it because he was so different from the fat King? Or because, as with girls, the first one you encounter . . . The major propped himself up to make himself more comfortable and looked at his emaciated hands.

"What can I tell you? I can't read Fred's mind. But it's not so complicated. Napoleon's return means that the others are leaving. And I kill myself trying to tell you that the Emperor will be what we make of him. . . ."

That was what he had said at Poix. But now he had gone back to thinking about his son: "A good youngster, I swear to you. Children like that are what the people need. A nation with children like that—"

"Don't you think it's just *because* he's young," asked Théodore, "and that he'll get over it?"

The major, breathing with difficulty now, shook his fist in the air. He wanted to say ten things at once: that he had confidence, that these youths of today would make wonderful men, that the world would change in their hands, that they were courageous, stubborn, that they would not flinch before the task; that they would carry on where the Revolution had left off; that in their hands, the colors of France . . . There were tiny red fibrils in the corneas of his discolored eyes, normally a faded blue but now feverish and bright. He was telling about his son at school, little everyday things, illustrating his generosity, his . . .

"Frédéric," said Aldegonde gently, "it's wrong of you to tire yourself like this; and besides, Monsieur Théodore doesn't know our son. He'll say to himself that of course the parents . . ." As she was speaking, she turned toward their guest. "It's true though that he's a good boy!" She put her forefinger to her lips . . . and as a matter of fact the major was dozing off, his mouth half open, his eyelids fluttering, his fingers outstretched on the sheet, fingers with big round folds at the joints, nails that looked crushed.

They went out on tiptoe.

"Listen, Monsieur Théodore," said the major's wife, "I think I've found just the thing. . . . Catherine told me. A cousin of ours, Machu, who is a coachman on the stagecoach—I think he's just about your size . . . he'll certainly have an old suit. No, really! I'm not going to let you ruin yourself at the old-clothes dealer's!"

The eyes beneath the closed lids, turning toward the future, toward the dream that could not be reduced to words. Behind the beige curtain with its big flower pattern the major drifts on a shifting current. Along the current of the years that he will never see again. All the wrinkles of his face, all the worries of the past, form the unknown alphabet of that future for which he has lived. Small skin marks, a scar on the lower lip, the texture of the gray beard which he has not shaved this morning, a bump of flesh at the edge of the right eyebrow, the moist furrow near the nose, which vanishes into the mustache. You tell a long, troubled story, the fate of a man who was a prey to chance, the disorder of contemporary history, the life of Major Degeorge as I imagine it to have been. But what is this life which is ending now, if not the beginning of what is to come, of that hope left behind it, of another existence reborn, young, quivering, with all the illusions of twenty-five years ago, and something more. . . . It is like the seasons that follow one another, the grass which disappears completely but comes back with the springtime. Die? What does it mean *to die?* A man does not die as long as there are the others. And what he has thought, believed, loved so strongly, so passionately, turns green again with those who come after, those children whose bodies and souls grow, respond in turn to the springtime air, to goodness, to the sweetness of evening.

The past, the past! It is an unchallenged convention that, at the moment of death, a man sees the past, his past, in a lightning flash as though the spool of memory were suddenly releasing its patiently wound thread. As though man were not the negation of the past, that which springs from it without ever returning to it, as though memory itself were not a transformation of the past, an image corrected according to the deep desires each man bears within himself! Man is not turned toward the past, and, even were you to stone me for this, I like to believe that at the supreme moment, when it is borne in upon the flesh how cruelly brief that very moment is, the soul looks forward, yearns to know more, seeks with the feeble strength of an eye whose light is failing to guess what lies ahead, beyond the turn in the road, the new horizon . . . the future.

I don't know, perhaps this book—my sixty-first year is drawing to an end as I write this, the same age as the gouty King Louis XVIII, with the swollen feet, who was carted about in a wheel chair—perhaps this book falsely, only apparently, turned toward the past, is only a great quest of the future on my part; perhaps it is only that last view of the world in which I merely need to burst my everyday clothes, the clothes of all my days. And perhaps that is why, as I progress from Palm Sunday toward Easter, one word is heard more and more often in my prose—a distant sound at first, like a striking of the ground transmitted by the earth, barely audible, a word ceaselessly repeated, which beats like an insistent drum, now muffled, now unmuffled—the future.

Perhaps I have picked up this strange old damask of history, assailed by doubts and certainties, following the crisscross threads of the fabric, the complex tapestry of men and colors; perhaps I have flung myself into the crowd of a vanished time in order to break away from that simplified, linear vision of the world in which I am completing a trajectory, to seek in the dust the multiple seeds of what I am, of what we are, and especially of what will spring from us, against us, above us, beyond us, that springtime of cemeteries which we call the future.

Perhaps it is because at this moment I measure the limited present that is still allotted to me, that with all my strength, with all my will power, with a mad labor which makes those about me shake their heads, I have foolishly undertaken to divert all the past toward the future.

I am that man in a house on the rue Serrée in Béthune, and from here only a bit of leaden sky is visible through the window. When the light of day begins to fade, is it day, is it life? I am that man whom a sudden illness—sudden at least for others, for each one alone knows his heart; the doctors themselves with all their apparatus and their instruments catch only its deceptive signs—I am that man whom a sudden illness interrupts in the everyday refrain, who in the bed where he still vaguely turns, has nothing left but that remote stare fixed wildly on the future.

The future is himself perpetuated, the delegation of his thinking to others, it is the energy of this body transformed, the light transmitted, the ardor communicated. The man who in his dreams never dies, the man who can understand everything, conceive everything except nothingness, if in the depth of the invading night he still has left a fragment of a star, a drop of consciousness, yes, when you think you see him returning to his past, it is to his youth that he appeals, and as he gradually fails, his youth becomes youth itself, the triumph, in its name, of everything that dies over that which inflicts death. At this moment, the future of the man is the youth that survives him.

Youth. . . . The young people who rise and bear the hope of the world for you. Like you, they will be deceived, scoffed at; like you, they will be exposed to a thousand snares, but no matter. They are life, they are renewal, let them, in the name of life, even laugh at you, at that which was your life, yours alone. That laughter avenges you for all your falls, your failures, your mistakes. Youth, old man, is your apotheosis . . . old man of the rue Serrée at Béthune, where the light is fading.

Yes, it is those rising young people who bear the hope of the world. It is not yourself that your already glazed eye now sees, not the past that is past, but your son, your sons, the future. Reject once and for all those lying legends, according to which the ancestor is greater than the grandson. On your last bed at Béthune, what inner light invades you? How could the degenerate children of the Revolution and the Empire light up with their faces the window of the room that is gradually turning dark? But at the window of your soul, this brightness is that of the new generations which lift you higher than you have been able to go. You refuse this judgment of their destiny that others seek to impose on you. Your son, your sons —they are your self enhanced, reaching for other stars. Try then to see the road they will travel. Do not listen to the philosophers and the historians of this century after you, full of contempt, full of lofty pity for this generation that succeeds you because they understand nothing of the continuity of effort, of man's devotion; because they mistake flash for greatness, even the flash of cannon.

There they are, your sons, man of 1793. Away with anyone whose heart is base enough to judge them by the piece, according to the law of the countinghouse, debit and credit, and arrogantly smiles before the everlasting conspiracies in which their lives are spent, their springtime is consumed. Count those who die. For a long time they will fling themselves into ventures which from the very first seem desperate in the eyes of History. Yet they will have believed in them sufficiently to stake all they have of youth on them and the tomorrow of their maturity. Every year, after the massacres succeeding the return of the Princes—the real Terror—will bring its harvest of ardor and bloodshed. And during this time the major's prophecy is fulfilled—for, just look: Napoleon vanquished, the people have taken him into their hands, have shaped him to their own measure, he has become what the people have made him, he is no longer the Emperor of Austria's brother-in-law, he exists through that *canaille* whose prisoner he was so afraid of becoming, exists through them alone, a prisoner of those kings whose courts he copied. And if he is the tobacco pouch of the half-pay soldier, the veteran's pipe, the picture on the wall in the peasant's thatched hut, Béranger's song on irreverent lips, most of those conspirators, throughout the whole of France, from Grenoble to La Rochelle, from Toulon to Lille to Paris . . . are republicans, men of the people, who go to their deaths for a gesture, without anyone's support, without a guarantee from the banks, betrayed by people in high places whom they had once thought to be allies—they are republicans and their conspiracies are no longer the daughters of intrigue, but a protest from the depths.

O patriots of 1816! See Tolleron who placed his wrist on the block on the Place de Grève and said to the executioner: "Cut off this hand which has defended our native land!" His companions in martyrdom were a leather dresser and a writing master. And if there were still doubts as to whom Jean-Paul Didier worked for that year in Isère, it is quite certain that his young accomplice, Maurice Miard, who at fifteen was a tailor in La Mure, died for liberty on the 15th of May on the Grenoble Esplanade. The following year Desbans, the quartermaster-sergeant's assistant in that same 2nd Infantry Division in which Major Degeorge and Fred served just after Leipzig, Desbans who had received the cross of the Legion of Honor from Napoleon's hands, rather than surrender it on the Grenelle drill ground, bent it and swallowed it in front of the firing squad and died at twenty-four with his twenty-two-year-old comrade Chayeux. When Frédéric Degeorge, the son, arrives at the Law School in Paris in 1818, the students no longer bear any resemblance to the volunteers of 1815.

Only that year, thanks to Richelieu, do the foreign armies evacuate French territory. And in 1819 your son, *mon commandant,* will go to prison for a brochure entitled *Ce qu'il faut faire, ou, ce qui nous menace* (what must be done, or what threatens us), at the time when his comrades in the Law School rise up to defend M. Bavoux, their professor, whom the dean has suspended, and the bayonets are called out against them. The School is shut by decree. That year the Abbé Grégoire, the regicide, is sent to the Chamber of Deputies by the people, and the King has his election annulled. The following year Frédéric is in front of the iron railings of the Tuileries on the eve of Corpus Christi when one of his comrades from the School, a student of twenty-three, is killed there by the troops. He is with the six thousand youngsters from the schools who march on the palace the next day, armed with canes. The day after, he is among the four thousand dressed in black who carry their comrade to the cemetery. And that very evening there is a riot on the Place Louis-XV, the rue de Rivoli, and as far as the Faubourg Saint-Antoine. Two days later Frédéric will be among those who shout *Vive la République!* between the Porte Saint-Denis and the Porte Saint-Martin, in the course of which demonstration one man is killed and fifty wounded. In 1821 the troops again have to be called out to disperse the Law School students.

But before this, Frédéric has joined the lodge of the *Amis de la Liberté* and is already on the road to conspiracy. The time has come, and 1822 begins the great tragic stories of that generation: a year of disturbances and duels, of plots and executions. . . . It is the year of the risings of Thouars and of Saumur, when General Berton is executed and when the Four Sergeants of La Rochelle go to the scaffold despite the attempts of the *carbonari* to rescue them on the way, to suborn the governor of the Bicêtre prison on the eve of the execution (and among those who give money is Colonel Fabvier, as well as Horace Vernet and his friend Théodore Géricault). There are further risings at the Law School, and the School of Medicine has to be shut down— Such were the youths of that day. Who, then, what blind romantics, from Stendhal to Musset, could speak of them as though they believed in nothing, as though all they knew was how to drink and smoke, corrupt girls and cash annuity coupons, as though they were inferior to the warriors of the Empire or to the *condottieri* of the Renaissance? Youths impelled neither by self-interest nor by the assurance of winning, gave ungrudgingly. Yes, you are right, old man, the sons of the Soldiers of the Year Two were worthy of their fathers. They were not merely the ladies' men of the Boulevard de Gand.

He was asleep, Major Degeorge—or could that difficult breathing, that violent perspiration, that fitful acceleration of the breath, followed immediately by an alarming calm, be called sleep? Come, try to see ahead, look. . . .

That child of whom you are proud, who like you bears the name Frédéric, went off to Spain where the republicans had got rid of the kings. For Frenchmen were needed on that frontier, when the Bourbons of Paris had decided not to tolerate freedom beyond the Pyrenees, when the army, the army of France, in which the memory of Valmy was not completely lost, marched against Riego. How many of them were there with Fabvier from Saint-Sebastien to Irun? A hundred and fifty at most, but all of them veterans of one conspiracy or another, like the young Delon who had gone to school with Victor Hugo and was condemned to death in the Saumur affair, as well as Gauchard, Pombas, and Cossin. And when the army advances on the Bidassoa, they shout to it: *Soldiers, where are you going? And who would recognize in this young army, under that dirty flag, the children of the victors of Marengo and Austerlitz? Your vanguard is composed of Capuchin friars and thieves, at your head are* émigrés *and traitors; your rear guard is made up of Austrians. You are going to destroy the liberty your fathers founded and paid*

for with their blood, and bring fanaticism and tyranny back to France.
What your leaders call "honor" and "discipline" is nothing but the
hateful principle of the demoralization and debasement of the nation.
A hundred and fifty—what could they do? The French cannon fired
on them point-blank. O first defenders of a new principle, the
solidarity of peoples, young heroes whose history is not taught in
school, you are founding here, at the Pas de Béhobie, that French
tradition which will some day win the world. Hail to you who will
be so well forgotten! Gratitude to you who, with Austerlitz on your
lips, have just effaced the dirty war of Spain, Napoleon's crime, that
blot on the French flag!

Try to follow him, old man, as you breathe and moan, lifting
your useless lid on a vacant eye, try to follow him, that son of yours
who is now here in Denmark Street in London, a small street in Soho
where a France-in-exile lives. Frédéric has been sentenced to death in
absentia. Look at him, among the outlaws. He speaks with Fabvier
who is here on a short stay with General Lallemand, the one whose
wife had hidden on the Géricault property in 1815 and who is now
leaving for America. Here with him are the survivors of the Thouars
and Saumur affairs, of the La Rochelle conspiracy, that of Toulon,
that of Belfort, and Martin-Maillefer whom we shall find again in
1834 with the Lyons silk weavers. . . . He is your son, the very one
who left the Lycée for the army upon hearing the news of the defeat
at Leipzig. And who is this lad of twenty who one day in 1825
pushes open the door in this house in Soho and falls into the midst
of the exiles? Look closely, don't you recognize him? He is your
own little Jean, the urchin you used to send to bed when the sandman
had passed. He has come here to see his brother, whom he will
resemble tomorrow—your second son. But try to follow only the
older one, who is now in France, where there is a price on his head,
and who is being hidden by Armand Carrel. . . . Wait a little, all
this is boiling and churning, something enormous is in preparation—
Do you hear the carts in the streets? the dead carried in the light of
torches? It is Paris, the barricades, and Frédéric is there on the rue
de Rohan, standing gun in hand amid the powder and the blood,
waiting, he says, for that for which he had braved death: *a govern-*
ment of the country by the country. . . .

Are they any less brave, the fighters of the Trois Glorieuses,* for

* See footnote, page 388.

having had their victory snatched from them? And under the crowned Robert Macaire* your son will continue straight on his republican path. Twenty-nine trials under Louis-Philippe, at Arras, where he has chosen to fight. And in this period, at Lyons—in France—the workers' flag has been raised for the first time in the world.

Ah, poor man, it is difficult for you to follow, with what little breath you have left, with what is becoming progressively extinguished in your head, and perhaps it is better that you do not see the sequel, the tragedy. Sleep, or if it is not sleep . . . I am looking beyond you at your son's destiny.

The tragedy. No man alone can change the world. All the forces exerted on the jack must come into play together in order to lift the old society for a moment and topple it forever. . . . Frédéric, of Arras, has made contact with a prisoner of state. A young man who has captivated him by the fire of his republicanism. He has a confidence in him that prison has fortified. He will open to him the columns of the newspaper that he has founded at Arras. Has not this prisoner fought with the carbonari in Italy? In the fortress of Ham this son of Queen Hortense, who bears Napoleon's name, is for Frédéric what the people have made him, and it is true that this Louis Bonaparte claims to believe in socialism, that he proclaims the rights of workers.

We are in a time when everything changes. Why not this man?

Everything changes, even the face of the country. We are in 1843, the Vicoigne company receives the concession of the Noeux mines which lie between Béthune and Lens. Prospectors are looking for coal everywhere, enter properties, make holes, soundings. It creates a fever. The naïve, listening to the stories that are told them, are ready to believe they have Peru in their gardens. Companies are founded. Spoil-banks rise. Men leave the fields for the bowels of the earth. We are in a period when everything changes. Landscapes and human beings. . . .

Already in November of 1847 when Frédéric comes to the gates of Béthune, to the Château d'Annezin, to that banquet at which David d'Angers, Hennequin, Crémieux, Charles Ledru, and Oscar Lafayette are present, together with four hundred and fifty guests,

---

* Robert Macaire: a fictional character in the play, *L'Auberge des Adrets*, played with great success by the popular contemporary actor, Frédéric Lemaître, and borrowed by Daumier who immortalized him in his caricatures. He personifies crookedness in respectable garb, and is a satiric portrait of the new class of *nouveaux riches* who became conspicuous during the monarchy of Louis-Philippe (1830-1848).

he no longer recognizes the horizon of his childhood from the windows. His native town, in the distance, no longer seems to be on a height; black hills have grown up round it. Little houses built of brick begin to form new centers of population, the children play in tiny gardens stained with black gold. Three months later Frédéric comes back here as a commissary of the Republic; it is he who appoints the new municipality in which I recognize an old man, that same Bellonet encountered on the rue Serrée in 1815 who had said to Théodore Géricault that not having found something to die for was having something to live for. . . . Your son, *mon commandant,* represents Pas-de-Calais in the Chamber of the Republic. A radical-socialist deputy. The hope which is that of all men is going to be compromised by haste. The workers are not reasonable, but whose side can I be on, if not on theirs? And—yes—men change. The republicans, his companions of thirty years, cannot understand the friendship that binds him to the prisoner of Ham. He defends Louis-Napoleon, the socialist. He believes in this man. And because of this he becomes suspect to his comrades. "But I swear to you, I know him, he is incapable of a bad action, he is a man of honor, *he is what the people have made him.* Believe me, Louis-Napoleon accepts the presidency, as he says, only to *strengthen the Republic and help it prosper.* Look here, I am not one to compromise! Was I on the side of Cavaignac* in June? We can count ourselves, those of us who don't have the people's blood on our hands. . . ."

But December 2, 1851,† reveals to Frédéric Degeorge what unfathomable depths existed in this man. The state of siege, the Assembly dispersed, the military masters of the street, the republicans arrested in the middle of the night, the dead on the Paris pavements, Lambessa, Cayenne.‡ Frédéric is as though struck by lightning. He will never recover, he has to be shut away in a lunatic asylum. Is he really insane, he who curses the assassins of liberty every day of the thirty months that he has left to live? Upon his death, in July of 1854, a republican subscription raises the funds

---

* Louis-Eugène Cavaignac (1802-1857), French general, who commanded the bloody repression of the working-class uprising in June, 1848, after the deposition of Louis-Philippe in February of that year.

† December 2, 1851: date of the *coup d'état* by which Charles-Louis-Napoléon Bonaparte, the son of Louis Bonaparte and Hortense de Beauharnais, seized dictatorial power, ending the Second Republic of which he was president, and inaugurating the Second Empire.

‡ Lambessa and Cayenne: penal colonies, in Algeria and French Guiana respectively.

necessary for that monument on his tomb. The Emperor is said to have contributed a thousand francs anonymously. And now this bronze head is all that remains of Frédéric Degeorge. His name had indeed been given to one of Béthune's avenues, near the station, when the railway was opened, when the ramparts and the gates were torn down and the town opened to the future. But this straight thoroughfare was later debaptized and renamed the Boulevard Raymond Poincaré. The children of Béthune—of Béthune, which was destroyed and rebuilt, and where the end of the rue Serrée on which the major lived no longer exists, and a pharmacy has taken the place of the forge of Tocquenne the blacksmith—the children of Béthune who play in the street and who are sent to bed when the sandman has passed, know nothing about little Frédéric who after school used to fight with boys twice his size, and his name means nothing to them. Nor to anyone. Just ask the tradespeople. All this has returned to the realm of the imagination.

But in the cemetery of Arras, year after year, the socialist municipality maintains an odd monument. On a column which has disappeared under the ivy—it is trimmed a little, that's all, and a few flowers are put around it—an emaciated man's head with hollow eyes, a nose curved like a beak. The head, pierced by shrapnel or shell fragments during the war of 1914, holds together miraculously over a gaping wound extending from the left shoulder to the right ear, and the birds pass through the torn throat and the clouds can be seen in the gap. . . .

Soon no one will remember who he was. Already forgetfulness is like the ivy, but no one trims that year by year.

The doctor came toward evening. He looked at the patient, shook his head, listened to the wheezy, whistling respiration, looked at the fingers that moved back and forth on the sheets, the vacant eye, and he said that in his opinion, barring a miracle, Major Degeorge would not live through the night.

Théodore had once again gone to Tocquenne's, wanting to see the well-spoken M. de Prat, and once again he had not found him. The Noailles Guard was spending all his time at the post of the Porte d'Arras. As for Géricault himself, no one in the midst of this disorder thought of giving him an assignment, a sentry duty. Nor did he volunteer his services—he was only too happy to lose himself in the crowd and rediscover solitude and meditation. He had remained a long time watching over the dying man while the two women remained seated as if stunned, their tears flowing uninterruptedly in the silence. Then Catherine had said to him softly, "Go and get some air, Monsieur Géricault," in a tone that could also have meant, "Leave us alone with him."

All Béthune gave the impression that someone was dying here. Everywhere the stroller felt that he was unwanted, that he was in the family's way. He thought of things he had said the day before of which he was ashamed now: "I found nothing to die for . . ." He had said that to the man who now was in his death agony. And also, when this man had asked him what was the secret of that indulgence that he felt for the members of the Household, whose youth should not have made him forget that they were the enemies of that very people from whom they were fleeing—for they were not fleeing from Napoleon, but from the people—Théodore had replied, perhaps with some levity, that even the enemy, even madmen or criminals, are first of all human beings. The major had looked at him then with that severity he sometimes assumed, and said, "It may be that you have neither anything to live for nor anything to die for, but to concern yourself with criminals and madmen you must at least have a good deal of time to waste!" At the time, this remark had struck Théodore as that of a somewhat simple man who saw things according to a ready-made pattern. Tonight it took on a quite different meaning—he who had uttered it yesterday was perhaps even then measuring the time that he could not afford to waste, this last day. . . .

It seemed to him that he could no longer accept Aldegonde's gift, and that he had better go and get that castoff outfit at the old-clothes dealer's. It was no longer there, and the pile of clothes that had been on display yesterday had singularly diminished. Quite naturally Géricault found himself at the Porte du Rivage where the Lancers had encountered the Royal Household. The sentry challenged him but let him pass on to the fortifications when he recognized him as a Musketeer. There was a kind of moonlight tonight which prolonged the day. From the lunette where he chatted with some comrades, Gray Musketeers who proposed a game of cards which he declined, the whole landscape of the canal and the small woods could be seen, as well as the walls stretching in both directions to the extremities of the town. Everything was quiet, mute. Was it possible—was the major right?—that there really was no one, that there were no troops besieging Béthune?

No, on this Saturday night the Imperial army was still a good distance from the town. If some regiments had passed on Friday, coming from Arras or Hazebrouck, it was by pure chance because military movements had not yet been co-ordinated; and the circle that Exelmans was drawing round Béthune to close the trap on the Royal Household was still incomplete, still open. That was because it was necessary for the King, then the Princes, to escape first, to discredit themselves and become quite obviously the playthings of the foreigner. And also because it was necessary for the escort which had accompanied them to the frontier to return into the trap, to Béthune, so that its capitulation could be negotiated at a single stroke. By what route they would return and how, at the point of this story that we have reached, is no longer of any importance. Concerning the region between Nieppe where Lauriston spent Saturday and the Grand'Place where the disbanding was going to be effected, the captain-lieutenant, in the light of his experience of the night of Holy Friday, had but one conviction, which was that it must be traversed by day. And so he would be seen re-entering Béthune only on Easter morning. Which meant that at that time the town was still not surrounded. Where, then, was Exelmans on Saturday night and Sunday morning? Still at Doullens, sixteen leagues from Béthune. Those sixteen leagues would be covered on Easter day by two Light Cavalry regiments. And Schmalz said to Arnavon: "No luck! We're going back to our garrison—billiards at the Hôtel du Nord, and *ting-ling-ling,* the chimes on the quarter, the half-hour and the hour. . . ." Until M. le Baron Denniée, the Household's quarter-master general, had received the Imperial order to assemble the horses of the red and the white companies and send them to Arras. As late as Sunday night another two hundred or more officers would escape in the direction of Belgium.

How did it happen that the mechanism functioned so slowly, and at the same time so precisely? How, if Exelmans, at his headquarters at Doullens, was not kept minutely informed of the movements of the Household and the morale of the men? The mice caught in the trap accused Lauriston (who would not serve the Emperor during the Hundred Days) and La Grange (who was said to have dined a few days later with Napoleon, by whom he was certainly confirmed in his rank). But Géricault could have had no idea of all this on that Saturday night. He felt this extraordinary calm of the darkness as a menace. Nothing stirred round Béthune. Nothing.

Yet a carriage was approaching. Over there at the advanced post of the gate, the driver parleyed for a long time, until in the end the drawbridge was lowered. It was a supply wagon coming from the countryside. Even at this hour, even at the risk of introducing a spy hidden under the tarpaulin, provisions had to be let in. But at the very moment when the drawbridge was lowered, a small group of seven infantrymen rushed forward. Did they really force their way through? The men at the post, those who a while ago had wanted to play cards, did nothing to bar their way; and behind them, five or six officers of the Household seemed about to make a dash for freedom. They were undoubtedly there awaiting a chance to escape. They were at the point of missing it, but the sentinel said to them, "You at least, messieurs, are not going to follow the example of those confounded volunteers. . . ."—as though he wanted to let them know that the opportunity was a good one. And since they still hesitated the commander of the post, who was pretending to have been outwitted by the volunteers, added, "Orders are orders, but I have only four sentinels at my disposal!"

So nothing was simpler, if a man wanted to, than to leave the fortress. Théodore would gladly have left in this way, without taking anything with him, leaving even Trick behind. He could not, because of what was happening at the rue Serrée. He returned there. He had thought of going on to the Porte d'Arras to see M. de Prat. I really don't know what held him back. It seemed to him to be somehow lacking in delicacy. Yet at this hour, he was perhaps the only man in the town with whom he could speak of painting, with whom he could speak of Italy.

The two women were still in the room, as though they had not moved—though Catherine had gone and put her little brother to bed. As Théodore entered he took her hand, and this no longer had at all the meaning that it might have had the day before. In a low voice the girl said, "He is dying . . ." There was no priest, no pious picture in the room, no crucifix on the bed. All this seemed natural to Théodore, or would have seemed natural to him if it had been himself. But he was impressed by the fact that it was so for these women. So there were other people for whom God had not sufficient reality to justify even a wager as to His existence, as a sort of game in the face of death. By the absence of all suggestion of Christian pretenses here in this last hour it was possible to measure the degree of de-Christianization the country had reached since the Revolution.

"Call me," he said to Mademoiselle Degeorge, and went to shut himself up in his room. He sat down on the yellow wood bed with its green serge curtains and its flowered counterpane. That a man should be dying in the next room was strangely appropriate to this last evening of Holy Week, to this Paschal vigil of the unbeliever. He reflected that that letter from the son which had arrived from Paris was the final point of this life, that the old man had lived until then, until he had received that letter, as at the theatre the actor waits for the scenic effect whereby the unfolding of the action begins. He reflected that among the seven volunteers whom he had seen fleeing toward Belgium was a tall lad who could only be the Paul Royer-Collard of the other evening. Thus Béthune was the dividing line for the men whom a capricious destiny had brought together there: some heading abroad, others going toward France, still others to oblivion. Suddenly he felt that there had been in him a kind of thirst that he had not recognized until then: to know what *follows*. Follows—after what? Was this not a stupid sentiment? Perhaps so, but he had it. A kind of anxiety, the eagerness for the next page, the morrow. To know . . . to see, to understand . . . To penetrate the reasons for what was inexplicable today, to put a new logic into things, to say to himself, So that was why this man, this woman, these people, behaved in such and such a way, what seemed pure chance, odd coincidence, insignificant, becoming involved and complicated, and it was like a story that was being written. They had come to Béthune as though a huge sack had been shaken over the town, from which fell ill-assorted beings, Moncorps, Lamartine, Houdetot, generals, that tall, lanky Royer-Collard. . . . All this was merely disorder, and here it was as it is for a disheveled sleeper in the morning: he passes his comb through his hair, and the strands turn this way and that, a part is made. To know the sequel . . . Tonight Théodore felt himself facing life as a painter faces his canvas: to paint is to create order. So is to live.

Alone in this room, he admitted to himself things he had not recognized until then. That when all was said and done, with or without reasons, he had a furious urge to live. Having reached this personal frontier where it was necessary to choose whether to pass to the other side, a stranger to life henceforth, or to turn back and plunge into it, he was suddenly caught as by a passion for the things to be done. He would have liked to meet the great David, speak with him deferentially about art, question him, tell him . . . He would have liked to travel, perhaps on foot, in sunny regions. Italy, where he would probe Michelangelo. Or in the northern mists—England, where he would interrogate Hogarth. And just Paris where nothing now would be the same, after this journey to the limits of the possible, this journey during which he had discovered so many unsuspected things. All this would have to be put into order, into art. All this would have to be given a meaning. Paris would no longer be a city through which he passed on horseback. Life, where men and women looked at one another, rubbed elbows without seeing one another, would assume a new place, in which nothing would any longer escape criticism, life of which the measure is man. And he would go and see Horace in his studio, he would talk with him in quite a new way of the same things, he would feel closer to Horace whose painting left him rather indifferent, because Horace Vernet was the living link with an underground world which he was not going to be able to do without. Horace, la Nouvelle-Athènes . . . and no longer the elements to be met in the Lorette district, the horsemen and the ladies who stepped down from their carriages before the mansions of one or another Court, groups attached to the King or the Emperor, but those who had nothing to lose, who could not turn their coats, who were always the victims, those who earned their bread and therefore knew its price, people encountered in the street, who dreamed by a milestone, who drove a cart to the quarries, to the plaster kiln, who curried the horses that others mounted, who carried the water in which others bathed, those from whom sprang the unruly children who were always darting about where they shouldn't and who got run over by carriages, those who died in war or fell from roofs, those who lived under one system or another, no one knew how, but badly, narrowly, always lacking something that they hoped for. And once again he saw la Nouvelle-Athènes, the dance halls, the puppet-master, the little scattered houses, the chickens and the rabbits, the tiny gardens tended in the evening after work, the lane of trees in which was the little Greek temple. He told himself that on his return he would perhaps know why, before he left, *it was necessary* for him to have found Caroline Lallemand, so feminine, so light in his arms, under the portico on the rue des Martyrs.

Thus he dreamed for a long time, waiting for someone to come for him. He had not relit the light when the candle burned itself out, and suddenly, in the dead, stunned town, outside, great peals rang forth. It was midnight, the bells were back from Rome, and in the churches the statues and the paintings were being uncovered after the Gloria of the Paschal vigil in the glory of the bells which answered one another from church to church, with that haste of the Resurrection which does not wait for the dawn when Mary Magdalene and the other Mary went to visit the Sepulcher. All christendom at midnight relinquished the long, unendurable silence that had begun on Thursday evening. The bells rang, life began again.

I shall give another meaning to the ancient myths. It is not the Angel of the Lord who has descended from heaven, with a great trembling of the earth, who has rolled away the stone and seated himself upon it. The one whose countenance here is like lightning, the one whose raiment is not white as snow, is Man, and let those who bear the sword gaze upon him and tremble! Man is reborn, the keepers have fled, life begins again, the life of every day, where there is no need for anyone to perform miracles, where a glass and a knife sing like a canticle on a table, a woman's hand suffices to make light at the curtain that she draws aside, and little violin players walk on the country roads, picking blackberries in the hedges. . . .

The door opened. It was Catherine. She did not wipe her tears. She said, simply: "Come, it is over."

Robert Dieudonné, whom Colonel Simonneau had just appointed captain at Doullens, had stopped outside Saint-Pol with his squadron for the noonday halt. Arms had been stacked, the horses had been put at the foot of the trees, the field kitchen was besieged. There was a pale sun, after a squall. As he was chatting with Riquet and Bouvard, the horseman Langlet came and reported to him that they had stopped a man in civilian clothes who was trying to escape by a side road, and claimed to be a carter going to Doullens with his horse. "But the animal was not a draught horse, the fellow looked as much like a carter as I look like a prince." Robert wanted to see for himself. In Langlet's opinion, it was probably an officer of the Royal Household who had escaped from Béthune. "And if it is, *mon capitaine,* the fellows are going to make him do a fine dance!"

In spite of the distance, the moment he saw the horse Robert wrinkled up his nose, and his freckles spread to form a single big one. No, that certainly was no draught horse! He found the suspect surrounded by the Light-Cavalrymen; they were plying him with questions, which the man did not answer. He was a tall fellow, with a rather worn brown leather coat, a felt hat, and boots that were too fine for those shabby trousers.

"You're lucky to have run into me," said the new captain. "My men were ready to give you a bad time. . . ."

And he gave a pass, signed with his own hand, to M. Théodore Géricault, painter, who was on his way to La Manche, to the house of his uncle, M. Siméon Bonnesoeur, barrister at Mortain. For Paris

was prohibited to officers of the Hoyal Household. And Cousin
Machu's suit of clothes was no guarantee.

"But tell me," said Dieudonné, perplexed, "by what insane chance
did you happen to get into this? Théodore, a Royal Musketeer! Well,
you've got something to brag about. But I say, he's not bad, that nag
they've given you . . . what do you call him? I'll buy him from you."
"Trick," Géricault replied, and he patted his mount. "He's my horse
. . . I wouldn't give him to you for a cannon ball."

There were Hussars who formed a column with the 1st Light Cavalry regiment. A captain, upon arriving, came and saluted his fellow
officer. He gave his name: Descrivieux. Did they know what was
happening at Béthune? He had a friend there whom he would have
liked to help, a neighbor in the country who was in the Royal Household. When he found out that this carter standing to one side happened to be a Musketeer who had escaped from there, he turned to
him eagerly and asked him if he hadn't run into a Lifeguard at Béthune
by the name of Lamartine. "M. de Prat?" said Théodore. "He was
lodging at Tocquenne's, the blacksmith's, on the rue Serrée. But to
find him you'd better ask for him at the Porte d'Arras post where he
spends all his time." Géricault was about to leave. Dieudonné embraced him. And, slapping him on the shoulder, he said, "If you are
really going to Mortain, do give the Regicide my greetings. . . ."

It was a funny thing: the road was no longer at all the same, now
that the sun was shining.

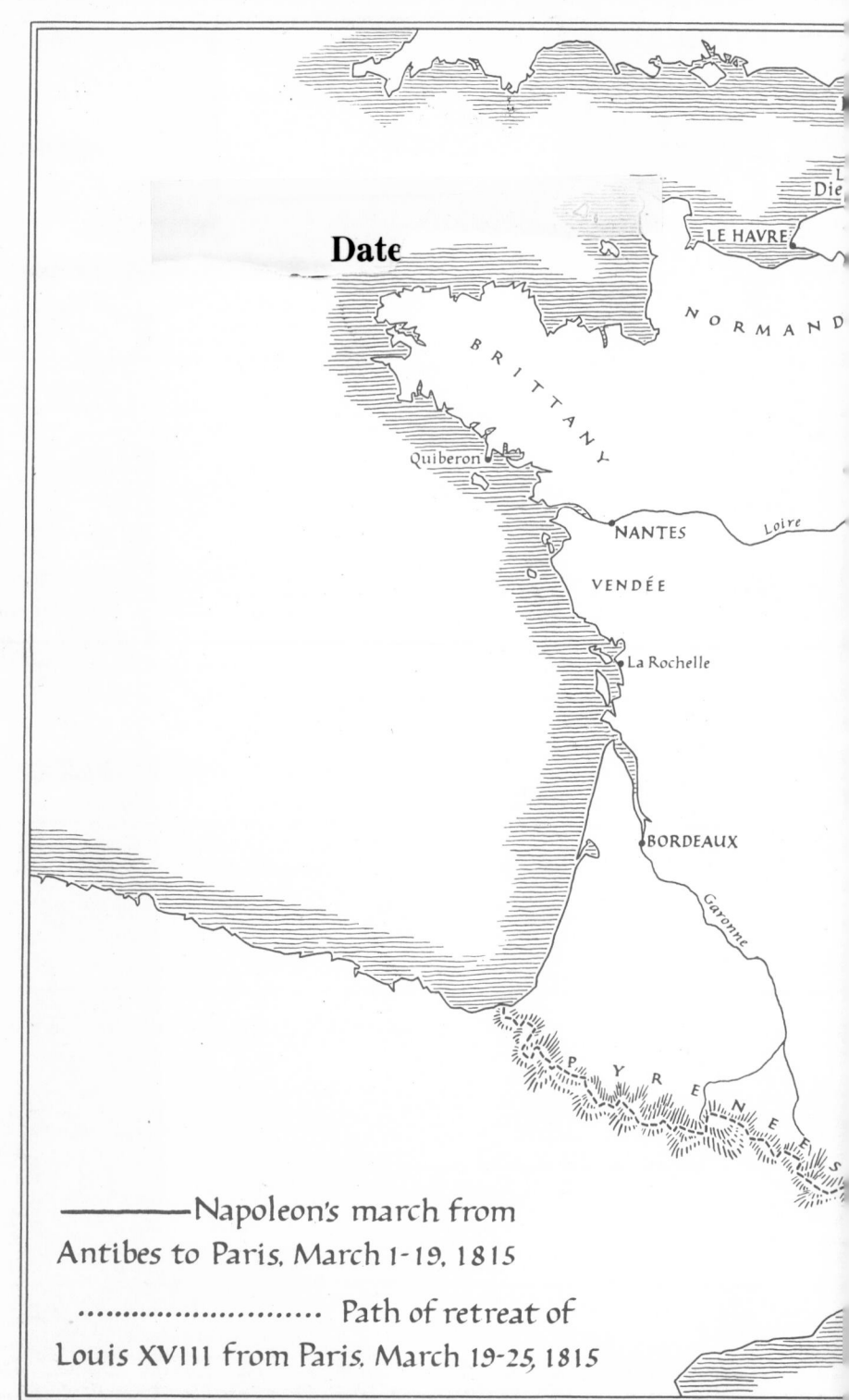

Date

Die
LE HAVRE

N O R M A N D

B R I T T A N Y

Quiberon

NANTES

VENDÉE

Loire

La Rochelle

BORDEAUX

Garonne

P Y R E N E E S

————Napoleon's march from
Antibes to Paris, March 1-19, 1815

·················· Path of retreat of
Louis XVIII from Paris, March 19-25, 1815